To this day I don't kn... make a confession to my ... though I was in accordance with Texas state law, I was in direct violation of the company's workplace safety rule.

"You know that no weapons at work policy?" I asked the twitching and growing hairy monstrosity. "I never did like that rule," I said as I bent down and drew my gun from my ankle holster, and rapidly fired all five shots from my snub-nosed .357 Smith & Wesson into Mr. Huffman's body. God bless Texas.

The creature that had been Huffman staggered back against the window. I turned and ran, empty gun in one hand, fingers of my other hand groping through my coat pocket for my speed loader of extra ammo.

Huffman's office door flew open with a bang. Long claws tore divots into the blue industrial carpet. Coarse black hair covered his body, and the wolf face was a nightmare come to life. Lips pulled back into a drooling snarl, revealing a row of razor-like teeth.

Running in the direction of the elevator, I snapped the cylinder of my revolver closed with five more Federal 125-grain hollowpoints inside.

I'm a very good shot. The tiny revolver was not my best weapon for accuracy, but I did my part. Aiming for the creature's skull, I pulled the trigger. My pulse was pounding like a drum.

I just killed a werewolf.

Then Mr. Huffman rose up and snarled at me.

Baen Books by Larry Correia

Monster Hunter International
Monster Hunter Vendetta
Monster Hunter Alpha
The Monster Hunters (omnibus)
Monster Hunter Legion

THE GRIMNOIR CHRONICLES
Hard Magic
Spellbound
Warbound

WITH MIKE KUPARI
Dead Six
Swords of Exodus (forthcoming)

To purchase these and all Baen Book titles
in e-book format, please go to www.baen.com.

The Following is an excerpt from:

DEAD SIX

by
Larry Correia
Mike Kupari

Available from Baen Books
October 2011
Original Mass Market Paper Back

Prologue: Cold Open

VALENTINE
Sierra Vista Resort Hotel
Cancun, Quintana Roo
Southern Mexico
February 17

There was an angel standing over me when I opened my eyes. She was speaking but I could barely hear her. Every sound was muffled, as if I were underwater, except for the rapid pounding of my heart. *Am I dreaming? Am I dead?*

"On your feet, damn it!" the angel said as she grabbed my load-bearing vest and hauled me from my seat. My head was swimming, and every bone in my body ached. I wasn't sure where I was at first, but reality quickly came screaming back to me. We were still in the chopper. We'd crashed. The angel was pulling me toward the door. "Can you walk? Come on."

"Wait," I protested, steadying myself against the hull. "The others." I turned to where my teammates were sitting. Several of them were still strapped into their seats, but they weren't moving. Dim light poured through a gaping hole in the hull. Smoke and dust moved in the light, but behind that there was blood *everywhere*. My heart dropped into my stomach. I'd worked with these men for years.

"They're dead, bro," Tailor said, suddenly appearing in the door frame. At least one of my friends had made it. "She's right. We've got to get out of here before they start dropping mortars on us. This isn't a good place to be."

Still terribly disoriented, I shook my head, trying to clear it.

"You're in shock," the angel said, pushing me through

MONSTER HUNTER INTERNATIONAL

Larry Correia

MONSTER HUNTER INTERNATIONAL

A Baen Book

Baen Publishing Enterprises
P.O. Box 1403
Riverdale, NY 10471
www.baen.com

ISBN 13: 978-1-4391-3285-2

Cover art by Alan Pollack

First Baen printing, August 2009
Sixth Baen printing, May 2013

Distributed by Simon & Schuster
1230 Avenue of the Americas
New York, NY 10020

Pages by Joy Freeman (www.pagesbyjoy.com)
Printed in the United States of America

This novel is dedicated to Bridget.

Acknowledgments

I want to acknowledge my original readers. I couldn't have done it without your encouragement. Thanks to Oleg Volk for his cover design for the original edition, Justin Otis for blog art, Bob Westover for proofing, and special thanks to my editor, Kathy Jackson, for all the effort she put into making this book work.

the door of our wrecked NH-90 helicopter. "What's your name?" she asked as we stepped onto a large, tiled surface.

"V . . . Valentine," I stammered, squinting in the early morning sun. "Where are we?"

"In a pool," Tailor said, moving up a steep embankment ahead of me. "Ramirez is dead. Half the team's gone." He dropped the magazine out of his stubby, short-barreled OSW FAL and rocked in a fresh one. "Hostiles will be on us quick. You locked and loaded?"

My head was clearing. I looked down at the DSA FAL carbine in my hands and retracted the bolt slightly. A .308 round was in the chamber. My good-luck charm, a custom Smith & Wesson .44 Magnum, was still in its holster on my left thigh. I was still alive, so it hadn't let me down. "I'm ready," I said, following Tailor up the incline.

Our chopper had crashed in the deep end of a huge, pear-shaped swimming pool that had been mostly drained of water. It sat at an odd angle, still smoking, the camouflage hull absolutely riddled with bullet holes. The walls of the pool's deep end prevented the chopper from flipping over, but it was leaning to the side. There were deep gashes in the tile where the rotor had struck. The rotor had blown to pieces, and fragments were scattered everywhere.

"What happened?" I asked. The angel didn't answer at first. I remembered then; her name was Ling, the one who hired us. She followed me up the embankment, clutching a suppressed Sig 551 assault rifle.

"We crashed," she said after a moment, as if I didn't know that. We cleared the top of the incline. A handful of armed people waited for us in the shallow end of the empty pool. Aside from Tailor and me, only three were dressed in the green fatigues of my company, Vanguard Strategic Solutions. I closed my eyes and tried to catch my breath. Ten of us had left on this mission. Half hadn't made it. *Goddamn it . . .*

"You alright, Val?" Tailor asked. "I really need you with me, okay?"

"I'm fine," I said, kneeling down to check my gear. "Just a little rattled." We'd crash-landed in the middle of a deserted resort complex. The city had once been covered in places like this, but now they were all abandoned. In front of us stood a cluster of white towers that must have been a luxury hotel once. About a hundred yards behind us was the beach and ocean as far as the eye could see. The place had probably been evacuated back when the fighting started. It was dirty from disuse and littered with garbage and debris. Several plumes of smoke rose in the distance. Cancun had seen better days.

Ling brushed the dust from her black body armor. "Mr. Tailor. You're in charge now, correct? We must keep moving." I believed she was from China, but there was no accent to her speech.

With Ramirez gone, Tailor had just been promoted to team leader. He quickly looked around, taking in our surroundings. "And where in the hell do you want to go? This part of town is covered in hostiles." His East Tennessee twang were more pronounced with his anger.

"Somewhere that is not *here*. I have multiple wounded," Ling said, nodding toward the rest of her teammates, all members of the same mysterious *Exodus* organization. Like her, they were heavily armed and dressed in black. They were clustered in a tight circle near the edge of the pool, waiting for instructions. In the middle of them was a teenaged girl being tended to by their medic. "We have to get her out."

"Look, damn it," Tailor exclaimed. "We'll save your precious package. That was the deal." He jerked a thumb at the young girl as he spoke. "Let me try to get help again." Tailor squeezed the radio microphone on his vest and spoke into it. "Ocean-Four-One, this is Switchblade-Four-Alpha."

While Tailor tried to raise the base, our team sharpshooter, Skunky, ran over to see if I was okay. He was a skinny Asian guy and was in his mid-twenties, same age as me. "Dude, you're alive."

"I'm fine," I said, standing up. "What happened?"

"They hit us with some kind of big gun right after we took off. It punched that hole in the chopper. The pilots were hit with frag. We made it a few miles, but it was too much damage. They were trying to set us down when the pilot died. That's how we ended up in the pool."

Tailor looked over at us, flustered. "I can't raise the base. This is bad, really bad."

"*Switchblade-Four-Alpha, this is Stingray-Two-Zero,*" a new voice said, crackling over our radios.

That was the call-sign for our air support. One of Vanguard's Super Tucano turboprop attack planes roared overhead and began to circle our position. Vanguard was one of the best-funded private military companies in the business. We could provide our own air support if we needed to.

"Stingray-Two-Zero, this is Switchblade-Four-Alpha," Tailor said. "What's your status?"

"*We were going to ask you the same thing, Four-Alpha,*" the pilot replied. "*We've lost communication with the airfield. It looks bad down there.*"

"We've got multiple wounded and multiple KIA. We need an immediate medevac. Five of us, six Exodus personnel, and the package. Eight confirmed KIA, including the crew of the chopper." Switchblade-Four was down to just me, Tailor, Skunky, Tower, and Harper.

As Tailor talked to the pilot, trying to figure out what was going on, I looked over at Ling and her people and at the young girl that we'd gone through so much trouble to acquire. I didn't know who the girl was or why Exodus wanted her so badly. She had to be important, though, since Ling had offered us an ungodly sum of money to go into Cancun, guns blazing, to rescue her. The fact that we'd be violating the UN cease-fire hadn't seemed to bother her.

Tailor let go of his radio microphone. "Pilot says there's an armed convoy headed our way up Kukulkan Boulevard.

Looks like Mendoza's militia. They saw us go down, I guess. Couple trucks full of guys and some technicals. He'll provide cover, but he's low on ammo."

"Just like us," Skunky interjected.

Ling put her gloved hand on Tailor's shoulder. "I need you to get your men moving," she said. "I'll contact my people to see if I can find out what's going on."

As Ling trotted off, Tailor turned back to us with a worried look on his face. "Val, Skunky, c'mon, we gotta go." Nodding, I followed him as he waved to the others. Standing away from the Exodus people, we huddled up. "Listen up, Switchblade-Four," Tailor said, addressing us as a team. "We're in some serious shit here. I don't know what's going on back at the base. I got a bad feeling." Tailor looked over his shoulder as an explosion detonated to the southeast. The Tucano had begun its attack run.

"This is the third time we've broken the cease-fire this month," Skunky said, anxiously grasping his scoped, accurized M14. "You don't think . . ."

"I know what *I* think," Tower, our machine gunner, said. Sweat beaded on his dark face. "I think they *left* us here."

That got everyone's attention. Being abandoned in-country was every mercenary's worst nightmare.

"It doesn't matter," Tailor said. "Everybody shut up and listen. I don't trust these Exodus assholes. When we start moving, y'all look out for each other. If we have to, we'll ditch these guys and head out on our own."

I flinched. "Tailor, they've got wounded and a kid. And where in the hell do you think we're gonna go?"

"Don't argue with me!" Tailor snapped. The pressure was getting to him. "We'll figure it out. Now get ready. We're moving out. Keep your spacing, use cover, and watch for snipers."

"*Get some!*" the rest of us shouted in response.

"Mr. Tailor, I've got some bad news," Ling said, approaching our group. She had a satellite phone in her hand. "I don't think anyone's coming for us."

"What?" Tailor asked, his face going a little pale.

"Something happened. According to my people, the UN shut down all of Vanguard's operations about an hour ago."

"The UN?" Tailor asked, exasperated. "But the Mexican government—"

"The Mexican Nationalist government dissolved last night, Mr. Tailor. I don't have all the details. I'm afraid we're on our own."

"All we have to do is get to the safe areas in the city, right?" Harper asked. Since the cease-fire, half of Cancun was controlled by UN peacekeepers.

Ling took off her tinted shooting glasses and wiped her brow on her sleeve. "I don't think that's wise," she said, putting the glasses back on. "All employees of Vanguard have been declared unlawful combatants by the UN. I'm sorry, but we need to go, *now*." We all looked at each other, and several obscenities were uttered. We were now on our own in a country where we'd made a *lot* of enemies.

"They sold us out," Tower said. "I told you!"

Tailor spoke up. "It don't matter. Let's move." He took off after Ling. The rest of us followed, spacing ourselves out in a small column. Ling rallied the Exodus personnel, and they followed her as she climbed over the edge of the pool. Two of them were always within arm's reach of the strange young girl. We quickly moved across the courtyard of the resort complex, heading for the buildings. The grass was overgrown, and the palm trees were untended.

Tailor tried to contact the pilots for an update but got no response. It was obvious something was wrong. The small attack plane zoomed back over the resort in a steep right turn, ejecting flares as it went. An instant later, a missile shrieked across the sky, trailing smoke behind it. The Super Tucano exploded in mid-air, raining burning debris into the ocean below. A Rafale fighter jet with UN markings roared overhead, turning to the east.

Our entire group froze in disbelief. This day just kept getting better and better. Beyond the noise of the fighter's engines, the distinctive sound of a large helicopter approaching could be heard.

Tailor grabbed my shoulder and pulled me along. "Move, move, move!" he shouted, breaking into a run.

"Into the hotel, quickly!" Ling ordered. Behind us, a huge Super Cougar transport helicopter descended past our crash site and set down in the courtyard. Like the fighter jet, it bore UN markings. More than twenty soldiers, clad in urban camouflage and blue berets, spilled out of the chopper. They fanned out and immediately started shooting at us. Rounds snapped past my head as I ran across the hotel lobby. I jumped, slid across the reception desk, and crashed to the floor below. I landed on top of Tailor. Harper landed next to me.

"What do we do?" I asked, climbing off of Tailor. The water-damaged lobby was illuminated by hazy daylight streaming through the huge, shattered skylight. The wall in front of us was pockmarked with puffs of plaster dust as bullets struck. The reception desk was heavily constructed out of marble and concrete, so it provided decent cover. The hotel interior was ruined from disuse and stunk of rot.

"Why are they shooting at us?" Tailor screamed.

Ling was crouched down next to Tailor. She shouted in his ear. "I *told* you, they declared you unlawful combatants. We broke the cease-fire. They're just following orders!" She then reached up, leveled her assault rifle across the counter, and ripped off a long burst. "Protect the child!" The Exodus operatives under her command obeyed her order without hesitation. The two men guarding the young girl hustled her, crouched over, to the very back of the room. The rest started shooting, causing the UN troops outside to break their advance and dive for cover.

I glanced over at Tailor. "What do we do?"

Tailor looked around for a moment, the gears turning in his head. He swore to himself, then raised his voice so he could be heard over the noise. "Switchblade-Four! Open fire!"

My team was aggressive to the last. Tower opened up with his M60E4. The machine gun's rattling roar filled the lobby, making it difficult to hear anything. I saw a UN trooper drop to the ground as Skunky took the top of his head off with a single, well-placed shot from his M14. Harper's FAL carbine barked as he let off shot after shot.

I took a deep breath. My heart rate slowed down, and everything seemed to slow with it. I was *calm*. I found a target, a cluster of enemy soldiers advancing toward the lobby, and squeezed the trigger. The shortened alloy butt-stock bucked into my left shoulder as I fired. One of the UN troops, much closer, tried to bolt across the foyer. Two quick shots and he went down. Another soldier crouched down to reload his G36 carbine. The palm tree he was hiding behind didn't conceal him well. The blue beret flew off in a spray of blood as I put two bullets through the tree.

I flinched. Something wet struck the right side of my face. Red droplets splashed my shooting glasses. Ducking back down, I reflexively wiped my glasses, smearing dark blood across them. Harper was lying on the floor, a gaping exit wound in the back of his head. Bits of gore and brain matter was splattered on the wall behind him.

I tugged on Tailor's pant leg. He dropped behind the counter. I pointed at Harper. My mouth opened, but I couldn't find anything to say. "He's dead?" Tailor asked, yelling to make himself heard as he rocked a fresh magazine into his weapon.

I nodded in affirmation. "We have to move! We're gonna get pinned down!"

"Got any grenades left?" Tailor asked. I nodded. He got Ling's attention. "Hey! We'll toss frags, then I'll pop smoke. They'll find a way to flank us if we stay here."

Ling shouted orders to the rest of her men. Tailor and I pulled fragmentation grenades from our vests and readied them.

"Frag out!" We lobbed them over the counter. The lobby was rocked by a double concussion as the explosives detonated nearly simultaneously. Dust filled the room, and the remaining glass in the skylight broke free and rained down on top of us. Tailor then threw his smoke grenade. It fired a few seconds later, and the lobby quickly filled with dense white smoke.

"That way!" Ling shouted, pointing to my right. At the far wall was a large doorway that led into the main part of the hotel. Her men filed past us at a run, stepping over Harper's body as they went.

One of Ling's men stopped. He was a hulking African man, probably six-foot-four and muscular, so broad that the rifle he carried seemed like a toy in his hands. "Commander, come on!" Behind him, a Chinese man fired short bursts through the smoke, keeping the UN troops busy as we fell back into the building. Then came the young girl, flanked by her two bodyguards.

The girl looked down at me as they hustled her by, and everything else dropped away. Her eyes were intensely blue, almost luminescent. Her hair was such a light shade of platinum blond that it looked white. It was like she was looking right through me. "I'm sorry about your friends," she whispered. At least, I could've sworn she did. I don't remember *seeing* her say anything, but I definitely *heard* her.

Tailor grabbed me by the arm. "Val, *go*, goddamn it!" It snapped me back to reality. He shoved me forward and we followed Ling's people into the building.

"You know what the difference between me and you really is? You look out there and see a horde of evil, brain-eating zombies. I look out there and see a target-rich environment."

—Dillis D. Freeman, Jr.
11/2/2001

CHAPTER 1

On one otherwise normal Tuesday evening I had the chance to live the American dream. I was able to throw my incompetent jackass of a boss from a fourteenth-story window.

Now, I didn't just wake up that morning and decide that I was going to kill my boss with my bare hands. It really was much more complicated than that. In my life up to that point I would never have even considered something that sounded so crazy. I was just a normal guy, a working stiff. Heck, I was an accountant. It doesn't get much more mundane than that.

That one screwed-up event changed my life. Little did I realize that turning my boss into sidewalk pizza would have so many bizarre consequences. Well, technically, he did not actually hit the sidewalk. He landed on the roof of a double-parked Lincoln Navigator, but I digress.

My name is Owen Zastava Pitt and this is my story.

◈   ◈   ◈

The finance department of Hansen Industries, Inc. was on the fourteenth floor of a generic-looking office building in downtown Dallas. There were ten of us accountants, placed in ten cubicles in a narrow patch of office sandwiched between marketing and the women's restroom. It was your standard professional office, complete with blue industrial carpet, motivational posters, Dilbert cartoons, and some dead potted plants. I was the new guy.

It was a pretty good job. The pay was respectable. The work was semi-interesting. Most of my co-workers were easy to get along with. It was my first actual serious career-type job after college, or at least my first job that didn't require heavy lifting or bouncing drunks.

Now I had a 401k and dental benefits. My plan was to work hard, find myself a wife, have some kids, and settle down in the suburbs. I was a young professional, and my future looked bright.

There was only one major drawback to my job with such a fine, established company. My boss was an angry idiot. Mr. Huffman was the worst kind of boss, incompetent and always able to find an underling to blame for his own screw-ups. Plus he was mad at the world, not really for any specifics, mind you, but more mad at the world in a general way for being mean to him. Despite his laziness and stupidity, his little pig brain just could not comprehend why he was never promoted beyond the same position that he had held for the last decade. It was obvious to him that the world was out to wrong him. After getting to know the man, I could not blame the world one bit.

As the newest hire in the Hansen Industries Internal

Auditing Department, I was the designated whipping boy for Mr. Huffman's fury. The previous newest hire had committed suicide, thereby creating the opening that I now filled. At the time I had not really made the connection between job satisfaction and the likelihood of taking a bottle of sleeping pills and washing it down with a fifth of scotch.

It had been another twelve-hour day, as had become my custom, always hopelessly behind, trying to learn as I went, and realizing that college really did not have much of anything to do with the real world. Since my supervisor, the vile Mr. Huffman, was supposed to train me, I was pretty much screwed from the get-go. Since I currently had no life outside of work (except for every Saturday when I worked on my hobby), I did not really mind staying late. Hopefully it would impress somebody important at the company, who might offer me a transfer to their department and out of Huffman's.

At least the month had been pleasant. Mr. Huffman had been on vacation camping at some national park or another. He had come back for a week, wherein he had stayed locked in his office, never speaking to anyone or returning any calls, and then went out on sick leave for a few more weeks. His annual vacation was usually my department's most productive time of the year. Go figure.

I glanced absently at my watch. 8:05 P.M. The surrounding gray-carpeted cubes were quiet. My stomach growled, signaling that the bag of Cheetos and the banana I had eaten for lunch had long since worn off. It was time to go. I logged out of my computer, locked up my files, and put on my coat as I headed for the door. Believing I was the only one there, I killed the lights on the way out. Then the intercom buzzed. It made me jump.

"Who's there?" The ponderous voice belonged to Mr. Huffman. That was a surprise. I had not known that he was back yet. *Damn.* I kept walking, deciding to pretend that I had not heard the intercom. If Huffman were here this late, then I did not want to get assigned whatever crap job he was working on, which, knowing what a lazy slug he was, was sure to happen. He would probably call it delegating, and pat himself on the back for being such a proactive member of the management team.

"Owen? Is that you? Come to my office immediately!" *Busted.* "Now, Owen. This is important!" He sounded as officious and pompous as usual.

As I sulked toward his office I had to wonder how he had known it was me. Probably a lucky guess. He must have seen the lights go out from his office. I started thinking of excuses to give him about why I needed to leave, but knew from long experience that he would just shoot them all down. Martial arts class? Nope, he already thinks I'm too militant, and he doesn't even know about my gun collection. Church? Fat chance of that. Date? I wish. Sick mother? Worth a shot, I thought. So I approached his office preparing the story about how I needed to tend to my ill mother. She lived three states away, but what Huffman didn't know couldn't hurt him.

When I entered Huffman's office, all thoughts of my mom's imaginary sickness disappeared. The lights were off, which was very weird. I could not see my boss, as the back of his leather swivel chair was toward me.

The city lights provided a small amount of illumination through the windows. I never could figure out how a toad like him had scored a corner office with a view. Perhaps he had some incriminating photos of the CFO with a hooker or something. His huge oak desk was a mess, and there was a stained paper sack sitting in the middle that must have been his dinner. Whatever was in the bag was slowly leaking a sloppy puddle onto the papers on the desk.

"Have a seat, Owen," Huffman rasped. His voice sounded strange. He did not turn around to look at me. From the top of his head it appeared that he was looking at the evening sky.

"Uh, no thanks, sir . . . I've really got to be going. My mom is sick and . . ."

"I . . . said . . . SIT!" he shouted as he spun around in his chair. I gasped, partly because Mr. Huffman had a look in his eyes like he was insane, but mostly because he was totally naked. Not something that I ever thought I would have to see. The lower half of his jowly face was stained with something dark and greasy, as if he had gone hog-wild at a barbeque.

Okay, that's certainly different. I raised my hands in front of me. "Look, sir, I've got to say that I don't swing that way. You do your thing. I don't care. Some guys would be flattered, but I'm out of here," I stated as I slowly backed toward the door.

"SILENCE!" he shouted, slamming his chubby fingers onto the desk hard enough to rattle it and knock over his dinner bag, spilling its contents. I froze, surprised at the fierce intensity of the command, which was unexpected coming from a man like Huffman, who had what could best be described as "jiggly man bosoms." "Do you know what tonight is, Owen? Do you? Tonight is a very special night!"

"Is it all-you-can-eat shrimp night at Sizzlers?" I replied calmly as I reached back and put my hand on the doorknob. It was official. Mr. Huffman had gone nuts. It looked like he was foaming at the mouth.

"Tonight I punish the wicked. A month ago I was given a gift. Now I'm king. I've seen how you and the others talk about me behind my back. How you don't respect my leadership." My boss's voice had lowered into a growl. His eyes darted about as if he were seeing exciting things in the dark corners of the office. "You're the worst, Owen. You're not a team player. You don't respect my authority. You want to steal my job. You want to stab me in the back!"

I didn't want to stab him in the back, but I was about ready to punch him in the face. My earlier assessment was right. He really was foaming at the mouth. Being attacked by fat, naked Mr. Huffman was not that much of a worry, as I was what could best be called a big fellow, and surprising for an accountant, knew how to kick some butt if necessary. The situation felt surreal and slightly amusing, but I knew that crazy people could be unpredictably dangerous. It was time to slip out and call for some professional help. I turned the door handle, idly wondering if our health plan covered psychiatric care.

"Just take it easy, Mr. Huffman. I'm not out to get you. I'm just going to step out for a second." Then I noticed what had spilled out of the dinner bag.

"Is that a hand?" I blurted.

Huffman ignored me and continued yelling and pounding the desk. Each strike made his layers of blubber ripple dangerously. It sure enough looked like a woman's hand, complete with painted nails, a wedding ring, and a jagged stump where the wrist bones were sticking out. *Holy crap!* My boss wasn't just a run-of-the-mill crazy. I was working for a serial killer.

The naked, crazy, fat man pointed out the window. "The time has come! Tonight I am a god!" he squealed.

His sausagelike finger was pointing at the full moon.

As I watched in the pale lunar glow and the yellowish backdrop of the city lights, that finger seemed to stretch. The hands began to elongate, and the fingernails thickened and spread. He looked at me, and I saw that his grin now stretched from ear to ear, literally, and his gums and teeth began to protrude menacingly past his lips. Thick dark hair was sprouting from his pores. Huffman screamed in pain and exhilaration as the popping and cracking of bones filled the room.

"Owen. You're mine now. I'm gonna eat your heart." His words were barely understandable through his dripping jaw and swelling tongue. His teeth were growing in length and sharpness.

For a second I froze, paralyzed by conflicting emotions as reason came to a screeching halt. The room was dark enough that the civilized part of my brain was trying to convince the primitive caveman section of my brain that this was just some sort of visual trick, a sick practical joke, or something else logical. Luckily for me, the caveman won.

To this day I don't know why at that moment I felt the need to make a confession to my rapidly mutating boss. Even though I was in accordance with Texas state law, I was in direct violation of the company's workplace safety rule.

"You know that 'no weapons at work' policy?" I asked the twitching and growing hairy monstrosity standing less than ten feet from me. His yellow eyes bored into me with raw animal hatred. There was nothing recognizably human in that look.

"I never did like that rule," I said as I bent down and drew my gun from my ankle holster, put the front sight on the target and rapidly fired all five shots from my snub-nosed .357 Smith & Wesson into Mr. Huffman's body. God bless Texas.

The creature that had been Huffman staggered back against the window, leaving a smear of blood and tissue as it slid down the glass onto the carpet. Some of the bullets had either missed or over-penetrated and cracked the thick window. Not staying to examine, I turned and ran, almost breaking my nose as I crashed into the door while trying to open it. I took the time to slam it behind me before sprinting down the narrow hallway, empty gun in one hand, fingers of my other hand groping through my coat pocket for my speed loader of extra ammo.

Huffman's office door flew open with a bang. The thing standing in the doorway was clearly more animal than man, but obviously not any normal animal. My supervisor's fatty bulk had been somehow twisted into a sleek and muscled form. Long claws tore divots into the blue industrial carpet. Coarse black hair covered his body, and the wolf face was a nightmare come to life. Lips pulled back into a drooling snarl, revealing a row of razorlike teeth. Now on all fours, he raised his muzzle and smelled the air, howling when he spotted me.

The blood in my veins turned to ice.

Running in the direction of the elevator, I snapped the cylinder of my revolver closed with five more Federal 125-grain hollowpoints inside. The creature was fast, much faster than an Olympic sprinter, and I was no Olympic sprinter. My lead down the hallway dwindled in seconds. I spun and fired as it leapt at me, striking the beast in the face. His snout turned on impact and momentum carried him into the wall, crushing the sheetrock. Immediately he started to rise, jagged fur bristling down his back.

I'm a very good shot. The tiny revolver was not my best weapon for accuracy, but I did my part. Focusing on the front sight, aiming for the creature's skull, I pulled the trigger. With each concussion I brought the little gun back down and repeated the process. I was rewarded with a flash of red and white as a .357 hollowpoint blossomed through Huffman's brain, but I kept pulling the trigger until the hammer clicked empty. I was out of ammo.

My vision had tunneled in on the threat. My pulse was pounding like a drum. The adrenaline running through my system had tuned out the horrendous muzzle blasts. I brought the gun down to my side. Huffman was dead.

I tried to control my breathing as I began to hyperventilate. Perhaps I was losing my mind, for lying not twenty feet from my cubicle was a dead werewolf. A monster from fairy tales, but somehow it was here, sprawled on the carpet, brains blown out. There had not been time to feel fear or any other emotion as the creature had been chasing me, but that all came out now as if a dam had burst. The uncontrollable shaking in my limbs was slow at first, but quickly gained in intensity as I got a better look at the beast on the floor. It was like being in a car wreck. The almost disbelief as the events unfolded. The lack of emotion during the impact. And finally the brutal realization of what had happened. *I just killed a werewolf.*

Then Mr. Huffman rose up and snarled at me.

The exposed brain matter pulsed back into his head, and with a crunching noise the plates of his skull rejoined. The creature stood on his hind legs somehow, even with knees twisted like a canine's. With one taloned finger he speared a chunk of tissue from his fur and tossed it into his maw, chewing his own discarded flesh. Returning gracefully to all fours he shook himself like a giant dog, splattering the blood from his wounds on the white walls and motivational posters in the hall.

The monster howled again, long and high-pitched, and the sound ignited some primal survival instinct buried deep within me. I turned and ran faster than I ever had before. Somehow I kept my wits, and rather than trying to outrun the creature to the elevator, I twisted hard to the right and through a doorway, slammed the door, locked it, and shoved a heavy desk in front of it. A computer monitor fell to the ground and sparked. I was in the marketing room. A poster with a kitten forlornly holding onto a clothesline had the caption: HANG IN THERE. *Thanks for the advice, buddy.*

There was no time to think. I kept moving, hoping that the door and the desk would slow Huffman down. It did, for a few seconds at least. In a cloud of splinters the werewolf began to tear the door apart, snarling, grunting, gradually pushing the desk out of the way. There was another doorway at the end of the office that led to a side corridor. I slammed the door behind me, but there was nothing there to block it with. *Weapon. Need a weapon.* My gun was still in hand, but it was empty, and a lightweight snub was definitely lacking as a club. I had a concealed weapons permit for defense against muggers and assorted scumbags. I had never thought I would need it to fight a creature from the SciFi channel. There was a fire extinguisher mounted on the wall so I pulled it down and took it with me. It was better than nothing.

Down the corridor was the door to my department, if I could get through it and I had a shot at the elevator. Legs and heart pumping, I heard the door behind me crash off of its hinges. Not sparing the time to look, I yanked open the door to Finance and rushed through, trying to pull it closed behind me. The door slammed into Huffman's claws and muzzle. I tried in vain to close the door but he was far stronger than I was. He swiped his talons down across my chest, tearing cleanly through my clothing and into me. *Pain. Unbelievable pain.* Screaming, I fell on my back and activated the fire extinguisher, directing the spray into the werewolf's gaping mouth and eyes. The creature howled, reared up on its hind legs, and covered its face. I lashed out with my foot, kicked the creature in the ribs and knocked it back into the corridor. Scrambling to my feet, I pulled the door closed and locked it.

My chest burned from the lacerations. The injury looked bad, and blood was soaking across my shirt, but the pain was now just something throbbing in the background behind the wall of adrenaline rushing through my system. The hurt would come later. I had a monster to worry about right now.

The werewolf punched through the wooden door, talons narrowly missing my flesh as he searched for me. I raised the fire extinguisher above my head and lashed out at the hairy arm, smashing it again and again with blows that would easily have broken ordinary bones. Finally the forearm shattered with an audible snap, but Huffman was not deterred. The claws kept swinging, and within seconds the limb had seemingly healed. Shouting unintelligibly, I continued bringing the extinguisher down on Huffman, the metal echoing with each hit.

We were at an impasse. He could not push through with me crushing his arms. His animal mind must have come to that same realization. As fast as it had appeared, the arm disappeared, leaving nothing but a gaping hole through the heavy oak door.

My breath came in ragged gasps from the exertion. Nothing seemed to hurt him. I had to think of something . . . *Silver.* That's what always worked in the movies. Where was I going to get silver in my office? But I knew the answer to that one immediately. Nowhere.

If I could make it to the elevator I would be home free, but to do so I needed to cover forty feet of Finance, and then about a hundred feet of hallway. Cradling the fire extinguisher in my arms I stumbled for the door. In the darkness, the green light from the exit sign was my beacon. The blood running down my stomach was warm and slick. I made it as far as my cubicle before Huffman got a running start and crashed into the room. There was no way I could escape before he would be on me, claws and teeth flashing, and I would be a dead man.

Flight wasn't working, so now it was fight time. At least I was on my home turf.

"Huffman, you son of a bitch! Come and get me!" I roared as I sprayed him with the fire extinguisher. "This is my cube!"

The werewolf swatted my improvised weapon away, breaking my left hand on impact. He rammed into me and hurled me straight into the air. The ceiling tiles barely slowed my flight and I rebounded off of a heating duct with a resounding clang. I fell onto the top of my cube wall. It was not designed to take the impact of a three-hundred-pound man. It collapsed and I slammed onto my desk.

Keep going. Groaning and trying to catch my breath, I tried to think of something, anything, that I could do. The werewolf's head rose at the base of my desk. I kicked him hard in the face. Huffman bit my shoe off.

With leg muscles like coiled springs, the werewolf easily hopped up beside me, claws clicking on the hard surface like fingernails on a chalkboard. I felt the instinctive twinge down my spine. I tried to roll off the desk, but Huffman effortlessly sunk a claw deep into my thigh, pinning me down. I screamed in pain as the talon pierced through the muscle. Grabbing the back of his hairy claw with my one working hand, I tried to pull it out. It wouldn't budge.

He had me. I lay there bleeding with my leg pinned to my desk. The werewolf seemed to be enjoying himself, taking his sweet time, savoring my pain. I wondered if somewhere deep inside that animal Mr. Huffman was there, enjoying this, loving the power, finally being able to strike back at the world he hated so much.

My fear was replaced with anger.

The shooting pain in my leg was unbearable, and all reason told me that I was a dead man, but I would be damned if I was going to die at the hand of that fat piece of shit Mr. Huffman.

The werewolf opened his jaws slowly, impossibly wide, and lowered them toward my face. His breath was hot, and stunk like rotting meat. He was going to eat me and somehow I knew he was going to do it as slowly and painfully as possible. Trying to be inconspicuous I reached into my pocket. Huffman licked my face. The tongue was damp and rough and I cringed in revulsion. Bastard probably wanted to see what I tasted like first.

My pocketknife opened with a snap the instant before I jabbed it into his throat. The three-inch Spyderco was not really a fighting knife, but I put it to the test. Twisting and pulling, I tried to do as much damage as I could. Blood geysered across my cube as I severed his jugular. He jerked his claw out of my leg, and I almost fainted as blood flooded out the gaping hole. I pulled the little blade back and stabbed it into his eye. My knife, slick with fluids, slipped out of my hand as Huffman pulled away, and it remained stuck in his face. He lashed out, striking me in the head. The claw tore down to the skull, opening my flesh, dragging down across my face. I felt it in almost clinical detachment, knowing it was bad, but beyond the point of feeling or caring. My whole life had dilated down to one simple thought: *Huffman must die.* Lights flashed in my eyes as my enemy roared.

"Regenerate this!" I bellowed as I grabbed my letter opener off of my desk and stabbed it repeatedly into his chest. Reversing my grip, I thrust it up through his bottom jaw, lodging it deep into the roof of his mouth, pinning his muzzle shut. Then I kicked him in the balls and smashed my chair over his head for good measure. He hit me with a backhand that knocked me across the room like a human cannonball. I crashed through a potted plant and rolled across the carpet.

Disoriented, I left Huffman swirling about like a tornado of death while I limped away, trying to staunch the massive bleeding from my leg. The werewolf thrashed, trying to pry one little knife out of his eye socket and a letter opener out of his palate. I had landed near Huffman's office so I pulled myself through the door. Options were running out. I was going to pass out soon from blood loss. The only thing sustaining me was anger and determination, and that wouldn't last much longer. I needed to think of something, and I needed to think of it quick. Taking stock, I saw filing cabinets on each side of the door. Chair. Desk. Golf magazines. Some lady's hand. But nothing that I could use as a weapon.

I could hear the werewolf raging, smashing apart my cube, destroying anything within reach, ripping and snarling, then gradually quieting as he caught my scent. He was coming for me again. I was waiting for him.

But not where he expected. As Huffman charged in, led at this point only by instinct and pure animal fury, I jumped from the top of the filing cabinet onto his back. We collided with a great deal of force and he crashed snoutfirst into his desk. Wrapping my arms around his neck, I choked him, straining as hard as

I could. "Let's see how tough you are without air!" I screamed in his pointy ear. We flipped over the desk but I stubbornly held on. His jaws snapped shut but I was safely under them. He reached over and raked razor claws down my back. We spun crazily and crashed into the already damaged window, shattering it and sending shards raining to the ground below. By some miracle we did not fall. Keeping my damaged left arm around his throat, I grabbed his muzzle with my good hand and wrenched it to the side with all of the strength and anger and fear that I had left. I grunted under the strain and roared. The beast's spine was like rebar. Somehow I pulled harder.

The werewolf's neck broke with a sickening pop. Severed from the impulses firing in his brain, the creature's body spasmed wildly. The claws dropped away from my ravaged back and he lay under me, flopping violently. I rolled off and dragged myself away, barely able to stay conscious. Pulling myself along with one arm, shoving with one leg, the other leg limp and leaving a wide trail of blood, I made it to the other side of the desk and collapsed.

I heard the scraping of bones again as Huffman's vertebrae realigned. In a second he would be back up, and I would not be able to fight him off again. With my good hand I struggled up so I could see over the desk. There was Huffman's dinner, and in my brain that was running dangerously low on blood and oxygen, it struck me as funny. "Need a hand?" I asked nobody in particular and giggled.

The werewolf was starting to sit up. In another few seconds I would be providing him nourishment. Then he would be off killing innocent people at every full moon. On the other days of the month I was sure that he would just keep being the worst boss in the world. I don't know which one made me angrier.

Huffman swiveled his from head side to side as he regained his senses.

"Not this time, asshole!" I said as I heaved all of my weight against the heavy desk. With a groan of protest it moved from its depression in the carpet. Desperately shoving, my one good leg straining for traction, made even more difficult because I was missing my shoe, I pushed the desk into Huffman, knocking him over, and before the werewolf realized what was happening I had pushed him and his damned desk out of the window.

CHAPTER 2

I could tell I was dreaming. Everything had that fuzzy, disjointed dream feel to it. First I had flashes of dragging myself toward the elevator, my belt being used as an improvised tourniquet on my leg. However, in my dream it didn't hurt a bit. Movement was slow as though I were underwater. There were glimpses of an ambulance and men sticking me with needles and pounding on my chest.

The next scene was weird, since I usually dreamed in a first person perspective. I floated weightless as I looked down and watched people in masks shock my heart with a defibrillator.

Back in the first person again. Now I stood in a field. A good, strong, green crop of some kind. My feet were bare and I could feel the wetness of the dew as I wiggled my toes. The sky was dark blue and the air smelled fresh and clean like after a summer rainstorm. A herd of cows grazed in the distance.

A man stood nearby. He was old and bent. His white hair was wild and he had a kindly smile, but hard eyes behind small round glasses. He leaned on his cane and waved.

"Hello, Boy." The old man had some sort of heavy Eastern European accent.

"Are you God?" I asked.

He laughed hard. "Me? Ha! Is good one. 'Fraid not. I just friend."

"Am I dead?"

"Almost. But you need go back. You have work to do. Yes, much work."

"Work?"

"A calling. Is hard, but is good."

"A calling?"

"From before you born. How you say?"

"Preordination?"

"More like you get short straw. Now go. No time. I send you back."

"Will we meet again?"

"Only if you are slow-witted boy and get dead again."

The nice dream ended and my world exploded in pain.

There was a steady beeping noise. It matched pace with my heartbeat. *Bump-bump.* Two black shapes stood over me.

"I say we waste him now."

"Not yet."

"No way he's clean."

"You know the rules."

"The rules are wrong. I could smother him with his pillow and nobody would ever know."

"I would know."

I went back to sleep.

◇   ◇   ◇

I awoke to the smell of hospital antiseptic. My eyes were matted shut, my mouth was horribly dry, and my tongue was stuck to the roof of my mouth. I had that weird, tingly, high on painkillers feeling, which I had not felt since the last time I had surgery years before. Forcing my eyes open and gradually adjusting to the muted light, I could see that I was in a hospital room. Hospitals make me nervous and uncomfortable, though right now it sure beat the alternative.

Trying to sit up, I realized that I had an IV running into my arm, bulky bandages placed on my chest, legs, and back, and my left hand was in a cast.

Wincing at the tightness in my scalp, I gingerly reached up and touched my forehead. There was no bandage there, and I counted at least fifty prickly stitches that ran from the crown of my head, right between my eyebrows, across the bridge of my nose, and ended on my cheek. I was thankful that I did not have a mirror. Being naturally curious, and of course fearless on a morphine drip, I lifted up the edge of the big bandage on my chest. They had used staples to close the deeper lacerations there. In my drug-induced stupor, it struck me as funny that the doctors had shaved my chest. That would probably itch bad later.

I did not remember how I had gotten here, or even how long I had been out. My watch could tell me what day it was, but it was missing, as were all my clothes. All I had on was a flimsy gown and a medical supply store's worth of bandages.

As my senses gradually returned, I started to remember what had happened to put me here. I had to admit that at first I blamed my strange memory on the drugs. Killer werewolf boss? Yep, whatever they gave me, it sure was some good stuff.

You imagined the whole thing, the logical part of my brain told me. *You must have been in some sort of accident, and woke up here. There's no such thing as monsters. Mr. Huffman didn't turn into a werewolf. You didn't push him out a window. Those can't possibly be claw marks. They're from a car wreck or something. The whole thing is a bad hallucination. Everybody at work will laugh when they hear your crazy story. Huffman is probably there now, complaining that you are out and running up workers' comp.*

Screw you, logical brain. I know what I saw.

There was one way to find out what put me in here. There was a call button attached to the IV. I pushed it and waited, trying not to dwell on the image of Huffman's face turning into an incisor-filled muzzle. Finally, after what seemed like an eternity, the door opened. Unfortunately, it was not a nurse.

"Mr. Pitt. I'm Special Agent Myers and this is Special Agent Franks. We're with the government." The two men flashed their credentials in my general direction. One agent was a dark brooding type, obviously muscular and grim of attitude. The speaker was older and looked more like a college professor than a Fed. They were both wearing off-the-rack suits, and neither looked very happy. They pulled up chairs. The professor crossed his legs, steepled his fingers, and scowled at me. The younger one pulled his gun.

"Move and I'll kill you," he said, and I did not doubt him for an instant. It was a Glock, and it had a sound suppressor screwed onto its muzzle. I did not know what caliber it was, but from where I was sitting the bore looked freaking huge. The suppressor did not waver. I did not move.

The professor spoke. "Mr. Pitt. Would you care to tell us what happened at your office?"

Speaking was difficult with my bad case of cottonmouth. "Msssph umm suh . . ." I told them. "Wah um fa?" They could probably tell that I was either asking for water or speaking in tongues. The professor hesitated and then obliged, taking a cup off of the dresser and pressing the straw to my lips. The cold wetness was the best thing in the world. The agent called Franks leaned slightly forward so he could still shoot me if necessary. That guy obviously took his job very seriously.

"Ahhh . . . Thanks," I croaked.

"You're welcome. Now tell us what happened before Agent Franks here gets cranky."

I paused, not really wanting to tell the FBI that my boss had transformed into a monster and tried to eat me, before I managed to snap his neck and shove him out the window. They would lock me up for sure if I said that, so I improvised.

"I fell down the stairs." Hey, I was on morphine. It was the best I could come up with on short notice.

The professor frowned. "Cut the crap, Pitt. We know what happened. We watched the security tapes already. Five days ago, your supervisor, one Cecil Huffman, transformed into a lycanthrope, a werewolf in this case, and attempted to kill you. You fought him off, and pushed him to his death."

I was shocked. The FBI agents seemed to not have a problem with the idea that my boss had turned into a werewolf. I was also surprised that I had been out for five straight days. But mostly I was surprised that Mr. Huffman's first name had been Cecil.

"It was self-defense. I'm the good guy here. Why the gun?"

"You know how people become werewolves, don't you, Mr. Pitt? That's one thing that the movies get right. If you're bitten by one you, too, will be infected. The DNA-altering virus lives in their saliva. If you're clawed there is a smaller chance that you can be infected, but it's still possible. If we had found a single clear bite mark on you, we would be disposing of your body right now. Under the Anti-Lycanthrope Act of '95 we're supposed to terminate all confirmed were creatures immediately. I'm sorry."

"I don't think he bit me," I squeaked. But I felt a lump of dread in my gut. He had mauled me pretty badly. Was I going to turn into a werewolf? Or was the FBI just going to shoot me first?

"Silver bullets," grunted Agent Franks. He kept the Glock centered on my head. I don't know what kind of Jackie Chan move he was expecting me to pull, but I wasn't planning on going anywhere. I could barely move. "Just in case."

"So now what?" I queried.

"We wait. A sample of your blood has been sent for testing. If it comes back positive you will have to be put down. If it comes back negative, you're free to go. We should be getting a call shortly."

He said "put down" like I was some sort of dog. This encounter was just strengthening my already strong anti-authoritarian tendencies.

"You'll just let me go?"

"Yes. Though if you ever speak of this in public you will be in violation of the Unearthly Forces Disclosure Act, and you'll be prosecuted to the fullest extent of the law."

Franks nodded and muttered, "Lead bullets." His conversation skills seemed rather limited.

Myers' eyes betrayed an emotion that I thought might have been pity. "Look, Mr. Pitt, this is for your own good. If you're infected, we're doing you a favor. Otherwise in three weeks you'll be eating little old ladies and babies. Hopefully the tests come back negative, and we forget this ever happened."

"So what now?"

"Just chill for a while," Agent Franks said.

"Easy for you to say."

A doctor came in and took my pulse and blood pressure. A nurse changed my IV and checked my bandages. The staff seemed intimidated by the Feds, and left without talking. Flowers were delivered. They were from Hansen Industries, with a card wishing me a speedy recovery. Along with the card there was also a letter on Hansen Industries stationary that informed me that I was fired for violating the Official Workplace Safety Code No Weapons in the Workplace Rule. If I did not want to risk an interruption to my Workers' Compensation, I had best not protest the firing. Hugs and kisses, Human Resources.

I pushed the button on the motorized bed so I could sit upright. Myers turned on the little TV and we watched *Jeopardy*. Watching television kept my brain occupied, and more importantly kept me from dwelling on the possibility of ending up dead, or even worse, like Huffman. Myers was pretty good, but I was destroying him. I'm a Trivia King. Franks kept the gun in his lap and sipped a Diet Coke. I tried not to think about the fact that the nice men from the government were here to shoot me in the brain with silver bullets. The feeling of helplessness was horrible. Alex Trebek had all of the answers. I just had questions.

"What is Constantinople? So, Myers, how bad was I injured?"

"You lost a lot of blood and technically died on the operating table for two minutes. No brain activity at all. You have about three hundred stitches and staples in you and some broken bones. If we don't have to shoot you, you should heal up just fine. But you won't ever be pretty. What is the Great Wall of China?"

The thought that I had actually been dead was interesting. That was kind of cool. I wondered if I could use that as a pickup line.

"Who is Ghandi? What happened to Mr. Huffman?"

"He landed on a Lincoln Navigator. The desk landed on him. He was pulped. Nobody else got hurt." He was frustrated. I was tearing him up in the Famous History category. I could tell the professor was used to winning. *Ha ha sucker, eat hot trivia death!* "What was the Magna Carta? Huffman didn't pull back together or anything did he?"

"Damn, you're fast. Nope. Lycanthropes can regenerate from just about anything other than silver, but it takes energy to restore tissue. There's only so much energy stored in one body, so if you inflict enough damage on them, they die."

"Fire," grunted Franks.

"Indeed, fire works great. Wait, I know this. What is uranium?" he shouted.

I made a buzzing sound. "Wrong. What is beryllium? Damn, Myers, I thought you had to have an education to be a G-man. You suck."

The senior FBI man changed the TV channel to CNN and sulked. Well, at least I had the satisfaction that if they were going to kill me, I had defended my honor on the field of useless knowledge. The news was saying something about a huge pipeline explosion in a remote part of Russia apparently caused by Chechen terrorists. I tuned it out and went back to harassing the Feds.

"Does this kind of thing happen all of the time? How did Huffman become a werewolf? Are there many more out there?"

"You ask too many questions," Franks said.

"My associate is correct, Mr. Pitt. This subject's on a need-to-know basis. You just need to know to keep your mouth shut." *Fine*. I figured I would just go back to sleep. Stupid Feds.

There was a knock on the door. It must have just been a mere courtesy knock because whoever it was immediately barged in. Franks barely had time to hide his Glock under an issue of *Martha Stewart Living*.

The man was of average height and lean, with short-cropped, sandy blond hair, probably in his mid-forties. With no really remarkable features, he was not a memorable-looking guy, but emanated an old-school toughness when he strutted into the room, an attitude like a Bogart or a Cagney from the golden age of movies. A cigarette hung lazily from the corner of his mouth in clear violation of hospital rules.

Myers grimaced and it looked like Franks gave some serious thought about pointing his gun at somebody else for a change.

"Well, if it ain't the junior danger rangers. How's the murdering witnesses business?" the man asked, reaching into the pocket of his leather bomber jacket and pulling out a business card. He stuck the card into the edge of my wrist cast. It stuck there, vibrating slightly.

"Screw you, Harbinger," Franks said.

"Situation's under control. No need for you here," the professor stated in a cold voice.

"I'll be ice-skating in hell before I believe that you federal weasels have anything under control."

"You better shut up," Franks growled.

"Or what?" the man said with calculated belligerence and just a touch of a southern accent. "Gonna arrest me? You might not like it much, but we're a legitimate business again. If you Feds hadn't booted us out of Yellowstone, that werewolf wouldn't have gotten away, that fat guy wouldn't have gotten bitten, and this guy never would have gotten attacked."

"National parks are our jurisdiction. Your people can't legally be armed in them, so you were out of luck. So you just need to calm down," Myers stated in a manner that suggested he was used to being obeyed.

The new guy sneered. "I need to calm down, Myers? Your bureaucratic nonsense caused this trail of bodies. You could have let us break a couple of stupid laws and you wouldn't have two dead people and this one." He jerked a thumb in my general direction.

"The rules are there for a reason. Not obeying the rules is what got you shut down the first time.

I think it was a mistake to ever let your kind back into business."

Needless to say, the atmosphere in the room was very tense. I was pretty much forgotten in my heap of bandages and bedpans. Myers and the interloper were locked in a staring contest. Franks looked ready to escort our guest out, preferably headfirst down the stairs. Anybody who made these guys that uncomfortable was all right by me.

"Umm . . . Not to interrupt this love fest or anything, but who are you?"

Finally Myers must have blinked and ended the stare off. The stranger looked at me as if he was sizing me up. His eyes were cold, blue, and intimidating. After a long unblinking moment he finally must have decided I passed muster, since he held out his hand to shake mine. Franks removed the *Martha Stewart* magazine to display his gun, just to remind me not to try anything.

"Name's Earl Harbinger. I'm with MHI."

"Owen Pitt. CPA." His grip was like iron. "MHI? Is that like some top secret government agency or something?" I asked.

Agent Myers snickered. "Not even close."

Harbinger just scowled at them. "No. If I worked with these idiots I would kill myself. We're a private organization. We're a for-profit business, and if I do say so myself, we're the premier leader in our field. One which I would say that you would probably be pretty good at. You did good back there."

"Thanks, but I don't think it's going to be good enough. These guys tell me that I'm probably going to end up turning into something like my boss." It was an ugly thing to say, and I could feel a great cold weight in my chest as I said it. "I don't want to end up like that."

The stranger shook his head. "Don't worry about it."

"Recruiting some fresh cannon fodder, Harbinger?" Myers interrupted. "Right now Mr. Pitt is in our custody, and he doesn't go anywhere until I say so."

"I'm not recruiting, Myers, but if you're looking I hear Wal-Mart needs a new door greeter," he responded. Turning back to me, he continued speaking as if he had never been cut off. "Have you asked yourself why every one of your injuries is bandaged except for that great big slash on your head?"

Subconsciously I reached up and touched the nasty pile of stitches that snaked down my face. All I knew was that it was going to leave a horrible scar.

"It's uncovered so they could watch it. If you had started to heal unnaturally fast, they would have dropped you dead in a heartbeat. From the amount of damage you sustained, I'm sure they were positive that you were going to make the change. I don't think anybody has ever been that torn up by a were creature and lived. I'm also guessing that since you haven't started to heal yet, they've sent out for a blood test to be sure, because they're probably itching to finish you. But they don't dare, just in case you're still human."

"They said they were waiting for a test."

"Damn right they are. But let me tell you something. I wrote the book on these monsters. If you haven't shown any signs after five days, I give you my word that you ain't infected."

"Really?" I felt the first real surge of hope since I had woken up in this antiseptic dungeon.

"You're going to be fine. Look, when these jerk-offs

get their test back negative, and you get out of here, give me a call. You have my card. We need to talk. Get some rest." Strangely enough, I believed the stranger's promise. He did not strike me as the kind of person to sugarcoat an ugly truth.

Harbinger stalked out, rudely bumping into Agent Myers on the way. The senior agent appeared ruffled but he did not speak until after the door shut and our guest was gone.

"You'd best stay away from that bunch, Pitt, if you know what's good for you. They're going to screw up some day and every last one of them is going to end up in prison or dead. They don't respect governmental authority."

Well, neither did I. I flipped the agents the bird. "You know what, I'm going back to sleep. I've had a crappy day. If your stupid test comes back positive, just shoot me and get it over with. If it comes back negative, get the hell out and leave me alone. Either way you don't need to wake me." I pushed the button to lower the bed back into a sleeping position. It wasn't as dramatic as a good door slam, but it would have to do.

It actually only took me a few minutes to fade out. My body was still wracked with painful injuries and the painkillers still hummed through my system, but I was careful to first safely cradle the business card in my hand.

The Feds went back to watching TV.

I had a strange dream. It was hazy and blurry, jerky and disjointed, violent and quick. Not like a normal dream at all.

There was a battle. I did not know when it took

place, but somehow I knew that it had occurred in the past. Details were obscured by billowing clouds of snow. Huge numbers of soldiers defended against a single unnatural being, trying in vain to keep him from his goal, and dying by the score. The only thing that mattered to him had been taken, and he had come to reclaim it. He was the Guardian.

There was an evil thing in the dream, even more sinister than the Guardian. It too was old, cursed and blighted, and seething with rage and hate. It was weakened by failure, and retreated as the Guardian approached. Its final minions fell before the immortal killer as the cursed thing fled into the ruins.

The last soldier waited for the Guardian. He had been the leader of the blood-drenched, elite force. He stood defiant in his black uniform, towering over the body of a frail human sacrifice, proudly shouting that his lord would return to finish what they had started. The soldier placed his pistol against his temple and ended his life.

The final moments of the dream had a small bit of clarity to them. I was able to finally see the Guardian. He was a giant of a man. Every inch of his skin had been covered in strange tattoos. The ink lines moved like living things. He looked right at me across space and time. His eyes were solid pools of hate-filled black.

"Thou shalt die by my hand."

I woke up with a start. What a freaky dream . . . I had no idea what that had been about. Weird shapeless evil things, tattooed killers fighting in the snow, and a bunch of soldiers screaming in German. I blamed it on the drugs.

A cell phone was blaring an annoying downloaded ring tone. I think it was "Take Me Out to the Ballgame." I kept my eyes closed and pretended to be asleep. There was some fumbling and then Agent Myers' voice. "Myers." I eavesdropped intently, hoping to get an early clue to my fate. By nature, I'm not a particularly religious man, but I found myself praying that the stranger had been right. Twenty-four was too young to die. I would miss my parents and my brother, and I wished that I had more time to fix my relationship with them. I wished that I hadn't wasted so much time on the little things. It was too late for that now. My life came down to the contents of a single phone call, and the trigger pull of a Glock.

"Uh-huh. Yep. Uh-huh . . . Okay . . . Sure . . . Bye."

Well, that end of the conversation sure didn't help much. I stiffened up and waited for the bullet to blow through my skull and mushroom in my gray matter. For a long moment I wondered if Franks was a good shot. The last thing I wanted was to end up as a vegetable. Would it hurt? I bit my tongue. There would be no begging; better to end it this way than twisted into something inhuman at the next full moon.

The wait seemed to last an eternity. There were a few whispers and a small rustle of movement, but no flash of gunpowder, no crack of muzzle blast. The only constant was the quiet *beep-beep* of the machine matching my heartbeat. That particular pulse was noticeably faster than it had been a moment before. It was hard to pretend to sleep when electronic devices were so ready to betray you. My lungs ached from holding my breath, and my stomach muscles were clenched painfully tight. Some sick part of me hoped that my exploding head would make a real nasty mess on their cheap suits. Dry-clean that, you jerks.

Finally I heard the agents move. The door opened slowly. I risked a quick peek as the two FBI men walked quietly from the room. Franks looked dejected, deprived of his chance to legally kill somebody, and surprisingly enough Myers appeared to be politely trying to keep the noise down. The door closed and they were gone.

Slow minutes passed as I made sure they weren't coming back, but all was still. The call had come. The stranger's promise had been true. I was not infected, was still human, and wasn't going to die. I laughed until I pulled something in one of the many lacerations in my back and then I cried in pain and then in relief. As I said earlier, I was not normally by nature a pious man, but on that night I sure was. I sobbed and heaved as all of the stress left me spent and wasted.

There were two final things to do before I went back to sleep. I grabbed the bouquet of get-well flowers from Hansen Industries and hurled it across the room. It had been a stupid job anyway. Then I pulled the business card out, brought it up close to my face, and tried to read it with my blurry eyes. I couldn't focus well enough to read the fine print, but I could read the heading.

Monster Hunter International
Monster Problems? Call the Professionals.
Established 1895

CHAPTER 3

Physical therapy sucks. Recuperation sucks. And the never-ending itching that comes from under a cast has to possibly be the worst form of torture known to man. The worst, unless you happen to have your parents invade your home in an attempt to comfort you. My folks had flown in when they had been informed of the "incident," and had immediately set about being a huge nuisance.

Before that, however, my hospital stay had dragged on for another week. Apparently, dying, even if only for a minute or two, could be quite a stressful event. The doctors had been impressed that I was even alive. When I had asked one of them approximately how much blood I had lost, he had responded wryly with "most of it."

Treatment had consisted of me trying to move around without tearing anything. Gradually my strength returned until I was able to hobble a few feet on my own and even digest some of the hospital food. Detectives from the Dallas PD had come out to interview me. They did not say anything about supernatural monsters or the FBI agents, and believe me, I did not bring them up either. Instead the cops were under the impression that Mr. Huffman had been some sort of deranged serial killer high on PCP and armed with a 14-inch bowie knife. I was sure that my new friends from the federal government had arranged the crime scene to show whatever story they wanted, and it certainly didn't involve werewolves. The police thanked me for ridding the world of a very bad man, and told me that their investigation showed a clear-cut case of justifiable homicide. There was no indication that I was going to be indicted for anything, and they even arranged to return my .357 once everything was cleared through the prosecutor's office.

The local papers had run stories about my heroic defense against the crazed serial killer Cecil Huffman. In an amusing note the cover story featured both of our employee pictures. I'm sure that most casual readers would conclude that my picture showed the insane murderer, since I was big, young, muscular, swarthy, generally ugly, and beady-eyed. Mr. Huffman looked more like the victim type, a fat, middle-aged, middle manager, with big sad eyes and triple chins. Looks could be deceiving. During my hospital stay I had repeatedly turned away reporters. The last thing I wanted to do was to make up a story, or screw something up and draw the ire of the FBI. I had even turned down a potential guest spot on Oprah. My mom had been royally ticked when she found out about that.

The folks had arrived right before I was discharged. Now, don't get me wrong. I honestly love my family. They are good people. Crazy, but good.

"Damn, boy, you look like shit," was the first thing that my father exclaimed when he saw my face.

My father was an upstanding citizen, a decorated war hero and member of the tight-knit Special Forces community, a man who was respected by his peers. At home, however, he was an emotionally distant and stern man who had a hard time relating to his children. When I was younger I had taken this to mean that he did not approve of us or even really like us much. I had dealt with that by trying to follow in his footsteps. My younger brother had dealt with that kind of thing by dropping out of high school and forming a heavy metal band. While I had become a CPA, my brother's band had landed a record deal and was always surrounded by hot groupies and wild parties. I think I got the shaft in that deal.

Apparently my father was a little ashamed that I had gotten so torn up by a corpulent schmuck, when I myself was young, fit, and—since I had been brought up right—carrying a gun. I imagine that if Huffman had succeeded in eating me, my father would have been more embarrassed that a Pitt had lost a fight, than saddened by my actual demise. The last time my father had been obviously ashamed of me was when the Army recruiters had turned me down because of flat feet and a childhood history of asthma attacks. That had been a tough day for him.

He had brought his sons up to follow in his soldiering footsteps. In fact, the idea for my first name came from the Owen submachine gun that he had used to save his life in the backcountry of Cambodia during a war that never officially existed. He thought the name had a nice ring to it, and the actual gun had come in handy for mowing down communist insurgents after he was trapped deep in enemy territory with nothing but an obsolete Australian weapon older than he was. Believe me, as kids, we had heard *all* of those stories.

"Oh my baby! My poor poor baby! How did this happen? You poor thing!" was the first thing from my mom. It continued like that for several minutes in a barrage of hugs, kisses, and dampened tissues. Mom was the emotional one in the family. She also showed her love by cooking, which is why I was always the chubby kid growing up. In my house, if you weren't eating, obviously you were not loved. Needless to say, the Pitts tended to be big people.

They had taken me back to my apartment, where to my surprise they promptly settled in for a stay. I tried to assure them that I would be fine, and that I would not need any help. Since I could barely walk and was still covered in bandages I don't think I made a very convincing argument in favor of my independence.

Weeks passed as I gradually healed. My strength was returning, and after a few doctors' visits, I was running out of staples. I had to admit that I loved my mom's cooking, and between the lack of exercise, atrophied muscles, and 3,000-calorie meals I was starting to put on some weight. The trade-off came in the constant questioning. "Why no girlfriend? When are you going to get married? When will you find another job? What are you going to do now?" These were always followed by invitations to move back home where I could find another job and meet a nice girl.

Friends came to visit several times. Mom rented

lots of movies for me to watch. I caught up on my reading, and checked the want ads for a new job.

Dad mostly played golf.

This whole time the business card that I had received at the hospital lay discarded in a drawer in my bedroom. I had thought about calling the number, but couldn't bring myself to do so. It was much easier not to think about a world where creatures like Mr. Huffman existed.

The hardest part was not being able to talk to anybody about it.

One night I received a phone call from my brother Mosh. His real name was David, but it had been a long time since anybody other than our parents had called him that. Since I was the only one in the family that he ever spoke with, and that was only on rare occasions, he had not known about the Incident until then. He had called as soon as he had found out. We spoke for a while, him wanting the blow by blow, and me giving him the FBI approved version. Of everyone that I had spoken with, he was the one I was the most tempted to tell the truth to, but I really didn't want the government to kill me, so I refrained.

I had asked how he was doing. His band, Cabbage Point Killing Machine, was doing well and they were going to release their next album, *Hold the Pig Steady*, in the next month. I made him promise to send me a copy, and VIP passes for when his tour hit Dallas. He told me he would, as long as I managed to not get murdered before then. I gave him my word that I would try.

The night before my parents were scheduled to fly out, my father took me aside for a conversation.

He waited until Mom was occupied in the kitchen cooking another four-course meal, then motioned me into the living room.

"Owen, we need to talk."

"Sure, Dad. What's up?" It was not very often that my father wanted to speak with me. He usually just spoke at me, but tonight he seemed rather agitated.

"Look, son, let me just come right out and say it. I know you aren't telling us everything."

"Huh?" This was a surprise. "What do you mean?"

"I've seen your injuries. I've seen knife wounds, hell, I've *given* knife wounds. Those aren't knife wounds."

He had me there. I didn't know what to say so I just nodded.

"Plus, I know what you did to put yourself through school, and I know that you never told us because you didn't want your mother to worry."

That made me jump. I had had no idea that he knew.

"What do you mean, Dad? I worked in a warehouse."

"Sure you did, for a while, except after that you bounced in a biker bar, and you used to compete in underground fights for money."

"How did you know?"

"Remember crazy Charlie from my office? He had a gambling problem. Old guy would bet on anything. He caught one of your performances one night. Called me the next morning to tell me how he had seen my boy kick the living hell out of some tough customers. So I did a little checking is all . . . Did it pay good?"

Early on in life, I had discovered that I had a remarkable gift for violence, which had been encouraged and cultivated by my father. That, coupled with my physical ability to soak up a beating, had enabled me to make some pretty decent money on more than a few occasions. It didn't have the perks of accounting, but I do have to admit that punching people in the face had its own certain charms.

"Twenty percent of the house if you win. Five if you lose. Very illegal. I did the bar gig for a while. I was the cooler; they actually just let me hang out in the back and do homework until they had a problem." I neglected to mention that we had had problems on an hourly basis and it was the kind of bar where the local paramedics had our address memorized. "I only did that kind of thing long enough to pay for school." That was a shameful lie, but I could never tell my father the truth about why I had quit. "How come you never said anything?" I asked after a time.

He looked a little sheepish for a minute. Confused by emotion he quickly turned up the gruffness. "Not my business, you were an adult."

I believe that was the closest he had ever come to giving me a compliment.

"But anyway, what I'm getting at is I'm guessing you've got experience handling guys with knives." He had no idea. My body had a lot more scars than just the new ones. "I want to know how that asshole managed to wipe the floor with you, break walls, smash furniture, get shot ten times, and still manage to rip you open?"

"Drugs, I guess," was the only response I could think of.

He continued, "I've seen wounds like that before. I saw a guy who'd been mauled by a tiger once. Looked like what happened to you. He got raked up and down, dragged around. The cat toyed with him for a while. Unlike you, he had the muscles on his back eaten right off, right down to the bone like we would eat a fried chicken, and that was 'fore he got flipped over, and cracked open so it could eat the sweet spots out from his guts." I remembered that story, if I recalled correctly. Dad had shared the long gory version as a bedtime story when I was about six.

"I don't know what to tell you, Dad."

He looked me hard in the eyes. He was still a remarkably intimidating man, physically and emotionally. "Look, I know there's some weird stuff out there. I've heard stories from people I trust. I've seen a few things myself back in the day that no rational man can explain." He shook his head vacantly as if he was trying to forget something. "I guess what I'm trying to say is that I know you didn't just tangle with a normal man. If you want to tell me the whole story, I'll listen."

I didn't reply.

He scowled, eventually tired of waiting, and left the room without saying another word, no doubt ashamed of me once again.

They flew out the next day.

I cursed and swore as I hobbled through my apartment, crutch banging randomly into objects as I tried to make my way to the entrance. The doorbell rang again, and this time they held it down, and wouldn't let up. It was a very shrill doorbell.

"Just a minute!" I bellowed as I stumbled around the couch. My leg was getting much better. That had been by far the worst wound, and it was still the most tender, especially when I tried to walk on it. The rest of my injuries were healing nicely, and even my hand cast had finally come off. I promised myself on my long journey across the living room that if the person ringing my doorbell was with the media, I was going to shove my crutch through the reporter's chest cavity and leave the corpse propped up in the hallway as a warning to the others.

Peering through the peephole, all I could see was darkness. The hallway light had burned out again. "Who is it?" I yelled through the door, ready to give the crutch treatment if they said anything about a newspaper or television station. The media were apparently drawn to my story like flies to garbage, probably due to the made-for-TV movie feel of the whole thing. Serial killer thrown from a high building? Sounds like a winner to me.

"Earl Harbinger," came the muffled reply. "We met at the hospital."

I had almost managed to forget about that business card. *Almost.*

"What do you want?" I shouted.

"I need help with my taxes, what do you think I want?"

I debated opening the door. On one hand I could go back to my normal life, find a job, pretend that the biggest dangers in the world were good old-fashioned bad people, and sleep well at night. On the other hand I could get some answers.

Curiosity won out in the end. I unlocked the two dead bolts and opened the door.

Harbinger had brought a friend.

She was beautiful. In fact she was possibly the most beautiful woman I had ever seen. She was tall, with dark black hair, light skin, and big brown eyes. Her face was beautiful, not fake beautiful like a model or an actress, because she was obviously a real person, but rather Helen of Troy, launch-a-thousand-ships kind of good-looking. She wore glasses, and I was a sucker for a girl in corrective eyewear. Since I was ugly it was probably some sort of subconscious reaction in the hope that I might have a chance with a cute girl who couldn't see very well. She was dressed in a conservative business suit, but unlike most women I knew, she made it look good. If I were to guess I would have said that she was in her mid-twenties.

"Mr. Pitt?" she asked. Even her voice was pretty. She was a goddess.

I tried to answer, but no words would come out. *Talk, idiot!* "Um . . . Hi." Smooth . . . *So far so good, keep going, big guy.*

"You can, um . . . my name is . . . Owen. My friends call me Z. Because of my middle name. It starts with a Z. Or whatever works for you. Come in. Please!" Well, so much for smooth.

She smiled and held out her hand. "Julie Shackleford, pleased to meet you." Her grip was strong, with surprisingly callused, working hands. Her handshake sent the message that she was no wimp. Had I found the perfect woman?

Her eyes widened when she saw my face. The scar. It was healing nicely, but I knew that it was still grisly. Once the swelling went down I was left with a massive red strip that evenly halved my forehead, split the bridge of my many times broken nose and ended up on my cheek. It was brutal.

She looked away. "I'm sorry, I didn't mean to stare." She had a small hint of a Southern accent.

"It's no big deal. Just a scratch. Think of it as Harry Potter on steroids," I said, trying to make her feel comfortable. "Come in, grab a seat. You need anything to drink?"

"No thank you," Julie said. Julie . . . Such a pretty name.

"I'll take a beer," Harbinger growled.

"Sorry, no beer," almost adding that I didn't drink, but not wanting to look like a wuss. The truth was after spending so much time working around drunks, I never touched the stuff.

Harbinger just grunted in disappointment. They both sat down on my thrift store couch. It took me a minute to get my crutch repositioned so that I could move gingerly to a chair. It's hard to impress a pretty girl when you're a big clumsy oaf balancing on a stupid padded aluminum stick. I flopped down and dropped the crutch.

"Feeling better?" Harbinger asked.

"Much. Doctors say I'm healing fast. I got my cast off, and I can start doing upper body exercise again as long as I'm really careful not to push too hard."

"You lift?"

"A little bit," I answered. In truth, before the Incident I had been pushing just over a 400-pound bench press. I didn't look it, but that was the disadvantage of being both tall and stocky. Because of the injuries on my chest and the amount of time off, I knew that it was going to take a while to get up to that weight again.

"Careful you don't hurt yourself. You got banged up good. In fact I've never seen anybody take on a werewolf like that and live. Not without some good silver weapons at least, but tangling hand to hand, that's crazy. You were lucky." He talked about were-wolves like it was a common and everyday item of no special interest. Like a normal person would refer to a vacuum cleaner or a toaster.

"Mr. Pitt . . . Sorry . . . Owen," Julie started, "what we're about to say may sound a little weird, but after your recent experience you of all people will understand that we're not crazy. Earl and I represent a company called Monster Hunter International."

"Okay. I'm listening." Julie could tell me that she was from the moons of Jupiter and I would give her my full attention. Less weird than that? Piece of cake.

"MHI is a private organization, and we handle monster-related problems. I guess you could say that we are in fact Monster Hunters."

"Sounds reasonable." I smiled. It didn't sound reasonable at all. It sounded wacky as all get out, but if I told a shrink about my Huffman experience I would be in a padded cell inside of fifteen minutes. So I listened.

"As you now are aware, monsters are very real. They're out there, and are a serious threat to the world. Our company specializes in neutralizing monster threats," she said.

"Good money in that?" I asked jokingly.

Harbinger reached inside his jacket, pulled out a plain envelope and tossed it to me. I caught it.

"What's this?"

"There's a federal bounty paid on undesirable unnaturals. It's called the PUFF," Harbinger stated.

"Puff?"

"Perpetual Unearthly Forces Fund," Julie answered.

"Teddy Roosevelt started it when he was president. PUFF is a tool for controlling monster populations. It's a big source of income for MHI. We make the rest in contracts set up with various municipalities, organizations, and private individuals with monster problems."

"Go ahead and open it," Harbinger suggested. "The Feds weren't going to tell you about it, but you killed a newly blooded adult werewolf by yourself. That makes you the sole recipient of any bounty for that particular creature. I took the liberty of doing the paperwork for you. I didn't think you would mind."

Inside the envelope was an ordinary-looking check. Sure enough it was from the Department of the Treasury, with PUFF stamped in green ink under their insignia. It was made out to one Owen Zastava Pitt in the amount of $50,000.

I think that the noise I made could best be described as a squeak, only less manly. This could not be real. My job, which I had been fired from so recently, had paid less than that in a year. "You have got to be freaking kidding me!" Fixing Julie with an incredulous look, I did my best to raise a single eyebrow.

"Nope," Julie laughed. She had a beautiful sounding laugh. "That check is totally legit. The bounties change depending on the severity of the monster populations, and the number of human casualties. In this case lycanthrope attacks are at an all-time high, and this particular specimen had already taken a few victims the night before. Now if he had been older, or had eaten more people, then you would be looking at a bigger bounty."

"So you're telling me that the government gives

people money for killing werewolves?" I was prepared to take her word for it, but I was definitely going to limp down to the bank and try to deposit this thing as soon as they left.

"Yes, and other types of unnaturals."

"Others? So what else is out there?"

She shrugged. "Lots of things, but I don't want to get too far off of the subject. If you don't agree to our offer then anything I tell you can never be shared with the general public, or the government will arrange for you to have a chainsaw accident or something equally bad, and I'm not kidding about that one bit. They have a strict policy of keeping all of this secret. So before I tell you what else is out there, let me ask you if—"

I cut her off. "Zombies? Are there really zombies?"

"Owen, please, I need to . . ."

"Yes, there are zombies. A whole bunch of different kinds. Slow ones, fast ones. Nasty bastards," Harbinger said.

"Vampires?"

"Oh yeah. And let me tell you, they ain't the nice charming debonair kind of thing you see on TV, those suckers are meaner than hell. Trust me on this one; pop culture makes them all intellectual and sexy, there ain't nothing sexy about getting your carotid artery ripped out. There're actually a mess of different kinds of undead."

Julie sighed as she gave up on her pitch. I was going to find out what exactly was real, and Harbinger was more than willing to talk. He seemed to be enjoying himself, and also getting a kick out of Julie's discomfort.

"Bigfoot, the Yeti?"

"Yep, but no bounties because they ain't really a problem."

"Chupacabras?"

"Goat suckers. They'll tear you up."

"Giant mutant animals?"

"Sure, but the Japanese have cornered that market."

"Sea monsters?"

"Yes, but only bounties on the evil kind."

"Wow, no kidding? Space aliens?"

"No intelligent little green men, if that's what you're thinking of. If those are out there we haven't ever dealt with them."

"Ghosts?"

"We have a strict policy: we only hunt things that have physical bodies. No physical body, no contract, and no way to collect a bounty either. We stick with things that are flesh and blood, or at least bone, exoskeleton, or slime."

We continued on like that for a few minutes, with me thinking of every creature from every horror movie I had ever seen, and Harbinger letting me know if it was real or not. Every answer he gave was in total seriousness. If he was making any of this crazy monster stuff up, I sure would hate to play a game of poker against him.

Finally after asking about the creature from the black lagoon and finding out that that was actually based on a true story, Julie had had enough and jumped in. She elbowed Harbinger in the ribs. "Sorry guys, back to business. Owen, we're looking for new Hunters. Because of the nature of what we do, we can't exactly advertise. Usually we meet people through our business who have monster experience, and who have handled themselves well."

"I did okay, I guess."

Julie laughed again. Harbinger smirked. She pulled a DVD case out of her purse. "Do you mind?" I shook my head and she stood up and put the disk in the player and turned on my TV. "I don't think you've seen this. As far as your former company is concerned, and as far as the Dallas PD knows, this doesn't exist."

"Put it on channel three. There you go."

It was a black and white security video of the four-teenth floor of my former office building. The screen was split into four squares, each with a different view. It was surprising where some of the cameras were pointing, as I had never been aware of any cameras in those locations. There was even one that had a good view of Huffman's office.

"They have hidden cameras all over the place. I guess you folks have a big problem with employee theft," Harbinger stated. I knew I should never have taken those Post-It notes home.

The video started. The digital readout showed the time as 8:05. I thought that I looked silly, as most people do when they watch video of themselves. There was no sound, but it unfolded pretty much exactly as I remembered it. Only this time I was surprised by how fast everything happened. The transformation that had seemed to take forever actually happened rather quickly when seen from a strange angle in clinical detachment. The entire battle had been over in a matter of minutes, yet for me time had dilated down so that each fraction of a second had been an eternity. The creature was not nearly as intimidating on the screen as he had been when his hot breath was straining at my face. The third camera winked into static as my body was put through the ceiling tiles. We combatants would disappear from the cameras for a moment, only to reappear jerkily in another frame a few seconds later. In black and white I was surprised how plain all of our blood appeared on the walls. Finally I watched as I snapped the werewolf's neck and pushed the desk out the window.

I realized I was breathing hard.

Julie quietly shut the TV off and carefully placed the DVD back in its case.

"You just did okay, huh? Looks to me like you put up an amazing fight. You could have given up a bunch of times. You would be surprised. Most people faced with something out of their nightmares will just freeze up. Their brains can't begin to process what they're seeing, and by then it's too late, and next thing you know something from the great beyond is flossing with their spine. Hunters don't freeze. Hunters fight."

"Listen, I'm just a normal guy. I'm an accountant even. It doesn't get any more normal than that!" I exclaimed in defense of my average life.

Julie pulled a manila file folder out of her purse.

"What's that?" I asked.

"Your secret file from the Department of Homeland Security."

"If the government didn't want it stolen, they shouldn't just leave it out where any master hacker can break in and get it," Harbinger explained patiently.

"Owen Zastava Pitt, age 24. Born in Merced, California . . . Zastava?" Julie asked.

"My mom's family is mostly mixed Czech and Serb. It's an old family name. Like the place that made those little cars," I answered.

"Little cars?" she asked.

"You know, the Yugo."

"Oh." She continued, "Black belt in two martial arts. You wrestled in high school and took the state championship heavyweight division two years in a row. Homeland Security has you flagged because you're considered a militant right-wing gun nut. You became involved in competitive shooting at eight years old, and have a master rating in International Practical Shooting. You've placed in the top five in several different national level three-gun tactical competitions. You were ranked as one of the top young shooters in the country, though you've slipped over the last few years."

"Working too many hours, hard to keep up the practice routine." My father had been more drill instructor than dad, trying to prepare us for some kind of future apocalypse that existed in his paranoid imagination. I could hit targets at a quarter mile with a rifle before I could ride a bike. When normal kids went to summer camp and made crafts out of beads and twigs, my brother and I had gone on miniature death marches with giant rucksacks. Other children got sports, I got hand-to-hand combat training. I suppose showing up in a government database shouldn't have been too shocking.

"You tried to join the Army but were turned down due to some minor health problems. DHS also notes that you've participated in illegal pit fighting and in illegal sports gambling organizations."

I cringed, it not being something I was real proud of now.

"It says here that you earned a bachelor's and a master's degree in six years total, top of your class, passed the CPA exam the first time. National Honor Society," Julie continued.

After coming within a couple heartbeats of ending another fighter's life, I had devoted myself to being as boring as possible, no more pushing the limits, nothing but normal. And what was more normal than an accountant?

"You speak five languages fluently, mostly because of your extremely varied family background, and know enough to get by in several others. Your psychological profile says that you're a pathological overachiever with severe overcompensating tendencies as a result of your relationship with your father, and the fact that you were always the picked-on fat kid while growing up."

"Does it actually say 'fat kid'?" I asked in total bewilderment.

"Actually it says it in some sort of psychological mumbo-jumbo about body image and self-esteem, but I'm just paraphrasing."

"I wasn't fat. I was big-boned." I leaned back in my chair and rubbed my temples. I was amazed that all of this was from some government database. Chalk up a few more points for my antiauthoritarian side.

"Look, Owen, you're not a normal person; none of us are normal, either. MHI is a family business, my family. My great-great-granddad founded the company, five generations of Hunters. You haven't seen weird until you've met my family, so don't feel bad." Julie patted my knee. She touched me! I perked right up.

"We're not looking for normal people. Normal people scream and run and get eaten. You have to be a little different to do the kind of stuff that we do. I mean, heck, looking at your shooting scores, I've been shooting pistols since I was a little kid, and your classifications blow mine away. Your National Match rifle scores are equal to mine, and I'm the team sharpshooter."

As Julie said this I realized that I had in fact met the woman of my dreams. Attractive, smart, and a shooter? *Wow.*

"I don't know. I don't have any experience with this kind of thing. Aren't you better off with soldiers or Marines or Navy SEALs and stuff like that? My gosh, I'm an office dweeb."

Harbinger answered this time. "We have all of those, and we also have former truck drivers, school teachers, farmers, doctors, a priest and a stripper, and pretty much anything else you can think of. It comes down to finding people who don't have a problem coping with weirdness. The best Hunters are people whose minds are . . . flexible."

"Well . . . the pay seems good," I said as I held up the check.

"Keep in mind that was for you on a solo bounty. When you work with a team you share bounties with the team, and the company. However, people who try monster hunting as individuals usually get real dead, real quick. Working with backup is the only way to stay alive. But with the amount of business that we do, the pay's good," Harbinger said.

"How good?"

Harbinger shrugged. "We have a real problem with our experienced people retiring and buying small countries."

"I'm guessing it's dangerous?"

Julie shrugged. "I won't lie to you. It's super dangerous. Our job is to go head to head with the forces of evil. We lose a lot of people, but with well trained groups that work together as a team, we do better than any other group of Hunters, and that includes the Feds."

I sat silently in thought. My visitors didn't say anything for a moment. Finally Julie tried one last thing.

"Look, I'm going to tell you the truth. We have the most insane job in the world, many of us die young, and sometimes in really horrible ways. But this is the best job there is. It's never boring, and you get to do something really worthwhile. We're the pros, the go-to people when all hell's broken loose. When the situation is totally hosed, we're the ones they call. We do the job that nobody else can do, and we do it good." She said this with deep and sincere emotion. Julie obviously had a passion for her work.

I absently rubbed my facial scar. A random thought popped into my mind and I instantly muttered it under my breath.

"What was that?" asked Julie.

"A calling. Is hard, but is good."

"What does that mean?"

"I don't know, just something an old man said to me once. Short straw." I thought about the strange dream that I had had in the hospital. Had it happened while I was technically dead?

"Huh?"

"Never mind." I had to admit, I was interested in what they had been telling me, and I was a real chump when it came to a pretty girl, especially one who was smart, and into guns, to boot.

This was crazy. I had spent the last few years trying to be average just for once, until my boss had tried to have me for dinner and life had pulled the rug out from under me. The smart thing to do would be to push this whole incident to the back of my mind, and forget it ever happened.

But I did need a job, and Owen Z. Pitt, Monster Hunter, had a certain ring to it.

Ah, what the hell.

"Tell you what, Mr. Harbinger, Ms. Shackleford. I'm going to go down to the bank and try to deposit this check. If it's real, and I don't get arrested for trying to pass a make-believe check, I'm going to believe everything that you said. I'm in, on two conditions."

They waited for my terms. I paused as I screwed up my courage.

"If at any time I think this job is totally insane, I'm out of there. No questions, no ifs, ands, or buts. Don't think I'm kidding either. I've been shafted already, and I'm not going to do that again. You screw with me in any way, shape, or form and you can color me gone."

"We wouldn't have it any other way," Julie said. "And what else?"

"You, uh . . . need to have dinner with me tonight," I stammered, surprising myself with my own courage. *There you go, Casanova.* I had no idea why I had said that, it had just kind of popped out.

Julie looked momentarily taken aback. I could not tell from her reaction if she was flattered or insulted by my lame attempt to ask her out. Earl rolled his eyes.

"I guess you ain't talking about me," he said.

"No, I . . . uh . . . well, I just thought, you know . . ." It wasn't exactly poetry.

She did not respond immediately. I think I took her by surprise. I knew that surprise was good in war, but it wasn't necessarily what I was going for here. I have never been very good with women. Actually, that's an understatement. I turn into a bumbling incompetent oaf around them.

"Was that a lame attempt to ask me out?" she queried. "It's usually considered bad form to do that in what is basically a job interview."

"Well, I just wanted to . . . maybe ask some questions. About, you know—"

Earl cut me off. "There's some more business that I need to conduct anyway. I've got to go. Julie can fill you in on the rest of the details." He stood up. "You kids have fun."

"Earl, wait a second, what about . . ." Julie started to stand. My heart lurched. Had I offended her?

"Julie, you know what I'm talking about. You know what tonight is. Stick around. Fill Owen in on the details of our operation." He adjusted his bomber jacket.

She slowly slid back down the couch. *Way to go, Earl!* I thought happily. Harbinger made as if to leave. I tried to grab my crutch so I could stand to see him out.

"Not necessary," he said as he shook my hand. "I look forward to working with you."

"Me too," I responded before wincing at the amazing strength in the man's fingers as he easily crushed my much larger hand. He was far stronger than he appeared. I tried not to visibly show how much pain he was inflicting. He bent down and spoke low enough in my ear that Julie couldn't hear.

"That took guts, but be a gentleman with her, or I'll be displeased," he whispered. I had no doubt that his displeasure would somehow involve me becoming seriously injured.

I nodded. He let go, grinned evilly and patted me on the back, before swiftly leaving.

Julie Shackleford sat on my bargain basement furniture in my rundown apartment in a bad part of town and examined me quizzically. I had no idea what she was thinking. It was an awkward moment.

Finally she broke the silence.

"Want to order pizza?"

"So you know all about me because of that file," I said after swallowing a blob of cheese and pineapple. Delivery had been relatively swift, the pizza was good, and surprisingly enough Julie seemed to be enjoying our conversation. After the first few awkward minutes she had warmed up to my attempt at flirting, and was at least tolerating me. Her smile was contagious, and I felt better than I had in weeks. The sun was starting to set, and long orange shadows were cast through my barred apartment windows.

"Scary, isn't it? How much they keep track of people," she said, trying to be polite and not talk with her mouth full, and failing miserably. "You should see what mine says. If you read it you would probably be scared to be around me. They think I'm totally nuts."

"Oh, I don't know about that," I replied, going for another slice, trying not to lean forward on my bad leg too much. "You don't seem nuts to me, except for the whole good versus evil zombie werewolf thing at least."

She noticed my predicament and helpfully shoved the box closer on my little coffee table. My furniture was sparse and mostly cheap junk, but at least the place was clean, even if it was only because my mom had visited recently.

"They think everybody in this line of work is certifiable. They even think that about their own guys that Hunt."

"Like the two that visited me in the hospital?" I asked.

"Myers and Franks? Myers isn't so bad. Believe it or not, he worked for us before the government recruited him, but that was a long time ago. He had a bit of a falling out. Franks on the other hand is a jerk. I'm surprised he didn't kill you just to be on the safe side. We have to deal with the Feds once in a while. They watch us like hawks. They're actually in a special unit in the Justice Department, the Monster Control Bureau, that deals with problems like you."

"Problems like me, gee thanks. Anyway, I don't want to talk about those guys." I really did not. I wanted to talk about her. "Like I was saying, you've seen my file, so you have the advantage. Tell me about you."

"Well, first off, I'm in a relationship if that's what you want to know," she replied mischievously. "I'm just here as a professional courtesy."

Ouch.

"Really, I wasn't trying to say anything like that," I responded quickly.

"Owen, you may be a great accountant, and one heck of a shooter, but you're a horrible liar."

She leaned back on the couch and put her feet up on the coffee table next to the pizza box. I noticed that she was wearing heavy-duty boots that did not really match her conservative suit. As she made herself comfortable and her jacket fell open revealing her fitted shirt, I realized two things: a) She had a great body, and b) she was carrying a gun in a leather pancake holster on her right hip.

Not able to comment on a) in a polite manner, I instead remarked on b).

"What are you carrying?"

"This?" She reached around, drew the gun, dropped the magazine, racked the slide and expertly caught the ejected round in her off hand. She then passed it over to me with the action open while she rattled off the stats only another gun nut would appreciate. "Commander-sized 1911, Baer slide and frame, match barrel. Heinie night sights. Thin Alumagrips. Bobtail conversion to the frame. All Greider tool steel parts. Trigger and action job. It's a good shooter. I've carried this one for a year now."

I examined her gun. It was a gorgeous piece of work. The slide was so smooth it felt like it was on rollers. It was obviously used hard, but well cared for.

"Mind if I try the trigger? I'm a 1911 guy myself."

"Go for it," she said with a grin. She was proud of her gun.

The break was clean and light with no detectable creep. It was a very good trigger job.

"Who did the work?" I asked. It was obviously a high quality custom build. Being a serious competitor on a limited budget I did my own gunsmithing. My stuff tended to be ugly but functional. This specimen was obviously functional but it was so well fitted that it was almost a work of art.

"I did most of it myself," Julie said with obvious pride.

"Will you marry me?" I blurted.

She laughed, and it was such a pretty laugh. I reluctantly handed her gun back. She reinserted the magazine, chambered a round, and then took the mag out to top it off with the extracted round she still had in her hand. She paused for a second and then tossed it to me. Reflexively I snatched it out of the air.

Examining the cartridge, I noticed it was a strange design. The case was normal brass, but the bullet itself was different. It was shaped like an ordinary .45 bullet, except that it appeared to be a standard jacketed hollowpoint, with a shiny metallic ball filling the cavity. The two pieces appeared to be sealed together into a solid projectile.

"What's this?"

"Contrary to the Lone Ranger, silver bullets really suck compared to good old-fashioned lead. Silver's too hard, and it doesn't fully engage the rifling. It's lighter than lead, so you get really lightweight projectiles with lousy accuracy. It's pretty useless except for one thing: it's the only thing that will kill some of the stuff we face."

"Why is that, anyway?" I asked.

"Nobody knows for sure, but we have some theories. Most popular is it is a violent reaction of evil creatures to the thirty pieces of silver that Judas was paid. The Vatican's Hunter team says that it is because silver is a pure metal that represents goodness, while lead is a base metal of the earth. You get other weird ideas from Wiccans and mystics, but even science is stumped why silver works so much better on bona fide evil creatures. All we know is that it does. Lycanthropes can't regenerate, and even vampires feel pain from silver."

"Looks like a Corbon Pow'r Ball." That was a type of regular defensive ammunition that I had used a few times before. It used a ball stuck in a hollow cavity designed to squish back to force expansion of the bullet on impact, thereby increasing the severity of the wound.

"Good call. That's who we stole the idea from. The ball in front is pure silver. It penetrates well, and as the silver is forced back it expands the traditional lead slug around it. Usually the silver fragments off after a few inches and leaves a separate wound cavity. Best of both worlds. Still works like a regular bullet, shoots like a regular bullet, but enough silver to do a number on evil. We have them made for us specifically. They cost a fortune, so we only make them in .45 for pistols and subguns, and .308 for rifles. When we need lots of silver up close and fast, we use a modified silver double-aught buckshot."

"Now you're talking my language." I held up the bullet. "So I guess that's what the Feds were going to shoot me with if I had been infected."

"Nope, they use a sintered metal. Silver powder encased in a polymer matrix. Neat stuff, but the company that makes it only sells to the government." She caught the bullet when I tossed it back. She loaded it back in the magazine, inserted that back into her 1911 and reholstered without looking.

"You really know your stuff."

"Thanks. I love my job . . . I really shouldn't have

another piece, but this stuff is great," she said as she went for another slice of pizza. "I think you'll fit right in at MHI. It really is a great thing that we do, and we're a good company to work for."

"So about this 'relationship'?" I used my fingers to make quotation marks. Julie rolled her eyes at me behind her glasses.

"You don't quit, do you?"

"Isn't that why you guys want to hire me?"

"Tenacity good. Stalking bad."

"Okay, agreed, stalking bad. Especially when the stalkee is packing heat. So are you and Earl an item?"

Julie snorted and started to choke on her pizza. I couldn't tell if she was trying to laugh or not die. So I didn't know if I should be in on the joke, or try to perform the Heimlich maneuver.

"Earl? You've got to be kidding me. No. Oh no. Hell no. We're related. This is a family business. Why would you even think that? Earl's much older than me."

"He doesn't look that old."

"Let's just say that the man has aged well. Earl has been like a dad to me. He pretty much raised me and my brothers." There was an audible trace of her Southern accent when she said that.

"Why?"

She thought about it for a moment, as if debating whether she should tell me or not, finally she shook her head in the negative.

"Never mind. It doesn't matter." It was obvious it did matter, but it was a sensitive topic and none of my business. On that subject she seemed to be wound tight as a spring. "Just know that Earl is probably the greatest Hunter alive. If he tells you something, listen."

"So is your boyfriend a Hunter too?"

"Yes he is, and if you ask me any more personal questions, I'm going to beat you to death with your own crutch." She was only half joking, and in my current physical condition, she could probably do it without elevating her heartbeat.

We finished the pizza as the afternoon slowly turned into evening. Julie gradually filled in the gaps in my knowledge about her company, though she was tight-lipped and uncomfortable talking about herself. I did learn more about this interesting woman as she talked about her work, because it was so obviously a big part of her. Julie had worked in this field since she was a child, and seemed to know it very well. As the daylight fled, she started to glance nervously toward the window. I did not ask why.

She was a veritable encyclopedia of monster-related knowledge, and she even let slip the fact that she had earned a degree in ancient history and a master's in archeology because it pertained so much to her life's work.

When I had asked why those particular fields, she explained that the battle did not start recently, and she left it at that. The open window kept drawing her attention. It was dark outside. Finally I could not help but ask, "So why are you so distracted? What're you looking for?"

Julie sighed, and brushed back her long dark hair, looking relieved. She yawned, stretched, and stood, adjusted her jacket and prepared to leave. She patted her gun to make sure it was properly holstered. "I've got to be going."

"Why?" I asked, puzzled by the sudden change.

"You don't realize what tonight is, do you?" she asked.

"Thursday?" I answered helpfully as I grabbed my crutch and pulled myself out of my chair.

"I wonder if we stole the right file, because for a genius you're not real fast on the uptake."

I shrugged. I had no idea. She grabbed my arm and helped me stand up. Julie looked me in the eye, and I could see my reflection in her thick glasses. Her brown eyes were beautiful.

"It's been one month since you were attacked. The test came back negative, but they're not always right."

She guided me as I hobbled over to the window. The full moon hung low and bright above the Dallas skyline. I realized now why she had stayed. Other than my still sore leg and healing muscles, I felt fine. I wasn't spouting any hair, at least not any more than my normal prodigious amount.

"So it was a test?"

"Nothing personal. We just had to make sure."

"Oh." I could not think of anything to say. She had been prepared to kill me all along.

We silently watched the sky. I realized that she was still holding my arm, standing close, and I could feel the warm, soft pressure of her body against mine. There together, in the light of the moon, just the slight tenseness of her hands on the muscles of my arm, I could feel her breath on my ear. It was a good moment. I wished that it could last forever. Unfortunately she was only holding me to help keep my pathetic crippled ass from falling down.

Once she was sure that I was stable on my crutch she let go. She reached into her purse, produced a card and handed it over. The card had a set of directions, a very basic map, and a picture of a green happy face with horns.

"We're putting together a training class. It's going to be brutally hard, because we only hire the best. Once you have had a chance to think about it, if you're still interested, be at the location on that card in three weeks." I put the card in my pocket.

"I'll be there," I promised.

"Good. Welcome to MHI." She shook my hand in a professional manner.

"Thanks."

"I'll let myself out," Julie said. She started to walk away, leaving me to watch the moon.

Julie Shackleford made it a few steps, and then surprised me by turning around and coming back. I felt her full lips brush softly against my cheek in a brief kiss. Luckily the crutch was well grounded or I might have fallen headfirst out the window in shock.

"You're a sweet guy, Owen. Thanks for the nice dinner. See you in a few weeks." Then she glided away.

At least I waited for the confirmation of my front door closing before grinning like an idiot. It had been a good day after all. I had gotten some of my questions answered. I had found a new job, one that at least sounded interesting, even if it was a bit of a career change on the insane side. I had, in theory at least, a check for $50,000 in my pocket. And best of all, a pretty girl had kissed me on the cheek. Yes, it had been a great day indeed.

I pulled the card and examined it. I was going to Alabama.

CHAPTER 4

The next three weeks had passed quickly. The PUFF
check had surprisingly enough cleared. And with a
bloated bank account, I had packed my bags, sold
or given away most of my stuff, broken the lease on
my apartment, and driven to the middle of nowhere,
following the directions that Julie Shackleford had
left me.

Everything that I still owned was stuffed into the
back seat and trunk of my rust-brown Chevy Caprice.
All I had was a couple duffel bags with clothing, my
laptop, a few other supplies, and about a dozen guns.
There was no way I was parting with those. It was
a good thing that a Caprice's trunk is big enough to
suit a Mafia don.

Julie's directions had been printed on a 3x5 card.
Her parting instructions had been for me to meet at
the location listed at a certain time and date. She had
told me that food and lodging would be provided, but
she had not given me any other details.

I had driven straight through from Dallas to Alabama,

thoughts of the absurdity of what I was doing nagging at me the entire time. WELCOME TO THE HEART OF DIXIE, the sign on the border had proclaimed. I stopped once in Montgomery to pick up a better map. According to the card's directions the place I was driving to was nothing but an almost blank green spot on the map with only one road and one small dot for a town. Cazador, Alabama.

It took another two hours from Montgomery to arrive in Cazador, but a good half of that was spent driving lost through the forest. The trees were dense and the underbrush was thick and still over the iron-red soil. The country around Cazador consisted of beautiful rolling hills interspersed with many streams and creeks.

The town itself was really more of a village. There were a few small stores, a Baptist church directly across from a Church of Christ, and a scattering of houses. The buildings appeared old and weathered. An old sign near the road read simply CAZADOR, ALABAMA, POPULATION 682. A slightly newer sign beneath stated that guided tours of the catfish plant were available from noon until four. I'm sure that was a barrel of fun.

I stopped for overpriced gas, a soda, and to scrape the bugs off of my windows at the only convenience store in town. A few locals made eye contact but nobody spoke to me. I overheard a toothless geezer murmuring to the cashier something about fresh meat. I didn't care to guess if he was talking about me or the lunch menu.

Following the final directions on the card, I had taken a small, barely paved road through some more hills and into even deeper woods. It branched and I

kept to the west for another mile. I almost missed
the gravel turnoff. My main indication that I had
found the home of Monster Hunter International was
a small sign painted with the letters MHI and a green
smiley face. The smiley face had horns. As my car
bounced slowly down the gravel road I took note of
the many NO TRESPASSING and TRESPASSERS WILL
BE SHOT warnings.

Finally I came to an open gate surrounded by
high chain link and razor wire. Near the gate, a man
sat in a folding chair under the shade of a large
umbrella, relaxed and apparently listening to a big
battery-powered radio. He waved lazily as I braked
and rolled down my window.

He was an interesting-looking fellow, weathered
to the point that it was difficult to guess his age, a
little shorter than average, with a shaved head, small
wire-rimmed glasses over a blunt freckled nose, and
a thick red beard that was absurdly long and pointy.
The end had even been braided with a few decorative
beads. He was wearing a Rush Tom Sawyer T-shirt,
cargo shorts, and Birkenstock sandals. He looked kind
of like a granola-eating environmentalist type, except
for the worn M4 carbine hanging idly from a tactical-
sling draped over his shoulder. He was spitting the
remains of sunflower seeds into a cup.

"Hi. I'm looking for MHI," I said.

The man adjusted his glasses and looked at me,
head tilted at a slightly strange angle as he smiled
absently. Suddenly he clicked his tongue and pointed
at me.

"Big dude . . . Scar face. You must be that guy Earl
found. Threw a werewolf out a window?"

"That would be me." I realized that the boom box was set to a talk radio station, and the subject was something to do with black helicopters and cattle mutilation. "Julie Shackleford offered me a job."

"She does that a lot. We're a little short-handed right now, but that's a long story. Drive straight in, park in front of the biggest building. You're a little early, but a few other Newbies are already here. The Boss said that he would say a few words to you guys, so just hang out."

"Newbie?"

"New hire. Greenies. Monster bait. Organ donors. You know. It's slang."

"Oh, okay . . . I'm Owen Pitt." I stuck my hand out the window.

"Milo Ivan Anderson. Jack of all trades, master of a couple. Call me Milo. If you live long enough I'm the guy that gets to teach you how all of the cool stuff works." He shook my hand and grinned. His beard stretched halfway to his shorts. "See you around."

I parked in the lot that Milo pointed out, locked the doors out of habit, and checked out the surroundings. The MHI property could probably best be described as a compound. The main building appeared to be the only permanent structure, being constructed of heavy red brick and steel. It was an office building, but with narrow windows, obviously thick walls, and iron bars. It looked like it could pass muster as a fortress if the need arose. I wouldn't be surprised if there had been a big pot, full of boiling oil, just out of sight on the wide flat roof. As I entered I realized that the main doors opened into a small room that funneled down to a smaller set of doors. Suspended overhead was what appeared to be a heavy portcullis that could be dropped to seal the secondary doors. Very interesting.

An older lady was seated behind a massive reception desk. She smiled at me as I approached. At least the staff here was friendly. She had to be in her sixties and looked plump and cheerful. She was wearing a matronly purple knit sweater, but the large-frame revolver in her shoulder holster was printing pretty badly through the fabric.

"Hello, dear. You must be here for the orientation," she said.

"Yes. My name's Owen Pitt."

"Oh, I recognize you. You're the one that kicked that werewolf's ass. That was some mighty fine brawling, sonny."

"Uh, thanks, I guess."

"No, thank you. Earl showed us all that video. It was right entertaining. I hate werewolves. Used to hunt the sons a bitches once my own self. Used to could do a fair job in my day, till one of the bastards took my leg. This one here is plastic." She knocked on her plastic leg for effect. It made a hollow noise. "My old one was made out of wood, but it would swell up when it got humid. I reckon it does get mighty wet in these parts. No place at all for a wood leg. Could be worse. Old Leroy had himself a wood eye. Painted it brown, same color as the other. Summer time roll around, damn thing would swell till it would get stuck pointing in one direction. Poor old Leroy. He was a good one. Oh well, sign in here."

My signature was quick and sloppy on the clipboard. As an accountant you have to sign your name a lot.

You try to keep a pretty signature when you have to sign it a couple hundred times a day. There were at least twenty names ahead of mine.

"My name's Dorcas. Some kids nowadays snicker at that name. But my ma said that it was a right fine biblical name, and it has suited me for close to seventy years. Any punk kids make fun of my name, I'll put my plastic foot in their ass. Got that, boy?"

"Yes, ma'am." That was my instinctive response to crotchety old ladies. Especially former Monster Hunters strapped with what appeared to be a .44 magnum.

"Good, go down the hall. Double door on the right. That's the cafeteria and meeting hall. Now scat. I got business to conduct."

"Yes, ma'am." I hurried away so Dorcas could continue her game of solitaire on the computer.

As I strolled in the direction the receptionist had indicated, something caught my eye. I paused in front of a wall of small silver plaques. There had to be at least four hundred of them and they took up quite a bit of space. Not all of them had pictures, but all had a name, a birth date, and a death date. The oldest plaques mostly lacked photos, and the birth dates started clear back in the 1850s. It was a wall of remembrance for fallen comrades. There was an inscription in Latin carved into a large polished board at the top of the wall. *Sic Transit Gloria Mundi.*

Being an auditor by trade I could not help but notice the curious fact that almost a hundred of the newest memorials shared the same death date: December 15, 1995.

Whatever had happened on that date must have been a black day for the Hunters.

Also strange, there was a span going forward from that day, with no new death dates until a few in the current year. The six-year gap was conspicuous by its absence.

A group was waiting in the cafeteria. There were a few small pockets of conversation, but mostly they had pulled up chairs by themselves and were waiting nervously. Not being one for socializing, I grabbed a metal folding chair and took up residence in the back of the room. The fellow to my right was snoring loudly. To my left was a young Asian man, warily watching the others. He shook my hand and introduced himself as Albert Lee. When I asked him how he had ended up here he muttered something about spiders. Big spiders.

More people gradually arrived. To pass the time I studied the others. I caught a few of them studying me back. The group was about eighty percent male, and I would guess that the average age was probably just under thirty. Most of the Newbies looked relatively fit, though surprisingly there were a few people I would call gravitationally challenged. The group was a good demographic cross section of America, with the biggest numbers being Caucasian, but also some Hispanics, Asians, Blacks, and a couple of people like me of indeterminate race. Don't bother to ask. My ancestors really got around.

Finally when I counted about forty others in the room, I heard a voice bellow for everybody to quiet down and take a seat. Earl Harbinger paced back and forth at the front of the cafeteria. He was wearing the same leather bomber jacket, and he had the same intense presence, as when I had first met him. Several other individuals entered and took seats behind him. I recognized Milo from the gate, and there was Julie Shackleford. She smiled when she saw me. My heart skipped a beat.

"Hello. My name is Earl Harbinger. Many of you know me already. I'm the Director of Operations here at MHI. Welcome to our new Hunter orientation. Let's get one thing straight right off the bat. We hunt monsters. That's what we do. Every one of you has had the experience to realize that there is a lot more out there than you've been led to believe. In the coming days I would just ask for one thing. Keep your mind flexible. Don't get caught up in what you're sure is real, because if you can't believe in them, you can't fight them."

Harbinger stopped speaking just as an older gentleman limped into the room. He was tall and gaunt. A black patch covered his obviously empty left eye socket, and the skin on that side of his face looked as if it had been badly burned at some point in the distant past. He had a stainless steel hook instead of a right hand. His hair was thick and white, and had been neatly combed. He wore an obviously expensive, dark Italian suit. He walked slowly, one foot slightly dragging.

"Ladies and gentlemen. Let me introduce Raymond Shackleford, President and CEO of Monster Hunter International." Harbinger quickly sat down. Most of us started to clap politely.

The senior Shackleford shushed us and waved his hook in our general direction. "Enough of that nonsense. I ain't no politician." He paused, folded his arms behind his back almost as if he was at parade rest and proudly addressed the room. He had the air of an old Southern gentleman. The boom of his voice did not fit his frail appearance.

"Welcome to Monster Hunter International. My name is Raymond Shackleford the Third. You can call me sir, Mr. Shackleford, or Boss. Today you are going to get a little history lesson, so pay attention." He cleared his throat loudly. "My grandfather founded this company in 1895. Raymond Shackleford the First, but around these parts everybody knew him as Bubba. Bubba Shackleford was born and raised in this very valley, here in the heart of Keene County. One winter the good folk of Keene County started to disappear: sadly, some of them even came back, only they were not quite human any more. My grandfather formed a group of concerned citizens, best could be described as an angry mob, and took care of the problem. The fault lay with what we now know to be a vampire. Grandpa Shackleford lynched the creature twice, and when it wouldn't die they finally, in frustration, burned it at the stake. One by one my grandfather's men found every newly created vampire, and destroyed each in turn, until finally the county and Cazador township was made safe."

The old man coughed, then pulled a white handkerchief from his suit coat and wiped his nose. It was plain to see that he was not in good shape, but it was obvious that he still maintained an amazingly strong will and presence. I had met a few people like that before, mostly at Veterans' Day functions. They were the kind of men that even my father saluted.

"Word spread across the state, and then across the South. Bubba's reputation grew. Turns out that there were many other towns that had their own supernatural problems. Grandpa was offered what was for the time princely sums of money to travel and dispatch other monsters. As time passed he assembled a group of strong men to assist him. They learned from their mistakes and they improved their methods. In December of 1895 they formed Bubba Shackleford's Professional Monster Killers. It has a certain ring to it, doesn't it?" he asked rhetorically.

"A contemporary of my grandfather was one Theodore Roosevelt. As luck would have it, Teddy, being an adventurous sort, had had a few monster encounters of his own—once as the New York City police commissioner, and then again in Cuba during the Spanish American war. When Teddy became President he was hell bent on the creation of some means to keep the forces of evil in check. Thus the Perpetual Unearthly Forces Fund was begun, or as we like to call it, PUFF. This was intended as a bounty system to award entrepreneurial brave men who would aid the nation by destroying dangerous monsters. My grandfather was the first person awarded a PUFF bounty.

"Since those early days this company has led the way in the fight against evil. After taking big jobs in Mexico for Standard Oil and in the Caribbean for United Fruit, the name was changed from Bubba Shackleford's Professional Monster Killers to something considered a bit more respectable: Monster Hunter International. Grandpa's company grew in stature and wealth, and he was even offered a position of some authority with the government's newly created Monster Control Bureau. He turned it down because he hated the government and had vowed never to work for any Yankees." There was some laughter at that.

"Eventually my grandfather died doing what he loved. His son, my father, took over the company at that time. He, too, was struck down. When I was old enough, I became the head of this company, and I have seen it change from a small operation into the premier monster hunting organization in the world."

He suddenly coughed again, this time with much greater intensity, a deep racking hack that sounded painful and wet. He covered his mouth with his hook, and Julie quickly stepped to her grandfather's side to offer assistance. He gently waved her away and, looking very concerned, she returned to her seat.

He continued as if nothing had happened. "For over a hundred years, this company has fought the good fight, the noble fight. We have always fought in secret because the powers that be don't want the sheep to be scared. We are the sheepdogs, and there are wolves out there, as all of you know firsthand. But things have changed. We have entered dark times indeed. For a brief time the fools in power, who should have known better, declared our business illegal. They caved in to monsters' rights groups, and the bureaucrats who assured them that federal agencies could handle the problem. There was an executive order. We were shut down, our assets confiscated, and any of us who opened our mouths were threatened with jail time. The damn nanny state couldn't handle the idea of private citizens taking care of *their* business." He was becoming visibly agitated. That explained the gap in the memorial plaques, but not what happened on December 15th.

"Ha! Ignorant bastards just had to have their fingers in everything. Monster attacks went up three *thousand* percent in the six years PUFF was shut down. The government has long had a policy to keep the truth secret. That is why so many of you here today were paid visits by agents and threatened with physical harm if you talked too much. But with incidents going through the roof, they were not going to be able to keep the lid on for much longer. Even with the full cooperation of the media, word was starting to spread. Not all of those crazy folks on that Internet thing are as crazy as you might think." He grinned widely, obviously amused at that thought. "Once enough voters were getting eaten, Congress had had enough and pressured the next President to reinstate PUFF and revoke the executive order that had banned professional monster hunting.

"So now we have restarted operations, and are trying to move past our dark days. Unfortunately we are short handed, and the monster problem is out of control. We are spread thin, with only small teams of experienced Hunters scattered around the country trying to put out fires. On the bright side, with so many attacks, it certainly makes finding and recruiting brave people like y'all much easier." He gestured at us with his hook.

"Thank you for coming. I look forward to working with each of you who make it through our training process. It will be hard. Earl here is gonna be a mean one, but it's for your own good. I must be going now."

We all stood and clapped as he shuffled out of the room. Judging by the man's injuries and attitude, I was willing to bet that he was a student of the lead-from-the-front school of management. His savaged appearance was sobering though, and I'm sure it made a few of the other Newbies question wanting to try monster hunting as a career.

Harbinger stood and addressed us again. "Every single person in this room was contacted after they survived some sort of monster encounter. Trust me, just surviving means that each one of you is statistically significant. We personally invited about double the number of people that you see here. Most of those decided not to come. That either makes you braver, or maybe stupider than the others." There were a few chuckles from the crowd.

"I ain't joking, people. I'm going to be flat-out honest here. I'm sure you all saw that wall outside. The one with all of the pretty silver things on it? Each one of those represents a fallen Monster Hunter. There is just over a hundred years of history on that wall. What we do is dangerous, sometimes stupidly dangerous, but it is necessary, more necessary than you might even realize for reasons that you'll come to understand with time. The only way that we win is if we work together as a team and be every bit as tough and ruthless and clever as the things we're chasing.

"Many of you will wash out of training, or get kicked out if you ain't up to snuff. That's fine, so don't get hurt feelings. This job is not for everybody. There ain't no shame in quitting. If at any time you decide that you want to quit, no problem. Talk to Dorcas, we'll write you out a check for your time and there are no hard feelings. Keep in mind, however, that if you talk about us in public, the nice men from the Monster Control Bureau, that most of you have already met, will probably kill you." Harbinger moved like a predator, eyeing the group with unnerving intensity.

"Your teachers will consist of experienced Hunters. Listen to them carefully. Read everything that you're given. Your life, or the lives of your teammates, may depend on your skill or knowledge." Harbinger pointed at the small knot of people sitting behind him. "We're not normally teachers. The folks sitting behind me are actually my personal team. I trust each of them with my life, and any of them would trust me with theirs. If any one of them decides that any one of you does not have what it takes to be a Hunter, then you're gone. That is all. Don't screw around with us. We're much better killers than we are babysitters." I knew Julie, and I had met Milo briefly, but I had no clue who the others were. One instructor had a giant mustache, looked like a cross between a cowboy and a truck driver, and reminded me of Kenny's dad from *South Park*.

"Some of you are here because you're tough, some are smart, some are warriors, some are not, it doesn't matter. Everybody will go through the same training. We recruited many of you because of your brains, and though you will probably never need to be on an actual hunting mission, you will still be trained to the same standards in weapons, tactics, and other skills. You need to understand the people you are supporting as good as you understand yourself. Those of you we recruited because you're fighters, you will need to learn every single bit of monster-related information that the smart folks learn. For those of you who think you are both smart and tough, don't get cocky because you will probably be the first one to get eaten." A few people started to snicker at that, but most of us realized that it was not meant to be funny. I was feeling rather sober and slightly intimidated.

"Training will last until we decide that you're good enough. After that you will be assigned to your duties. Some of you will be assigned to Hunter teams. We have teams stationed all around the country. Those teams respond to crises as they develop. Other people will work in direct support of the teams. We will go into greater details about how this entire thing works as training progresses. Every employee will be paid bimonthly according to your position. Any PUFF your personal team earns will be shared by the whole company, with your team getting the largest percentage. Think of it as profit sharing. That means that if your team wins a huge bounty you don't get to keep it all. Be careful not to bitch too much about that, however, because the next week it will probably be some other team that wins the big one and not you. Don't worry, though, the lowest paid employee we have probably made more than most of you did in the last year. Our business is monsters, and business is booming." He showed a lot of teeth when he smiled. It almost reminded me of when Mr. Huffman was about to eat me.

"Any questions?"

It was quiet. I was positive that there were many questions, but everyone was afraid to ask. I debated for a moment, but once again, curiosity got the better of me and I hesitantly raised my hand.

"Pitt." Harbinger pointed at me.

"What happened on December 15th, 1995?"

The instructors looked at each other uneasily. The pause was unnaturally long, and I realized from the creaking of folding chairs and the rustle of forty separate adjustments that the whole room was looking at me.

"How did you know something happened on that day?" asked one of the instructors in an accusatory tone. He was a handsome man, and was dressed more stylishly than the others. I immediately didn't like him.

"Lots of plaques with that date. Beginning of the big gap," I answered.

"Are you a detective or a reporter or something . . ."

Harbinger held up his hand and the other instructor shut up.

"Worse, he's an accountant." Harbinger nodded in my direction. "Very astute of you, Pitt. I'll answer your question, but not today. Most of you in this room are not going to make it through training. Those folks get to walk away from this place and never look back. They don't need to know. Trust me, they don't want to know. For those of you who make it, I'll tell you the story personally, because I was there, and it affects every single Hunter. It was the straw that broke the camel's back and got us shut down. It was the one hundred year anniversary of the founding of the company, and it was one hell of a Christmas party."

The room was quiet.

"Any more questions?"

No one else said a word.

"Okay, everybody grab your crap and follow me. I'll show you where you sleep, and then we get started. We have work to do."

CHAPTER 5

Over the last week I had become very familiar with the compound. There was the two-story office building/fortress, and several smaller buildings that served as barracks, classrooms, workshops and armories. A few hundred yards away was the hangar, housing one medium plane and one strange-looking helicopter of foreign origin. Behind the asphalt runway, just far enough away so that the noise would not be distracting, were the shooting ranges. Bulldozers had pushed up huge berms of red clay soil to serve as backstops. A razor-wire-topped chain link fence stretched around the entire property, intimidating and sharp wherever it had not been overtaken with kudzu vines.

At that moment I was standing in front of a small group of other recruits on one of the shooting ranges. Ten yards away were five eight-inch steel plates, each one about a yard apart. Snugly tucked into my shoulder was the rubber butt pad of a slicked up Remington 870, pump-action, 12-gauge shotgun. The muzzle was kept at the low ready, and my trigger finger was extended safely along the receiver. I could sense the instructor standing behind me, holding the PACT timer right behind my head.

"Shooter ready?" he asked, voice slightly amplified through my electronic earplugs. The MHI-issued plugs were the most advanced that I had ever used. Totally comfortable, and wired into a communications net, they would block all sounds over a certain decibel level, while normal conversation was perfectly audible, even if slightly directionally distorted. I nodded.

"Stand by," the instructor said mechanically. I waited.

The timer beeped. This was the moment I lived for. In one fluid motion I deactivated the safety and pulled the shotgun into position. Leaning forward with my center of gravity one with the shotgun, I focused on the plates and willed them to be shot. I had no conscious thought of controlling the trigger. Having practiced drills like this thousands of times, the muzzle automatically sought out the plates. With each shot my arm pulled the pump without thought or hesitation. The barrel rose slightly only to settle almost instantly on the next plate. I absorbed and rolled with the heavy recoil of the double-aught buckshot. I knew that each shot had been clean even before the last payload of shot had impacted the steel surface. I lowered the gun as the last two plates fell with a clang.

"Holy shit." The instructor's voice was incredulous as he glanced at the electronic timer. It was designed to pick up the sound of each shot and digitally record it. It was a very handy training device. "One-point-eight-seven seconds. You did a Dozier drill in one-point-eight-seven with a pump shotgun and full power buckshot. That was unbelievable."

I stayed facing downrange. My personal best on this particular drill had been several years earlier in a match at 1.75, but that was with one of my personal guns that I had worked over myself. Contrary to popular myth, a shotgun pattern is not a huge room-clearing boulder of death; at ten yards it is usually smaller than a basketball. The real key is learning how to be one with the recoil. I had been doing stuff like this since I was a little kid.

"It sounded like it was full-auto," one of the other newbies said.

"Fluke," said another voice that I had seriously grown to dislike. "Have him do it again."

"Okay," said the instructor, a former U.S. Navy SEAL turned Monster Hunter named Sam Haven. He was our main weapons and tactics instructor. Sam was a the walrus-mustached man, a burly guy with a penchant for western wear, rodeo belt buckles and Stetson hats. He was also a bad mo-fo, whom I would never on my best day want to mess with. "Load up."

Somebody else pushed the button to activate the pneumatic target system. The five plates reset themselves with a hiss. I decided to show off a little for the crowd. Since the action was open, I quickly plucked a spare round of buckshot from the elastic sidesaddle mounted on the shotgun's receiver. I dropped it into the chamber, and instantly slammed the pump forward. Instinctively my support hand moved to the bandoleer of spare shells strapped across my chest. Grasping four cases, I palmed them under the loading port and rapid fire shoved them in as if my hand itself was a

spring-loaded mechanism. *Snick, snick, snick, snick.*
Four shells loaded in under two seconds.

It was a trick used by three-gun competitors. We
would often shoot in long field courses involving rifles,
pistols and shotguns. The shotgun portions sometimes
consisted of twenty or even thirty separate targets.
Since we were scored according to our total time,
and since shotguns are low capacity weapons of five
to nine shots (with some exceptions), the winners were
the people who could keep their weapons loaded the
fastest. Combine large groups of hyper-competitive type
A personality gun people, and I guarantee you will see
some amazing and creative ways to do things.

I heard another Newbie say something about a magic
trick. Not magic my friend, just the result of practicing until my thumbs were a mass of nerve-deadened
scar tissue. I tucked the shotgun back into the correct
position, positioned my feet, and squared off against
the targets. I indicated my readiness to Sam.

He leaned in close and spoke loud enough that
he knew I would pick it up, but quiet enough that
the rest of the class would not. His breath smelled
of Copenhagen chewing tobacco.

"You're gonna have to show me how you do that
loading trick."

I grinned, and answered, "Shooter ready."

Beep. This time I was really in the zone. The five
shots came out as a continuous thunder of buckshot
pelting steel to the ground. I lowered the smoking
muzzle.

Sam paused before saying the time. "One-point-
eight-two seconds. Hot damn."

I could not help but gloat a little as I smiled for

my nemesis. Grant Jefferson. The smug bastard had only been able to do it in 2.5, which was still pretty respectable, but not even close to as fast as mine. And the best part was that he knew it. He was the one who said my first run had been a fluke. Grant was not used to being bested at anything. I enjoyed watching as he stomped off in frustration. He did not like me, and the feeling was mutual. I handed the shotgun over for the next shooter.

Grant was no Newbie. He was a full-fledged member of MHI, and also one of our instructors, though he was the junior man on Harbinger's team. He had only come out to shoot in the hopes of showing us poor folks how it was done. Grant was totally my opposite. Lean and handsome, witty, charming, a product of the finest schools, and descended from the oldest established (as in super wealthy) New England families. He even had nice hair. He was the type of person everybody liked, and everybody wanted to be liked by.

I wouldn't trust him as far as I could throw him. I thought he was a pompous ass from the moment I had met him, and I felt the primal and instinctual need to beat him up and take his lunch money.

But the real reason that I hated his guts was that he was Julie Shackleford's boyfriend.

Julie and I had only spoken briefly since my arrival at the compound, and that had been mostly a "Hi, how are you" kind of thing. I had been totally swamped with training, and she was always occupied with one piece of business or another. It wasn't like she had ever even given me any sort of indication that she liked me as anything other than as an employee, so I don't know why the thought of her dating a jerk like

Grant bothered me so much. As much as I hated to admit it, I had a horrible crush on her.

Sam interrupted my reverie. "Pitt! I want you to tell everybody else how you shoot like that. I've told y'all what I know, and most of you still can't shoot for shit, you damn bunch of worthless derelicts, so let's get a fresh perspective. The pump is not your main weapon, or even your first choice, but there're times when it is the absolute best thing you can have. We have a lot of specialty rounds that won't run through a semi. Every one of you needs to know how to use this thing because one of these days it might save your life." Knowing how to do things because they might someday save your life was the mantra of our experienced Monster Hunters.

The former SEAL spit a mighty wad of tobacco juices into the gravel. That was good. I noticed that most of the time he just swallowed the stuff. That could not be healthy.

"Okay. Um . . ." I looked over the group and thought about what to say. "What I'm seeing from most of you is that you aren't really familiar with your weapons yet. You need to get to the point where your gun is an extension of your body. You don't think about shooting, because if you're thinking then you're going too slow. You just let the shot happen. Shotguns are more of an instinctive weapon than pistols or rifles. Some of you guys need to relax and let it flow."

I pointed at one of the other Newbies, a muscular black man with dreadlocks. "Trip here is a great example. When he uses the pump, it's shoot, dramatic pause, pump, pause, shoot, pause, pump. You're thinking too hard. Thinking takes time. It's just boom and go. Like playing an instrument, you don't think about the notes, you just play." He nodded in understanding. Trip and I had hit it off, and he was currently my bunkmate in the barracks. His real name was John Jermain Jones, and he was at a loss to explain what his folks had been thinking when they had come up with that combination. The nickname that had stuck was Triple J, and after a week, most of us just called him Trip.

Trip had been recruited by MHI after a voodoo priestess had placed a curse on his small Florida town and caused some of the recently deceased to rise from their graves to feast upon the brains of the living. He had solved the zombie problem with judicious use of a pickax. He was a great guy, and so far his only real challenge in training had been his lack of exposure to firearms, though he was coming along really well with the subguns. They just suited his personality more. Considering that a year ago he had been a high school chemistry teacher, he was actually one tough dude.

"Then the other problem I see is that some of you are just kind of recoil sensitive, like Holly." I pointed out the next Newbie. Holly Newcastle was an attractive young woman with bleached blond hair and an amazing boob job. She never told the rest of us how she ended up at MHI, but apparently she had worked as a stripper, or as she preferred, exotic dancer, before being recruited. The rumors were that it had involved a hot lesbian vampire, but I'm pretty sure that that was just wishful thinking by most of the guys in the barracks.

As far as I could tell she had exactly zero experience with any sort of firearms, but she was coming along gradually. She really surprised me when it came to the class portion of our training; she had an amazing ability to soak up knowledge and monster-related trivia. She may have looked like the stereotype, but she was no dumb blonde. I had no doubt that whatever she had done to get herself recruited by MHI, she had done very well.

"Holly, the shotgun kicks, but once you master the correct form, you learn to just flow with the recoil and it's no big deal. It's all about proper fit, and how you hold it. If you're doing it right it doesn't hurt at all."

"So what you're saying, Z, is that it's kinda like sex. If it hurts, you must be doing it wrong?" She smiled seductively and winked. I blushed. Everybody else laughed, including Sam the instructor.

"Pretty much." I had a sneaky feeling that Holly wanted me to help her with more forms than just her shotgunning. It's kind of a bummer that for a person with such a dark complexion my cheeks turned red so easily. "Seriously though, fit is very important; we need to find you a stock that's a couple of inches shorter." I hurried along before anybody thought to make a nasty joke about that comment.

I continued my demonstration to the other new recruits. We were an odd collection. Ages ranged from mid-forties all the way down to barely old enough to drink. We had people from all parts of the country and all walks of life. We had everything from an Army Ranger to a taxi driver, from a narcotics cop to a librarian, and we even had a plumber. Take my word for it, you do not want to hear the detailed account of his first monster encounter.

Despite our differences, we all had a few things in common. Every single one of us had come face to face with something from mankind's darkest imagination, and every single one of us was a survivor.

At the beginning of our training we had been informed that not all of us would make it, and they had not been kidding. The experienced instructors made judgment calls as necessary, and many a recruit was sent packing with an extremely generous severance check and an admonition not to talk too freely about what they had learned. Other Newbies quit on their own. Some could not handle the physical stress, others, the mental. There was no real shame in quitting. Anyone was free to leave at any time, and many did. I thought about it a few times myself.

I was too stubborn to admit it to anyone, but every day that I had been here, I had struggled with the idea of what we were doing. I was torn, part of me loved the idea and the challenge, but the part of me that had sought to be normal for so long was having a real hard time adjusting to the fact that I was learning how to kill monsters for fun and profit.

The physical training was difficult, though according to our former Ranger it was a total sissified cakewalk. Personally, my leg was still tender and weak, and the running was killing me. I hate running. I was still walking with a limp, and I had despised running when I was totally healthy. Running is for skinny people.

Weapons and tactics was my favorite segment. Not just because it was what I had done for fun for most of my life anyway, but also because I excelled at it. Many of the Newbies struggled through, while others would never have what it took to work as a well-coordinated team, armed with lethal weapons, operating seamlessly together under intense pressure. That was fine. We had been told early on that not all of us would end up as the tip of the spear, on an actual fighting Hunter team. There was plenty of other work that also needed to be done—research, support, admin, technical stuff, and other jobs—but every employee of MHI was to be proficient enough that they could stand in as an emergency replacement if needed.

Out of our current group I was guessing that about half of us would be assigned to Hunting teams. Not bad considering that we had started with forty recruits and now we were down to only twenty. There were a few I was not sure about, who could probably go either way, and then there were the last few, who personally I was not comfortable with even having loaded weapons anywhere near me. Some people just did not have the proper mindset to ever rise above mere proficiency with a firearm.

The classroom sessions were by far the most educational for all of us, because regardless of what kind of bizarre background somebody might have hailed from, the things we were being taught were guaranteed to be new material.

Earl Harbinger sat with his feet up on the desk. In one hand he held the remote control for the slide show, and the other held a yardstick that he used to point out interesting things. The photos on the slide show were disturbing to say the least.

"There's many kinds of undead. Undead is basically a catchall term for any being that's scientifically dead, yet still animated. They range from your basic zombie, which is nothing more than a flesh-eating corpse, all the way up to your virtually invincible master vampires and pretty much anything you can think of in between. You'll need to know them all—their strengths and especially their weaknesses." *Click*. This slide showed a large number of chewed-up corpses littering a suburban street. It could have been in any town in the country. Some of the modest ranch-style homes in the background were on fire. "Undead are our bread and butter. In North America alone we average at least one incident involving them a month. Factor in South America and the Caribbean and we probably have a Hunter team working an undead outbreak at any given time. With your basic lower-level undead, the key is a swift response. They multiply like rabbits, and the denser the human population, the more danger there is."

Click. The next slide appeared to have been taken with a cheap disposable camera at a really bad angle. The subject was a woman lunging with filthy hands outstretched toward the unseen photographer. Most of her face was missing, and her lower jaw consisted only of exposed bone, but she did not appear to notice. Her eyes were wide and hungry.

"Zombie. The walking dead. Not very fast. Not very smart. They'll head straight for you, they never stop, they feel no pain, they never tire, and they never quit. Luckily they're about as creative as broccoli. The real danger is their bite, as the guy taking this picture found out. A single bite is infectious and the victim's destined to end up a zombie themselves. The worse the injury, the faster you die, the faster you come back. George Romero was an optimist. Yes, head shots work, but you've got to really damage their brains for a reliable stop." We had learned that oftentimes cultural and entertainment ideas about monsters had some basis in fact.

"Where do they come from?" one of the class asked.

"Voodoo," muttered Trip. The twenty remaining Newbies sat on metal folding chairs behind rickety plastic tables. We were in a small room located in the main building. The air conditioner kept us alive in the freshly arrived Alabama heat.

"That's one possibility, and a good thing to keep in mind. If you can bag the person that animated the dead to begin with, by all means do it. Animating the dead is a serious felony, and the Feds usually pay a good reward for renegade witch doctors or mad scientists. I've got to keep going, though, because we have a lot to cover. All of this information is in your packets, and I'll get to specifics later, today is just the overview. Last thing on zombies, PUFF is usually about $5,000 a head, depending on the severity of the outbreak."

Click. The thing in the picture had obviously once been a person, but was now a hunched and rotting pile of rags and jagged edges and pointed teeth. The creature held what appeared to be a human leg in its mostly skeletal hand. It looked as if its lunch had been rudely interrupted by the flash of the picture. "This is a ghoul. Think of it as a super zombie on crack. Much smarter, much faster, way harder to stop. Luckily they're rare, which is a good thing because the one in this picture soaked up about two hundred rounds before it finally quit kicking. Head shots don't usually work, though they tend to slow them down. Your best bet is to hammer them until you break down their skeletal structure to the point where they just can't fight anymore. Then burn them to be sure. They're usually found around cemeteries, as they're carrion feeders. PUFF for a ghoul runs around 20K."

Click. "This is a wight. Toughest of the zombie family. One of old Europe's least popular exports." This picture took me by surprise. Sure the creature was as nasty as expected, appearing to be a normal man except for his horribly distorted visage, sharp, black teeth and red eyes, but this picture caught my attention because it was an action shot. Julie Shackleford was in the corner of the frame, with a long spear in her hands, keeping the creature at bay while it clawed at her. She was wearing some sort of strange body armor that I did not recognize. Her dark hair had been captured flying wildly around her head like a halo, and there was an intense look of fear and concentration on her face. She was frozen in midmovement, gracefully lunging toward the claws of the undead beast. It was like a cover shot from *Sports Illustrated* only this time the sport was Mutant Tag and the penalty for losing was painful death.

I studied her face. She was much younger, far too young to be doing what she was doing. Not as gorgeous and distinct then as she would turn out to be, but obviously filled with courage. She was wearing her glasses, but I could still see her brown eyes, and her teeth were a hard white line in her face. My heart knotted at the sight of her in danger, though obviously that incident must have turned out just fine. She was beautiful.

I'm such a sap.

I snapped out of my reverie and tried to pay attention to Harbinger's lesson. I had missed part of what he had said, but I did not dare ask him to repeat it. He was finishing up on the dangers of facing wights.

"Their touch causes immediate paralysis, even through armor. It wears off quickly, but by then it's usually too late. They can be insanely strong. So don't screw around against these without backup and heavy weapons."

"What happened?" I blurted.

"Huh?" he answered.

"In the picture, with this . . . wight."

Harbinger paused. Probably debating whether he should rip me for butting in, or just tell the story. He was notorious amongst the Newbies for not telling the stories behind their adventures, as opposed to Sam or especially Milo who seemed to love it. Finally the internal battle was ended and he decided to share. However, the look he fixed me with let me know that I would be running laps until I puked because of the interruption.

"Outside of Sandusky, Ohio, October of '95. Just before Halloween. Crazy time of year in this business. My team was taking care of a ghoul problem at an old cemetery, when this one surprised us. We didn't expect a wight. It popped out of the ground right in front of our vehicle, crushed the whole front end with its bare hands, and smashed through the window like it was nothing. I was in the passenger seat and it was on me so fast that it was a blur. It hit me and all of my muscles locked right up like I was frozen. Milo was driving. It nailed him too. Julie was in the back seat. She opened up right between us with her pistol, surprised it apparently, because it quit trying to kill me and Milo. The wight jumped on the roof and started peeling it back to get her. She bailed out with that spear." He paused and chewed on his lower lip for a moment.

"Make a note, it was a good thing she didn't just keep using her gun. Firearms will stop a wight eventually, but *eventually* is the key word. See, the longer an undead like the wight exists, the stronger it becomes. New ones are pretty easy to kill, but this particular son of a bitch dated back to the Civil War. They can take forever to quit, so you work in teams, hold them off you while you pour fire into them. The rest of the team heard the commotion on the radio, and they were coming fast, but not fast enough.

"So anyways, Julie gets out and uses the spear to hold it back. Every time it moved, she would stick it. You can see in the slide that it has a catch past the blade to keep creatures from slipping down the shaft to get you. She kept sticking it and basically played keep away. It couldn't reach her as long as she kept stabbing it, but there was no way that spear was going to put it down. The guy that took the picture was no help. He was just some bozo bystander. Great shot though. Finally the feeling returned to my limbs enough to flop out of the Suburban and I lit him up."

"Lit him up?" somebody else asked.

"Flamethrower. Don't fight high-level undead without one. Once its flesh was on fire it was only a matter of time before it ran out of steam. Julie pinned it to a mausoleum door and held it there until it quit kicking. Took forever. Mean sons o' bitches."

"How old was she?" Holly asked.

Harbinger thought about it for a moment.

"She had just turned eighteen."

"Damn."

"It runs in the family." He returned to the lesson.

Sawing off a human head is harder than it looks. The body tends to flop around every time you hit it, and it makes a really nasty mess. Once goo gets on the handle of your knife, it gets even worse, and the next thing you know, your blade is glancing off of bones that you didn't even know were there. I grunted as I strained the blade against the rubbery flesh.

"Damn it, Pitt, don't saw. This ain't gardening. It's killing. Chop it!" Sam shouted at me. Sam always shouted.

Responding to the order, I raised the heavy knife over my head and brought it down with as much force as possible, this time chopping completely through the tissue and breaking the vertebrae. The cadaver's head rolled off the table and landed on the floor with a damp thud.

"Much better!" the instructor bellowed. "See that, class? Don't screw around with them. There are some things that don't quit until you take their heads off. If you have got to do it, do it quick. Solid whack like you're chopping wood. Don't pussyfoot around. And remember the fresh ones squirt more!"

Our class of remaining Newbies was slowly shaping up into a coherent team of Hunters. Currently we were standing in a small refrigerated room near the hangar, known as the Body Shack. MHI had saved the most disgusting lessons for the last of us. I'm sure that staking and beheading corpses was practical training, but I believed that the main reason we did this was to weed out the trainees who couldn't handle the sheer nastiness of lopping off a human head.

It probably would have been more efficient to do the horrific stuff first, as it really took out anyone with a weak stomach. According to Milo the reason we saved it for this late in the training was that it was hard to get a good supply of medical school leftover bodies. By saving this part until most of the trainees had washed out he had to scrounge up fewer corpses. Milo was a pretty efficient guy.

"Next team. Newcastle and Mead," Sam said to Holly and Chuck, the next people in line, as Milo used a hose to spray down the floor. Several of the other Newbies had lost their lunch on this exercise. Mingled fluids coagulated around the central drain.

Placing the gore-splattered knife on the table, I stumbled away to wash my hands. They were shaking badly and I felt a strong urge to vomit. Trip was already at the sink scrubbing furiously.

"Dude, that sucked," he hissed.

"Next time I stake, you chop," I replied.

"Hey, you called heads. Not my fault."

"At least it wasn't the Gut Crawl."

He frowned at me. "Come on, man, I'm already trying not to barf as it is, don't bring that up."

The Gut Crawl had consisted of a single Newbie wiggling through a long section of pipe filled with cow entrails. Between the dark, the smell, the heat of the pipe and the horrible *squishiness* of it all, it was probably the worst experience of my life, up to and including actually dying. Supposedly it had been

a test of our ability to deal with disturbing surroundings and still keep our wits. Personally I thought it
was Harbinger torturing us. Two of our class had quit
rather than do it, and when I had been stuck halfway
down that dark pipe, covered in slime and feces and
intestines, I had envied them. One other trainee had
made it halfway down the pipe, only to suffer a panic
attack and lock up. All three of them had been given
fat severance checks and sent home.

There were only a dozen of us left. Judging by the
standards of our instructors, it was no surprise that
MHI was currently short-handed. Harbinger had been
very up-front about it though. He was a firm believer
that the harder we sweated in practice, the less we
would bleed when it was for real.

Holly finished her staking and came over to wash
up. She seemed unperturbed by the minor fact that she
had just used a hammer to drive a sharpened wooden
shaft through what had once been a real live person's
rib cage. I had been surprised by our former stripper.
Nothing ever seemed to faze her, and she attacked
every job with a vengeance. We still had not learned
her story, but it was obvious that she well and truly
hated the other team, and she was looking forward
to exacting some payback. If that required crawling
through guts, or chopping off limbs, no problem.

"That wasn't so bad. Chuck got stuck with the head.
Poor guy, he brought it on himself though," she said,
flashing us with a wicked grin.

"How?" asked Trip, still washing his hands. I had
news for him, no amount of water was going to make
us feel clean after what we had just done.

"He always goes rock. Never paper or scissors.

Dumb ass." She examined the old blood staining her nails. "By the way, I overheard Dorcas talking to Milo. Harbinger's pretty happy with how we're doing. We're going to get the whole weekend off."

"Awesome," I exclaimed. We had been training hard for a solid month. I'd be more than ready for a break this weekend. With the prospect of an actual couple of days off, I suddenly didn't mind so much being covered in gore. "It'll be good to get out of here."

"No kidding," she replied, then turned toward Trip who was adding more soap and giving it another try. "Dude, Trip, you need to hurry up, the rest of us need a turn too."

"Ugh, you have no idea what kind of bacteria is in something like this," he said. "You've got to do a good job sanitizing."

"Weren't you a science teacher?" Holly asked.

"Chemistry, and I subbed band, and I was the assistant football coach. It was a small school." Being his roommate, I knew his story well. Having to cave in some students' heads once they had joined the ranks of the undead really tended to mess up a teaching career.

"I figured with all of the frog dissecting you wouldn't be so damn squeamish. Hey, you have some blood or snot or something in your dreads." As he reached up in disgust, Holly cut in front of him to wash her hands. "Sucker."

With a thwacking noise and a flourish Chuck took his cadaver's head off, and Sam bellowed at us the fact that we did not do too bad for a bunch of derelicts, thus ending another day of training.

◈　　　◈　　　◈

My breath came in ragged gasps. I had long since passed the point where I could control it. The muscles in my legs were on fire, especially where Huffman's talons had pierced me, and my feet and knees ached with each footfall. Blinking away the sweat in my eyes, I pushed on, trying to once again find that point of oblivion where the pain didn't matter. I hate running. All big men hate running. Sure, I could sprint, but you don't see very many three-hundred-pound marathoners for good reason. Only crazy people run for fun.

The last mile of forest trail was the worst. It had the steepest hills and the most rutted path of the whole trek. But I took comfort as I made my way up the red dirt road, as we were almost done for the day. It had started just after dawn, with hours of physical training, tactics, armed and unarmed combat practice, monster class, and now the sun was down and we were limping in from a six-mile run from hell. Finally the trees thinned, and I even managed to smile as we passed the kudzu-covered chain link fence to enter the compound. Most of the Newbies had already arrived and were crashing out on the available benches or stretching on the grass. The good runners like Trip, Lee, and Mead looked almost relaxed and refreshed from the little jaunt. Trip's good natured thumbs-up made me want to beat him to death.

"About time, Pitt," Grant Jefferson shouted. He glanced at his stopwatch in disgust. "Pathetic. Just pathetic." He had led the run and had made most of the rest of us look bad. Of course, some of us came out looking worse than others. One of the other Newbies stumbled off to the side to puke. Grant just smirked. "All right. We're done for now. Stretch out tonight, because we're doing this twice tomorrow." Everyone groaned.

I sat on one of the empty benches and put my head in my hands. I knew that I was supposed to walk around and gradually let my heart rate subside to avoid muscle soreness, but man, I just needed a break. I excelled at everything physical except for this. Gradually my panting turned to normal breathing, and my heart was no longer pounding away. The other Newbies began to wander off toward the barracks for some much-needed sleep. I stayed on the bench to enjoy the cool twilight.

"Hi." A lovely voice spoke from behind me. "Mind if I have a seat?" It was Julie.

"No. Yes. I mean, of course," I stammered, sliding over so she could fit. She dropped down next to me with a smile. She was wearing shorts and looked like she had been working out. I tried not to stare at her well-muscled legs. I was suddenly very self-conscious about my sweat-soaked T-shirt. I bet I stunk.

"So how's everything going?" she asked.

"Fine, I'm doing okay. Except for that." I jerked my thumb toward the cross-country track. "That sucks."

She laughed, hopefully with me, and not at me. "I know it. I hate it too. Not all of us are like Grant." She pointed across the field. A lone figure stood a hundred yards away, throwing punches at invisible foes under the lights of the obstacle course.

Grant Jefferson had stuck around after the Newbies had left. He had stripped off his shirt and was practicing what appeared to be some extremely difficult martial exercises. I hated to admit it, but the man was a near-perfect physical specimen. If monster hunting didn't work out for him, I was sure he could get a gig as an underwear model.

"So . . . how long have you guys been dating?" I asked, trying not to sound jealous. I don't know if I succeeded.

"A couple months," she answered as she looked at me suspiciously. "Why?"

"Oh . . . I don't know. He just seems a little . . ."

"Arrogant?"

I paused, not quite sure how to answer that. "Uh, yeah, I guess. He just doesn't strike me as your type is all."

"And you know my type how?" she asked, studying me carefully. I swallowed, wanting to shout "Me." Thankfully she continued before I had to answer. "Yes, I know Grant comes off a little arrogant, but he really is a great guy. He's smart and ambitious. He was in Harvard Law School when we recruited him."

Figures, I thought to myself. "The CPA exam is way harder than passing the Bar," I muttered.

"What?"

"Uh . . . nothing."

"We hit it off when he arrived here. Grant's traveled the world. He's sophisticated, cultured, educated. He's done a lot of really interesting things. So he's kind of . . . confident. That comes off as cocky sometimes."

Comes off as an ass. I bit my tongue. I knew the truth. I bet he drowned sacks of puppies for fun. In the distance Grant had dropped down and started doing pushups.

"Well, good for you guys . . . I've got to get some sleep." I stood up to leave.

"Goodnight, Owen."

"Yeah, 'night, Julie." I wandered off. It figured that I had finally met the perfect woman, only to find out she wasn't interested in me. I kicked over the garbage can outside the barracks. Screw it. I was tired.

"What're you doing?" Trip asked me as he entered our tiny barracks room. The windows were open and loud insects chirped and whistled in the darkness outside.

"I don't know," I answered honestly. I was sitting on my bunk, suitcase open on the floor in front of me. My right hand ached from the impact it had taken an hour earlier. "Thinking about packing, I guess."

"You didn't strike me as a quitter," he said simply. "That was an accident with Green. You didn't mean to hurt him. Milo says he'll be out of the hospital in a week. It's just his collar bone and a concussion."

"I only hit him once."

We had been practicing going hands-on. Never a good choice against a monster, but a necessary skill to have nonetheless. They had paired me up with Green, a muscle-bound former narc. It had gotten kind of competitive.

"Stuff happens," Trip shrugged. "Don't be a baby about it."

"Sam said I wasn't being aggressive enough."

"He probably shouldn't have said that to somebody who beat up a werewolf." Trip sat on his bed. "When Green wakes up, he'll be cool. It was an accident."

I shook my head. "No. It wasn't. I got angry. I didn't hold back. Look, man, this is why I should probably go. When I get mad, when I lose control, people get hurt."

"You make it sound like you're the Hulk," he laughed. "You're training to be a Monster Hunter. We're supposed to hurt things. Come on, dude, what's the deal?"

Trip had become a good friend over the last few weeks of training, and I could tell that he did honestly want to help. I stared down at the open suitcase. "You know I used to fight for money, right?" I continued, not looking up. "A few years ago, I had a big one. My last one. Lots of cash on the table. The other guy was supposed to be a real badass. Supposedly he had killed a couple of people in prison. There were no rules, and it wasn't supposed to stop until one of us couldn't fight anymore. Last man standing got paid."

"Why would you do that?" he asked, sincerely perplexed. Trip was a good man, and the idea of inflicting violence on another human being for no good reason was truly foreign to him.

I sighed. "You've got to understand. My whole life, my father tried to prepare me for something. All he did was push. He had some sort of fucked-up vision of the future, and he wanted me to be ready for it. I guess I just needed to prove that I was as tough as he thought I was."

"So what happened?"

"The other fighter really *was* a bad dude. Meanest I had ever dealt with. I couldn't take him. He just wouldn't quit. Then, something happened . . . Something snapped, broke loose. No pain, just focus. Like when Huffman tried to eat me. Next thing I knew, I had blood up to my armpits and I was kneeling on this guy while I hit him until my knuckles broke."

Trip looked shocked. "You killed him?"

"Almost, and I would have, but the promoters pulled me off. They managed to stitch his skull back together, but he lost an eye, and I've heard he's still all messed up. . . . I would've killed him. And right then, I *wanted* to kill him, and for what? How stupid is that?"

"Pretty stupid."

We sat in silence for a while, Trip not really knowing what to say. I knew from our talks that he was a devoutly religious man and was probably trying to think of how to politely tell me that I was surely going to hell. Finally I spoke. "You know why I became an accountant?"

"Pays better than teaching."

"I picked the most straight-laced, stereotypically boring thing that I could think of. My entire life I'd been taught to be a killer, but after that night, I just wanted to get as far away from it as I could."

"But you still carried a gun everyday?"

"I didn't go looking for trouble, didn't mean I wasn't ready for trouble to look for me," I answered.

"Beats hitting zombies with a pickax . . ." he muttered.

"And now here I am. In this place, where all the things I've spent the last few years trying to distance myself from are not only encouraged, they're mandatory. And it seems like I might actually be pretty good at this. But I'm worried . . ."

"That you'll hurt somebody who don't need hurting?"

"Yeah, something like that." I clenched my scarred-up fists. My hand throbbed from where I had slugged Green. It had only been a brief instant, a flash of anger, but that was all it took.

Trip thought about it for a few long seconds, absently chewing on his lower lip, then stood. "The way I see it, we're here to do good. I don't know about you, but

I came here to stop monsters from hurting folks. The Lord's given you a gift, a weird one, but still a gift, and the fact that you're worried about misusing it means that you're not a bad guy. So put that suitcase away, man up, and let's get to class before Harbinger realizes we're late. He kind of scares me." He thumped me on the shoulder, and walked out the door.

I waited a moment, listening to the angry buzz of the insects crashing against the window screen. Then I pushed the suitcase back under my bunk and went back to work.

I thought I understood discomfort and heat. I had lived in Texas for a few years, and I had grown up in the San Joaquin Valley of California. One was miserably hot and windy, and other was muggy from all of the open-air irrigation. But summer in the Heart of Dixie was a whole new type of evil. So hot that you couldn't think, and so wet you could almost drink the air. Summer had come to Alabama.

So of course this was the day when we were issued our body armor. It was heavy, and though well designed to be comfortable and breathable, during summers in Alabama a pair of shorts and a tank top were considered warm clothing. I was sweating profusely, not that that said much, considering that men of my bulk usually started sweating at room temperature, but this was particularly bad. Thankfully the armor came equipped with a CamelBak water bladder and drinking tube. As their ad so eloquently stated: Hydrate or Die.

Milo Anderson paced back and forth in front of the assembled Newbies. Today he was wearing a Violent Femmes T-shirt and his red beard had been braided into two separate forks, both seemingly long enough to rappel from. Occasionally he would stop before a Newbie, examine them critically, and then pause long enough to adjust some strap or buckle. He was the creator of the suit, as well as many of the other devices the Hunting teams used.

Grant Jefferson watched us smugly in our discomfort. He was wearing his armor, which had been tailored to suit him better. Holly had said that he was dashingly handsome, and even she, being so very jaded and cynical about men because of her background, found him very charismatic and charming. She told me that it was easy to see why Grant and Julie had hooked up. He was young, smart, good-looking, knew how to talk to people, and everybody loved him. I still wanted to kick his ass.

On Grant's shoulder was a patch with the green smiley face with horns that was the unofficial company logo, which only Harbinger's personal team wore. We had been told that the other teams made up their own logos. The only other team logo that I had seen here at the compound had been a fire-breathing warthog that Dorcas had engraved onto her plastic leg. Grant wore the smiley face with pride—apparently it was a real honor to end up on Harbinger's team. I had learned that he had only been a Hunter since the business had reopened, but he had shown so much potential in training that he had been picked to fill a void on what was considered the best team.

"You will learn to live in these suits for days at a time. This suit will save your life. This suit will become like a second skin to you." Grant was lecturing us, gesturing at his own gear. Milo stopped in front of me with a scowl and adjusted the webbing around my torso. Apparently Milo had never had to make a suit for somebody as big as I am, and it had been a bit of a challenge to come up with Kevlar sheets for a sixty-two-inch chest.

"Psst . . . Milo," I whispered. "Since these are supposed to be like second skins, where's yours?"

"Screw that. It's hot," he answered.

And he invented the darn thing. *Testify, brother,* I thought.

"One time this suit saved my life. You can see right here where I was clawed by a golem. See, right there on the abdomen. Surely this would have been a mortal blow, but I was able to shrug it off and stay in the fight. I dispatched the monster and was able to rush to the aid of my team and save them from certain death," Grant told us, lifting up the front of his armor so we could all see his sculpted abs. The man must do crunches in his sleep to look like that. Grant had been talking forever, and unlike the other instructors, did not have a drop of humility in his soul. I was about ten minutes from a heat stroke, and we were stuck suffering in the sun while our teacher blathered.

Milo rolled his eyes and went back to adjusting straps. "Some golem. It was three feet tall," he muttered under his breath so it was barely audible to just me, "ass."

The armor was a modular system that could be configured by the user depending on what kind of threat we were going to face. A thick layer of stab-proof Kevlar covered the vital organs. Though not much heavier than regular thick clothing, the sleeves and pant legs had the same fibers sewn into the fabric. There was a neck guard that could be raised to resemble a turtle neck to protect against bites. Most of the threats we would face would involve teeth or claws, so unlike regular body armor, ours was designed for that rather than for bullet resistance. Milo informed us that the torso was rated the same as a traditional level IIIA bulletproof vest, able to stop most pistol rounds. There were pouches on the front and back designed to hold ceramic plates that could stop rifle rounds if the threat warranted it, and if the user didn't mind the extra weight. The system incorporated load-bearing gear and pouches for magazines, weapons, tools, medical kits, or whatever other useful things the Hunter might need.

There were two different types of gloves that came with the suit. One was a basic shooting glove that offered a small amount of protection, but still allowed good dexterity. And the other was a heavy armored gauntlet for when you needed maximum protection and just had to wade in and crush some heads. The heavy units could be attached to the end of the sleeves. There were also two types of helmets. The first was simply a modified hockey helmet, good basically to keep you from banging yourself in the skull when blundering around in the dark. The second, an armored monstrosity that looked kind of like a motorcycle helmet with a full visor and face shield, could be attached to the neck guard. With the heavy gloves and big helmet, a suited Monster Hunter could become a chew toy for a pile of zombies and come out gnawed on, but unbitten. Unfortunately for me, Milo did not have a helmet that would fit my enormous head so he had special-ordered one. Hopefully nothing would try to eat me before then.

The armor had lots of extras designed just for the people in our peculiar business. A CO_2 cartridge was carried in the shoulder harness. In case of emergency it could be activated and the harness would inflate. Handy if you got dumped into deep water, because it was difficult to swim while strapped with piles of gear. My understanding was that Sam, our former SEAL, had insisted on that device. Each suit also had a GPS unit for navigation, which occasionally came in handy to locate a Hunter's body when the bad guys won.

The armor could be ordered in whatever color you wanted, as long as it was black, olive drab, or coyote brown. There was not a lot of use for festive colors in monster hunting, nor were there a lot of suppliers of heavyweight military strength Cordura in any other colors. I had gone with brown. Grant had gone with black. He probably thought it made him look tough. I thought he looked kind of like a silly version of Darth Vader. I took comfort in the fact that he had to be cooking in the sun right about now, though the bastard did not even give me the satisfaction of looking uncomfortable.

"Pay attention," Grant snapped at me. Milo rolled his eyes again. I snickered. Grant stormed toward us like a bulldog.

"Pitt. I don't like your attitude."

"Trust me, Grant. It's mutual," I snapped back.

"What did you say?" He poked me in the chest with his trigger finger. I couldn't feel a thing through the armor, but that did not change the fact that I did not like getting poked. It was hot, I was tired, and frankly in no mood to put up with any nonsense. Milo wisely moved aside.

"I said it's mutual. Meaning I don't like your attitude either."

"I'm trying to teach you Newbies how to stay alive."

"Then teach. All I'm hearing is stories about how great you are. I came here to learn how to kill stuff, not to join your fan club."

He stabbed me again. "I'm a pro. You need to shut your stupid Newbie mouth. You think you know so much. I saw that video. You got lucky with that werewolf, and now you think you're hot shit."

"You had best take that hand off of me," I said. The rest of the class was gradually spreading out around us. The group could sense trouble brewing and were ready for some entertainment. Apparently I was not the only one in a foul mood.

"Or what?" And he poked harder. It was really kind of a useless gesture considering the armor could stop a battle-ax. With years of experience bouncing rowdy people from bars, I had a good sense of when somebody was itching for trouble, and Grant was itching bad.

"I'll take it off and feed it to you." I smiled at him and winked. That really seemed to anger him. Grant's movie star face turned bright red. He was as tall as I was, but not nearly as big or as strong. I had no doubt that I could beat him mercilessly.

"I could have you kicked out of here like that." He took his hand away long enough to snap his fingers, then he went back to poking me.

"For what?" asked Milo, arms folded, studying the

other instructor. Milo was by far the senior in experience, and in the amount of respect he received from the trainees. That was easy though, Milo Anderson was a likable guy. Grant on the other hand . . .

"Insubordination," Grant hissed. "One word to the Boss about your attitude and you're gone."

"If I'm going to get kicked out, believe me, I'm going to have some fun doing it." I felt my body tense as the adrenaline began to flow. If Grant wanted a piece of me, I was prepared to give that preppie piece of trash what he wanted.

"Grant." Milo spoke quietly. "That's the stupidest thing I've ever heard. You're picking a fight with somebody who outweighs you by a hundred pounds of muscle. Insubordination my butt. You say anything to the Boss and my side of the story will be that you were trying to commit suicide by accountant."

"I could take him," the junior instructor stated coldly. "He isn't as tough as everybody thinks."

"Grant, I could kick your ass. Pitt would make you his bitch."

That took the wind out of Grant's sails. I could see the realization dawn in his blue eyes, the realization that I could probably turn him into pulp. I just kept smiling, still prepared to mess up his pretty face and give him the opportunity to digest some of his perfectly white teeth. He had already pushed too far, though. He could not back off now without looking bad. He leaned in close and whispered in my ear.

"Stay away from Julie, you son of a bitch. I've seen you looking at her." I was surprised. So that was what this was all about. I had barely even seen her since training had started.

"Bite me," I replied.

"Enough!" Milo shouted. "Class is over. It's too hot and everybody's tempers are short. You've been working hard. Go grab some lunch."

Grant stepped back and glared at the little man. Milo met his gaze evenly. I think that my nemesis quickly realized that the other instructor had just given him a window of opportunity to back out of his potential beating and not look like a wimp in front of the others. Grant Jefferson may have been a prick, but he was no dummy.

"Fine. Class dismissed," Grant sneered. "I'll be seeing you around, Pitt." He spun on his polished boots and haughtily strode away.

"Looking forward to it," I rumbled under my breath as the group began to disperse. Milo shouted for all of us to turn our suits in to his workshop for adjustments before we left the compound for our weekend off. There were some relieved sighs as the Newbies unceremoniously began to remove their armor. I stomped away to avoid speaking to anybody.

Not that it did me much good. One person followed me. Trip patted me on my armored shoulder to get my attention. "Have I ever told you how much I respect your professionalism and restraint?"

"Some people just need a good beating."

"I agree. The man's a jerk. But last night I talked you out of quitting, so I don't want to see you get fired today," Trip said as we started toward the cafeteria, new suits creaking. Hopefully they would break in and soften up. My friend continued speaking as if I was one of his former ignorant teenage students. "You know why he hates you, right?"

I had spoken about my infatuation with Julie Shackleford to Trip. He was my roommate after all. "I suppose I do."

"Well, then, you would be wrong."

"Huh?"

"You think it's because of the girl. Grant probably thinks it's because of the girl too. That's because you're both idiots."

"Gee thanks, Trip." We continued walking slowly, talking quietly so the others wouldn't hear our conversation. "Well, if it isn't because of her, what's his problem?"

"You're his problem. I've seen this before. Grant is the golden boy. He came in here last year and tore stuff up. He's the best at everything. Even the big dogs took him under their wing. I bet he has won at everything he's ever tried. You come along, and you're naturally better than him at some things, so immediately he doesn't like you. It is all about pride, my friend, and Grant is stuffed so full of it it's a wonder he doesn't burst."

"Okay, I can see that."

"And you do keep staring at his woman like a slobbering moron."

"Slobbering?" That hurt.

"And you're a smart ass who can't help but show him up every chance that you get."

"Fair enough."

"And you can't handle losing just as bad as him. You're both torn up with pride and, like the Bible says, pride is the sin that will drag you down faster than anything else."

"Where does it say that?"

"Luke chapter . . . something or other. Well, that's what my mom said about it anyway."

"Thanks, Pastor Jones. I'll be sure to keep my pride and my slobbering in check from now on." I laughed. He was not that much older than I was, but somewhere along the line Trip had gained a lot more wisdom than I had.

"That's Father Reverend Elder Jones to you . . . heathen. Now let's get some lunch. We got the whole weekend off, and we're going to need our energy. I've got an auntie who lives in Wetumpka, up past Montgomery, and we're gonna have us a party. Have you ever had chitlins? Bona fide Southern delicacy."

"Can't say that I have. What the hell's a chitlin?" The way he said it, I didn't know if chitlins were a delicacy or a form of torture. Probably could go either way, depending on your perspective.

"Then you're going to have yourself one hell of a weekend, Z."

CHAPTER 6

I was dreaming. I found myself in the same field as I'd been in during the strange dream that I had experienced in the hospital. Once again, the crop was lush and green, and my feet were bare. The air was cool and fresh, so I definitely was not in Alabama. The sky was darker and thick black rain clouds were collecting on the horizon. It looked like it was going to be a terrible storm.

The Old Man was there also. This time he was sitting on a small grassy mound. His hair was still wild and white, his cane sat on the ground next to him, and he was absently polishing his small round glasses on a white handkerchief.

"Hello, Boy. Welcome again here." His accent was still thick, reminding me somewhat of my grandparents on my mom's side of the family. A deep Eastern European sound, but not from any of the languages that I spoke.

"What am I doing here?" I asked, sitting down on the grass next to him. We watched the storm front approach. The wind was beginning to pick up and the crop was waving under the onslaught. "I thought you said that we wouldn't meet again unless I did something stupid and got killed."

"I was wrong. I new at this too," he answered. "Is closer now. So I help more easy."

"What is closer now?"

"You will see. It comes." He pointed at the storm roiling across the distant landscape.

"What comes?"

"The storm. I show you when can. I help you if can."

"Help me with what?" This was a confusing dream, not helped at all by my host's mangled English.

"The evil comes. The Cursed One brings. You will stop, if can. If not, time will die." He stated it as if that cryptic information was a simple fact.

"Who are you?"

"I told you. I am friend. I here to help." He spit on his glasses and continued to polish them. I noticed that he wore a small Star of David around his neck. His clothes were old and simple, and appeared to be sewn by hand.

"What's your name?"

"No one ask that for long time."

"That doesn't answer the question," I replied.

"My name not matter now, Boy. I am just Old Man."

He held up the glasses and examined them, nodding in satisfaction before placing them on his face. "Is good. Help me up, please." I stood, and then lent him a hand as he slowly rose to his feet. I retrieved his cane and handed it over. The polished wood was surprisingly heavy and dense.

As I looked up I realized that somehow the storm

had drawn impossibly close. The blue sky was blotted out and the wall that was approaching was a swirling mass of darkness, clouds, and lightning. The sky had taken on a green halo and I could feel the energy crackling through the ground. The crop was lying down or being torn out of the soil as powerful gusts struck us.

"We go now. I show you what I can. I need your help."

"Okay," I answered, not knowing what else to say.

"You help me. I help you. No can promise it will work, but I will try." He grasped my wrist. His cold hands were frail and arthritic.

He adjusted his glasses and watched with hard eyes as the storm approached. It was moving across the land like a tidal wave now, closing on us with what seemed like malevolent intent. As it grew closer I could see that there were shapes in the clouds—warriors, monsters, death, plague, famine, suffering, pestilence and war. My pleasant dream was changing into a nightmare. The roar of wind and crashing of thunder and wails of something else washed over us. The wall of black hit us, and we were swiftly engulfed.

Still dreaming. Only now, I was somehow above the MHI compound. I had no body, but somehow I could see, and not only that, I could see everything. Walls meant nothing to me. Maybe seeing wasn't the right term. I was aware of everything. I was not limited by the information that my eyes could register or that my brain could process. I found my body sleeping peacefully in the barracks. Trip, in the bunk above, was reading some pulp fantasy novel as he did every night. The man was a fantasy book addict.

The rest of my fellow trainees were sleeping or pretending to. In the women's barracks I was not surprised to learn that Holly Newcastle slept in the nude. As interesting as that sight was, I moved on. I was no Peeping Tom, or in this case a peeping ghost.

The office/fortress was totally open to me now. It was much larger than any of us had realized, with a huge underground level that was a complete secret to the trainees. In the dark corners I glimpsed that not all of the other employees were human. *What a strange dream.* On the top floor our instructors were holding a meeting around a huge table. Julie, Harbinger, Sam, Milo, and Grant were arguing about something. I focused in on that, and somehow my presence joined them in the room. Movements were cloudy, and the voices were indistinct and muffled because of all of the other sensations I was receiving without my normal faculties.

"No other teams are available. Just us and the Newbies. Boone's team's in Atlanta. They just finished a case, and they can meet us on the way. I can send them the schematics." Julie was speaking.

"We'll need extra men," Sam said, his voice echoing strangely. "Freighter that big is too hard to cover with just two teams. And we don't have an effing clue what we're facing."

"The Newbies aren't ready," Milo stated flatly. "Most of them would get killed if it gets hairy."

"Who do we have who's ready then?" Harbinger asked. "We can keep them in reserve. They don't need to be in front."

"Mead, Lee and maybe Triple J," Grant said. "Green could, except that oaf put him in the hospital."

"Newcastle can handle support," Milo added.

"Agreed," stated Harbinger.

"What about Pitt?" Julie asked.

"No way. He's out of control," Grant replied hotly.

"He's also the best shooter we have. I hate to admit it, but he's even better than I am," Sam said. The big cowboy banged the table for emphasis.

"Pitt's a hothead. He'll blow it," Grant retorted.

"He is a natural leader, however." Milo stuck up for me. "Put him in charge of the Newbie squad. The others will follow him."

"I vote that he goes," Julie said. "You heard the French. They lost a whole team on that boat. We don't know what's out there. We need every shooter we can get."

"I don't like the Frenchies, but their Hunters are first rate. I'll give them that," Milo said. "If something on that ship took out their team, then I'm guessing that it's bad news. I've got a feeling we're going to need trigger pullers."

"Done. Wake up Pitt, Jones, Mead, Lee and Newcastle. Let's move, folks. Clock's ticking," Harbinger ordered. Grant sulked and the rest of the team sprang into action.

Cool, I thought to my disembodied self. *This was an interesting dream.* Harbinger jumped as if somebody had startled him. He turned and scowled at the corner of the room that held my consciousness. Before he could act, my presence was suddenly jerked out of the room, through the roof, and into the night sky, leaving the man scowling in puzzlement at the now empty room. I heard the mysterious Old Man's voice.

"Sorry. Lost you for minute. I not done this before."

The ground flashed by below as my awareness sped through the air at what had to be a thousand miles an hour. The darkness was interrupted by the occasional lights of human activity, and finally a mass of lights on an otherwise dark coast came into focus as we appeared to slow. I could sense masses of people, most sleeping, a smaller number awake. The ocean stretched black and unrelenting before us, while above, unfettered by normal human senses, I could make out literally billions of stars. It was beautiful.

Then I was on a dark beach. Behind me was a patch of swampy forest, lit by incandescent gasses and teaming with life. Out to sea, something approached. I could sense the shape of men in a small lifeboat. The boat moved soundlessly toward the beach, propelled not by wind, oar or engine, but rather by some force that even in my dream state I could not understand. As the boat approached, the sounds of life behind us were suddenly silent as every living creature either fled or hid. Somehow I knew that even the fish in the water were swimming away from the boat in a panic. They knew something in their simple brains that all of the sleeping humans nearby did not. An unnatural fog, somehow icy in the humid southern air, swirled around the small craft.

"He comes," said the Old Man.

"Who is he?" my dream self asked.

"I know him as the Cursed One."

There were multiple shapes in the boat. Some appeared to be human, and were crouched low in the hull, red eyes scanning the beach, noses sniffing the air for prey. I recognized them from Harbinger's lectures. *Vampires*. The kings and queens of the undead, and from the vibe that I was getting from them, these were ancient and powerful beings. Master vampires. According to my lessons, masters were solitary creatures who had never been known to work together. Apparently the lessons had been very wrong. My dream was getting ugly.

Standing in the midst of the creatures was some *thing*. At first it appeared to be a man. Cloaked in a huge robe, only the reflection of what appeared to be a polished steel breastplate and helmet could be made out through the unnatural fog. The armor reminded me of the type that the conquistadors had worn. A sense of pure evil emanated from the cloaked being, an icy feeling of dread that I could feel piercing through my consciousness. I could not imagine how horrible it would have been if I had been there in my physical body instead of in this dream. As the image drew closer I could see a mass of withering blackness glistening between the creases of the armor and under the helmet. I could not comprehend what it was, but it certainly was not flesh. Somehow the twitching movement brought back memories of the boxes of live earthworms that my father used to fish with.

It looked almost like the famous painting of Washington crossing the Delaware, only this time featuring a host of evil undead, and some hideous monstrosity in the place of the great general. There was a name painted on the side of the craft. *Antoine-Henri*. The lifeboat glided up onto the sand with a crunch, and the vampires immediately sprang out and formed a protective circle around the *thing*. Some splashed out into the surf to cover that direction. There were six of them, both male and female, and they were unnaturally graceful and swift. They were evil and savage, but somehow beautiful at the same time. A seventh vampire remained in the craft with its master. If the *thing* was the commander, then that vampire was its lieutenant. I felt a seething hatred around me. It was coming from the Old Man, and it was directed at that seventh and final vampire in particular. It was a tall, pale thing with a hatchet face, slicked back hair, and a dark trench coat that it wore like a uniform. The vampire actually stood at attention as the armored monstrosity glided onto the beach.

When the *thing* touched the sand, the whole universe jolted. A blast of discomfort rippled through every living being for hundreds of miles. You may have felt it yourself; an unexplained shiver, a sensation of fear that had come out of nowhere, a crawling feeling in the pit of your gut, a jolt that tore you out of sleep. That was the Cursed One setting foot on his new land.

The lead vampire announced something in a foreign language. It took me a moment to recognize it as Portuguese, or a dialect thereof. I knew enough of the language to understand.

"Welcome home, Lord Machado," the creature crowed, bowing deeply. All of the other vampires forming the perimeter immediately bowed as well, the ones in the surf submerging themselves completely in the saltwater waves. It did not matter to them. They did not need air. The abnormal fog drifted up onto the beach, serving as the fanfare for the abomination before us. "Your kingdom awaits."

The *thing* was silent. It slowly rotated, taking in the sight. Beneath the cloak and armor I could not tell how it moved, but it was black and damp and slithery. It turned until it looked right at us. I could feel its gaze sweep across us, and if I had been in my body I would have been trembling. I could not see eyes, but somehow it knew we were there. Instantly the vampires jerked up and followed their leader's gaze, somehow locking onto the Old Man and me. I felt fear greater than I ever had before. Greater than when I had died. Greater than anything I could imagine. The creature did not want my life. It wanted my very soul and the soul of every person I had ever loved.

"Hello, Byreika." The lead vampire smiled, revealing pointed incisors. "My, it certainly has been a while, hasn't it? I see you brought a friend."

The Cursed One raised a strangely jointed, cloaked limb and pointed at us. I could feel the flash of panic from my incorporeal companion. With an explosion of sand and seawater, several massive shapes crashed into the surf around us. I had not sensed them circling above. Giant horrific things with massive wings beating, they surrounded us, and moved toward us, murder in their blank eyes. They were enormous clawed beasts, horns and talons glistening with sea spray.

"Get us out of here!" I screamed.

The world jerked wildly around us as my consciousness was pulled again through the night sky, faster this time than before. The winged monsters below us sprang into pursuit, blasting holes through the ice fog with their gargantuan wings, but they were limited by their physical bodies and we were not. Far more terrifying than the monsters was the feeling of the Cursed One somehow trying to latch onto us to keep us from escaping. It was as if a net of blackness were being thrown, and we were the target. The creatures beneath us rapidly shrank from view. Somehow we slipped through the evil grip as my consciousness screamed across the sky at unbelievable speeds. I had one last view of the MHI compound before I flew through the roof of the barracks and slammed back into my body.

I awoke screaming, tearing at my sheets, and crying for the Old Man to save us from the Cursed One. Trip was standing at my bedside, shaking me.

"Owen! Dude! Wake up. It was a dream. Calm down."

Gasping for air and lying back on the sweat-stained sheets, it was only a dream. The storm. The Old Man. The Cursed One. The vampires. It was all a dream. Everything was fine.

"I had the worst nightmare," I gasped.

"No kidding. You were really freaking out. Everybody was. Just a couple of minutes ago everybody in the barracks woke up. Like the whole place was having a nightmare or something. I get the feeling that something really bad just happened."

Then our door opened. Earl Harbinger and Sam Haven were standing in the hall, both were suited up in full armor, bristling with ammunition and weapons.

"What's the racket?" Harbinger asked.

"Just a bad dream," I answered.

The Director of Operations frowned at me. He had felt the strange sensation as well. "Both of you. Grab your stuff. Get over to the armory and get suited up. We have a mission. Consider the weekend cancelled," Harbinger ordered, as he slung an ancient Thompson submachine gun over his shoulder.

"We have a ship to catch," grunted Sam, while twirling the ends of his mighty mustache. "Think of this as a field trip."

CHAPTER 7

The small boat rolled on the harsh waves, leaving me with a slightly nauseous and uncomfortable feeling. I held onto the guardrail until my knuckles were white, or at least I'm sure they would have been if I could have seen them through my gloves. I had been uncomfortable since the coast had disappeared. The ocean stretched as far as my eye could see. The sun had risen shortly before we launched, and now cast a golden light over the blue surface. I'm sure that if I wasn't mentally preparing myself to go into battle I might have found it a stunning sight. I had never really been out to sea before, other than brief trips on tourist boats off the California coast. I'm sure some of my father's islander ancestors would have scoffed at that.

There were ten of us Hunters on the small boat, the *Brilliant Mistake,* which Harbinger had hired to transport us to our target. I did not take the name of the boat as a good omen, but once the captain had been given a large wad of cash, he had assured us that the name was in reference to a favorite song and not to any flaw in his boat's design or crew. I still did not like it either way. It was a rusty, old, creaky thing, but it had been available, and even better, the crew didn't look like the type that talked too much.

We had assembled before midnight at the compound, burdened with all manner of equipment and weaponry. Most of us had been loaded into MHI's cargo plane, an old but serviceable former U.S. Mail carrier. It did not look like much, but it got the job done, and it could haul a ton of gear. Then we had flown first to a small airstrip outside of Atlanta, where we had picked up another team of Hunters, before arriving at our final destination, another small airport on the Georgia coast. The rest had taken the slower, but necessary for this mission, helicopter and rendezvoused with us there while Harbinger was securing us a boat. The team leaders had spent the flight memorizing diagrams e-mailed to us from a French shipyard.

In Georgia we had broken into two groups. The larger group boarded the *Brilliant Mistake* under cover of darkness and the smaller group took the helicopter. The plan was for the airborne unit to fly over our target to scope it out, and then to drop some of the Hunters onto the ship. That unit would secure a rope ladder for the rest of us to climb up, while the helicopter provided covering fire if necessary. Both vehicles would stay nearby in case we needed a quick escape route.

It sounded simple enough. My job was to do exactly what the smart people told me, and carry lots of extra ammunition.

Trip stood beside me at the railing. Unlike yours truly, he did not appear to be feeling seasick at all, but rather seemed to be enjoying himself. He was descended from Jamaican fishermen, so he must have been more in touch with his ancestors' seafaring genes than I was. I had told him about my dream.

"I still have nightmares. I think most of us do," he told me. I knew that some of the zombies that he had been forced to dispatch had been some of his friends and former students. Something like that is bound to weigh heavy on a man's mind. "Something weird was in the air last night."

"But I heard the instructors' meeting about us. I knew about this mission before they came to get us. Explain that."

He shrugged. "You know how it is when you wake up confused. Your brain chemistry's all screwed up. Your unconscious mind just fills in the blanks as needed. We found out about this right after your dream. Seems like the logical thing to me."

"Seems to me that if you want to be logical, you sure did go into the wrong line of work."

He ignored that. "And six master vampires working together? That isn't supposed to happen either."

"Seven," I corrected him. I couldn't forget about the one in the boat, the sharp-faced one that had so enraged and terrified the Old Man.

"Either way. That has never happened. They're too powerful, and too territorial. According to Harbinger there probably aren't that many Masters in the whole world. Besides, how could you tell they were so powerful? All of them look the same." That much was true. From what we had been taught all vampires looked pretty much human, unless you caught them feeding.

"I don't know how I knew. I just did. And there were huge winged monsters, but I didn't get a good look at them. But the other thing, the thing in the boat. That was the scariest. I mean it was the worst thing I've ever seen." I nervously checked my Remington 870 for the twentieth time. It was still there.

"Quit worrying about your dream, man. We've got real stuff to worry about. Let's put our game faces on." He slugged me in the arm, hard. Damn football players.

Sam Haven had us gather at the rear of the boat for a briefing, away from the ears of the crew, who I was positive were already really curious what the ten strangers in body armor and carrying guns were doing on their boat. Lucky for us, fifteen thousand dollars in cash for one day of work was considered good enough money to put up with all manner of weirdness. Of course it was half up front, the other half after they picked us up. Since we were the waterborne team, Harbinger had placed our former Navy man in charge. Thus Sam was even louder than normal. He and Milo were on the boat with us, and the rest of their team was in the chopper. One of the Newbies, Chuck Mead, a former Army Ranger, was up there as well. He knew how to rappel and that was a handy skill to have for this mission.

"Listen up, folks. Here's the deal." Sam began to brief us as he methodically unloaded, checked each round and reloaded his rifle. The rear of the boat smelled like fish. "A few hours ago we were contacted by the French corporation that owns the freighter. It was destined for the USA carrying an extremely valuable cargo. The freighter lost contact a week ago in the Atlantic. The last transmissions indicated some sort of supernatural problem."

"What did they say?" asked one of the Hunters out of Atlanta, whom I had not met.

"Unknown. Mostly gibberish. They did say monsters, but they didn't say what kinds. But this was an experienced crew so it is doubtful if they did something stupid." Sam's personal weapon was a very strange choice. It was a Marlin .45-70 lever action carbine. Very slow to reload. Low capacity. Slow rate of fire. But as he had pointed out while boarding, the 450-grain hard-cast bullets he was shooting could go through a buffalo longways. That was no small comfort, just in case the freighter had been taken over by militant evil bison.

"What's the ship's name?" someone asked.

Sam shrugged. "Something French. Hell if I know."

"Why did they contact us? The frogs hate hiring American Hunters." That was from the man named Boone. He was the leader of the other team, and from what I had seen so far, he was a serious professional. According to what I had heard on the trip, he had recently gotten off of active duty with the Army Special Forces in Afghanistan, and had been eager to get back into hunting when the company reopened. Boone was a lean and good-natured guy, and his team was ready to follow his lead into anything. I took that as a good sign. He had a stubby Russian Krinkov slung from his chest, and apparently his team's logo was a mini-lop bunny armed with a switchblade.

"We weren't their first choice. The day after they lost contact a French team was dispatched to intercept. They flew out to the freighter, and their l transmission indicated that they'd landed and were starting to clear the ship. They haven't been heard from since."

"Well, that's great," Boone said.

"Wait, it gets better," Milo Anderson interjected. "Jean Darné was the leader of the French team."

Several of the experienced Hunters began to mutter. Boone swore.

"Who is this Dar Nay guy? And why is that bad?" I asked.

"He was the best that they had. Probably the best team lead in Europe. You know they didn't do anything sloppy. Whatever is on that boat is serious," said one of the experienced Hunters, a South African immigrant named Priest.

"So we're going in hard and fast." Sam worked the lever on his Marlin and chambered a round. "Since we don't know what's on that freighter we're coming ready for anything. Everybody is armed with something that shoots silver, even if it is just your handgun. We have every specialty round for the shotguns that we can think of. Big fifties. RPGs, flamethrowers, thermite, C4, and I even have a chainsaw around here somewhere. The Hind will stay airborne and provide covering fire if we need to bail out."

"Mission parameters?" Boone asked.

"Don't hurt the cargo. Cargo is boxed in the hold. Apparently it's priceless art or some shit. So no bullet holes or fire in the hold. Rest of the ship is open game. If we can save any crew or the French Hunters, do it. Don't sink the ship."

"What's the contract worth?" Boone again.

"Julie negotiated it, so of course it's a good deal.

We got a million up front. If the cargo is unharmed then MHI gets another 3.5 mil. The more the cargo is damaged, the less we get. If we sink the ship then we don't get nothing. So let's not sink the ship."

We continued to cover details. There had been thirty crew, a ten-man security detail for the cargo, and a dozen French Hunters. So if we were dealing with an undead infestation we were looking at over fifty potential hostiles, not including whatever started the infection to begin with. The Hunters hazarded guesses about what we could face on the ship, including weird, but not unheard of things like Saughafin, fish-men, or just a plain old giant killer mollusk. As we continued toward our target we tried to iron out details and figure out any potential problems. Luckily for us, radar indicated that the freighter had stopped moving last night, so it must have dropped anchor. At least it would not be steaming toward land any longer, but it also raised the question what exactly had dropped the anchor.

"The freighter was headed for points northward. Two days ago, it turned south and has been paralleling the coast. GPS transponder is still working, so we know right where she is," Sam told us over a spread-out blueprint of the ship. "When we pull alongside, just try not to fall off the ladder. The fall probably won't kill you, but we ain't got time to screw around fishing you out."

Finally we could see the freighter. It was a massive gray construction, with superstructure rising high into the air. It was a beautiful summer morning, but I could not help but feel an ominous shiver when I looked at the otherwise-normal-looking ship. I knew from the briefing that the mammoth ship was just under 600 feet long and displaced over 15,000 tons. Sam had assured us that the ship was not as big as it appeared, since most of the interior was open cargo space, but it was still going to be a beast to search.

Suddenly there was a massive roar as the bulbous helicopter flew low over us and charged the freighter. Wind and salt spray buffeted those of us at the railings. A figure manning a door gun waved at us as they passed. "Show offs!" Milo yelled and waved back.

MHI's helicopter was a surplus MI-24 Hind. Harbinger had picked it up for next to nothing after the collapse of communism. It was possibly the ugliest thing ever designed, but it was considered a flying tank for a reason. Utilitarian in comfort, it was nonetheless reliable and versatile. It was missing its missiles and rocket pods because the Feds would not allow it in the country that way. Instead the pylons had been replaced with storage compartments for gear and extra fuel. It was big enough to carry eight of us, and could carry enough weight and had enough fuel that the entire team could be evacuated on it if necessary, provided we did not mind hanging off of the wing pylons. It was fast, but it lacked maneuverability at low speeds.

In its original communist paint job it had been a strange enough sight that the company had avoided using the Hind during daylight hours over populated areas. A few flights had resulted in calls to the authorities that Red Dawn was happening for real. To combat this, Harbinger had ordered the chopper painted white and red, so now it was usually mistaken for a med-evac or search-and-rescue helicopter instead.

They had, however, taken the liberty of painting a huge pair of sharp-toothed jaws around the cockpit. That was a nice touch.

The chopper swept quickly over the freighter, banked hard, and made another pass. It slowed until it was hovering and then lazily rotated over the center of the ship. Sam Haven stood nearby, listening intently into his earpiece. All of us were on the same radio net and could listen along. We had been warned to stay off of the radio unless absolutely necessary, except to check in every five minutes once we were onboard.

Julie Shackleford's voice crackled over the radio. She had been the waving door gunner.

"This is Julie. I see no movement. Deck looks clear. No bodies. No signs of damage. French chopper is still on the pad." We were a small enough group that we just used our names on our secure radio net.

"Chopper One. This is Boat One. Can you see into the bridge? Over." Except for Sam, of course. He did not get to be in charge very often, and was not going to waste his chance to use correct radio jargon.

The Hind gradually changed position until it was directly in front of the superstructure. Julie leaned out the door, secured only by bungee cords clipped to her harness. She mounted her rifle and used the scope to scan the windows.

"Negative, Sam. We have a ghost ship."

"Roger that," the big cowboy radioed back. He nudged Milo in the ribs and gave him a Copenhagen-colored grin. "Did you know my middle name was Roger?"

"Yes, Sam, I know," Milo responded. Great guy, but a little bit of Sam went a long ways.

Harbinger's voice came over the radio next. "Let's do it. Front of the ship is clear. We're going to rope down and set up a perimeter. We'll send down the ladder. Front, left-hand side."

"Chopper One, this is Boat One. It's the prow, damn it. Left is port. The front of the ship is fore and the back is aft. Over," Sam responded in consternation.

"Roger that. Front, left-hand side. Ladder is going to come down near the anchor chain. If nothing comes out to attack us we will throw down a second ladder. Signal us when you're in position," Harbinger radioed back.

"Damn Army pus-nuts."

"Navy dumb-shit," Boone said as he flipped Sam the bird. The cowboy grinned and spit a huge gob of chew on the deck.

Directions were given to the captain and the *Brilliant Mistake* motored into position. Orange bumpers were thrown over the side to protect us from the much larger vessel. Luckily for us the ocean was relatively calm, or at least that is what they told me. I was having a hard time standing up without holding onto something. The deck was slick and the steel-gray wall approaching us was intimidating as hell. I was not looking forward to climbing a wet ladder while wearing forty pounds of gear, but it could be a lot worse. The freighter could be moving. The waves could be higher. Sam had told us that before they had a helicopter, they used to board ships by actually climbing up the anchor chain.

"Chopper One, this is Boat One. We will be in position in one minute. Over."

"Roger that. We're heading down."

From the boat we could not see the five Hunters in the Hind as they rappelled to the deck. Gradually our boat bumped its way into position. We waited breathlessly. Nothing could be heard above our own engine, the roar of the chopper beating gravity into submission, and the crashing of waves.

Our only indication of success was when a chain ladder came hurtling toward us, rattling violently as it unrolled down the freighter's hull. Sam lunged forward, grabbed it, and gave it a mighty tug. Nodding in satisfaction, he turned to us and stabbed his finger upward. Milo led the way; he was the best climber of the bunch, since he free climbed mountains for fun. The smaller man grabbed onto the chains and pulled himself up effortlessly. With his long red beard, and bristling with firearms and knives, he reminded me of a pirate. A very mellow pirate, but a pirate nonetheless. Sam went next. Though burly and not as graceful as his predecessor, he had the most experience at this kind of thing, and was still remarkably fast. A second ladder came crashing down, and Boone's team started to clamber up them as well. The Newbies were to go last. Except for Holly Newcastle. She had been given support duty. That meant that she needed to stay on the *Brilliant Mistake* and send up any of the special gear that ended up being needed that was still on the boat. We would send down a cord and she would tie it to the necessary equipment. She got to stay where it was the safest, and she did not like it one bit. In fact, she had been royally insulted.

"This sucks," she said as I waited my turn at the ladder. I was extremely nervous, but I tried not to let it show.

"It's an important job. Somebody has to do it," I replied. "We don't know what's on this thing, and we can't haul all of this with us. Who knows what might come in handy."

"Blow me, Z," she retorted.

"I'm gonna have to take a rain check on that one. Thanks, though." Conversation was good. Conversation kept me from thinking about what I was going to have to do in about thirty seconds.

"You know what I mean. I should be up there with you guys. I can handle this."

"I know you can. Don't worry. You'll get your chance. Hey, me, Trip and Lee are just guarding the escape route. That isn't very heroic."

"Don't matter. We still get paid!" Trip shouted over the noise. It was his turn. Lee was already halfway up the first ladder. My friend let out a mighty rebel yell—"Yee Haw!"—and started climbing. It was strange to hear a black man shout a Confederate battle cry. Hey, whatever worked.

It was my turn. Lee was almost over the bow. It looked to be at least a twenty-five-foot climb. Dangling from the side of a ship. On a slippery metal ladder. Hanging over the open ocean. Fun. I checked to make sure my 12 gauge was securely slung and that all of the pouches on my load bearing gear were still closed. It was go time.

As I hit the ladder I realized that at that moment I was well and truly beginning my career as a professional Monster Hunter. I was prepared. I had recovered from my previous injuries, and I had been working out harder than I had in years. I was in excellent physical shape. I was scared and nervous, but I was actually looking forward to this. *This is it.*

I had been the last one up the ladder because I

was the heaviest, probably the strongest too, but I had to pull a lot more weight than the others. There is a reason you don't see very many big, muscle-bound guys as mountain climbers. The ladder was as bad as I feared, and it was difficult to get my big boots on top of the narrow rungs without twisting them. A sudden wave crashed against the freighter and splashed cold salt water on my face. I spat it out and kept going. By the time I was halfway up I could feel the muscles in my biceps and calves burning. I passed a small porthole, but it had been blacked out from the inside. I focused on the gray painted hull inches from my face and pulled myself up as fast as I could. Radio banter had started above me as the teams moved into position. They were waiting for me and I wasn't going to let them down.

A huge painted letter A gradually appeared as I made my way up the hull. I froze, blinked hard, gasped, and had to catch myself as I almost fell off the ladder into the waiting ocean below. Stenciled in black block letters directly in front of my face was the name of the ship.

Antoine-Henri.

"Holy shit!" I exclaimed.

I had not been able to see it from the angle of our approach, and when we had been directly under the letters, I had been too preoccupied to notice. It was the same name that had been printed on the little boat of evil in my dream.

Trying not to panic, I keyed my mike. "This is Pitt. I need to talk to Harbinger, right now!"

"Pitt. What's wrong?" crackled the response in my ear.

"We have to get off this ship, fast."

"Why? Say again."

"There are seven Master vampires onboard, some giant flying monsters, and a super-evil armored *thing*. Or at least there were. I think they might have gone ashore last night."

"How do you know that?" said an amused voice. Grant Jefferson.

"I dreamed it last night. I saw them." I knew that everyone was listening to me.

Somebody laughed at me over the radio net.

"He's panicking on the ladder. Big dummy. Told you guys. Pitt, go sit in the boat," Grant ordered.

"Grant, you stupid son of a bitch, shut up and listen. I saw the name of the ship in my dream. The monsters came ashore in a lifeboat with the name *Antoine-Henri* painted on it."

The radio net was silent. I hung from the ladder. Twenty feet below, Holly stared up at me incredulously. Five feet above, the Hunters were assembled and either scoffing at me, or hopefully, pondering what I had to say. The stenciled letters on the ghost ship taunted me.

Finally Harbinger's voice came back on. "Pitt, get your ass up here."

I climbed the rest of the way as fast as I could, clambered over the railing and slipped and sprawled onto the gray-painted deck. I leapt to my feet and looked for Harbinger. The Hunters had spread out, using whatever cover was available, and had secured the front of the ship. The Hind roared overhead, tearing at us with wind.

"What's going on?" Harbinger asked. He held a

Tommy gun in his hands and there was murder in his eyes. He angrily glared at the chopper and made a whirling motion with his finger. Julie was still in the door, she gave him a thumbs-up, shouted something at the pilot and the chopper backed off enough that we could converse.

"I had a dream last night. I saw you guys talking about this mission. You were picking which Newbies to go. Then I saw a lifeboat land on a little beach by a swamp; the boat had the name *Antoine-Henri* on it. There were seven Master vampires on board, and some sort of dark evil cloaked thing that was wearing armor. They were taking orders from it. Then it saw us and some winged demon-looking things attacked. I woke up after that."

The Director of Operations studied me carefully. I could not tell what he was thinking. Several of the other Hunters were glancing nervously our way. This episode was costing them valuable daylight. Finally he keyed his neck mike.

"Julie, do another pass around the ship. Check for missing lifeboats."

"Got it, Earl," crackled in my ear. The Hind took off in a burst of speed, nose suddenly down as it headed toward the rear of the freighter. He kept watching me. I readied my 870 and studied the deck. We had thirteen Hunters armed to the teeth, and Julie with a sniper rifle overhead. I did not feel safe at all. Sam and Grant detached themselves from the perimeter and trotted over to join us.

"What the hell is going on?" Grant demanded. His black armor was still polished bright, and somehow not dirtied from the rappel down. His personal weapon was an extremely expensive, customized, suppressed Knights SR25 .308 carbine. "We don't have time for this nonsense, Harbinger. Send him back to the boat. Pitt can't handle it and he's freaking out."

"Shut up, Grant," I snapped.

Harbinger held up his hand, cutting us both off. Julie had come back on the radio.

"I don't think there were any lifeboats mounted. Looks like they have inflatable rafts for that." Her voice was distorted with static.

My spirits sank. Grant laughed at me. Harbinger frowned. Sam spit a glob of chew overboard. I suddenly felt very stupid. Maybe it had just been some weird fluke coincidence of my subconscious.

Not a chance.

"You saw me. In your meeting last night. You at least sensed me somehow. I thought something, and it surprised you. I was in the corner of the conference room," I told Harbinger desperately. "Then I was gone, and that's when the monsters landed. When the big one touched the ground, that's when everybody got that weird feeling."

As I have said before, Harbinger was not a man that I would want to play poker with. He did not normally display his emotions, but right now they were as easy to read as the name on the side of this cursed ship. His jaw dropped open, and his eyes widened. That had shocked him.

"How in the hell—"

He was interrupted midsentence as Julie came back on the radio.

"Earl. I take back what I said. Looks like they had a motor launch or something. There is a pulley system rigged near the end of the ship. Looks like it was used to lower or haul something out of the water. It's empty and the cables are dragging in the water, I repeat it is empty and the cables are in the water. There was a boat of some kind, but it is gone."

"Thanks, Julie. Keep your eyes peeled," he responded, took his hand away, thought better of it, and then keyed his mike again. "Boone, get over here. We need to have a little meeting."

Sam clutched his .45-70 warily. "No way, Earl. Seven Masters? That don't sound right. They don't work together. At least they never have."

"Are you guys crazy? The Newbie is full of it. He needs—"

"Grant. Get back on the perimeter," Harbinger stated flatly.

"But I—"

"Go," the Director snapped. Grant angrily complied.

Boone joined us with a worried look. Harbinger gave him a quick rundown. Julie had told me that Harbinger was much older than he looked, but right now he appeared to have aged a decade right in front of us. Boone looked at all of us as if we were crazy.

"So are you supposed to be like a psychic or something?"

"Not that I know of. I'm an accountant."

"We've seen weirder things, Boone," stated Harbinger. "Remember, flexible minds."

"No shit. But this is weird even for us," Boone replied. Then turning towards me, he asked, "All right, big guy, how did you know they were Masters?"

"I don't know. I could just tell. But they worked together, like a military unit."

"Come on, Earl. That's impossible. If vamps worked together, they could have taken over the world by now. It's been twenty years since there was a confirmed report of a Master."

"Closer to thirty. I know. I'm the one that killed it," Harbinger answered. "But Pitt is right on one thing. Something surprised me last night. I couldn't see anything, but there was something in the conference room with us. How else could he have known that?"

The four of us jumped when the radio sprang to life.

"This is Priest. You lot aren't going to believe this, but I've got signs of life. Somebody must have heard us arrive."

"What?" Boone responded.

"Listen, I'm going to put my mike on it. I'm getting this through a duct."

Every Hunter on the ship strained to hear. It was a series of seemingly random clicks, repeated over and over. I did not immediately recognize it. Sam picked it up first.

"Morse code," he translated. "SOS . . . T R A P P E D space E N G I N E R O O M space D A R N E space SOS."

"Priest, send a message back," Harbinger ordered.

"No can do, chief. Don't know Morse code."

"On it, Earl," Sam responded and hurried off in that direction.

- Harbinger got back on the radio. "Okay, folks. Mission parameters have changed. This is now a rescue." He released the mike. "Boone, gather your men. Let's clear this ship!"

"Won't be the first time Americans have saved the French," the Special Forces vet shouted over his shoulder as he ran to rejoin his team.

I waited for my boss to address me. I could not tell what he was thinking.

"Pitt."

"Yes, sir?"

"Cut the 'sir' crap. Can you think of anything else from that dream of yours that might help?"

"Not really. If the dream is right, then the really bad dudes have disembarked. So do you believe me then?"

He did not answer my question directly. Instead he got back on the radio.

"Holly, send up every stake we have. We need to kill us some vampires."

"So is that a yes?" I asked again.

"Come on . . . We're burning daylight. Nobody's ever killed a Master in the dark."

CHAPTER 8

Vampires are one of the most dangerous forms of undead—brutal, swift, and smart. No Hunter in the world takes one on lightly. They vary greatly in ability, with the weakest being only super dangerous, while Masters are virtually unstoppable, perfect killing machines. Unluckily for us, anyone who is killed while being fed upon by a vampire could rise as one the next few nights, so we were potentially looking at fifty enraged bloodsuckers on the freighter. Luckily for us, newly created vampires tend to be confused and disoriented. The longer the creature exists, and the more blood that it has fed on, the greater its power would become.

Once again, literature and the movies got the story partially correct. Vampires *are* creatures of the night. Indirect sunlight can burn them. Direct sunlight will kill them. Their cells can regenerate almost instantly, but a stake through the heart will paralyze their advanced circulatory systems, and shut them down long enough to take their heads off. Even in our line of work there are not too many things that could survive getting their brain housings severed. Holy symbols like crosses and blessed water occasionally have an effect, but are dependent upon the personal faith of the user. Most Hunters opt for violence over faith; we're kind of like soccer fans that way.

I took small comfort from that fact as I hauled a case of fragmentation grenades up from the *Brilliant Mistake*. They could be destroyed, and we had the means to do it. I grunted as I set the heavy case down on the deck, unclamped the cable, and threw it back over the side. Holly waited below for our next request. Trip and Lee stood nearby, scanning for any threats. We were the security detail. Julie was in the Hind, still on overwatch, and the ten other Hunters had broken into two raid teams and were making their way gradually toward the engine room.

"This is Harbinger. Still haven't seen anything."

"Boone's team. All clear. Stay frosty."

We had sent a coded message down the duct. The French Hunter tapped back that most of his team had been taken out by vampires, and they had sealed themselves in a compartment, were out of ammo, and were hiding.

"Newbie team. All clear on top." I cradled my Remington and watched the deck. Nothing was moving except for the French flag flapping in the breeze. Since we were standing in broad daylight, and worried about creatures that burst into flame when they got too much sun, there was not a lot for the Newbie team to do other than keep a sharp eye on nothing. The Hind circled lazily above.

"How come Chuck got to go inside, and we're

stuck out here?" Albert Lee complained. He was a small-statured man of Asian descent. He had been a librarian once upon a time, before a colony of giant mutant spiders had taken up residence in his archives and started sucking the fluids out of his clientele. Unlike your average librarian, however, he had put himself through college on the GI Bill, and had been a demolitions specialist in the Marine Corps. His giant spider problem had met a fiery end, thanks to diesel fuel and ammonium nitrate fertilizer. Sadly, the library had burned down as well. He was sharp, and unlike many of the Newbies had already known which end of the gun was the dangerous one. I was glad that Harbinger had picked him to come along.

"Chuck has more CQB training," I answered. CQB stood for close quarters battle, and Mead had a lot more experience in it from his Ranger days than the rest of the Newbies. Lee just shook his head and we went back to waiting. Time passed slowly except for the occasional radio check-ins. The two assault teams were converging on the engine room from separate corridors.

"This is Harbinger. Galley's clear. Buckets of blood on the floor. There was a struggle here."

"This is Boone. We're above the boilers. More blood. Lots of shell casings. This must be where the French bought it."

"This is Julie. Deck is clear."

"Newbie team. All clear on top," I said again.

"This is the 'support' team. I've got stupid sailors trying to hit on me and this damn boat smells like fish guts," Holly reported.

I checked my weapons again. The 870 had an 18-inch barrel and a two-shot mag extension, giving me seven total shots in the gun. It was a personal favorite of mine. I had owned this particular unit since I was fifteen. I had replaced the fore end with a Surefire high intensity flashlight, mounted a glow in the dark XS bead sight on the rib, attached a side saddle that held an extra six shells, and added a nylon butt cuff that held six more. My load-bearing gear was heavily laden with extra shells: silver buckshot, silver slugs, flechettes, armor-piercing quadrangle shot, internally suppressed buckshot, Milo's special magnum breaching charges, and even a couple of Penguin tear gas rounds. I had strapped on everything but the kitchen sink, and I'm sure that they had a specialty round for that as well.

My handgun was also an old friend. At MHI, Hunters are able to customize their kits to suit them, and any handgun is allowed as long as it is a .45 that is reliable with our special silver bullets. My pistol was a Kimber/BUL polymer-framed double stack 1911 that I had been shooting in three-gun matches for years. The fat magazines held 14 rounds of .45, and I had six extras on my belt. I had customized it with huge tritium Ashley Express sights, that gave up a little precision for a whole lot of speed, which suited me just fine. I had over 10,000 rounds through that pistol, and I had won more than a few trophies with it.

There were several grenades on my webbing, a few sharpened stakes, and other miscellaneous tools. The enormous knife strapped to my chest completed my ensemble. Being a big guy, I had taken one of the biggest knives in the armory. Milo had said that it was a kukri from Nepal, the weapon of choice of the renowned Gurkha troops. It was curved deadly steel, with a fat heavy end designed for maximum chopping power. The version I had strapped on was called a ganga ram, and it was longer than my forearm. If I had to chop any heads off, I wasn't going to screw around. Most of us were wearing the lightweight hockey helmets, as the big ones were too bulky for the close quarters of the ship.

I was as ready as I could be. I felt like I had in the minutes before a big money fight. Every one of us had been training hard, both physically and mentally. The Newbie team was ready to rumble. The others were armed with Heckler & Koch .45 subguns. I wasn't particularly impressed with the guns, and thought the whole German engineering thing was really overrated, but Milo had gotten a good deal on a couple dozen, so they were passed out to most of the Newbies until they were proficient enough to pick their own gear.

The radio crackled again. The deeper the teams moved into the bowels of the ship, the greater the distortion. We were using top-of-the-line communications equipment, but there was only so much that radio waves could do through layers of steel plate.

"Boone here. We have movement ahead. Five yards from the engine room."

"This is Harbinger. Movement ahead."

"Shit. They're behind us too."

"Incoming. They're coming through the grates."

"Under the floor. Coming through the floor." Gunfire erupted in the background.

"Ambush! It's an ambush!"

The radio cut out. I couldn't hear a thing. The three of us on deck stared at each other in confusion.

"Earl, come in Earl. Boone. Anybody hear me?"

Julie asked over the radio from the circling helicopter. She sounded worried.

I looked up to see her holding her hand to her neck, sniper rifle dangling from its straps. She was shouting something at the pilot, then she looked at me, and quickly snapped her rifle to her shoulder.

"Newbie team. You have incoming!" she shouted over the radio as she fired right past my head.

The supersonic crack could be felt in my eyeballs and eardrums as the bullet whizzed by, mere inches from my helmet. I spun in time to see a hideous undead face fall away from the ship's railing, an extra hole in its gray forehead. Gore-stained men in rags were coming up over the sides, and charging with fast loping gaits, directly toward us.

No time for emotion. Training kicked in.

Without any conscious thought I raised the shotgun, flicked off the safety and caressed the trigger. I slammed a creature to the deck with a load of double-aught to the chest. Before it had even fallen, I had pumped and fired at the next creature in line, tearing off its jaw in a spray of black ooze. It kept coming, arms outstretched and clawed hands grasping for me. I cranked off two more rapid shots and it stumbled and fell over the railing. The *chunk-chunk-chunk* sound of suppressed subguns opened up as Trip and Lee fired their H&K UMP .45s.

Grabbing shells from my vest I rapid-fire shoved them into the loading port as I searched for more targets. The ashen undead were pouring over the sides of the ship, and spilling out around us in a confused mass. I fired at them as fast as I could, the gun an extension of my will. I put twelve silver pellets through the brain cage of a creature closing on Lee, and dropped a slug through the chest cavity of another charging Trip. I felt a cold wet splash as the head of an undead that had appeared behind me was vaporized by a .308 round from Julie's rifle.

"Close ranks. Get back to back! Back to back!" I shouted at my team. Somehow in the confusion they heard and ran toward me, all of us firing simultaneously in different directions. Some of the monsters that had been put down were already standing up again. I punt-kicked one as I passed, a move that would have broken every rib and probably killed a human. All it did was send the creature to its feet faster. It opened its maw in a soundless roar and lunged. I stuck the 870's muzzle under its sternum at near-contact distance and blew a softball-sized hole out its back. It stumbled away momentarily, but then changed its mind and kept coming. I crushed its skull with the butt of my gun, and kicked its legs out from under it.

Lee screamed in pain as a bone claw struck him in the leg, and he collapsed to the ground. Trip stitched the monster through the face, grabbed Lee by the drag handle on the back of his armor, and pulled him to safety. I emptied my shotgun into the throng of undead, trying to take head shots, and then dropped it when it clicked empty. My tac sling kept it from hitting the ground. I instantly transitioned to my Kimber, centered the sights on the closest target and started firing. Bits of meat and bone flew from the creatures' heads as the bullets struck home.

The three of us clustered together, shooting and reloading wildly. Lee lay prone on his stomach, firing his UMP upwards. More bullets cracked past us as Julie fired into the crowd. The slide of my 1911 locked back empty just as a creature was almost on me. My hand flashed toward a new magazine in a speed reload, but Trip was suddenly past me and took the monster's arm off at the shoulder with his hatchet. With its remaining arm the creature brutally swatted Trip to the deck. I slammed the fresh mag home, dropped the slide and shot it through both eye sockets.

Lee was reloading, struggling to get a magazine out of his chest pockets while lying on them, his legs paralyzed beneath him. Trip wasn't moving.

There were only two creatures still up, but they were coming our way fast. One was wearing what used to be a sailor's uniform, and the other was wearing some sort of security coverall. Their eyes glowed red, and their teeth were broken and black. Sharpened bones appeared through the torn ends of their hands. I hammered two quick rounds into the first creature's head, and it spilled forward onto the deck.

I shot the former sailor in the face. Its claws slashed out toward me as I threw myself down in an attempt to avoid them. My back hit the deck, sliding through the spilled fluids, firing upward into the creature still relentlessly pursuing me. Its neck erupted in a spray of black as Julie nailed it, temporarily slowing the monster. I pulled the massive ganga ram from my chest and swung at the creature's legs. The big knife tore through the monster's knee, severing the limb. It fell beside me and I cleaved the top half of its skull off, spilling pink brains and black fluid onto the painted deck.

The front of the ship was littered with steaming

gray bodies. Some of them were still moving, and a few were already starting to rise. I raised the huge knife over my head and shouted in rage. I hacked wildly at anything that twitched, spraying fluids and meat with every swing. Lee struggled to his feet shakily and shot .45 caliber holes in anything that looked suspicious. The Hind dropped altitude, and roared over the side of the ship.

"Owen! The undead are coming out the portholes. They're crawling up the sides of the ship. Holly needs help."

Shit. I slammed the still sticky knife back into its sheath, holstered my pistol, retrieved my shotgun and started loading it with slugs as I ran toward the chain ladders. Julie was dangling from the Hind, firing at the side of the ship below me. A ricochet sparked upwards and struck my body armor. Ignoring the painful but not dangerous hit, I leaned across the railing to look down at the deck of the *Brilliant Mistake*. Holly was firing her UMP at the monsters dangling unnaturally from the slick steel hull. They were crawling along it somehow, in violation of gravity and common sense, heading directly toward her. There were at least five of them, and they were soaking up bullets without much effect.

I put the bead on a creature directly below me. It was an awkward angle, and I had to lean over so far that I was afraid I was going to end up in the ocean. I stroked the trigger and put an ounce of silver through the first undead's shoulder blades. Arms limp, it slipped from the hull and fell into the waves. I pumped the action and took aim on the next target.

Then a cold feeling surged through my body, starting

in the center of my back, and spreading out into my limbs, so very cold it burned. My legs went numb, and buckled beneath me. My 870 slipped from my grasp and dangled on its sling. I was jerked around like a rag doll. An undead sailor held me by the straps of my armor. Its touch had caused instant paralysis. I looked into its clear, blood-red eyes as it opened its mouth impossibly wide, black razor teeth glistening. I tried to move, but all I could manage was a weak flopping of my arms, twitching the muscles of my face, and a small tingle of my fingers. I was about to die.

Suddenly the top of the creature's head opened up like a cantaloupe stuffed with firecrackers. Julie had fired right past my limp body. The bullet actually grazed my helmet. It was perhaps the best shot I had ever seen. The creature fell, lifeless claws trailing away from me. I could see Trip and Lee heading my way, trying to reach me before my limp body went over the rail. Trip dived recklessly over the near headless undead, arms outstretched like I was the winning end zone pass.

He did not quite make it.

I fell the thirty feet into the ocean soundlessly. Not because I was too brave to scream, believe me. I was screaming on the inside, but my throat was too frozen to make any sound. I hit the waves with a huge splash. Immediately the weight of my armor and weapons dragged me down. My limbs floated numbly around me. I was at least able to close my mouth, but water started to rush relentlessly down my nose. I tried to move. I willed my arms to move. Nothing was happening. I tried to struggle. I raged soundlessly at my helplessness as I spiraled into the depths.

The light was dwindling above. I did not know if that was because I was putting some serious distance against the surface, or because my brain was running out of oxygen. The water was cold, but my body felt colder still. Lights began to pop behind my eyes as water expanded into my lungs. I knew that soon they would lock up in desperation, and I was screwed.

What were the undead that paralyzed you at their touch? We had discussed them in class . . . There had been a picture of Julie fighting one. *Wights*. Wights could paralyze you. How long did it last though? Lee had gotten up pretty quick, and Trip was moving around when I slipped over the edge. A minute? Maybe two? Unfortunately I didn't have a minute or two. My depth was increasing, and I was starting to panic from lack of air. Terror without the outlet of movement is a real bummer. I kept trying to move, willing myself to respond with all my might. My fingers wiggled slightly. Not enough.

It had been fun while it lasted.

Then I stopped. The Old Man from my dream was in front of me. I could see him clearly in the dark water. He was perfectly dry as fish swam past his bony shoulders. He shook his head sadly.

"Boy, we have to stop meeting like this."

He reached out with his heavy cane and stabbed the emergency button on my armored harness. The CO_2 canister erupted with bubbles, instantly inflating the shoulder portion of the armor, and giving me positive buoyancy. I started to rise.

"Up you go now. Your friends need help. You not very good at this. No more getting dead!"

As my armor carried me toward the surface in a

cloud of bubbles, I could sense the feeling returning to my body. It was an awful, tingly pain. Combined with the screaming, air-starved agony in my chest and the explosive pain in my head, it was horrible. My legs began to kick and my arms began to tear at the hard water, forcing myself ever faster toward the light and a breath of precious, precious air.

My head broke the surface. I somehow gasped and filled my mostly liquid-distended lungs, and simultaneously violently vomited salt water. That hurt. Immediately one of the fishermen started to wildly strike me in the helmet with a pole.

"Kill it! Kill it!" one of them shouted.

I tried to swat the pole away, but my limbs were still regaining their strength. "Stop it! I'm human, you idiots," I croaked as they tried their best to shove me back underwater.

"He's on our side. Quit hitting him, damn it!" I heard Holly order. "Pull him in."

I did my best to grab the end of the pole and I was dragged to the *Brilliant Mistake*. Rough hands grabbed me by my harness and pulled me aboard, soaked, shaking, gasping and still vomiting. There was sudden movement in the waves as one of the wights broke the surface and did a savage impersonation of dog-paddling toward our boat.

"You can whack that one," I gurgled, as my numb fingers tried to grasp my still-secured shotgun.

"I've got it. Fire in the hole!" Holly shouted. I heard a plopping splash, and a few seconds later a thunderous roar as the frag grenade detonated. The ocean erupted. Water and miscellaneous undead bits rained down on the little boat.

"That's the last of them," Holly reported. "Are you okay?"

I rolled onto my side and retched and coughed horribly. My chest was racked with spasms of pain and I was seeing double.

"Yeah, I'm cool," I gasped.

"Sure, you're the picture of health. Come on, Z." She tried to help me up, but I was far too heavy to budge. I struggled to my knees as she pulled at the drag handles on my armor. There was a large scorch mark on the hull of the *Antoine-Henri*, with a small jagged crater torn through the metal in the center. She saw me looking at the hole in puzzlement.

"What? You thought you guys were going to leave me down here with all of the cool stuff and I wasn't going to use any of it?" She pointed at the spent RPG launcher lying on the deck. Next to it was the head-less body of a still-twitching wight. She had pinned it to the wooden deck with a boathook.

"They need help up top," I said as she helped me to my feet. I had to stop and vomit once again. It still hurt but it was getting easier. That one had contained my dinner from the evening before. Nachos.

"I'll go. You stay here. The captain is casting off. They're going to get the hell away from this demon boat, and I can't say I blame them. They'll pull back and wait for our signal in case any more of those things come squirting out the portholes."

"I'm going," I stated.

"You almost drowned," she pleaded.

"And I didn't even get any mouth to mouth. We're wasting time." I grabbed onto the ladder as the *Brilliant Mistake's* engine turned over with a cough and ejected a cloud of diesel smoke. Holly shook her head in consternation and grabbed the second ladder. We started climbing as the little boat pulled away. If I had thought that it was hard the first time, doing it after almost drowning was infinitely more difficult. My boots and armor were soaked, and had seemingly tripled in damp weight like giant Cordura sponges. Holly easily outpaced me—her lighter weight and excellent muscle tone surely helped—and she went over the top first. Trip and Lee were waiting for me, and helped drag my carcass the last few feet.

"Ugh," I grunted as I fell onto the deck for the second time. "I hate that stupid ladder."

"It's easier than upside-down pole dancing, you sissy," Holly stated as she unslung her UMP. Surveying the deck, I could see that my companions had been busy while I had taken a little swim. Every wight had been hastily chopped into its component bits. Some gray arms were still pulling themselves along, and a few severed heads were glaring and gnashing their teeth. The Hind was still circling above us. Surprisingly, my radio still worked.

"I popped a couple climbing up the other side. I think we're clear," Julie's voice said. "No response from the assault element. I'm coming down."

The chopper stopped directly above us, a rope was thrown out the side, and Julie unclipped herself from her bungee cords. She expertly fast-roped down, dropping swiftly to the deck. As soon as her boots hit the surface she was heading our way, helmeted head pointed down to avoid the harsh blast of the rotors. The Hind immediately gained altitude and banked hard and away.

"He can stay for another twenty minutes, tops, then

he needs to refuel," she shouted as she approached. "Is everybody okay?"

"Good to go," Holly stated. The rest of us nodded.

I suddenly dry-heaved and went to my knees coughing and choking. Once it passed, I shakily lumbered back up. "Just peachy," I said giving a big cheesy grin and a thumbs-up.

"Good. We're going in," Julie ordered. She dropped the partially expended magazine from her accurized M14, and replaced it with a full one. "Assault team has been out of contact for a few minutes. They probably need help. Let's move out."

She trotted toward the entrance to the belly of the beast. The rest of us followed obediently. It had been felt that the Newbie team had not been ready for the brutal close quarters battle that was monster hunting in a claustrophobic ship's interior. That didn't matter now. We were the cavalry and we were coming to the rescue. At least Julie knew what she was doing.

"Take grenades. But be careful how you use them. We're going to be inside a steel tube. Back pressure from an explosion can kill. Don't hose shots. Everything ricochets down here. Watch your muzzle and be aware of where the rest of your team is. No flames. The ship is metal, but everything onboard can burn, and a ship fire is bad news. If anything moves, and it isn't human, shoot it. Questions?"

Nobody said anything. We stopped in front of the massive metal door. Julie grabbed Holly by the straps of her armor and looked her in the eyes. "It's going to be dark in there, Holly. Just like the hole. Are you going to be okay? You don't have to do this if you aren't ready."

"I'm fine. I hate vampires. Let's kill these assholes," she replied angrily. Julie nodded and smiled. I had no idea what that was about.

"We're going to move fast. We're not going to stack at each entrance. We're not going to do a full clearing. Keep moving. Watch above you. Watch floor grates. Lee, you bring up the rear, watch behind us. I'm on point, then Pitt, Trip, and Newcastle. Got it?"

"Let me take point," I suggested.

"Why?"

"I've got the shotgun. You've got a sniper rifle with a scope on it. Plus I'm expendable. If you're in front and you die, then the rest of us are screwed." I wasn't being chivalrous. For conversational distance a shotgun beat the pants off of a long rifle with a magnifying optic.

She thought about it for a moment, then nodded. "Pitt on point, then me. Any questions?" It probably made more sense to put one of the other three with the suppressed subguns next in line, but I did not think Julie was real confident in their shooting abilities at that point.

We were quiet, each of us preparing ourselves in our own way to enter the dark. Trip was obviously mumbling a prayer. Lee had his eyes closed and appeared to be doing controlled breathing. Holly was wearing an evil predatory grin. I made sure my shotgun and pistol were fully loaded and my magazines and knife were in place. At least my quick dip in the ocean had cleaned most of the wight juices off of me. The rest of the Newbie team was coated in them.

Julie slapped me on the back of my soggy armor. "Go."

❖   ❖   ❖

The first floor we covered was still lit with fluo-
rescent lights, but by the time we hit the stairs for
the next level down, we were forced to switch to our
helmet-mounted night vision monoculars. Something
had systematically smashed every light. Glass crunched
under our boots as we quickly made our way through
the narrow steel corridors. I had a pair of lights on
my shotgun, one a super-bright white light, and the
second cast a brilliant beam that was invisible to the
human eye, but lit up the whole world in green through
my monocular. The rest of the team was similarly
equipped with infrared lights on their guns as well.
Since we were fighting undead, the thermal-imaging
gear had been left on deck. It was not very useful
against things that were already room temperature.

We swiftly passed through what had been the galley.
I kept the shotgun at the low ready, elbows tucked
down to keep from banging them on the walls. Meals
lay half eaten and rotting on the tables. The walls
were splashed with a thick fluid that was indeterminate through night vision, but my gut told me that it
had once been bright arterial spray. I bumped into a
wine bottle with my foot and sent it spinning under
one of the tables. The doors were basically watertight
hatches, and I had to carefully step over a steep sealing lip on the base of each portal as I passed. So far
all of the hatches had been open.

The crash of gunfire echoed through the corridors
and ductwork. That was a good sign that our friends
were still alive. My small team quickened its pace.
According to the blueprints we'd studied on the
way to the ship, we needed to go down one more

flight of stairs, through some quarters, down a long corridor, and then we would be right on top of the engine room. We all flinched as an explosive *whump* vibrated the whole freighter and rattled the utensils in the galley.

"Bomb?" Trip asked.

"Hard to tell," Julie answered.

"I hope we don't sink," Lee grunted.

Our boots rattled on the metal stairs as we double-timed it to the next level. The time for stealth had passed. I turned the corner into the crew quarters, light probing ahead, shotgun butt ground tightly into my shoulder pocket. The long narrow room was filled with double bunks. Pornography had been crudely taped to the walls, and it looked strange in the glowing green light. Blankets and trash were strewn everywhere. It was a veritable warren of hiding places. Jerking my fist up, I signaled the team to freeze. I had sensed something.

Julie drew against me, her rifle at the ready. I could hear her breathing. There was a clank as another member of our team tripped on the doorway. Something was in the room with us. I could feel it.

Nothing happened.

The group continued to shine our invisible lights around the room. I could not put my finger on what I was feeling, but something was waiting for us.

Julie must have felt the same thing. "Everybody, NVGs off. Go to white light," she commanded.

I flipped my monocular back and complied, pushing the button that activated the 120-lumen Surefire light on the forearm of my 870. Brilliant, scalding light suddenly filled the room from five waving points.

A night vision monocular has some advantages over a similar pair of goggles that cover both eyes, but it also has its disadvantages. On the plus side, with the single lens, one pupil will be fully dilated for natural human night vision, and the other eye will be looking at an already bright green world. The human brain, being the amazing thing that it is, superimposes both lighted and unlighted images together. You get electronically enhanced vision, with one eye still able to see as well as any human could in the dark if the device gets lost. With two-lens goggles, you have better night vision capability, but if your device goes out, you're pretty much screwed until your eyes adjust to the dark. Great as our monoculars are, there's a disadvantage inherent to them as well. When you suddenly flip on bright lights, one of your eyes is immediately blinded.

So the five of us were down to one sort of functioning eye and one dazzled eye when the Surefires kicked in. That was probably why the image of the vampire crawling down the ceiling toward us was extra surreal. As I had been told, it did in fact look like a normal person. This one looked like a regular sailor. Pale and defying gravity, but human.

I reacted a fraction of a second before the rest of the team. In that moment I was able to pump two silver slugs through the vampire's chest and pelvis. The concussion of the shotgun was deafening in the confined space, but nothing compared to the sonic crack of Julie's M14. Her bullet clipped the vampire through the shoulder. The creature dropped to the floor, and both of us hit it again on the way down. The rest of the team did not have a clear shot through us.

The vampire screamed inhumanly as Julie and I simultaneously dropped to our knees. The three Newbies behind us opened fire over our heads. The suppressed weapons shuddered as .45 bullets stitched the creature, with plenty of other bullets missing and hitting the walls and bunks. It shook and staggered, but kept coming. Impact holes puckered in the monster's pale skin, only to instantly close. I emptied the rest of my slugs in a continuous burst, nailing the monster from the crotch to the forehead, the last shot snapping the vampire's head back violently.

I dropped the smoking Remington, drew my handgun, and fired two shots before I was swatted aside. My body armor cushioned the blow, but I was hurled through the air and slammed into the steel wall. Pain surged through my ribs and I lost my pistol on impact. Julie dropped down and rolled under a nearby bunk, narrowly avoiding the vampire's foot as it smashed an indentation into the metal floor. Illumination from five different flashlights pointing in strange directions created a hellish and confusing scene.

The rest of my team emptied their subguns into the creature as it closed on them. Holly and Trip started to reload and Lee drew his knife and swung wildly. The vampire moved so quickly that it was hard to track visually. It side-stepped the blow, grabbed Lee by his arm and tossed him across the room. I heard the smaller man skid roughly across the floor. The vampire was distracted from Trip and Holly as heavy .308 bullets struck it in the feet and legs.

Julie's cover was torn away as the sailor thing grabbed the bunk and ripped it from the wall, easily breaking the heavy bolts. It reached for her but I got there first. I swung my ganga ram with all of the fury that I possessed. Somehow it sensed me in midswing, and started to move. I had been aiming for its neck, but instead my blade sunk deep into its shoulder, breaking the collarbone and grinding out against the top of the monster's ribs. Black fluid sprayed everywhere like a pierced hydraulic cylinder.

Spinning away, the creature ripped my blade from my grasp. The vampire flew backwards, and stuck to the wall like a spider. Screeching in anger, it reached up, grasped the hilt of the massive Nepalese blade and drug it out of its back. The noise of steel scraping on bone was sickening. The blade dropped to the floor with a clatter. I heard the near simultaneous dropping of bolts as Trip and Holly got their UMPs back in action. Julie was reloading. Lee wasn't moving. I reached for a specialty 12 gauge round, dropped it into the open chamber of my 870, and ran the pump forward.

The wound was already sealing. It hissed something obviously profane in French.

"Parley-vous this, mother-fucker."

It leapt at me, launching itself like a demon frog missile. I brought the shotgun up and pulled the trigger as the muzzle contacted the vampire's chest.

A regular breaching round is used by police to safely break the locks or hinges on heavy doors during raids, which fragments without endangering any bystanders. The 3-inch magnum 12 gauge sintered magnesium/tungsten breaching charge that I had just fired had been designed for blowing through hinges suitable for bank vaults. Milo had told me that, during testing, this special breacher had put a basketball-sized hole through a side of beef.

The recoil was amazing, even by my standards. The noise was going to leave all of us with ringing ears for a week. The vampire's torso exploded in a black mist.

The creature's momentum carried it into me, we both crashed to the floor, rolling and thrashing. Entrails were spilling everywhere. Its legs were kicking on the ground, but its top half kept fighting. I pushed it off as it clawed at me and rolled away. Trip and Holly responded by pouring two full magazines of .45 caliber silver into the thrashing monstrosity, riddling it with holes. As soon as they ran dry, Julie charged the torso. She placed one heavy boot on the creature's neck, raised a sharpened stake high over her head and, with a cry, slammed it through the evil black heart.

A fountain of black ooze shot into the air and the hideous shrieks pierced us to the bone. Julie was splattered, but undaunted. The vampire was twitching, but could barely move. She held her hand out. "Big knife."

Grabbing my ganga ram from the floor I limped over. I handed it over hilt first. The knife was huge, but she was a strong woman. She swung it back with one hand like she was clearing brush with a machete, then struck. There was a thud and the screaming finally stopped. The head rolled free. She kicked it in disgust.

"Reload. There's more where that came from. Lee, you still with us?" Julie said. She wiped the knife blade on her leg and handed it back over, mouthing the word "thanks." She looked deadly serious covered in vampire gore and illuminated by powerful flashlights.

"I'm okay. Ow, damn," Lee said as Trip helped him

to his feet. He sounded weak and raspy. "I think I broke a rib."

"Take it easy for a sec. Holly, cover the other doorway. Keep it on white light. Our vision is shot, and the lights disorient them."

"That was disoriented?" Trip asked.

I speed-reloaded the shotgun. I did not dare load any more breaching rounds since they were useless past contact distance. "Anybody see my pistol?"

Lee handed it to me, scuffed, but undamaged. I changed magazines and reholstered. The bunk I was leaning against had a picture of a sailor's wife and kids standing in front of the Eiffel Tower. I shined my light on the vampire's body. The flesh was slowly bubbling and melting into a tarlike substance, leaving only sticky bones. The eyeless skull appeared to be watching me.

"So that's a Master vampire. They aren't so tough," I said.

Julie surprised us all by laughing. It was a genuine sound of merriment, and was totally out of place in the splattered crew quarters. She paused in cleaning the slime off her prescription goggles long enough to look at all of us poor befuddled Newbies. She shook her head and smiled.

"That was just a baby." All of the Newbies had some choice words at that. Holly swore so creatively that it was almost poetry. "Masters can move so fast you can't hardly see them. They can eat a stack of Bibles and wash it down with a lit Molotov cocktail. This guy was probably turned in the last week. Abnormally quick regeneration, but the more powerful the creator, the stronger the creation. Whatever started this mess was one bad son of a gun. It would have to be to create those wights to serve as daylight guardians too."

Satisfied that she could see again, Julie pointed toward Holly and the passage to the engine room. "Owen on point again. Trip, stay by Lee and help him if he needs it. Holly, you bring up the rear. If we come across more vamps, stop, then throw in some grenades first. All right, let's move."

I took my place at the door, light stabbing ahead, searching for targets. Julie took the second position. She spoke softly in my ear.

"Parley-vous, mother effer?"

"It sounded good at the time," I shrugged. "Hey, if we don't die in the next few minutes, are you doing anything for dinner tonight?"

She thumped me in the shoulder to indicate that it was time to move out. I took that as a no. I moved quickly, the light from the flashlights behind threw my hulking shadow down the hall. I had pulled something in my leg in the struggle with the vampire. My head and chest ached from my earlier adventure in the water. My stomach and throat hurt from all of the heaving. My nerves tingled with adrenaline and terror-induced endorphins. I was still seeing purple ghosts in one semi-blinded eye, and I was covered in vampire juices. I was having a great time and had never felt more alive.

Finally a voice came over the radio. It was Harbinger.

"Lights coming near the engine room. Who is it?"

"Hold your fire. It's me and the Newbie team," Julie answered.

"Stop where you are. There's a mess of hostiles about thirty feet from your position through the door on your left. We're at the end of the hall on the other side of that. Why ain't you up top?"

It was good to hear Harbinger's voice. I pointed my shotgun at the indicated compartment. Anything that came through that portal was going to get a snout full of buckshot.

"We lost radio contact after you got ambushed. The deck got swarmed with wights. We killed them, but the boat crew wasn't going to stick around, and the Hind was low on fuel. The Newbies did good, only minor injuries. We decided to come find you guys. I thought for a minute we had lost you, Earl," Julie answered.

"Nope. But Boone lost a man. Roberts got swarmed in the ambush. We have some others wounded, but nothing critical. It was bad. There had to be at least twenty vamps. And they rigged the lights to blow when they attacked." His voice sounded tired and ragged.

"That doesn't sound right. Undead don't coordinate," she said.

"These do. It was planned. We killed most of them, and the rest are holed up in that engine compartment. There are at least five."

"Fire?" Julie asked, sounding hopeful.

"Negative. Fuel storage is through there. Same with explosives. We set anything off in that room and we're swimming home. Plus the room that Darné and his men are locked in is on the other side of where the vamps are."

"Plan?" she asked.

"I haven't figured that out yet. We can go in shooting. But if we do we might hit a steam line and cook us all, or we might hit the boiler and blow a hole in the bottom of the ship. Either way we're running out of time. We got another coded message from the French Hunters. The vamps are trying to break into their compartment—wait a second."

I did not turn to look. I kept my muzzle on the door. We had a great position. Both groups of Hunters could fire with impunity into the doorway, and the angles were such that the chances of ricocheting a shot into the other team were virtually nil. Trip and Holly both squeezed around me so that they would have a shot as well. The injured Lee watched our backs and Julie stayed on the radio. The walls and floor vibrated slightly from the powerful engine nearby. The air smelled of diesel and rubber and rust and the faint copper smell of blood.

While we waited for Harbinger to get back to us, I could not help but ask, "Did any of you guys know Roberts?"

"He was the tall, skinny, blond guy on the boat," Trip said. "Seemed like a good guy."

"He was a great guy. Brave. A little crazy, but he was a dang good Hunter," Julie told us. "Roberts has been with us since we restarted. First batch of Newbies we had. He'll be missed. I think he had an ex-wife and some kids in St. Louis."

Harbinger's voice crackled in my ear piece. "Sam says that he found something on the schematics. We're directly under the main cargo bay. There's an escape hatch there that leads into that engine compartment. Sam says that we can put somebody through it, and they can pierce a steam pipe in the vamp's room, and then close the hatch before they get cooked. The steam will fry the undead, or at least flush them into the corridor where we can blast them."

"Won't that kill the Frenchmen also?" Julie asked.

"Sam doesn't think so. Might raise the temperature a little, but judging from the schematics they should be fine. I'm sending Sam, Grant and Mead up to do it."

"What about Boone's team?"

"My team's a little occupied, Jules," Boone replied over the net. "Your uncle Earl neglected to mention that we have at least two more of the bloodsuckers pinned down by the shafts. One of them is the son of a whore that bit Roberts."

"Roger that." She released her mike. "Wait for the cookout."

"I could place some claymores down the hall. Give them a surprise when they come running out," Lee offered helpfully. Just like a former demo guy, always looking to blow something up.

"No, we're too enclosed."

She was probably right. But judging by the number of projectiles these things could soak up, I sure was not looking forward to five of them heading our way at the same time. There had been an FN MAG machine gun brought on board from the *Brilliant Mistake*. I had left it behind since it was so long and unwieldy inside the tight confines of the ship. However, 200 rounds of belt-fed .308 full auto firepower would have been great right about then.

"I've got some smaller stuff. It should do the trick with minimal damage to us, but it'll turn anything that comes through that door into hamburger." For emphasis, Lee patted a pouch that was clipped to his webbing. "I'm hurting pretty bad, so I don't think I could throw it far enough, but one of you guys could probably land it right outside that hatch. It's radio detonated."

Julie thought about it for a moment and then nodded at Trip. Lee unclipped the pouch, opened it, made a few adjustments, zipped it back up and handed it over. Trip gently bounced it in his hands a few times to test the weight, then he underhanded it with perfect accuracy, landing it on our side, just in front of the targeted hatch.

"Good throw," Holly said.

"I helped coach the girl's softball team too. Slow pitch." All of us gave him funny looks. "It was a small school," he added defensively.

Time passed. Harbinger informed us that the captive French were sending more messages. The vampires were slowly battering their way in looking for fresh blood. Sam checked in to tell us that the three of them were almost in position. Boone's team was down to four, and two of them were injured, and they had problems of their own. Harbinger and Milo were in position, but since there were only two of them they were in for trouble if all of the vampires headed their way. We were spread awfully thin. It was going to be tight.

"This is Sam. We're in place. Main cargo bay appears empty. But there's a mess of Conex containers up here, it's hard to tell. We're gonna pop the hatch. You should know if this works. Over."

"Go get them, Cowboy," Julie whispered under her breath, while tightening the grip on her M14. We were positioned so that anything stepping into the hall was going to get a big surprise. A bit of high explosives and four of us that were able to provide direct fire.

Julie and I were even pretty decent shots. Who was I kidding, I was pretty good, but from what I had seen up on the deck, she was amazing. I glanced surreptitiously her way. Her brown eyes were focused through the lens of her ACOG scope. Her gloved finger was resting easily just alongside the trigger guard. She was leaning against the steel hull to steady herself. Her features were strong, and somehow she was still attractive in her relatively unflattering green body armor despite the scratches and slime all over her face. Julie Shackleford was the girl of my dreams.

In the distance the sound of banging metal could be heard and then a rapid series of gunshots and another clang of metal on metal. Trip was prone on the floor, so he felt the vibration first. "Here we go!" he shouted.

A metallic screeching tore at our ears, as a wall of white vapor poured out of the open hatchway. The noise was a bastardized version of the world's greatest and most terrifying teapot. Even from where we were, the temperature rose dramatically as the scalding mist began to fill the hallway. Just under the onslaught of noise could be heard other equally inhuman screams, this time from the engine compartment's resident vampires.

Something moved in the hatchway. First one, then two, and finally a third vampire stumbled into the corridor. The steam was boiling their fluids and peeling their flesh far faster than they could regenerate. One of them turned malevolently toward us with blind, molten eye sockets and screamed.

"Hit it, Lee!" Julie shouted. Our demolitionist librarian complied and compressed the clacker in his gloved fist.

The small charge detonated. The explosion was more of a muted thump than the expected fireball. In the open, Lee's little bomb might not have been very impressive, but in the narrow metal space, the energy of the C4 tore through the undead. Their bones were smashed into powder and their bodies were disseminated into their component materials. We were thirty feet away but we were still peppered with a fine mist of vampire.

Two more creatures spilled from the hatchway, just having missed the bomb. One moved in our direction, the other turned toward Harbinger and Milo. Six weapons opened fire. The creature heading our way was blind, burned, and torn. Some of its internal organs had expanded under the intense, wet heat, and the creature appeared lopsided and ungainly. Our bullets tore into it, rupturing through fluids and tissues, breaking bones, and spilling the vampire's unnatural life onto the floor. It fell to its knees under our onslaught, dragging itself inexorably toward us. One scalded claw was torn completely off by my last round of buckshot, and it still somehow continued trying to pull itself on its one functioning limb.

It fell silent as we ran our guns dry. My ears were partially protected by the high quality earpieces, but even with that my head swam from the barrage in the tight echoing chamber. No gunfire could be heard from the other Hunters' position.

"Earl. Come in, Earl. Are you okay?" Julie dropped her spent M14 mag, and inserted another, letting the bolt fly forward to chamber another round. "Can you hear us?"

"Got it. Our vamp is down."

"We're coming around the corner to finish ours. Hold your fire."

"Roger that."

The vampire was torn asunder, but already it was beginning to heal. This time Trip and Holly did the honors while I covered them. Holly put her boot down on the creature's spine, and slammed a stake through its back with a vengeance. This vampire was too damaged to scream. Trip grimaced as he pulled out his hatchet. I suppose that the correct term was tomahawk for the Vietnam-era weapon that he had picked out of the armory. My friend raised the little ax and brought it down swiftly. The vampire had been shot through the neck so many times that it did not take much effort. The tomahawk slipped through with enough force to raise sparks on the floor. Immediately the tissue began to dissolve and drip through the grating, leaving only a black, damaged skeleton with abnormally long teeth.

The noise of the escaping steam died off as the ship's emergency systems took over, shutting down the boilers, and locking down specific valves. The white mist in the hall slowly dissipated. The temperature had risen at least twenty degrees, and I could feel the sweat rolling down my body.

"Julie, that should be all of these. When it cools down enough, get in there and rescue Darné and his men. Milo and I are going to help Boone."

"Roger that, Earl."

The Newbie squad waited patiently. Lee was hurting bad, and Trip was doing his best to help the smaller man walk.

"Are you going to make it?" Julie asked him softly.

"We grab the French and we head back up top. We should be almost about out of undead."

"I'm just having a hard time breathing is all," he grunted.

"Whatever doesn't kill us, only makes us stronger," Trip stated solemnly.

"Remember that when I'm kicking your ass later," Lee laughed, and then grimaced in pain.

The vampires that had fallen prey to Lee's bomb were reduced to pulp and bones. There was not even enough left to put a stake through. As I entered the engine compartment, the intense heat made my head swim. The air was thick with damp, hot vapor. A bit of residual steam hissed from the giant ruptured pipe that Sam had shot. Water dripped from everything. It was as if it was raining from the ceiling. The room was like a sauna, only worse, as all of the exposed metal pipes and fittings were hot enough to burn us. I could feel the heat of the floor through my boot soles. I took another swig from my Camelbak. The room was lit by red emergency lights. I turned off my flashlight to retain my batteries. Overhead, water dripped from the ladder and the hatch that led to the main cargo bay.

I paused in front of the heavy metal door that held the French survivors. I tried the wheel. My gloves provided enough protection to touch the metal, but not for long. It was stuck. I pounded on the door. The fist falls echoed loudly.

"Anybody know Morse code?" I asked. Everybody shook their heads in the negative. Not a whole lot of former Eagle Scouts on my team. Julie shoved past me and struck the butt of her rifle against the door. *Dum-du-du-dum-dum.* Shave and a haircut.

We waited a few seconds. *Dum-dum*. Came the response. Two bits. The wheel began to turn. I sighed in relief and tried in vain to wipe the sweat and moisture from my face. I could hardly wait to get out of this sauna. The door opened.

The famous French hunter Jean Darné stood before us, tall and imposing in his black body armor that differed only slightly from our own. He was a legend. Considered one of the greatest Hunters the Europeans had, he had hunted more monsters in more places than probably anybody but Earl Harbinger. His team was well respected, and he was considered by many to be the best of the best.

He was also currently dead. As were the four other members of his team standing to his side.

"We have been waiting for you," the vampire said.

CHAPTER 9

None of us moved. The vampire and his four wights stood separated from the Hunters only by one narrow doorway. Julie and I were closest. For some reason the vampire did not move. The wights made chewing motions and stood tensed, ready to pounce. Their red eyes studied us hungrily. They were all wearing the same black body armor. Darné smiled at us, showing off his elongated incisors. He absently rapped his knuckles on the metal hatchway. S-O-S.

"Well, if it is not little Julie Shackleford. My, how you have grown up," Darné said. "You are the image of your mother, an absolutely lovely woman. What a pleasure."

"The pleasure is all yours, Jean," she answered. She shifted her rifle slightly. The two of us were blocking the doorway. The undead were close enough to smell. I did not think I could move fast enough to get away. It would only take a single touch from one of those wights to end up paralyzed.

"Now, now, little girl. Do not try anything hasty.

The only thing holding back my 'men' is my will. They are bonded to me. If I lose concentration for an instant your team is doomed." He would have been a very handsome man when he was alive, suave and distinguished with just a touch of gray at his temples and in his thin moustache; his English was impeccable. I'm sure he could have been quite the charmer except for the whole evil vampire thing and the four undead pit-bull equivalents standing beside him.

"So why didn't you make your move? You could have just charged us immediately and taken us by surprise." I could tell Julie was stalling for time. But I wasn't sure what exactly she was hoping for.

"Americans have no flair for the dramatic. You are almost as bad as the Germans. No romance in your souls. Always straightforward." He snapped his long fingers. "I want to make a deal."

"We don't deal with vampires," she stated flatly.

"But you have made deals with monsters before. The truth of that is undeniable. I want to make a deal with you. I will let you live, and I will give you important information, in exchange for safe passage from this ship after sunset."

"Except the monsters that we have made deals with don't leave a trail of bodies wherever they go. I can't do that to the world," Julie spoke softly. One of my teammates moved slowly behind me.

"So naïve, girl. Your father would be ashamed. He was such a practical man. He would make a deal with the devil for the right cause. Order your man to stop what he is doing or I release these wights. You don't want to try to toss a grenade in here. There are thousands of gallons of fuel and vapor in these pipes. You would kill your whole team and the others as well."

Julie shook her head. "No explosives. Okay, Jean. Let's talk. But leave my parents out of it."

"Fair enough." The movement behind me stopped. The vampire continued, "Your team will go to the bridge, pull up the anchor and set course for the mainland. Then you will leave this ship."

"How do you know we won't walk out of here and just sink the ship?" Julie asked.

"Because I will keep you as a hostage. Your uncle is running this operation. He will do anything to protect you. I will let you go free when we run aground."

Julie laughed coldly. "And I'm supposed to believe you? You would bite me as soon as the helicopter lifted off. Screw you, Jean."

"Now, young one, please, I did not choose this path, but I am a survivor. I just want to live."

"If you can call that living."

"Do not be so quick to judge. You of all people must wonder about this life. It is marvelous. I fought the darkness for so many years. I did not know what I was missing. I can see everything, Julie. I can feel your pulse from here. I can feel the world. The heartbeat of the very world. It is ecstasy." The vampire was beginning to wax poetic. I had to try something.

"Hey, Jean," I interrupted. "The girl's hardheaded. I'm willing to talk business."

"Your standards are slipping. When did MHI start hiring gorillas?" the vampire asked wryly, glancing in my direction. His red eyes bored into me.

"Owen? What are you doing?"

"Shut up," I snapped at her. "I don't want to die here.

You can keep the girl. I'll go up and pull up the anchor and point this barge at Florida. Old man Earl isn't going to want anything to happen to this chick. We will leave."

"A sensible one. You must be new, yes?"

"Yeah, I'm just a mercenary. I'm just in this for the money," I lied. Moisture dripped onto my helmet and rolled hotly down my spine.

"Ahh, good." The vampire steepled his fingers.

"Now you said you had some valuable information. Just what are we talking about, Frenchy? Valuable means something that I can use." I had no idea if vampires were good judges of character.

"I can tell you about the six old ones, and their leader. They are on your country's soil now."

"And what about the Cursed One?" I ordered.

The four wights shrieked in chorus. Darné cringed.

"How do you know of Lord Machado?" The vampire hissed the name.

"Me and him are old pals. Now if you want the girl, I want to know what he's here for."

"Very well then. But it is your doom. Lord Machado has the artifact. He will take it to a Place of Power and he will use it. You cannot stop him. No mortal can stop him."

"Look, Jean, I don't want to stop him. I just want to make sure I end up on the winning team. Know what I mean?"

The vampire smiled. "I can help you then. You do not want to be on the wrong side when Lord Machado rules. Do we have a deal?"

Julie interrupted angrily. "Owen? What the hell are you thinking? No deals with vampires; he'll kill me as soon as you walk out the door."

"Shut up, bitch!" I snarled. I move very fast for a big man. In the next second, I dropped my shotgun, letting the sling catch it. I lifted my right hand as if I was going to backhand her. Julie's eyes widened in shocked surprise. The vampire's eyes followed my uplifted hand, as my left hand lifted a grenade off of my webbing. I brought my hands together smoothly. Instead of throwing my fist, I stuck my finger through the safety pin and pulled. The sound of the pin landing on the steaming floor was exceedingly loud.

"Run, Julie. Run now." I held the live grenade up next to my face. The only thing keeping the grenade from exploding was the thin spring-loaded metal spoon that I was holding down with one finger. If I relaxed my grip the fuse would ignite. Five seconds later it would explode, and possibly ignite the engine room in a massive explosion. Julie did not say anything. She nodded and then retreated. The rest of the team followed quickly. I shouted one final instruction: "Get ready to abandon ship!"

"You idiot!" the vampire roared. The wights hissed and thrashed in unison. "You will destroy us all!"

"Better my way than yours, you snail-eating bastard." I started slowly backing away. The wights exploded from the room and spread out in a skirmish line, snapping and clawing at the air. Jean Darné stepped through the portal and strode forward. In the residual steam and in the red emergency lights he looked like the traditional versions of the devil. So this must be hell.

"Give me the grenade," he ordered. Darné locked his eyes on mine. Shivers ran down my spine, though the room temperature was running around a hundred and thirty degrees.

"Oh, I'll give it to you all right."

"I compel you. Hand me the grenade, safely." The red eyes bored into mine. The words repeated themselves in my conscious mind, and burrowed into my subconscious like tendrils. I felt myself starting to comply. The wights began to inch closer. My vision began to darken.

"NO!" I shouted, shaking my head wildly. The wights shrank back.

"You have a strong will, ape man, but it won't do you any good. Give me that grenade. You do not want to die."

"Neither do you! Stay back!" I waved the grenade in front of me. A pound of high explosives was my holy symbol.

"Maybe I should just take it. I am greater than you can understand. The greater the creator, the greater the creation. My creator was the greatest of them all." Darné's devil visage continued to advance.

"If you think you're fast enough, come and get it." I backed into something solid, the escape ladder leading to the cargo bay, forty feet of iron rungs standing in the middle of the crowded room between me and safety. I knew that Darné would never let me make it to the corridor.

"You are not leaving me with any choice, human," the vampire hissed. He stopped, less than ten feet away. His wights stopped alongside of him, two on each side. There was about a yard between each of the creatures. An image of black steel plates popped unbidden into my mind.

It had to be fate.

I kept my left arm extended with the grenade. I

reached down with my right and grasped the stock of my shotgun. I had fired this gun hundreds and thousands of times, practiced until my fingers had bled and my shoulder formed thick recoil calluses. My father, the ruthless perfectionist, had driven me hard when it came to shooting, because he sensed that I had a gift and would not settle for anything less than perfection in his sons. The wood was worn smooth under my glove. The Remington glistened darkly with moisture from the steam. I brought the butt into contact with my shoulder. My life came down to this instant. I needed to beat my record.

"Catch!" I tossed the grenade to Darné. The spoon released with a metallic *sproing*, igniting the fuse. The vampire moved as a blur to snatch the grenade out of the air. The wights mindlessly tracked the moving object. For me, time ceased. The gun and I were one seamless melding of man and machine. The safety was released as my finger knowingly sought the trigger. The muzzle rose perfectly. The trigger was pulled. The sear released. The hammer fell. The firing pin struck the primer. The powder burned.

I was bringing the muzzle onto the second wight's head before the buckshot struck the first. Fire. Work the action. Repeat. Five shots. Faster than I had ever gone before. The fusillade was a continuous roar without pause. I did not miss any of the five undead craniums.

Dropping the shotgun onto its sling, I grabbed the ladder and started to climb as fast as I humanly could. I did not wait to watch for results. I heard thuds as some of the wights fell to their backs, or collapsed to their knees.

Darné had been a Monster Hunter for longer than I had been alive. He knew what to do with live ordnance in a bad place. He had caught, and then immediately launched the grenade with a pitch that would have made any major league pitcher proud, right through the doorway and into the corridor. He did that even as my silver buckshot pellets penetrated his skull.

The grenade hit the corridor wall and rolled away, now belching orange signal smoke. It was a harmless smoke grenade.

Darné screamed as the silver burned him. "Kill him! KILL HIM!"

Two of the wights shrugged off their shattered skulls and damaged brain tissues, leapt to their feet and charged. The first began to climb after me as the second jumped onto one of the engines and began to climb up the metal surface like a spider. One wight had its eyes put out and stumbled blindly for the ladder, searching for me by smell. The last had its spinal cord severed and was flopping wildly as random impulses fired from its undead brain. I climbed as fast as I could, legs pumping, arms grasping and pulling with all of the desperate strength I could muster. The wights were far faster.

I was halfway up the ladder when the first wight clawed at my boot. Grabbing the shotgun, I fired a single round straight down between my feet. The creature's hand exploded on impact and it fell toward the ground. The blind wight quickly took its place, scurrying after me. The wall crawler matched my pace, and launched itself at the ladder. There was barely time to swing around to the other side as it crashed into the slick steel bars. I dangled over the floor as it wildly tore at me. One paralyzing touch and I was dead. I swung the shotgun like a club, smashing the wight in the face. It tore my weapon away, ripping through the sling as it fell to the deck. I slipped on a wet rung, and then forced myself to start climbing again.

Darné caught my Remington in one hand. He expertly pumped the weapon, aimed it at me and fired. The buckshot slammed into my armored chest, knocking me back. I grunted in pain, but the silver pellets stopped against the woven Kevlar. My gloves slipped on the wet steel, and I toppled backwards in flailing panic. My knee wrenched painfully as I crashed upside-down into the ladder. I hung suspended, my boot wedged under one rung, and my knee bent over the top of another, like an insane trapeze artist. The blood rushed to my head, and I watched as Darné pumped the shotgun, aimed it right between my eyes and pulled the trigger.

Nothing. The click was the loudest sound in the world. That had been my seven shots.

The blind wight surged upwards, sensing my warm blood. Still facing down, I swung my fist and shattered its undead face. The creature was knocked aside and fell. Instantly my hand went numb, and coldness rippled up my arm. I grunted as I did an upside-down sit-up, grabbed the rung above me with my left hand, and pulled. My right arm hanging limply and my knee throbbing in pain, I kept pulling myself along; push up one rung, lean in, reach up for the next one, repeat. My shotgun shattered as it ricocheted spectacularly off of the rail next to my head. Darné had a good arm.

"That was my favorite gun!" I bellowed as I kept inching nearer to the hatch. I now had a wight on the ladder below, rapidly gaining, and two more scaling the wall to pounce on me. The hatch was still ten feet away.

"You should have taken my offer," the vampire roared.

He jumped impossibly high and landed on the ladder directly below me. The metal shook under the impact. Hot water droplets flew off and struck me in the face. Three wights and a vampire in striking distance in the next few seconds. I just kept climbing because that was my only option. I was pretty much screwed.

Then the hatch opened, directly above my head. It was my savior.

It was Grant Jefferson.

"Grant! Help me!" I screamed, clawing my way toward him.

His eyes grew wide as he saw the undead creatures swarming upwards. He started to hold out his hand to me, and then he apparently decided that he did not have time before the creatures would be on him as well. I could see the fear register on his face as he did the math. They were too close. Grant stood in his polished black body armor, bristling with useful weaponry, and said two words: "Sorry, Pitt." He looked right at me as he slammed the hatch.

"Arrgghhhh!" I shouted unintelligibly. Darné laughed below. I stuck one of my legs through the ladder to lock myself into position as well as possible. I reached across my body and drew my pistol with my left hand, sighted on the closest wight spider-crawling upward, and shot it in the head four times before it slipped from the wall and fell thirty-five feet onto its back with a bone-jarring crunch. The other wall crawler leapt, and I just barely had time to align the front sight on the monster before impact, firing a silver slug through the monster's brain. The wight's momentum carried it forward where it struck one of my legs. It fell away screaming in rage. Darné easily avoided the falling undead, but the blind wight underneath was not so lucky. The two monsters collided and fell the rest of the way to the hard metal floor. This time they did not rise. My now-numb leg buckled, and I only barely held on.

Now it was just me and Darné. He flew up the ladder. I fired the remaining ten rounds as fast as I could pull the trigger. I hit him repeatedly but with almost no effect. I dropped the pistol, and he swatted it out of the air. I watched hopelessly as it flew into multiple pieces. I grasped wildly for my knife, but it was too late. He was beside me on the ladder.

His clawed hand clamped around my throat like an iron vise, choking off my air. A bullet hole in his forehead closed and squeezed out a mushroomed .45 slug like some disastrous pimple. I learned a few things right then. Vampires did not breathe, and I was in fact still afraid of dying. I was surprised that I was thinking about Julie. I just hoped that she made it.

"Tell me just one thing, you poor brave idiot," the vampire ordered as he shook me. "How did you know about Lord Machado? How?"

"I went to France once," I gasped.

"And what does that have to do with anything?" Darné asked, fangs extending as he prepared to feed on me. I wondered if I had the strength to break free long enough to fall to my death. It beat the alternative.

"My family went there to see where one of my grandpas was buried. He died on Utah Beach."

"How touching. Now, if you tell me how you learned about Lord Machado, I'll make your death painless."

"I learned that the people in the countryside were pretty nice. But the people in Paris were a bunch of stuck-up, self-righteous pricks. I'm guessing you're from Paris."

"Idiot." Darné's jaw distended as his mouth opened like an anaconda about to eat a goat.

"Darné!" a voice shouted from below. It was Earl Harbinger. He strode into the engine room through the swirling orange smoke.

The vampire's mouth slowly closed. "Hello, Earl. It has been a while."

"Come down here and face me. You know you're not going to get out of here alive. MHI controls the whole freighter. Your goons are all staked. It's over."

"I have your man as a hostage. Let me go, or I kill him," the vampire hissed.

"You know the rules. You helped write them. Let him go and come down here and fight me. You know you've wanted to prove something for a long time. Let's go. Either way you're going to die. At least this way you get the satisfaction of seeing if I am as good as they say."

"And what if I just kill this piece of *merde*?" He squeezed so hard that the vertebrae in my neck popped. I cringed in pain, and involuntary tears rolled from my eyes.

"Then I'll have my men at the hatch above you throw down buckets of holy water. I'll just stake you while you're laying on the ground and sizzling. Or even better, I'll tie you up and drag you into the sun. You've seen it. You know how much that has to hurt. I swear that if you kill that Hunter then I'll drag you out of here and nail you to the superstructure and watch you burn. I figure you can probably go a while before you finally quit kicking." Harbinger unbuckled his armor straps and set his weapon harness on the deck. "Just you and me, Darné. One last go-round."

"How do I know you don't have ten Hunters waiting in the hall?"

"You don't. But you know my reputation."

"I do. Fine, Earl. Let us see who the best Hunter really is." The vampire released me and I dropped, barely managing to grab a rail. Darné let go and fell swiftly to the floor, landing as if it was nothing.

The two combatants squared off in the red light and steam. I watched in amazement as Harbinger began to circle. He was just a normal man, maybe two thirds of my weight, and in training he had never given any indication of having any sort of special fighting skills. On the other hand, I had just watched Darné perform several superhuman feats and smash my pistol into bits with his bare hands. This did not look good for Harbinger.

The hatch creaked open above me. Strong hands reached through and grasped the handles of my armor. The smell of Copenhagen told me that it was Sam Haven. He hung upside-down through the hatch and scanned the room. He saw Harbinger and Darné preparing to fight.

"Oh hell. We've got to get out of here!" Sam blurted. He tugged on me and grunted. "Help me, you hare-lipped derelict! You're too damn heavy."

"What about Harbinger?" I asked in a panic.

"Don't worry about Earl. He'll be fine. You don't want to be around him when he gets into one of his moods. Now move, damn it!" I struggled up the ladder with Sam pulling me. More hands grasped my arms and helped. Chuck Mead was there as well. The two burly men pulled me into the cargo bay. Sam threw the hatch down and spun the wheel to seal it behind us.

The cargo bay was much cooler. The steel of the floor was cold under my face. I lay there for a minute, panting, as the feeling painfully returned to my arm and leg. I could not understand what had just happened. Earl Harbinger had just given up his life for mine. I was sure that Darné was tearing him to pieces as we sat here uselessly. I gradually pulled myself to a sitting position, my back resting against a sheet-metal shipping container, my stomach clenched in agony, and my knee twinged as I moved it.

"We have to help him."

"Trust me, Pitt. Earl's fine. Too late to do nothing now anyways. Let's get up to the weather deck."

"What's a weather deck?" Mead asked with a blank stare. The big Ranger was splattered with blood, and there appeared to be claw marks on his M249 Squad Automatic Weapon.

"Fricking army. The top. The top part of the ship. The part that can see sky."

"Oh, okay. Sunlight would be good."

"I'm unarmed. Darné broke my guns," I stated as Mead pulled me up.

"And that's a sorry state to be in. Here. Take this thing. The French guys don't need it no more." Sam handed me a French FAMAS bullpup assault rifle. It was a slightly unwieldy and strange-looking weapon, but it would have to do. "The crew, security team and Hunters have all been accounted for. We should be clear, but you never make no assumptions in this business. Let's get."

As we made our way out of the cargo bay, I could not help but ask, "Where is Grant?"

Sam scowled, his handlebar mustache scrunching in consternation; he finally spit a nasty clump of chew and shrugged. "Reckon I don't know. Probably in the light."

"He left me to die," I said hotly.

"Yep. I figured as much. Some folks are brave when others are watching them, but it is harder to be brave when there ain't no witnesses. Grant's never flaked on us before. He probably figured you were dead anyway, no use getting killed for no reason. I reckon that Earl will want to talk with him about that."

"Yeah. Me too." I cracked my knuckles. I had murder in my heart and it must have been obvious to Sam. He just smiled.

"Just don't kill him. We're short-handed as it is," the former SEAL pointed out. "Plus then Julie would probably shoot you, and you don't want to mess with her." Sam pointedly went back to his radio traffic, warning the others that we were coming out. I could not listen along. Somewhere along the line my radio had been broken.

The daylight was beautiful. The breeze was cool and refreshing. I was surprised at how low the sun was on the horizon. We had been in the dark bowels of the ship forever. It felt good to be alive. Almost all of the Hunters were milling around on the deck. Boone's team was somber near the sheet-draped body of their lost man. My team was there. Holly and Trip rushed to me, hugging me and slapping me on my back. Lee was lying on some blankets, his shirt off and thick bandages encircling his chest. He shouted my name and clapped. Julie was there as well. She quit giving orders long enough to run over and grab me by my armor.

"I'm sorry we couldn't come back for you. There were more of them in the corridor waiting for us. We got jumped. I'm sorry. How did you make it?" She looked really happy to see me. The feeling was mutual.

"Earl saved me. I think he's dead."

"Nope. I just talked to him on the radio. He is on his way up and he has Darné's skull as a souvenir."

"How?" I asked in surprise. My spirit lifted upon hearing that bit of news.

"Like I said. Earl is the best Hunter alive. Don't worry about it. I'm just glad you're okay. I thought for sure that you were dead . . ." She paused. "That was really brave. Stupid, but brave. Thank you."

I blushed. "No big deal."

She patted my arm. "I've got to go inspect the cargo and make sure nothing is damaged before I contact the clients. You stay here and get some food and something to drink. You look like crap."

She signaled for a few of the others to go with

her. Nobody was going to go anywhere alone on this tub. I watched her walk away. Even coated in dried vampire juices, she was the prettiest girl I had ever known. Trip interrupted my reverie by handing me a Gatorade and a power bar. I scarfed them down as he gave me the blow by blow of their last vampire encounter. I sat on a crate of grenades and listened to my friends. What it all came down to was this: it did not matter what high tech gear we had, or what weapons, or even what training. It came down to the friends that stood by our side, and our will to fight for them. It felt really good to be alive right then, I would stand with these people any day, and I knew that they would stand by me.

I started to tell them about my close encounter with Darné when I heard a voice. I stopped instantly, leaving the others regarding me curiously. Lumbering to my feet, I limped with resolute purpose in the direction of that voice. That smarmy, prideful, movie-star voice. I bent my head from side to side and cracked my neck and back, an old habit that I had picked up in my bouncing days. I used to do that before beating down rowdy drunks.

"Hey, Grant," I said cooly as I approached him.

"Pitt. I'm glad you made it. Look, I'm really sorry, but—"

I cut him off. I was closing distance. I did not want him to run because I didn't think I could catch him.

"Grant. You left me to die."

"Wait just a second." He lifted his hands defensively. "It isn't like that. They would have gotten me too. If I left that hatch open, we would both be dead."

I tried to look nonviolent. That is difficult when you are a hulking, scar-faced brute of a man. I kept slowly closing distance. The Hunters from Boone's team that had been speaking with him sensed serious trouble and backed away.

"You left me behind." I was directly in front of him now.

The railing was to his back and he had nowhere to go. He must have sensed what was coming because he tried to duck. It did not work. I felt great satisfaction as his nose broke with an audible crunch under my meaty fist. His legs buckled and he started to fall.

I grabbed him by his neck guard and jerked him around until he was facing me. Blood was streaming down his face. He tried to perform an aikido wrist lock to break my grasp, but I was far too strong and angry to fall for that. I slammed him backwards into the railing.

"Do you know how to swim?" I asked coldly.

"Pitt, it wasn't my fault, please wait . . ." he begged. I punched him solidly again, this time in the mouth, smashing his lips and cracking a few teeth. My cup was not exactly overflowing with mercy.

"I said: Do. You. Know. How. To. Swim?"

"No, please. I'm sorry."

"You had best be a quick learner then," I said as I lifted him off of his feet, and heaved him over the railing.

I stepped away, not even bothering to watch him hit the water. That had felt really good. I was not worried about him drowning. In a moment of unusual kindness that surprised even me, I had hit the button to activate the emergency flotation device on his harness before tossing him. I can be a jerk, but I'm no monster.

Boone moved in front of me. He did not look happy. All of the other Hunters had come running to see what the commotion was about. From the looks on their faces I was guessing that they had seen Grant take his plunge.

"What the hell was that?" he demanded.

"He left me for dead back there. He left me in a room with a vampire and some wights. He slammed the door in my face, and he apologized before he did it. Son of a bitch is lucky I didn't just shoot him in the head."

The former SF man studied me. He signaled one of his men. "Throw Jefferson a rope."

"He isn't going to drown. I turned on his CO2 before I tossed him over."

"I'm not worried about him drowning, fucktard. I'm worried that all of the wight meat in the water has riled up the sharks and they're going to chew on his pompous ass."

Crap. I hadn't thought about sharks. *Oh well.* I went back to my Gatorade.

The sun was setting over the bow of the *Antoine-Henri.* The fourteen surviving members of the MHI teams were gathered on the deck in a rough semicircle, illuminated in our ragged exhaustion by the fading golden rays. Grant Jefferson had been safely retrieved from the water and was standing as far away from me as was possible, with a giant, white cotton swab shoved into each nostril. Harbinger had not been happy, and had promised to talk to both of us later. I was not looking forward to that, and I just hoped that it did not end up with me being terminated.

Julie had cataloged all of the valuable cargo. None of the artwork had been lost. The others had found her excitedly browsing through an open cargo container filled with priceless art. Not being a connoisseur of painting, all of the French artwork looked like bunches of colored dots to me. She had not been very happy when she had heard about what I did to her boyfriend. The look she gave me had been oddly similar to the one that she had given that first vampire before she had shafted it through the heart.

All of the crew and French Hunters had been accounted for. Tissue samples had been taken from each individual creature to be sent to the PUFF offices for confirmation and to begin the bounty paperwork. Between the huge PUFF reward and the fulfillment of the French contract, it had been a very lucrative day.

But it had its price.

The body of Jeremiah Roberts had been laid upon an unzipped body bag on the cold steel deck. His neck guard had been torn away, and unlike the neat little puncture holes that most people seem to imagine for vampire bites, the Hunter's throat was missing a massive chunk of flesh, leaving a hole from his trachea to his spine. Boone's team stood the closest to the body. This was their business. The rest of us were mere watchers. The man they called Priest said a few words. As it turned out, they called him that because he had been one once upon a time. This was a Hunter's funeral, and it was as sacred as any service inside a church.

"He was the bravest amongst us. So fearless that

regular people would think he was crazy, but not us. We understood him and loved him for it. Jerry was afraid of no man or beast on Earth or from Hell. I am alive because of him. Our whole team is alive because of him. He is here because he took the brunt of the attack to protect the rest of us. And today was not the first time he did that, just the time that his luck ran out. We are taught, *Greater love has no man than this that he lays down his life for his friends.* My friend. Our friend. May you rest in peace. Until we meet again in the better place. Amen."

"Amen," chorused the group as one.

Boone stepped forward. His face was streaked where tears had run through the grime on his cheeks. He looked somberly down at his fallen teammate, and then he slowly knelt at his side. The warrior gently touched his friend for the last time.

"I'm sorry I failed you, Jerry. I'll be seeing you around."

I had to avert my eyes because of what I knew was coming next. I was not the only one. The sound of Boone's fighting knife being drawn from its sheath seemed to go on forever. Roberts had been bitten by a vampire. It had to be done.

When Boone was finished the rest of his team helped him to his feet. He cleaned his knife on a rag. Priest zipped up the rubber bag, and the Hunter's funeral was over.

CHAPTER 10

Harbinger summoned me to the cargo bay. There were only a handful of us left on the freighter. The Hind had taken the most injured of the Hunters, and the *Brilliant Mistake* had been signaled to return to pick up a few more men and our gear. Surprisingly, the little boat's crew had stayed nearby to help us. Harbinger gave them an extra $20,000 for their trouble and the admonition to never talk about this unless they wanted the government to pay them a very unpleasant visit. He must have been feeling generous due to the big haul. The Director also gave them business cards, along with instructions to contact us if they ever heard of any more monster problems. Since we could not advertise, much of our business came in the form of referrals. Representatives of the French shipping corporation were already en route to retrieve their valuable cargo. The remainder of our fee was to be wired to us upon receipt. The Hind was to return for its last pickup shortly.

I limped painfully down the stairs into the vast

central bay. Each bootfall echoed hollowly through the cavernous room. I had been paralyzed, drowned, beaten, shot with my own gun, partially paralyzed and choked, and I was hungry, tired and saddened by the loss of some of my favorite guns. If anybody should have been put on that chopper it was me. However, it seemed that Harbinger wanted to speak privately first. That was not a good sign. Even Grant had been sent back to land to get his nose and teeth checked.

Earl Harbinger, Sam Haven, Milo Anderson and Julie Shackleford stood before a giant orange container, the heavy-duty kind that could be picked up through the opening in the deck by a giant dock crane and set onto a semitrailer or train. The sheet-metal double doors were hanging open, and the four experienced Hunters were gathered at the opening.

"Hey," I said as I approached, not that they did not hear me coming, but I couldn't think of what else to say. None of the four looked up. Julie had her arms folded and she appeared rather cross. Harbinger pointed inside the container.

"What do you make of this, Pitt?" He shined a flashlight into the interior. There were seven wooden crates inside. Each was long enough and deep enough to easily hold a person. I ducked my head as I entered, pulling out my own flashlight to get a closer look. The air tasted stale. The lids for the crates had been set aside, and the interiors seemed to be filled with nothing but dirt. I ran my hands through one; it was a thick black loam. Another was white particulate sand, and yet another looked almost like Alabama red clay.

"Coffins," I said. "For the seven Masters in my dream."

"Yep," Harbinger said. "And I'm willing to bet that the dirt is soil from their native lands."

"What does that mean?" Julie asked. "I know I've heard about that in the folk tales, but we've never seen evidence of vampires actually needing to sleep in soil from their homeland."

"Beats me. But this is really a weird bunch. I've never seen anything like this before, and I've never even heard or read about anything like this either."

"We don't know for sure that they are really Masters, Earl," Sam said. "We haven't actually seen any of them yet."

"The stronger the creator, the greater the creation. Some of those sailors we killed were way too powerful to be that young, but they were. Plus creating wights as daylight guardians? Darné was as powerful as a hundred-year-old bloodsucker, and he has to have been turned in the last week. Whoever turned him was one bad dude. So there is at least one Master in this gang. I would bet on it," Harbinger replied.

"So how did you beat Darné anyway?" I asked. The other Hunters glanced at their team leader, curious to hear his response.

"Later. It isn't important right now."

"He was a good guy when he was human," Sam said. "Losing him is a damn shame."

"People change when they are turned. It doesn't matter what they were like before. No matter how good they were, when they turn, they come back as pure evil . . ." Julie trailed off, and then changed the subject. "We probably need to alert the Feds. Seven high-level vamps on U.S. soil? They would shut us

down in a second if they found out that we knew
and didn't tell them."

"I hate Feds." Milo spoke for the first time. Sam
spit on the floor.

"Me too. But they need to mobilize. They're somewhere in Georgia, and heading who knows where.
I'll call Myers," Harbinger told them with a look like
he had just bit into something sour. "They probably
won't believe us though. Hell, I don't believe what
I'm saying."

I looked in the other coffins. Thicker sand, rich
topsoil, alkali dirt, and finally broken shale and gravel.
I noticed something as I shined my light in the back
corner.

"You guys seen this?"

"What?" Harbinger asked as he entered and came
up next to me. I squatted and pointed at the ground.
Something had dissolved all of the paint in the corner. A dark substance coated the floor. I sure as heck
wasn't going to touch it. It felt unnatural from where
I stood, and I had a visceral feeling that it was some
sort of secretions from the cloaked and armored monstrosity from my dream. Harbinger knelt and studied
it. "Ichor. Looks like snot from somebody with real
bad allergies. Let's take a sample."

I breathed a little easier once I was out of the
claustrophobic box.

"But wait, there's more," Sam stated. "I saw this
earlier when we were getting set to blow the steam
pipe. Check this shit out."

He took us to another shipping container. This one
appeared normal until we circled it and saw what was
on the other side. The steel walls had been pierced

and peeled back from the inside. I touched one of the edges. The steel was a quarter-inch thick, and the reinforced tubing around the edges had been easily bent.

"Wow," Milo said, stroking his beard absently, "no sign of explosion or cutting torch, or anything like that. Something just punched its way through. Isn't that special?"

"Yeah, it just fricking warms my heart," Sam said. "Why can't we ever fight cute, helpless monsters? Like the ones on Sesame Street?"

"The big things from my dream," I said. "They could have done this. They had to be at least ten feet tall. And they could fly, they had huge wingspans. They were ugly, and they had horns and big teeth and claws. That was about all I saw because I was just moving too fast."

The four Hunters surrounded me.

"Now start from the beginning and tell us the whole story about this dream," Harbinger ordered.

"So that's why you brought me down here. I thought you were going to yell at me for beating up Grant," I replied cheerfully. Julie folded her arms and glared.

Harbinger shook his head. "Oh, don't worry, I'll get to that. But business first. From the beginning, tell us every single detail you can think of. Even things that you might not think are important."

"We might as well get comfortable. This is going to take a while." I told the whole story. Starting with my initial dream in the hospital. I tried to convey the weirdness of it, and probably failed. I went into as much detail as I could about the next dream. I did not, however, tell them about seeing the Old Man when I had been underwater. I was still not sure if that had actually happened, or if it had been a panicked trick of my oxygen-starved brain. When I was finished the others began to drill me with questions, only some of which I could answer.

"The head vampire called the Old Man, Bar Eeka?"

"As near as I could tell. Something like that."

"Could he be a wraith? Maybe a revenant even?" Julie asked. "No wait, those have bodies. How about a shade?"

"Beats me."

"There is a possibility," Harbinger stated. "I've heard some weird stories since I've been doing this kind of thing. He could be a ghost, and he could have hooked up with you while you were dead on the operating table. You might have actually met him on the other side and brought him back. Now he's using you somehow. Problem is, we don't know jack about ghosts, so how do we figure out why he's trying to help you?"

"Be sure to ask him that the next time you see him," Milo told me.

"Except I only see him when I'm dead, or about to come close to death," I added sardonically.

"That will be convenient for you then. You're a Monster Hunter now. Plenty of good opportunities to die all of the time!"

The ocean rushed by below. The interior of the Hind was very loud, and that was not helped by the fact that our pilot felt the need to blare heavy metal through the intercom. Excellent selection though. Disturbed, Slip Knot, Rob Zombie, and even the latest

single by my brother's band. I figured I would have to
let the pilot know that I knew Cabbage Point Killing
Machine's guitarist once we landed. I had not met the
pilot yet, and all that I had been told about him was
when Milo had jokingly said that he had been included
in the purchase of the chopper. I had no idea what
that was supposed to mean. All that I had seen so far
had been the back of his helmeted head.

I had never ridden in a helicopter before, and it
was kind of exciting, loud and with painful vibrations,
but still fun. Almost like a roller coaster ride with the
added advantage that it could shear a bolt and kill
you in a matter of seconds.

We were sitting in the cramped crew compartment. The Hind had originally been used to move
Russian infantry, though this particular specimen had
been tweaked and customized extensively by MHI. It
was still tight, but I was given to understand that it
was downright plush compared to what it had once
been.

Almost all of the other Hunters had immediately
gone to sleep. They understood the basic principle of
sleep when you can because you don't know when you
are going to get to do it again. I couldn't do it, so
I passed the time by picking silver buckshot pellets
out of my armor. I made a mental note to add Milo
Anderson to my Christmas card list.

I held up one of the silver pellets, now deformed
from the impact, and studied it, deep in thought. I
had almost died today. Now that the adrenaline had
left my system, I found my exhausted brain once
again pondering just what the hell I was doing, and
truthfully, I didn't have an answer.

Julie's head was rolled to the side and she was snoring. She had hardly spoken to me since she had found out about my little altercation with Grant. I was not about to apologize. He had left me to get eaten, and I did not like that one bit.

Harbinger opened his eyes. He had been awake. He checked to make sure Julie was out, and then unbuckled his seatbelt and moved next to me, flopping solidly into the uncomfortable chair. He turned and shouted in my ear.

"I wanted to talk to you about Grant."

"Okay," I shouted back.

"I know about what happened."

"He left me behind to save his own skin."

"I know," he yelled. It was hard to have a conversation by shouting. "Grant says that he didn't think he could save you . . . That you would both have been killed."

Perhaps. I did not respond, not knowing what to say, and not wanting to admit that Grant very well might have been right, and honestly not really knowing what I would have done if our situations had been reversed.

"Don't ever let something like that happen again. I'm the boss. I take care of discipline. You undermined my authority."

"That's it? You aren't mad at me for hitting him?"

"Oh, if I was mad, you'd be swimming home."

"Serious?" I asked.

Earl sighed and rubbed his face.

"What are you going to do with him?" I asked.

"Huh?"

"What are you going to do with Grant?" I said, turning up the volume.

"I don't know yet. Maybe Grant's right, and he would've died keeping that door open, and I don't believe in committing suicide to prove a point."

"Sam said something about it being easier to be brave when others are watching you. Maybe Grant isn't so tough when there aren't any witnesses," I insisted.

"Yeah, Sam's a regular philosopher," Earl responded. "You can face some really scary shit, and be just fine, as long as you're doing it for your team." He grew suddenly serious, and I had to look away from those cold eyes. "Either way, it ain't none of your business now. Don't ever do something like that again. Hunters can't lose control. Got that? You never lose control. Do you have a problem with that?"

"No, sir."

We sat in silence for a few minutes, listening to the rotors beat the air, and some amazing guitar playing by my brother. From the expression on Harbinger's face, I don't think that he cared for metal. I refrained from banging my head in deference to his tender sensibilities.

"What about Julie?" I asked.

"What about her?"

"Does she believe that Grant abandoned me?"

"None of my business. She's a grown-up." The look he gave me told me to shut it. He quickly changed the subject. "Let me ask you this, Pitt. You've been with us for a few months. You've gone on exactly one mission. Could you leave now and go back to your spreadsheets and your tax forms?"

I did not answer. Did Earl know how much I was doubting the path that I was on? He was the experienced one, maybe he could see what I could not.

"Well, you'll probably need to."

My heart sank. So this was it. Was he going to let me go because of my rash actions? If he felt he could not trust me then I would be out. Did he think that I was too hotheaded and impulsive to be a member of the team?

"I got a letter yesterday. The IRS is going to audit us. I'm gonna need your help; our books are a mess. Once we handle this little vampire problem, of course."

I grinned. That I could handle.

"I can deal with the IRS. They're a little easier than vampires. Not much, but a little."

"Will sunlight banish them?"

"Maybe. I haven't tried that before."

"That's just the tip of the iceberg though. OSHA is crawling all over us for—I kid you not—workplace safety violations. As if there is anything safe about what we do at all. The EPA is angry about some of the pollution we have caused by burning certain kinds of monsters. Fish and Wildlife wants to fine us for killing a giant mutant Tennessee River catfish because it was endangered. Sure it had just crawled up on land and eaten some teenagers, but it was still an endangered species. We're in trouble with the BATF for some missing compliance paperwork for the machine guns and explosives—paperwork which they lost. And Immigration is investigating us for employing some illegal aliens."

"Are we?"

"Sure, but who doesn't? Do you think you just put an ad in the paper for people who can fly Russian attack helicopters?"

"Why are the Feds hammering us?"

"We've pissed a lot of people off in Washington. Our company was shut down for a long time. PUFF was only reactivated by the slimmest of margins. There are a lot of bureaucrats who are itching for us to fail. They're making it damn near impossible to get our jobs done."

"So what are we going to do?"

Harbinger grinned savagely. "From the amount of money we made on this job, I'm going to buy me some congressmen, maybe even a senator."

I was shocked. "Are you talking about bribery?"

"Why? Does that offend you?" he asked.

"Oh hell no. I'm a libertarian at heart. Screw 'em."

CHAPTER 11

That night I dreamed again. But it was not about my apparent friend, the Old Man with the poor English. Nor was it about the Cursed One and his gang of abominations. This was something different.

A lone mountain rose out of a bleak, dead forest. The side of the peak had been torn asunder in some sort of huge explosion. Trees had been shattered, stripped of their bark, or bent to the earth. Rock was charred and broken, the very foundations of the mountain had been cracked, and the face of the mighty peak had collapsed in an avalanche.

Amongst the shale and gravel was a low spot where the rubble had settled into what had once been a natural cavern or perhaps an underground structure. In the deepest depression, small bits of gravel and dust began to stir as something pushed against them from underneath, gradually and laboriously moving the weight of the earth above. Finally a dirt-encrusted hand thrust its way into the air, followed by a massively muscled arm. The torn and bloodied fingers clenched into an angry fist.

It was covered in black, swirling tattoos.

I woke up the next morning, groggy, sore, and cranky. We were staying at the bug-infested Radio City Motor Lodge in some little Georgia town that made Cazador look like a thriving metropolis. It had been the closest lodging to the dirt strip that passed for the local airport. It is hard to sleep when roaches keep skittering across your body. My understanding is that since roaches can't shift into reverse, if one of them crawls into your ear canal it can get really nasty and potentially kill you. Sleep on that.

The injured Hunters had been dispersed to seek medical care. The cargo plane had dropped off Boone's two injured men at their home city of Atlanta. Roberts' body had gone with them. The plane had then continued west, delivering Albert Lee and his fractured rib back to Alabama. Grant Jefferson had flown the plane. He had been sent back to the compound supposedly to take over and continue the Newbies' training. I figured that I probably needed some medical care as well, but Harbinger wanted to keep me around because of my dreams, and also possibly because he worried that I might murder Grant once I was left unsupervised.

So that left ten of us in coastal Georgia. Eleven if you counted our mysterious helicopter pilot, who had apparently slept in the chopper. I still had not seen the man without his face-shielding helmet, and he never seemed to speak. The experienced Hunters seemed used to the odd behavior and did not even bother to remark upon it.

There had only been three available rooms. The ladies had taken the nicest one, meaning that the toilet worked, and there weren't as many unidentifiable spots on the walls. I had bunked with Trip, Mead and Milo. Taking pity on me because of the beating I had received, they gave me one of the twin beds. Milo had seniority so he got the other. Trip had won a game of rock, paper, scissors (of course Chuck went rock) to get the couch. Mead got to sleep on the carpet with the mystery stains.

We gathered in Harbinger's room not long after dawn. A large map of Georgia had been purchased and was stuck to the wall with someone's throwing knives. Julie and Boone both had powerful laptops open and running. Boxes of our gear and munitions had been hastily piled into the corners. We had hired a flatbed to move it from the docks to here.

The group was sitting around in their shorts and T-shirts, all except for the Newbie squad who had not known to bring any clothing other than our armor. Holly had borrowed some clothing from Julie. Trip and Chuck had stolen some from somebody else. Since I was the only 4XL I stood in the corner wearing my boxer shorts and a towel for modesty. I had hosed the undead juices off of my armor. The suit was still drying in the shower.

"Pitt. This is an informal meeting. You shouldn't dress up so much," Sam told me. At least he didn't try to steal my towel and flick me with it. I could tell he was tempted.

"Okay, everybody. Here's the situation," Harbinger began, a cigarette dangling unlit from his lips. "We have seven very powerful vampires, possibly Masters, that landed somewhere near here, along with some other monsters of unknown type. They must have arrived sometime in the last three days. If they launched as soon as the freighter turned south down the coast they would have arrived near Myrtle Beach, South Carolina, though my gut feeling's that they didn't do that. The ship dropped anchor off this coast for a reason. If they came straight to shore they would've landed in this area east of us." He put his finger on a spot of coastline. There were a lot of islands, peninsulas and inlets under that fingertip.

"If they started moving as soon as they landed, then they could be almost anywhere. They could still be on foot, or they could have secured some transportation. If they're in a vehicle then they could be in Florida, Alabama, or South Carolina by now."

"Vampires can drive?" Chuck asked blankly.

"Yes, Mead. Vampires can drive. Just not during the daylight. If they secured a truck with a trailer, it would give them a place to sleep during the daylight hours too."

"What if they split up?" Milo asked.

"They won't," I answered. Nine heads swiveled in my direction. I tried to cover myself with the towel as best as I could. I was a little self-conscious, especially with all of the thick red scar tissue on my chest and back. "They're like a protective detail. The Cursed One is their principal. They're guarding him. Wherever he goes, they go."

"Yeah, about that. I've been meaning to ask, how do we know you aren't just bloody nuts?" Priest asked. "No offense intended."

"None taken. To be honest, I don't know. But the seven coffins is a pretty good indicator."

"Fair enough," he answered.

"What about this Cursed One? Do we have anything on record about that?" Milo asked.

"Negative. I can't find anything. Lots of things with curses, but not that match this one. Nothing comes up in a search, and nothing under Lord Machado. No entries about anything wearing a suit of armor either. I've got a bunch of folks hitting the books back at the compound looking for something. There might be something in the old archives that hasn't been scanned in yet." MHI kept meticulous records of all known monster encounters, and also drew upon a massive library of information gathered from around the world. The stuff that we dealt with did not just pop up during a Google search.

"Maybe if we had a better description it might help," Julie said coldly. She was still pretty mad at me.

"Sorry, I was incorporeal at the time."

"Machado is a Portagee last name. It means ax. Like the kind that an executioner would use," Sam told us. His useful information was a bit of a surprise. His teammates regarded him strangely. The cowboy spent a lot more time busting heads than he did studying monster history. "What? I had a master chief with that last name. He thought the ax thing was pretty cool."

"We're listening to the local police bands. If we're lucky somebody will see something and call it in; if we're unlucky, somebody is going to end up as lunch. So we are also listening for any missing persons reports. This is Boone's turf so he's trying to contact some of the locals who might be first in line for information."

"First in line?" Holly queried.

"Cops, coroners, reporters. In this case, I'm going to contact hookers, pimps, and drug dealers. Also some backwoods hillfolk that I've dealt with before. When vampires feed, they will usually go after the underbelly of society. They keep off the radar that way."

"How often do they need to feed?" Trip asked.

"Unknown. The usual low-level vamps that we deal with seem to do it every chance they get, with probably a minimum of about once a month. I know that the Feds have captured a few in the past and done testing on them, even starved a few, but they don't share that kind of info with us," Julie said.

"Speaking of the Feds, I had to call them," Harbinger said sadly. He paused during the inevitable cursing long enough to light his cigarette and take a long drag. "Didn't have much choice. We're still short-handed. We have to face the fact that we might not be able to tackle all of them, especially if they're roaming together."

"What did they say?" Milo asked.

"Nothing basically. They said thanks for the tip. That was it. I think they thought I was nuts."

"We can handle them, Earl. We don't need no Feds," Sam said.

"Maybe if we catch them while they're sleeping and toss in a couple hundred pounds of C4. Facing them while they're awake? No way." There was some murmuring at that. We were a testosterone-charged, confident, well-trained team. "No offense, but I'm the only person here who has actually killed a Master. I'm one of the only people alive who has even seen one. And I was just lucky. Trust me on this one. We're good, but we ain't that good. If we find them, we wait until they hole up, and then we blow it to hell with bombs or napalm or something. Face to face, no thanks."

"Who else can we call in?" Boone asked.

Julie played with her laptop for a minute. "Closest other Hunters are Hurley's team out of Miami, but they're on a case in the Bahamas."

"Lucky bastards," Sam grunted.

"Nope, they're tracking a luska." She shuddered.

"Oh, never mind," he said quickly. I did not know what a luska was, but if Sam or Julie did not want to mess with one, neither did I.

"After that the only other MHI personnel in the south are Boone's guys, and then the Newbies and a few others at the compound. I don't think we want to call up Grandpa or Dorcas. Going out from there we have two teams in the northeast, both on cases right now in New York and Baltimore. Next closest after that is Phillips, who's currently dealing with some devil monkeys in St. Paul. Only five other teams left, and they're out west or out of the country. Every single team is working a case."

"We need to speed up the training process," Milo suggested.

"I know, I know. But it doesn't do any good to train them fast if they just get killed on their first mission. Julie, send every team a message. Give them a brief summary about what we're probably facing and tell them that if we beep them, they need to drop whatever they're doing and get here as quick as they possibly can. This case takes precedence over anything."

"Because of the danger to people?" asked Trip, always looking out for the little guy, being the team's resident good Samaritan and idealist.

"No, because the bounty on a Master vampire is fricking huge," Sam said.

"How huge are we talking about?" asked Holly. We had been told that our next bimonthly check would probably hover around $20,000 for our cut of the action from the *Antoine-Henri*. I couldn't wait to see what the year-end bonus looked like.

"Like we could buy Idaho kind of money."

"Back to business. Here's the plan. We break up into groups. One group stays here at base, monitors communications and checks all of the gear. Boone will take a group and start hitting up his sources."

"Priest can take a group also, he knows the same people I do. We can cover more ground that way. Some of these folks are not the kind of people that you can just get on the phone."

"Good. Final group takes the chopper. I'll head up and down the coastline looking for that little boat or where it might have possibly landed. Pitt comes with me and we will see if we can't identify anything from his dream."

"Uh . . . what do we do about cars?" Mead asked.

"Head into town. Buy some from the locals. Let Milo do it. He's our best scrounger. We have two suitcases full of money, so try to get something nice." And I had wondered why we had IRS troubles. We threw cash around like the Cali cartel.

"Oh, and somebody, for the love of all that is holy, buy Pitt a pair of pants."

The Hind sat on the broken tarmac, looking like a squat and angry amphibian. I jumped out of the back of the pickup, and just barely had time to grab my gear before the truck roared off and sprayed me with gravel and dust. Milo was having entirely too much fun with the jacked up 4x4 that he had just bought off of a local named, and I'm not making this up, Cooter. There were even naked lady silhouettes on the mud flaps, and a little sticker of Calvin peeing on a Ford symbol in the back window. Harbinger and I headed toward the chopper.

We were wearing normal clothing, concealing only handguns, with our more serious gear shoved into the duffel bags that both of us were lugging. The pistol that I had under my shirt had belonged to Roberts. It was a big, stainless steel, Smith & Wesson 4506. Not my style, but it was available, and he was not using it anymore. It sure beat being unarmed. Milo had picked me up some regular clothes at the nearest country store. The only shirt they had in my size was lime green and was emblazoned with the deep philosophy of "No Fat Chicks."

Our pilot was waiting for us. I finally got to see him without his helmet. Unfortunately he was wearing a black balaclava and tinted goggles. Harbinger waved as we approached. The pilot waved back.

"So what's the deal with the pilot?"

"What do you mean?"

"I mean, it's already eighty degrees out here and he's wearing a ski mask."

"Oh. He's just shy is all."

We stopped in front of the chopper. I held out my hand and introduced myself. The pilot tilted his head to the side and studied my hand. I gradually lowered it, and finally put it my pocket, slightly embarrassed.

"Well, he's foreign. Weird customs, you know, a bit antisocial."

"Right. Nice to meet you, Mister . . . ?"

The pilot grumbled something guttural and incomprehensible. It sounded like gibberish to me. I looked to my boss.

"It means Skull Crushing Battle Hand of Fury in his language. We call him Skippy." Harbinger seemed to be enjoying himself. "Saves on time that way."

"I was told he came with the chopper?"

"Kind of. It's a long story. I met him in Uzbekistan. His tribe came from there. MHI is kind of his tribe now. He has himself a little place just outside the compound. Skip here is one hell of a pilot, however, and keeps this bird running great too."

"You have great taste in music, Skippy," I told him slowly. "One of the bands you played, CPKM. My brother plays guitar for them."

"You . . . are . . . blood of . . . Mosh Pitt?" The pilot's voice was very deep, and he seemed to struggle with the unfamiliar words.

"Yes. He's my little brother. I can probably get you some backstage passes when his tour comes through town. I think they're playing Birmingham in September."

He dropped to his knees. I stepped back in surprise. Skippy prostrated himself on the ground and bowed until his balaclava was touching the asphalt. He said something else in his strange language.

"Skip, please, you're making a scene," Harbinger said as he grabbed the pilot's arm and stood him up. The airport manager was watching us through his trailer's miniblinds, and another pilot, putting fuel in his Cessna, stared at us strangely.

"Sorry, Harb Anger . . . I not know . . . that big scarface Hunter . . . how you say . . . *Grzystilikz?*"

"What? Royalty? Oh hell no."

"Huh?"

"He thinks you're from a royal family. Uh, equivalent to a great war chief or something like that." He shrugged. "I've never seen Skippy bow to anybody before."

"Wow. Uzbekistan really appreciates their heavy metal. No, Skippy, I'm not royalty. This is America. And I'll still get us some VIP passes, okay?"

"Great honor . . . great honor on my tribe." The gravel voiced pilot seemed positively giddy.

"All right, let's get in the air. We're burning daylight." Harbinger tossed his duffel bag into the crew compartment. Skippy bowed a final time, not quite as deeply as before, and then he ran for the pilot's compartment. From the horrible noise he made, I think he was trying to sing the chorus from "Hold the Pig Steady." I work with the strangest people.

We spent the next hour flying over the coast around St. Catherine's Island and then to the east of Sapelo Island. We were not having much luck. There were lots of places where a little boat could be landed, and there were a lot of boats in the area as well. But none of the spots we flew over matched the little patch of sand from my dreams.

"It's possible that the boat washed back out to sea. Weather report says the tides have been pretty low the last few days, but you never know."

"I hope not," I replied. Skippy was blasting my brother's CD loud enough to be heard over the rotor. He had one heck of a good sound system installed in this thing. Harbinger kept cringing every time the music got particularly good. There is just no accounting for taste.

"We can either head toward Brunswick or Savannah next. I would guess Brunswick, since it's smaller," Harbinger shouted over the noise, pointing at the map. "They're probably staying away from population centers."

I shook my head in the negative. "In my dream there were a lot of lights nearby. From overhead it was pretty big. I say Savannah."

"Okay, then." He keyed the intercom button. "Skippy, take us north, hug the coast. Stay low. If the ATC hails us, let me know."

"ATC?"

"Air Traffic Control. They have a real airport. Everybody else is shafting us with fines, I don't want to piss off the FAA."

"Does he even have an actual pilot's license?"

"Beats me."

"You can't fly without a license."

"Sure you can . . . just not officially." He shrugged and went back to looking out the window. And before I worked here, I thought that I had a bad problem with authority. I fit right into this gang of misfits.

The area was beautiful from a hundred feet and a hundred miles an hour. Homes would appear between the dark green trees, only to quickly vanish as we soared past. Miles flashed by, lots of little boats and little beaches, but not the one that we were looking for.

"Ossabaw Island," Harbinger announced.

It was difficult to tell in the daylight. Everything looked different after dark. We flew over the nature preserve, and then turned inland, back toward the intercoastal waterway. There were lots of boats in the area. Most of them appeared to be for shrimping. The chopper ate up ground fast, and we flew low over a historic fort and recreation area, but I still had not seen anything that looked right. More homes began to appear as we neared Savannah.

"Whoa. Have Skippy flip a U-turn."

Harbinger gave the order, and our pilot pulled a maneuver that left me dizzy. I searched again for the spot that had just flashed by. It was a small patch of sand, with deep swampy forest surrounding it.

"Bingo." I pointed at the small white boat. It was still grounded on the sand. "This is it."

The Hind circled the area. There was a single home set back into the trees a few hundred feet from the landing spot. It was a nice home, two stories with an attached garage, a red-shingled roof and a big chimney. It was a gorgeous piece of property. The nearest homes were a considerable distance away.

"Are you sure?"

"Yeah. Damn sure. I can feel it in my bones."

My boss nodded and punched the intercom, cutting off a good drum solo. "Skippy, can you get us down on that beach?"

We approached the boat cautiously. The Hind tore away, heading farther out to sea to hover and wait. It was broad daylight, but after my experience with the wights, I knew that didn't mean squat. I held Jerry Robert's FAL carbine at the low ready. Earl nonchalantly cradled his Thompson.

"They ain't here."

"How do you know?" I asked.

"I can smell vampires," he answered. "Plus birds are singing in the trees. If your ten-foot winged things were here, I don't think there would be birds singing or squirrels playing."

"How do you know? Maybe they really like squirrels?" I kept my weapon pointed toward the boat. Sure enough, it read *Antoine-Henri*. It was empty.

"More of that slime," Harbinger pointed out. "Same stuff from the shipping container. Your Cursed One was here. Boogery thing, ain't he? I hate monsters that leak all over the place."

There were no visible tracks in the sand. Any sign left by the creatures had been obliterated by wind or surf. The forest was alive with noise and light. Not at all like the night in my dream. It was good to have the final piece of physical evidence washed up here at my feet. This proved that I was not crazy. Well, maybe not that I wasn't crazy since I was standing on a beach with a battle rifle talking about vampires, but at least not certifiable.

"Let's check the house," he said.

"What if somebody's home?" I raised my rifle to accentuate my point. I had a bag of spare magazines slung over my lime green T-shirt. We did look a little odd.

"There's nobody home."

"How do you know?" The house was half a football field away through the trees.

"I don't hear anything. I don't see any lights. It's hotter than hell and the air conditioner isn't running. If they can afford that house, they can afford to run the air conditioner." I had no idea how he could tell that from this distance. From all of my years of being around loud guns and louder rock music, I could barely hear our conversation. "I want to see why this place is special. They turned that ship a couple hundred miles off course to land here, and I want to know why."

There was a small path through the thick vegetation. I tried to move silently over the packed earth, without much luck. I'm not built for stealth. Harbinger moved like a ghost. He held up his hand for us to stop. He quietly pointed at a spot on the house's roof. There had been some damage to the shingles in a few spots, and one of the corners had been broken cleanly, with the rain gutter dangling into the yard. Something heavy had landed on that roof, a few heavy things actually.

The back door was ajar. A muddy pair of boots had been set aside, as well as a fishing pole and a small plastic tackle box. A welcome mat was slightly askew on the porch.

Harbinger entered first. The door creaked on its hinges as he opened it fully. I had never done anything like this before. It was like a scene out of a bad cop movie, except we were private citizens. We were merely breaking and entering.

I leaned in close and cupped my hand over my mouth. "Are you sure nobody is home?"

"Hello! Anybody home?" he shouted. We waited. There was no response. "Happy?"

"I guess."

The back door entered into the kitchen. The interior was uncomfortably warm. My suspicion had been right; this was the home of an affluent person. All of the appliances were top-of-the-line stainless steel, and the counters were made of real marble. There were dried mud footprints on the otherwise spotless floor, several pairs of them.

The living room was much the same. The fine furniture could have been found in any upper-middle-class home in the country. There were dirty footprints running across the thick carpeting, and running up and back down the wide staircase. Huge polished book-cases lined the walls, filled with thousands of books. Most of them appeared to be history books: Ancient American archeology, Meso-American art, mound build-ers, Native American religion. There were stacks of magazines and scholarly periodicals, *Archeology*, the *Smithsonian*, *BYU FARMS* newsletter. All of them were addressed to their subscriber, Dr. Jonas Turley. I noticed that many of the books had his name on the spine. The doctor was a prolific writer.

We proceeded to the next floor. I began to touch the banister and my companion stopped me. "Don't leave fingerprints." I nodded. We had not been upstairs yet, but already we both knew that this was shortly going to be considered a crime scene by the local authorities. No need for complications.

The door to the master bedroom had been smashed into kindling. As I stepped through the wreckage, my nose was assaulted by the smell of decay and small biting flies buzzed around my head. We had found the Turleys. Tissues break down rapidly in the warm humidity of coastal Georgia.

"Do we need to cut their heads off?" I asked hesitantly. The old couple had been savaged and torn. Blood had coagulated and dried on the sheets. I tried to sound confident to the more experienced Hunter, but desecrating the bodies of old folks in their own bedroom was a lot more wrenching than doing it to a creature that had just tried to take my life.

"No. They're dead. Really dead. They ain't coming back. The vamps didn't bite them, they beat them to death. I wonder why?"

"Maybe they didn't want him coming back. Why this guy? What makes him so special?"

"I don't know. Search the place. Look for papers. Journals. A diary. Find his computer. Anything." The doctor's office had been ransacked. Pieces of ancient North and South American art had been pulled from the walls and smashed. The computer had been pulverized. Papers and books were strewn everywhere. In the far corner a small wall safe had been ripped from the studs, and the door had been torn open. The contents, a stack of fifty-dollar bills and an old .38 special, had not been disturbed.

"This is going to take hours. There's got to be thousands of pages of notes here."

"We don't have hours. We've got company." Harbinger craned his head back and closed his eyes. "Helicopters. Lots of them. Low and fast . . . Feds. Damn it." He must have had freakishly good hearing. I could not hear anything other than the creaking of the floorboards. "We don't have time to meet with the Hind. No need for Skippy to get dragged into this." He pulled a radio out of his pocket and clicked the transmit button three times. The response came back with two clicks in the affirmative. Our chopper was heading back to the airport.

By the time that we reached the living room even I could hear the drumming of the multiple helicopters.

There were at least four UH-60 Blackhawks, and two Apache gunships to provide cover. They surrounded the Turley home and multiple teams of black-clad men rappelled to the ground.

"Wow. Isn't this a bit of overkill?"

"That there is your tax dollars at work. Best throw your guns down in case one of the storm troopers has an itchy trigger finger." He placed his Thompson and his snub-nosed 625 on the loveseat. I carefully put Roberts' FAL and Smith on the couch. We both stepped to the center of the room, away from anything that could be considered dangerous. Harbinger placed his hands on top of his head. That seemed like a good idea so I copied him.

"Should we open the door for them?"

"Nah. The Feds are going to blow it open anyway. Best close your eyes and stick your thumbs in your ears. Open your mouth a little, that will equalize the pressure. This is gonna hurt."

I had no idea what he was talking about, but they proved to be good instructions. Almost simultaneously half of the windows in the house shattered into tinkling glass as flash-bang grenades were tossed in. The concussions were horrendous, the noise was amazing, and I was dazzled even through my closed eyes. Harbinger was laughing.

The black-suited Feds came crashing through the door, piled on top of each other, each one taking a section of room and covering it. They began to scream commands at us. I went to my knees, and kept my hands on my head. It didn't matter because somebody moved behind me, kicked me in the back with a heavy boot, forced me down, and ground my face into the carpet. My arms were jerked behind me and I was placed in handcuffs. They really cranked them on tight, biting the steel deep into my wrists. The boot was placed back on my spine, and I had no doubt that the trooper's muzzle was aimed at my head.

I stayed there, with my face shoved into the carpet, while the Feds secured the home. They entered each room by tossing in more distraction devices, clomping around, and then shouting "Clear." After a few minutes the noise died down a bit, and the radio chatter started up. A slightly scuffed, black leather wingtip stopped inches from my nose.

"Hello again, Earl. And if it isn't Owen Pitt, CPA. I warned you not to fall in with this crowd."

"Hey, Myers. How's it hanging?" I mumbled through my mouth full of high quality rug fibers. He barked an order and my arms were yanked in a vain attempt to get me up. The Fed doing the pulling couldn't deadlift me, and I wasn't feeling particularly cooperative. Another one grasped me, and with a grunt they jerked me to my feet. I was about ten inches taller than my old friend that I had dubbed the Professor. Agent Franks stood behind him, now in his black body armor and carrying a brand new FN F2000 with grenade launcher. The stone-cold killer looked far more comfortable in his combat gear than he had been dressed up at the hospital. Myers was still in a cheap suit.

"Franks. What's up, my brother? Kill anybody interesting lately?"

"Tons."

"Good for you," I said cheerfully.

The muscular Fed read the message on my lime green attire. "Nice shirt."

"We're not doing anything illegal, Myers. We called and let you guys in on this case as soon as we knew how big it was. We're totally in our rights." Harbinger had a thin smear of blood next to his lip. Apparently one of the Feds had felt the need to help him to the ground.

"You are at a crime scene related to that case and you haven't bothered to call. That could be construed as withholding information concerning a monster menace," Myers stated in a smug and condescending manner, "which is very illegal."

"We just got here. We were meaning to call. My cell phone wasn't getting a signal," he lied.

"I bet. So tell me how exactly did you find this place?"

"We flew down the coast until we spotted the motor launch missing from the freighter. The same launch I told your people about last night."

"So you just happened to fly around until you found it? And you just picked it out of the ten thousand other boats around here."

"Pretty much."

"I'm supposed to believe that?"

"Come on, Myers. How else do you think we found this place? Do you think we have visions or magic dreams or something? Okay, I give up. You got me. We called the psychic friends network, they gave us the coordinates." My boss certainly turned into a smart-ass when dealing with federal agents.

"So what are you guys doing here?" I asked.

Myers started to answer and then caught himself. "None of your damn business."

"You got our call last night about the seven vampires

and the Cursed One, and within a few hours you end up right here. That has got to be an amazing coincidence."

"Yes. Pretty amazing coincidence, Mr. Pitt."

"Ironic," Franks said, patting his Belgian assault rifle tenderly.

"Yeah, silly me. Never mind I said anything."

Myers' phone rang. He still had that annoying ring tone of "Take Me Out to the Ballgame." "This is Agent Myers . . ." He listened for a minute, then he covered the receiver and spoke to us. "Earl, get your crew and take them home. This is no longer your affair. If I see a single Monster Hunter poking around Georgia I'll shut you down so fast your head will spin."

"I've got Hunters that live in Atlanta, Myers."

"Well, they better not be doing anything involving this case. At all. Period. I want you and your freak show back in Alabama immediately. You're lucky you caught me in a good mood. I don't want to hear about you doing anything with these seven vampires, or anything related to them. This case and everything pertaining to it is a federal matter. Got that?"

"Understood. Mind if we call a cab or something?"

"Get them out of my sight." He went back to his phone call.

We were shoved rudely out the front door. Franks stopped us on the porch long enough to undo our handcuffs. I rubbed my tender wrists. My boss leaned in close and whispered a single word.

"Stall."

I raised a single eyebrow incredulously. What the heck was I supposed to do? Talk about the weather?

"Hey, Franks?"

"What, Pitt?"

"What about our guns?"

"They're evidence."

"Evidence of what?" I had the urge to punch the morose man in the snout. He was one ripped son of a gun, he even had big veins bulging in his forehead and neck, so at least I would get a good fight out of it. Except the other forty Feds would probably shoot me. Scratch that stalling plan.

"Crime."

"What crime?"

He shrugged.

"Dude, that FAL and that 4506 belonged to the Hunter that got killed yesterday. Have a little heart. Give them back and I'll deliver them to his sons. Give them something to remember their dad by."

"No."

"Why not?" I knew that there was no way that was going to happen. The Smith was legal, but the full-auto FAL had to be the property of MHI, because it would be too illegal to own without the special paperwork and permissions. Stupid laws.

"Evidence."

"Listen, you monosyllabic moron. Let me spell this out. You can't just go around confiscating private property. There's a fourth amendment. Maybe you heard of it?"

"Did you just call me a moron?" That was possibly the longest sentence I had ever heard from him.

"Yeah, I did. I'm using my right to free speech to call you a moron. That falls under one of those other amendments."

Franks handed his FN to one of the other Feds.

He tapped his radio. "This is Franks. Are there any cameras or witnesses in the immediate area? Over." He listened for a moment and then smiled.

He hit me harder than I have ever been hit before. His fist was like lightning, striking deep into my gut. The air exploded out of my lungs in a rush. I have fought in dozens of brawls and underground fights, and won most of them. I've been hit by bikers, construction workers, crack heads, karate experts, and semiprofessional boxers, and just yesterday I had been hit by a vampire. Franks must be dropping some serious 'roids, because none of the others held a candle to him.

I fell off of the porch and landed in the flowerbed. I jumped up, and turned to face him just in time to catch a hammer blow to the side of my head. I tripped backwards over the small white fence and landed on my back. Some of the other Feds stepped forward to give me a little stick time, but Franks just held his hand up to dismiss them. This was his gig.

He waited patiently for me to stand up. I dropped into a fighting stance, legs bent, arms up, hands open and loose. The pain was displaced by my anger. I was ready. "Come get some."

"Okay."

Franks moved faster than I thought possible. I blocked his first two punches, and narrowly ducked under the third. His dark face was emotionless, and his eyes were unblinking. I threw a fast jab and then a hook. He dodged them easily, and then kicked me in the chest. I was rocked backwards in shock. He followed with a spin kick, again hitting me in the stomach. I grunted as my abdominal muscles absorbed the blow.

I'm extremely fast for my size, unbelievably fast.

I threw a flurry of punches, and then followed with elbow and knee strikes as the range closed. I did not manage to hit him once. Franks swatted my blows aside with bone-jarring force. He dodged under my elbow, blocked the knee, and then head-butted me in the face.

With eyes watering I dove for his waist. I had been a wrestler. If I could take him to the ground I would have a chance. He pushed off against my shoulders, avoiding my trap, and broke some of my teeth with a hook. He followed that by kicking me in the sternum. Good thing I'm padded with muscle or that one would have killed me.

"Enough!" Myers shrieked.

Franks instantly stopped. He was not even breathing hard. I was panting and bleeding. I spit a blob of blood and half of a molar on the ground. The Feds that had been watching moved aside to let Agent Myers through.

"Striking a federal agent? This is a new low even for your thugs, Earl."

"He didn't hit me. Too slow," Franks stated.

"I'll try harder next time," I gasped.

"Look forward to it."

"Get off this property now before I have you arrested," Myers ordered. Harbinger put his arm over my shoulders and led me away. We walked down the driveway, more like my boss walked and I weaved. My head was throbbing, my eyes were watering, my nose and lips were bleeding, my chest and stomach burned in pain, and I felt at least two broken teeth with my tongue. I had not gotten my ass handed to me in a one-on-one fight like that since I was fifteen.

He waited until we were well away from the helicopters and perimeter of armed guards before speaking. "Good stall. Not exactly the tactic I would have used, but letting Franks beat you up was great."

"I didn't *let* him."

"Good job anyway." He pulled a handkerchief out of his pocket and handed it to me. I held it tightly under my nose.

"So what was the purpose of that little exercise?" I asked. "What was I stalling for?"

"I was trying to listen in on Myers' phone call. He was standing right in the living room."

"Do you have superpowers or something?"

"Nope. I just have good senses," he smiled. "And I know how to pay attention."

"So did you hear anything?"

He was quiet for a long moment as we crunched our way down the long gravel lane. "Not really. He was talking way too softly. And there were helicopters overhead."

"So I took a beating for nothing?"

"Pretty much. But it was entertaining."

We called for help and Milo retrieved us an hour later with the jacked-up Chevy. We drove south in silence. Our mission was at a dead end. The Feds were running us off. Harbinger was in a bad mood as we stopped for gas in a small town. Milo apologized, but apparently the newly purchased truck got about three miles to the gallon.

Back at the Radio City Motor Lodge, the rest of the Hunters were not particularly thrilled either. The ten of us were gathered in our improvised command center, sweltering in the humidity. I passed the time by flicking pennies at the roaches scurrying up the walls. A few of the bugs were big enough that they shrugged off the impacts and one particularly impressive specimen even latched onto the coin and kept it.

"This is bullshit!" Sam said as he kicked a hole in the sheetrock.

"If we took all of them down it would be the biggest PUFF bounty in history," Boone added. "Seven high-level bloodsuckers, and we would be set for life."

"Myers doesn't bluff. We're on thin ice as it is." Julie was the voice of reason. "We have to go home."

"I don't like it at all, people, but we ain't got much choice. We're leaving. Boone and Priest can head back to Atlanta. You can take whatever gear that don't fit in the Hind."

"I'm short handed, Earl. I'm down a man, and it's going to be a while before the other guys are healed up," he said.

"You guys earned the vacation. Spend some time with your families. Get some rest. We won't send any missions your way until your team is up and running. As for short-handed, you want some Newbies? I think we can consider these graduated from basic training."

The Atlanta team leader critically studied Chuck, Holly, Trip and me. It reminded me of when we used to pick teams in grade school. I sucked my stomach in and tried to look tough. He looked each of us in the eye individually, and nodded in satisfaction.

"Earl. I would be honored to have any of them. From what I understand each one of them did good on that freighter, and that was some hairy shit. If they can keep it together through that, they'll be just fine. I've been running with only five men, and five is a pretty small team to start with. I would take them all if you would let me." I took that as quite the compliment.

"I can't spare them. I'm going to need to spread them around. I've got other short-handed teams, and we need to put together a new team based in the intermountain west. Sam's gonna lead that one."

Sam quit angrily putting holes in the walls long enough to stammer something in surprise. I believe that he used the F word as noun, verb and adjective all in the same sentence.

"Team Haven?" he said. "No way."

"We need another team. You're the best man for the job. Congratulations," Harbinger said. The former SEAL slowly sat on one of the beds in shock. Milo patted him on the back. The rest of us voiced our congratulations. "We'll work out the logistics and the details when we get back to the compound. I've got to spread around my experienced people."

"Good for you, Sam. You'll do fine. As good as any Navy guys can be expected at least. So who do I get?" Boone said.

"I could send you Grant," Harbinger suggested.

"Only if you give me Pitt too. Grant would end up at the bottom of the Chattahoochee within a week. I could deal with that," Boone said. He grimaced as Julie slugged him hard in the arm.

"Roberts was a gunman. You need a gunman. You get Mead. I watched him shoot that SAW on that freighter and he was hell on wheels. He'll do you proud."

"Aw, shucks," said our big simple Ranger.

"Chuck, say hello to your new boss. Don't screw up."

"Yes, sir!" he shouted. Boone shook his hand, welcoming him aboard.

"Okay. Now for the rest of us, here's the deal. We're leaving, but we ain't quitting this case. We keep working our sources. We put out the word to every team, every informant, and every sewer-dwelling mutant out there. As soon as these things show up on the radar we're going to nail them. I'll call in every single Hunter in the country if necessary. Feds be damned. We started this and we're gonna finish it."

"So if we do track them down and destroy them, how do we keep from losing our charter?" Milo asked. "I mean, if we get them, won't the Feds just shut us down for nosing in on their case?"

"Not if we just 'blunder' into the seven while we're working on something else."

"Groovy."

We were dropped off at the little airport. The sun was gradually setting over the Georgia countryside and mosquitoes and little evil gnats swarmed over our bodies. The Hind was prepped, and we made our way toward it, carrying duffel bags and heavy cases. The airport manager sat in a lawn chair in front of his little rusted trailer, an old gray dog curled at his feet. He waved at us lazily.

I was at the rear of the group, lugging a heavy wooden crate filled with all manner of controlled destruction. The big guy always gets to carry the heavy stuff. Julie broke away from the others and stopped in my path.

"Owen, we need to talk for a second."

"Sure," I grunted as I set the crate on the ground.

"First off, I appreciate all of the hard work that you have done. And I really appreciate you risking your life to save me and the others. That was very brave."

"Look Julie, I'm sorry, but—" She cut me off.

"But what you did with Grant was over the line."

"You can stick up for your boyfriend all you want, but he left me behind. He left me to get killed by Darné." My cheeks flushed hotly in sudden anger. I wasn't about to be told that what I had done was wrong.

"I know. That wasn't right, but Earl will deal with it. Not you."

"Wait a second. You're mad because I stepped outside my authority, and not because I punched out your boyfriend?" I was confused.

"And you threw him into shark-infested waters, don't forget the shark part. Your temper will get you killed in this job. It only takes one stupid decision to get you or your team killed. You need to keep the emotions in check."

"Like you," I said pointedly.

"I guess." There was a long and uncomfortable pause. "Look, I just . . . I don't want you to get hurt. You seem to do that a lot already." She lightly touched my bruised and swollen face. Her fingertips were surprisingly gentle. "Damn. Franks really did give you a beating."

"I am sorry. I'm not sorry about hitting Grant or even the swimming with sharks part, but I'm really sorry about . . . you know. I don't want you mad at me." I took a deep breath. "I felt like I betrayed you, and that's what I'm sorry for."

"I'm fine, but I've got one request. Stay out of my business. What happens between me and Grant is between me and Grant. Not you, not Earl, not Milo, or Sam or anybody else who feels the need to harass me about it. I know how you guys see him, but I know him better than that. I'm sure he had a reason for what he did."

"Are you going to dump him?" I asked, suddenly hopeful. "Because he panicked and left me behind?"

"What did I just say?"

"Stay out of your business?"

"Right." She must have realized that her fingers were still on my cheek as she reflexively snatched them away. She lowered her voice to just barely over a whisper. "Owen, look . . . I know that . . . well, I know how you feel, and I—"

"Brother of War Chief!" Skippy rumbled as he interrupted her. He was still covered from head to foot, the mirrored visor of his flight helmet was down, showing only my reflection. I was a little perturbed. *Skip, you have lousy timing.*

The pilot fell to his knees and bowed again, until his helmet hit the ground. "Hind is . . . she ready to fly . . . Noble One." His voice sounded like rocks being poured into a cement mixer. He sprang quickly to his feet.

"Noble One . . . no carry . . . he no carry." He made that horrible noise that represented his real name as he grabbed the handles of the heavy crate and bucked it up onto his knees. He clucked when I tried to take it from him. "Skip carry . . . Bring honor to tribe."

The black-garbed pilot waddled with the heavy load toward the waiting chopper. Julie's brown eyes were wide behind her glasses. I shrugged. It didn't make a lick of sense to me either.

"Noble One? What the hell? He's not your own personal porter, Owen," she said as she turned and stalked away. The moment was gone.

I took one last look at the sunset, swatted a mosquito, muttered something suitably profane, and followed Skippy, who was once again trying in vain to sing. It sounded particularly horrible when he tried to grumble-hum the sounds of the instruments.

"Hold pig steady . . . dum dum dum . . . ra ra ra . . . yeah. Pig. Pig! PIG!"

CHAPTER 12

That night I slept in my comfortable and familiar bed at the MHI compound. The barracks were clean and roach free. I passed out within minutes of getting home.

My dreams were confusing. I saw an enormous cargo plane take off from an airfield somewhere far in the bleak north. It was a giant, unfamiliar, four-engined monstrosity, bellowing smoke and noise. Inside, the plane was packed with boxes, cargo and even some recently butchered livestock. A man stood near the rear door of the huge cargo plane. He did not need to hold onto anything, despite the uneven vibrations and turbulence, and I knew that he would stand the entire long trip. Unmoving, arms folded, legs wide, thick fur cloak covering most of his features, black eyes staring unceasingly in the direction of his destination.

His face was a mass of black tattoos, giving the illusion of a leering skull. In my dream the ink on his skin moved.

❖   ❖   ❖

I got back from Montgomery in time to catch most of the meeting. The dentist had fixed my two broken teeth. Half of my face was numb and tingly with Novocain and I could not help but poke at my cheeks to feel the weird pressure. They were using the conference room from my dream. All of the experienced Hunters were there, including Raymond Shackleford III himself. The few Newbies, who it had been felt were ready for action, were sitting around the huge wooden table. Holly Newcastle smiled and gave me a little wink as I tried to sneak in. I sat as far away from Grant as I could. Grant and his nose bandage studiously ignored me.

Julie was speaking. She stood at the head of the table to give her briefing. "Dr. Jonas Turley was considered one of the premier experts on the religion, art and history of the ancient civilizations of this continent. He wrote over twenty books on those subjects, and has done research and been a major part of archeological digs from Alaska to Argentina. I got to hear him speak once at in Birmingham. The man knew his stuff."

"So why did the bad guys go directly to his house and beat him and his wife to death? They tore apart all of his possessions looking for something, something important. I've got an idea as to what." She let slip a brief moment of pride as she made us wait for the answer. "While Pitt was bluffing that he was going to blow up the *Antoine-Henri*, Darné said that this Lord Machado had some sort of artifact and that he was going to take it to a Place of Power to use it. Dr. Turley had done a lot of research concerning ancient religious sites. His last book was about that very subject, and the word in the academic community was that his next paper was going to be an exhaustive catalog of sites and what their importance was. My theory is that the bad guys went to his house for information. They are looking for a particular place, this 'Place of Power,' so they can use their artifact."

"What does this artifact do?" the senior Shackleford asked.

"I'm the historian; ask the psychic." She pointed at me.

"I'm no psychic. I just have a strange old Jewish man that visits me in my dreams and takes me on wild and crazy adventures—hey, that sounds like a children's book."

"What does the artifact do?" repeated the head boss patiently.

"I don't really know. But I was told that the evil comes. The Cursed One will bring it. We stop it if we can, if not time will die."

"Time will die?"

"That's what the Old Man told me. I saw a storm coming. It brought Armageddon with it."

"I see. That would probably be bad. Carry on, Jules," Mr. Shackleford ordered.

Julie continued, "We need to figure out what this Place of Power is. Then we can get there first and set a trap."

"For seven Master vamps? How are we going to pull that off?" Sam asked. "We got any nuclear weapons stashed?"

"Well, actually—ouch!" Milo started to speak and Harbinger painfully kicked him under the table. *Whoa.* I had no idea what we had stashed in the basement, but I wasn't even willing to consider that. I forcefully banished the thought of Milo Anderson armed with a thermonuclear weapon out of my brain.

"We will think of something, but right now we need to gather information. We need to find out where Turley's places are, and which one is the right one. We need to keep an ear out for any sign of these monsters, and we need to keep searching the archives until we find out who Lord Machado is and what this artifact does."

"No luck with the search yet," Albert Lee told us. In the last few days he had become our unofficial librarian. "There are a lot of books down there, and no offense, but your cataloging system absolutely sucks."

"And a lot of the archives got burned in '95," Sam said.

"About '95? When do we get to hear the story?" I asked.

Harbinger shook his head. "We'll get to it, but later."

"There is one person who knows all the stories in the archives better than anybody," Milo suggested. "We could go ask him. If anybody would know who Lord Machado is, it would be him."

The experienced Hunters gave each other incredulous looks. Milo's suggestion went over like a lead balloon.

"No way," Harbinger ordered with some force.

"I forbid it," Mr. Shackleford said.

"Milo, don't be stupid," Julie snapped. She visibly paled at whatever the red-bearded man was suggesting. I had never seen anything shake her like that before.

"But if this artifact is really going to end time or blow up the world or whatever, don't you think it is worth the risk?" Milo argued. "This isn't just a normal case. We're talking about some serious stuff. He's mad at all of us, but he would talk to Julie."

"But I don't want her to talk to him. He's dangerous," Harbinger stated flatly.

"Earl, he's still her dad. He wouldn't try to hurt her."

"I've got ninety-seven dead Hunters that say otherwise. End of discussion, Milo. Don't bring it up again."

Milo leaned back in his chair and rested his palms on the table. "Fine. Forget I said anything. Just don't blame me when the world blows up." The conference room was uncomfortably silent. Julie just stared at her hands. And I had thought that my family had problems.

"We do have other options." Harbinger broke the silence. "We can talk to Turley's colleagues. See if any of them know anything about a Place of Power. He had to confide in somebody. We'll need to be discreet though, or the Feds will find out. When I called and told them about the seven vampires, they knew right where to go."

"They could have tracked us there," I said. "The Hind does stick out a bit."

"Possibly, but I don't want to assume that. Even if they did, they're probably in the same boat we are and they will be interviewing the same people. Word gets back to Myers and we're screwed."

"We could knock Pitt out, and see if he has any more dreams," Grant offered.

"Or I could try to divine the future with your entrails. I hear that works with chickens," I replied. He glared at me. Julie shook her head in resignation. I had never promised to play nice.

"There are some other sources we can go to though. There are others out there who are more in touch with . . . uh, I guess you would say the magical world and all of this Place of Power mumbo jumbo. Or if Lord Machado is evil enough, they may even be able to sense his location," Milo suggested. "We could pay a visit to the Elf Queen."

"Not a bad idea. If we bring a good enough offering she may speak to us," Julie said.

"Whoa. Back up. Wait just a minute. Are you trying to tell me there are really elves?" Trip said.

"Yes, Trip. There are elves," she told him. I refrained from asking if they lived in a magic tree and made delicious cookies.

"Like as in J.R.R. Tolkien elves?" Trip asked again. His eyes lit up in wonderment like a kid who still believed in Santa on Christmas morning.

"Old JR was quite the character. He learned from a few British Hunters who knew their stuff. Always hanging around them and picking their brains about languages and whatnot," the senior Shackleford wheezed. "He did tend to romanticize things a bit in his writing, however."

"I can't believe it," Trip told us. "It's just that this whole time all I've learned about is horrible ugly things. Evil things and dead things that hurt people. I mean I understand that our job is to fight them, so we have to know them, but I didn't know that there were good and magical things too. This is great!"

"Son, just remember. Old JR did tend to exaggerate to spin a good yarn. Real life ain't always like the books or the movies," Mr. Shackleford warned. He glanced at his antique watch. "We got time. Sounds like somebody is taking a trip to the Enchanted Forest. Go with them if you must, Mr. Jones. Milo, it was your idea so you're in charge. Take Pitt too, I reckon he's the psychic."

The Hind set down in Booneville, Mississippi, a few hours later. Our target was actually closer to the town of Corinth, but Skippy refused to land any closer to the Enchanted Forest than we had to. He did not share his reasons, and Milo Anderson, who was leading our little expedition, did not feel the need to argue about it. Luckily for us there was a place in town to rent a car. Sadly, the only available choice was a Ford Escort station wagon. The air conditioning wheezed, hissed and died before we had gone five miles heading north on 45.

"Now when we get to the Enchanted Forest, don't speak unless spoken to. And try not to stare at them. They find that insulting."

"Because they're so beautiful?" Trip asked.

"Uh . . . probably something like that." Milo was driving. I was in the passenger seat, knees crushed uncomfortably into my chest. Spacious interior leg room my ass. Trip and Holly were in the backseat. When it came to monster research or interviewing Dr. Turley's associates, most of the Newbie squad was pretty useless at the compound. Lee was having a great time exploring and organizing dusty books and journals back at the archives. He had found his niche. As for the rest of us, we were still working on that. I decided that the hole in my gums was done bleeding and I spit the wad of gauze out the window. The Novocain had worn off and my face hurt.

Milo continued speaking, stroking his beard absently. Today he had removed the beads and was going with just a simple braid. He had dressed up for the occasion with a purple paisley shirt and green pants. "Let me do the talking. Etiquette is very important to their people. If they ask a question, answer it, but don't try to make small talk. They can be very touchy and secretive."

"I bet it's because they're so ancient and wise," Trip said. Holly put her finger in her mouth and made a gagging noise.

"Hey, laugh all you want, but I grew up poor in backwoods Florida, with an immigrant, single mom. I'm the only person in my family who learned to read, and that was only because of comic books at first, and then fantasy novels and an active imagination. I got addicted to them when I was a kid and read like crazy. I must have read thousands of them. So I've been reading about elves and that kind of thing for twenty plus years. I can't help it if I'm excited."

"You were a geek," she said.

"Well, I guess."

"I bet you played Dungeons and Dragons in a friend's garage."

"Well, yeah."

"Nerd."

"Hey now," Trip protested.

"Since you were such a nerd, how did you manage to get so buff?"

"Well, one day I learned that I could run really fast with a football, paid for college."

"Still a nerd at heart though, aren't you? Oooh magic elves." She actually mimicked him rather well. "Happy fairy magic wonderland."

"Holly! Quit picking on the nerd!" I shouted.

"You should talk, spreadsheet boy."

"You kids, don't make me stop this car!" Milo said as he turned on the radio and cranked the volume as high as it would go. The channel was Spanish language love songs, but it succeeded in finally drowning us all out. The miles flashed by. Deep green trees and farms, cows and goats, interspersed with patches where out-of-control kudzu vines had managed to kill off all of the native vegetation. Kudzu was the real monster of the South. The open windows only served to circulate the hot damp air. Sweat rings formed in my armpits and spread down my chest, quickly soaking through my dress shirt.

We stopped at a Piggly Wiggly in Corinth. Milo did not explain what we were doing. We three Newbies bought sodas and tried to stay in the air conditioning as long as possible. Milo purchased a shopping cart full of supplies and loaded them in the back of the station wagon while a large fan distracted the rest of us. He had to honk the horn to get our attention.

Milo drank a Sprite while we headed out of Corinth. He pointed out a spot on the map. "Here is the Enchanted Forest. The locals pretty much know to leave it alone. Now for future reference, this area over here is known as Natchy Bottom. Do not *ever* go there. MHI has had a few cases in the Bottoms over the last hundred years. There are some places on Earth that you just shouldn't mess with, some out west, a couple in Maine, one in the New Jersey pine barrens, places that are just pure evil. That is one of them. That place is just plain bad. The people that live out there are pretty strange and keep to themselves. Heck, they didn't get electricity until the late '90s. There is some crazy stuff back in those woods that you just don't want to mess with." He did not elaborate further.

We took a series of turns, heading deeper and deeper in the hills. The few scattered houses we passed became shoddier and older as we went. The last few houses we saw were so dilapidated that it was surprising that anyone was able to live in them, but lights were on, and dogs roamed the trash-filled yards. The woods grew thicker, older and darker. It rained briefly out of the clear hot sky. The rain was warm, and quickly passed, serving only to increase the already brutal humidity.

Finally we stopped in front of a small sign. It read ENCHANTED FOREST in big letters, and TRAILER PARK in smaller letters underneath.

"Probably a trick to keep outsiders away," Trip told us. Milo sneezed loudly as he had an allergy attack. The Escort's tires crunched over pea gravel as we entered the Enchanted Forest.

It looked like a trailer park to me, and a rundown one at that. The trailers were rusty and old. Cardboard served as windows in places. Garbage and beer cans were strewn everywhere. Milo swerved around what appeared to be a pile of used disposable diapers. There were a few old cars, but it had been a long time since they had been mobile. Most of them were up on jacks or cinder blocks, tires long since rotted away. There was no life to be seen other than a couple of mangy dogs trying to stay in the shade. I could hear the sound of televisions through some of the open doors. Somewhere a baby cried.

Milo stopped the car in front of a double-wide trailer with a no-longer-used giant satellite dish rusting in front. A rudimentary porch had been built out of scrap lumber. A recliner and a big faded couch were on the porch, and a fat, greasy dog was sleeping on the cushions. We exited our little vehicle. Heavy black flies landed on us to check if we were edible.

"Wha chu want?" a voice shouted from inside.

"We bring gifts," Milo replied.

"I didn't order no free Bible off o' the TV, so git," the voice replied.

"We are here to speak with the Elf Queen."

It was quiet except for the sound of a professional wrestling match blaring on the TV. Trip looked hopeful. Holly adjusted her pistol under her shirt. She still wasn't used to packing heat, and she kept touching it nervously. Finally the owner of the voice appeared in the doorway.

He was tall and very skinny, wearing a stained wife-beater tank top and a puffy trucker hat. His blond hair was long and stringy. His fingertips were stained yellow from nicotine, and his teeth were crooked when he smiled. His features were fine, and sharply pointed ears stuck out from under his mullet. "Well, if it ain't some Hunters. Come to see the Queen. Well, she be busy, so git, 'fore I sic the dogs on ya." He pointed at the fat dog on the couch. It regarded us sullenly, but it must have decided that it was too hot to growl.

"We have brought gifts," Milo said casually. He opened the back of the little station wagon. The trailer park elf regarded us with suspicion in his beady blue eyes before he stepped off the porch and looked at our purchases from the Piggly Wiggly. He whistled when he saw the contents. Milo had bought several cases of Budweiser and ten cartons of Marlboro lights.

"I'se go get her. See if she wants to speak at chu." He grabbed a carton of cigarettes, stuffed it under his tank top, and headed for the trailer. We could hear him yelling from the yard. "Rondel! You'se got company."

Trip's face had fallen a bit, but he still looked hopeful. "It's all just a trick to keep away outsiders," he assured himself.

"Dude, he looks like Kid Rock with Mr. Spock ears," Holly whispered. "He sure ain't no Orlando Bloom."

The elf returned. He was unnaturally graceful and long limbed, but other than that and the ears, he made a convincing redneck. "The Queen will be out in a sec. Y'all have a seat," he said, pointing at the couch. The dog didn't move. It had gone back to sleep.

"Git offa there. We's got guests." He kicked the dog with his bare foot. It woke up, stood, and urinated all over the cushion. He kicked it again and it scurried off of the porch, tail between its legs. "Sorrys 'bout that," he said as he flipped the couch cushion over so we could sit on the dry side.

Milo gestured for us to sit. I reluctantly sat on the old couch, so as not to offend the elves, but leaned forward as much as possible to keep a minimal amount of contact between my pants and who knows what. Trip, who was a mild germaphobe, did not look so good.

"I think I'll guard the car," Holly stated. Milo shook his head sternly, and after a moment's hesitation she sat next to me. Our elf host excused himself and went back into the doublewide. Milo, being the experienced and wise Hunter that he was, sat on the steps. He sneezed violently.

"Well, this is a little different than what I expected," I said cheerfully.

"It's got to be a diversion," Trip whispered.

"The elf keeps staring at my chest," Holly said coldly.

A few humid minutes passed. A bright blue electric bug zapper noisily executed some mystery critters. I noticed a few sets of eyes checking us out through cracks in various trailers' miniblinds. Our host returned. He passed by us, crunched across the gravel in his dirty bare feet, opened the back of the Escort and started unloading beer and cigarettes. He grabbed a few cases and took them into the house.

"Queen Ilrondelia will be out in a sec. Y'all want a beer?" That was a mighty generous offer considering that we had just paid for it.

"No thanks," said Milo. The rest of us followed the experienced Hunter's lead and turned him down as well. Trip really looked like he could use one though. I think the ugly truth was just sinking in. Kind of like when you are young and you eventually learn that your heroes are only human, only I imagined that this was probably a whole lot worse.

The Elf Queen appeared in the doorway. Perhaps filled the doorway would be a better description. She was probably pretty close to me in weight, but about two feet shorter. She was wearing a flaming red muu-muu and white bunny slippers. Her arms dangled fat rolls, and I stopped counting chins at number five. Her blond hair was up in curlers, and her blue eyes were beady between layers of lard. Other than the pointy ears, there was not much magical here. She was a definite candidate for gastric bypass surgery.

"Presenting Queen Ilrondelia. Ruler of the Elves of the Enchanted Forest. Mistress of all she sur-vaaays. Y'all have a good un." He popped a Budweiser and went back into the trailer to watch wrestling. The Queen waddled over to her Lazy Boy recliner/throne and flopped into it with a satisfied grunt.

"Your Majesty. We have come to ask for your wis-dom. We seek knowledge," Milo told her.

"I don't do spells no mo. I'm on disability. I done hurt my back. Get me a check from the gubmint, says I can't do no spells no mo," she said in a very plump and semiliterate voice.

"Well, Your Majesty, that's fine. We aren't looking for any spells. We're looking for some information. Elves are long-lived and wise, and you pass down the wisdom of your forefathers."

"Yup. I'll be a hunnert an' fifty in August." I did a double-take at that. She looked to be in her forties. Milo did not seem to question it.

"So, Your Majesty. Since elves are so much more in touch with the spirit of the earth, we need to know if you have sensed a new evil in this land."

"There be plenty of evil in this land, Hunter. Y'all know that." She smiled in satisfaction as the bug zap-per electrocuted something particularly large.

"Yes, but something landed on the coast in the last few days."

"Oh, him? Yup. Felt it clear to the Enchanted Forest. He's a bad un a'ight. I figured he was why y'all came to call."

"Do you know who he is?" Milo asked excitedly.

"Nope. But he's been here before. Back 'fore he got hisself cursed, he was jus' a man. Came here before the first elves settled in these parts, back when we all lived in Yur-Up. He was some high an' mighty type general or sumpin. Cut a deal wit the Old Ones, down in wha' y'all call Bra-Zil nowadays. Got hisself cursed for it real good."

"How long have elves been on this continent, your Majesty?" Trip asked.

"Oh, my grammy brought our people over, four, maybe five hunnert years ago. Back in them days, the Enchanted Forest was a heck lot finer place." Her jowly face broke into a wide smile.

"I bet," Holly muttered under her breath.

"What kind of deal did he make with the Old Ones, Your Majesty?" Milo queried.

"I don't rightly know. You know how the Old Ones is. Everythin' black and dark and scary evil like. It was sumpin to do with messing wit time. No mortal man can mess wit time, but he wanted to turn it backwards. He lost his love, and he wanted to make it right."

"His love?"

"I ain't be knowing the story, jus' wha I gets from my cousins over in Yur-Up, but they don't ever call no mo. This noble's wife or lady friend got herself kilt, he went too damn far trying to get her back. 'Bout all I know."

"Do you know why he is here now?" Milo asked. She shrugged her meaty shoulders. Her muumuu had ranch-dressing stains on it. "Can you sense where he is now?"

"No, but I reckon right now he's near water. Cain't say why I know, but I know."

Fat lot of good that did us. You couldn't swing a dead cat in the South without hitting a body of water.

"Do you know about an artifact that can kill time?"

"Lots of artifacts out there I reckon. I'd have to see it to tell y'all."

"Do you know about a Place of Power nearby?" I asked.

"Boy, don't y'all go messing wit that. Humans ain't equip-ed to deal wit that stuff."

"He's looking for a Place of Power."

"They are all over the place. Especially this land, can't go no place wit out being someplace right powerful. Good thing they ain't active mos' of the time. Only some times when the sun or the moon or the stars is just in the right spot and that only happens so many times in a life, an' I ain't talking 'bout no short little human life. Stuff gots to line up jus' right to have a Place of Power."

"Do you know where the next one is going to be?"

Another shrug. "Y'all about done? *Wheel of Fortune* comes on in a minute."

"Well, that is what we came for, your Majesty. Thank you for your time," Milo said.

Suddenly there was a horrible high-pitched screech. I jumped, startled off of the urine couch. Something the size of a bird was stuck in the bug zapper. Blue flashes and sparks fell to the porch as the device swung wildly from its chain. The Elf Queen took off one of her bunny slippers and hurled it against the zapper. The slipper hit true, and what appeared to be a tiny human with butterfly wings buzzed hurriedly away. "Damn pixies! Stay offa my porch!" the Elf Queen shouted as she shook her blubbery fist in the air.

Milo gingerly picked up the slipper and handed it back.

"Y'all be careful. I don't know whas coming, but I can feel it. Sumpin big is coming. If it ain't stopped, then I figure we all done in." She put her slipper back on, and leveraged herself to her feet. She lumbered into the double-wide while we excused ourselves and stepped off of the porch. She stopped in the doorway, turned and shouted.

"Which one of y'all is the dreamer?"

Milo nudged me to respond.

"I guess I am, ma'am."

"You seen the tattoo man. The one with the ink?"

"Yes, ma'am. I have." That was a surprise. I had just thought that was a normal dream.

"If'n you see him fo' real. Run. He ain't nothin' but the spirit of hurt and revenge."

"What do you know about him? Who is he?"

"I don't know, but I seen him in my dreams too. Y'all run. Run fast as y'all can go. He ain't on nobody's side, not good not evil." She started to waddle away, but then thought better of it.

"Dreamer. One last thing. Y'all got a mission. Don't screw up. Or we all git dead. This here is serious, and I ain't just funnin' ya." She regarded me solemnly. "As Queen of the Enchanted Forest, I order y'all not to fail. Kill the bad un, or it's all over."

"What's all over?" I asked.

"Everything . . . Now git. *Wheel of Fortune* is on." She turned away and the red muumuu swished. An argument started up immediately between the residents of the double-wide over game shows versus WWF.

"Let's get the hell out of this hole," Holly said. We all agreed. Trip almost looked like he could cry.

We drove back into town to grab some lunch and call in our findings to headquarters. We stopped at a Subway in Corinth. It felt good to be back in civilization. People were friendly, the cars weren't on jacks, and I was relatively certain that nothing had urinated on my seat. Trip had not spoken since leaving the Enchanted Forest. We ordered our sandwiches and sat in a corner booth. Milo stepped outside for a little privacy while he called headquarters.

"That really sucked," Trip finally said around a mouthful of food.

Holly was serious for once. "I really am sorry. Forget about the nerd teasing. It's tough when your illusions get shattered. I know about that. Trust me I do, but you will feel better."

"It's just that I got my hopes up. You have to understand, I loved my life. I loved teaching kids. When it all went to hell, I just couldn't go back. Once I found out what ugliness was out there, the magic was gone. Everything became bleak. So when I got the chance to fight evil, I took it, plus—don't get me wrong—the massive pay raise helped too; I'm not fighting evil for free or anything naïve like that. But come on now, with so much secret evil in the world, I thought for just a minute that there might be a secret good. I just got really excited. Maybe the magic was still out there, you know?"

I nodded. Personally I was still trying to wrap my brain around the fact that I had just seen a pixie and was apparently having visions. I looked at the mushrooms on my sandwich suspiciously.

"I'm sure there is a greater good out there that offsets the evil, Trip. You will find it someday, just don't give up hope. You have seen the dark, but for every dark thing, there is light," Holly said, and patted him on the back of the hand. That was possibly the kindest and most upbeat thing that I had ever heard out of Holly Newcastle. Of course she immediately followed it with, "But if I have to deal with another stupid elf and their mystic crap I swear I'm going to shoot them all in their stupid inbred hick faces and burn their stupid trailer park down."

Milo came back and slid into the booth. He tore into his sandwich with a vengeance. "Don't let me forget to pick up a sub for Skippy too. He loves tuna salad," he mumbled with his mouth full.

"Milo, I've got to ask. Why did Harbinger and the Shacklefords freak out so bad in the meeting this morning?" I asked.

He hesitated. "I probably shouldn't answer that. It's Earl's job to tell the story about '95. I'm just the gadget guy. It's a touchy subject is all, what with all the death, and unimaginable horror, and rifts in the very fabric of reality, and whatnot."

Now I was really curious. "Come on, Milo. You're way more than just the gadget guy."

"True, I'm the guy that takes care of all of the little things. Hey, Milo, we need to make det cord pretzels.

Hey, Milo, where can we find a thousand gallons of Holy Water at two in the morning? Hey, Milo, hurry up and build some new device that we need right now out of old junk A-team style. Hey, Milo, cast out these evil spirits. That kind of thing. But when it comes to a good suggestion, No, Milo, we won't go with your idea, because we're *sensitive.*"

"Everybody takes advantage of you," I said.

"Ha. Nice try. I'm still not talking. You want to know about the Shackleford family and what happened at the Christmas Party, you got to talk to Earl. He saved my life when I was only fifteen years old. I've been with them ever since." He chewed his food for another minute.

"You really rebuke evil spirits?" Trip asked. "Cast them out like in the Bible?"

"Sort of. Hey, I'm a Mormon. Every team has to have at least one person with a little faith. Not all problems can be solved by shooting the heck out of them. Well, most problems can. If not, then high explosives can really be your friend, but every now and then you just need to put your faith against the bad guys. For most Hunters that's a losing proposition, so that's why company policy is that if it don't have a physical body, take it up with the religious authority of your choice. Sometimes we don't get a choice in the matter though. . . ." He slurped noisily from his straw. "Look guys, back to the subject, I grew up in Idaho, the youngest of fourteen kids. So family's important to me. When most of them got eaten, MHI became my family. And I'm loyal, so if Earl doesn't want me to tell you about '95 then I'm not gonna do it."

"Fair enough," I said. We all went back to our

food and studiously avoided talking. Milo appeared to sink into his beard, deep into thought, chewing contemplatively.

After a few minutes of actual relaxation, Milo signaled that it was time to move out. We refilled our drinks and prepared ourselves to move back out into the stifling heat. Our group got a few looks from the locals saying that we obviously weren't from around them parts. I picked up a sandwich for Skippy and another foot-long meatball for myself. The senior Hunter waited for the other two to walk out the door before catching my arm.

"Owen." He looked to make sure nobody was listening. "I know you like Julie and that's why you're so intent on finding out what happened to her family." He pulled off his little round glasses and wiped them on his horribly ugly shirt.

"No, it's not that at all," I lied.

"Whatever. I didn't fall off the potato truck yesterday. Look, all I'm saying is that if stuff heats up, and this Cursed One turns out to be as bad as my gut tells me he's going to be, I'll fill you in on the details—provided you do me a couple of favors."

"And those would be?"

"Help me talk Julie into speaking with her dad. He might be the only person in the world who knows what's really going on. I don't want to go behind Earl's back, but this might be the only way. She might listen to you."

"Really? Why would she listen to me? Did she tell you she liked me?" My hope spiked temporarily. Milo quickly brought me back down.

"No. But she thinks you have visions."

"I'm not going to lie to her."

"I don't want you to. But if the choice comes down to having the world blow up, or having a painful Shackleford family reunion, personally I would rather have the reunion."

"Why don't we just go speak to him ourselves?"

"He's real particular who he talks with," Milo whispered. Holly sounded the horn. She actually held it down for a full ten seconds. "Just stop by my workshop tonight, and we'll talk then. And I've got a piece of hardware I want you to try out. I think it might actually suit your personality."

"Little green book-keeper visor that clamps to my helmet?"

"Nah. Full auto, magazine-fed, 12-gauge shotgun."

My earlier hunch had been correct. Milo Anderson was a mad genius.

The drive back to Booneville and the return flight to the compound were uneventful. The rest of the Hunters were busy reading through old books or making phone calls. I helped give a short debriefing about the information we received from the Elf Queen. At the end of the little meeting I was taken to task for not telling the others about the Tattooed Man from the dreams.

"You should have said something. We could have been researching him too. Who knows what clues that might have turned up?" Julie snapped at me. She was tired and discouraged from a long day of research. I couldn't really blame her.

"Sorry. I didn't know. I thought they were just normal dreams."

"Yes, but your dreams are somehow tied to this case. I don't know how, but until we figure it out, you need to report every single dream you have." She pushed away from the table and stood to leave. "I'll go see if I can find any records matching the Tattooed Man's description. If you will excuse me, I've got a hundred years of dusty garbage to read."

After she stormed off, Harbinger assigned me to go to the range and help coach the remaining Newbies with their pistol shooting. At least there was one thing that I was good at. I stopped by the armory and picked up another pistol on the way. I needed to replace my poor broken Kimber. Stupid vampire.

There was an absurd number of weapons to choose from. The armory was actually a concrete bunker with a bomb-proof door, filled from floor to ceiling with weapons. I could spend hours in that room fondling and drooling over the various guns. There was a wall dedicated to just .45 caliber handguns: Colt, Springfield, Kimber, H&K, CZ, Sig, S&W, Beretta and other lesser known brands. I picked out a lightly customized CZ 97B. I was always a sucker for a big .45. Ten rounds in the mag, plus one in the chamber. I could carry it cocked and locked; it would not be in the armory if it had not passed the reliability test with our ammo. I took the CZ, an inside-the-waistband holster, and several extra magazines. Dorcas would make sure that it came out of my check.

That evening I stopped by Milo's workshop. It was a corrugated steel building located behind the main office. All manner of tools and gadgets were hung on the walls. Drill presses, welders, machine tools and worktables filled almost every square foot of the large space, leaving only narrow foot trails to navigate through the mess. A large American flag was taped up on the far wall. Huge speakers mounted in the corners were playing Oingo Boingo. Sparks flew as Milo used a grinder on some sort of massive device that appeared to be a harpoon launcher. He lifted his plastic face shield when he saw me coming.

"Ooo-wen. What's up, my man?" He bobbed his head to "Only a Lad."

"Milo, what the hell is that thing?"

"Harpoon launcher."

"What for?"

"In case we need to harpoon something."

I nodded slowly. I think even by the bizarre standards of Monster Hunters, there were still a few of us who marched to the beat of a slightly different drummer. In another corner there was a stuffed head mounted on the wall. It looked kind of like an alligator, but it had antlers. I did not dare ask if it was real.

"Check this thing out. We can still hit the range while there is a little bit of light left." He led me to a workbench where a strange-looking gun was mounted in a vise.

"Saiga?" I asked. That was a Russian shotgun that was based upon the action of an AK.

"At first. On this one I mounted an adjustable ACE stock, with recoil pad of course, FAL pistol grip, holographic sight system, EOTech in particular, night vision compatible. Full rail system, so you can mount lights or IR illuminators, or as you can see here, a Tula 6G15 40mm grenade launcher, front-loading, single-shot. The barrel has been cut down to twelve inches, modified choke, gave it the Vang comp treatment also so the patterns are good and tight and recoil is softer. I modified the trigger group, so top position is safe, middle is full, bottom is semi. I've got the gas adjusted so you are looking at about 700 RPM on full."

He was speaking my language. "Don't these only come with five-shot magazines?"

"I've got a bunch of nine-round box mags, and two twenty-round drums. I've tested them all, all are reliable, but on full you can run through the nine rounder in a second, so use it sparingly. Go ahead, check it out."

I gently picked up the massive weapon. It was short, but it was thick and heavy, and that was while it was empty. Add almost a box of shells and a grenade and it would be even more so. I worked the action. The bolt was slick and the spring was powerful. Milo had thoughtfully added a shelf to the safety so that it could be operated with the trigger finger. It pointed better than it looked when I snapped it into position.

"What about specialty munitions?"

"There is a gas regulator at the end of the hand guard. I machined a new one so that it now has three positions. If you have the regulator in the right spot for the right ammo, it isn't going to malfunction."

I ran my finger along the regulator, and found detents for the different power levels. There was also a mystery button. When I pushed it a hinge unlocked, and an eight-inch, heavy-duty bayonet was released. The blade was absurdly sharp and thick. With a flick of the muzzle it locked into place with a snap. It was not the world's best-balanced spear, but I wouldn't want to be on the receiving end of it.

"No freaking way. That is awesome."

"I got the idea off of Czech CZ52, but I improved

it. It folds to the side, out of the way of the grenade launcher. You don't hardly even know it's there until you need it. Bottom edge is good cutting steel, on the top edge is a silver inlay. You stick this in a lycanthrope and it's going to know it."

"Why did you paint it brown?" I asked as I slowly turned the monstrous weapon over in my hands. It felt good. I realized I was grinning like an idiot.

He shrugged. "I'm tired of black guns. Everybody has black guns. I wanted this to be a little different. Plus black gets hot in the sun. I tried to give it kind of a desert-tiger-stripe thing. So do you like it?"

"Milo . . . This is the coolest gun I have ever seen in my life. And I've seen a lot of guns. How does it shoot?"

"Let's go find out. From what I've seen from you in practice, and from what Julie told me about your shooting on the freighter, I have been waiting for somebody worthy of Abomination."

Abomination? That was just too cool. Milo handed me a sack of loaded magazines. "Okay, just one more question. Exactly how many gun laws does this break?"

Milo's red eyebrows scrunched together in thought. He started to count on his fingers, and then thought better of it.

"All of them."

The Abomination shot far better than I had expected it to. It was not sleek, it was not stylish, it could never be considered pretty. But it was reliable, and it was amazingly fast. The front-heavy weight swung quickly, and the heft helped keep the barrel down as I poured shell after shell into the targets. The holosight was

amazingly fast. At close range you just put the target
into the giant floating circle and pulled the trigger. I
knocked down steel plates, I dusted clay pigeons out of
the sky, and I put slugs into pie-plate-sized targets at a
hundred yards with ease. The mag changes were so fast
that it put my old reloading trick to shame. If I felt the
need I could keep the rate of fire high enough to melt
the barrel off of the mutant shotgun from hell.

I even got to run through a dozen flour-filled practice
grenades, and even a handful of high explosive shells.
Shove them in the front of the stubby launcher until
they click, pull on the absurdly heavy trigger, and launch
a blob of deadly high explosive out to the end of the
range. The explosions threw clouds of red Alabama clay
high into the air. What's not to love about that? By the
last grenade I had figured out the approximate amount
of holdover necessary to get hits out to two hundred and
fifty yards. Well, perhaps not hits, but like the old saying
goes, close only counts in horseshoes and hand grenades.

By the time I had emptied all of the magazines, it
had been dark for hours, and I was standing in a sea
of spent plastic hulls. My clothing reeked of unburned
powder, and the muscles in my face hurt from smiling.
What can I say? I'm a gun nut.

"Oh my gosh. That is so cool," I gushed. "I have
to have one of these. This thing is going to rock
against undead."

Milo was obviously proud of his latest creation.
I had no idea how much he was paid by MHI, but
whatever it was, he certainly deserved more. "Go
ahead and take it. It's yours."

"For real?" I said, putting the warm gun over my
shoulder.

"Yeah, you get to be the beta tester. If any other Hunters want one I can build more. Personally, I'm going to stick with my carbine. Abomination is a little on the clunky side for me."

"Thanks, dude." Christmas had come early for Owen Z. Pitt.

"You can consider it bribery. Remember what I was talking about earlier? About that . . ." He drew in close. I felt rather conspiratorial. "Look, here's the deal, after Julie's mom was lost on a mission, her dad kind of withdrew from the world. He spent all of his time down in the archives. He read and studied every book we had, and then he started gathering more from all over. It became his thing. You think Julie is smart? She gets that from Ray. He was probably the smartest Hunter we have ever had. If anybody has heard of this Cursed One it would be him."

"What happened to her dad? Why the falling out?"

"From all of his studying, he learned things that no human should have ever learned. It was stupid. Ray loved his wife and tried something desperate to get her back. It did not go according to plan."

"So why doesn't Julie want to speak to him, and why does her grandfather and her uncle freak out at the mention of his name?"

Milo jumped about a foot off of the ground when he heard Julie speak. "Because my dad is dangerous and insane." We had not heard her approach. I stupidly removed my ear plugs. I had shut down the amplification to avoid wasting the batteries. I found myself wishing that I had left them on.

"It didn't go according to plan?" Julie snapped at Milo. She strode between us, and stopped directly in front of him, arms folded. She was quite a bit taller than he was. "Didn't go according to plan? Don't you think that's a bit of an understatement?"

"Well . . . I suppose that you could say . . ."

"According to plan? According to *plan*? Milo, all hell broke loose. *Literally.* Ninety-seven Hunters were killed, and it was only a miracle that we didn't suck all of Alabama into another dimension. Even then the government shut us down, and put all of us out of work. Monster attacks on innocent people went through the roof because we weren't around to stop them, and Dad is responsible for that too." Milo shrank a little in the face of the onslaught. She whirled and faced me. "And you. What did I tell you before we left Georgia?"

"Stay out of your business?" I answered, feeling like an idiot.

"Do I need to put that on flashcards? Do I need to have it branded on your forehead? I could have it put on backwards; that way you could read it in the mirror." She was seething. "Were you two going to try and get me to talk to Dad? What the hell were you thinking?"

"Julie, listen. The bad guys want to destroy time. That sounds like a bad thing. We have seven Masters tromping around working as a gosh-darn team for heck's sake, and it has even scared the elves *and* the Feds. If the bad guys get to the Place of Power and turn on their evil gizmo, we could be screwed. Ray can probably tell us where that's going to be," Milo asserted.

"Yeah. What he said," was my addition to the argument. Julie gave me the evil eye.

"Owen. Listen to me very carefully. You have no idea what level of trouble we are talking about here. The reason Milo thinks my dad is going to know where this evil place is, is because it is similar to the insane stunt that he pulled. He risked the lives of every living person for thousands of miles."

"He did it for a good reason," Milo insisted. "He was crazy with grief. Your dad was desperate."

"He risked the lives of millions to try to bring back one single person who was already dead. That is the definition of insanity!" she raged, grabbing Milo by the shoulders and shaking him violently. "Don't you get that? My dad did evil things. He is one of the bad guys. If I had known just how far gone he was I would have shot him myself."

"Ray did evil things, but he wasn't in his right mind. I'm not saying that we should let him out, just that you should talk to him. Get information, prevent another big problem. If he could help us stop the Cursed One, then it would be a way for him to make up for some of what he did," Milo shouted back. "He is our best chance. We could still be screwing around in the archives when they set off their evil gizmo."

Julie dropped her hands and kicked some shotgun hulls angrily. Her face was drawn tight, and she was frowning. She tucked an errant strand of dark hair behind an ear. "I know," she muttered.

"And another thing!" Milo started to yell, and then stopped abruptly. "You know?"

"Yes. I know. That was why I was looking for you, you idiot. The situation has gotten worse. We just got word from Boone. He's been keeping tabs in Georgia. About forty-five minutes ago there was an attack on the home of another university professor, strong vampires, at least a couple. Right in the suburbs, just after sunset. They were looking for something.

Unfortunately the prof was throwing a party at the house at the time. The place is crawling with the Feds' reaction team, so Boone couldn't get a good look, but he was guessing at least twenty dead."

"Let me guess. A colleague of Dr. Turley?"

"Yep. She was on our list to contact. A Ph.D. in anthropology, religion specialist."

"Smart vamps don't hit parties in the suburbs," Milo said. "That brings too much heat and attention. Vamps feed on the outskirts. It doesn't make sense."

"Unless the payoff is worth the risk," Julie said. "My guess is they're looking for the when and where to use their artifact."

"You think we're running out of time?"

"Why else would they risk having the Feds track them? The Monster Control Bureau guys are not the most efficient bunch, but they have resources we can only dream about. Vampires, especially old ones, don't pull stunts like this. That's how they lived to be old to begin with," she said with authority. "I don't think we are running out of time—I know it."

"So who's the idiot now?" Milo queried, somehow managing to look both smug and innocent at the same time.

"Don't push it. Milo, tomorrow you cover for me. Grandpa and Earl can't know what I'm going to do. Pitt . . ." That was a good indicator that she was not happy, she almost never called me by my last name.

"Yes?"

"Try to dream something useful tonight, because tomorrow you're going to meet my dad."

"Sounds like fun."

"It won't be."

CHAPTER 13

Dreaming. Pleasant dreams, just the normal disjointed clearing of the human subconscious. I slept deeply, able to tune out Trip's snores from the other bunk, and my only visions were good ones. Julie's beautiful smile and full-auto assault shotguns.

Then it changed. Events came into focus. My consciousness shifted gears. The pleasant normal dreams evolved into something sharper, with seemingly real physical sensations. Cold snow under my bare feet, and the smell of smoke in the air.

I was standing in the remains of a small town. The nearby buildings had been shelled into rubble. A light dusting of snow covered the broken stone, shattered wood and rusting metal. There were a few signs and torn advertising on some of the crumbled walls. I did not recognize the language, but it seemed familiar. The style of the art was simple and old-fashioned. A gray winter sky loomed fat and heavy overhead. The world was totally and impossibly silent.

The Old Man leaned against a piece of rubble, cane

in hand. He took a pocket watch out of his homespun coat and examined it absently when he saw me.

"You are late, Boy. Much work to do."

"Sorry."

"No, I the one that is sorry. Almost killed, I got you last time."

"When the Cursed One saw us on the beach?"

"Too dangerous to take your spirit out of body. I not know what I doing. I new at this. Too, how you say . . . stupid to do again. But I had to show . . . show Cursed One to you so you know what I know. Too dangerous. No more out of body."

"What would have happened if he had caught us?"

"For me, probably stay same. For you, you end up like me. Something else probably come and take your body while it empty." He shivered when he said that, drawing his collar up against the winter cold. "Would be bad."

"Something would inhabit my body?"

"Yes, there are things that not have body of own. They are, how you say . . . jealous. We not leave your body again. Not safe. I have to find new way to show you things."

"So where are we right now?" I gestured at the silent town.

"In your head, Boy. Where did think?"

"I don't know. I've never been here. I've never been to that field we met in before either."

"In your head. But from my memory. I am friend, I am guest here. I can show you thing that I know. Is hard to show, but I getting better. For smart boy, you are sometimes dumb."

"Hey now," I said defensively.

He laughed deeply. "Is fine. I forget. Real world is different where I am. Rules change. Come, I show you." He pointed with his cane, and walked away through the snow. I followed.

The church had been old and battered even before most of its roof had been blown off by artillery. The stained glass windows had been shattered, and small parts of the walls were charred ash where the church had caught fire. It was obvious that it had been a simple but beautiful structure at one time.

"What is this?"

"Is church. Got blowed up." He made an explosion noise and opened his hands, pantomiming a bomb. "I not know name, I go to synagogue own self."

"I can see that. I mean, what are you trying to show me?"

"Is Place of Power. Cursed One brought ancient artifact here. Under this land was place where old kings make sacrifices; before man, other things use this place. This is last place that Cursed One used to try to destroy time. Time is his enemy. Lucky for us, his learning was not right. He was not ready for such bold move. He failed." We continued toward the building. The stone stairs were cold and slick with ice. "Lucky that time."

"What would have happened if he had succeeded?" I ducked my head under a broken beam in the doorway. The interior of the church was just as damaged. Pews were smashed or knocked over. There was an altar at the far side of the room. "What does it mean to destroy time?"

"He not want to destroy. Cursed One thinks he can control. He has old device. Older than world. When matter was organized to create this world, the artifact was already there. Not meant for this world. It can torture time. Turn it . . . backwards. Make it stop for some. Go for others. Is bad. Very bad. Cursed One is vain, full of pride, nobody can control time. Will destroy world."

"The Elf Queen said that he is trying to get back his lost love."

"Yes. That was first reason. Now I think he is so much twisted with evil and hate I not know. I will try to show you. If you understand him, maybe you can stop." He reached up and put his cold, arthritic hands alongside my face. "I try to show. I not take you out of your body, but I can maybe show you Cursed One's memories."

"Wait. What is your name? The vampire called you Bar Eeka."

"Byreika," he corrected. "Not important who I am. Now shush, is hard to show. Must concentrate."

"Are you a ghost?"

"Ugh. Quiet, Boy. Time is short. Maybe is ghost. I not know." The Old Man squeezed my head. He wore an intense look of concentration.

"What is this place?"

He took one hand away, and brought it back with a surprising slap. It stung.

"Always with the questions. Respect your elders. Now shush!"

The Old Man closed his eyes in concentration. The church and the smoldering town began to darken and fragment. Falling snow froze in midair. The world he had created began to fall apart without his attention. I could see my reflection in his glasses. As I watched, my face changed into someone else.

◆   ◆   ◆

Confusion, resolving itself into a hazy vision from long ago.

The jungle road was hot. My horse was exhausted by the heat and lathered with foam. My plate was splattered with the blood of my enemies, and my helmet and plume sat heavy on my sweat-drenched brow. The air was thick with smoke and the acrid smell of powder. I rested my battle-ax across my saddle and passed my matchlock to my secondary to be reloaded. Large carrion birds circled overhead, eager to have their chance at the carnage on the jungle road.

My men were following after the routed, scattering enemy, cutting down as many as possible. Worried about possible counterattacks, I signaled my northern mercenary captain to call the men back. When the undergrowth became thick, the advantages of our muskets and plate were negated. The big man spurred his horse forward, shouting for the men to rally at his position.

I dismounted my steed as a prisoner was brought struggling before me. My men shoved him to his knees. The prisoner was obviously a man of some importance, adorned with gold jewelry and wearing complex armor made of hide, and crowned with a helmet constructed from a jaguar's skull. The prisoner babbled in his incoherent pagan language. I took my helmet off and waited patiently for Friar de Sousa.

The priest came. As a man of many letters, he had made a study of the enemy's language, and was able to communicate with them in a very rudimentary fashion. I waited as the priest and the pagan spoke in a mixture of words and hand signals.

"He is a leader of his people. He says that a great ransom will be paid for his return," the priest said. Shots echoed through the jungle as my men happened upon a few other stragglers. "His city is wealthy and the very streets are paved in gold."

That was more like it, for gold was the very essence of this conquest. Legends of the natives' *Dorado*, their land of endless gold, were what kept my men focused. "Where is his city?" I asked. The priest translated. The prisoner pointed down the road and said something, holding up a pair of fingers.

"Two days' march."

"Excellent . . . Why take a ransom when you can take the whole city?" The priest understood and stepped away to avoid splattering his robes. I casually raised my ax and brought it swiftly down on my captive's head.

NO!

Calm down, Boy. It is not you. These are Cursed One's memories. You see world from his . . . how you say . . . perspective.

But I just killed a man. I couldn't stop it.

No. Cursed One killed him. Killed him five hundred years ago. He is . . . I think you would say, mean son of bitch. We just observing.

How?

I am attached to him. Hard to explain. I have gone back too far in memory. Must go forward.

The jungle road faded away, only to be replaced with a city of giant stone buildings and massive pyramids. The city was wedged between jungle-covered peaks and surrounded by a swift river. Brilliant scarlet streamers hung above the roads, and trained jungle birds sang from cages hoisted over the intersections. The vision was jerky as the Old Man tried to control what I saw. If I was truly viewing the Cursed One's memories, that would explain why I somehow understood medieval Portuguese.

It was a strange and unnatural sensation, to see through another person's eyes, to smell the odors of a city long since gone, to hear the voices of people dead for hundreds of years, even to feel the sensations through another's skin, like wearing an all-encompassing suit made out of human senses: it was perhaps the strangest thing I had ever experienced. And worst of all, I could hear his thoughts—not truly hear them, but hear them as though they were my own, only not under my control.

The scene was slightly distorted. Less important details were fuzzy or incomplete, leaving gray patches on the otherwise brilliant landscape. Time moved quickly, only to drag to impossible slowness. Sounds were distorted. Conversations of less interest were merely buzzes of background noise. Of course, memory is an imperfect recording device.

The occupants of the city lined the street. Almost all of them bowed in fear. I ordered my men to kill the few who did not bow as a warning to any who would dare challenge their new rulers. My small army had penetrated further into the interior of the continent than any previous conquistadors and I intended to claim the riches of this city as my own. I led my men toward the central palace, lances up, muskets ready. Many of the people averted their eyes rather than see us in our armor and upon our horses. Bah . . . primitives.

The people of the city were right to be afraid. We

had ground their entire army into the earth only a few hours before. I had lost seven men and a few hundred native conscripts. They had lost over a thousand. Their army had been for ceremonial purposes, full of show, and probably good at raiding small villages to take slaves and sacrifices. My army was made up of hardened warriors, good at nothing other than killing and looting. Isolation rather than strength of arms had been this city's real protection, but no longer.

The priests were happy. We were going to send souls to the Lord, one way or the other. My men were content. There was more plunder, gold and women than they could have ever imagined. It was only through fear and loyalty to me that I had kept them from immediately looting the city. My troops worshipped me, and an entire country feared me. It was a good day.

I had a dream. Dare I say a vision? I saw myself riding forth at the head of a great army, conquering all of this land and making it my own. Returning home in glory, not as a failed merchant, not as just one of the many sons of a nobleman, but rather returning home in my own glory and with my own riches. I ordered no messengers to be dispatched to the sea. This was going to be my bounty, and mine alone. King Manuel would learn of this only when I was ready for him to learn.

My troops marched toward the city center, where the largest palace loomed. I called a halt as we entered the central courtyard, and had my men set up the cannon just in case a trap had been prepared, for surely not all of these backwards people could think that we were gods.

The royal entourage met us in the courtyard. They were brilliant in their finery. A contingent of jaguar-helmeted guards surrounded the royal family. Scores of priests and priestesses, wives and concubines, scribes and courtiers filled the square. A man stood at their head. His skin coated in gold dust, his raiment a robe of brilliant feathers, surely this was their king. He was frail and weak with age. The king approached, ahead of his personal bodyguard, and laid his staff upon the ground in front of my horse's shoes. His eyes were the sad eyes of a broken man. I summoned Friar de Sousa to translate.

"In the name of his Royal Highness, King Manuel the Great of Portugal, your kingdom has been conquered, and must pay tribute. I am General Joao Silva de Machado. My word is law in this land. You will provide gold and treasure as I see fit. You will provide food, lodging and clean women for my soldiers. You will provide able-bodied men to join my army in the continuing pacification of this land as I see fit. Your people will learn the true Catholic faith and receive the blessings therein. Failure to follow my orders will result in your death and the deaths of your people. Trickery will not be tolerated. For each of my men attacked by your people, I will kill five hundred of yours. For any of my priests attacked by your people, I shall kill five hundred of your priests. If any of you tries to harm my officers or me, I will raze this city to the ground until no two stones stand upon another. I will kill every man, woman and child, feed your flesh to our hounds, and salt the earth so that nothing will ever grow upon this blighted land ever again." I waited for the friar to catch up. He spoke loudly so that the whole crowd could hear. I imagined that de Sousa's gift of languages would only carry him so far, but as long as the heathens understood the fundamentals of what I was trying to convey, I would be satisfied.

"But do not think that you can harm us. For we are gods to you." The priest stuttered a bit as he translated that bit of blasphemy. "You have witnessed the power we control. I can call fire from the heavens and smite you to dust. You cannot harm us, but you can try. If you try, you will be punished. Is that understood?"

The priest finished and the king bowed before me. The royal party did so as well. Jaguar helmets touched the ground as their army followed suit. I could grow used to this.

All bowed except one, a dark-skinned woman in the opulent robes of a priestess. She alone met my gaze. She stood proudly as the other members of her strange priesthood cowered. I had not seen such beauty and poise since I had been banished from the royal courts so long ago. I gestured for two of my men to seize her and bring her forward. She held up a hand to stop them, and approached of her own volition.

The king glared at her as she made her way across the courtyard, and hissed something at her in their incomprehensible language. I spurred my horse forward. With a snort and flared nostrils, the mighty beast knocked the king roughly to the ground. The royal party gasped in astonishment as the old broken man scurried away from my war-horse's iron-shod hooves.

"Who are you and why do you think you should not bow?" She was a beautiful wench, and it was going to be a waste to kill her as an example, but the pagans could not be allowed to see weakness from my army. My fingers drifted toward the handle of my ax. Regardless of the answer I planned to take her head, though perhaps if she amused me I would have my way with her first, and I would do it in front of the royal family. Friar de Sousa hurriedly translated.

She cut him off. "I am Koriniha, High Priestess of the Temple of Neihor."

My hand moved away from my ax. "How do you speak our tongue?" Many of my priests and soldiers began to murmur at this surprise. We were the first civilized Christians to make it this far into the interior of the continent, that we knew of at least. Had some of the blasted Spaniards beaten us here?

"There is power here, untapped for generations. I have learned your language in preparation for this very day. The spirits burned your words into me so that I may speak with you," she boldly retorted. "I have been waiting for you. Your coming was prophesied by the Old Ones. Your men come here, searching for riches, like pigs, simple in their greed. Your priests come for souls, numbers to feed their machine. But you, my Lord Machado, you are different. Your quest is for power. It is what you seek in your heart. I can offer you power. Power beyond your dreams."

"She is a witch," exclaimed Friar de Sousa. "Kill her, Lord Machado, the devil has given her our speech."

"Silence, priest. Do not presume to tell me what to do." The friar bowed his head in submission. I was interested. Something about the beautiful priestess provoked something deep in the back of my mind. "What do you speak of, woman? Make it good or I will be most displeased by this interruption."

She bowed slightly. "I can offer you much, Lord Machado. With my help I can keep this city docile and willing to serve you."

"They will do that now," I stated.

"But only out of fear. You are a wise general. You know that eventually they will rebel. Brave ones will rise up, as they always do. I know that you are only men. Mighty and wise men to be sure, but you must sleep, and you must eat our food, and your flesh can be pierced by an assassin's blade when your guards are not alert. You need not rule this city out of fear, if I can make this people serve and worship you. Why plunder one country, one people, when you can instead bend that city to your will and use it to build your own kingdom out of this land?"

I found myself intrigued by the ruthless cunning of the witch.

"Tell me more, Priestess."

I blinked and the vision was gone. I was no longer an unwitting passenger in the Cursed One's memory. We were back in the destroyed church, except now the make-believe world was no longer in sharp focus, there were blank spots around us filled with *nothing*. The Old Man was losing his concentration. He was sitting on the steps of the altar, pale and wheezing. His hands were shaking. I sat down next to him.

"Sorry, Boy. Can only do for so long. Is very difficult."

"What were you trying to show me?" I felt unclean from seeing the world through the Cursed One's eyes, feeling his pride and his calculating mind, hearing his thoughts, and experiencing his casual brutality.

"Can't explain. Must show. I will try again if there is time, but now am weak. Very weak."

"How are you tied to Lord Machado?"

The Old Man was silent. He gently tapped the hard wood floor of the church with his cane, apparently lost in thought.

"How are you tied to him? I want to help you."

"Don't worry about me, Boy. I am trapped. I am no matter."

"Do you know where he is? Or where he is going? Can you show me a current memory?"

He laughed tiredly. "You can see his old memories from when he was man, but now? One look in his head and you either dead or go crazy." He used his finger to make a swirling motion around his ear. The universal sign of insanity. "Maybe I can send image. Maybe like photograph from what he sees. I will try . . . after I rest."

"Thank you." I thought for a moment. "One last thing."

"Hurry."

"What about the tattooed man?"

"Guardian of the artifact. Do not trust. He wants one thing. Just one thing. Get in his way—" The Old Man dragged his bony finger across his throat and made a *gack* sound. "You go now. Help your lady friend. Keep her safe. She is good girl. You two make cute babies someday." He patted me on my arm.

"Huh?"

"Go, stupid boy. Try not to get dead!"

I awoke with a start. My alarm was buzzing with all of the gentleness of an air-raid siren. I pounded the snooze button and jumped out of bed, alert and breathless. The sun would not rise for a few more hours, but I had to tell the others about my dream immediately. I still did not understand exactly what was happening to me, but somehow I was being given some serious knowledge about our adversary. I threw on a T-shirt and a pair of jeans, and rushed out of the barracks, not even bothering with shoes. I crashed into Trip on the way out the door. He swore as he spilled his coffee. I shouted an apology as I sprinted for the main office building.

The MHI library was located in the basement. It was a massive room, tight with shelves and dusty tables. All of the company's monster encounters had been logged and documented for the last hundred years. In addition, books of topical value had been brought here by more scholarly-minded Hunters the entire time. In total there was a century of accumulated paper moldering away in that room. It was probably the world's biggest collection of actual monster lore, but it was a daunting task to find any one particular thing.

I found Earl Harbinger in the archives, staring vacantly at a heavy old book. From his appearance I could not tell if he had gotten up really early, or if he had never gone to sleep.

"Another dream? Did you learn something?" I nodded in the affirmative. "What did you get?"

"It was weird, but I got his whole name, General Joao Silva de Machado, and I know a lot more about him. He was an evil bastard when he was human, and apparently he has just gotten worse with age."

Harbinger smiled tiredly. Apparently that was the

best news he had gotten lately. "Good work. With that I bet we can pin him down. I'll go get the others," he said as he left.

I pulled out a chair and sat down tiredly. Whatever happened when I had these dreams, it certainly wasn't restful. I put my head down on the old wood table. I closed my eyes. The minutes ticked by. I did not feel so good.

Then the vision began. The Old Man had been true to his word. Once he had recovered enough he attempted to bring me a more recent memory from the Cursed One. This was merely a visual snapshot, just a single image that might help us locate the enemy, nothing more.

However, it came from such a tortured mind, so filled with hate and darkness and pain, that just the brief second I felt the connection was enough to knock me to the ground and leave me gasping for air in a blind panic. The Old Man must have made a mistake. I could feel the Cursed One as he sensed me intruding. I could feel his anger, and his promise to destroy me and the very fabric of my world. He sent me a message. I screamed in agony and clutched my face as I was wracked with spasms of unspeakable pain. Crashing out of the chair, I twitched wildly as thousands of invisible blades stabbed at my flesh. Tears streamed from my eyes as I thrashed about, trying to evade the pain. Everything went mercifully black.

The others were standing over me. Julie was kneeling at my side, her hand gently resting on my forehead. They all looked very concerned.

"What happened?"

"You were having a seizure or something," she said. "How do you feel?"

"Like crap. That wasn't a seizure. Lord Machado sensed me. I had another vision."

"While you were awake?" Harbinger asked sharply.

"I requested it. Last night in my dream. I asked for a picture, a current memory . . ." The other Hunters looked at each other in confusion. "I'll explain later, look . . ." I tried to sit up but I was too dizzy. I gave up and embraced the cold floor. "I saw one of his memories. I saw the world through the Cursed One's eyes. I don't know from when, but it was a recent memory."

"Owen, take it easy. Tell us what you saw." Julie's voice was soothing and relaxed.

"He was in some sort of vehicle. It was dark. I just saw the road illuminated in the headlights. They were approaching a sign . . ."

"What did it say?" Julie asked.

"Welcome to Alabama."

CHAPTER 14

The Appleton Asylum was located on the banks of the Alabama River. It was an isolated location, far off of the main road, nestled deep into the thick surrounding trees. According to the map it was only sixty miles from the MHI compound, but the barely paved route to the asylum was so circuitous that I think we had to go twice that far. The nearest actual town was Camden, and to call it close was a stretch. The afternoon air was still thick with dew. Spanish moss dangled over the roads, dappling them in shadow, and dragged along the roof of our van.

The asylum itself was an enormous, four-story gothic construction, gray and stern, surrounded by a high, wrought-iron security fence. The narrow windows were barred, and the building emanated a quiet bleakness. The sign above the entrance said APPLETON. I had almost been expecting it to have a quote from Dante's *Inferno* instead.

Julie and I had slipped away after the morning debriefing. I had given as much detail from my dream as I could to the other Hunters. None of us really knew what it all meant, but we knew that the Cursed One and his minions were now on our turf. Unfortunately, as near as we could figure, there were at least a dozen roads along the border that had a sign like the one I had seen, plus we had no idea how old the memory was. Reports had begun to drift in that the government had activated all of the National Guard units in the southeastern U.S., including units that had just gotten back from long deployments overseas. The morning news had a report showing tanks and trucks parked at the Pharr Mounds in Mississippi. Reports indicated that there were also troops protecting Civil War battlefields, Indian burial grounds and historic monuments. The spokesman from the Department of Homeland Security explained that it was merely an exercise to prepare for potential terrorist threats. Apparently the Feds were nervous as well, and trying to cover any spots that might potentially be the Place of Power.

Julie Shackleford was silent as she drove up to the gate. She had barely spoken during the drive. Her lips were set in a hard line, and she wore a look of concentration similar to the one that she had before we had stormed the bowels of the *Antoine-Henri*. She tapped her fingers nervously on the steering wheel. She was not looking forward to speaking with her father.

"It will be okay, Julie. Don't worry about it," I said, in an inane attempt at comforting her.

"Are your parents weird?" she responded, still staring out the window. She had stopped beside the security intercom, but she had not yet hit the button.

"Mom thinks that if we don't eat all of her cooking we don't love her. When she gets excited she forgets to speak English. My dad made us kids call him Sergeant."

"Well, Owen, that sounds like *Leave It to Beaver* to me. My mom disappeared on a mission and my dad locked himself in a library for a few years. He twisted forces of ancient and unspeakable evil to his will and tore open a rift in the fabric of space and time to bring her soul back from the other side. He failed, and a horde of rampaging demons from a different dimension killed most of the friends I have ever had. Now Mom is still dead, and Dad's insane . . . so don't think that you can tell me that it is okay."

"Got it," I answered. So much for being helpful. Another minute passed in silence. Finally, with a dejected sigh, she rolled down the van window and pushed the intercom button.

"Who is it?" asked the tinny and static-laced voice of the intercom.

"Julie Shackleford. I'm here to visit my father—Raymond Shackleford. He is a patient of the Doctors Nelson." There was a long pause before the heavy, iron gate creaked open under hydraulic pressure. We drove through.

"Doctors Nelson?"

"Lucius and Joan. Husband and wife team. One is a psychiatrist, the other is a psychologist. I can't remember which is which though."

"What's the difference?"

"Beats me. I was a history major. You're the trivia nut," she replied. "They are actually both retired Hunters. They bought this place from the state when they left MHI. They're good folks. I've known them since I was a kid. They are getting up in age, but they do really good work here. The Nelsons have done some great research. They help a lot of people with special problems."

"Special problems?"

"Mostly they work with regular mental problems, like any treatment center, but they specialize in people who have had monster encounters. Not everybody has a flexible mind like those of us who become Hunters," she answered.

I had never thought about that. I was still internally freaking out about the things that were happening to me. I could only imagine how some people would react from that kind of trauma. Apparently here was my answer.

We parked in the near empty lot under a large tree. Thick leaves dangled across the windshield. Julie cautioned me to make sure the door was locked. Her suggestion made sense considering that there were crazy people roaming the lawn, and we had something like a dozen firearms, grenade launchers, a flamethrower, edged weapons, and several pounds of high explosive in the back of our huge Ford passenger van.

The grounds around the asylum were immaculate. The lawns were green, and comfortable chairs had been placed in various strategic locations for the patients to make themselves at ease. A group of casually dressed people were sitting in a circle, listening to one of their own tell a story. The woman was very animated, and obviously distressed.

"They would bite me, and it would hurt, and they would suck on me until I was so weak I was almost dead. But they would never kill me. They would just go until they got full, and then they would just stick me in the hole with the others. They would throw enough food down the hole to keep us alive. It was always dark, so we couldn't tell what we were eating, but it was always raw meat. But we were so weak and hungry that we had no choice." The woman was crying and shaking. She was twisting the bottom of her Winnie the Pooh sweatshirt violently. She was young, and had been probably been very pretty once, but was now prematurely aged from stress. "Sometimes, when one of us would finally get too weak, and . . . and . . . and finally die . . . Then the next day there would be more food. So we knew what it was. But we were too weak to fight. Some of us went crazy. Crazy. Waiting for them to come back and drag another one of us out of the hole to feed on. It went on and on and on like that. I don't know how long because it was always dark. So dark." She finally broke down in deep pitiful sobs.

An older woman who was obviously a doctor stood and comforted her, hugging her and telling her that she was so brave, and that it was all going to be okay now. The group echoed the sentiment, congratulating the woman for sharing. The crying patient returned to her seat.

"Vampires," said a man who had stopped beside me.

I had been so distracted by the patient's story that I had not heard him approach. He was a short, pudgy gentleman with huge, thick glasses and wild hair. His pants were hitched up over his belly button and kept there with a giant pair of suspenders. If I were to guess I would have to say that he was in his sixties.

"One of the ways that they stay off the radar. Abduct some poor folks, and keep them locked in a pen, like cattle. Rotate through, feeding just enough to keep them alive. They don't need to take as many victims that way. Keeps them from drawing the attention of Hunters. Saddest part of all is that even if a victim has only been bitten once, even if it was years and years before, when they die, they will return as a vampire themselves. That's the real reason we embalm people nowadays. Keeps them from coming back. Even though this poor girl survived, she has to deal with that knowledge the rest of her life."

"Dr. Nelson!" Julie exclaimed. She hugged the man. He grunted as she almost lifted him off of his feet.

"Ah . . . little Julie. You have grown so much. My gosh, let me have a look at you." He studied her for a moment at arms' length. "My dear, you look just like your mother. Susan was a beautiful woman too."

I swear that Julie the fearless Monster Hunter blushed. "Thanks, Doc. I'm told that a lot. Everybody loved Mom."

"Yes, we did. She was a shining light to all of us knuckle-dragging hooligans. She kept us in line, kept me and Joan alive on more than one occasion as well. How is your grandfather? Still a cantankerous old bastard I hope? Is he well?"

"Of course, on the cantankerous part. Health wise? He's getting older, but he's tough."

"Good, good. And Earl? Staying out of trouble? He needs to call more often to check in. I would love to write a paper about his condition if he would just sit on my couch long enough for an interview."

"Earl is good. I'll tell him to call . . ." She changed

the subject. "This is Owen Pitt. One of our newest Hunters."

The doctor shook my hand. His grip was strong for an old man. His grin was infectious.

"Nice to meet you." He pumped my arm vigorously. "Considerable facial scarring. Claws, yes?"

"Werewolf," I said, self-consciously touching my face. "I pushed him out of a tall building."

"You must be the lad from Dallas then. Good show on that one. I knew as soon as I saw the report that you would become a Hunter, though I would not have minded having you here for my research—werewolf encounter, survivor's guilt, and a near-death experience, all in one patient. My, but that would make a splendid paper. Perhaps if you have the time you could give me a blow-by-blow account, maybe tell me about any psychosomatic problems you have faced since, obviously not lack of appetite. Ha!" He punched me lightly in the stomach. "Perhaps bad dreams or sexual dysfunction then?"

Julie snickered at my discomfort. Luckily I was spared any further quizzing by the arrival of the other Doctor Nelson. She was a small, thin, birdlike woman. She was probably about the same age as her husband, but the main thing that they had in common was the enormously thick glasses. She also hugged Julie, but before they could even converse, Doctor Joan called the group of patients over.

"Look, everybody. These two people are from Monster Hunter International. They are real live Monster Hunters." I waved sheepishly. Some of the patients oohed and aahed. Others held back, and sullenly smoked cigarettes.

"You are so brave."

"Hunters saved my life."

"You were my savior."

"Thank you."

Probing hands grabbed at me. I was hugged and kissed on the cheeks, and tears fell onto my clothing. I was stunned by the outpouring of emotion, and mostly tried to keep my hands on my concealed weapons. I did not want to find out if any of the patients were feeling suicidal or homicidal. Finally the crowd drew back, leaving Julie and me disheveled and tear-stained. It was a strange experience to be thanked by total strangers for things which I had never done.

"Where were you people when my kids were getting torn apart?" one of the patients snarled. He was a middle-aged man who did not look comfortable in casual clothing.

"Now now, Barney. The Hunters are only human. They can't be everywhere. They can only do their best. We can all learn from that example." The female Doctor Nelson clapped her hands. "Okay, everyone, the sharing circle is done for today. It's lunchtime. Today we are having meatloaf."

"Bah." The man named Barney spit on the ground in my general direction and stormed away. The group dispersed.

"What's his problem?" I asked.

"He must not like meatloaf," Lucius Nelson answered.

The interior of the asylum was much warmer and friendlier than the gothic exterior. The Nelsons had remodeled the building until it looked less like a state-run ward, and more like a comfortable and relaxing place to live. The walls were painted warm colors, and the staff was courteous and friendly. Julie had gone with Doctor Joan to see her father. She had understandably not wanted my company for the painful meeting. If we were needed, Doctor Lucius had his beeper.

I was getting the tour. "Those patients you met are some of the more well-adjusted people we have staying here. Most of them are on the verge of really dealing with their issues. Hopefully some of them will be able to return to the world soon. We also, I'm afraid, have others who are not doing so well. This common area is made up of people who are no longer really a danger to themselves or others. The other sections have greater security."

"Which one is Ray Shackleford in?"

"Maximum security. He is actually a ward of the state, and only released into our custody because of the nature of our facility. We are required to keep him locked up and guarded."

"Is Julie going to be safe?" I could not help but ask.

"I saw that girl beat an Indonesian blood fiend into submission when she was sixteen years old. I'm not worried. But just in case, Ray has been restrained. I would have administered drugs, but I'm guessing that you want him lucid." He adjusted his suspenders. "I wish that MHI would have called and warned us you were coming."

"It was kind of a surprise decision." I shrugged. Some of the patients were playing Ping-Pong. One of them had scars that made my own look miniscule.

"Well, I'm glad that Julie is finally speaking with her father. I just hope that she has prepared herself for this. It could be potentially traumatic." He chuckled softly. "That is why my wife went with her instead of me. She is the loving one."

He pointed at other patients as we continued walking. "Part of the problem we face here is the whole government-mandated secrecy about monsters. Many of our patients were put into regular mental health facilities after their encounters, before we were able to find out about them and bring them here. Unfortunately, when a severely traumatized individual is taken in for treatment, and they are already struggling with the reality of what they have experienced, regular doctors are not much help. Can you imagine going to a normal psychologist and explaining that your boss turned into a werewolf and tried to eat you?" He did not wait for me to answer. "They would think that you were delusional and they would pump you full of drugs. You know what you saw. They don't think that is possible, so after a while the sane and healthy patient begins to doubt their own memories, that leads to insecurity and that snowballs into all sorts of mental problems. If you can't trust your own memory, what can you trust?"

"I got security camera video," I replied.

"Ha. Like most of these poor people get to see anything like that. Damn quacks can ignore piles of evidence, because they are sure that monsters are only figments of our subconscious. I've read huge textbooks explaining how the werewolf and vampire legends, that date back to the dawn of recorded civilization and span every single culture on the planet, are neatly explained by mass hysteria, religious fervor, vain attempts at understanding natural pathological psychoses, or even hallucinations caused by ergot in bad rye bread. Ha.

Joan and I were staking vampires while we were still in medschool, so our methods are a little unorthodox in the scientific community. Learn this, Mr. Pitt, there are three kinds of people in the world: people who can't believe in anything, suckers who believe in everything, and a few of us who can face the truth."

We stopped in front of a large security door. A hulking orderly nodded at us, and Doctor Nelson scanned his badge to get us through. We entered a long corridor, lined with steel doors with small window slits. Screaming, crying and gibbering nonsense echoed through the hall. It gave me shivers.

"This ward is for people who have had serious monster trauma and are not coping with it well. They are suicidal, violent, or unable to distinguish reality from fantasy." We stopped before a door. I peered through the slit. A man was sitting cross-legged in the corner. He was wearing a straitjacket, and he was softly beating his head against the padded wall. He was humming "Mary Had a Little Lamb" over and over again. Drool was running down his chin, and forming a puddle on the floor.

"Believe it or not, Carlos here was a Monster Hunter. He worked for MHI up until about fifteen years ago. He was one of our team leads in New England. Brilliant man, great Hunter, good leader."

"What happened?" I asked softly. Carlos cocked his head to the side as if listening to something very far away. After a few seconds he went back to humming.

"Have you ever read any H.P. Lovecraft, Mr. Pitt?"

"Please, just call me Owen. I read a little bit when I was a kid, why?" I did not say that his stories had given me nightmares.

"Lovecraft was no Hunter, but he heard the stories, and he did his research. He had a pretty good idea of what was out there. If you remember, a common theme in his work was the protagonist's gradual descent into madness over a period of being exposed to the darkness of the other side. There are things out there which man is not meant to ever see or understand. Poor Carlos here is a perfect example."

"What did he see?"

"Nobody knows. His whole team went missing, and he was found wandering in the countryside, naked and confused. Just keep that in mind as you continue your career, Owen. There are some things that are best just left alone."

We exited the ward, leaving Carlos and the others to their songs.

Lunch was filling, and the meatloaf was surprisingly edible, considering it was mass-produced in an insane asylum's cafeteria. Doctor Joan called at one point to tell us that Ray was finally speaking a little bit to his daughter. I overheard part of the conversation. He was coherent, but the Shackleford family reunion was not exactly a joyous occasion.

After we ate, the tour continued, terminating on the back lawns of the Appleton Asylum overlooking the sluggish Alabama River. A high fence ensured that none of the patients decided to take a swim. It had rained briefly, and this time it was enough to break the humidity and lower the temperature to an almost comfortable degree.

As we walked along the lawns, many other patients came up to speak with me. Some wanted to touch my hands, or give me hugs. Many of them thanked me for what I did with heartfelt emotion. I was not used to such attentions.

"They are trying to give their thanks. Of course, I find out about many of my patients from your organization. Many of them would not be alive if it weren't for MHI or your competitors," the good doctor explained. "They see people like you as saviors, as heroes, as champions."

"I'm no hero," I replied. "I'm not even particularly brave."

"It doesn't matter. Everybody needs something to believe in. So for those who have been hurt by evil, they need to have champions of good to offset that in their minds. For the victims, they see people like you as Batman or the Lone Ranger. It keeps their worlds in balance. Mankind needs our heroes."

"I'm not sure exactly what I am, but I'm nobody's champion."

"Don't be so sure. I've been around Hunters longer than you have been alive. It is a job that requires bravery to the point of insanity. Everyone has their own reasons. Some of us are just in this for the money, others are in it for the thrill, others because they need a place to vent their violence in a manner that is not only legal but encouraged. Some do it out of a thirst for revenge. Some, like Julie I'm afraid, do it because it is the only world they know or really fit into. And then there are the few, the very, very few, who do it because they really are heroes, and they don't have it in them to be anything else."

I thought of Trip when he said that. My friend was in this for the right reasons. He just wanted to do good and help people. Guys like him were the heroes. I was just an accountant with a gun.

"So why are you doing this, Owen?"

"You going to psychoanalyze me now, Doc?"

He laughed. "I'm just a curious man by nature."

"Honestly, I don't know. I'm still not sure this is right for me."

"Why?"

I scratched my head. "Well . . ." He was a shrink after all. "Growing up, my father had this weird apocalyptic idea about the future, and he wanted me to be ready for it. So he pushed me into being something that I didn't really think I wanted to be. Then when I got older, I felt like I let him down, so I did something really stupid, lost my temper, and almost killed somebody who probably deserved it, but that's beside the point. So when I tried to distance myself from that kind of thing, and tried to be normal, I find myself involved in something even worse than before. Monsters are real, and it looks like maybe my father was right all along, and the future really is bleak, and I'm supposed to be a violent brute, and it's good that I'm good at killing things. But I still lost my temper and almost killed another Hunter, who once again, probably deserved it, but at least the sharks didn't eat him, so I'm still managing to screw stuff up. Now I'm having visions and hearing voices."

"Okay . . . I'm going to need to bump a few appointments from my calendar this afternoon to squeeze you in . . ."

"No time for that, since it looks like some super monster is trying to destroy time, and somehow I'm tagged by fate or the universe or something to fight him. But when this is over, if I live, I really need to figure out, do I really want to do this kind of thing? Or is it better to just forget this ever happened, and go back to my normal life?"

Doctor Nelson digested my ramblings for a few moments while we strolled along the walk. "Ehhh . . ." He shrugged. "Normal people are lame. Stick with monster hunting."

We stopped as another patient came up to shake my hand.

"Thank you for what you do," he stated vacantly. "The screaming killer frogs done ate my whole family. But y'all came and saved the rest of the town. Thank you. Thank you."

"You're welcome," I said. I did not have the heart to tell him that I did not even know what a screaming killer frog was. "Our pleasure. You just get some rest and get to feeling better. Okay?"

He thanked me a few more times before letting go of my hand. He had some more information to share. "There are some killer frogs flying around. Big ones. These ones are shaped like men. But bigger. And they have wings and horns, so I reckon they ain't really frogs. But you know how that goes. I done saw them in the trees by the river, watching the place. If you get a chance, Mr. Hunter sir, you should probably go kill them or something."

"Thank you for the information, Travis. We will look into it." The doctor patted the young man on the shoulder and sent him on his way. We watched as he ambled off. "Poor boy. He has spent more than half of his life here and he is still delusional. That's too bad. He has not been seeing monsters for quite some time. I'm afraid he may be relapsing. I'm going to have to adjust his meds."

The doctor sat down tiredly when we came to the next bench. We had a good view of the forest, the river, and the back of the asylum. "It has been a long day. I need a little break, and then I'm going to have to return to my duties. And my door is always open, when you take care of your current monster problem. I'm afraid Joan and I don't get many visitors. I do realize that many people find this place kind of depressing."

"Just a little," I lied. I stretched my legs and studied the intricate architecture of the building. It was a remarkably depressing structure considering how much good the Nelsons were trying to accomplish. The building was hideously dark. The walls were thick blocky stone, with carved designs on the edges, and the look was completed by the pair of massive stone gargoyles that sat on the building's roof. "Maybe it's the setting? This place looks more like a haunted castle than an institution dedicated to helping people."

"That it does. But you should have seen it before we bought it from the state. Joan and I wanted to put our earnings from MHI to good use. This facility is perfect for what we do. Though I will agree, it does bring to mind *The Hunchback of Notre Dame*."

"Yeah, it looks like what insane asylums look like in horror movies. Sorry, mental health facilities," I said. "Heck, you even have gargoyles. Isn't that kind of a bad idea with patients who are scared out of their minds by monsters?"

He adjusted his absurdly thick glasses and studied the roof.

"Hmm . . . I may not need to change Travis's medication after all."

"Huh?"

"Our building doesn't have gargoyles."

We watched as one of the giant statues swiveled its horned head as if it was analyzing the air. The other creature slowly and ponderously stretched one of its wings.

"Oh shit," we said in unison.

CHAPTER 15

"Julie! We have gargoyles on the roof. At least two of them," I shouted into my cell phone as I sprinted around the property for the van and our stash of weapons. Doctor Nelson had left to sound the alarm to lock down the facility.

"How big are they?" she asked.

"Freaking huge. Probably ten or twelve feet tall. I think they're the big monsters from my dream." I leapt over a bench, surprising a patient who had been napping. "Get inside! Run!" I shouted at the patients as I went past. Just as I said that a horn began to blow. The alarm. "What do we do? I haven't learned about gargoyles yet."

"Grab big guns. Explosives. Gargoyles are stone golems. Animated creatures. If you have to engage with small arms, go for the joints—those are fluid. That's how they move. I'll call Earl." She hung up.

I made my way to the parking lot in an all-out sprint, fumbling in my pocket for my keys. I looked up in time to see a third gargoyle land on the front roof of the Appleton Asylum. The roof splintered and cracked as the creature settled its weight. Its wingspan had to be forty feet across, and it nearly blotted out the sun. There was a whooshing noise as the monster gently flapped its wings. It settled deeply into a powerful crouch, talons digging into the roof tiles. Massive arms dangled at its sides, ending in pointed claws. Long horns extended from its head, and continued down its back, terminating in a stubby tail. The beast was gray, and had the texture of poured concrete. It swiveled its head and studied me with blank stone eyes.

I crashed into the van, keys in hand. I picked out the correct one, but before I had a chance to insert it, the gargoyle spread its wings and leapt downwards, covering the four stories in an instant. There was no natural explanation for how such a big thing could glide. It landed on the roof of the van, crushing the center, shattering every window, and compressing the shocks. I jumped aside as the van rocked wildly. The gargoyle swung an absurdly long arm at me, and I barely had time to fall backwards as the claws dug long furrows into the asphalt.

Patients were screaming, falling to the ground and covering their heads, running or hiding, and a few were just standing there mumbling to themselves. I ran for the entrance, and seconds later heard the concrete stairs break behind me as the creature jumped from the roof of the van. Not looking back, I jerked open the double door and entered the asylum. It closed automatically behind me.

Doctor Lucius was there, pushing his way through the panicked crowd. He was breathing hard and his

face was gray. The retired Hunter knew to fetch us
some hardware, though. The doctor shoved a rifle
into my hands, and then shakily lifted his own. They
were old M1 Garand rifles from WWII. He handed
me a few 8-round en-bloc clips that I dropped into
my pants pocket.

"Armor piercing .30-06. That should get his attention. It's already loaded," he gasped, and then added,
"I'm really far too old for this kind of thing." Patients
and staff were moving around us in confusion. "Get
out of the main hallways. Get to your rooms, or get
to the basement!" he ordered.

I stuck my finger in the trigger guard to remove
the safety. I pointed it at the door and waited. Nothing happened. The doctor continued to bellow orders
over the screaming and hysterical crying. Since I had
a moment, I took my electronic earplugs out of my
shirt pocket and stuffed them into my ears. If I lived
through this, at least I might keep some of my hearing. I quickly studied my surroundings. A large open
room, some Ping-Pong tables and couches, there was
no real cover to use in the common room. Nothing
that a giant stone creature couldn't just bull its way
through.

I interrupted the doctor's shouted orders. "You
better get out of here. Get your people and go. I'll
hold it as long as I can." I kept the old rifle pointed
at the door. I did not know what the creature was
waiting for.

"No way. This is my home. No monster pushes
me around."

"Then we stick and move. Fall back when I tell you
to." *Had the creature taken back to the sky? Could I*

risk returning to the van for some bigger weapons? I caught the doctor nodding out of the corner of my eye. Good, the last thing I wanted was for him to stay here and get turned into paste. Then I heard the noise as stone talons clicked rapidly toward the entrance.

There was a tremendous crash as the gargoyle threw itself against the doorframe. Mortar rained from the wall under the impact as the wooden doors broke inward. The heavy wood flew, crumbling into splinters. A horned head appeared through the cloud of dust. The creature tried to crawl through the entrance, but its shoulders were too large. The doctor and I opened fire.

I fired my eight shots in a few seconds, the empty clip ejected with a metallic *ping*. Dust rose from the gargoyle as the bullets struck. The impacts made small craters in the stone, but the creature was seemingly unfazed. It pulled its massive bulk back, and crashed into the frame again, dislodging several heavy stones and knocking them to the floor.

"Fall back, Doctor!" I shouted as I reached into my pocket and pulled out an en-bloc clip. I thumbed it into the open action, narrowly avoiding getting my thumb pinched as the bolt flew forward. The doctor obliged and I lost track of him as he retreated toward a side hallway. I took careful aim at the creature, trying to find a joint. The monster's giant stone face opened, showing a throatless mouth filled with huge blunted teeth. It was a roar, but no sound issued forth. The gargoyle drew back for another run, crashed into the stones, and then backed up to come again. A few more tries and it would be inside. I placed the front sight carefully on the gargoyle's massive neck and fired. The bullet struck high and ricocheted off. I adjusted my aim and shot it again. This time there was a flash of molten liquid as the .30 caliber round punched into softer material. The thing reeled back. It had felt that one. I shot it in the armpit when it tried to cover its throat, and was rewarded with another splash. The monster flinched as if in pain, and leapt straight into the air and out of my view. I could hear the powerful beating of wings as it soared upwards.

"Doctor Nelson! Are you okay?" Nobody answered. I heard whimpering and crazed babbling from some of the patients who were too confused or paralyzed with fear to run. "Anybody seen the doctor?" I shouted again.

"He's over here. I think he's hurt," someone called.

Doctor Lucius had made it a few yards down the hallway before he had fallen. He was clutching his chest and his face was contorted in a grimace. A female patient was cradling his head and an orderly was trying to help him.

"He-he-heart . . ." the doctor said. Sweat was rolling off of his forehead and he had lost his glasses.

"Aw hell." For all I knew the gargoyle could be coming back any second. "Get him out of here. Drag him if you have to. Find a doctor or a nurse or something." The orderly and the patient complied.

There was a loud crash from above, and dust fell from the ceiling. *Julie!* I sprinted back into the common room and up the stairs. I barely reached the second floor when the entryway exploded in a cloud of stone, wood and debris. Pieces of furniture were hurled clear to the second-floor balcony.

The gargoyle had not retreated at all. Rather, it had

taken to the air to build momentum. The thing rolled crazily through the foyer, turning furniture into kindling. I had no idea if all of the patients had evacuated or not, though I doubted it, and I had no time to find out. The unnatural creature stood on its crooked hind legs, and somehow I knew it was searching for me. Its wings unfurled outwards, filling the big room and shattering many of the barred windows.

The Garand barked as I fired down on the beast. The gargoyle folded one huge wing over its body like a shield, and the bullets shattered against it. The empty en-bloc clip automatically ejected, and I reached for a new one as I resumed running.

The center of the Appleton Asylum was one large room, with stairs that circled clear to the top. I knew from my conversation with Doctor Lucius that the maximum-security ward was on the top floor. I pushed myself as fast as I could go, fervently wishing that I had spent more time on the company Stairmaster. Unable to spread its mighty wings inside the confines of the asylum, the gargoyle clambered up the stairs after me. It crawled rather than walked, long arms extended. The stairs and support boards cracked as each stone claw came crashing down.

So far, the creature appeared to be ignoring the patients and concentrating on me. I did not know if the gargoyle was targeting me because it somehow knew I was a Hunter, or because I had the nerve to shoot it, or because it recognized me from my dream.

The gargoyle paused as something struck it from behind. It swiveled at the base of the stairs. A patient was standing defiant, holding Doctor Nelson's rifle. It was the man who had not liked Hunters. I believe his name was Barney. He held the rifle at his waist, pointing it in the general direction of the monster.

"I hid from you demons last time while you ate my kids. But not this time! Die you son of a bitch!" *Blam!* He jerked the trigger. The first shot fragmented off of the monster's wide chest. The next shot impacted the wall four inches from my head. The patient laughed in glee. "I'm free. I'm finally free!" He shot the creature in the foot.

"Barney! Run! Get out of there!" I shot the gargoyle in the back, but the armored wings covered all of the vulnerable joints.

The creature absently flicked one long arm, talons spread wide. Barney exploded in a red haze. His lifeless torso bounced off the wall, leaving a huge stain of blood and entrails on the bright paint. He slid to the ground, almost cut in two. Having dealt with the annoyance, the monster turned and regarded me with lifeless eyes. I ran.

Third floor. The gargoyle was directly under me and gaining fast. It was cumbersome, but it was impossibly large and covered a lot of stairs with each lunge. I leaned dangerously far over the edge and fired at it. The creature barely slowed as most of the bullets bounced harmlessly off of its stone body. I was going to need a bigger gun if I wanted to do anything other than just piss it off.

"Owen! Up here, quick!" Julie shouted from the fourth-floor balcony. She had her pistol in one hand and was guiding a strait-jacketed man with the other. Doctor Joan was behind them, aghast at the destruction being visited upon her facility. I clambered up the stairs toward them. I heard Julie order the doctor to take her father, and then gunfire broke out as she tried to slow the climbing gargoyle.

"Down that hall." Julie gestured with her head as I reached her position. She was inserting a new magazine into her 1911. She dropped the slide. "Elevator. Hurry." My pursuer was about to reach the fourth floor. More noise rang out from the opposite corridor as another gargoyle tore its way through the building's walls.

I ran a few yards down the hall, gunshots banging away behind me as Julie tried in vain to slow the monster. I took up position, and waited for her to leapfrog past. She fired until her pistol was empty, and then turned and sprinted past me. At least three thousand pounds of unnaturally animated, living-stone destruction and pure evil came bearing at me, blank eyes wide, stone mouth gaping. I slowed it down as I placed bullets into its knees and elbows, splashing molten rock onto the walls, which immediately began to smoke and smolder under the superheated fluid.

The monster stumbled, limbs temporarily buckling, and face planted into the balcony floor. The sudden blow brutally shook the fourth-floor balcony. The old wood structure tore away from its supports with a dust cloud and a screech of bending nails and breaking boards, spilling the gargoyle over the edge. It clawed at the ledge, but the thing was far too heavy, and its talons pulled through the building materials. It fell silently, lacking the room to spread its huge wings, and a second later I was rewarded with a massive echoing crash as the gargoyle smashed through the floor tiles and into the basement.

"So long, sucker!" I shouted as I ran for the elevator. There was still another gargoyle on this floor. I could hear it breaking its way through the narrow halls to reach us, and there had been a third one on the roof that could be anywhere by now.

The ceiling exploded. A porous rock claw grasped at my head. I dodged under it and dived into the waiting elevator. Doctor Joan stabbed at the buttons frantically as Julie fired on the monster's arm. We had found our third gargoyle.

"Going down?" I asked as I rolled over and patted my pockets searching for another en-bloc clip. I was out.

"You got a better idea?" Julie asked. It was taking the doors forever to close. The nearest gargoyle was battering its way in from the roof; tiles and wood splinters rained down as it applied its bulk and fury against the feeble barrier. We only had seconds.

Gradually the door closed. Pulleys whirred as the elevator started down.

"What happens if it comes after us while we're still stuck in here?" I asked absently as I pulled myself to my feet and drew my pistol from inside my waistband.

"Have you ever stepped on a ketchup packet?" Julie asked rhetorically. "Kind of like that, but a whole lot nastier." She kept her 1911 pointed at the roof of the elevator car. Not that that would do us an iota of good if the gargoyle made it into the shaft. Dropping several thousand pounds of animated stone onto the car would probably kill us all instantly. It was a tense moment. I thought about telling the doctor about her husband's apparent heart attack, but I refrained. It wasn't like she didn't have enough other problems to worry about right then. Soothing instrumentals played over the elevator's sound system.

"Kenny G?" I asked, also keeping my CZ .45 pointed upwards in a futile gesture.

"John Tesh," answered Doctor Joan. *Great.* Not exactly the music I would have chosen as the soundtrack for my death. I had been hoping for something a little more dramatic. And with drums. It had to have drums. The elevator continued down. Crashing noises echoed down the shaft.

The third floor gradually passed. "Why aren't we stopping?"

"The door is stuck on that floor. We were going to have it fixed," the doctor explained patiently. "Really, we were meaning to get around to it." *Wonderful.* Our getaway vehicle was the slowest elevator in the world. We all jerked upwards in surprise as small bits of debris began to rain on our metallic roof. I did not think we were going to make it.

Ray Shackleford sat on the floor, staring blankly off into space. He was a surprisingly big man. In his prime he must have been nearly as muscular as I was. His nose was hooked, and had been broken many times. His hair was prematurely gray, long and unkempt. His face reminded me of the senior Shackleford, and vaguely of Earl Harbinger. Julie must have taken after her mother. Thank goodness.

"Since we're about to die together, my name's Owen. Nice to meet you," I told him.

He regarded me sullenly for a moment before responding. "And I'm Napoleon Bonaparte. Nice to meet you . . . Chill out kid, just kidding. I'm not that kind of crazy. Julie, please tell me this moose isn't your boyfriend."

Julie kept her eye on the ceiling. "No, Dad."

"Good. Damn, he's ugly. Now will somebody get me out of these restraints? I can help here."

"Not a good idea," Doctor Joan stated.

"Joan, you old biddy. I'm not gonna wring your neck. You and Lucius have been right kind. But I can help, damn it." Something heavy rebounded off the top of the car, shaking all of us, causing the lights to flicker and the easy listening music to stop. *Finally.* I shot two quick rounds through the roof. The sound from the silver .45 slugs inside the narrow confines was brutal. I was glad that I had put my plugs in.

"Hold your fire! That was just the doors coming down. Cut him loose, Doc. Get ready to bail," Julie ordered. The doctor moved to unlock Ray's restraints. The digital display stopped at 2. A chime sounded. I knew that at any second, several thousand pounds of gargoyle were going to land on us. The doors gradually began to slide back, not fast enough. I wedged my body between them and forced them to open faster.

"Go!" We spilled into the hallway. A horrible screech of metal on stone came from the shaft as one of the gargoyles finally forced itself into the narrow passage. The elevator car was crushed as the massive creature smashed into it. The car and the monster disappeared down the shaft, hurtling toward impact in the asylum's basement. Dust billowed up as car and monster collided with the concrete floor.

"They're after my dad," Julie said as she glanced down the now-open shaft. The dangling cable jerked wildly. "Crap. Monster's already starting to climb. Wish I had a satchel charge."

"I think one of them is after me," I said. "They seem to be ignoring everybody else who isn't shooting at them. If we can get out of here they'll probably follow. The van got stepped on, but it should still be driveable."

"Let's go." Julie quickly led us to the main room balcony. The stairs curved down to the common area and our escape. There was a huge hole in the floor from where the first gargoyle had crashed from the fourth-floor balcony. "Clear," she said after a quick scan revealed no giant monsters. If the sound coming from behind us was any indication, the elevator gargoyle was almost free.

We ran down the stairs, jumping carelessly over wreckage. Doctor Joan gasped when she saw her dead patient, Barney, nearly cut in two. But she was a former Monster Hunter, and she did not shake easily. I stopped her with a firm hand on her shoulder.

"You need to tend to your husband. He's down that hall."

"What do you mean?" Her eyes widened and her head bobbed as she swallowed in surprise. "What happened to Lucius?"

"I think it's his heart."

"But, but . . ." she stammered. Her eyes blinked in confusion. She was wearing bright blue eye shadow. "Not Lucius."

"You'd best go." She nodded and ran in the direction I was pointing. She was fast for an older lady. I sure hoped that her husband was okay, and I also hoped that this worked and these damned evil things followed us out of here and away from all of the defenseless patients.

I ran around the edge of the massive hole in the floor. Wild sparks flew from severed electrical cables and water poured from busted pipes. I saw a slippered foot sticking out from under some wreckage. Not all of the patients had run after all. Damn. Julie was at the smashed doorway, with her father standing right behind her. He was breathing heavily, not used to the physical exertion.

"I don't see any of them. Let's head for the van."

"I'll drive," Ray offered.

"Oh, hell no," she responded.

I felt it before I heard it, a deep rumble as a stone body rubbed on walls. A claw, as big across as my torso, crawled up over the edge of the hole. The monster pulled against the floor, trying to heave itself up and at us. A second gargoyle appeared above us on the ragged edge of the destroyed balcony. The elevator shaft gargoyle smashed its horned head through the wall on the second floor. Three pairs of blank eyes fixated on our position.

"We got company," I said. All three creatures exploded forward at once.

We reached the van in record time. Ray tripped on the broken stairs, and almost fell. I caught him by his arm and pulled him along. Julie headed for the driver's seat. I had lost my keys, so I reached through the already shattered window and unlocked the passenger side door. I hurled Ray in headfirst, and I squished myself in beside him. Between our twin bulks, I was not even able to close the door.

Julie turned it over. The powerful V8 caught with a roar. She slammed it into reverse and stepped on the gas. The nearest creature leapt off of the stairs and lumbered at us on its squat legs. I pushed Ray out of the way as I fired my pistol out the front window. The van whipped around in a squeal of rubber.

My neck snapped back painfully as the rear end smashed into a parked Lexus with an MHI Alumni bumper sticker. Julie put the big vehicle into drive and floored it. The van roared past the nearest gargoyle. It swung a claw at us and with a screech of metal and sparks the creature tore the sliding door completely off the side of the van. Julie swerved around the next monster as its talons ripped a huge gash through the sheet metal on the driver's side.

We escaped in a spray of gravel. Ray flopped into the back seat. I pulled the door closed. In the rearview mirror the gargoyles spread their huge wings and with powerful legs launched themselves into the sky.

"They're airborne," I warned.

"I bet they can't do a hundred," Julie replied. The van tore down the Appleton Asylum lane at reckless and dangerous speeds. She continued to accelerate as we approached the gate.

It was a very heavy-looking gate.

"Julie. Gate. Gate!" I pointed. Wind rushed through the broken windshield.

"I know. Buckle up. This is going to hurt."

"Honey, I don't think that's a good idea."

"Shut up, Dad."

I quickly fumbled around for my seat belt, snagged it on my holster for a panic-filled moment, and then got it buckled. The gate approached far too quickly. I closed my eyes and braced for impact. *Crash*. Our front end crumpled. The van shuddered, but our momentum tore the heavy gate from its rusted hinges. Julie turned hard to the side and we slid onto the open road.

"That was awesome," was all that I could think to say.

"Yeah, that was cool," Julie said as she picked her glasses out of her lap and put them back on. "I don't see them. Are they following . . . ack!" She struggled against the wheel as something huge collided with our roof.

I turned in time to see a stone talon pierce the sheet metal over the rear of the van. More claws appeared as the creature wedged its way in and began to peel our van open like a ripe banana. I tried to get up, realized I was still strapped in, and then hit the button to set myself free. I fell into the back seat beside Ray and groped on the floor through the various gun cases. The van shook wildly as the gargoyle's weight shifted. I found the case I was looking for and unzipped it. I lifted the heavy weapon, inserted one of the huge magazines into the gun's side and worked the heavy bolt. It was so long that it was difficult to turn the gun from the horizontal to point toward the back of the van in the tiny space available.

"Cover your ears!" I shouted. Ray obliged. Julie was driving and I just hoped that she had put her plugs in, otherwise the blast from the Coke-can-sized muzzle brake on the end of the .50 BMG was probably going to blow her drums out.

The Ultramag 50 was equipped with a 10X scope for precision fire at extended ranges. It had not been designed to be used inside the confines of a moving vehicle. I stuck the butt stock under my armpit and pointed the muzzle in the direction of the gargoyle. At this range the barrel was halfway there.

BOOOOM!

If the windows had not already been shattered, I had no doubt that the concussion of the 750 grain bullet would have done the job. The enormous slug impacted the monster at nearly 2,800 feet per second. Stone fragments imbedded themselves into the seats, hot fluid sprayed the interior of the van, and I yelped in pain as some splashed on my unprotected arm. The back seats caught on fire. The gargoyle flinched as the massive chunk was torn violently from its arm. It did not, however, let go.

"Get off my van!" I had four more where that came from. I worked the heavy bolt, ejecting the smoking brass case and shoving another huge armor-piercing round into the chamber. I elevated the muzzle slightly and fired again. The gargoyle fell from the van as the second bullet pulverized its face. It pulled the rear doors clean off of their hinges. Monster and metal fell, clanking and clattering down the asphalt, pieces flying everywhere. We kept accelerating.

"Damn! That was loud!" Ray exclaimed.

"Julie, are you okay?" I shouted.

"Fine. Hang on." She pumped the brakes, and somehow managed to keep the van on the road as we careened around a corner. The van was not a sports car, but it did manage to stay on all four tires. She accelerated out of the turn. "If I can build up speed I can lose them, but the roads are too curvy. If I push it we'll end up in the trees."

"Is there a straightaway around here somewhere?"

"Son, you're in rural Alabama. Just how many straight roads do you think you're gonna find?" Ray asked rhetorically.

I swore, climbed over the center seat, and positioned

myself in the back cargo space. I scanned the skies through our new gargoyle-supplied sunroof.

"I don't see them," I shouted over the roar of the wind. I held on as Julie slalomed our boxlike van around another bend. "Ray, pass me that OD green case. The stubby one," I ordered. If we couldn't outrun them, we would outfight them. I spotted a huge black spot in the clear sky, heading right for us.

There had to be some sort of explanation for how the creatures were able to fly so fast. They were huge. They were heavy. But they flew like birds. When this one folded its wings and dived, it came out of the sun like a Stuka dive bomber. I yelled a warning as I planted the rifle against my shoulder. The .50 weighed thirty-two pounds, most of that towards the muzzle. It was designed to be fired from a prone position with a bipod. I was about to use it while kneeling in the back of a wildly moving vehicle. Not the best recipe for success.

Julie shouted something, and I was flung against the wall. I lost my balance and almost fell out the open rear of the van. Pavement rushed by, painted lines and a trail of fluid leaking from our damaged radiator, all a foot under my face. I scrambled to grab onto something. An air horn blew in protest as Julie swung us beside a loaded logging truck. We were in thick forest on a curving hillside road. This was not a good place to be stuck trying to pass somebody. If another truck came around the bend, we were going to be road pizza.

I pulled the heavy weapon up, searching for the diving gargoyle. I spotted it above us, losing altitude quickly. I snapped the rifle to my shoulder, struggling to find the creature in the narrow field of view of the scope. One of the world's most powerful sniper rifles had never been meant to be used like a skeet gun. I shot. Missed. Worked the bolt. Shot. Missed. The recoil pounded me each time, but I did not have time to notice. Last shot. The creature was larger now, looming above the logging truck and heading our way. It spread its wings to control its descent, aimed directly at us. It flashed black through the scope, I raised the muzzle and let the heavy weight bring it down. I fired as something darker than sky filled the lens.

The .50 BMG did a real number on the gargoyle's wing. A hole appeared in the stone membrane, molten stone splashed as one wing dipped and the creature crashed onto the top of the logs. The heavy chains kept the load in place. It lashed out with its talons, sinking them deep into the wood, and anchoring itself to keep from falling. Blank eyes locked onto our van, and it immediately began to slink toward us.

I dropped the now-empty rifle to the floor, reached around to take the green soft case from Ray. He was one step ahead of me. He had removed Abomination and held it out for me to grab. The gargoyle was moving, ready to leap onto our van. Julie was trying to get away, but the truck was swerving in panic. We were in range of the gargoyle. I reached forward and pulled the heavy trigger on the under-slung grenade launcher. My aim was a little off. The 40mm shell struck under the gargoyle, but it was close enough. The explosion was more of a muted thump, turning green logs into kindling, and snapping heavy safety chains. The gargoyle fell back, hanging onto the load now by one talon.

The trucker laid on the horn, confused by our gun-fire and whatever the hell was landing on his trailer. Julie had not been able to pass on the narrow, curvy road. The driver must have decided we were the threat, because the truck drifted into our path. Julie would have made a great NASCAR racer; she braked, dodged the trailer, then took us onto the shoulder and partway into the grass to avoid the oncoming tons of steel and wood. The van thumped and rattled over the ruts and potholes. An unfortunate armadillo blundered into our path and was sent on its way to armadillo nirvana.

Unfortunately our loss of speed put us right next to the gargoyle clinging to the trailer. It launched itself, smashing into our van with the force of a car wreck. I lost my balance and flopped about in the cargo area. Claws pierced through the side wall as the gargoyle latched on. I shouted for another grenade and Ray thumbed through the case. When he found one of the yellow painted shells he handed it over. I could not use the grenade against a target so close, and the shotgun shells would be virtually useless. The van swerved back onto the road behind the weaving trailer. Julie looked in the mirror, saw me loading the grenade and shouted something.

"What?" The grenade clicked into place. Farmland and forest flashed by. One stone arm came searching for us, tearing through the van like it was made of tinfoil, ripping through the still smoking center seat and sending foam bits into the rushing wind. Ray pushed himself as far away as he could without falling out the opening where our sliding door had been.

"Hang on!" She stepped on it, and we pulled behind

the accelerating semi. She timed it perfectly, waiting for the end of the trailer to sweep past, red-flagged log ends only feet from her open windshield. The van pulled alongside the rear of the trailer, and Julie swerved toward it. She was going to attempt to scrape the gargoyle off. I pushed myself against the far wall as claws swept past. The arm was still stained with red. It was the gargoyle who had gotten poor crazy Barney. The van shook as Julie played bumper cars with the eighteen-wheeler.

Ray looked at me with wild eyes. "I taught her how to drive," he said.

Julie leaned on the wheel, forcing the gargoyle into the rear set of trailer tires. The van screamed in protest. Truck tires popped in a moving cloud of smoke and rubber. The giant claws were sucked away from my face as the gargoyle was pulled and partially crushed under the trailer. Much of our van was peeled away with it. We swerved from the trailer, back onto the shoulder, but then back again as our monster-side tires blew and sent us out of control. Somehow the gargoyle was still hanging on. Chains snapped and logs spilled onto the narrow road.

For an instant, time seemed to stand still as we tilted, then it sped forward as we rolled onto our side in a fury of sparks and tearing metal. I fell as down changed to sideways. Somehow I managed to hold onto the back seat for dear life, a torn opening gaping below me, hard pavement flashing by.

Luckily we only rolled onto our side and no further. The van gradually slowed as our remaining energy was spent against the pavement. The seat cushion tore in my grasp and I slipped from safety.

Crying out, I fell through the gap and onto the road. Rolling, pain, tearing, everything a wild flashing of movement, cracking myself against the pavement and leaving inches of skin behind. I slid and flopped to a wet stop.

I lay there in the road.

It hurt to think.

Excruciating agony. I looked at my hands. Blood. All down my arms, a bloody road rash. Bits of gravel were imbedded deep into my skin. I tried to sit up. I realized that my clothing hung in ragged tatters, torn away by the gripping pavement.

"Son of a bitch! Worthless fucking monster bastard asshole!" Blood splattered as I shook my fist in the air. I forced myself to stand. Grimacing against the road rash, I stumbled down the road. The van was thirty feet away, resting on its side. The logging truck disappeared around the bend, torn tires flopping madly. The driver was no doubt glad to be away from the crazy people who had been shooting at his load. A few huge logs lay splintered, blocking the way. A tranquil and cozy farmhouse stood a hundred yards to our side, behind a small pen full of goats. I concentrated on putting one foot in front of the other. I had to reach the van. There was still one uninjured gargoyle somewhere and I was fresh out of big guns.

The van's wheels had stopped turning. The engine had died. There was an eerie silence punctuated only by ticking noises coming from the hot engine. A green pool of antifreeze was spreading. As I approached, my pain-fogged mind realized why the van had not kept rolling when we had flipped on our side.

The gargoyle was wedged underneath. Its massive

bulk was partially crushed into gravel, silver liquid poured from its interior, steaming and smoking on the pavement. One of its arms was missing. The other ended in a jagged stump. Its lower half was trapped under the driver's side. It continued to stab at the roof with its stump, searching for Julie and Ray.

My hand flew to my holster, only to discover that at some point of my road-rash roll my CZ had been knocked loose and lost. I spotted the .50 lying in the road, scope shattered, scuffed and battered. It looked operable, but it was empty. I picked it up to use as a club. The gargoyle shoved its pointed stump through another spot in the roof directly over where Julie would have been buckled in. I heard a scream of pain come from the van. The stump came out.

The jagged end was splattered with blood.

The pain stopped. My anger focused like a laser beam.

"Hey!" I shouted, limping toward the wounded beast. Its gray eyes turned in my direction. "Yeah. I'm talking to you." It tried to move against me, but it had been hopelessly damaged by the truck. It did not matter. I was coming for it. I was not going to let it get the others.

I raised the heavy rifle over my head and charged. It swung its stump. I stepped out of the way as it crashed into the asphalt. I smashed the rifle into the stump, again and again. The butt stock broke off, so I shifted it in my hands and used the barrel like a bat. I pounded the stone arm until it quit trying to move, and then I stepped over the dusted remains and with a cry of rage swung at the monster's head. I struck it again and again. The barrel bent, and my hands bled as I swung at the unyielding rock, steel bar against stone face, over and over. Muscles straining, I continued to shout as smoking fluid spilled from the creature's broken face and splattered me with burning bits. "Die! Die! Die!" I raised the barrel and drove it forward like a pack bar. The creature twisted its powerful neck and I lost my weapon. I spotted something else that had spilled from the back of the van. I left the creature for a moment, retrieved the tire iron, and then went back to work. I hammered the creature as it twitched and thrashed.

Finally it quit moving. The molten stone that served as the creature's blood formed a smoking puddle, and then gradually solidified as it cooled. Cracks formed in the stone body. Perhaps it had never truly been alive, but it was certainly dead now.

"Can anybody hear me?" Gasping, shaking, I went to the front of the van and knelt before the shattered windshield. Julie was trapped on her side, and there was blood on her shirt. Far too much. "Are you okay?"

"I whacked my head. Then got stabbed." She gestured weakly at the hole the monster had just punched through the roof.

"How bad?" I asked frantically as I tried to gently pull her through the window.

"Hurts . . ." She had her hand pressed against the top of her shoulder. "I can still move."

I pulled her out and helped her sit. The entry wound appeared to be through the flesh above her collar bone, and into the muscles of her back. It was bleeding, but not very fast. I did not know squat about anatomy, and I had no idea how deep it had penetrated.

"Dad? Where's my dad?"

"I don't know. Just keep pressure on it." I kept scanning the sky. There was one gargoyle left somewhere.

"Find him, please."

"What about you?" I asked.

"I'm fine. I don't think it's that bad. Find him, Owen. Keep him safe . . ." Her eyes rolled back, and her head dipped forward. I caught her.

"Shit. Julie. Julie! Come on. It's going to be okay. Julie!" I shook her. She did not respond. Blood rolled out of her hair and down her cheek from her head wound. I rested her on the ground and went through the window for the first aid kit that was stored under the passenger seat. I tore a wider opening in her shirt. I pulled out a package of Quick Clot, ripped it open, and poured it into the hole in her shoulder. I stuffed a bandage over the top of that. It wasn't much, but it was the best that I could do at the time.

I felt the rush of air before I heard the beating of stone wings. The final monster did a pass overhead, slowly circling. Wings spread, it landed twenty yards away and perched on top of one of the many spilled logs. The huge wings folded and the creature put its long forearms down until its clawed fists rested on the ground. It began to crawl toward us. It was the size of a compact car. All I had was a tire iron.

I flung the tool at the creature. It ricocheted harmlessly away. I abandoned Julie; no matter how much I did not want to, I did not have much choice. I dived into the van, searching for a weapon—any weapon—but preferably a really big gun. Stone feet crunched as it made its way closer.

"Hello there, big fella. I think I'm the one you're after." *Ray.* Julie's dad appeared out of nowhere. Looking a little worse from the accident, he limped calmly toward the monster. The gargoyle stopped, seemingly confused by having a human not run from it or shoot at it. "No reason to kill these others. You want me, you can have me."

The gargoyle turned away from the van, and started for Ray. He made no effort to evade the monster. He spread his arms and walked straight toward it.

"Come on. That's a good monster. Yeah, that's a good boy. Just kill me and get it over with."

But the gargoyle had not been dispatched to kill him. The Cursed One was looking for information. The monster reached out and grabbed him around the waist with one gnarled claw, easily lifting him into the air. The creature spread its massive wings, preparing to leap into the sky.

My hand landed on Abomination. Somehow the brutal, stubby shotgun/grenade launcher had not been tossed out of the vehicle. I hugged it against my bloody chest and crawled for the exit. There was no way I was going to be able to make it in time to save Ray, but I was going to try.

The monster crouched, building energy in its powerful legs, wings spread a full forty feet across the road. Ray was tucked easily under one arm. The man was not even struggling. Julie was still out. I pulled myself along, trying to think of something, anything, which I could do to stop the monster.

The gargoyle shook as the heavy bullet struck its head. The weight of the impact was enough to jar it. The boom followed a split second later as the sound caught up. I pulled myself out of the van, shotgun lifted ahead of me. I had no idea where the bullet had come from. The second mystery shot collided with the creature's upper arm, splattering liquid stone from a pierced joint. It spasmodically dropped Ray Shackleford to the pavement. Ray lay there, unmoving.

I flipped the selector to full-auto and dumped twenty shells of alternating slugs and buck into the monster as I charged it. The shot was mostly useless, except for the few pellets that struck joints. The slugs, however, carried quite a bit of energy, and disoriented the creature further. I snagged Ray by his arm, and dragged his limp form away from the monster. If I could get him far enough away, I could use my grenade. The mystery shooter fired a third shot, striking the monster in the neck. The gargoyle raised its hands to the injury as rock splashed forth.

I dragged Ray back by Julie and dropped him. I turned toward the monster and aimed Abomination, fingers seeking for the 40mm launcher's heavy trigger. I did not know for sure if we were safely out of the minimum safe range for the blast radius, but I did not have much choice. The gargoyle reared up, wings spreading in a roar. I pulled the trigger.

There was barely enough distance for the grenade to achieve the rotations necessary to disarm its safety mechanisms. The heavy shell impacted just under the gargoyle's chin. The thump of the explosion shook me and I was pelted with stone and bits of superhot liquid. The gargoyle fell backward in a cloud of dust and fragments. Its chest was ragged, blasted and scorched.

It shrugged off the impact and wobbled to its feet.

"Aw, crap."

It took two hesitant steps, weeping cracks spider-webbing across it, before it shattered like a dropped glass, stone clattering onto the pavement in a spreading pool of silver.

I knelt beside Julie. She was breathing, and the clotting agent and the bandage seemed to be working. Her pulse was decent, not great, but decent. Her head wound looked pretty ugly. Ray was mumbling something and waving at the air.

"Hey hey we're the Monkees, and we like to monkey around!" he sang. I resisted the urge to put my size 15 boot through his head.

"Are you folks okay?" a voice called. The man was older, and had a thick southern accent. He came walking tentatively from the nearby farm, an embroidered NRA hat on his head, and an enormous bolt action rifle in his hands. "What in the hell was that thing?"

"Gargoyle. Animated monster. Bad mother."

"Damn." He saw Julie, bloodstained and unconscious. "My wife called the cops and told them to send the paramedics. They're coming out of Camden, but they should be here right quick. Brother, you look like you need them your own self. You look like hell."

I looked down at my road-rashed arms. Blood was welling from several spots around embedded gravel and there were a few spots that appeared to be totally devoid of skin. It really stung. Thus far I was showing a bad tendency to get my ass kicked in this job.

"That was some good shooting back there," I told him. "You saved us. Thanks."

"Yup. I was in my living room when you crashed. I saw it right out my window. Saw the big monster

thingy hanging on the side so I grabbed my big gun."
He shook the heavy rifle. "Four-fifty-eight Winchester
Magnum. And to think my wife told me, Carlyle, you
don't need no damn expensive elephant gun. What're
you going to do with an elephant gun? Harumph.
Women . . . Showed her."

Amazingly enough my wallet was still in my pants.
I thumbed through it until I found the business card
with the little green smiley face with horns. I had not
had the chance to get my own made up, so Harbinger's
would have to do.

"Tell you what, Mr. Carlyle. If you ever get tired
of farming and want to kill monsters for a living, give
this guy a call. Tell him Owen Zastava Pitt sent you.
I'm gonna pass out now." I wearily slumped down next
to Julie, ignored Ray's babbling, and settled in to wait
for the ambulance. I was unconscious in seconds.

CHAPTER 16

The Old Man was waiting for me on the steps of the bombed-out church. He was whittling away at a small block of wood with a tiny pocketknife. The world of the destroyed town was once again whole and complete. Battle damaged, but at least there were no gaps of *nothingness*. Snow crunched under my bare feet, yet it was not cold. In my dream, I was not in pain. I received a scowl and a firm finger-shaking as I approached.

"Boy. You not very good at this job. Werewolf scar you. Wight paralyze you. Fall off boat. Vampire beat you. Policeman beat you. Gargoyle chase you, and now you fall off car. Moving car at that. Maybe I think we should have picked some other person." He continued shaking his finger. He reminded me of my Czech immigrant grandfather—easily exasperated, and often having a hard time expressing it. "You can no seem to help. You are like, how you say . . . punching bag. You say, hey monster, here I am. Hit me in head."

"Look, I'm pretty tired of getting my ass kicked too.

You want to pick somebody else to bug, feel free." I sat down beside him on the steps. I could not tell what he was carving. One thing was for sure, he did not appear to be very good at it.

"I need to get back. Julie needs me. I need to wake up."

"Sorry, Boy, not can do. You are hurt. Need time for body to rest. You must take time for other things now."

"I've got an idea then. How about some straight-forward answers for a change?"

"Bah." He spit in the snow. "You want answers. I give you answers. I try to help you, Boy. Some thing I not can say, I can only show. Is hard to do, you know."

"Why did the Cursed One go after Julie's dad?"

He shrugged. "He is just like you. Always wants the straight answers. Just like you, even has the same questions."

"Where's the Place of Power and when's he going to use it?"

"See. What did say? Same questions. How am I supposed to know this thing?"

I picked up a rock and hurled it against some rubble. I was rewarded with a crash.

"Boy. You are mad, yes? Very angry?" I nodded. The Old Man paused in his carving for a moment and patted me gently on the arm. "You are mad because girl is hurt. Old doctor is hurt. And some of crazy people get smooshed by gargoyle, yes?"

I did not respond. After a moment he got tired of waiting for my answer.

"Hunters must learn, not can save everyone. Sometimes not can save own self even. Is just how it is . . ."

He trailed off. "Bah! Enough talk. Time is short. You wake up soon. I try to show you more memories."

"Not anything recent, I hope," I said fearfully. My brief encounter with Lord Machado's mind had left me very uneasy about that idea. I did not want to risk that again, because I had a sneaky feeling that I might not wake up from it.

"No. Is old memory again. Much safer. He probably not know about this. I not strong enough to try new memory. Too dangerous. Put worms in your head. Eat your brain out."

I did not dare ask for an explanation of whatever the hell that was supposed to mean.

"Listen, Boy, hard to explain. This Cursed One, I not can show you things that are in his mind now, for he will know. But these other things, they are long ago in his past. Buried like body in ground. He not pay attention to them now anymore. So we sneak in for look, he not know. You shut up and learn."

"How can you do that?"

He scowled as he searched for the words. "I stuck here, because of stupid artifact. Because of Cursed One, I not can move on. Trapped for long time. Cursed One forgot about me. But he—how you say?— underestimates things I do to try stop him. I sneak chance to talk to you, to help. He not expect that. Now shush. See what you have done with questions? Waste much time."

He set aside his carving, folded his knife, carefully put it away, and placed his hands on my face.

"Let's do this thing," I said, with more courage than I actually felt.

The blasted town faded away.

❖   ❖   ❖

Lord Machado's memories. I settled into them like an actor taking on a role. I was immersed into the senses of a man who had long since ceased to be a man. The memories were hazy, fragmented, but the important things had engraved themselves deep into the Cursed One's mind.

The priestess Koriniha led me deep beneath the pyramid. I followed, hoping to find answers to my questions. My reign over the city was a success thus far. Treasure filled my coffers, and my small army was training a much larger army of local conscripts. She had been good to her word: the city did not just abide me as a conqueror with an iron fist. They were treating me like their true king, and perhaps, dare I say . . . their god. I could grow used to being worshipped.

She had told me of her dark and secret knowledge. The priestess' offer had been intriguing. Eternal life and strength. An immortal army under my command. Powers so great, that not only could I control this new land, but I could return to my old, and take upon me the very birthright that was taken from me. If the words of Koriniha were even partially true, I could return home and take the very crown, and the crown of any kingdom I desired.

I desired all of them.

King Manuel the Great? I would show him who the great one really was. Philip and his blasted Spaniards would be next. After that, why not all of Europe, forcefully united under my banner. If a fraction of the dark secrets the priestess had whispered to me were true, then all of that would be a simple task to accomplish. And from the signs that she had shown me, I believed her to be telling the truth.

I followed her farther into the darkness. The priestess' hips swayed beneath her thin robes. She was a wanton creature, beautiful and cunning, wise in many arts unknown in my homeland. I had already taken her as my concubine, as was part of our initial agreement. It had been a very beneficial arrangement indeed. It had legitimized my rule over this people, and I enjoyed the benefits befitting a man of my station.

The torch in my hand flickered and spat as damp winds traveled down the tunnel. I had a brace of pistols in my belt, fresh matches stored in a wax-tight pouch, and the very ax that was the source of my family name slung over my back, yet somehow I still felt uneasy. There was darkness under this pyramid, not just darkness of the eyes, but a darkness of the soul.

Friar de Sousa had attempted to warn me away from the priestess and her strange cult. I had discovered him trying to send a messenger back to our ships on the coast. The note had been intercepted. The Jesuit had been worried that I was descending into madness and following a pagan religion, and especially damning, he wrote of the riches of the city and how I had thus far kept our expedition a secret from both the crown and the church. He had been a kindly man, wise and merciful, and his knowledge of languages had been a valuable tool of conquest. It had saddened me momentarily when I hsd ordered him burned at the stake. Of course to keep that fact from the men, I had blamed it on the locals and had had five hundred of their priests executed, supposedly in retribution. Appearances had to be kept up, after all.

Some of the men had been suspicious, but as long as I kept them supplied with riches, I was not worried about their loyalty. Sacks of gold would satisfy even the most pious amongst them. The crown's military governor had no knowledge of our expedition's location, so my troops were effectively sealed from the outside world. My secrets were my own to keep.

We walked for what seemed like hours, always down, always descending. The walls changed from stone and mortar into natural rock, and then finally into something else. Something that I had never seen before. Slick, soft and oily, almost pulsing with its own strange energy. Out of the corner of my eye it would sometimes seem as if the very walls were moving.

Finally we entered a huge space, deep in the bowels of the earth. I could not tell how big it was, but my meager torch could illuminate but a small portion. The floor was smooth and slick, and I had to be careful to maintain my footing. Water drizzled down from above, splashing upon my armor. The air was heavy, and did not taste like air that should be breathed into the lungs of men. It was salty, and the cavern smelled faintly of decaying fish.

Koriniha led me toward the center of the vast darkness. We walked for miles. I realized that if she had so desired, she could have run out of the circle of torchlight, and I might not have ever found my way out. A lesser man might have felt fear at that, but not I. The temperature dropped until I could see my breath. The floor became softer, and my boots left impressions in the oily surface. The priestess halted in front of the first landmark we had happened upon in the otherwise featureless room.

It was an obelisk of black metal, tall enough to disappear into the darkness above, yet so thin that I could not comprehend how it could stay upright. The object had been inscribed with strange writing. Not like the now-familiar picture writing of the civilization above, but something rather far more complex. The runes appeared to move under the flickering light of the torch. A small, unadorned stone box sat in a tiny alcove of the obelisk. It hurt my eyes to look directly at it, as if I had stared into the sun.

"What is this thing? Is this the key? Tell me now," I ordered.

She smiled at me wickedly, dark eyes flashing red in the torchlight. "Yes, Lord Machado. This is the key to unlock infinite power. The very power of the Old Ones themselves, and they have been waiting for one such as you."

"Such as I?"

She placed her delicate hands on my bearded cheeks and her eyes bore into mine. They seemed to flicker unnaturally in the light of the sputtering flames.

"Yes, my lord. The Old Ones left this device. It is ancient. Older than this world. It is an item of such power that it was never intended to be used by mortal man. It is a device intended for the service of what you know as angels or demons, and even then best left alone even by them. Yet every five hundred years, a man will be born, a mortal with the power to use this device and bend it to his will. You are this man, you are the one who has been prophesied by the Old Ones." As she spoke, I felt the air rush past as if something incomprehensibly huge had just taken a breath.

"Tell me this prophecy, woman."

She took her hands from my face and gestured at the obelisk. The runes changed, and were now written in the Latin letters I had learned as a youth.

He will come
    Son of a great warrior
    Taught in the skills of the world
Yet drawn to the sword
His very name taken from
The weapon of his fathers
Given a quest by the crown
To defeat an impossible foe
Possessor of visions
Ally of dark forces
Friend of monsters
Leader of men
    Only he will have the will
    And the power
    Through his love of another
To break time and the world

The words resonated with me. I was the one meant for the power and the greatness. My family name came from the very ax now strapped to me, the very weapon used by my forefathers. My father had been a great general. As one of the younger sons, I had been sent away for an education, expected to manage the family fortune, yet I had failed, and become a soldier and eventually a commander. My task was to pacify this land for the crown and deliver its treasure unto my king and its inhabitants' souls to my mother church. I had visions of leading my host to glory. As for darkness, I had no doubt that my concubine and her cabal of heart-removing priests and their rivers of sacrificial blood would serve that purpose.

"So what does this mean? What must I do now?" I asked. The priestess did not answer. She reached into the alcove and removed the small rectangular box. She shouted something in her language, and the rush of air changed direction as if something massive had just exhaled. I held out my hand, and she placed the box gently in my palm. It was small, but unnaturally heavy. I shuddered as cold shivers pulsed down my arm. "What is this?"

"It is the key, my lord. Alone, it is an object of mighty strength, capable of great magic, but when you are prepared, I can take you to the proper place, a Place of Power. There you can utilize it to inflict your will upon the entire world. No one shall stand in your way. The world will be yours."

"Is that all?"

"There is but one last thing to fulfill the prophecy, my lord. You must do it through love of another. You are a lover of power, but not of people. You must do so to utilize the artifact. Love is a notion of the weak, yet through it great power can be unlocked. It is a tool to be used as needed."

"I have a wife and children in Lisboa, will that not suffice?" I did not have time for weak notions such as love or mercy. Not when there was plunder to be taken, and lands to be crushed. A wife of good blood was a political necessity and a way to produce heirs, nothing more.

"Perhaps not, my lord. But I will provide a way." The priestess untied the front of her robes and let them fall to the slick floor. "I can be your love. Together we can rule the world."

The damp wind picked up again, almost as if the cavern itself was filling unseen lungs, far greater in intensity this time. My torch was blown out, plunging us into darkness.

❖   ❖   ❖

I was sitting on the steps of the church, once again in my own body, and seeing the world through my own eyes. Reliving the Cursed One's memories left me feeling unclean. The Old Man had gone back to his carving, gently flicking the blade of the knife over the small block of wood. Chips were falling onto his homespun pants. Even if the clear winter sky around me was a figment of my imagination, it was a far nicer place than the mysterious unnatural cavern.

"Why are you showing me these things?"

"So you understand. Is important."

"What is important? That Machado was an evil bastard when he was human, so bad that even the Aztecs or the Incas or whoever they were prophesied him coming, and that some mysterious Old Ones wanted to give him a magical whatchamacallit to blow up the world?"

"You not have name for that people. They are gone. World not know about them today. Is probably for best. But there is more, Boy. You must pay attention more."

"Pay attention to what more? He was about to score with the evil priestess chick. That was pretty hard to miss," I replied.

"Young people. Mind always in gutter. No, more important things to learn."

"How about you just tell me how to kill him?"

He shrugged. "I not know."

"Who are the Old Ones? The Elf Queen mentioned them also."

"Very bad. Very much bad. I not know. But they here long before us. Not supposed to be. But they are—how you say?—trespassers. They want nothing more than to kill world. They kill anything they not can have."

He used his coat sleeve to brush aside the snow on one of the steps, creating a clear spot. He placed his carving on the smooth surface and spun it. The little top made it only a few turns before flopping over. It looked like crap and was horribly unbalanced. He was not very good at whittling.

"Your top is broken."

"Is not 'top.' Is dreidel. Fun little game. Should be made out of clay. But I try wood." He picked it up and went back to carving. "No laugh, Boy, is harder than it looks. Time for you to go. You wake up now. Be careful of big red thing. No want to crash."

"What big red thing?"

"You see."

I woke up disoriented and confused. I was lying on some sort of gurney, and I cracked my face painfully into a white metal cabinet when I sat up. Julie was a few feet away, also lying on a stretcher. Her shirt had been cut away, and a much better bandage had been placed on her shoulder. She was still out. A siren was blaring. We were in the back of an ambulance.

"What the hell?" I said, as the ambulance turned far too sharply and I bounced off of the wall. Mad laughter came from the front.

"Hang on, kid. It's been a while since I've driven last. You know, with being locked up and all that." Ray Shackleford honked the horn and screamed out the window. "Watch out, moron!"

I squeezed my way through the narrow space and into the passenger seat. I had to push aside a big black duffel bag. I was glad to see that it was the bag that held my armor and personal gear, including spare magazines and grenades for Abomination. My shotgun was sitting on the dash, sliding crazily back and forth as Ray jerked the wheel. The speedometer showed one hundred and five miles an hour. I had not known that an ambulance could go that fast.

"What happened?" I shouted over the siren. Ray's gray hair was flapping madly in the wind from the open window. He was grinning maniacally, and having far too much fun for an escaped lunatic.

"You passed out. Can't say I blame you. You look like shit. Julie had a cell phone in her pocket. It started ringing so naturally I answered it. It was Earl." The crazy man laughed. "Old son of a bitch was a bit surprised to find himself talking to me. Didn't expect that one bit. Well, anyway . . ." He swerved around a truck and into oncoming traffic, dodged a station wagon, and jerked back into the correct lane. I cringed. "As I was saying, Earl called, said that the Feds were heading this way fast. They put out an APB on me and both of you. He said not to go to the hospital because the Monster Control Bureau guys were already en route, and not to go back to the compound because the place was already crawling with Feds. So I'm supposed to take us someplace safe to hide out."

"You didn't kill any of the paramedics did you?" I gestured at Abomination.

"Oh no. I've never killed a human being . . . on purpose at least, so I ain't gonna start now. I bluffed our way out. Told them I was an escaped mental patient."

"Gee whiz? I'm surprised they believed you." I had not realized, but he was wearing sweats, and a bathrobe.

With the matted hair, and the unkempt beard, he looked the part. Plus when I had passed out he had been singing the theme song from the Monkees.

"I know. Imagine that." He scratched himself as we tore down the road.

"Julie needs medical attention."

"Earl has arranged for some. Don't worry. We're going home."

"But the compound is covered in Feds."

"Nope. You'll see. Earl said 'Go to your house, Ray. You can remember how to get there. Just go home.'"

Ray turned to look at me as he explained. Crazy people must use the Force to drive or something. "We're going home. It'll be just like old times. All the kids, Ray the fifth, Julie, even little Nate, they can play in the tree house. And Susan will be there too. It'll be great. We can have a barbecue."

"Ray. Watch the road." I noticed flashing red lights ahead. He was no longer living in the same world; instead he was taking a little trip down memory lane.

"Maybe there'll be an Alabama game on today. Roll Tide. That would be fun. Maybe even the Alabama versus Auburn game. Best game of the year. Yep, I lost a lot of money on that one last season, I tell you what." I realized that the flashing lights originated at a train crossing. The crossing arms were coming down.

"Train. Ray, brake. Hit the brakes!"

He turned and studied it absently. "Yep, train. How about that? You like hotdogs or hamburgers? Susan might have even marinated some steaks if we're lucky." I watched in horror as the train came into view. The engine was enormous and red. We were not going to make it in time.

I shoved my way over into the driver's seat, squishing Ray painfully into the door. I stomped my boot down on the brake and I fought for control of the wheel. The tires locked up with a squeal, leaving behind plenty of rubber and smoke. Ray tried to fight me. I elbowed him violently in the forehead, snapping his head back against the seat.

Keeping the van under control while braking and fighting for the wheel against an insane man while barreling toward a train is not a pleasant experience. Luckily the ambulance had some decent brake pads installed. We broke through the wooden safety rail with a slow crack, and skidded to a halt, our front bumper inches from the sparking train wheels.

"Car-jacking! Car-jacking!" he shouted in my ear as he tried to stick his thumb in my eye.

Ray kept fighting, unaware that I had just saved his life. He tried to choke me with the seat belt, so I elbowed him in the face until he stopped moving. It took three good blows to his noggin to put him out. I'll admit, I enjoyed that part. I put the van in park and crawled back out the passenger door. I went around, deafened by the roar of the train only scant feet away, opened the door, after a moment found the switch to kill the highly annoying siren, pulled Ray's unconscious body out of the driver's side and set him on the gurney in the back. There were straps to hold down thrashing patients, and I applied them snugly.

Julie stirred. Her eyes fluttered open.

"Owen. What's going on?" she mumbled sleepily. "Wait a second," as she realized that her shirt was cut open and she was only wearing a bra beneath. "Pervert."

"Hey, blame the paramedics. Listen, Julie. I don't have time to explain. We need to get you someplace that your dad called home. Earl is going to have help for you there."

She was obviously high on painkillers or something that the paramedics had given her. She smiled absently. "Hey, what happened to Dad?"

"Uh, he got sedated. Look, can you give me directions? Earl said for us to go home, not the compound, but someplace your dad would think of as home."

"Sure . . . I can find home. Where are we?"

"I don't know. Look, I'm going to help you to the front seat. You just stay awake and tell me where to go, okay?"

"Okay. Can do. And look, next time you want to see me naked, just ask. Don't cut up my clothes. That's creepy . . . and I liked this shirt." Her eyes closed and she went back to sleep.

I carried her to the passenger side, as gently as was possible, careful not to disturb her wound or bandages. I buckled her into place as the last of the train cars passed. Julie stirred and mumbled something.

"What?"

"I know this place. We're near Greenville. Just keep going." Her speech was slurred, but she did not appear to be losing any more blood. I decided that if she started to look any worse I was going to take her to the nearest town and doctor. Keeping from getting arrested was not worth her life. Hopefully I would not have to make that choice.

I put the ambulance into drive and continued down the road.

CHAPTER 17

The home that Ray Shackleford had been referring to was an enormous old plantation house nestled in a beautiful patch of woods and streams. It was far off of the main drive and isolated from the rest of the world. The home had been opulent at one time, but had fallen into disrepair. Thick Doric columns, cracked with age, lined the front porch. Moss and vines were growing up some of the walls, but it appeared as if some recent efforts had been made to paint and restore the old place. There was a black sedan parked near the dry fountain in front of the home.

I parked the van near the entrance, honked the horn, and jumped out to help Julie. She had remained semilucid for the remainder of the short trip, but she was pale and did not look very good. Despite her feeble protest that she could do it herself, I picked her up in my arms and carried her onto the porch. She was not light by any means, but rather heavier than she appeared because of lean muscle. She winced in pain as the pressure changed against her wound. The main door was open, leaving only a screen.

"Hey! Anybody there? We need help," I yelled.

"Z. Thank goodness." It was good to hear Trip's voice. The screen door opened and he stepped out. A smaller figure stood behind him, totally cloaked in what appeared to be a black burkha. "Come on. We have a spot ready. Earl said Gretchen here's as good as any doctor." The robed figure nodded. Only a small patch of her face was showing through her hood, and even then her eyes were covered with large mirrored sunglasses. She gestured for me to follow.

I cradled Julie's limp form against my chest as we hurried down the entry hall. The interior of the home was undergoing serious renovation. Flooring had been pulled up and was in various states of repair. Some walls had been painted, while others were a work in progress. Sawdust and miscellaneous tools littered the floor.

Gretchen led us across the spacious parlor, through a huge dining room complete with chandelier and twenty-foot table, down a small hallway, and into what was probably meant to be a guest bedroom, though right now it looked a bit like an extemporaneous field hospital. A small table had been moved into the room, covered by a white cloth, and littered with strange surgical-looking implements and jars filled with unknown fluids. Gretchen nodded toward the bed and I placed Julie down as gently as possible.

Julie's eyes peeked out from under heavy lids.

"I can't see," she said.

I began to panic. The blow to her head . . . had

it blinded her? Was Julie going to lose her sight? She was a lover of art, and an amazing marksman. Going blind would kill her. I grabbed her hand and squeezed.

"Don't worry. It's going to be okay. I'm here for you. I'm sure your sight will come back."

"Owen." She closed her eyes and sighed. "You big dummy. Of course my sight will come back. My glasses are on the floor of the ambulance. Be a dear and grab them for me . . . Is that Gretchen?" The robed woman came over and patted Julie's forehead. I had not noticed that the strange woman was wearing surgical gloves. "Hey, Gretchen honey. I'm glad you're here. I'm going back to sleep now . . ." she mumbled as she drifted off.

Gretchen took her gloved hand from Julie's head and immediately started to remove the blood-stained bandage. The petite robed woman examined the injury. The wound path actually started behind the point of Julie's shoulder and traveled down into the muscles over her shoulder blade. It was a nasty puncture. I had seen a few knife wounds like that while I had been bouncing, but never one that big or at such an angle. The mysterious woman must have then realized that I was still in the room. She looked up until I saw my reflection in her mirrored shades and she made a shooing motion.

"Me?" I pointed at myself. She nodded and kept waving her hands at me. "Sorry." I backed out of the room and gently closed the door behind me. Trip was waiting for me.

"Don't worry. Earl said Gretchen's the best. She's supposed to be able to fix any injury. Milo and Sam swear by her. I guess we're supposed to leave her alone to do her thing."

"Any relation to Skippy? They share the same fashion sense."

"Yeah. They said she's one of his wives. I think she's like the tribal healer," he said.

"Wives? With an S? As in plural?" That was a bit surprising.

"Sam said he's got like five of them. Hey, different cultures. Whatever works, I guess."

"Dang. I don't even have a girlfriend and Skippy has extra wives," I replied.

"No wonder. You look like shit," Holly said from behind me. Between her sultry looks, her swimsuit model's body, and the .308 Vepr in her hands, she looked like she should have been in a James Bond movie. "You're bleeding all over the carpet. What the hell did you do to yourself this time?"

I turned to regard her and smiled broadly. "I fell out of the van. While it was moving."

"You should stick with accounting. Holy crap. You have gravel stuck in your arms. Sit down, I'll grab some iodine. Trip, get a towel, and by the way, the property is clear. I didn't see anybody out there."

"Julie's dad is strapped down in the back of the ambulance. He's out cold. You should probably see to him first," I told them as I studied my shredded arms. They looked almost as bad as I felt.

"Is he hurt?" Trip asked. "I'm no Gretchen but I know first aid."

"Mildly concussed probably. Crazy son of a bitch tried to drive us into a train so I clocked him in the head until he quit. Watch him. He's nuts. Find a room to lock him in, and keep him tied up. Preferably chained to something heavy."

"You really are a people person, aren't you? Give me the keys too, I'll hide the ambulance around back." I tossed them over. He left to retrieve Ray.

"I'm not kidding. Lock him in the attic if we have one," I shouted after him. "And check the room to make sure there aren't any weapons in it."

Holly forced me to take a seat in the kitchen while she raided the extensive first aid kit. I sat next to the marble sink with my shirt off while she painfully removed each piece of bloody gravel with a pair of needle nose pliers. The kitchen was also under construction, someone had pulled down most of the cabinets to be restained, and a pair of sawhorses and some plywood served as the kitchen table. Mercy was not Holly's strong suit, and after violently ripping each piece free she dropped them into the sink with a clatter. It was not a pleasant experience.

She told me about how after Julie had called from the asylum, Earl had immediately loaded up a response team in the chopper to come to our rescue, only to be intercepted and forced to return to the compound by the Monster Control Bureau's helicopters. While the Feds were watching them land, Earl had called to check on our status and had gotten Ray instead. Since Holly and Trip were considered mere untrained Newbies by the Feds, and not really important in the grand scheme of things, he had given them directions to the Shackleford family home and had them sneak off with Gretchen.

"What's this stuff? Looks like you got splashed with slag from a cutting torch or something," she asked as she removed a chunk of metal from my arm. It left a small hole that immediately began to well up with blood.

"Gargoyles bleed molten. I beat one of them to death with a fifty barrel. It kind of got on me."

"No kidding?" I flinched as she jerked out a particularly pointy piece of asphalt.

"No biggie. It only had one arm. And it was stuck under the van. It was the bastard that stabbed Julie. I lost the barrel, so I finished it off with a tire iron. When I cracked its head it kind of just squirted everywhere."

"You rushed a giant monster with an empty gun to save her?" She jabbed me with the pliers.

"I guess. Ow. Careful." I grimaced as she grabbed a chunk of flesh instead of rock.

"Hold still, you big sissy . . . Look, Z, let me be honest here. I'm getting a little worried about you. Seriously." Holly sounded earnest. She paused to wipe her brow. It was uncomfortably warm and stuffy in the kitchen. "Back on the freighter you were willing to play chicken with a vampire to save Julie. And now you take on a damn ten-ton gargoyle with a stinking tire iron to protect her?"

"It wasn't that big. And on the freighter I pulled that grenade to save all of us, not just her."

"Sure . . ." She did not sound convinced. "Z, I'm not stupid. I can see how you get all dopey around her. Whatever. I don't want to see you do something stupid and get killed for her is all."

"Nothing that I wouldn't do for anybody else," I said defensively.

"I don't doubt that either. You would probably do something stupid to save anybody. You and Trip both.

Idiot wannabe heroes who would probably run into a burning building to save kittens or some shit. I'm surrounded by idiots."

"I didn't know you cared." I grinned. She stabbed me again.

"Trust me on this one, Z. There'll come a time when you're going to have to make a choice. Somebody who you can't save, no matter what. And then you're going to have to choose, you can either save yourself, or you can die trying. Sometimes the choice is between running like a coward, or fighting like a fool." Holly sounded angry as she said that.

"What are you trying to say?"

"Just something I learned the hard way is all. You know, before . . ." She trailed off, then changed the subject. "I think that's the last of it. I'm going to put some iodine on this now. You're missing a ton of skin, so this might sting."

"Before what?" I pressed. "You're the only Newbie who has never told us how you got into this business. Everybody knows about my werewolf, or Trip's zombies, or Lee's spiders. Holly, you're tough as nails, and you don't take crap off of anybody, but you're buttoned up so tight about your past. What happened before? You know you can tell me any . . . Yeeaaarrrgghhh!" I screamed as horrible burning pain ripped through the raw nerves of my arms.

"Oh, my bad. That wasn't iodine. That was rubbing alcohol. All your babbling distracted me. Now shut the hell up," she ordered.

I did as I was told. I wasn't going to push it while she still had that bottle of liquid pain. Damn, that hurt. The iodine stung, but it was nothing in comparison.

Trip returned after he had secured Ray and had hidden the stolen ambulance.

"What did I miss?" he asked. "Holly, you don't look happy."

"Nothing," she replied stonily. "Hold still. Some of these holes are going to need stitches."

"Gretchen could do it, probably?"

"She's busy. Julie has a real injury, this is just a boo-boo. Besides, I know what I'm doing. This won't hurt a bit. Well, actually it'll probably hurt like a son of a bitch. Bite down on something," she suggested.

Trip pulled up a chair and sat down next to the improvised table. "I put Julie's dad in a bedroom upstairs. I checked the room for weapons, found this. I think Julie has loaded guns stashed in every room of this place." He placed a .45 Beretta in front of him. "Don't worry though. I've got him handcuffed to a wrought-iron bed frame. He isn't going anywhere."

I thought about that for a moment. It beat thinking about the needle that Holly was running thread through. I hated getting stitches. I had done it plenty of times without local anesthesia. Illegal fighting rings did not exactly have the best insurance. "Where exactly did you get handcuffs?"

He shrugged. "They were in one of the gear bags."

"They're mine," Holly said. Trip jumped. She looked up at us in consternation. "Get your mind out of the gutter. Damn, I am supposed to be the support person, remember? I was just thinking ahead. Earl said we had a dangerous crazy guy to baby-sit."

"Sorry," Trip said.

"Bible thumper," she muttered under her breath as she stuck the curved needle through my skin.

"No really, I didn't mean—"

"Whatever, Trip. Just because I danced naked for money doesn't make me a whore."

"Sorry. That wasn't even what I was thinking," he replied, raising his hands defensively. Holly was quiet as she continued stitching me up. Trip was too dark to blush, but he was obviously embarrassed. "I'll go check on Gretchen." He left the room in a hurry.

I watched as the tear in my flesh gradually closed. She did good work. I felt the need to defend my friend. "I don't think Trip was judging you. He's real religious, but he isn't that way at all."

"I know." She continued stitching. "He's probably the nicest guy I've ever met. And he's real innocent at heart. At least as much as somebody can be in this job." She finished closing the gash.

"You're pretty good at that. I should know . . . I've been stitched up plenty of times. I've even done it to myself when I didn't have help," I told her.

"Thanks." She tied off the end. "I learned how in nursing school."

"You were in nursing school?"

"Yeah . . . don't act so surprised. You think I took a degrading job because of the quality people I got to hang around? I needed to pay bills, you know."

"I'm not. I understand."

"I was at UNLV. I only had a couple of semesters left is all . . . And don't ask."

"Got it." I understood. There seemed to be no shortage of Monster Hunters with secrets in their past. She finished stitching me up and wrapped clean gauze over my arms.

"That's about all that I can do," she said. "You

need to get some rest, and you probably need to eat. I saw some food in the fridge. Trip and I will keep watch tonight."

"Thanks," I told her. She stood and stretched, then retrieved her rifle and slung it over her back. She paused on her way out of the kitchen.

"Think about what I said earlier. I don't want you getting killed for no reason."

"I promise I won't," I replied.

"Whatever . . . Stupid heroes." She left the room. "Sweet dreams, Z."

I picked one of the many bedrooms on the top floor. The plan was for all of us to sleep in the same general part of the house. Splitting up seemed like a stupid thing to do considering that we did not know how safe we were here from the Cursed One's minions.

It was a small room, and the walls were bare sheet-rock, but the bed was soft and I was exhausted and still in pain. I popped a handful of Tylenol and hoped that it would help. There were plenty of stronger pain-killers in the ambulance, but the last thing I wanted to be was groggy. It took me a few minutes to find a comfortable spot on the bed where nothing was rubbing a scabbed-over patch of missing skin. That was rather difficult considering the extent of my road rash.

The Cursed One was coming. I knew that. I could feel it in my bones. I knew that he was close, I was not aware of how I knew that, but somehow I knew. Ray was the key. Something in the man's head was the secret that Lord Machado was looking for. Some bit of knowledge gleaned from his own forbidden studies in breaking the laws of nature and bringing back the dead. I would kill Ray Shackleford myself before I let him fall into the hands of the enemy. I did not relish the thought of murdering a human being, but it beat the alternative.

I was asleep in minutes.

My dreams that night were brief. The Old Man did not pay me a visit, and thankfully I did not have to see the world through the lens of the Cursed One's memories. For most of the night I slept like a normal man, not bound by strange visions or plagued with old prophecies and mysteries.

I had a brief nightmare, a panicked, disjointed chase through the halls of the Appleton Asylum. This time the gargoyles were much faster. This time I could not save Julie from them. They took her from me and tore the life out of her with their stone claws. A well of rage and hate opened up inside of my soul. Every bit of anger that I had ever possessed was uncorked and unleashed upon my enemies. I crushed the massive unnatural beings into dust with my bare hands as if they were nothing. My rage continued, until finally in my wrath I destroyed everything around me, leaving nothing but a smoking wasteland of death.

I slept.

I woke up late the next morning, sunlight streaming through my window. I felt remarkably good considering how badly beaten up I was. Despite my hectic schedule over the last few weeks, and my total lack of down time, I felt downright refreshed. Rolling out of bed, I could already tell it was going to be a great day.

A horrible odor assaulted my senses. My bandages were missing and had been replaced by something foul. A green, tarlike substance was smeared all over my arms. It stunk of dead road kill and body odor. I gagged reflexively as it hit my nostrils like a hammer.

"Hey! There's something going on!" I bellowed at the top of my lungs. Considering the weirdness we dealt with in this business, I figured that if you woke up to find yourself coated in strange secretions, it was probably best to alert your co-workers. Unlike most polite jobs, of course.

Trip burst into the bedroom, subgun at the ready, scanning for threats. He must have been right outside the door.

"Something slimed me." I held up one goo-coated arm.

"Dude, you about gave me a heart attack."

"What the hell is this?" I shook my arms and some of the stuff splattered onto the sheets. We were probably going to have to burn them later.

"Don't worry. Gretchen checked on you when she was done working on Julie. After she saw your injuries, she made that paste in the kitchen, came up here and smeared it on you. I'm guessing it's supposed to be some sort of salve or something."

"I didn't hear a thing," I stated suspiciously. I could not believe that I had slept through that. And certainly not while sober.

"If you haven't noticed, she moves kinda quiet."

"What's in it? It smells terrible."

"If I tell you, you're either going to puke or straight up shoot her. So I'm not saying anything. Just remember, she's supposed to be the healer . . . But according to my knowledge of chemistry, I can't think of a thing that it is supposed to do other than reek."

"I'm gonna shower. If you see ninja doctor tell her thanks for the slime." I grabbed my bag and stormed down the hall. At least I had learned from previous mistakes and had packed some extra clothing along with my armor and weapons. A man should always have access to emergency pants.

I found a bathroom, eagerly stripped out of my torn clothes, and jumped into the scalding shower. I had not thought that anything could be grosser than the wight and vampire fluids I had been sprayed with on the freighter, but I had been very wrong.

Under closer examination the stuff appeared to be vegetable-based, except for the particles that I hesitantly identified as ground bones or teeth. Skippy's wife was one weird chick, not that he was exactly a bastion of normalcy himself. As I was scrubbing the filth off under the stream of hot water I realized a few things. First, I should have been in intense pain from the water striking my injuries. Second, I wasn't in any pain at all.

As the stuff was sluiced away, I discovered that rather than being inflamed and scabbed like my arms should have been on the day after such an accident, they were mostly clear, with only smaller spots of scabbing where the very worst of the injuries had been. The gashes that Holly had sewn shut looked like they had been stitched a week ago instead of last night.

Stepping out of the shower I held my arms above my head in amazement. Other than the discoloration and missing hair, the formerly destroyed patches were well on their way toward healing. I turned my arms over, disbelieving what was directly in front of my eyes. It was a miracle. I quickly dried off and dressed.

I found the others in the kitchen. The smell of coffee was strong, and Holly was frying some eggs over the stove. Trip was leaning against a counter, subgun still casually slung and steaming mug in his hands. Gretchen was nowhere to be seen. Skippy's people did not seem particularly social. Surprisingly, Julie was out of bed and sitting at the improvised table, laughing and talking with the others. She had a small bandage on the side of her head, and there was a larger bandage peeking out from under the edges of her shirt. She smiled when she saw me enter, and she looked a thousand times better than when I had brought her here only twelve hours ago. Other than the fact that everybody was armed, and there was a flamethrower sitting in the corner, it looked like a breakfast commercial.

"Good morning, Owen," Julie called happily.

"Breakfast will be ready in a few minutes," Holly added. " 'Bout time you rolled your carcass out of bed. Thanks for all the help with cooking. Both of you."

"Hey, I'm on guard duty," Trip said as he patted his H&K.

"Whatever. I was wandering around the halls with night vision watching for gargoyles until three A.M. so forgive me if I don't cry you a river. Make yourself useful and grab some plates."

"Sorry to interrupt the breakfast club here, guys"—I held up my relatively healthy arms—"but what the hell is going on?"

"Holy shit!" exclaimed Holly. She flung her spatula aside and ran over to look. Trip gasped and dropped a stack of disposable plates on the ground. "This is way better than it should be. The ones I stitched are about closed."

"I told you guys. Gretchen knows her stuff," Julie said.

"No way, man," Trip said as he examined me. "I saw what she boiled up in that pot. It was just a bunch of weeds, dirt and some teeth. She even put a dead raccoon in it. There's no way. Just no way."

"Screw Monster Hunting. Let's sell this and get rich," Holly said.

"We've been trying to talk her into bottling her tribal cures for years. She won't do it. Says that they have to be specifically prepared for each person. On the spot," Julie answered as she sipped her orange juice.

"How's your shoulder?" I asked.

"Much better. I'm sore, and I can't lift my arm above my head yet, but give me a few days and I'll be fine." She reached into her pocket and pulled something out. She dropped it onto the center of the plywood. It was a jagged three-inch piece of stone. "Souvenir. Gretchen pulled this out."

"Damn," all three Newbies said in unison. She was lucky to be alive, let alone walking around in a pleasant mood.

"Seriously. She works magic. All of Skippy's people have gifts. He can do things with that chopper that aren't possible according to the laws of physics. Wait until you meet the rest of his family. They will probably introduce themselves to you when they're comfortable."

I pulled up a chair. "They aren't normal people. What are they?"

"It really isn't my place to say. That's up to them."
She changed the subject. "Eggs are burning."

Holly cursed and returned to the stove. Trip put
the plates and some forks on the table. "What about
your dad?" he asked.

"As far as I care he can eat spiders. Old house has
plenty of them," she said coldly.

"I'll take him a plate," I answered.

"Suit yourself," Julie stated as she returned to her
juice. I did not know what had transpired between
father and daughter while I was taking my tour of the
asylum, but obviously it had not been pleasant.

"He didn't run off when you two were unconscious. Do we really need to leave him locked up?"
Trip asked.

"My dad may seem fine sometimes, but don't let him
fool you. He saw some things that the human brain
isn't wired to deal with. His reality is all screwed up.
He's dangerous. Doctor Joan told me that he's tried
to escape a bunch of times, and he damn near beat
one of their orderlies to death. We let him loose and
he'll be trying to raise the dead or something stupid
in no time flat." She shook her head. "I sure as hell
am not going to let that man loose on the world. I
fight monsters, I don't help them."

"So what's the plan?" I said. My stomach grumbled
loudly. The food smelled great. "After we eat, of course."

"Sit tight. Heal up. Stay low," Holly said. "That's
what Harbinger told us at least. We're supposed to
keep Ray safe and away from the bad guys. He's going
to call us as soon as they work out the problems with
the Feds."

"And he's mad at you," Trip added helpfully.

"What about me?" I asked. I had gone along with her after all.

"I think they think you're just a big protective dupe is all," Holly said. "At least that's the impression I got when he said that you were just a big protective dupe following Julie around like a dumb puppy."

"Oh good."

"Then the Feds were crawling all over us. They want Ray and they want him bad. There had to be like fifty of them at the compound."

"I wonder why Earl didn't just turn Dad over?" Julie mused. "It isn't like there's any love lost there. If the Feds just want to keep his knowledge out of the hands of the Cursed One, then they are way better equipped to baby-sit him than we are."

"He didn't say, but I've come up with a theory," Trip said. We waited. "Well, who all knows about Ray Shackleford and his research? Just MHI and the Feds. It isn't exactly public knowledge, I'm guessing, what with all of this being secret and all. The professors who got attacked in Georgia were both well known for their knowledge on esoteric anthropology; vampires can read books too. Ray was just another inmate in an asylum. How did they know what he had in his head? How did they know that he was so important?"

"You think one of the Monster Control Bureau agents is talking to the CO," Holly said.

"CO?" I asked.

"Beats saying Cursed One over and over again."

"Yeah," Trip answered. "If it's only us and them that know about Ray, somebody must have told the bad guys. How else did they know who he was or even where he was?"

Julie thought about it for a moment. "Good point. Humans have worked for evil forces before. Especially vampires—they have a way of enthralling the weak-willed."

"And there is something else. While you were gone yesterday, Lee found some stuff in one of the old journals. Some Monster Hunter who died back during World War Two. We think it was about the Cursed One. I didn't get to see it, but the experienced Hunters were all freaked out. I mean really scared. Harbinger, Milo, even Sam. They were freaked. They wanted to show you, and that's when they found out that you had taken off."

"Those three don't scare easy," Julie stated.

"This journal scared them. Harbinger was talking about the apocalypse," Holly said as she dished out the scrambled eggs.

"So that's why I think Harbinger is having us hide your dad. Something he knows is the key that unlocks the gate for the Cursed One, and it's very bad news. Like the-end-of-life-as-we-know-it kind of stuff. And he thinks some Fed is working for the bad guys. He's scared to death that they're going to get their hands on your dad." He finished his theory and dug into his breakfast.

Holly sat down, looking slightly uneasy. She hesitated before speaking. "There is one other thing . . . Trip? You want to tell them?"

My friend did not reply. He contemplated his food. Holly did not appear eager to tell us either. Julie broke the silence.

"Let me guess." She leaned back in her folding chair. "If the bad guys find us, we're supposed to kill my dad ourselves rather than let him fall into their hands? Correct?"

The two Newbies nodded. Finally Holly spoke. "I'm sorry. That's what Harbinger told us. He wanted to make sure that we could do it if we needed to. He really accentuated how serious this is."

Julie nodded. "Yeah. I suppose so . . ." She trailed off.

"I'm sorry," Trip said.

"It might be a moot point. How likely is it that the Cursed One's minions are going to find us here?" I asked. I was not particularly surprised at Harbinger's direction to kill Ray if necessary, having already decided the same thing myself. At least now the others were beginning to understand just how serious the Cursed One was.

"This is the old family place. My great-grandfather bought it way back when. It has always kind of been isolated. Legally speaking, nobody lives here. As far as the outside world is concerned, this place is pretty much a forgotten relic. It was sold a long time ago to the Heart of Dixie Historical Preservation Society."

"Who are they?" I asked. The mansion was obviously a landmark of some kind, and somebody had been working at restoring the building.

Julie raised her hand. "I'm the Heart of Dixie Historical Preservation Society." She smiled wickedly. "Since it's a non-profit organization, all a perfectly legal front, and I technically don't live here, it sure does save me a bunch of money in property taxes."

"So you're a tax evader too?" I mumbled around a mouthful of eggs. "Groovy."

"There are only a handful of people who know about

this house, and most of them wear a green smiley face on their armor or their last name is Shackleford." She went back to eating. Julie appeared to be starved, and she should be considering how much blood she had lost yesterday. She paused, swallowed and continued, "And I've got this place rigged with one hell of a security system. If anything drives, walks, slithers or lands on this property, we'll know. There's also a hidden armory in the basement stocked with stuff that would have been confiscated when we got shut down last time, and the compound is only about fifteen minutes away. If we get attacked, we'll just need to hold out that long."

"Will your security system detect vampires?" I asked.

"Probably. As far as we know they still need to walk like anything else. There has never been any actual documented case of them turning into bats or mist like in *Dracula*, only superstitions say that they can shape-shift. But remember, they can't come into a home unless they're invited. That's the rule."

"Why is that anyway?" I asked. "I mean, I've seen it in the movies, but that doesn't really make any sense."

"Nobody knows. But it seems to be a rule with vampires. Other undead don't seem to care, but it does affect vamps," she said. "Unless you let them in, they can't enter."

"But they came into Dr. Turley's house and killed him and his wife. And he was still in bed. They couldn't have been invited. Or what about the attack in Atlanta?"

"Atlanta was a party. All it would take is a single

invited guest to let one in. You guys have only seen newly created vamps. The old ones can be pretty darn charming, and they look just like humans unless they're about to feed. As for the Turleys, who knows? Any indication of invitation would probably do." She forked another piece of egg and dipped it in ketchup. "Did they have a door mat or any signs that may have said welcome, or something like that?"

I nodded as I remembered the Turley home's open rear door, along with the mud stained welcome mat. I swore that I would never own one of those things again.

"Gargoyles?" Trip asked.

"I've got a Barrett .50, a 20mm Lahti, and some grenade launchers in the armory. Also an RPG and for the worst-case scenario, a Spig 9. After we eat, I'll break those out and dust them off. I'm going to need help getting the Spig up the stairs," Julie said. I did not know what a Spig 9 was, but if it was in fact a gun that she needed help to even move, I was very excited.

"What about the CO?" Holly asked. I did not like the abbreviated name. After having seen him, and feeling a taste of his power, calling the evil creature something so innocuous seemed a little silly. The residents of Tokyo didn't call Godzilla "Big G."

"Unknown quantity," Julie stated. "We have no idea what would work on him. It could be something as simple as just shooting him full of holes, or lighting him on fire, or blowing him up, I don't know. Some monsters are hard to kill." She looked at me for help.

I shrugged. "Beats me. The Old Man won't or

can't tell me that. I'll say this though. I don't expect him to go easy. I've got a feeling that he's going to be one mean son of a bitch."

Julie finished her breakfast and pushed the plate away. I dished myself a second helping. Trip sipped his coffee. Holly made sure her sidearm was still there.

"One last thing," Julie said. She was fully confident, and back in command mode. "If they find us. If we get attacked. And we can't beat them or hold them off until help arrives. If and only if the bad guys are about to take Dad away, then we have no choice. Kill him. And do it in a way that they can't bring him back. Shoot him in the head, and burn him." She said this casually, as if she was telling us about the weather. "It's one thing to kill monsters, but it's another to have human blood on your hands . . . If we have to do it, if possible I'll do it myself. My family, my business . . . Everybody okay with that?"

The rest of us nodded dumbly.

Julie scooped up a plate of rapidly cooling eggs and sausage and passed it over to me. "You had best take him some food. He's probably starved. Tell him I send my regards."

Ray Shackleford was sitting on his bed, one wrist handcuffed to the wrought-iron headboard. He regarded me sullenly as I entered. His gray hair was wild, and he had a black eye and bruises from where I had hit him. At least he seemed coherent now.

"I brought you some food," I said. I did not add that I had only supplied him with a plastic fork.

"Let me loose, kid," he ordered.

"Can't do that. This is for your own protection."

"Fine, then I'll take a dump on the floor."

I had not thought about that, but then again I had never kidnapped a crazy person before either. I set the food down on a dresser and removed the handcuff key from my pocket. There was an attached bathroom, there was only one way in, and the window over the shower was too small to squeeze out of. I checked the bathroom for any hidden weapons (this was Julie's house after all), but found nothing.

"Okay, fine. But if you try anything stupid, I will beat you down. I'm just itching for a reason to get my violence on. Got it?"

"Fine. Just hurry up." I unlocked the cuffs and waited patiently as he made his way to the bathroom. He closed the door behind him. I opened it.

"Nope. I don't trust you."

"Fine. Suit yourself . . . freak."

I waited while he took care of business. Once he had washed his hands and pulled back his hair, I escorted him back to the bed and put the cuffs back on. He gave me no trouble. I passed the food over and he gobbled it down messily.

"You knocked me out," he said between bites. "If I was in the shape I used to be, I would have kicked your ass."

"Whatever you have to tell yourself," I said.

"Don't get cocky. I've been around guys like you. I know your type. You're hired muscle. Just a trigger puller. I bet Earl brought you on because you're good at hurting things. You know what? That don't make you special. Hurting things is easy. Understanding them is hard."

"I don't like to complicate things. I see the monster.

I shoot the monster. There. Nice and simple," I said.

"Let me let you in on a little secret, kid. Guys like you are a dime a dozen. A real Hunter understands his prey. He knows how they think. He succeeds where others fail because he knows the monster better than he knows himself. I was the best Hunter we've ever had because of that."

"Whoever fights monsters should see to it that in the process he does not become a monster . . ." I said.

"And when you look long into an abyss, the abyss also looks into you. Ahh . . . an educated man. Well, you're not as stupid as you look. Don't quote Nietzsche at me, kid. That German crackpot wouldn't know a real monster if it bit him on the ass."

Actually I hated philosophy. I had memorized the quote from the intro of a video game. "You about done?" I asked.

"Julie told me a little about you. You're the dreamer. You've been having visions. You want what I've got up here." He tapped the side of his head with his fork, leaving ketchup in his hair. "You want me to help you find Lord Machado."

"Pretty much."

"I can do it, you know. The other Hunters can read those old books forever, but they ain't gonna answer your questions. It isn't what you read, it's putting the information together in your head like a puzzle. Only when you're all done can you really see the picture. I've had lots of time on my hands for the last six years. I've sat in a padded cell all day long with nothing to do but put those puzzles together. I can see the whole picture now. You fools are still trying to find your corner pieces and sorting them out by color."

"Is there a point to this, or are you just trying to get me to punch you in the head some more?"

"Here's the point: I can help you. I can tell you where and when Lord Machado is going to use his artifact. I can tell you what to do. I can tell you how to stop him. I can even tell you how to kill him. The dead guy in your head can't answer those questions, but I can."

"So why don't you just tell me what I need to know?"

"Because, kid, what's in it for me?"

"The world doesn't get destroyed. That sounds kind of beneficial don't you think?"

"I tell you. You tell Earl. You guys kill Lord Machado and the seven. You save the world, cash big fat checks. You get to be heroes. I go back to Appleton and rot in a cell until the day I die. You want my help, you let me go and I'll tell you everything I know."

"And I'm just supposed to let somebody who opened a gate to hell in the middle of Alabama walk free."

"I learned from my mistakes. I won't do that again. I'm not as crazy as everybody thinks I am. I know the score. Let me loose, I promise not to meddle in that business again; I'll just disappear off the radar and nobody needs to know where I went. I've got money, fake IDs, passports, all stashed. You let me go, and nobody ever hears from me again. I'll go down to Mexico and sip margaritas on the beach with pretty senoritas."

"I'll run that past your daughter."

"Julie's squeamish. She's a goody two-shoes like her mother. Believe me. I've learned from my mistakes. I'm done. Earl will tell you no. My dad will say no.

They don't trust me. My offer is to you, kid. Think about it." He smiled hopefully. I did not trust him as far as I could throw him.

"How about you give me a little information up front? Let me see if what you know is worth it."

"I give you enough pieces of the puzzle, you'll figure it out yourself. You won't need me and I go back to Appleton. On good days maybe I get to play Ping-Pong in leg irons with Dr. Nelson. Look out the window while crazy people whine about what monsters did to them. Like those pussies know jack squat about real torment. Whoopee. No way, kid. I talk. I walk. That's the deal."

"Screw you, Ray." I took his empty plate and walked away.

"Wait!" he cried. I paused with my hand on the doorknob. "You have to understand. I can't go back there." I opened the door. "Stop. Listen. I tried to bring my wife back. Is that so wrong? I loved her. I know I made a mistake. I was desperate. You would do the same. I loved her too much to let her go. I know not to try again. I saw things in that rift. Things you can't even begin to understand. I know what's out there. My mind is scarred worse than your face. Believe me. I promise that it won't happen again."

"Good-bye, Ray. I'll send somebody up around lunch for a bathroom break." I stepped out the door into the hall.

"Wait! Don't leave me alone! You want some information. Fine," he shouted. I paused. "There is no real Place of Power. It isn't a fixed piece of geography. There's a nexus of magical energy. The place is where those lines intersect. They are always moving. They are always changing. But I know where and when they are. Those professors that got killed, it's because some of the dead cultures they studied had their fingers on the puzzle. They maybe had bits and pieces. I can see the whole puzzle. I can see the picture. I can even see the box the pieces came in. It's going to happen at the full moon."

"Tell me more, Ray."

"You have three days before the concept of linear time becomes obsolete. Lord Machado thinks he knows what he's doing, but he's wrong. The world you know is going to cease to exist. Billions will die, and the handful that survive are going to be nothing more than cattle living in a blinded stupor. Mankind is going to be nothing but food and entertainment for the Old Ones. You had better think about my offer, kid. The clock is ticking. In three days it stops. Forever."

"Your dad made me an offer," I told Julie when I found her on the main floor. She must have gotten bored after cleaning and hauling up all of the interesting weapons from the basement, because she had busied herself by returning to her renovations.

"Make yourself useful and hold this." She handed me the end of a tape measure. "Put it against that edge there." She walked a few steps and lowered the tape to the floor. She took a pencil from behind an ear and marked a spot on the floor. "I need more flooring. I've got enough to finish the front hall, but not the main entryway."

"You don't want to hear his offer?" I asked. I think that I already knew the answer to that one.

"Let me guess. Let me go. I promise to be good.

No more demon summoning. Blah, blah, blah. I'll tell you what you need to know." She let the tape measure snap closed in her hand and dropped it into a pocket.

"Pretty much. But he did say that the Cursed One is going to strike on the full moon. That gives us just three days."

"Not much time. Figures. Bad stuff always goes down on the full moon. How did this get here?" She bent down to pick up a belt sander that was lying on the floor. Grunting in sudden pain, she paused, and slowly stood back up. "Forgot. Big hole in my shoulder. Would you grab that for me? I need to put it away."

I picked up the sander. "You should take it easy."

She shook her head. "I can't. I'm a little tense. My insane dad is upstairs, in the home that I grew up in. It's just a bit awkward is all. . . . I like working on the house. It keeps my mind off of things, you know?" I nodded. "It helps me to keep busy. I feel better when I'm improving something."

The whole mansion was torn apart. Every room that I had been in so far had some project begun in it, but very few had been finished. Apparently Julie had a lot of things that she did not want to dwell on.

"You seem to be pretty good at it," I said. That was true enough. The work that was finished appeared to be meticulous and professional. Which was not really a surprise considering what I knew about Julie Shackleford's nature.

"Thanks." She paused uncomfortably. "Enough about my dingbat father. I'm just glad he didn't stab you with his plastic fork."

"I did check the bathroom for guns before I let him go."

"Beat you to it." She reached into her back pocket and pulled out a .38 Detective Special. "Bathroom number three gun. I've got them stashed all over."

"You really are my kind of girl."

She smiled. "Thanks. Most regular people think I'm insane."

"Screw regular people. They suck." It was good to hear her laugh again. "Since you're too injured to lay floor, how about a tour of the Heart of Dixie Historical Preservation Society headquarters?"

"That I can do. And by the way, I never said thanks for saving my life from that gargoyle. That was a little too close." She absently touched the bandage on the side of her head.

"No big deal. That was some pretty good driving."

"If that jackass in the truck would have just let us pass, I could have lost them."

"Jerk," I agreed.

"Tour?" she asked.

"Gladly."

CHAPTER 18

The Shackleford ancestral home was an imposing structure. Once one of the finest of the great antebellum homes of the Old South, it was the crown jewel of a once-massive plantation. Ages ago it had been the center of thousands of acres of timber and farming cut out of the woods of Alabama. The original builder's heirs had sold the home and the property to the first Raymond Shackleford nearly a hundred years before.

"You can see out this window where the slave quarters used to be, the kind of empty spot right there. You can still make out the foundations. They were pretty rickety and busted up by the time I was a kid." Julie pointed out the back windows off of the main corridor. "I burned them down when I was twelve."

"Why? Some sort of protest against the injustice? A young girl trying to right the wrongs of the past?" I asked.

"Nothing so noble. Me and my brothers were learning how to make homemade napalm. Styrofoam packing peanuts dissolved into a bottle of gasoline. They make the best Molotov cocktails. I let one of mine get away from me. I'm just lucky that it didn't spread and burn the house down. . . . Those were the days."

"I can understand. I did something similar once when I was a kid. My brother and I built a pipe bomb. Big thing. We smuggled powder out of my father's reloading room for almost a year so he wouldn't notice. Mixed it with a whole bunch of other ingredients. Detonated it in the backyard when my folks weren't home. It was a little bit bigger boom than expected though, dug a four-foot trench in the yard, cut the gas main and forced the neighborhood to evacuate."

"No wonder the ATF has your name on file," she said. "I wonder if all future Monster Hunters blow stuff up as kids?"

"Probably. The ones that live that long at least." I shrugged. "Hey, I was an upstanding citizen until I met you guys."

"I bet. . . . Anyway, I was sad when the old slave quarters burned down. I was just a little girl. I hadn't really understood what they stood for. I mean, I knew what they were, but not why they were important."

"Lot of history in the South," I stated.

"Don't go getting high and mighty because of slavery. You grew up out West, you have no clue about the South. My family might own this house, but that doesn't mean that we approve of the kinds of things that happened here. I had ancestors who fought for the Confederacy, but I would be real surprised if any of them had two nickels to rub together, let alone owned a slave. People think that the South is racist, and it was, and some parts still are, but for the most part, we've dealt with our history. The biggest racists I've ever met aren't here, they're in politics, and they are smug bastards. They're the ones that are quick to play the race card, the ones that pimp poverty. Those are the real bigots."

"Touchy subject."

"I guess. But Bubba Shackleford employed black Hunters in his very first group of Professional Monster Killers. Remember 'Flexible Minds.' He made that little credo up. That's not just about the unnatural, it's about how you look at the world. He only cared if they could fight, and that they kept it together when strange stuff started. They were some pretty tough Hunters too. You don't want to know what happened to the Klan boys that messed with them."

"I can guess." I could only imagine that after dealing with werewolves and vampires, yokels hiding under white sheets were not that big of a deal.

"Rumor has it that a bunch of night riders ended up buried in the back forty. Great-great-grandpa never had much trouble from those folks after that." She changed the subject. "Let me show you the ballroom. This is probably my favorite room in the whole house." She pushed open some double doors and led the way into a huge space. The floor was vast and open, ornate antique chairs lined the walls, and an opulent crystal chandelier hung from the ceiling. Most of the walls were mirrored, with old-fashioned and slightly distorted glass. A large stage filled the back corner of the room, complete with carved pillars capped in brass. Staircases spiraled around and upward to the second floor, perfect for the Southern belles of old to descend for their grand entrances.

I walked into the room. My boots echoed on the worn smooth wood, stirring up small clouds of dust. I could imagine the parties of bejeweled women and men in Confederate gray, royalty of a forgotten time and kingdom. "Impressive."

"I haven't done any work in here. I don't really want to. I'm just going to leave this one alone. We never used this room growing up. If this old place has a soul, it would be in this room. So I leave it closed." I watched her reflection in one of the many mirrors. She awkwardly placed her hands into the pockets of her jeans. "I know it sounds silly, but that's how it is."

"I understand," I said, not really, but it seemed like the correct answer. Even though there had not been any music played in this room for generations, I had to resist the urge to ask her to dance.

"Um . . . Through here is the formal living room. Now this one, we used a little, for guests and that kind of thing." I followed her through another set of double doors into a much less lavish room. This one was under drastic construction. Tarps had been thrown over the furniture, and sawdust covered almost everything. Only one wall was not in the process of being stripped and repainted. It was covered in painted portraits of Julie's ancestors.

"Five generations of Monster Hunters," she proclaimed, "and a few who decided to stay out of the family business, but we still love them too. Even if they are strange." There were dozens of paintings. Most done in a classically formal style, kind of stuffy, and not really befitting the homespun, slightly insane, good nature of the family as I knew them. The first painting was of Raymond "Bubba" Shackleford, followed by a picture of his wife and children, and then each of the succeeding generations after that. There was a single blank spot on the wall where Raymond II was missing, but other than that there were a lot of pictures up there. In totality it created a beast of a family tree. The last of the pictures were of people I recognized. The Ray Shackleford IV that I knew as a wild-eyed lunatic was captured on canvas as a handsome, square-jawed man. His wife, Susan, had looked almost exactly like Julie did today. My tour guide's portrait must have been taken when she was younger. I did not feel that the painting had done her justice. She looked slightly artificial. I felt for the painter, capturing something like Julie's beauty had to be difficult. You could get the technical details correct, but how did you convey the spirit?

"Lot of Raymonds. Must be kind of hard to keep track of them."

"It's a bit of a tradition. Oldest son got the name. I'm the oldest in my family, so it went to my younger brother." She pointed at one of the last of the portraits. He resembled his father.

"Where's he now?"

"Dead," she said sadly. "It's been a few years."

"I'm sorry."

"No. He died well. You can't be sorry for somebody that brave. You can be sad, but not sorry. He earned his plaque at the compound. Even the best of us get it eventually."

"What happened?" I don't know why I asked her, but I did. She hesitated only briefly before speaking.

"1995. At the Christmas party, Monster Hunter International's one-hundredth anniversary. He was one of the ninety-seven Hunters killed that night. He was just a Newbie, but he fought like a champion. You should have seen him. He sure was something."

"I've never heard the whole story."

She gestured at one of the tarp-covered couches. I sat, and she sat next to me, under the watchful painted eyes of her ancestors. We sunk into the deep cushions with a rustle of plastic. I could taste the sawdust in the air.

"It was a great party. Hunters know how to throw a great party—you know, live fast, party hard, die young. That kind of philosophy tends to grow amongst people with such a dangerous job. Everybody who wasn't in the middle of a case was there, so most of us at least. Well anyway, it was at a resort near Gulf Shores, right on the beach. Beautiful spot, Dad had picked it out, reserved it for us. At the time I was just glad that he seemed to be coming out of his mourning, coming out of the archives, and participating with the living again. I had been worried about him for so long. Little did I know that he had picked that spot because it was the right place and the right time for his damned summoning." She brushed aside some dust. "I should have seen it coming."

"You couldn't have known. Nobody could have."

"I know, but that doesn't change the fact that it was my job to know. I'm the historian. I'm the researcher. I'm supposed to be the one with the answers. That's my job, and this one was right under my nose. I knew Dad was sad about Mom's death, but I never expected him to do something like this. The resort was his Place of Power. We didn't know until later that it was built on top of what used to be some tribe's sacred ground. It was his chance to bring her back. While the rest of us were gathering down at the resort, he planted a bomb in the archives. None of us ever learned the real logic behind that. He had the information he needed stored in his head, so he probably wanted to destroy the books that had the information on how to stop him, just in case. That's my guess anyway. Burned a big chunk of it down."

She sighed, apparently studying her father's portrait, trying to discern reason behind the painted mask. She continued, "Every Hunter that could be there, was there. Even the retired ones. Lots of wives, husbands, girlfriends, boyfriends, dates, it was a great big party. Even the caterers and the bartenders had been picked from people who knew what was up. People who knew about monsters and who and what we were. We could let our hair down. There weren't any secrets being kept in that room. I don't know why Dad wanted such an audience, but he had it.

"At midnight, Dad went to the center of the dance floor, splashed some blood in a circle, and said a few words. I think most of the folks near him thought that he was just drunk or something. I saw him doing it, I didn't understand, but I knew that it was wrong. I knew that something bad was about to happen. His voice became louder, almost like he was talking with a megaphone. I've heard about every language there is, but not this one. Whatever it was, it wasn't meant to be pronounced with a human tongue. The blood caught on fire and the floor under him disappeared, it just kind of opened right up. I was far enough away that I didn't get to see *where* it opened to, but some of the others did. They died first."

"What was it?" I asked.

Julie appeared shaken as she recalled the memory. "A rift. To someplace else, we don't really know where. We say hell, but that isn't really right, that's just our way of explaining something that we don't understand, but it was not on Earth, that's for sure. Things came out of that rift, bad things. I can't even begin to describe them. They tore through the party like the Hunters were made out of tissue paper. Dad's plan had gone wrong. Bad wrong."

She unconsciously clenched her fists, the muscles in her jaw contracted, and her eyes narrowed angrily at the memory.

"We fought. We fought hard. But we had been caught unaware, and these things were tough. More and more of them kept pouring through the hole every second, and they weren't going to stop. We held them, we killed them until their husks were piled waist-deep. We couldn't retreat, because they just kept flooding out the rift. If we gave up at the gate then these things would have filled the country, don't ask me how I know that, but somehow we all did. Every inch we gave up was one more inch that would no longer belong to our world, it would belong to them. Everybody stood and fought. No Hunter ran."

I reached over and grasped her hand. She was shaking.

"We didn't have armor—hell, all I had was a cute little black dress. All we had were handguns, of course everybody was packing, I mean, think about the crowd that we're talking about here. Some Hunters made it to their vehicles and grabbed heavier weapons and came back, others had been thoughtful enough to have some already stashed at the resort. After the first few minutes I was out of ammo and down to using a table leg as a club. My brother Ray stood with me, all he had was a broken beer bottle. I watched . . . watched as something pulled his intestines out and painted the ceiling with them. I killed it, but I was too late. I didn't even have time to see him die. I was too busy fighting."

Silent moments passed as she regained her composure. She lifted her glasses and wiped under her eyes. "Sorry."

"No . . . no, that's okay," I said.

"Right after my brother was hit, something big bumped against the rift. Unbelievably big. It's hard to explain, but all I saw was its pupil, but that was bigger than this house. The rift was growing. It was coming through into this world. Grenades and rockets just made it blink. If it came through, then this world was gone. We all knew it. Earl saved us. He made his way *into* the rift. He killed anything that came near him. He came out a second later with my dad slung over his shoulder. When Dad was pulled through, the rift collapsed. We had beaten them. Whatever they were.

"Then we had to run. The resort had caught on fire, the building was coming down. I carried one of my wounded friends out, and by the time I made it outside she had already started to convulse . . . Poor Piper. Apparently the monsters from the rift were poisonous. She died in my arms. The building burned. It was still burning when the Feds arrived. It burned for three straight days. Nothing could put it out. When it was done there was nothing but ash, and charred bones that weren't human."

She stared off into space, reunited once more with the memories of her fallen family and comrades. I did not speak.

"Three quarters of us were dead. And some who had been too close to that rift just walked away and never came back. Ninety-seven dead Hunters and forty dead guests and resort staff. Within a few days an executive order was issued and we were shut down. The Feds took my dad away. The news reported that an oil tanker had run aground and caught fire. I went to a lot of funerals."

"Julie. I don't know what to say."

She put her head down and cried softly. I put my arm around her and waited for her to stop. She sobbed a few times as she was temporarily overcome with emotion.

"I'm okay." She raised her head, sniffed, but then pushed away and stood proudly. "And now you know about us. You know the whole story. And you know why I don't give a shit if that son of a bitch who claims to be my father lives or dies. It would be better for a whole lot of people if his damned black heart quit beating, but if he lives, I think that Appleton is far too nice a place to hold him. If I had my way I would have left him in that rift. He's caused too much pain. He isn't my father. He's nothing but a monster. And I'll be damned if I'm going to let him be taken to help some other monster unleash that kind of terror on my world again."

"I know."

"Good." She stopped. "I loved my brother. I miss him still. And I lost friends, people I've known since I was a kid. I hold *him* responsible for this. So that's why I've been acting the way I have. I'm sorry if I've been harsh, but I'll kill him before I let him go free."

"If anything, I think you've shown remarkable restraint. Thanks for telling me the story." She was an interesting woman to say the least. I was still curious. "What did you do next?"

"What do you mean?" she asked.

"After the company was shut down, until we started back up. What did you do?"

"Well . . ." She sat back down next to me with a creak of plastic. I don't think that she had expected to continue her story. "I went back to school. Finished up my degrees. I tried to be normal for a while."

"Normal?" I had been struggling with the concept myself, doubting myself, my choices, and my abilities. It was strange to hear Julie, super Monster Hunter Julie Shackleford, say the same thing. Strange, but comforting.

"You know. Not a crazed monster killer. I didn't fight evil. I didn't do anything like that. I went to college. I went on dates. I got a job. I didn't really need the money, but I wanted to be like everybody else. I started working on this house as a hobby. I painted."

"You paint?"

"A little," she answered sheepishly.

"Can I see them?" I asked.

"They're not very good. Maybe another time."

"I bet they're fine," I assured her. "Another time then."

"Earl kept hunting. Only now he had to work out of the country and had to compete against established companies, with more assets and the backing of their respective governments. Milo and Sam and the others like them kept hunting free-lance overseas. They would contact me, invite me to come work with them, but I always turned them down. I wanted to pretend that world never existed."

"I can see why."

"Grandpa got sick. The shock of what his son had done almost killed him. He actually came and lived here for a while with a nurse. You can imagine how well he did without Hunters to boss around. I tried to help him, but even he encouraged me to go work with Earl and the other survivors. I turned him down too, and I think it made him even sicker. I vowed that the family legacy was going to die with me. No more Shacklefords were going to hunt monsters ever again."

"So what happened?" I asked. I could not imagine having gone through the things that she had. It made me put my own family relationships in perspective. Nobody in my family had ever summoned any demons. At least as far as I was aware.

"I was in school. Students started disappearing on campus. Young girls. The police said that it was a serial killer. The whole community was scared to death. But I knew what it really was. I could recognize the signs. I ignored it at first. It was somebody else's problem. That world didn't exist for me anymore. I was just a grad student working on my thesis. I pretended that it was just a normal human killer, and that the authorities would handle it."

"It didn't work out did it?"

"It never does. . . . A friend of mine was next. Got nailed while coming out of the library late one night. They never found her head. She was a nice kid. Freshman, from a little town in Illinois if I remember right.

That one was my fault, don't try to disagree, you of all people understand, Owen. I tracked the vampires down. I found their lair. They were sloppy new creations. Weak, stupid and hungry. I went in alone, first time I've ever hunted solo. I spent the whole day staking and chopping. Going from one coffin or hole to the next. Finally I thought that I was going to run out of daylight before I had found them all, so I used some of those homemade Molotovs and burned the science building down. The killings stopped and the cops figured that their imaginary serial killer had moved on. Police never caught the arsonist." She smiled weakly. "I finished my dissertation the next week, boarded up this house, and joined Earl and the others on a case in Uruguay. A few years later, we're back in business. I've never looked back."

"Are you glad?"

"What do you think?" She snorted. "I was deluding myself in school. Normal is an illusion. Normalcy doesn't exist." She gestured at the wall of paintings. "That is normal. These people are real. All that stuff I told you back at your apartment, when we were trying to recruit you. Yes. I do actually believe that. I believe in what we do. It's more than just the job. It's more than the PUFF check."

"It's a calling," I said.

We sat in silence beneath the pictures. We had an understanding.

"You have another brother?" I asked, pointing at the last picture. He looked more like Julie.

"Nate," she laughed. "He wants to kill monsters so bad he can taste it."

"Where's he at now?"

"Seattle. He went through the last class of Newbies.

He's doing okay from what I hear. I made sure that he's with a great team who'll keep him alive long enough that his enthusiasm gets tempered with experience. He's nineteen. You'll like him. He's just insane enough to be entertaining . . ." She put her hand on my knee. I could not tell if she had done it on purpose or if she had done it without thinking. Either one was fine with me. "Well, that's pretty much the tour. Sorry I got all blubbery and emotional on you."

"Julie. If you didn't get emotional about that, then you wouldn't be human. Thanks for the tour. I can tell you love this house."

"I can't say why, but I do. One of these days I'm going to get it all fixed up. I could probably hire professionals to do it and just get it over with, but that doesn't seem right. There are a lot of memories here . . ." She suddenly snapped her fingers. "Wait a second, I've got something for you." She jumped up, and walked quickly to the door. "I'll be back in a minute, I've just got to find it."

I sat on the plastic covered couch and waited. After a few minutes I grew restless and decided to check out the portraits more closely. The Shacklefords were one interesting group—heroes, villains and everything in between. I stood close to the wall and examined the intricate paintings. Julie's grandfather had been a handsome man before he had lost his eye and been so disfigured. I could see the resemblance to his son, and they both looked slightly like Earl Harbinger. I was not exactly sure how he was related, but there was no picture of him on the wall, and there were no Harbingers listed at all. Looking at the other pictures, I decided that Julie was very lucky that she took after her mother. Besides the lack of glasses and the slightly outdated hairstyle, they could have been the same person. I would imagine that a historian would be able to compile quite the entertaining book about this family. Of course the government would probably end up sending somebody like Agent Franks to the author's home to shoot him in the brain.

The one blank spot on the wall was interesting, but I did not dwell on it for long. Even an auditor's curiosity only runs so deep when there are other matters at hand.

Julie returned with a dust-covered, wooden case. "Found it." She sat it on the tarped-over table and opened the metal clasps. "Now you are going to appreciate this, Mr. Gun Nut." She opened the box with a flourish. Inside the molded case were two pistols. One was big, and the other small, a matched pair, down to the finishes. "Go ahead. Check them out."

The guns were custom. STI frames, the full-size had an extended, threaded barrel, and was complete with a rail for a mounted light. The smaller one was a custom chopped version, cut down in every possible dimension for concealment. For a competition nut like myself, these pistols were the kind of thing that I dreamed about. Normal men had pornography. I had gun magazines. They were beautiful.

"Twenty-eleven frame, fourteen rounds of .45 in the big one, twenty with the extended mags. Ten in the little one, but it can take the full-size mags, they just hang out a bit. I worked them over so they're reliable with our silver bullets. Match barrels, these are scary accurate. But clearances are loose enough that these should be able to get really gunked up and still work fine," she told me proudly. I pulled back the slide to check the chamber, and it glided as smoothly as silk. I checked the trigger. The hammer fell with a snap. It was possibly the nicest trigger I had ever felt on any weapon, ever.

"These were made for somebody with mutant hands, notice even the long trigger. Extended safeties for shooting high thumb; beaver tail, small mag release so big-handed shooters don't release them by accident; you guys don't need to shift your grip to change mags anyway."

"Sweet. Did you do these yourself?"

"They were an old project."

I gently put the guns back in the box. "They're beautiful. Much nicer than my old one. I've gone through quite a few guns this week."

She closed the box, snapped the clasps closed, and shoved it over toward me. I looked at it in confusion for a moment.

"You'd better be more careful with these then. Lose them and I'll kill you."

"But, but . . . you're just giving these to me?" I asked. "Why?"

"I have these lying around the house. They don't fit me at all. Some Hunter with ham fists needs to put them to good use, and you currently don't have a pistol at all. My little brother won't use them. He's a Glock nut. The poor deluded bastard. Plus the way these things shoot, they need to be in the hands of a real pistolero. You'll have to do." She smiled. "Consider it my way of saying thank you for saving my life."

"Thanks," I said. It was the nicest gift that anyone had ever given me.

"Look, I've got to go," she said, sounding almost sheepish. "I need to take care of some things."

"Thanks," was all that I could think of to say.

"Don't mention it." She winked at me and walked away.

I watched her leave the room before opening the case and examining the fine weapons again. I did not want to look like a total dweeb in front of her, but for me, Christmas had come real early. Grinning like an idiot, I field-stripped and checked the guns. The case even came with a cleaning kit. I lubed the guns, and did several practice draws, adjusting my grip each time, until the sights snapped unconsciously into place. Finally I forced myself to put them down. I needed to take over for Trip on the perimeter. It was my turn to stand guard.

I noticed something as I started to shut the case. The foam in the top half had come slightly undone. Between the foam and the wood was an envelope. The envelope was blank, but it contained a small handwritten note.

> *Dear Ray,*
>
> *I hope you like these. After that luska ate your other guns, I thought I would do something nice for you. I built these up just the way you like them. Milo's been teaching me everything he knows about gunsmithing, and I think that these have come out really good.*
>
> *Dad's doing better. He's been really excited, looking forward to the 100th anniversary party. Should be a blast. Nate's*

bummed he can't come. Earl is doing good.
Piper Cavanaugh has been dying to talk to
you. I think she has a crush on you. She's
cute. You two should hook up. See you at
the party.
    I love you, Bro. Hope you like the guns.
                                    Julie
                                12/2/95

I carefully refolded the note, placed it in its envelope, and put it back in the case.

Trip was waiting for me on the porch. We were
not taking any chances, and were taking turns with
one heavily armed and armored Hunter outside to
watch the skies for more gargoyles. Of course all of
us were wearing our radios, and the person patrolling
the outside checked in constantly. If there had been
more of us available, we would have worked in pairs
and had a better rotation, but as it was, there were
only the four of us on our little baby-sitting detail.

"Holly is watching the video feeds. Julie has one
heck of a system installed here. Don't go more than
twenty yards from the building or you'll probably activate a sensor. Check in with her every few minutes."
He handed me the RPG. If anything suspicious landed
on the property, we weren't going to screw around.
The huge rocket-propelled grenade would take out
an armored vehicle, so a gargoyle would not be a
significant problem. "You learned how to use one of
these, right?"

"Dude . . . please." I patted the lethal tube gently.
If third-world goat herders could figure out an RPG,

I wasn't worried. Even though I had not shot one yet, Milo had trained us in their basic use. I was looking forward to firing one. And if the target happened to be a ten-foot-tall, animated chunk of rock, that was fine by me.

"Never mind. I forgot I was talking to the combat accountant. I haven't seen anything except for bugs and a cottonmouth."

"Like the killer snake cottonmouth?" I asked, glancing nervously at the ground.

"Yeah, but it was just a baby. You should have seen the ones we grow in Florida. They climb trees, and drop on you. When you're on the river fishing, they will swim out to your boat and climb in. Mean little bastards," he told me this with a straight enough face that I was not quite sure if he was making it up or not. "Anyway, if you need me, I'll be on the radio."

"Okay." He started to walk away. I stopped him. "Hey, Trip, one last thing . . . Thanks for coming out here to help me and Julie," I told him. "I appreciate it."

"Dude, don't worry about it. Harbinger needed somebody not very important to the Feds, is all."

"Still. Thanks," I said. He shrugged and went back into the house. The screen door clattered behind him. I shifted the RPG to one shoulder and started my patrol.

The afternoon air was thick with humidity, and moisture gleamed on the surrounding foliage. The once-cleared farmland that had surrounded the plantation had been retaken by swift-growing plants, including the evil nemesis of all that was good in the plant world—kudzu. It was stiflingly hot in my armor, and sweat ran freely down my back. I had left my hockey helmet behind in favor of a simple ball cap to keep the sun out of my eyes. I sipped constantly from my CamelBak. Big guys dehydrate fast in the summer.

I did not see anything of note as I passed the time. Holly checked in every few minutes to make sure that nothing was trying to kill me, besides the bloodthirsty clouds of gnats of course. So far I liked the South. I liked the people and their attitude, but I sure could do without all of the damned gnats, mosquitoes, chiggers, ticks and other things interested in eating me.

As I approached the remains of the old slave quarters, I noticed one solid piece of construction not destroyed down to its foundations. It was a tiny building, slightly lopsided from settling over time, probably only ten feet across, but constructed out of thick-mortared stones. There was a very heavy door, but it was hanging open on massive rusty hinges. I debated it briefly, but decided to take a look inside the old relic.

It must have been some sort of prison cell for the slaves so long ago. The interior of the room was empty, but the few small windows were blocked with thick steel bars set deep into the stones. Thin shafts of light pierced the gloom, but not nearly enough to see by. The inside of the door was banded with iron slats, and the door itself was constructed of ancient pieces of wood, almost big enough to serve as railroad ties. It was a construction far heavier than possibly needed to keep anyone from escaping. There was a latch on the doorframe where a big crossbeam could be set to keep the door closed, probably held in place by a long-since-missing chain and padlock. The air was stale and damp with mildew.

I entered the cell. It was dark. I blinked a few times, but my eyes were adjusted to the summer sunlight outside. Raising Abomination slightly from its tac sling, I activated the powerful weapon-mounted flashlight. The room was instantly flooded in brightness. *Much better*. The texture of the stone walls was strange. It took me a moment to understand exactly what it was that I was looking at.

Scratches. Tens of thousands of scratches. Some sort of hard and sharp implement had scratched every reachable surface. The only clear spots on the walls were more than ten feet high, but even then there were a few marks above that where the creator must have gotten a running start. I looked down. Even the floor was torn with a patchwork of deep marks. The marks were deep, as if struck into the rock with great force.

An involuntary shudder passed down my now-cold spine. I did not understand what had made the marks, but someone had spent a whole lot of time tearing at the tiny prison. It had to be hundreds of hours' worth of either methodical work, or perhaps savage frenzy. Now uncomfortable, I left the flashlight on until I was back out in the sunlight.

Holly relieved me on guard duty a few hours later. I took a turn watching the security cameras. It was a monotonous job, but somebody had to do it.

At least the little room with the monitors had a ceiling fan. The central air had died, and none of us had been able to fix it. The security system was impressive: motion detectors, pressure sensors, and video in regular and thermal images. The most paranoid recluse would be proud to own this system. Very fitting for the home of a Monster Hunter.

Holly appeared on one of the screens. I was glad to see that she had paid attention to her lessons in tactics and was varying her route to keep any tunneling creatures from being able to set up an ambush. My earpiece crackled as she checked in.

"Nada. I almost wish that something would attack. This is boring," she told me. On the monitor she moved the RPG to her other hand. "I would love to blast something. These things are awesome."

"It worked pretty good for you back on that boat."

"Yeah, you missed it since you were busy drowning. Turned those wights into chum. RPGs rock." She went back to her patrol. I went back to my monitors.

An alarm sounded and a red light on the control panel started to flash. "We have company," I said into the radio as I checked the appropriate camera. "A car is coming up the lane."

Julie's voice came over the radio. "Can you tell who it is?"

"Negative."

There was a brief pause as she digested the information. "Everybody assemble toward the front. Except for Gretchen, stay back in case one of us is wounded. Holly, use the corner of the house as cover. Trip, you and me, front porch. Owen, second-floor balcony. Be ready for anything."

"It's daylight. At least it can't be vampires," I said as I left the control room and headed for my assigned area. I swung Abomination around my back, and grabbed the flattop AR-15 that was mounted over the doorway. If I needed to engage targets off the second floor, the .223 rifle would be better suited for that task than my relatively short-range shotgun. I chambered a round. I loved Julie's idea of home decor. She had a weapon stashed every ten feet.

"It could be anything. We didn't know the CO had gargoyles either," Julie said. Now even she was using the abbreviated form.

"What if it's the Feds?" asked Holly. "I've got an RPG," she added helpfully.

"Hold your fire," Julie ordered.

Somehow, I did not find that comforting. I found a spot on the balcony overlooking the front approach. I left the window closed. If I needed to shoot, I could do so through the glass, and there was no need to give away my position beforehand. I grabbed a nearby dresser and pulled it into position to use as a rest. I gazed through the 4X magnification of the Trijicon scope. The car was a new, black Mercedes, and it was approaching rapidly, spinning up a cloud of dust behind it. I put the illuminated reticle on the car's windshield.

"I only see the driver . . . No visible passengers. But the windows are tinted. Hard to tell."

"Roger that," Julie responded. "Everybody get ready. I'll walk out to meet them. It might just be somebody lost, or a salesman, or the Jehovah's Witnesses or something."

"J-Dubs huh? Like I said, I've got a perfectly good RPG . . ." Holly offered.

"Mercedes is at two hundred yards and closing."

"Mercedes?" she responded hopefully.

"Yes. A new black one," I replied through my mike.

It was quiet. I watched the car pull into the courtyard and stop next to the dry fountain. The scope vibrated slightly as I waited for the driver to exit. We waited as the driver took his sweet time putting his sunglasses away and checking his hair in the interior mirror.

Finally the door opened and the driver's expensive Italian shoes touched down on the gravel. I exhaled slowly, perfectly balanced, ready to shoot. Julie's back appeared in my field of vision, quickly approaching the Mercedes. The man unfolded himself gracefully out of the vehicle. He was tall, handsome and wearing a finely tailored suit. Julie hugged the driver, and I watched her kiss him through 4X magnification.

Shit.

It was Grant Jefferson. The insufferable little ass-clown.

I put the safety back on the rifle, and moved the muzzle into an upward direction. I swore and violently kicked the helpless antique dresser. Grant Jefferson. Monster hunting legend . . . in his own mind at least. Brave hero who didn't think twice about leaving me to die. Perhaps the most stuck-up prick I had ever met, and worst of all . . . Julie's boyfriend.

I would have preferred vampires.

"Hello, Pitt." Grant greeted me as I stomped down the stairs. "I'm glad to see you were able to escape those gargoyles." He lied easily enough. I knew that if I had been pasted all over rural Alabama he wouldn't have shed many tears. I resisted the urge to snap-shoot the scumbag right between the eyes.

"I bet you are," I grunted.

"Owen saved my life," Julie told him. "If it hadn't been for him I'd be dead. He beat one of them to bits. Saved my dad too."

"Really? Good job . . . Newbie," Grant said. Trip entered behind them and rolled his eyes when he saw Grant.

"We had a little help." I thought of the farmer with the NRA hat and elephant rifle. "Some folks aren't too chicken-shit to risk their lives for somebody else."

"Owen!" Julie snapped. "We don't have time for that right now."

Grant surprised me then. I had not known that the man had any humility in him at all. "No. That's okay. I'll admit, I made a tactical error. I didn't think I could save you, so I retreated to a more advantageous position. It seemed like the prudent thing to do at the time." He draped one arm casually over Julie's shoulders.

I figured that was probably as close to an apology as he had ever mustered. I bit my tongue to keep from saying anything further. Holly entered from the back and Gretchen glided silently in from the kitchen. Julie shrugged out from under Grant's arm and sat down. She was back to business.

"So what's going on back at the compound?" Julie demanded. "And more important, how's Doctor Nelson?"

Grant adjusted his silk tie as he spoke. He did not like being ordered around, but he knew his place. "The doctor's going to be okay. He suffered a coronary, but he's stable." I breathed a sigh of relief.

"As for the compound, Myers and the Monster Control Bureau agents are still there. They want your father, badly. APBs have been issued for him, you and Pitt. They're making life difficult. All of our personnel have been grounded until Ray Shackleford is found. "

"That sucks," Julie said.

"There is good news, though. There have been undead attacks all over Georgia, Alabama and Eastern Mississippi. Looks like the seven split up to cause trouble. Over the last two days, newly created vampires, wights and zombies have wreaked havoc."

"That's good news?" Trip said incredulously.

"Sure is. The Feds are jumping, trying to contain the outbreaks, and still watch the spots they think are Places of Power. Local law enforcement doesn't have any idea what's going on because the Feds are keeping them in the dark. Every National Guardsman and Reservist in the South has been called up on emergency duty. Local officials are panicking. The news is reporting it all as terrorist attacks and Homeland Security has moved most of the Southeast to condition red."

"I'm still not grasping the 'good' part of that," Trip replied.

Grant sighed in exasperation, as if baffled by the ignorance of Newbies. "Harbinger's put the word out to all of the local officials who are on our side. The Governor's office, state legislatures, even Congress and the Senate, pretty much every pro-Hunting politician." I imagined that some of our bounty from the *Antoine-Henri* job had been used to grease a few palms as well. "They're putting pressure on Myers to let us go so we can do our jobs. We have contracts with these states that we can't currently fulfill because of the Feds. Lots of people are getting ticked off, and the worse the crisis gets, the more their complaints get heard by Myers' bosses in Washington. The last thing that they want is for it to get so bad that the truth can't be contained from the general populace."

"So you think they're going to let us go?" asked Holly. "The Feds are just going to back off?"

"I think so," Grant said smugly. Which I took to mean that Harbinger thought so, and Grant liked to be right. "If there are more attacks tonight like there were last night, then they aren't going to have much choice."

"I'm surprised they're doing this. It isn't like vampires to provoke confrontation with humans. They're powerful, but there are lots more of us than there are of them. Direct confrontation with the living usually gets them staked and chopped in short order. Why all of these attacks?" Julie mused.

"Because in three days, it isn't going to matter," I told them. "The seven are only here to help the Cursed One. They know that we're onto them. They have nothing to lose. They attack. They create more undead. They cause confusion and spread human forces thin. That's what they want."

"Three days?" Grant asked in confusion.

"That's when my dad says that they will use their artifact," Julie said. "Come on, what else?"

He continued, "Harbinger doesn't want to turn your dad over. He thinks the Feds have a leak. How else could the CO have known about Ray? The only people who know about him are us and them." Grant seemed saddened that this news did not shock us.

"I told you so," Trip said. I golf-clapped for him. He flipped me the bird. All in good fun of course.

Our visitor ignored our antics. "We learned some more things while you've been away." He nodded in my general direction, not quite willing to actually mention any contributions I have made, but needing to emphasize the source of their intel. "We found the name Byreika. We think we know who he is, or maybe I should say, was."

"The Old Man?" I was shocked.

He pulled a piece of paper out of his suit pocket. He carefully unfolded it and read. "Mordechai Byreika. Born in Lodz, Poland, in 1874. Freelance Monster Hunter. Did rather well for someone who worked solo, mostly in Eastern Europe. Last whereabouts were when he was arrested by Nazis in 1941, he was sent to a concentration camp, escaped, was recaptured, sent to another camp in 1943, and never heard from again." Grant handed the paper over to me. There was a single, grainy, black-and-white photograph photocopied under the information.

It was him all right. Slightly younger, not quite as worn down by age and time, but still with the same hard eyes behind small glasses. I was sure of it. In the picture he was standing, with a rifle in hand, in front of the corpse of some sort of massive scaled monster. It was a trophy shot, the kind that you took as proof to collect on a bounty.

"Is that the man, Owen?" Julie asked, standing up, and crowding next to me to see the picture. Trip and Holly followed closely, also curious to see. Gretchen was inscrutable under her burkha and shades. She wandered off toward the kitchen, probably bored and looking for something to eat.

"This is him. I'm sure of it. How did you find him?"

"His journal is in the archives. It was found on a contract mission to Prague back in the '80s."

"We collect information from old Hunters every

chance we get. We aren't any smarter than the old-timers, we've just learned from their experience," Julie explained.

"Lee found it. He was cross-referencing everything in the archives, and the name stuck out. He remembered Pitt saying that name from his dreams."

"Remind me to give Albert a fat bonus when we get back," Julie said. "What's in the journal?"

"Years and years of hunting, but if you skip to the end, he was after the CO. It was kind of like a quest for him. Killing that particular monster was his Holy Grail," Grant told us. I found that a slightly ironic turn of phrase to use about a Jew. "Byreika studied him for years. He was sure that the creature's physical body was someplace in Europe. His search led him to believe that the Nazis were in league with Lord Machado."

"In league for what?" Holly asked.

"Complete and total control over time."

"Sounds familiar," I said.

"It's worse. Byreika studied this for years. He was convinced that the CO had the ability, and the insanity, to do it. The only thing holding him back was that he needed a certain artifact that was protected by some sort of ancient guardian. Once it was taken from the guardian, it had to be taken to a certain place, at a certain time, and activated with a special blood sacrifice. The journal went into a lot of details about what he thought would happen if the CO was successful."

"How bad?" all of us asked in unison.

"I don't know, haven't read it yet. But Harbinger absolutely freaked out. Said that we should shoot your dad rather than let anything come near him, including the Feds. Milo read it, and then he had to call the general authorities of his church. Even Sam didn't look so good, and I didn't even know that man's brain was wired to understand fear. I mean, I've never seen those three scared of anything before, ever."

"I've only seen them scared once," Julie stated. I thought of her story, with the giant pupil looking through the rift into our universe.

"Literally the end of the world," Grant told us as he adjusted the lapels of his expensive suit. "I mean, seriously, I'm a little nervous about the whole thing myself."

Holly cleared her throat. "This might sound bad . . . and I'm sorry to be the one to bring it up, but if it's that serious, why don't we just kill Ray right now?"

"Holly!" Trip sputtered. "That would be murder."

"Hey, I'm trying to be practical here," Holly retorted. "Whole world dies, or one nutcase buys it, no offense, Julie . . ."

"None taken," she said.

"Then I'm siding with the whole world. It's a pretty sucky place, but I like it not destroyed. Let's just plug Ray and bury him in the backyard," Holly said. I reminded myself to stay on her good side. Trip looked disgusted. Grant seemed impressed by her logic. I was morally ambivalent, but it was too damn hot to have to dig a deep enough hole to hide a body.

"I've thought of that myself," Julie told us. "But there's one problem. Dad is probably not the only way for them to find their Place of Power. I mean, Dad found a way, so that information is out there somewhere. And on the other hand, he is *our* only way to find out where the Cursed One is going to be . . ."

"So we can be waiting for the son of a bitch," I finished for her. My hand instinctively moved to the grip of my shotgun. "We need to make Ray talk."

"Stick Holly in with him for ten minutes," Trip said in disgust.

"Can I borrow your car battery and some jumper cables?" Holly batted her eyelashes innocently. "I've got fifty bucks says he talks."

"Damn, woman, you have serious issues," Trip said.

"Anything else, Grant?" Julie asked.

"Just one thing. The blood sacrifice to turn on this evil artifact . . . Byreika said that it had to come from a hero, a protector, a mystic champion."

Apparently none of us had a clue what that meant. I shrugged. Personally I had had about enough with the mystic garbage.

"The blood has to come from the heart of a Monster Hunter."

CHAPTER 19

The paper plate of ham and cheese grits was slightly heavy and oily in my hands. Needlessly polite, I knocked on the door.

"Ray, I brought you some dinner."

He snarled at me from his bed, and jerked on the handcuff, but the heavy railing snapped his arm back. He was not having a good moment. His hair was wild, his skin was pale, and his eyes were unfocused. He looked as if he was listening to something far away.

"Ray? Are you with me, buddy? Hello . . . anybody home?" I set the plate of grits next to him. Once again, all I gave him was a plastic utensil, and if he could take me out with a spoon, he deserved to escape.

Gradually his face returned to normal. His eyes focused on the food, and then he looked up at me.

"Sorry. I was having an episode." He sounded slightly confused.

"Not a problem." I had no idea what medications he had been on at the asylum, but we had nothing to help him with here. "I brought you dinner."

"Thanks." He took the plate and dived into the food with gusto.

"Have you given any thought to telling us some more information, Ray?" I asked politely.

"Have you given any more thought to letting me go?"

"We're talking about it," I lied. "If you gave us a little more to go on, a little something to show good faith effort, we would probably be more inclined to just turn you loose."

"I'll tell you everything I know as soon as I'm free. I'll call you from a payphone or something," he answered as he swallowed his food without chewing. Bits of grits ran into his facial hair. "Honest."

"Sure. I believe that."

"No, really. Look, once I'm free, having the world destroyed doesn't exactly fit my plans. I can't hang out with the pretty senoritas if the clock for the universe isn't ticking. I'm talking about a win-win situation."

I tried a different tack. "We found Byreika's journal. We know all about the Cursed One. We're going to figure it out without you, Ray. We'll figure it out soon enough. You help us now, you get on our good side, and then we can try to help you out."

He laughed at me. "Do you think I'm stupid? Jeez, kid. I may be a little crazy but I still have an IQ of 160. I've read that book too. All you know now is how serious your problem is. That old Jew had a lot more questions than answers. Besides, he's stuck in your head anyway, so you should already know all of this stuff."

"Why is he stuck in my head? How can he communicate with me?" I pressed for any information that I could, hoping that he would slip.

"You can't be serious? Really? Damn. My first impression was right, you are stupid. Earl must be hiring strictly by the benchpress now. If you haven't figured out how that Old Man is trying to help you, then you really are up a creek. Even if I told you where to meet the Cursed One, you wouldn't know what to do when you caught him."

"What do you mean?"

"No mystery here, kid. I'm not Hannibal Lecter. I'm not trying to play mind games with you. I'm just surprised is all. You don't even know who you are, do you?"

"I know exactly who I am."

"If you did, then we wouldn't be having this conversation." He laughed at me again. "Oh shit. The world is screwed. Good night, kid. Shut the lights on your way out. Talk to me when you have a clue."

I was heading to bed when I heard the raised voices. I hurried toward the noise, thinking that it might be some sort of emergency, but slowed down when I realized it was Grant arguing with Julie in her room. She sounded rather calm, but he sounded upset.

Probably should have kept walking, but showing a real lack of character, I decided to eavesdrop through the door.

"—could have at least tried."

"Darné and his wights were right there. I swear, there was nothing I could have done except die along with him," Grant pleaded. "I don't like him, but you know I would never abandon another Hunter if there was a chance to save them, but there was no chance!"

"Well, he made it, so apparently you were wrong."

I suddenly felt very smug.

There was an awkward pause on the other side of the door.

"I know . . ." Grant sounded tired. It was the first time I had heard genuine emotion in his voice. "I've been dwelling on it every minute since it happened. I misjudged, and that mistake left a man to die. I left a fellow Hunter to die alone . . ."

Was he crying?

"Grant, it's okay, everyone makes mistakes."

"I don't . . . Sorry. I've got to go. See you in the morning," Grant said. I moved away from the door as fast as I could remain silent, and made it about ten feet before the door opened. I spun around, as if I had been coming from the other direction.

Grant was in fact wiping his eyes as he closed Julie's door behind him.

"Evening, Grant."

"Pitt." He nodded, then walked quickly in the other direction, his pride not able to show weakness to a rival. Especially a rival whom he had accidentally condemned to a horrible death, but I could tell by looking at him that it wasn't an act. He really was torn up by his failure. Torn up, and hurting.

I didn't feel so smug anymore.

Grant stayed the night. I still didn't like the man one iota, but it was rather nice to have one more person to pull guard duty. While it was dark, it did not do us much good to have somebody on patrol outside, so instead, we all clustered in one suite of rooms centered around Ray Shackleford's little prison. One person was awake at all times to walk the hall. The sensors had been rigged to alert us if anything bigger than a rabbit came within twenty feet of the house. We could have moved that perimeter back, but the number of deer in the woods would have been setting off alarms all night long.

Julie had taken extra precautions with Ray's room. She had put motion detectors all around his bed. If he even thought about making an escape we would all know.

Personally, I didn't think we had anything to really worry about. Nobody outside of Julie's immediate circle of friends and family knew about the home. The Heart of Dixie Historical Preservation Society was an effective front, so even if the Feds did have somebody leaking information to Lord Machado, they didn't know about this place.

I turned in for the evening. I put my armor on the ground next to the bed, weapons sitting on top. If I needed to find them quickly in the dark, it would not be a problem. I even left my pants on in case I needed to move in a hurry. My watch wasn't until 2:00 A.M. I heard Holly's boots echo in the hall. All of us were close enough that if anything bad happened, we would all know. The only people who slept far apart in a situation like this were the suckers in the horror movies.

Before I drifted off to sleep, I comforted myself that at least Grant was sleeping in a different room than Julie. I had no idea if that meant they weren't as close as I feared, or if their relationship was currently on the rocks, like I hoped, or—worst-case scenario—Julie was just trying to be polite to the rest of us. I did not really know why or how I had fallen so hard for Julie Shackleford, but I had. She was by far the most interesting, smart and attractive woman I had ever known. I cringed when I remembered seeing her kissing Grant through the rifle scope. Now that was an unpleasant thought to fall asleep on.

"Hello again, Boy," called the Old Man. He was still sitting on the stone steps of the crumbled and partially burned church. "Watch this as it goes now." He spun his little carved toy on the steps. This time it stayed upright for nearly two whole seconds before it fell over. "See, is much better this time," he said with obvious pride.

"Bravo," I said as I walked through the snow toward him. Once again I was barefoot, but the cold was not uncomfortable beneath my soles. "And I always thought ghosts floated around in white sheets and rattled chains."

"Ha. Boy thinks he is funny man now."

"You are, or were, Mordechai Byreika. Born in Lodz, Poland. Monster Hunter." He did not betray any noticeable reaction when I said that.

"Is good name. I not hear whole name in long time."

"I guess. If you were alive you would be almost a hundred and thirty."

"Is all? Time pass so slow when is stuck."

"So you're not alive, but you're stuck. Just what are you?"

"I say before. Is no important. I just friend." The Old Man scooped up his little makeshift dreidel and placed it in my hand. "Here, you take. Give to your childrens some day. Maybe they play with, and say, oy is fun."

I held the little toy in my palm. It really did look awful, but I did not have the heart to tell him since he seemed so proud. In his defense, he had been dead for sixty years. I imagined that would make a man's carving skills a little rusty. "Thanks." I tucked it into my pocket.

"Welcome. Now for me, you not worry. You stop Cursed One, you help me just fine. Maybe I get not stuck." He shrugged his narrow shoulders. "Who knows?"

"That was your mission in life. Stopping the Cursed One."

"Is hard to remember." He tapped one bony finger against his cranium. "Few things I know. Some I only think I know. But I know for sure one thing that is true. Time is short."

"Ray Shackleford says three days. I suppose two now."

"Yes. Sounds right. You must learn much very fast. Is up to you, no one else, Boy."

"I know," I answered. At this point, arguing about my purpose in life seemed rather silly, especially against the ghost in my head. "If you don't mind me asking, how did you die? Last anybody heard, the Nazis had taken you."

He hawked and spat a wad of phlegm into the snow. "Bastards. Some monsters are just men. Sometimes, worst kind of all is men. How I die? Is hard to say, is not important now."

"Did it hurt?" It seemed a stupid question.

"Is stupid question. Of course hurt. Hurt when you died, yes?"

"Yeah, I guess." Even in my dream state, the scar

tissue that coated so much of my body was still thick and coarse. I thought that I had understood what pain was, until that day in my office showed me that I still had a lot to learn.

"You no guess. You know. Hurts to get cut open . . . Fine, I tell story, but is hard to remember. Nazis thought they could use Cursed One. Helped him . . . tried to do then, what he trying to do again now. Cursed One was weaker then, his body was not solid yet. He was like you, want to hurry, not want to learn. He could not get artifact himself, made deal with Nazi bastards. They stole artifact, hurt the Guardian, thought they kill, but not realize he not can die. Took to Place of Power. Here, this place, in my time." He gestured around the church.

"What happened?"

"Cursed One was fool. Time was wrong. Artifact not work. Tattooed Man came, fought here in the snow, destroyed them, took back artifact." That explained the strange dream that I had had in the hospital while I was waiting for Myers' phone call.

"He hid the artifact again. This time vampires help Cursed One. They steal artifact. Bury Guardian under mountain, but even that not kill him."

I shook my head. I had dreamed that. "No, I mean you. What happened to you?"

He shrugged. "I not important, Boy. Important thing is beat them now."

"We will," I promised.

"Only before, they wrong. They fail, and they die. Guardian kill them. Now Cursed One is smarter and stronger. He not mess up again this time. . . . Enough. I must show you more of his memories."

"I hate seeing through his eyes. It's like I'm not myself. It's like I'm actually in his head. I don't like it at all."

"Is . . . how you say . . . necessary. I understand, Boy. Is shitty feeling to be stuck in some other body's head. Now shush. You must learn."

At this point I knew the drill. I bowed down so he could place his hands on my head.

"If any consolation, inside your head is much nicer than his."

"Thanks."

Lord Machado's memories.

A giant pyramid, deep in the jungle. The midnight moon fat and heavy over us. The climb to the top of the huge, ancient thing, covered in strange, faded carvings, leaving us sweat-soaked and exhausted beneath our armor. Far removed from the conquered city, nearly two weeks deep into the trackless wilderness, and this lone edifice was the only thing to be seen.

This was the Place of Power.

The sacrifice was prepared.

Tonight was the night. Tonight the ceremony would be comp—

The vision suddenly ended. I was sitting on the steps of the church. The Old Man jerked his hands back in surprise. His eyes widened behind his glasses.

"What happened? Why did the memory stop?" I felt as if I had been on the verge of learning something. I did not know what, but something important about stopping the Cursed One.

"Boy. You must go. Great danger comes!" He grabbed

his cane, holding it in his frail hands like it was a weapon. The reaction seemed purely instinctual.

"What?" I jumped to my feet, but the imaginary world of the battle-damaged village was still as unnaturally quiet as ever. "What comes?"

"Go!" he shouted.

I woke with a start and flung the sheets aside. It was dark inside the little guest room, but I knew right where I had left my weapons. I reached down and grabbed Abomination, my finger flipped the selector down to semiauto, and I waited. The room was quiet except for my breathing and the pounding of blood in my head. I listened. The house itself was eerily silent.

"Owen."

I pointed the shotgun at the voice but froze before my finger moved to the trigger. Julie's form was silhouetted in the faint light coming from the window. I gasped and moved the muzzle aside.

"Julie? I almost shot you." I was surprised. I had not sensed her until she had spoken. She glided across the room toward me. In the dark, I could barely make out that she was wearing nothing but a small nightgown that stirred slightly in the breeze.

"What are you doing here?" I asked. It was a stupid question.

"Shh." She climbed onto the bed. She brushed the shotgun aside as she crawled over my legs, hiking up the flimsy nightgown as she went. Julie's lips sought mine, found them. She pushed me down, kissing me, running her face down my neck. Her hands pulled at my shirt, caressing the lines of scar tissue across my chest.

I responded. Clumsily I rubbed my hands over her body, feeling the silky gown slide about over her skin. I forgot about my dream, I forgot about the warning. Ever since I had met her I had wanted to be with her, but I had doubted that it would ever happen. I doubted, but apparently I had been wrong.

I was in love with Julie Shackleford, and she had come to me in the night. I did not care about anything other than that.

The breeze stung the sweat on my arms.

Breeze?

Why was my window open?

I froze. She did not stop moving against me. She licked my neck hungrily, excitedly. My throat was damp. I could not feel her breath.

She was not breathing.

Realization hit me like a ton of bricks. "NO!" I shouted as I twisted away.

Seemingly surprised at the interruption, she fought me, pushing herself down against my throat. I took my hands from her body and grabbed her by the hair. I tried to pull her head away from my neck. She was stronger than I was, impossibly strong. Using my weight and a whole lot of desperation, I rolled off of the bed and took her with me. We crashed to the floor.

Razor-white teeth flashed in the moonlight. She was still trying to bite me. I struggled, shouting for help, and she swatted me in the face. My cranium bounced off of the floorboards.

In the last minute, I had been asleep, surprised, confused, then horny, followed by terrified, but now I was just pissed off.

I hit her again and again. She jumped off of me with unnatural speed, landing on her feet. I kicked at her, but she caught my bare ankle, picked me up as if I was a child, and swung me violently into the wall. I impacted sideways, broke several boards and fell painfully to the floor.

She grabbed me by the back of my neck and jerked me to my feet. I grasped her much smaller hands and tried to pry them away; it was a futile effort. I might as well have been bending steel bars. The voice was definitely not Julie's.

"Quit fighting. You belong to me now."

The lights came on. She twisted me around so that I faced the door.

The real Julie Shackleford stood in the doorway, pistol in hand. I looked directly down the .45 caliber hole in the barrel as I heard the safety snick off. This Julie was dressed, armed, and she looked really mad.

"Stinking vamps. You heard him. No means no." She braced herself against the doorjamb, looking for a clear shot. The clamplike grip around my neck moved me into position as a human shield. I felt another hand grab onto my shoulder as the vampire peered around me. The pain was incredible, and the threat was unspoken. If Julie shot, then the undead would snap my neck.

The grip on my neck intensified, cutting off some of the blood flow to my brain. The vampire spoke. The voice sounded almost like Julie with a more pronounced accent, but somehow dusty with age, as if not used to speaking often.

"Hi, honey . . . I'm home."

Julie's jaw dropped open in surprise. She blinked several times, and shook her head. It looked like she was about to pass out from shock. The muzzle of her 1911 dipped slightly as her shooting stance fell apart.

"Mom?"

Not good, I thought to myself.

"Julie. You're all grown up. Look at you."

"Mom?" Julie refocused, the gun moved back into position. "But, but you're dead."

The vampire moved me slightly as she conversed with her daughter. "I'm not dead, honey. I'm right here. Everything is going to be just fine."

Holly appeared in the doorway, she raised her rifle and pointed it at my head as well. Now that made me real nervous. Though she was training hard and getting better, she was still a pretty lousy shot. If I had to choose between the emotionally stunned sharpshooter or the Newbie, I knew which one I wanted to take the shot. I managed to grunt out one request.

"Hol . . . let . . . Julie . . . shoot . . . ugh." The vampire shook me like a rag doll.

"Shut it, blood bag," the creature hissed. "I'm having a conversation here."

"Let him go, bitch," Holly commanded. She tucked her face down tight against the stock and peered through the sights. "Or I'll blow your brains out."

"You can't be here. You haven't been invited," Julie said. She sounded rather confused.

"This is my home," she replied. "I don't need an invitation."

"Mom. Please. This can't be happening. You disappeared. We thought you were dead."

"Come on, honey. You had to have suspected this. You knew what I was working on when I left. You never found my body." I could hear the gentle smile creep into the creature's voice, trying to once again be the loving parent. "I'm just here for your daddy," the vampire said soothingly.

"Julie, you have one fucked up family," Holly stated.

"Ack . . . Ugh . . ." I agreed.

I heard rapid speaking in the hallway, a desperate call for help. Trip stepped quickly into the room behind Holly. He still had his cell phone in one hand. He moved off to the side as he raised his subgun. Now I had three weapons pointed at my head, and the triangulation of fire was giving the vampire less room to hide. She backed up, dragging my heavy bulk along easily. We were backed into a corner.

"Mom. How could you become . . . become one of them?" Julie asked plaintively.

"I didn't have much choice, dear. But once you get used to it, it is wonderful. I can do things that you can't even imagine. I can feel things that would stop your heart if you experienced them. I have eternal youth and beauty. Come with me. . . . We can take your daddy. The change will be good for him. It will fix his mind. We can be a family again."

"Never," Julie said with determination. Her brown eyes narrowed as she concentrated on her front sight.

"Suit yourself, dear. But it beats being a rotting piece of meat . . . like your boyfriend here is going to be if you don't back the hell off of me." She picked me up off of the ground. I cringed as my vertebrae popped. All pretenses of motherly love vanished. "I didn't want to kill you, honey, but if you push me, then I don't have a choice. I'm taking your daddy back no matter what."

"You got three guns on you. Kind of stupid to be making demands," Holly said. The vampire hissed at her. "I hate vampires, sister, give me a reason."

"I'm a Master now. I'm a queen in my world. You can't even begin to understand what I can do. This is your last chance."

"You're too young to be a Master," Julie stated calmly. She stayed framed in the doorway. The other two slowly began to spread out even further. Holly looked angry. Trip looked scared but determined. Fingers moved onto triggers. Somebody was going to shoot at any second. I could feel it. I tried to make myself as small a target as possible. That is very difficult if you happen to look like me.

"Too young? Am I now? Poor kid. Just like your dad. Nose always in a book, thinking that you understand what's really going on. I was a Hunter once myself. I know what you know. And let me tell you, you're wrong. It isn't about time, honey, it's about the blood. The power is in the blood that makes you, and in the blood that you take. I was made by the strongest of them all, and I've taken so much blood and so many lives that you can't even begin to understand. I have swum in rivers of it. I've torn the life out of ten thousand beating hearts, and *you will be next*. Now give me your FATHER!" She shouted so loudly that dust shook from the ceiling and all of the humans in the room flinched.

Gretchen appeared in the hallway, short and cloaked in her burkha, armed only with what looked like a stick. She pointed at me and said a single word in a rumble almost as deep as her husband's. "Pocket."

I reached down, cringing against the pressure on my neck, trying hard to focus and maintain consciousness, my hand touched my pants pocket. There was something inside. I reached in. My fingers felt the lumpy texture of poorly whittled wood. The Old Man's handmade toy.

It could not be there, but it was.

Without thinking, I pulled the impossible little carving out, and stuck it firmly against the hard fingers pressing into my neck. The toy disintegrated in a flash. The undead thing that used to be Susan Shackleford screamed when it touched her, an unbearable howl of burning agony. I was dropped to the ground as her hand burst into blue flames. I hit the floor and rolled away as the other three Hunters reacted and started pulling triggers.

It was the first time that I had seen more than a darkened silhouette of my midnight visitor. She really did look like Julie, but possibly even more hauntingly beautiful, ethereal, even stunning. Pale skin, dark hair, eyes that you could drown in, but then the resemblance stopped. For vampires were unnatural creatures, and right now this one was distracted by a burning hand, long fangs revealed in a frozen scream. A split-second snapshot of confusion and pain, and then the bullets hit.

Impact after impact tore into the creature, spraying black fluids across the room. Holes appeared in the wall behind as bullets passed through tissues and shattered bones. I scrambled for my shotgun as the uninhibited blasts assaulted and damaged my hearing. I grabbed Abomination, swung it around, and still sitting on the floor, fired a nine-round magazine of buckshot into the creature. One hundred and eight silver pellets struck her body in less than a second and a half, and at that limited range, most of them were still impacting as a solid penetrating mass.

The room was filled with drifting smoke from burning flesh and gunpowder. Brass tinkled, steel and plastic thumped on the floor as the four of us simultaneously dropped our spent magazines. I fumbled toward my armor and ammo pouches. Susan Shackleford was pressed solidly into the riddled corner, torn asunder, leaking black fluids, and broken by the carnage that we had unleashed. The flame on her hand gradually died down as she studied it through her shattered visage, seemingly in fascination. The creature stood upright. Her flesh had been pulverized and stripped from her bones.

She laughed at us. A long hard laugh, as if we had provided some serious entertainment. "Hunters are even more pathetic than I remember. I'm a *Master* now. Don't you understand what that means?" Almost instantly her flesh was whole and white. I blinked, trying to understand how exactly that worked according to the laws of physics. She smiled widely, fangs gleaming. "You can't kill me."

"But we can try," Julie answered as she dropped the slide on a fresh magazine . She snapped the pistol up and shot her mother right between the eyes. The creature's smiling face rocked back briefly. I locked in a fresh magazine of buckshot, but before I could fire, the vampire moved in a blur of speed, crossing the room in a split second, almost too fast to track. Holly was knocked easily aside. Julie's hands were jerked over her head as the vampire grabbed her.

"I offered you immortality, honey. That was not a choice. I'm going to give it to you whether you want it or not," the vampire said in her sweet Southern belle voice. I snapped my shotgun up, but stopped, fearful of striking Julie. Trip's UMP was reloaded, and he had a clean angle. He lifted the gun to fire, but it was torn out of his surprised hands. The vampire had moved so quickly that I had not even seen it strike. "You can either come back as a dimwitted slave, or you can partake of my blood and taste of my power."

Julie struggled to release herself. "Never!" she shouted.

A small black flash charged in from the hallway. Gretchen screamed some sort of battle cry. She shook a narrow stick above her head, complete with feathers, leather braids, and what looked like a shrunken head. The vampire hissed, let go of Julie, and retreated back into the room. Gretchen pursued, still shaking her totem and shouting in her strange gravel-voiced language. The vampire fell back, cringing and recoiling, until it struck the wall.

"Holy symbol!" Holly shouted as she aimed her Vepr and pulled the trigger. The roar of the .308 was tremendous in the enclosed space. If I lived through this I was probably going to be deaf. The bullet tore into the vampire's side. The rest of us followed suit, firing over and around Gretchen, who continued to wave the stick and hold the vampire back. I emptied my second magazine in a heartbeat, and grabbed another one. My hands were a blur as I reloaded. Our lives depended on putting some hurt into the evil thing, and I moved faster than I ever had before.

Abomination barked again and again as I put solid silver slugs into the monster.

Susan Shackleford disappeared. More holes were torn into the already damaged wall before we realized and stopped shooting. One moment she had been there, the next she was gone. The shredded nightgown fell to the floor and lay in a puddle of black ooze. A thick gray mist spiraled slowly out of the open window.

"Did she just turn into fog?" Trip asked.

"I didn't know they could really do that," Holly said.

"We didn't think they could," Julie answered. "Hey, that was my nightie."

"What?" I shouted. I was the only poor fool who had not been wearing their electronic earplugs.

"Reload. She's going to go for my dad."

That I understood. I did not have time to put on my whole suit of armor, so I threw the chest webbing on and buckled the pistol belt over that. At least I was going to have lots of ammo and a big honking knife. Gretchen pulled a leather pouch from under her burkha, dipped her gloved finger in and pulled out a blob of purple goo. She stuck it into my ears. It was cold and disgusting. After seeing what she had done with the road rash, however, I wasn't going to protest.

"I called Earl. Help is on the way." Trip kicked his broken UMP. "We're gonna need bigger guns."

"My room's on the way. Let's go." Julie led the way into the hall, gun outstretched. "Where's Grant?" she shouted back over her shoulder.

"Haven't seen him," Holly answered.

"His turn to be on guard. She probably killed him

already. Bitch. Damn it!" Julie raged. "Come on." I had thought that I had seen her angry before, but I had been wrong. "Trip, grab some hardware out of my room. Hurry."

"What should I get?"

"Use your imagination! Now go!" She sprinted down the hall. I was right behind her. I was barefoot. The hardwood was cold under my soles. I pushed past Julie as we approached the door to her father's room. There was no time for subtlety. I lowered one shoulder and with a roar I smashed into the heavy portal. It flew open as the frame broke under the impact.

Some *thing* was waiting for us, standing on the bed over the still form of Ray Shackleford.

Julie's mother had changed into something horrible, something out of a bad nightmare. Her false cloak of humanity had been shed and now we could look upon the true face of a Master vampire. Her body had twisted and elongated, gray skin stretched tight over twitching muscles as she swiveled her long neck toward us, her eyes were solid red, and her mouth opened to reveal incisors as long as fingers and sharper than knives. Her beautiful features had contorted back, ears lengthened and swept up, I could see how the vampire legends had come to include bats.

She had Ray by the wrist, she tugged and the hand-cuff chain snapped. She snarled at us as we entered. "You don't learn, do you?" Her voice had changed, becoming deeper and more animalistic. I raised my shotgun and fired. The slug struck her in the chest and exploded out the other side. I fired again as she hopped off of the bed, dragging Ray with her. The vampire grabbed the heavy wrought-iron frame and effortlessly hurled it toward us, several hundred pounds of furniture turned into a missile. The bed struck and I was hurled backwards into the hall. I crashed into Julie, and we both sprawled to the floor.

I opened my eyes. Julie was lying inches away, profile crushed painfully against the floor. "We have to shoot my dad," she cried as she tried to rise. "Don't let her take him."

"Got it," Holly stated as she stepped over us. The bed was lying sideways, blocking the doorway. She raised her Vepr over the obstacle and fired wildly into the room, emptying the twenty-round magazine in an instant. I surged to my feet and pushed the bed out of the way, Abomination held in one hand, ready to shoot as soon as I had a target.

There was nothing but a hole in the floor. Boards had been pulverized into sawdust, and the creature had dropped through, taking Ray with her.

"Aw hell," I said. If Ray fell into the hands of the Cursed One, the world was pretty much screwed. I could see no movement down the dark hole.

"Don't let her take him. Do whatever you have to do," Julie ordered. She stepped to the edge of the ragged hole, knelt down, and without hesitation began to descend. Tactically it was a stupid move to crawl blindly after a superpowerful undead, but we did not have any choice other than pursuit. She looked up at me before she dropped into the opening. I could not tell if her features were betraying fear or sadness. She disappeared into the dark hole.

"Clear!" she shouted.

I followed. My torso barely fit through the jagged opening, I leveraged myself down as best as possible, dangled from my fingertips, and then bent my knees and dropped the last four feet. I landed with a thud. Julie flipped the lights on. We were in the guest bedroom that had served as Gretchen's hospital. We were alone.

"Split up. Find them," she shouted up through the hole. "You three take the stairs."

"But if we split up, we're easy targets."

"Doesn't matter, we just need to stay alive long enough to kill Dad." She sounded desperate. "I'll head for the kitchen, you take the family room. Hurry."

"All right." I wanted to tell her to be careful. I wanted to tell her to stay alive. I wanted to tell her to be reasonable, and let me stay with her. But there was just no time. I fled the room, turning the lights on as I went. The mansion was huge, and the impossibly fast creature could be anywhere, or she could have already have fled.

No. She was going to stay and finish her work tonight. She had said that she was going to take Julie, and give her the gift of twisted immortality. Somehow I knew that Susan was still here in her ancestral home. She was here. I could feel it, and she had the one person who could help the Cursed One. I had to kill Ray before he could talk.

The doors to the family room crashed open when I kicked them with my bare foot. I swept in fast, shotgun at the ready. I activated the flashlight. I had no idea where the light switch was in the large room. Dozens of Shackleford faces stared down at me from their portraits. I stabbed the beam quickly into each corner, across furniture and construction in progress, and remembering my lessons from the *Antoine-Henri*, I shined the light on the ceiling as well. Nothing.

I ran for the next set of doors. The ballroom. I did not really know what I was going to do if I stumbled across the enemy. She had moved so quickly that I could scarcely believe my own eyes. Hopefully I would have time to blow Ray's brains out before Susan tore my head off. I really wished that I had Gretchen and her faith right about then. I knew that I did not have time to gain religion in the next few seconds, but it sure would have been nice.

The doors opened. I stepped quickly into the ancient ballroom. I heard a noise, something wet and slurping. I shined the Surefire light across the walls. The old-fashioned mirrors reflected the brilliant beam, over and over, refracting seemingly without end from all of the reflective surfaces. Even the chandelier was briefly lit. My reflection stared back at me from twenty mirrors, but there was another reflection as well. Ray Shackleford was in the center of the room, legs sprawled on the floor, head tilted back and mouth lifelessly open, torso slowly rocking, unsupported at an impossible angle as if he were held up with wires. I turned to face the center of the dance floor.

He was not unsupported at all. Vampires just didn't cast reflections. His wife held him, cradled in her arms. She was in human form again, squatting, with her naked back toward me. She was feeding from Ray's neck. She stopped drinking when the beam struck her. Susan lifted her dripping face and kissed her husband tenderly on the forehead, leaving a crimson lip imprint, before letting him drop limply to the ground. She looked at me and smiled. Her eyes reflected the light like a cat. She licked the blood from her lips.

"We have some unfinished business, you and I."

She wiped her forearm across her face, and smeared blood down her bare chest. She strode wantonly toward me. I was terrified. I snapped Abomination to my shoulder, aimed at Ray's brain cage, and squeezed the trigger. It might have been murder, but the fate of the world was at stake.

Nothing happened.

I could feel the texture of the metal beneath the joint of my finger, but it wouldn't respond. I concentrated, but I could not force myself to pull the trigger. My hand would not respond to my brain. I could feel her presence, boring into me, her iron will testing itself against mine. She walked right into the gun, putting the muzzle directly between her breasts and over her heart. I could not fire. My body was frozen. I could not even move.

"You are a strong one," she told me, "but your human will is no match for mine." She dragged one fingernail under my eye, opening the skin and spilling blood down my cheek. A black presence pushed against my conscious mind, probing it violently, relentlessly. "Tell me, how did you hurt me? How did you burn me? Nothing can inflict pain upon a Master, but that did."

I tried to speak through rigidly clenched jaws. I fought a battle inside my skull, a fiercer fight than anything I had ever experienced before, a struggle for the very control of my body. The black weight pressed down hard, and unfortunately for me, this was an unfamiliar battleground.

"Tell me your secret, Hunter. Tell me and I will give you a gift. I can see it in your mind, the very thing you desire most." She smiled seductively. "Let go of your secrets, join me, and I will give you my daughter. She can be yours forever."

The blackness encroached into my vision, I could feel the tendrils of her power crawling deep into my mind, and I was powerless to stop it. I did not know how to defeat something with no physical body. Pain began to emanate from my skull, rippling down my paralyzed spine, and searing every nerve in agony. I fought on, I did not know how, but I knew that I fought.

"I just have to say, Hunter, you have the strongest will of any mortal I have ever encountered. You'll make a good servant for Lord Machado." I watched in horror as her razor fangs extended. I knew what was going to come next. She would rip me open and drain my blood. Either she would let me just die to rise again as a near mindless undead, or she would open her own veins and force me to partake of her blood, and I would become a horrible beast in her image. I despaired, but I fought on.

Boy. Let me help.

I heard the comforting voice of the Old Man. Suddenly I had hope. Something else joined my internal struggle, another presence took up the fight, the blackness paused, and was then overwhelmed and pushed aside. I gasped in relief as my muscles unlocked.

Susan stopped, her teeth hovering centimeters from my throat. "How—"

Abomination cut her off as a solid ounce of silver exploded through her black heart. She stumbled in surprise. I felt the Old Man's presence leave my body to continue his assault against her mind.

"You want my secrets?" *BOOM. BOOM.* I shot her

twice through the face. "You really want to know?" *BOOM. BOOM.* I shot her in the throat and chin. "There is no secret. . ." *BOOM.* A slug pierced through her brain, rocking her back. "I just hate monsters!" *CLICK.* I released the silver bayonet. It locked into place with a snap. "So go to hell . . ." I slammed the broad blade through her torso and released the shotgun as I reached for my knife. "And die . . ." *THWACK.* The ganga ram's blade embedded halfway through her throat, lodging against her hardened spine. Black fluids and fresh red blood geysered forth. "You evil bitch!" I wrenched the big blade violently free.

She grabbed my shotgun and pulled the blade out. Abomination was still slung to my body. She swung it around and I was dragged along. I was launched hard across the dance floor. I crashed and skidded, coming to a stop next to Ray Shackleford. The big, red lip prints on his forehead would have looked silly if our situation had not been so deadly serious.

Susan twisted her head around as her wounds closed. I had not even slowed her down. She changed right before my eyes, lengthening, thickening, twisting into the gray killing machine that we had seen upstairs. Her brown eyes, so like Julie's, filled with blood and turned into red pools of hate. I could feel the Old Man's presence in the room with us, but after his initial surprise, he had nothing to offer against this creature.

I got to my knees as I pulled my STI and placed the .45 against Ray's temple. He looked up at me weakly, and nodded. The vampire paused, pulsing and seething in its killing rage.

"Stop or I'll waste him. Even you aren't that fast." I had about two and a half pounds of pressure on the three-pound trigger. I felt her will intrude against my own, but this time I was ready. I knew what was coming. I cannot explain the mechanism of it, but her attack was thwarted. This time my will was mine and mine alone.

"Mom!" Julie called from the entrance. An ominous hum emanated from the lit flamethrower in her hands. "Your invitation has been revoked. Get the hell out of *my* house!" She depressed the trigger.

The vampire was engulfed in a spray of pressurized napalm. The stream of jellified gasoline exploded in a wall of intense heat, setting the floor afire, and shattering several of the antique mirrors under the assault. I grabbed Ray by the collar and pulled him away as burning fuel splashed in every direction.

Trip appeared on the balcony above. "Run, Z!" he shouted as he leveled the grenade launcher at the inferno. He at least waited long enough for me to be out of the blast radius before launching a high explosive round into the floor at the monster's feet. The concussion was horrendous. The priceless chandelier fell from its mounting and crashed to earth, flying into millions of separate shards.

Susan's burning body was flung against the far wall, shattering the glass doors to the veranda. Julie kept up a constant spray of napalm. Even the mightiest queen of the undead could not regenerate under that onslaught. The vampire smashed through the glass. I picked up Abomination and fired a grenade after her. My aim was off, but it was close enough to shred the burning flesh from her bones.

I heard Trip shouting. "Backblast! Backblast!" I looked up in time to see Holly steadying her RPG over her shoulder. Firing that with her back against a wall would probably be immediately fatal.

"Oh yeah," she said, "damn it!" She threw the rocket-propelled grenade aside and retrieved her rifle. And she had been so looking forward to blasting something with it.

Julie followed her mother, keeping up the onslaught of fire and burning fuel. The ballroom was burning now, and it was spreading up the walls and toward the ceiling. The house was going up. She finally stopped, and the flamethrower's stream died off to a small flame.

Her mother was on the burning veranda, a charred and curled skeleton, flesh turned to ash. The creature crumbled as it tried to move, revealing blackened and twisted bones. She slowly stood, ash falling away, new flesh and tissues already pulsing underneath.

"Won't you just die already?" Julie screamed. She was crying. My heart went out to her. Her home was burning down, and her undead mother was intent on drinking her blood. It was a really crappy evening by any standard.

Then something strange happened. One second the room was burning, fire licking around us, scalding us with intense heat, and the next second it just stopped. The flames were extinguished, leaving only smoking embers. The temperature dropped at least seventy degrees almost instantly, as if we had just stepped into a walk-in freezer. My breath came out in a cloud of ice vapor. The remaining mirrors fogged up and cracked.

"What the hell is happening?" Holly asked quietly, her voice trembling.

I did not know. But I took the opportunity to reload a fresh grenade into Abomination's underslung launcher. My fingers fumbled clumsily, suddenly nerve-deadened by the cold. I shivered, and my teeth began to clatter together. A horrible feeling of dread traveled down my spine.

"Who's that?" Trip asked. His tone betrayed his fear.

I looked up in time to see a second figure appear on the veranda. This one was a gaunt man, with greasily slicked back hair, and a narrow hatchet face. He was wearing a full-length trench coat. His bearing was ramrod straight, his movements were unnaturally sharp and crisp. The tall man paused beside the scorched vampire. He stood at parade rest. It was the lead vampire from my dream. Lord Machado's lieutenant. Susan's blackened form bowed before him. He placed one gloved hand on her head.

"You have failed me, Susan. I am most displeased." His voice was deep and had a precise German or Austrian accent.

I could still feel the Old Man's presence in the ballroom. The ghost surged with anger toward the new intruder.

"Forgive me, Jaeger," she rasped. Her vocal cords had been burned seconds before, and she could barely speak. "I didn't kill them. But I have learned of the Place. My husband told me."

"Excellent." He patted Susan on the head, scattering ashes from her skull. Then he turned his attention on us. "You are in luck that I do not have an invitation. Be warned. Do not trifle in our affairs. Or it will be your death." The Master vampire looked upwards as he heard something. The perimeter alarm sounded.

Helicopter blades beat in the distance. Company was on the way.

He glared at me in particular. "If it isn't Byreika and his oafish friend." I could feel the hate emanating from the Old Man toward the vampire. It was almost a physical thing. "You are out of your league, *Juden*. I am surprised at your resourcefulness. None of the others that have been used have been able to come back to this world. You ever surprise me, but in the end, you are nothing."

We will see, Nazi bastard son of bitch.

The hatchet-faced vampire smiled, showing us his razor teeth. "You amuse me, Old Man. Your kind always has. . . . Come, Susan. We have much work to do." He faded into the darkness and was gone. The temperature slowly began to climb to normal levels.

Susan Shackleford was whole once again. She brushed back her hair, knocking the remaining ashes free. The beautiful vampire was savagely angry.

"You will be mine again, honey. Just you wait."

"Don't call me honey. You're not really my mom."

"Whatever you have to tell yourself to keep the nightmares away, honey. I love you." She slowly backed into the shadows, fading away until only her eyes were visible. She blinked and they too were gone into the night.

CHAPTER 20

I knelt at Ray Shackleford's side. He had been savagely bitten and torn open. I pressed my hands against his neck to try to staunch the flow of blood, but it just kept pouring out.

"I'm sorry," he rasped.

"Just relax. You're going to be okay," I lied. His pulse was very weak. "Gretchen!" I screamed.

"Susan. She took it from my mind. I couldn't stop her." He groaned in pain.

"Dad." Julie fell to her knees, the super-hot flame-thrower clattering to the floor next to her.

"Oh, honey, I'm so sorry." He coughed, and blood bubbled from his lips. "I never wanted to hurt anyone. I just loved her so much. I couldn't let her go."

"It's okay, Dad," she gasped, grabbing his hands. Tears cut a path down her soot-blackened face.

"I didn't know . . . vampire . . . that's why the spell failed." He was growing weaker. "Forgive me."

"I forgive you," she cried. "I forgive you. Just hang on."

Gretchen appeared. She pushed me aside and pressed a cloth against Ray's savaged throat. She wiped away enough blood to get a good look and then she immediately went to work with a small kit of primitive tools. I backed away, so as not to disturb the healer in her work. Trip and Holly were standing back, watching the veranda, weapons at the ready. The helicopters were louder now.

"We have company," Holly said. "Feds."

"Listen . . . the Place . . . Natchy Bottom."

"Mississippi?" I asked. Milo had warned us briefly about it during our trip to visit the Elves.

"Yes . . . Deep down . . . Hidden . . . Talk to the Wendigo." He closed his eyes. Gretchen looked up at Julie and shook her head slowly. "Julie . . . I love you." His voice was barely audible. "I'm so sorry."

"I love you too, Dad," she whispered. Only minutes before, she had been prepared to kill him, but now at the moment of his incipient death, she had to confront her feelings for her father. My heart ached for her.

The helicopters were overhead. Searchlights stabbed down onto the property as federal agents fast-roped onto the grounds. A loudspeaker boomed as directions were shouted at us. "Drop your weapons. Do not move." An Apache hovered low, beating the air, causing the broken remains of the veranda doors to rock closed. The 30mm chain gun was aimed directly at us.

We had no choice but to comply. I removed Abomination and pushed it away, then unbuckled the pistol belt and set it aside as well. Trip and Holly did as they were told. Julie was still holding her father's hand.

"Julie. Toss your gun." I did not know if the Feds would just blast the whole house, but I didn't want to provoke them. "Hey. Julie. Listen to me." She snapped out of it and angrily slid her pistol away. Black-clad troopers were approaching rapidly, guns leveled at us, flashlights pointing into our eyes.

"What do we do?" Trip asked. Julie did not answer. She just looked sullenly down at her dying father. I did not know what was going through her mind.

"Do what they say."

I had a feeling it was about to get ugly.

The Feds hit the house hard and fast. Windows shattered as flash-bang grenades were thrown in. Doors were smashed open with handheld battering rams or blown off their hinges with shotgun breaching rounds. The Monster Control agents swarmed over us, shouting orders, and forcing us to the ground. I fared a bit better than the last time I had encountered them. The boot placed on my neck was not nearly as heavy as the last one.

"We have an injured man," shouted one of the troopers. "It's Shackleford. Send the medic."

Gretchen howled in pain as one of the Feds booted her aside.

"Hey! She's a doctor!" Trip shouted. He pushed against the Feds that were trying to handcuff him. The first blow landed directly behind his ear, sending him sprawling back to his knees. He was clubbed to the ground in a flurry of rifle butts, and then stomped and kicked into submission. *Assholes.*

A trooper who must have been a medic dealt with Ray. From my position on the ground I could make eye contact with Julie. She was sobbing, looking at her father's still form, years of pent-up emotion all let free in a horrible moment of violence.

"Building secured," stated one of the troopers. "Opening up the perimeter." The noise level died off as the helicopters banked hard and away, covering more area, searching for vampires. I knew that they weren't going to find anything.

"We have another Hunter in the house. He's probably dead or injured," Julie shouted at the Feds, thinking of the missing Grant.

"Lieutenant, medevac Shackleford out of here. Get this one up," ordered a familiar voice. I was pulled up so that I could look into the stern face of Special Agent Myers. His personal attack dog, Agent Franks, stood behind him. Once again Myers was dressed in his cheap suit. The other agents were geared up in all of their body armor. "Pitt, what's going on here?"

"Vampires. They came for Ray," I answered truthfully, as Ray's limp form was carried out on a stretcher to a waiting Blackhawk. He did not look good, and if he was not already dead, I knew that he soon would be. If his injuries didn't kill him, standard operating procedure that I was well familiar with meant the Feds would take care of him.

"Where is the Place? Did you learn about the Place?" Myers shouted at me.

I did not know if I should mention it. I had been mistreated at their hands enough times that I had real doubts about how much I could trust them at all. On the other hand, somebody had to stop the Cursed One, and they were probably better equipped to do it than us.

"Talk," he ordered. "This is serious business."

"I know, Myers. Damn it. It's in . . ."

"Owen. Don't tell them!" Julie shouted. One of

the troopers kicked her in the ribs. She cried out in pain.

"Stop that!" I shouted. Franks brushed past Myers and slugged me in the side of the face. It was brutally hard. My head snapped back on my neck, and I was only kept from falling by the Feds that held my arms.

"Tell us where, Mr. Pitt!" Myers shouted. "We're at condition red. None of you have any civil rights at this moment, so we will beat it out of you if necessary. The clock is ticking." Franks punched me in the stomach. My abdominal muscles seized up in agony and I wheezed for air. The man could certainly throw a punch. I swear that he had to beat on sides of beef like Rocky or something to develop a punch like that. I did not know why Julie did not want me to tell them about Natchy Bottom, but if she said not to, I trusted her. I knew this was going to hurt.

"Kiss off, Myers. I ain't telling you shit," I gasped. WHAM. That hit compressed my stomach back into my spine. He hit me hard enough to make my dog bleed. And I don't even own a dog.

"Myers. You were MHI once. You can't do this," Julie pleaded.

"Why not, Julie?" he retorted. "Don't you understand what is at stake here?"

"The fate of the world," she answered. "Yes, we know."

"So just tell us where to go and we'll be waiting for him." He sounded very reasonable. I couldn't breathe.

"Sanctuary," she answered.

Myers scowled. Franks' dark features drew up in

confusion, obviously an emotion he didn't like so he hit me again just to be on the safe side. I wheezed in agony.

Franks pulled back and cracked his knuckles one-handed. At least I had succeeded in making his hands sore. "What's sanctuary?"

"They cut deals with some monsters," Myers answered. "Sometimes they find something they decide isn't really bad, even though it's on the PUFF list. They let it go. They even hide them from us. Grant them sanctuary if you will. Like this thing here." He gestured rudely toward Gretchen. "Her kind are fair game."

"If you hurt her, I swear I'll kill you," I told Myers.

Franks raised an eyebrow, ready to make good on the organ donor sticker on my driver's license. Myers put one small hand on the other agent's thick arm. Franks looked disappointed.

"No need, Mr. Pitt. I'm no monster. She isn't any threat." He sounded sincere. "I'm just a man trying to serve my country. Right now you people are standing in my way of doing that." He addressed Julie. "Listen, I'll give you my word. Whatever you have living at the Place, we'll leave it alone. We're just after Lord Machado."

Julie appeared to think about it. She winced under the weight of the Feds pushing down on her and put aside the pain of her new knowledge about her mother's fate and her father's apparent death. Finally she spoke, and when she did she was utterly calm. "I'll tell you everything I know. But you have to leave MHI alone. Get out of the compound. Let us do our jobs. You can have the Place, you can be ready for the Cursed One. Give me your word that you'll leave

the sanctuary alone and you're welcome to the rest."
I could see why she was the one that took care of
the company's contract negotiations.

"No," Myers stated flatly. "Your gang of misfits is
done as far as I'm concerned. Aiding and abetting a
fugitive. Nope. MHI is finished. Once again, Monster
Hunting is a government responsibility, just like it
should be."

"You bastard," she spat. "We didn't turn my dad
over because we thought you had a leak to the Cursed
One."

"That's absurd," he replied. Which was true enough.
The bad guys did not need information from us or
the Feds to know about Ray, not when his own wife
was working for the other team. Fat lot of good that
knowledge did us now. "Look. I don't like this at all.
I'm not a violent person, but we don't have time for
your games." He nodded toward his subordinate with
obvious distaste. "Agent Franks. Do what you have to
do. We need to know where the Place is."

"Yes, sir." The dark man looked at me emotionlessly.
It was going to be a long night. Just then Myers'
radio crackled.

"Delta team. This is Bravo. There's a car approaching,
high rate of speed. Should we fire on it? Over."

"Negative. Intercept at the gate," he replied. "Expecting company?" he asked Julie.

"No. Just the vampire that ransacked my home and
killed my dad," she stated flatly.

The radio again: "Sir, it appears to be some of the
Hunters from the MHI compound."

"Who?" Myers asked.

"Earl Harbinger and a few others. He's out of

the vehicle and approaching the entrance. Moving to intercept."

"Arrest them," Myers responded. "Be careful; Harbinger is extremely dangerous."

Julie made eye contact with me. She mouthed the words, "Get Ready." I nodded slightly. I did not know what was coming, but I was not going to let her down. I was not cuffed, but I had a Fed on each arm. So far I had not resisted, and they were merely holding me up to be Franks' punching bag. There was another trooper by Julie, one by Gretchen, and as far as I could tell, three on Trip and Holly. All of them were well trained, heavily armed, and looking for an excuse to shoot us.

Everyone was startled as automatic gunfire erupted from the front of the house. Franks looked in that direction as his hand moved toward his holstered Glock. He did not see my bare foot sailing towards his crotch. I kicked him hard. Too bad he was wearing armor. I brought my foot down, and used my leverage and brute strength to swing the two Feds holding my arms into each other. They collided in an armored mass. I smashed an elbow into the first one's jaw, and broke the second Fed's nose with a left jab. They both went down.

The room exploded into confusion. The agent kneeling on Julie screamed in pain and fell over. Franks recovered with a small grimace and charged me. The other Feds went for their guns. We were about to get killed.

The door exploded inward and two agents were hurled through, landing and rolling painfully across the floor. Harbinger came in fast, charging directly into the agents standing over Trip and Holly. He went swiftly into the path of their rising muzzles. He attacked, dodged between the guns, struck the agents down with his bare hands, batted aside a rifle, grasped the final Fed by his web gear and slung him back into the wall with a horrible crash.

I had never seen a man move that quickly.

Distracted by Harbinger's superhuman display, I did not see Franks' movement. He forced his palm into my face, pushing me off balance. He bladed off, protecting his right side, going for his pistol. I struggled forward, trying to reach his gun hand. Time slowed down. The pistol came up and out of the holster.

"Stop! Stop!" screamed Myers.

Franks froze. His Glock held in a tight, low, retention position. Finger on the trigger. Indexed directly at my sternum. His eyes were locked on mine. If I moved at all, I was dead.

Julie was still lying on the floor, but had rolled far enough to reach the flamethrower. It was humming, pointed at Myers' legs. The agent that she had knocked over had pressed his pistol into her back. Harbinger stood over the stunned forms of the other downed Feds. The Fed by Gretchen was holding his leg where her totem stick had stabbed him. Unfortunately he had raised his G36 and it was pointed at Gretchen's head. I could not see most of the Feds' expressions behind their black balaclavas, but I imagined that they were about as tense as I was. If one person twitched wrong, a whole bunch of us were going to get shot or immolated. It was the most screwed-up Mexican stand-off I had ever seen.

Another Fed entered the room, hands held above

his head, Sam Haven pushing close behind with the muzzle of his pistol screwed into the back of the agent's neck just under the helmet.

"Nobody move or I'll waste this punk!" Sam shouted. He paused as he studied the complicated situation, before shrugging and spitting some tobacco juices. "Oh . . . never mind. Y'all are ahead of me." He sounded rather disappointed.

"Don't spit on the floor, you ape!" Julie ordered. It may have been scorched and blasted with shrapnel, but it was still her house.

Harbinger's hands were empty of weapons, but after the display of physical prowess I had just seen, nobody was in a hurry to mess with him. Five Feds lay on the ground moaning or whimpering. He shouted down the hallway he had entered from, "Milo! How you doing?"

"Hurry up. There's like a hundred Feds coming this way. And they looked pissed!"

"Myers. Turn on your damn phone," Harbinger commanded. "Do it now."

The Fed complied. He slowly reached into the pocket of his suit, pulled out the phone and turned it on. Immediately we all heard that annoying "Take Me Out to the Ball Game."

"I hate that ring," I said, as I looked over Franks' Glock.

"Me too," he agreed, not letting the gun waver at all.

"I shut it off when we landed. It's kind of distracting on a raid," Myers said defensively as he pushed the button to answer it. "This is Agent Myers."

"Yes, I will hold for . . ." The senior agent sounded

surprised. "Oh . . . Hello, sir . . . Sorry . . . I apologize . . . Yes, sir . . . Yes, sir . . . But this is outside the regular chain of command . . ." We heard half of the conversation. Myers seemed remarkably collected considering Julie had the flamethrower pointed at him. The agent pointing the rifle at Gretchen looked a little shaky. I hoped this did not take long. "But, sir . . . But . . . But . . . We can . . . But . . . Yes, sir . . . I understand . . ." We waited for the conversation to end. "Understood . . . Good-bye, sir."

He refolded the phone and dropped it back into this pocket.

"Stand down," he shouted. "Everybody stand down." The guns in the ballroom slowly began to lower. Sam pulled his Sig 220 out of the back of the agent's neck. Julie set the flamethrower down.

"Tell the guys outside that too!" Milo blurted from down the hall. "There's a big black helicopter looking at me!"

Myers spoke into the radio. "Stand down. All units stand down. That is an order."

Tense moments passed as everyone complied. Franks was the last to do so. With the Glock still pointing at my heart he told me simply "I'll get to kill you one of these days." He slowly lowered the weapon and reholstered.

"Take a number," I replied.

"Well, Harbinger. I'm surprised," Myers said. He looked flustered and angry. He still reminded me of a professor, only now he looked like one who had just found out his tenure had been denied. "That's outside the chain of command, but you know I'm not going to go against a cabinet-level appointee."

"You heard him," Harbinger stated shortly. "We have a truce. Y'all can get the hell out of here."

"For now. As soon as I get orders from the Director, he's going to be overridden, and then I'm going to arrest every single one of you for assaulting federal agents and aiding and abetting a fugitive."

"I figure that will probably take more than forty-eight hours. So by then either the world is going to be destroyed or this is all a moot point. Until then you have your orders," Harbinger said coldly. "You can take the Place. We clean up the local infestations. We tell you what we know. You leave us alone."

The senior agent appeared to mull that over. The idea seemed to leave a bad taste in his mouth. "Fine. For now . . ." Myers said coldly. "We'll see about that in the long term, Earl."

I moved to help Julie stand. She looked shaky. Her wound had reopened, but there was not too much blood. She pushed me away. "I'm okay," she said.

"Bull," I stated. "Let me help you." I took her by the arm.

"All units. We're clear. Hold your fire. Prepare to pull out," Myers ordered into the radio. The Feds attended to their injured. The five men that Harbinger had attacked were all stirring, though some looked to be nursing broken bones. "You better not have seriously hurt any of my men," he told Harbinger. "I don't care how important some people think you are, Earl, I'll personally make sure your special status is revoked, and I'll see to it you rot in prison forever."

"I didn't hurt them too bad," Harbinger said simply. He spread his hands innocently, though he could not mask his predatory confidence. Somehow he had moved, weaponless, through a crowd of ready and armed men, and beaten down any of them that stood in his way. "They shouldn't have tried to stop me."

I remembered how Harbinger had saved me from Darné. At the time I had assumed that it had just been some sort of pro Monster Hunting trick, but after watching him dispatch the Feds with relative ease, I knew that something else was going on. "Just what the hell is he?" I said softly into Julie's ear. Somehow Harbinger heard me from across the room. He winked.

"It's a long story," she replied brusquely. "Earl, Grant's missing. Dad's dead."

"No," Harbinger said. His face fell. "Aw hell."

"My men have not reported any other Hunters on the premises," Myers said. "They probably took your man."

"Milo?" Harbinger shouted.

"I'm not getting Grant's signal on GPS. It's either broke or disabled. . . . He was wearing his armor, right?"

"Yes. He was on guard duty," she shouted back down the hall.

"Sorry, Julie. I've got nothing."

"He will be avenged," Sam told her. The big cowboy was solemn. "I promise."

"If it's any consolation, I'm sorry. But we're wasting time," Myers stated. "I need a Place, and I need it now. You have my word. Whatever *thing* you have hiding out there, we won't bother it."

"Deal," Harbinger said. "Julie?"

"Somewhere inside Natchy Bottom, Mississippi," she told the room after an instant of hesitation. She would have to grieve later. "You know about it?"

"Yes. We know it," the senior agent replied. "Bad place. Where though? That's a lot of swamp to cover."

"Dad said that it was hidden. You need to talk to the Wendigo to find out where."

"Impossible," Myers said. "Those are just Indian fairy tales."

"Nope," Harbinger said. "The Bottoms belong to him. We have an understanding."

"Fine. We'll handle it. You and your thugs can clean up the local undead outbreaks," Myers snapped. "We'll set up on the Place and blow the Cursed One to kingdom come."

"One problem," Julie said. "The Wendigo isn't going to talk to you. You're going to be wandering around the woods for weeks. You know what the Bottoms are like. The rules don't apply there."

"Let me guess," Myers said. He exhaled slowly, apparently trying to control his anger. "This thing will talk to you people though."

"He'll only talk to me," Harbinger said, before adding with a note of barely concealed disgust, "looks like we're going with you."

Myers cursed. The man had a remarkable gift for creative profanity.

"Looks like we get to work together," I told Franks cheerfully.

The silent brute just nodded as he patted his Glock, doubtlessly contemplating the moment he would finally get to use it on me.

"This is it," I said. "We know where the Cursed One is going to be. We finish this tomorrow—one way or the other."

"About time," Sam said. "Grant was one of us. That slimy bastard is gonna pay." The big cowboy kicked at the gravel.

"Yeah," Milo added with what was for him, unusual somberness. He wore his night vision monocular and scanned back and forth across the property.

The three of us were standing in the darkened driveway of the Shackleford ancestral home near the vehicles. We were waiting for the others. Gretchen was applying some first aid to Trip after the little bit of "stick time" he had received. Holly was grabbing some gear. Harbinger and Julie were standing about a hundred yards away, talking quietly between themselves. Apparently Julie had a few things that she needed to speak with him about privately. The Feds had left, quite a bit worse for wear after the beating that some of them had received from Harbinger.

"What do you think they did with him?" I asked. I did not like the way that we were talking about our companion as if he were already dead, but I could not realistically see much hope for the alternative.

"The Old Man's journal said that they needed to sacrifice a Hunter to use their device," Milo said. "I'm guessing that poor Grant is going to get himself sacrificed."

"Sucky way to die," Sam agreed.

"Do they need to keep him alive until the full moon? There is a possibility he could be alive still."

"Maybe," Milo said. "We can hope." He sounded doubtful. Most of the seasoned Hunters' missions involved search and destroy, rather than rescue.

Having eavesdropped on Grant's contrition earlier made him somehow more human now, and made his being taken that much more difficult to stomach. But a tiny, ugly part of me hated him even more now, because I could see that Julie was taking his disappearance hard, and I found myself somehow jealous of someone who was probably already dead. We sat in silence for a few moments. In the distance I could see that Julie and Harbinger were arguing. She looked rather angry and animated as the senior Hunter tried to explain something.

"What do you think they're fighting about?" I asked.

"I'm guessing she wants to know if Earl knew that Susan was a vampire," Milo answered as he looked upward through the night vision. "I can never get over how many stars you can see through one of these things."

"Did he know?"

"Beats me," Sam answered. "We had our suspicions, of course. We had never found her body, and they had been hunting a vampire. I mean, I guess we all kind of thought about it, but none of us wanted to think it was a real possibility. You gotta understand, we loved Susan. The idea of having any of us turned to the other side . . . well, that . . . That just ain't no good."

"I've got a chainsaw with my name on it in my workshop," Milo told us happily. "If I'm ever killed by undead, I want you guys to chop me up with it. It's a good chainsaw."

"I reckon it is, Milo. I would be honored to chop your head off," Sam said. I worked with some interesting folks.

The lights in the house were extinguished. Trip, Holly and Gretchen joined us a moment later. Since we had blown holes in the ballroom, and the Feds had kicked in all of the doors and many of the windows, we could not even lock up anything other than the vault. I just hoped that nobody came up here and looted the place while we were gone.

Trip was limping and did not look very good. "Now I know how Rodney King felt," he said through swollen gums. One eye was matted shut, and Gretchen had smeared him with some sort of foul-smelling cream.

"Yeah, but you ain't gonna get no million dollar settlement to blow on hookers and crack like he did," Sam said wryly. "We're just waiting for the boss and we can get out of here. We got us some monsters to kill."

Julie and Harbinger continued fighting for another minute, before finally coming to some sort of terms. He hugged her as she sobbed on his shoulder.

"She's had a tough night," Milo said simply. Estranged father dead. Boyfriend missing. Mother revealed to be undead. Milo Anderson was a master of understatement. None of us disagreed.

"I've got a question," Trip asked. "How come Grant didn't sound the alarm? I woke up when I heard Owen shouting."

"Probably snuck up on him," I lied. In truth I had a pretty good idea of what had happened. Probably something similar to what Susan had tried on me, only Grant had probably not realized what was going on until it was too late.

Holly knew the truth. "Vampires can be seductive. You saw what she was wearing. She probably floated in as mist, put on some of Julie's things, and bit Grant when he thought he was going to get lucky.

Then she tried the same thing on Z here . . ." She pointed at me. "So did you score with your friend's dead mom?"

"It sounds gross when you put it that way." It didn't do me much good to lie at that point. "I got to second base before I realized she wasn't breathing," I stammered with no small amount of embarrassment. "Hey, I thought she was Julie." And then I felt really stupid for saying that. Luckily she was still standing far enough away to have not heard.

"Way to go, Big Guy." Sam punched me in the shoulder. "If you had been a little dumber, you could have put a whole new meaning to 'staking' vampires."

"That's horrible," Trip said as he pressed a bag of ice against the side of his head.

"Whatever. She would've bit you next," Holly said.

"Probably not. I would have sounded the alarm," he answered.

"Sure you would have . . . church boy."

"No really, I've never . . ." He caught himself. "Uh . . . never mind."

"No way." Holly sounded stunned. "Are you saying . . . No way. You're what? Twenty-seven?"

Trip looked very uncomfortable.

"Saving it for marriage?" Milo interjected, looking alien with his massive beard poking out from under his night vision. "Good for you, Trip." At least he had the Mormon contingent's approval.

"I didn't know you Rastafarians did that kind of thing," Sam said. "I figured you all partied."

"Baptist," Trip said quickly.

"Oh, I just figured with the funky hair and whatnot. You should shave that thing then. You would look good." Sam spat into the gravel. I made a mental note never to listen to the fashion advice of a man with a mullet and a puffy trucker hat.

"Yeah, you would look like Shaft," I added helpfully. "Not the old one, the new one."

"Chicks dig that on a black dude. Be sure to get yourself laid then, kid," Sam told him with great confidence.

"But . . . Wait . . . It's a personal choice, damn it," Trip sputtered.

"Okay guys. Here's the plan." Thankfully Harbinger interrupted. He lit a cigarette as he approached. It was back to business. Julie looked sad, but resolute and determined. The director just looked angry. "Back to base. Gear up. We will form an assault element. We're going to meet the Feds in Natchy Bottom in the morning. Milo, load up everything you can think of. Julie, Sam, you two contact every other team in the country. Have them drop whatever they're working on and get back here now. Our team hits the Bottoms, everybody else hits the local outbreaks." He pointed at me. "Newbie squad, take a car. Take Gretchen back to her people."

I had almost forgotten about the small woman. She was so quiet, and cloaked in her shapeless robes she nearly disappeared in the shadows. Harbinger bowed toward her in a sign of sincere respect, and said something in her language. It sounded like gurgles and clicks to me. She replied, gravelly and deep.

"Thank you, Gretchen. You bring great honor to your clan," he said and turned back to me. "Get her home. She isn't a warrior, but she performed like one tonight. MHI will always be in her clan's debt. There is a little road just north of the compound. Follow it. She'll show you the way. Don't get jumpy if they get weird on you, remember they're our friends."

The group dispersed to their tasks. I grabbed Julie by the arm. "Wait." I didn't know what to say, but I needed to say something.

She turned around, great dark circles under her eyes. "What? What is it, Owen?"

"I'm sorry about your parents, and I'm sorry about Grant . . ."

She raised her hand and cut me off. "No. No you're not."

"No, I . . ." I stammered.

"You wanted Grant dead, didn't you?" she snapped. "Well, looks like you got your wish." She spun and walked away.

The compound was not that far away from the Shackleford home. We took Grant's car. The interior was immaculate and the XM stations were all pre-programmed for classical music. At least I could hear again; Gretchen's purple goo had worked well. Trip and Holly were in the back seat, and Gretchen rode up front. I passed the lane leading to the compound, and slowed down as Gretchen pointed out a tiny path cloaked in trees and moss. The narrow road was so overgrown with vegetation that the headlights only cut a small swath before us.

"This is it?" I asked her. She nodded, a movement barely perceptible beneath her robes. It was just after 3:00 A.M. but she was still wearing her mirrored shades. The Mercedes bumped through the foliage, and the undercarriage scraped as we dipped into the deep ruts. I rolled down the window. The chirping of insects was rhythmic and strong. A trio of cow skulls had been tied around a tree with leather cord. I knew that it was a sign that we were on Skippy's property. "I love what you've done with the place."

Gretchen clicked approvingly. We continued down the lane, deeper and deeper into the dark woods. Though the compound was only a few miles away, we seemed totally isolated from the world. The trees here were tall and the forest primeval. Glowing eyes reflected back at us as raccoons scurried away.

"This is kind of creepy," Trip said.

"It isn't so bad," I answered. Then something huge sprinted across the road through the headlights. It was massive and covered in black fur, and it was gone in an instant. "What the hell was that?" I shouted as I stomped on the brakes. The Mercedes halted on the packed dirt, leaving us in a cloud of red dust. I rolled up the window without thinking.

"Deer?" asked Holly.

"That wasn't no damn deer," I said. It had looked more like a scurvy bear crossed with a lion. Maybe I had not been getting enough sleep. Gretchen said something unintelligible and made shooing motions for me to continue onward. Apparently, whatever the animal had been, it was of no serious concern to her.

Flickering lights appeared in the distance. Campfires. Big ones. We slowly rolled forward until we saw the structures of a tiny community. Perhaps village would be the best word. The little houses were clustered tightly together into a rough semicircle. Surprisingly enough the homes looked nice and well cared for, despite the strange decorations of skins, bones, hides, antlers and feathers that decorated all of them. The fires emanated from large basins that had been set at the compass points around the village. There was a central area between the homes, with what appeared to be some sort of shrine or religious stage.

A black-clad figure appeared in the headlights and waved as we approached. I recognized Skippy from his gait. Other figures appeared from the homes, all of them shorter than average, and several squat ones that must have been children. Many of them were hurriedly pulling on their masks or hoods. I parked the car next to some older-model pickup trucks. Before I had even shut the engine off Gretchen had bailed out of the vehicle and went running toward her husband. He picked her up and swung her around as they joyfully embraced. Several of the others joined them in a massive group hug.

I stepped out of the car. The air smelled of delicious roasting meat. The sounds that I first thought were angry noises, actually were laughter coming from the reunited tribe. Some of the children began to play a game, running and chasing after each other. Skippy left the group when he saw me. Many of them studied us curiously from behind their tinted goggles or mirrored shades.

"Noble One . . . Thank . . . you . . . bringing . . . *Grtxschnns* . . . Gret chen . . . Home." He bowed down until his balaclava touched the ground. I bowed back.

"Thank you, Skippy. Gretchen saved our lives tonight. She healed our many wounds. And her faith and bravery turned away a Master vampire. If it wasn't for her, many Hunters would have died."

"She . . . brings honor . . . to clan?" He rose and spoke loudly in his language. There were some gasps of astonishment as they stepped away from Gretchen, and then bowed to her. I could not see her features, but by her mannerisms, I was guessing that she was slightly embarrassed by the display. After a few seconds they rose and went back to their merry greetings. Finally Gretchen was able to break away and approach us, the rest of the tribe following closely behind her, until finally the whole group was assembled quietly in front of the three of us.

Gretchen pointed at Trip, and said something to the others. There was much oohing and ahhing, and then they bowed toward him. Skippy's people were big on the bowing.

"Uh . . . what's going on?" he asked, running one hand through his dreads nervously.

"Dark Hunter . . . you fought . . . gub mint . . . agents . . . to protect Gret chen?" When he said government, the tribe booed.

"I guess," he answered.

"Agents beat you . . ." He pointed at Trip's face. "For protect her?"

"Yes. Really, it was no big deal . . . I—"

Skippy cut him off. He turned back to the tribe and loudly proclaimed: "*Smrslal! Smrslal Aiee!*" then to us, "Dark skin Hunter, Brother of War Chief, and . . . Girl. Bring great honor. My clan . . . you one with . . . us. With honor . . . No need for hide."

Skippy reached up and removed his glasses, revealing bright yellow eyes sunk deep into grayish-green tissue. He carefully folded and put the shades in a pocket, and began to remove his balaclava. One by one, the others did so as well. Even the little children removed their hoods, some needing the help of their mothers.

We had gained the trust and respect of the tribe. Honoring us as equals, they revealed their true selves. Their skin was bumpy, mottled, mostly green, some gray and some brown. They were either bald, or some with wispy white hair. Their lower jaws protruded, and tusklike teeth stuck past their lips. Most of their noses were squat, though some were raised up more like snouts. The eyes were yellow or pale blue, set under thick bone ridges and short foreheads. Their ears were long and pointy, and most if not all of them had facial piercings of bone or gold.

"Holy shit," Holly mumbled.

"Orcs," Trip said in awe. "I don't believe it."

Skippy's pointed teeth ground together above his wide jaw, in what I believed was a smile. His yellow eyes twinkled as he clapped his hands above his head. "*Urks!* Yes. Clan of *Gnrlwz,* fist of North. Spear of . . . Doom. Now clan of . . . M H I. Harb Anger . . . give us home. Give us work. Now are family. Join us . . . eat meat . . . dance." He pointed at one of the others, who immediately turned and ran for what I thought was a shrine. The younger orc knelt and fiddled with something on the backside of the edifice, and massive hidden speakers started blaring. Metal. The orcs were playing heavy metal.

"JBL. Kick Ass . . . Sound system," Skippy grunted at us. "Come! Party!" The entire tribe began to either bang their heads, dance wildly, or jump up and down with their hands extended above their heads, pointer and pinky fingers extended in the devil horns of classic rock. The children formed a mosh pit and began to slam each other about. The mothers looked on approvingly.

"Skippy, I wish that we could," I shouted back over the sounds of Static X. "But we have a mission. We need to fly to Natchy Bottom in the morning." The orcs danced. Giant wolves howled in the nearby forest. Of course, that explained the thing that had crossed the headlights. You can't have orcs without wargs.

Skippy nodded. "Skip understand. I be there . . . Together . . . crush foes. Must take . . . care of clan . . . Then come. To fly into battle." He bowed again. I returned the honor. "Thank you . . . Noble One."

"Great honor, Skippy. Thank you." We parted. I returned to the car.

Holly climbed into the front seat. Trip stood transfixed at the rear door, staring at the clan in wonder, as some of the giant wolves wandered out of the treeline and into the light of the fires. Little green children ran to crawl up on the horse-sized animals, playing with what to them were basically family pets. Pets with jaws that could snap a deer in half, but pets nonetheless. Skippy returned to Gretchen and they knocked their tusks together in what was probably the orcish equivalent of a kiss. I started the car. Finally Trip broke away from the sights and got in.

We drove down the lane. The raucous music died away as the distance increased. We did not speak. Trip stared out the window in silence. The Mercedes bumped and scraped as we bottomed out. It would take a pretty dedicated explorer to bother with this back road and now I could see that that was by design. It was a strange and secret community, but obviously one built upon strong family bonds of love. My spirits were lifted from my brief visit to Skippy's people.

Finally Holly spoke. "Well, Trip. Satisfied now?"

"Huh?"

"Remember when we met the elves?"

He did not answer. But none of us could forget his disappointment on that day.

"Remember when you said that since there was so much secret evil, there had to be some sort of secret good to balance it out?"

"Yeah," he answered slowly. I could not see him in the darkened car, but from his voice I could tell he was smiling. "I guess there is . . . I guess there really is."

"See, I told you so," Holly said in smug satisfaction.

We assembled in the meeting room. Harbinger was preparing to brief us. We would be taking off within the next half hour. It was 4:00 A.M. Every available Hunter was assembled, including the untested Newbies, all of Harbinger's team, Dorcas and the senior Shackleford. The conference room was crowded. Every other member of MHI in the country was currently en route.

I sat down at the conference table next to Milo. He grinned when he saw me. The man was always in a good mood.

"So did you get to meet Skippy's people?"

"Orcs," I answered. "That was pretty cool."

"Yeah, they're good folks. *Homo-Ogrillion.* We were hired to go into Uzbekistan and eradicate them. Turned out that they weren't so evil after all, so we brought them all home. I'm glad we did."

Harbinger called the briefing to order. It took a

few moments for the group to quiet down. Apparently word of the attack and all the gory details had spread quickly. Julie was sitting next to her grandfather, and his burned face was drawn into a tight grimace of pain and anger. I could not imagine how the man felt. Even if you had distanced yourself from a child who committed horrible crimes, he was still your child. And now he had lost that son.

Harbinger cut right to the chase. "Everybody knows about what's going on, and you've already heard about what happened earlier tonight. One former Hunter is dead. One current Hunter is missing. Turns out that one of our own is a Master vampire in the service of the Cursed One. We have a deal with the Feds. One team is going to go with them to Natchy Bottom to deal with the main bad guys. Every available Hunter is on the way. As they arrive, the rest of us will break into groups and handle the following undead outbreaks." He pointed at the map of the Southeast that had been taped to the wall. It was dotted with red tacks.

"Auburn, Gadsden, and Forestdale, Alabama; Columbus, Georgia; Pulaski, Tennessee; and Pensacola, Florida. Those are all confirmed vampires or wights. Boone's team just cleared out some new creations in Atlanta. I felt bad calling them up since some of his men are still hurting from the freighter, but they rose to the occasion. And we have unconfirmed reports in Florence, Tupelo, Dothan, Fayetteville, Russellville and Demopolis, though those might just be regular missing persons, but I wouldn't bet on it."

He paused long enough to take a drag off his cigarette. I had not seen him smoke indoors around the other Hunters before, but I was guessing that he was under more stress than normal.

"As other teams arrive they will be diverted to those trouble spots. This is our turf, so local law enforcement knows us and is helping out. National Guard, same thing. Mostly they can be used as perimeter security, but if you think you can trust them, press them into service as well. We don't have time to screw around, so if you find where the vamps are sleeping, just blow it straight to hell. We don't have time to stake and chop and all that. If they're in a mine, collapse it. If they're in a building, burn it down. If you need to, borrow a tank from the National Guard. If they're inside something that you can't justify blowing up, then do what you have to do."

"How many threats are we talking about?" Sam asked.

"Potentially hundreds." There was some murmuring and swearing at that, from everybody except the untested Newbies who had not yet seen a real undead. "We always thought that vampires were limited in the number of new creations they could make. That was always our theory on how come they didn't just bite everybody and overrun us. Looks like we were wrong, at least when it comes to Masters. We're looking at a few different threats here, so let me break it down. Somehow the CO is able to bring people back as wights. Then we have two kinds of vamps, the regular new creations, where somebody is just killed and comes back as one, and apparently a stronger, smarter type, made by biting the victim, and then giving them some of the Master vampire's own blood and power."

"Like Darné?" I asked. The former French Hunter

had been amazingly fast and seemed to be in full control of his faculties, unlike the more animalistic creatures that had been the other vampires.

"Most likely. So we're talking about some serious bad asses. Plus we know that he can animate gargoyles as well, though there have not been any sightings of those since the ones that Pitt and Julie killed. Nobody knows how long it takes to create one of those, or even how many he brought over to start with."

"What do we have?" Milo asked.

"Counting us and the Newbies, we have about twelve teams of Hunters. Six people in the hospital or on medical leave. Seventy total personnel available," Julie answered.

"Seventy-one," her grandfather said from the head of the table. He pulled a well-oiled S&W 1917 from under his sweater and put it on the table with a clunk. "I ain't sitting this one out."

"But, Grandpa . . ." Julie said.

"Whoever thought I would get to live this long anyway, kid? This old man is looking for a fight. These bastards killed my boy, even if he was a crazy son of a bitch himself. Monsters don't get to kill a Shackleford and get away with it. It sets bad precedent."

"Seventy-two," Dorcas added, her grandmotherly looks not quite matching the steel in her voice. "Try to stop me, you'll be tasting my plastic foot. I can still run a machine gun with the best of them."

"We help," said a gravelly voice from the doorway. I had not heard Skippy approach. "Ten warriors . . . Five who heal . . . Ride to battle . . . Slay many foes."

"Skippy, you don't have to. Your people are so few in number as it is," Harbinger said.

"Harb Anger deny us . . . honor . . . of battle?" Skippy asked. His voice sounded extra distorted through his flight helmet's face shield.

"No. Of course not." The Director bowed his head. "My clan thanks you for your brave warriors."

"Eighty-seven total staff then," Julie said. "Against probably double that number of powerful undead and who knows what, spread from one corner of the South to the other."

Eighty-eight, said the voice of the Old Man in my head. I wished he would stop doing that. It freaked me out. I may have a weird job, but that doesn't mean that I liked hearing voices in my head.

"Who's going to Natchy Bottom?" Sam asked.

"Feds are going to be the ones doing all of the fighting, and we can let them be the muscle. So we'll just take the Hind. Skippy flies of course, and one can ride co-pilot. Then we can fit eight plus gear."

"I'm going," Julie said.

"No. You're injured, and I need you here to coordinate the arriving teams."

"Bullshit," she snapped. "This is personal."

"I know, and that's why you ain't going," Harbinger stated.

"Wrong. I'm on that helicopter or you can have my resignation right now, and I'll drive up there myself." Julie stood up from the table. "Don't push me, Earl. She's going to be there, and she isn't going to rest until she gets me too."

Harbinger slowly nodded, his cigarette dangling from his lips. "Fine," he said. "Julie, Sam, Milo, so my whole team. Pitt, he knows the bad guys better than anybody. That leaves four volunteers. Keep in mind, this is probably going to be real dangerous. Most likely all seven of the Masters plus whatever powers that the Cursed One himself has."

"I'm going," Trip said, surprising no one.

"You feel up to it?"

"What, this?" He pointed at his battered face. "Just a scratch."

"I'm in," Holly stated. "Any excuse to kill something."

"Me too," Albert Lee offered.

"Nope. Your ribs are still jacked up. No offense, Lee, but if anything, you're going to run support for a local team. Sorry. Two more." He pointed at Dorcas. "Oh hell no. Don't even think about it. If Julie's going, I definitely need you here to coordinate. Once that's done then you can go get yourself killed all you want."

The older woman slowly lowered her hand.

Lee raised his hand again. "Mr. Harbinger, sir. I can do it. I feel a lot better. I won't slow us down, plus I've been doing nothing but studying the archives for the last week. Maybe something I learned can help." You had to admire our demolitionist librarian. It took some guts to stand up to Harbinger's overwhelming presence. "It wasn't even a real break, just a minor fracture, and Gretchen gave me some stuff, said that I'm good to go."

Harbinger scowled and thought about it for a moment. "Fine, Lee. You're on."

"I could go," stated Julie's grandfather. She gasped. "But I'm afraid I would just slow you down." There were a few relieved sighs at that. I could not imagine that Harbinger could order around the president of the company.

"Brother . . ." Skippy said. *"Exszrsd,* Edward, Ed . . . great warrior. Much honor clan to go . . ."

"The dude with the swords?" Milo asked. He mimicked swinging swords around his head.

"Yes. Ed with swords. He go too."

"Hell yeah," Sam said. "He's one bad dude."

"That's a full chopper," Harbinger said. He glanced down at his watch. "Hurley's team is due to hit Pensacola shortly. Boone's en route to Gadsden. Scramble the others as needed. Boss, Dorcas, shuffle the Newbies off to any teams that are shorthanded. It's all yours. This is it. For you Newbies who have not fought yet. Don't worry, you've been trained. You know what to do. Stick with your team leads, and do what they tell you. You'll be fine. Now let's go to work. The world is counting on us."

"Good luck, everyone," Julie said. "You know what to do."

"I taught you guys how to fight. Don't screw up," Sam ordered the Newbies. Everyone stood up from the table and began to disperse. He shouted one last set of instructions for his parting charges. "And if the going gets tough, and you get the urge to quit, just remember that we get paid real good for this shit!"

"We finish this today," Harbinger stated to no one in particular.

I hoped so. It was Thursday morning. Friday night was the full moon and the end of the world. I wondered if I would still be alive to see it.

I waited for Julie in the hallway, standing nervously in front of the wall of memorial plaques. A bright new one had been set on the wall for Jerry Roberts.

I was wearing my full armor, festooned with weapons and ammunition. I was ready for war.

But I was not ready for what I needed to do next.

Julie strode down the hall, also fully armed for battle. Her M14 was slung over one shoulder, and a row of sharpened stakes was lashed to her webbing. Her long hair had been tied up beneath her hockey helmet, and she had replaced her glasses with shatterproof prescription goggles. She was angry and determined, and no vampires or cursed conquistadors were going to stand in her way.

She saw me, and attempted to smile. She failed miserably.

"Hey, Owen. Look, I'm sorry you had to see me freak out back there at the house, and I'm sorry I snapped at you. That was just a lot of emotion for me, you know. Grant's probably dead, or worse. Dad is dead, and I didn't think that I would mind that, but I do, and Mom . . ." She shrugged.

"I know," I said simply. "If Grant's alive, we'll find him. And I'll help you deal with Susan."

She changed the subject. "How are your ribs? Franks beat the hell out of you."

"Fine," I lied. It hurt to move. Plus I had huge bruises on my neck from her mother. "How's your shoulder?"

"Fine," she lied. I grinned. That got her to smile.

"Look, Julie . . . I just want to say . . . you know . . . in case I don't make it . . ."

"I know," she answered sheepishly. "Don't talk like that."

I reached down and touched her hand. I very gradually took it into my own. "I . . . I . . ."

She squeezed back. "I know. I really do. But I can't deal with that right now. Too much other stuff going on. Besides, we're going to live through this. Right?"

I looked down. I was not so sure. The others had not felt the power of the Cursed One like I had. They did not really understand the evil that he contained. I had a bad feeling that we were not going to win.

She leaned in close and kissed me on the cheek. "Thanks," she said.

My heart skipped a beat. "Okay," I said. Not being a very eloquent man, that was the best that I could manage. She must have realized what she had done, but she did not move away. Instead she came a little closer. We stayed like that for a few seconds, neither of us knowing what to say.

"See that?" She nodded at the sign above the memorial wall. "Do you know Latin?"

"No." I had seen the plaque my first day here, but I had not understood what it meant.

"*Sic transit gloria mundi.*" She explained, "When Caesar would address his people, in all his glory, in his splendor, with his armies, and his riches, there would always be a functionary standing by his side, whispering that saying in his ear. It's a reminder. It means: The glory of man is fleeting. Do you know why we have that carved here?"

"Because we can get killed anytime?" I answered. "It keeps us humble?"

"Pretty much."

"That's a hell of a philosophy."

"It really is. It means that all of our glory, all of the good we accomplish, we had better enjoy them now, because we are one heartbeat away from losing it. We live fast, and we usually die young, but it sure is glorious while it lasts. Monster Hunters don't have time to waste."

"What are you trying to say?"

"You're not real bright for a genius, are you?" Julie stood close to me, armor against armor. She turned her head slightly and closed her eyes. "Shut up and kiss me."

I did.

It was glorious.

I took her in my arms, weapons clanking into each other. Time ceased to exist. The whole universe consisted of just her and me. Life was good. The kiss seemed to last forever.

"Ahem." I was jolted away from her soft lips. "Time to go, kids," Harbinger stated as he walked past us. "Helicopter is prepped. Feds are already en route."

"Yes, sir!" I shouted, very embarrassed.

"Be right there, Earl," Julie said, looking flushed. She waited for him to disappear. "I need to sit down."

"I don't want to feel like I'm taking advantage of you with all of the stuff going on and, and your parents, and Grant, and . . ." I stammered. She kissed me again, quicker this time.

"This isn't about any of them. Don't talk about it. . . . We had better get out of here."

"Sure." I didn't want to let go of her.

"Go, I've got to grab something. I'll be right there." We parted. She smiled. I grinned like an idiot. I walked away, looking back over my shoulder the whole time. She did the same. I finally had to quit when I walked painfully into the drinking fountain. I waved stupidly.

She disappeared around the corner. I started to run. It turned into a sprint. I could not help myself.

I passed Harbinger through the double doors, ran the few hundred yards to the runway without slowing, vaulted through the open door of the Hind and took a seat. Milo and Sam were sitting across from me, already strapped in. I gave them a big thumbs-up.

"Let's kill us some monsters!" I shouted over the already turning rotors. The two seasoned Hunters just looked at each other and shrugged.

The distant sky in the east was beginning to turn orange. Dawn would be here soon. It was going to be a great day. I could tell.

CHAPTER 21

We lifted off from the compound and headed northwest at over a hundred and twenty miles an hour. Even at that speed, we had about two hours of flight time. I sat next to Julie. She had winked at me when she had strapped in, but did not say anything that the others could hear. Harbinger studied us stonily, but after a few minutes of uneventful flight, he used the opportunity to get some sleep. Trip and Holly stared out of opposite windows, apparently lost in thought. Milo and Sam argued about what Sam's new team logo should be, either a frog or a walrus. Either way it was going to have a cowboy hat. Lee read a book until he became violently airsick, then he too went to sleep. Skippy left the music off of the intercom, probably in deference to the early morning hour, not that the internal engine noises of the chopper weren't already deafeningly loud. His brother Ed took the co-pilot's seat. He was dressed like a ninja, except for the tinted Bolle goggles.

When nobody was looking, Julie reached over and took my hand. She held it for most of the flight.

I did not know if she felt the same way about me as I felt about her. Looking at it logically, she barely knew me, and in the last twenty-four hours her world had been turned upside down. Was this sudden affection for me the result of feelings that she already held, or were they instead caused by her need to have some sort of anchor?

Either way, I was fine. I could deal with being an anchor. I was certainly heavy enough. Screw logic. It had no place in relationships anyway. I just enjoyed holding her hand.

The rhythmic strumming of the helicopter made me tired. I could understand why, since I had only had a few hours of sleep that night. And it had been a stressful night to say the least—check that, it had been a stressful week. On Saturday I had been drowned, beaten and shot. Sunday I had been slapped around and had some teeth knocked out. On Monday I got to go to the dentist and, sadly, that had been the most relaxing time of the whole week. Tuesday had resulted in a van wreck and road rash, and I had gotten my ass kicked last night by, first, a vampire, and then used by Franks as a punching bag. Who knew what today would bring? Interestingly enough, the full moon was going to be Friday night. Exactly one week from when this all started. It had an interesting sort of symmetry to it, or it probably would if I lived to enjoy it.

A week ago I had been ready to quit. Scared that I was doing the wrong thing. Scared by the violence that I kept leashed up inside. But those things, that darkness, it was what had kept many of us alive over the last few days. My pursuit of a regular life was a lie. I could see that now.

My place was here. I was a Monster Hunter.

By the time we flew over Hayneville, I was asleep.

I saw the mysterious Tattooed Man. He was driving a car down the nearly empty freeway. The person sitting next to him had been the vehicle's previous owner, neck snapped like a twig when the Tattooed Man had decided he needed transportation. His bare foot was on the gas, and he kept it just under the speed limit to avoid attention.

Black eyes stared straight ahead, fixed in the direction of his target. He drummed his fingers absently on the wheel. He was close. Very close. The anticipation of regaining his charge was great, and the excitement of approaching battle was building in his ancient soul.

He knew I was watching him. He was close enough now for that. The tattoos on his face withered as he spoke, knowing all too well that I could hear him despite the barriers of space and time. His archaic form of speech was thick and accented.

"I care not about thy war. The artifact is mine to protect, and do so I shall."

Who are you? I thought.

"Look upon me and see thy doom, cursed man. Thou shalt die by my hand."

Why?

He paused, the unnatural ink swirling around his blunt features. He seemed surprised by my question.

"Thou knowest not?"

No.

"Thou knowest not of thy fate? Of thy place in this world?"

Nope.

He laughed at me. A booming hearty laugh. It was without real emotion, as any human feelings that had once inhabited this hardened creature had passed a long time ago. Rather, the laughter was an ingrained reflex at hearing something so seemingly preposterous.

"Surely thou hast some knowledge?"

No. I'm getting pretty sick of this myself.

"Then I shall be saddened to take the life of a warrior whose heart is without guile. Alas, it must be. For that I am sorry, but thou must surely die by my hand. I shall do my best to make it swift and glorious."

I don't want to fight you.

"Thou hast no choice," he stated flatly. "'Tis my duty."

I had my fill of people and monsters threatening to kill me.

Bring it on, bitch.

His face cracked into a wide grin, the swirling markings formed a sympathetic jaw around his lips. "Ahh, there be the spirit. We shall wage us a fine battle."

He continued driving as my spirit lifted from the moving vehicle. The sun was rising on the freeway behind us. I recognized the city in the background.

Montgomery.

The dream world.

"Hello, Boy." The Old Man greeted me as I approached the destroyed church. "Hurry, hurry. Time is much short. Cut off last time." He looked agitated, limping toward me, using his cane as support in the light but slick snow.

"Mordechai, who the hell was that joker?" I asked as I stepped over some rubble and scattered bricks. Either I had not noticed before, or perhaps the Old Man had not put them there before, but there were thousands of shell casings scattered on the ground or pocked into the snow.

"Who?" he asked, perplexed.

"That big tattoo-faced guy. The Guardian of the artifact or whatever."

He hurried over, his face drawn into a look of concern. "You spoke to this man?"

"Yeah, just now. Didn't you see?"

"No." He shook his head, his Star of David bouncing wildly off of his thin chest. "He is here? Now?" The Old Man sounded very worried.

"I think so. I think he's in Montgomery."

"Is bad. Much much bad."

"He said he has to kill me."

"Afraid of this I was. Listen to me, Boy. You are brave and strong, but no match for him. If he comes, run."

"So let me get this straight, you've got no problem with me taking on the Cursed One and seven Master vampires, and gargoyles, and wights, and who knows what else, but you want me to turn and run if I see this tattoo-faced, funny-talking freak?"

"Yes." He shook his head happily. "Glad you understand, Boy. Now come, time is short, and still much you have to see. I will do what can, but not know if have time enough."

"Why is he so dangerous? How can he be any more dangerous than Lord Machado?"

The Old Man put his hands alongside my head.

"Not him who is dangerous. I worry about you who is dangerous."

"Huh?"

He squeezed my head and looked me in the eyes. I think he was trying to convey the seriousness of his advice. "Never mind. See him. Run away. Not strong enough to face. Bad things happen. Now shush. Much memory to show before fight."

The dream world faded away.

Lord Machado's memory was sharp and refined for this night, etched deeply into his mind.

This pyramid was much larger than the others, but had been partially buried by earthquakes and mudslides in the distant past, and then mostly reclaimed by the jungle. The stones were crumbling with age, and the once-intricate carvings were weathered to the point that they were no longer clearly recognizable. Now the pictures looked more like squid and crab things going about their business, than the pictorial people that they must have been at one time. The remaining architecture seemed unfamiliar and somehow alien.

Many months had passed while the priestess had instructed me in her dark arts. I had learned much, and seen things not meant for human eyes. I had communed with dark forces, and my education had continued until finally I felt ready to unleash the power. The time had come for me to reclaim my birthright and fulfill the prophecy. I was ready. The priestess Koriniha was at my side. A small contingent of her selected priests led the way up the steps. A squadron of my most trusted and loyal soldiers remained to guard the base of the pyramid.

The priestess leaned in close and spoke softly into my ear. "Your men are scared, Lord Machado."

"They do not understand what we do. But they are loyal. They will do as they are told. They would follow me into the very pit itself if ordered, for I am their general. And they know their place."

"That is good. But not all of your soldiers are so loyal. There has been no word of your chief captain." She sounded mildly worried. "We cannot afford an interruption during the sacrifice. The Old Ones would be offended."

She was right to be concerned. A small group of men, led by one of my best captains, had disappeared, most likely deserted. The giant of a man, called Thrall, had hired onto the expedition as a mercenary. He was from some small country to the northeast, and had barely even spoken our language at the time of our embarkation, but he had proven himself to be a fierce warrior, whom the men would follow without hesitation. I had been reluctant to promote him, but he was far too capable to have been wasted as a mere musketeer.

Unfortunately, his primitive upbringing had made my own superstitious men seem like philosophers in comparison. He had been against my initial conscription of the native forces, and he had been adamantly opposed to staying in the city, rather than sacking and burning it to the ground. I had my suspicions that he had been in league with the now departed Friar de Sousa as well. The divinations of the priestess had confirmed his treachery and the fact that he had been a holy man amongst his forgotten people. Doubtless my consorting with dark forces had driven him away.

It would not matter, even if the captain had fled for the sea. By the time he would be able to send a message of my treachery back to agents of the crown, it would be too late. My powers would be granted tonight. "No need to worry, my love. The good captain is no threat to us." I had dispatched a force of soldiers and conscripts to chase the deserters down and execute them. "It is under control."

"Excellent, my lord, but should it prove necessary, I summoned some protectors for our ceremony tonight."

The top of the ancient structure was flat except for a single raised dais. The altar had a funnel protruding from its base, giving some clue to its dark history. Giant braziers of flaming coals had been placed on the corners, illuminating us with flickering light. The pagan priests went immediately to their respective stations. Large stone demons squatted around the altar. One of the carved statues turned its head and regarded us with blank stone eyes. Dust shook from it as unnaturally long arms flexed nonexistent muscles. It was a mighty beast.

"What manner of creature is that?" I hissed.

"They are here to protect you, Lord Machado. Once you unlock the power of the Old Ones, you will be able to create these animations as you see fit." The stone creature turned away, satisfied that I was its new master. I could only imagine the army that I could command with creatures constructed from the rocks of the earth itself.

A small group of the feather-robed men were already waiting before the altar. They stood aside and kneeled as we approached. One of the priests said something in his language to the priestess.

"The sacrifice is ready, lord," she told me. A young man was stretched upon the altar, his wrists and ankles bound with heavy cords. Rather than fearful, the man appeared defiant. He said something in their strange language. I could tell he was cursing me.

"He is a hunter of the *Ewaipanoma* of the jungle and the *Ahuzoitl* of the rivers, a protector of the innocent, and a great warrior. The Old Ones demand such a sacrifice."

"What do I need to do?" I ran my finger down the worn wood shaft of my ax. I would show this hunter of monsters what I thought of his curses.

"Are you ready, my Lord of the Ax? Are you prepared to be a vessel for the very power of the ancients?"

"I am ready to take my rightful place as ruler of this world."

She looked deep into my eyes. The world condensed down to just the two of us, shutting out the chanting priests, the cursing and spitting Hunter, and the screaming of the jungle. "You are he who has been prophesied. Warrior, son of a great warrior, your very name taken from the weapons that have shed the blood of your family's enemies. Sent by a king on an impossible quest . . . A leader, a visionary, an ally of darkness . . ." She stroked my cheek as I recalled the prophecy of the black obelisk. "And of monsters . . ." She gestured at the hulking demon figure standing guard over us. "Truly you are the one, five hundred years since the last, five hundred years until the next, the only one amongst a thousand generations of man with the key to unlock the power over time . . . There is but one more thing."

"What is that?"

"The Old Ones said you must have love." She pulled herself tight against my armor, like a parasite, or a barnacle upon the hull of a ship. She needed me more than I needed her now. "Tell me, my lord, is it so?"

"Of course," I answered truthfully. I loved her as much as a practical man such as myself could love anything. I had found in the dark priestess an equal in ambition, desire and lust for control. If the Old Ones required a weak emotion to unlock the secrets of ultimate power, I could think of worse choices than the wanton evil creature before me.

"If I were to die, would you return for me? Would you bring me back from the other side?" she implored. "You alone will have the power, but you will need my guidance to use it."

Of course, that was her key to staying in my graces. The Old Ones had not revealed their secrets to me like they had to her. They only saw fit to give me a glimpse into the darkness and a taste of their unimaginable dominations. I needed her guidance. "I give you my word, Koriniha. I shall not allow you to perish so long as I live. And with this"—I pulled the bag from my waist—"should you die, I shall bring you back."

The priestess laughed again; it was the shrill cry of a harpy. "Then let us begin the ceremony, my lord."

The priests and sorcerers formed a chain around the altar, leaving Koriniha, the bound Hunter, and myself in the center. I was directed to remove the artifact from its bag and place it upon the stones. A burst of cold traveled up my arm as my gauntlet closed around the small rectangular box. It did not reflect the moonlight, rather it seemed to absorb it hungrily, leaving a greater darkness than was possible. For the first time, markings could be seen on the black surface. They began to glow and gain in strength, withering tendrils, seemingly alive and searching.

I placed the box near the head of the trapped Hunter. He shouted and spat at me, but his words were drowned out by the increasing hum of the chanting priests. The coldness in my arm did not dissipate, but began to travel deeper into my core, chilling my blood, and forming crystals of ice vapor in my lungs.

The priestess studied the moon. "The time is upon us. I must call upon the Old Ones in their speech. When I am done, remove the heart of the sacrifice. Drink some of his blood and pour the rest upon the artifact."

I pulled my battle-ax from my back, released the leather cover from the ancient sharpened head, and cast it aside. The shaft was smooth and polished with use, strengthened with bands of iron and had been replaced countless times over generations. The blade itself was ancient, made of an unknown metal that cut like the finest steel, yet had somehow survived in the possession of my family since the time of Alexander. It had taken many lives, and the sacrifice tonight would be but another, though it had never been used in so dark a pagan ritual.

For me there would be no reconciliation. There would be no forgiveness. After tonight there was no looking back or turning away from the dark path I trod. My people, my country and my God would all forsake me for the acts I was about to commit.

So be it.

I twisted the deadly weapon in my gauntleted fists. "I am ready."

The priestess began to speak, her voice low and guttural, descending somehow into tones not produced by human beings, and in pitches never meant to be heard by mortal ears. Swirling black clouds drew over the pyramid, moving at speeds greater than the greatest storms of the seas. Lightning cracked down into the surrounding jungle. Thunder boomed and echoed off of the mountains, deafening in its fury. Raindrops the size of babies' fists pelted down upon us in an intense deluge. Within moments the pyramid was drenched, and torrents of water spilled down the causeways and stairs. The memory became disjointed and the foundations of the world cracked.

You not listen to this, the Old Man whispered.
Why?
Is for best. Not to have such things in head. Drive you mad.

The memory flashed by impossibly fast. The ceremony continued. The priests gave dark signs. The priestess continued her impossible litany.

Time returned to normal.

Better. Now worms not eat your brain when wake up.

"Now take his heart and feast upon his blood!" The priestess screamed over the roar of the wind and rain. The artifact was floating now, inches above the stone. It was absorbing all of the available light, seeming to surge and gorge itself with every continuous lightning strike. The etchings on the artifact had detached themselves and were swirling in the air, growing and spinning, crackling with black energy.

The Hunter met my eyes. He was beyond fear and

prepared for his death. I brought the weapon down on the center of his chest, severing the muscles, and cracking the sternum. I stopped before it pierced his heart. I could use my ax with surgical precision. He screamed in agony. I twisted and levered the blade in, using the handle as a pry bar. I shattered the ribs, and pulled the ax free.

He was still alive as I reached into the cavity, pushed through the remaining flesh and welling fluids and grasped his beating heart with my gauntlet. It pulsed as I curled my fist around the organ and tugged. The Hunter screamed and spasmed as I tore the heart free.

"Drink." The priestess commanded.

No. I tore myself free of the vision.

You must watch, the Old Man insisted. *You must learn.*

Not that part. Hell no.

Good, Boy. Hope for you yet.

I tossed the still-warm heart aside. My mouth tasted coppery and my stomach roiled against the unfamiliar sensations. The fluids that I had poured into the artifact had seemingly disappeared, swallowed up and taken to another, darker place. The artifact was spinning now, the black lines of power twirling around like streamers, twisting with the physical presence of snakes.

"There is only one thing left, my lord," the priestess said, "and the power over time itself is yours."

"Tell me what I must do!" I raged into the storm. I was so close.

The booming of the thunder continued, but my battle-hardened senses picked up another sound—the explosions of gunpowder.

"You must take the final—" She stopped, glancing down in surprise. Koriniha reached one delicate hand between her breasts and probed with her fingers. Her hand came away from the hole as a trickle of blood ran down her rain-soaked robes.

I turned in time to see the armored figures appearing over the lip of the pyramid. Most of their matchlocks misfired as the fierce rain soaked their powder or extinguished their smoking cords, so they used them as clubs. Captain Thrall led the charge. His sword cleaved downward and tore one of the priests in half. Behind him were all of his men, and I was surprised to see many of the men that I had sent in pursuit of the deserters. Even my most loyal troops that I had left to guard the pyramid had turned against me.

The demons rose and lumbered into the fray, swatting aside the conquistadors with heavy stone limbs. The scene degenerated into a mob of confusion as rain fell and lightning flashed. The artifact still spun in its web of black tendrils.

"Koriniha!" I shouted as the priestess fell to her knees, vomiting blood from her open mouth. I knelt at her side, and caught her before she went facedown to the stone. I shook her. "What now? Tell me!"

"My love . . . Bring me back . . ." She foamed at the mouth, and died. Her eyes rolled sightlessly back into her head.

"No! No! Damn you! Damn you all!" I screamed as I dropped her soulless form into the rushing water. My plans were ruined. Without the priestess I did not know how to commune with the Old Ones. All of my treachery, throwing away my command, throwing away my generalship, all for naught. I howled in rage and hatred.

I had to reach the artifact.

Now the memory shifts, flailing forward in jerks and spurts.

"Stop him! Kill the general!" bellowed Captain Thrall. He was locked in battle against one of the fearsome demons. With his great strength he sent it tumbling backward over the pyramid's edge. "Kill him!" the brute screamed in a berserk rage.

Soldiers moved to block me. I killed one of Koriniha's priests that stumbled blindly into my path. I waded into the troops, ax humming through the giant water droplets. The troops fell back under the fury of my onslaught. My skin was like ice and my blade moved as quickly as the lightning. I could feel the power of the artifact. So close, so very close.

I crushed a soldier's skull and batted him aside. A sword tip streaked across my armor as I stepped clear and hammered the man to the earth. I wrenched out my ax blade, dripping with blood. Rage cascaded over me. How dare these men betray me after all that I had done for them? I swung my ax, killing or dismembering with each blow. I used the blade, spike and butt of my weapon to bring down my troops. Flailing limbs and blurred sword blades surrounded me as I poured death into my newfound enemies.

Pain flashed through my thigh as a blade pierced me. I broke free and spiked the soldier through the face. The water running off the top of the pyramid was running red with blood. The backdrop of the light-sucking altar and its spinning black tendrils were so close. I had to reach it. Razorlike steel cut through my back, breaking the coat of mail, and splattering my blood into the rain.

"NO!" I bellowed, turning and striking down the soldier who had dared to touch me. "YOU CAN NOT KILL ME!" The power of the artifact was thick upon me. I killed two others in one mighty swing. More wounds were inflicted on my flesh. I fell to my knees, but continued fighting. I cut a soldier's leg off, and finished him when he hit the ground.

That was all.

I pushed myself up. Slowly. Shakily. Bleeding from many punctures and lacerations. Dozens of bodies sprawled upon the pyramid top or across the stairs. My soldiers, my countrymen, all of them dead or dying. A few feet away, the final stone demon crumbled and flaked away into the rivers of blood and rain. Captain Thrall knelt upon its back, broken sword still clenched in one hand. His massive chest heaved with the exertion, and blood drizzled down his face from his lacerated scalp.

"Lord Machado," he said.

"Captain Thrall," I nodded.

We both looked at the darkness of the artifact, and then back at each other.

" 'Tis not meant to be, my General. 'Tis not meant for men to use such a black thing." His skull was visible through missing parts of his face.

"With it I can rule the world."

"Thou art lost without thy witch," the giant stated simply. The priestess' body lay nearby, partially submerged.

"I will bring her back," I hissed.

"My ancestors came to my dreams and told me of thy plans. Thou was destined to fail and to open the way for the return of the dark forces of the ancients through thy failure. My people are gone. I am the last. Yet I have not forgotten our sagas." The giant captain gradually heaved himself to his feet, shaking from the many grievous wounds on his body. A lesser man would have just lain down and died. "Ye shall not pass."

"Never." I used my ax to lever myself forward. "It is mine."

"I have made a vow to the spirits. I will protect this artifact until the end of time. No man will look upon its evil and live." The captain turned and stumbled toward the altar.

"It's mine!" I screamed as I hurled my heavy ax across the distance. The blade sunk deeply into his back. It was a lethal blow.

The captain fell forward into the swirling bands of crackling black energy. He bellowed in pain as the evil tore into his flesh. Searing him. Burning him. He was turned over and spun in the maelstrom of darkness. The bands sunk and bonded into his very skin, like a twisted inking, an evil living tattoo.

"I . . . vow . . . to . . . keep . . . it . . . from . . . you . . ." He was engulfed by the power. The whites of his eyes disappeared, to be replaced by solid inky blackness. He screamed in agony.

There was an explosion of color and energy as lightning struck the top of the pyramid. Pain and heat surged up through my armor, burning me and hurling me aside. I fell upon the stairs, rolling and tumbling, through the torrents of water, down, down into the darkness.

I gasped as the Old Man removed his hands from my head. I was once again myself. The jungle pyramid and its unholy storm were gone, replaced by the eerily silent 1940s Polish town.

"Holy shit!" I said. I felt terribly weak. "What happened?"

"In his mind too long," the Old Man said softly, "is great strain."

"The captain. Thrall. He is the Tattooed Man."

"Yes. Cursed like the rest of us. Always there is a catch with these things. How you say—I think . . . He got screwed."

Indeed. Cursed to guard an evil artifact for the last five hundred years. I could think of lots better ways to pass the time.

"But there is more?" I asked. There were still questions to be answered. "Lord Machado failed. That evil priestess chick got shot before they could finish the ceremony. Yet somehow he's still alive today. How did he become the Cursed One?"

"There is small bit of memory left. Only short time while he is still human, I think. Still that I must show you."

"You have to show me now, Mordechai," I pleaded. "If I can know how he became what he is, then I can know how to defeat him."

"Not yet. Too much strain. And rest I must."

"I can do it," I answered. "I have to be ready."

"No, Boy. Not ready. You wake up. Be ready for fight. Big fight for you today."

"Big fight?"

"Yes. Much big." He pointed his fingers and made shooting noises. "Much fight."

"You got any more little wooden carvings you want to send back with me?" I asked hopefully. "In case I need to roast any vampires?"

"Sorry, Boy. I surprised that work my own self."

"How could it anyway? I'm no expert of physics, but how can I take an immaterial thing into the material world?"

"Boy, much you have to learn. Even spirit is matter. Just much finer . . . Much simpler time when I used to hunt monsters. Shoot them with gun. Bang. Dead monster. Nice and simple. Monsters nowadays all complicated and hard to make dead."

"So any chance you might be able to scrounge up some toys then?"

He shrugged his thin shoulders. "I try. When time comes, I have something for help. Now go." He shooed me away. I turned to leave. "One last thing."

"Yeah?" I stood barefooted in the snow while I waited for him. He seemed to be trying to find the words. "Spit it out, Mordechai. Apparently I've got monsters to kill."

"Boy." He regarded me solemnly. "On this day. Try very hard not to get dead."

"I will try," I promised.

The Hind tore across the sky at rapid speed and dangerously low altitude. I awoke to the thrumming of the blades, the deafening roar of the engines, and the piped-in music from the Doors, "Riders on the Storm." Julie's head was resting on my shoulder. A lock of her hair had strayed from under her helmet and draped down her face. I brushed it back. She woke up and smiled tiredly.

She was still holding my hand.

Harbinger signaled for all of us to put in our earpieces so that we could communicate and do a radio check.

"Wake up, sleepy heads. We're only ten minutes out. Skippy is swinging wide around Corinth. His people have an agreement with the elves. No orcs on elf land. No elves on his. We'll be coming in from the south and will be setting down in a designated clearing. Feds have already gotten us on radio, and are even tracking us for surface to air missiles. Seedy bastards."

"I hope they don't get twitchy," Milo said.

"I hate the government," Sam stated coldly. "Remind me again why we're working with them?"

"They need us. We need them," Harbinger said.

"Not to be a jerk about it, but how exactly do we get paid for this?" Holly asked. "Saving the world don't pay the bills."

"Government representatives don't get to claim PUFF. By being here we will get at least an assist. Even that is worth a small fortune on a Master." Harbinger pulled his revolver, checked the rounds, spun the cylinder and reholstered. "Only I talk to the Wendigo. Everybody else stay way the hell back. He ain't friendly. When we go after the Cursed One, let the Feds go in first. At that point we're just observers. Let them do the bleeding. Pitt?"

"Yes, sir?"

"Damn it. Call me Earl. 'Sir' is the Boss. Have you learned anything new? Is Mordechai Byreika still in your dreams?"

"No and yes. I've seen things. But I don't know what's going to be able to help us."

"Give us the short version," he ordered.

I quickly told the others about the human Lord Machado and his army, about the ancient city, about the evil priestess Koriniha and her dark priests, about the artifact, the ceremony, the sacrifice and, finally, the Tattooed Man.

"I've spoken with him," I said, "just now, in my dream. It was real. He was heading toward Montgomery. He's coming for the artifact, and he swears he's going to kill me."

"I don't care how bad everybody thinks this guy is, MHI don't roll over and take it from no five-hundred-year-old pukes," Sam said. "If he shows up, we cap his trash. That simple. Fricking magic tattoo bullshit. I've got a magic tattoo. It's a frog with a banjo and it's on my ass. I got it in Singapore."

"Classy," Holly said.

"Wanna see it sometime?" he asked as he removed his can of Copenhagen from his armor and snapped his wrist repeatedly.

"I'll pass, thanks."

"There was something else. The Old Man warned me. He said we're going to have a big fight today. He didn't say what, but I got the impression it was going to be bad."

"Figures. Anything else?"

"Nope."

"Lee? Give everybody the rundown on what we've gotten from the archives," Harbinger ordered, "anything that might prove useful."

"Sure." The diminutive Hunter cleared his throat.

"There were no records of a conquistador general named Lord Machado anywhere. There were, however, some signs pointing to what was called the lost expedition. Early in the 1500s, the very first group dispatched into the interior, same basic area where Orellano would later discover the Amazon, but this group was never heard from again. All of the records about this expedition were destroyed by the military governor at Isle of the Cross, which is what they called Brazil back then. Even Walter Raleigh mentioned this lost expedition in his writings about El Dorado. Looking at what Owen has told us, I'm betting that was Lord Machado's group."

"What about the artifact or the Old Ones?"

"Just vague references to great and terrible evil. Lots of old Hunters have mentioned it in their writings, but I get the impression that none of them really knew what they were. Byreika's journal had the most about them."

"And?"

"Eldritch horrors, to paraphrase some Lovecraft. Horrible things that date back to before mankind, real serious, evil bad stuff. About the artifact itself? Byreika thought that it predated this world and was from somewhere else. I was kind of lost on that part. The journal was in Polish and I had to use a computer translator. It can be kind of hard to understand."

"He isn't much better in person," I mumbled.

"The first people recorded to have had it were the ancient Midianites, followed by the Assyrians. How it wound up in South America is anybody's guess. Supposedly it grants the user the power of the Old Ones. Control of time, space, energy, matter, that kind of thing. Anybody who tries to use it dies, unless you are one of the special people."

"Special?" Holly asked. "Like they ride the little bus to school?"

"No, I can't think of a better word for it. Once in a while someone comes along who has the ability to actually use this thing. Since the world is still here, we can assume that none of them have been successfully united with it yet. Except, of course, Lord Machado."

"The prophecy from my dream," I thought out loud. Just thinking about the black obelisk in the unnatural cavern made my skin crawl.

"Anything else?" Harbinger asked.

"Just that if this thing is activated by the right person, which we've got, and the right time, which is apparently tomorrow night, at the right place, which according to Ray Shackleford is right here, then we're pretty much boned. Stop them, and we save the world."

"Good thing," Milo said as he spit some sunflower seeds into a paper cup. "I like the world. It would suck to blow it up. Especially since I'm engaged now."

"What? Get out of here!" Harbinger said. "No way." Most of their team had a similar reaction.

"Who?" Julie asked. "I didn't even know you were dating."

"I bet I know," said Sam. "I bet it's that hot little scientist chick we rescued when we killed that mutant shrieker lizard in Guatemala. What was she again? A crip-to-whatsist?"

"Cryptozoologist," Milo said. He looked slightly embarrassed at the attention. "Shawna studies undis-covered animals. It's been a long-distance relationship.

I kind of popped the question. She said yeah. You know . . ."

"Why didn't you tell us, man? That's great news," Harbinger said.

"I was a little distracted, what with the forces of evil, and the freighter, and the undead, and the elves, and the gargoyles, and the Feds, and stuff."

"Land . . . Gub Mint below. Land now." Skippy's gravelly voice came over the radio. "Good Milo. Find wife . . . Now should get . . . more wifes . . . only one wife . . . make for . . . lonely warrior."

"I'll take it under consideration, Skip," he said cheerfully.

"Take her down," Harbinger ordered. "Okay team. This is it. Stay frosty. Keep your cool around the Feds."

"Look who's talking," Sam murmured.

The Feds had set up a command post that could best be described as a tent city. And they had done it all this morning. In the distance, dozens of Mississippi state troopers blocked off the road. The members of MHI were greeted by uniformed National Guardsmen and led toward an enormous green tent.

The inside of the command tent was climate-controlled and sealed against chemical, biological and radioactive agents. It smelled faintly of new rubber and was bigger than most middle-class homes. An entire wall was covered in giant flat-screen televisions. Rows of computers were manned by military personnel or armored federal agents. Some of the screens showed real-time satellite imagery of the area in normal and thermal views. I could make out our helicopter parked on the grass. It was glowing bright yellow and red. Dozens of cameras must have been dropped over the Bottoms, showing several different shots of the swamp. Agent Myers was directing the circus, and for the first time since I had met him, he had ditched the suit and dressed for battle.

"Check the feed from the Predator drones. Send another one to parallel the Hatchie River. Have the AWACs divert all air traffic out of this area. I want those bombers in the air now. I want some with napalm, and some with penetrators if they're underground. Where are those Abrams?"

"They are on Seventy-Two, ETA fifteen minutes, sir," answered one of the Feds as he tapped away on one of the many computers. "They're passing through the town of Walnut."

"Good. We may need to steamroll something," Myers said as he nervously tugged at the straps on his armor.

"Sir? What about 'final option'?" asked one of the agents at a computer.

"Tell the Pentagon to scramble the B1. Have it ready. What's the payload on that?"

"We are cleared for low tactical yield. Five kilotons. Minimal radiation."

"Civilian casualties?" he asked.

"Within an acceptable level. This area is sparsely populated."

"Excellent," he said slowly.

"Holy shit. They're going to nuke Mississippi," Holly said.

Myers turned around. The National Guard lieutenant that had led us in saluted.

"Sir. Here are the guests you were expecting."

"About damned time, Earl. Where the hell have you been?"

"If you wanted us sooner, Myers, you should have sent a jet," he explained casually. "Are you really authorized to go nuclear?"

"I'm authorized to tow the moon down here and crash it into Earth if I think it would help," Myers answered sharply. "If you haven't noticed, somebody is planning on destroying all life on this planet. The President is willing to do what it takes to solve this problem, so as a last resort, yes, I'm ready to go nuclear."

"Say . . . when did they put you in charge of the Monster Control Bureau anyway?" Harbinger asked. "When I saw you in Texas you were still just an assistant director."

Myers fixed my boss with a look that would have killed most people. I didn't know what it was, but there was certainly some bad history between these two men. "Last Friday," he answered sullenly. "I'm just interim director until the President appoints somebody else. I received the call, and a few hours later I hear from you that seven Master vampires just touched down. It's been a hell of a week."

"So that's why you've been cranky," Harbinger answered wryly.

The senior agent sighed. "Look. Are you going to take us to this Wendigo thing or not?"

"I'll do it. No vehicles, though. He isn't going to come out if there are vehicles, and you'll need to pull the air cover back."

"I guess I don't have much choice." Myers gestured toward one of the screens, a real-time satellite feed of the Natchy Bottom area. Most of the picture, including the area that we were currently in, was perfectly and surprisingly clear. The center of the screen, however, was fogged. "A billion dollars in equipment, and I can't get a clear picture of the interior of the Bottoms. No cameras will work more than thirty feet into the swamp. I'm reduced to talking to Indian fairy tales."

"You know how Natchy Bottom is. It don't obey the same rules as the rest of the world."

"I know. All right then, let's get this over with."

The roof of the tent began to rattle as the rain started.

"It was clear five minutes ago," Lee said to me anxiously.

"Welcome to Mississippi," I answered.

The Monster Control Bureau men were honed and ready. Picked from elite military units and trained to a standard far surpassing our own, every one of them appeared to be chiseled from solid muscle and rock-hard bone. They made my team look a little dumpy.

"Agent Franks, ready the men," Myers ordered as we approached the waiting group.

Franks gave me a slight nod of recognition when he saw me. He emotionlessly returned to his men. "Listen up!" Franks shouted. The thirty black-armored men snapped to attention, weapons bouncing in their slings, magazines and explosives clanking. They regarded us with steely eyes. Some were bruised from their brief encounter with MHI the day before. Harbinger ducked under an overhanging tarp and nonchalantly lit a cigarette. The cold drizzling rain quickly soaked us all to the bone.

"Pay attention, men." Myers spoke loudly, but rather than resembling a military leader rallying the troops, he still made me think of a college professor giving a lecture. "We are going into Natchy Bottom. This is possibly one of the most dangerous places in the world. Once we get into the swamp, you will need to keep your wits about you. Things are not always what they seem in the Bottoms. It is an intersection of all that is wrong in the universe. Do not fire until I or Agent Franks order you to do so. We are searching for the Cursed One and seven Master vampires."

Some of the men began to mutter and shift nervously. I was glad to see that. They may have been hard-charging warriors, but at least they weren't stupid about it.

"Don't worry, men. We are not going in looking for a fight. Right now we are going in to speak with one of the creatures in the swamp. It will provide us with the location of the enemy, and they will be dealt with using overwhelming force," Myers assured them. "Even Masters are not so tough when you carpet-bomb them."

"We might have a man in there, Myers," Harbinger said coldly.

"Then you are more than welcome to go in and rescue him before the air strike," Myers answered. "Nothing personal, but I'm not risking thirty good men for one of yours." The agent continued, "The ten individuals standing behind me, some of you already may have made their acquaintance—" A few of the bruised Feds nodded sullenly. One of the men that had beat down Trip made a thumping motion with his fist. "—are from MHI. They are here to make contact with the swamp creature and extract information. After that, they get out of the way. Earl, if you would tell us about this creature, please?"

Harbinger tossed his cigarette to the ground, giving up because of the soaking rain. "It's a Wendigo. If you see something ten feet tall and real scary looking, don't shoot at it. You'll make him angry."

"Any questions?" Myers asked.

"Sir, how are we supposed to work with these people? We've got three men in the hospital because of them." The agent who asked that had a bandage over his nose. He glared at me when he spoke. It wasn't my fault he didn't know how to block.

"You will do as you're told," Myers said coldly.

One of the agents raised his hand. "What about sensor arrays?"

"They don't seem to work in the Bottoms. We will take our portable gear, and hopefully we will get some reception the deeper we get, but I would not count on it."

Another agent asked, "How about the robots?"

"Same thing. We can't count on electronics in the Bottoms. The last thing we need is for one of their sensors to mistake some of us for undead and blast us. The recognition software only runs ninety-eight percent in optimal conditions."

"Air support?"

"Not until after we speak with this Wendigo thing. We can call them in if we have an emergency."

"Armor backup?"

"Abrams are en route, and will arrive shortly. However, they will not be able to operate in most of the terrain. Ground is too soft."

"What a bunch of babies," Sam whispered to me. "We don't ever got none of that cool stuff."

"Jeez, Milo, how come we don't have killer robots?" Julie asked.

"You write the check," he answered.

"Attention team. Form up. Franks has operational command. I will remain at the command center in radio contact." Myers signaled toward his second in command. "Which way, Earl?"

Harbinger pointed towards the heart of the swamp.

Natchy Bottom was a still and unnatural place. The small amounts of ground were soft and treacherous. Long patches were covered in dank, fetid water, thick and overgrown with gnarled trees and thorned vines that grabbed and clutched at you. Roots and other unknown items were always underfoot, waiting to cause the unwary to stumble. The rain dripped down through the thick canopy of trees. It was early in the morning, but it was dark inside the Bottoms.

"Welcome to Dagobah," Trip joked.

"You are such a geek," Holly retorted.

I swatted a mosquito that landed on my cheek. It splattered bloodily. It was as big around as a dime. I swore under my breath.

"Just wait until we get done and you check for leeches," Sam said. "You can have hundreds of those suckers on you and not know it."

"And ticks. Don't forget the ticks," Milo added.

"Don't pay them any attention," Julie said. "The leeches and ticks here are big enough that you'll feel them when they latch on."

"Good," I answered. "I don't want to waste my

time with wussy insects." I adjusted Abomination and forded on into the waist-deep muck.

The agents had broken into three teams, with MHI bringing up the rear in a rough diamond pattern. The agents moved like ghosts through the trees. They communicated totally with hand signals, and had drilled to the point that each team was a seamless blending of skill. I had to admit, they were impressive in action.

Then there was us.

"Wow. Did you see the size of that snake?"

"That wasn't a snake. It was a log."

"Hey, are there crocodiles here?"

"Alligators, moron. Crocodiles are in Africa."

"No, they aren't. Those are in Australia."

"Well, actually they're in both."

"You can tell the difference by the snout. I saw that on *Animal Planet*."

I idly wondered if the Monster Control Bureau were hiring.

Harbinger tapped me on the shoulder. "Do you sense anything?"

"No. It's just creepy. Why?"

"You've felt the Cursed One. You know him better than the rest of us. I just hoped you would know when he's near."

"Oh . . . Hey, Earl," I whispered. "I've got a question for you. How come we don't move like the Feds? All quiet and fast. We're just kind of clumped up and shooting the bull."

"Seems kind of unprofessional in comparison, don't it?" he asked. I nodded. "Well, let's look at this for a moment. I've been doing this kind of thing for a real long time, so I'm going to let you in on my philosophy." He lowered his Tommy gun and ducked under some puncture vines. "See how those guys are all intense? Real quiet like?"

"Yeah."

"All of them learned how to fight against human beings. Monsters are different. I bet most of those guys are multiple-combat vets. Were we to fight them, we would get our asses kicked, because they know how to fight people."

"You got them pretty good last night."

"Element of surprise, Owen. If I were to try that again they would pump my guts full of lead. Now here's the thing. They're moving like they're up against things with the same senses as them. I've got bad news, if the Masters are in this swamp, they already know we're here. And as far as being quiet so they can't sneak up on you, if a Master wants to sneak up on you, they are going to do it. Doesn't matter who you are. Well, with a few exceptions." He nodded toward Skippy and his brother Edward.

They were slightly apart from the group, heads cocked as they listened intently and sniffed the air. The two orcs were dressed in black and wearing their balaclavas, though they had ditched their glasses. Their yellow eyes studied the trees and the murky water with great interest. Skippy cradled an old AK47, adorned with feathers and small animal bones, while Edward's hands were empty, but with a pair of short swords strapped over his back. He looked like a ninja.

"How come Ed doesn't have a gun?"

"He's a lousy shot. . . . Anyways, now those boys. They're our early warning system. Ed goes for his sword. Get ready. Orcs sense things different than us."

"And what about you?" I asked seriously. Obviously Harbinger had some gifts that were not normal.

"Me? I've just got more experience is all . . . Don't dwell on it." He chuckled. "Back to your question, now here's the real difference between us and the Feds. They always act like that. We're not creatures of habit. We can tailor our behavior for the situation. If we need to be quiet, we can be quiet. If we need to be fast, we can be fast. But have you noticed the biggest difference between us and them?"

"They're jerk-offs?"

"Besides that."

I thought about it for a moment. I watched as one of the Feds scurried behind a patch of stunted trees. He scanned around him nervously, the barrel of his stubby F2000 poking around quickly as he heard the splash of a small swamp animal. Relieved, he quickly moved on.

"Some of them are terrified," I answered.

"Bingo. They're quiet. But that means they can't talk to their team. That means that their minds are totally on their surroundings. And if you ain't noticed, we're strolling through one of the most evil places in the world. A place like this gnaws at your mind. You start to see things out the corner of your eye. Pretty soon you're seeing ghosts, and I ain't talking about the friendly kind like you've got riding around in your head. I mean the bad kind that are jealous of the living, and want you to be just as miserable as they are. While those Feds are getting nervous and jumpy, their minds playing tricks on them, when it comes time to throw down, we're going to be just fine. That's why you see my team shooting the bull."

"It keeps their minds off of all this." I gestured at the drizzly blackness. As I concentrated on the swamp, I could feel the chill, the cold, the eons of hate, and the ancient evil that lay under the murky water. I looked away and turned back to my team. "I'm with you."

We continued on, drenched by the splashing mud and the drizzling rain. It was summer, but it was probably only forty degrees inside Natchy Bottom. I was shivering beneath my heavy armor. I did not envy the smaller Hunters who lacked my insulating body fat. Who's laughing now, skinny people?

The deeper we got into the swamp, the darker and more sinister it grew. After an hour of walking, the radio finally crackled. We had previously tuned into the Feds' secure frequency. "This is Alpha team. We have a contact. There are some huts on a little island. One hundred yards south of us. They appear to be inhabited. Huts have some sort of light source, and there are some cooking fires. Over." Our team halted, waiting for more information. I used the opportunity to spray more bug repellant onto my exposed skin.

"This is Delta," replied Myers. "Investigate. Proceed with caution. Over."

Harbinger scowled and his nostrils flared as he sniffed the air. Our leader looked uneasy as he studied the surrounding swamp. He looked to Skippy and Edward. The orcs studied the air. Skippy shook his head in the negative. Harbinger got on the radio.

"Belay that order, Alpha team. Do not make contact."

"MHI, get off my radio net," Myers snapped.

"What color are the lights in those shacks?" Harbinger asked. "I bet they're green."

"Uh . . . This is Alpha. The lights are green. I repeat green. Over."

"Fall back, Alpha. Fall back unless you want to get the marrow sucked out of your bones."

"This is Delta. Alpha, ignore that order and check out those structures. Over."

"Myers, you dumb ass. Pull your men back or you're going to lose a whole team. And then we're going to have to waste a day messing with the things on that island, and they don't have anything to do with what we're after. Alpha team, listen up. If you step foot on that island, you're dead men. By the time we get over there, they'll have skinned you and eaten your eyeballs right out of your heads." He let go of the mike, and then thought better of it. "Over," he added.

"What are they, Earl?" Julie asked with some concern. He just held up a hand and waited for Myers' response. A minute passed.

"This is Alpha. What should we do, sir? Over."

Finally Myers responded. "Fall back, Alpha. Ignore the structures for now. Mark them on your GPS for future investigation. Over."

"It's your funeral," Harbinger said into the radio.

"What are they?" Trip asked nervously.

"Humboldt Folk," he explained. Most of the Hunters looked at each other in confusion. Only the senior Hunters nodded in understanding. "They just want to be left alone is all. Alpha team is lucky they didn't set foot on that island. The Folk don't let trespassers leave. Ever."

"No, Earl. You forget something. We're real lucky our team isn't the one that happened across it," Julie corrected him. "They wouldn't leave their circle to attack Alpha. They're all male. For us they might have made an exception."

"What do you mean?" Trip asked quietly.

"The Folk tend to run real short on fertile females," Julie answered. She quickly checked her weapons. "Holly, if you get attacked by some strange-looking people with a green glow about them . . . save your last bullet for yourself." She was not joking.

"What are they?" Holly asked. She held her .308 Vepr and scanned the surrounding trees.

"What were they is a better question," Harbinger responded, "and that's a story that I'm going to save for when we're standing in a warm sunshiny place. Come on, team, we're wasting daylight."

Somewhere in the distance strange animals cried.

CHAPTER 22

Hours passed as we trudged deeper into the heart of the evil swamp, yet we had not gone very far. The going was slow in Natchy Bottom. It was afternoon, and the rain had not let up. The water level had risen, and walkable land was becoming scarcer. All too often we were forced to wade through the murk, unseen things grasping at our boots, mud sucking us down. At this point we were all so coated in filth that it was becoming difficult to tell who was who.

The shorter Hunters had it particularly bad, often having to wade through water that came up over their chests, and being forced to hold their weapons above their heads. At one point Lee slipped and disappeared beneath the water, and did not come up immediately. Sam dived under and retrieved him, bringing the other Hunter up sputtering and choking. Lee swore that the roots had not wanted to let him go.

I noticed that the mood of the group had become darker and more somber. The further we went into Natchy Bottom, the more it seemed to suck at a person's happiness and will to live. It really was a bad place. I could feel that something was watching us. Unknown insects crawled or slithered inside my clothing.

"Stop," Harbinger ordered, The team complied, weapons at the ready. "This is it."

I looked around. It looked just like every other patch of gray-and-black muck and mutant trees that I had been looking at all morning. I would certainly hate to get lost in here.

"Yes. Everybody stay quiet. No sudden moves. Don't point your weapons at the Wendigo." He got on the radio. "Franks. Call a halt. This is the place. I'm going to make contact."

"This is Delta. I want my men there with you. Over." Myers' voice was distorted, and hard to hear through the static.

"Alpha, Bravo, set up a perimeter. Charlie with me. Hold up, MHI. Over," Franks stated over the radio.

"All right. My favorite person in the whole world," I muttered. "My good buddy Agent Franks gets to hang out with us." My tongue unconsciously probed the gaps in my gums from where he had smashed out my teeth.

"He ain't so bad for a bureaucratic killing machine," Trip said.

"I heard he once burned a bus load of nuns 'cause he thought there was a zombie on board," Sam added.

"No, those were orphans," Milo corrected.

"He's actually kind of cute in a psychopathic way," Holly said.

"Eww," I responded. "That's sick."

"Hey, some girls go for that side-of-beef thug look." She winked at Julie. I could tell our sharpshooter's cheeks turned red beneath the coating of grime. Personally, besides the muscles, I did not think that I looked like Franks at all. I was, after all, much better looking. Well, in my opinion at least.

"I said quiet," Harbinger admonished. The team settled down. Charlie team materialized out of the mist a few minutes later, moving like ghosts. Franks looked like Swamp Thing, coated in mud and moss. He made a few rapid hand signals and his team disappeared into the trees.

"Okay," he grunted as he knelt in the mud amongst my team.

"Y'all sit tight. I'm going over there." Harbinger pointed out a small clump of land, almost tall enough to be dry. "I'll be right back. Franks, you'd best keep your men under control."

"Don't worry," the quiet man stated. Harbinger nodded and moved quickly away, sloshing through the mud, stepping on roots and semisolid land whenever possible.

"How's your stomach?" Franks asked as he studied the terrain.

"Sore. How're your nuts?" I whispered back.

"Fine." He shifted his gun in his big hands. "I killed the last guy who tried to kick me like that."

"Hey, asshole, if we're comparing notes, I think you've hit me a lot more times than I've hit you."

"Will you two shut up?" Julie hissed.

Harbinger had reached the island. He hung his Tommy gun in the branches of a tree, set down his revolver and grenades, and finally stabbed his bowie knife into the trunk, leaving it there vibrating slightly. He left his weapons behind and walked slowly up the mud hill. At the summit he sat down cross-legged, back toward us, and waited.

"Probably a stupid question at this point . . ." Trip whispered. "But what's a Wendigo exactly?"

"A shaman who was cursed for committing an unforgivable act, usually something cannibalistic. Doomed to walk the Earth forever, guardians of the land and its original inhabitants," Julie answered softly. "It's a horrible fate."

The swamp grew still. The rain stopped. The constant croaking and chittering of amphibians and insects abruptly died. The tiny bit of light that we had been getting through the canopy went away, leaving us in near darkness. A shiver ran down my spine. It felt almost sterile and impossibly lifeless.

An eerie illumination slowly rose from the other side of the hill, highlighting Harbinger as he sat perfectly still. Something moved in the unnatural light. Something huge. Impossibly tall, but startlingly lean. All we could see was a silhouette of billowing skins, ten feet tall, with antlers like a deer rising from the center of its elongated head. An alien figure out of nightmares. It was not of this world.

The thing stopped before Harbinger. Our team leader did not move. I realized I was holding my breath.

The antlered being was motionless. Its long limbs folded tight against its body, giving us no clue as to its unnatural structure. I could not see the Wendigo's facial features, and for that I was thankful. If they were conversing we could not tell. Other shapes moved on the island, giant hulking things, bristling with hair and mud, just outside of the circle of pale light. A horrible smell drifted across the water. I gagged involuntarily.

After a few minutes of silence the Wendigo turned and drifted off of the island. The hairy beasts ambled away, disappearing into the swamp. The gray light died. The rain began to pelt us again. Gradually the light returned to its natural levels and frogs began to croak. The swamp returned to normal, or at least as normal as a place like Natchy Bottom could be.

"That was the Wendigo," Julie told us. "The other things were skunk-apes. Swamp Sasquatches. It protects them, keeps them away from our world. They are why I didn't want your people"—she nodded at Franks—"to just come in here and blow the whole place up."

"Just big monkeys," the Fed grunted.

Julie started to reply, but then bit her tongue. Arguing with Franks would be like beating your head against a block of granite.

"Uh-oh," I said, "that don't look good." Once the mysterious being had gone, Harbinger leapt to his feet and slid down the hill, grabbed his weapons, and came leaping across the water, splashing toward us as fast as he could.

"It's a trap!" he shouted in our direction.

"Alpha, Bravo. Go hot," Franks ordered.

Harbinger skidded into us, breathing heavy. He looked like he had seen a ghost. I suppose in a way he had.

"The Cursed One ain't here. The vampires ain't here. But they summoned something else. Something is waiting for us. It was a trick." He turned to Franks. "We need immediate extraction and air cover."

The silent Fed did not argue. "Delta, this is Charlie. We need immediate evac. Over."

Nothing.

Franks repeated his request. Still no response. A regular man would have looked concerned at being stuck near the crossroads of all badness, in the middle of an ambush set by creatures of unspeakable evil. He shrugged, apparently unperturbed.

"The signal isn't getting out," Julie said. "How could it be a trap? My dad told us . . ." She trailed off. "Oh no."

"He told us what Susan wanted him to," Harbinger snapped. He kicked a tree stump. "Damn it! I should have thought of that. We have to get out of here."

"Alpha, Bravo. Come in," Franks said. "Nothing." He stood up and pointed at some of his men. He made several rapid hand signals and pumped his fist in the air. They nodded, leapt to their feet, and sloshed in the direction of the other teams. "We fall back to the extraction zone."

"Can you call in air cover with flares?" Sam asked.

"Already done," he answered as something boomed from the direction of Charlie team. A few seconds later, red flares erupted high above us and slowly drifted toward the thick canopy of trees.

"I just hope they see them in the bad visibility," Milo said, looking up at the rain and the roiling clouds.

From the distance came a sound like the blowing of a horn, a deep rumbling that we all felt in the pits of our stomachs. The low note continued for several seconds and then trailed off. Another horn blew to our south, and then another to the east.

"Earl, what did they summon?" I asked. All I knew

was that if they had been brought here by Lord Machado, they were not going to be friendly.

"I don't know." His face was streaked with mud and his eyes narrowed dangerously. "But the Wendigo said to get out. He said it's beyond his power. So it's bad. Real bad. I told him to get his people out of here. So if you see something that ain't human, shoot it."

More horns sounded. Now they were all around us. Several rang out between us and the way that we had come from. "Sounds like they're not going to let us retreat." Julie snapped her M14 to her shoulder and scanned through the scope. The MHI staff began to fan out, weapons at the ready, looking for defensive positions.

Deprived of his radio, Franks started to bellow orders to his men. "Dig in. Claymores. Hit them when they come for us. At my signal push through to the south." That was our end of the diamond. "Your men up to being the tip of the spear?" he asked Harbinger.

"Of course," our team leader answered with far more confidence than I felt. Ed's swords flashed silver in the low light as he pulled them smoothly from their sheaths. The blades were short and thick and wickedly sharp. He cracked his neck and vertebrae. The rest of us were armed with a variety of firearms, plus each person was packing along some form of heavier ordnance: RPGs, grenade launchers, and Milo had some sort of homemade lightweight flamethrower. It hummed ominously when he switched it on, heavily pressurized with napalm.

"Find cover," Harbinger ordered. "We don't know what they are, so hit them with everything." The squad complied. To our left, Charlie team dug down. To our right was Alpha. Bravo was behind us. Franks moved amongst his men, giving orders. Pointing out problems. Assigning areas of responsibility. Offering reassurance while the rumble of unnatural horns sounded in the distance. He may have been a violent bloodthirsty scumbag, but he was a good leader.

"Get lower, Trip," Harbinger suggested as he paced amongst us. "Holly, you have a clear area behind you, so you can use the RPG if we need it. Lee, don't hug right against that tree, it limits your mobility. Step back a bit and you still have cover." We had a great leader as well. "Looking good, Hunters. It ain't gonna be nothing we can't handle."

"I hate the part when you don't know what the bad guys are," Sam said quietly as he pressed his bulk behind a mound of tree roots. The low rumbling horns stopped. The rain slapped against the water.

"Harb Anger," Skippy grunted. The orc swiveled his head from side to side as he sniffed the air. "They come."

"What are they, Skip?" Julie asked.

"Not know," he answered. "Smell . . . smells not from . . . here."

The ten of us were spread out over a forty-foot area, holding low behind trees, roots, logs and mud. Each of us was scanning the swamp for threats. The rain and mist made it difficult to see very far. My area of responsibility was a confused mass of light and shadows, vines and trees, moss and mud. Nothing moved. The swamp was quiet except for the noises of small animals and the occasional bubble of mysterious organic gasses creeping to the surface.

Gunfire and explosions erupted to the north. Bravo team had made contact. Some of the Newbies jumped at the sounds and began to turn.

"Hold!" Harbinger shouted. "Watch your area! That's their problem. Deal with yours!"

I forced myself back into position as the supersonic cracks of rifle bullets and the duller whumps of high explosive filled the air. Bravo team was unleashing hell upon something. After several seconds the initial salvo died down until there was only a sporadic firing of weapons. Then nothing.

Franks' deep voice drifted through the trees, shouting orders and commands to his men.

"Bah. Whatever they are, they ain't so tough," Sam said as he spit into the water.

Harbinger held up his hand for quiet. He closed his eyes and listened intently, almost as if he was meditating. Suddenly he stiffened and swore quietly.

There was a whistling noise from the direction of Bravo. Then another, and another, until the swamp echoed with dozens of the strange sounds, and then the damp thuds of hundreds of separate impacts. Wails of pain and human agony followed.

"What was that?" Lee blurted, a hint of terror in his voice.

He did not get an answer. Harbinger snapped his Tommy gun into position and squeezed off a long controlled burst into a patch of black water. The .45 slugs tore into the muck and geysered upwards. The surface exploded under the impacts as something sprang upward through the mist.

I got a brief glimpse of the first creature before it was torn to pieces in the storm of hot lead and silver, orange fluids spraying into the surrounding foliage. It was about the size of a man, only hunched and misshapen. Insectile in its joints and extra limbs, the creature seemed all unnatural angles and claws, with two sets of interlocked jaws, and dozens of red eyes set into a blunted skull of a face. It ruptured open as the bullets pierced its carapace, almost as if its internal contents had been under great pressure. The torn thing thrashed about, falling backwards into the muck, finally lying still.

It was only because of my hearing protection, and its electronic amplification of sound, that I was able to hear Julie talking to herself. She sounded terrified and shaken. Julie Shackleford did not scare easily.

"Not them. Not again."

"What was that thing?" Holly shouted. None of the experienced Hunters answered. I lifted my cheek from my stock, looking over at the others. Milo blinked slowly, as if in disbelief. Sam stared silently into the distance. Julie had begun to shake uncontrollably. Harbinger changed magazines, looking down at his weapon instead of us. In the background more screams and random gunfire erupted from Bravo. Finally Harbinger pulled the bolt back, regarded it solemnly, and finally answered us.

"It's the things from the Christmas party."

"God help us," Milo said.

"This time we're armed, though," Sam answered. "It was hand-to-hand then, now we got guns."

"So do they," Harbinger replied sadly. "So do they."

"Incoming!" Julie shouted as she fired into the swamp. Orange-and-red shapes appeared from the murk or came charging out of the fog. Once again I heard the whistling noise, only this time it was closer, much closer. Something impacted the mud inches from my face, spraying my goggles. It appeared to be a long bone spine, dripping in dense orange fluid. I aimed at the source, a hunched insectoid demon thing, and stroked the trigger, blasting a slug through its thorax. More spines flew into our position, thudding into our cover like a volley of medieval arrows. The creature I shot stumbled, righted itself, hunkered down, pointed its crest in our direction, and launched another spine, cracking it deep through the bark of the tree I was hiding behind. I hit the creature with two more rapid shots, bursting some sort of internal fluid sack, and sent it back into the mud.

Spines landed all around me, each one impacting like a spear. The demons bobbed and crawled through the trees, closing the distance for their primitive weapons. They appeared to have no concept of fear, charging straight into our position, bodies exploding and breaking, limbs tearing off and being left behind, alien eyes pushing onward.

"Milo! Light 'em!" Harbinger ordered. Milo dropped his rifle onto its sling and scooped up the flamethrower. He fired a ten-second burst through the swamp, igniting the creatures, engulfing them in flames, sending them crackling back into the water. Some of the creatures reappeared, still burning, the water not being able to extinguish the lethal chemical mixture. They thrashed about, launching spines randomly until they expired.

Then it was still. There were no more moving orange shapes, only exploded and burned husks, charred and opened like overmicrowaved hot dogs. In the distance horns sounded as the demons regrouped, preparing to attack again.

"Everybody okay?" Harbinger shouted. One by one we shouted back in the affirmative. Somehow our team had gotten through the skirmish uninjured. Judging by the cries coming from Bravo's position, they had not been as lucky.

"They ain't so tough," Sam bellowed angrily as he shoved more massive shells into his .45-70.

"Sorry, Cowboy. Those were just scouts," Harbinger answered. "They were just probing us."

"How do you know?" I asked. "You don't even know what these things are."

"I can just tell. The ones we fought in '95 were just workers or drones. Mindless things with just claws and teeth. These things are the soldiers. They're gonna come again. That was just a test."

Explosions rocked from the direction of Alpha team as their position was attacked. We waited in anxious silence as the battle raged on without us. Sure enough, after a few minutes of fighting, Charlie team was attacked in turn. A stray bullet pulped a tree branch above my head. Other bullets whipped around us, sounding like angry bees.

"Watch your field of fire, you derelicts!" Sam shouted uselessly.

"MHI! I'm coming in," Franks shouted as he splashed toward us. He pushed his way to Harbinger's position and squatted in the mud.

"How's it going?" our leader asked.

"Two dead. Two wounded. One critical," the stoic man answered. He did not bother to ask about us. "We need to push out. Head for extraction."

"Negative. They can breathe under water. We could walk right into an ambush. If they get in close, those spear chuckers are gonna own us," Harbinger stated flatly. "We need to hold here."

"They are feeling us out for a rush."

"You saw how fast they move. We can't ditch them through the swamp, and with no cover, they're gonna tear us up."

"We have to fire and maneuver," Franks insisted.

"Listen, we're not fighting people. This ain't the army," Harbinger insisted. "We move out and we're dead."

"We're moving with or without you," Franks said. "Two minutes. We'll send up flares." The federal agent swiveled and moved away. "You can stay if you want."

Harbinger watched him go. "Shit."

"Earl? What do you wanna do?" Sam asked.

"We ain't got much choice. Without them, we get flanked and we're dead. We have to stick together." He changed the tone of his voice so that we could all hear. "Okay, team. When we see the flares, we move back the way we came. Lay down fire on anything that looks suspicious." He tried to rally us. "We can do this. We *are* the best. We've beaten these orange bastards before. I'm on point, then Skippy and Ed. We have the best senses. If we fire on a position, follow suit, it means we saw something." He switched magazines. "I'm loading tracers. I'll mark it, you kill it. Everybody get ready."

Flares rose into the rain-drenched sky. A cold weight shifted in my gut. The swamp before us was vast with shadowed hiding places.

"Move out!" Harbinger ordered.

◈   ◈   ◈

We set out toward safety, moving as fast as possible in the unforgiving terrain. Mud sucked at us, clung to us, increased our weight and tried to drag us down. The muscles in my calves burned at the exertion of double-timing it through the syrupy surface. To our sides and slightly behind us, the Feds moved through the trees. Even with their impressive physicality and despite their intense training, they could move no faster. The rain increased in intensity, hammering us, bouncing from the water below until it seemed as if it was raining from two directions.

It was still bone-numbingly cold, but we were all overheated and labored with the exertion of trying to move quickly through the muck. I did not take the time to brush the mammoth mosquitoes from my face. They were not the only things after our blood.

We crossed through the steaming carcasses of the destroyed demons. A closer look showed that the internal workings of the creatures were totally different than anything from this world. Their insides appeared to be a complicated series of bags and tubes, all orange, yellow or bright red. I stepped quickly over one creature, its two mouths open in a final death snarl, rows of jagged teeth and extra tongues hanging out haphazardly, a dozen dead eyes open and collecting rain.

I could feel a dark presence in the air. Not just the alien, skin-crawling sensation inherent in the haunted swamp, but rather an oppressive heaviness that seemed to further burden us. I recognized it.

The Cursed One was watching us.

His physical body was not here, of that I was certain, for surely I would have known it. But, rather, he watched us from afar. Somehow his presence was here amongst us, watching the trap which he had set encircling his enemies. Son of a bitch was enjoying this.

The evil signature of the accursed ancient artifact was on this endeavor. I did not know what the demon things were, but I knew that they had been ripped from their home world and brought here through its power. The artifact was the key.

We had made it less than three hundred yards before we made contact again.

Harbinger moved quickly, faster than the rest of us, somehow able to find traction where none of those following could. He froze in place, snapped his archaic subgun to his shoulder and fired a burst of tracers into the water below a fallen tree, splashing up gouts of water. Before the rest of us could react, he had aimed at another spot and fired more bright streaks into it.

The line of Hunters erupted. I lifted Abomination, aiming at the first spot. The hidden demon leapt upwards, intersecting with my buckshot, tearing its body asunder and taking its life. Other creatures rose beside and behind it, and I struck them down as well, Abomination merely a flawless extension of my killing will.

Then all hell broke loose.

Orange shapes tore through the pounding rain, scurrying at us from every direction. Insectoid horrors were coming out of the gnarled tree branches, erupting from the mud, launching their deadly missiles at us, trying to close the distance to use their claws and dripping teeth. Our advance stopped, the federal agents bearing down around us into the streaming horde of orange and red. The scene was utter chaos.

I emptied my shotgun, learning quickly to aim for the point where the creatures' heads intersected with their hardened bodies. It was a weak point, and beneath was some sort of fluid bag that would burst like a water balloon, putting the demons down hard. I dropped the spent magazine and instantly slammed a new one home. A spine whistled through the air, missing my face by inches. A Fed stumbled in the muck beside me, firing his FN into a charging monster. The .223 bullets punctured the body, but did not drop the creature.

"Aim for the neck!" I shouted as I chambered another round. He aimed higher and the creature exploded in a shower of gore. The body splashed into the water only a dozen feet away.

"Thanks!" the nameless man shouted. He raised his gun to engage another target, but stopped, looking down curiously at the alien spine embedded through the armor of his chest. "Shit!" he shouted before another spine nailed him squarely in the face, killing him instantly.

I caught the falling body and knelt behind him. It would be a lie to say that I did so to help, but rather it was an instinctive need to find cover as more spines sailed toward us. The limp form fell against me, heavy with sodden murk and spilling blood. I found the demon hunched down, launching spines at us. I aimed over the dead agent's shoulder and fired at the creature until it was dead. More creatures took its place, swarming over the fresh carcass and charging toward me. I fired my grenade, striking a tree and tearing three of the creatures asunder in the blast of hot shrapnel.

More spines struck the agent's twitching body. Abomination clicked dry. I dropped it onto its sling and grabbed the Fed's unfamiliar bullpup carbine. I raised it one-handed and sprayed the rest of the magazine in the direction of the creatures, the empty cases flying out the front of the weapon. When it was empty, I dropped it, sprang to my feet, and ran, searching desperately for cover, reloading my shotgun as I went.

Julie was kneeling behind a log. I dived over the top and splashed facedown in the mud next to her. I came up choking and spitting out the fetid taste. I rolled over and joined her. With each supersonic crack of her rifle, another demon went down. She hunched behind the log. "Reload!" she shouted as she searched for a fresh magazine. Spines impacted into our cover with wet thuds. I went over the top, spotted the demon hurling bits of itself toward us and swiftly killed it. More and more of them were pouring through the gray trees, a garish swarm of Mardi Gras color.

The tableau disappeared in a wall of brilliant flame as Milo ignited the swamp. "Clear out! Keep going!" he yelled at us as he put down a blanket of destruction. I knew that his portable weapon only had so much fuel, and demons were already closing from other directions, flashes of bright color betraying their positions all through the swamp.

Something shifted behind Milo. A single point opened in the rainy air, almost as if a giant hand had pulled back an invisible zipper. The sky on the other side was a dusty red, and flames licked the air when the alien atmosphere touched our own. A single demon dropped through the rift and splashed down. The opening snapped closed, leaving only pale sky. The creature raised a multijointed limb over its head.

"Milo!" Julie screamed as she fired at the creature. The bubble under its lower jaw exploded, sending it sprawling, but too late as its claws came down. Milo Anderson grimaced in pain as the sharpened bones pierced and shredded his arm. He went to his knees in a shower of crimson droplets.

Julie and I leapt to our feet, struggling forward. I grabbed Milo and hoisted him up. He kept the flames spraying into the swamp, beating back our foes. The intense heat washed over me and scalded my eyes. I could see flashes all across the terrain as other portals opened briefly and more creatures dropped into our world.

We were in a running battle against an endless foe, and there was only one possible outcome.

I pulled the bleeding and shaking Hunter across the water. The flamethrower sputtered and died. Julie was by my side, firing at the onrushing horde. She reached to her webbing, pulled a grenade and tossed it into the trees. The resulting blast shook me to my teeth. I made my way toward the rest of my team as fast as I could.

"Duck!" Harbinger shouted as I approached. I did so without thought, pushing Milo and myself down. He fired over our heads, cutting down the creature that had gated in beside us. The heavy husk fell on my back, a pointed, superheated, squishy weight. Pushing myself up, I kicked the segmented body aside.

Other types of demons were appearing now, smaller, swifter things, without any sort of distance weapon. They moved effortlessly across the terrain, faster than a human athlete could on dry ground. I watched as one leapt onto the back of a Fed, tearing at the man with its bone claws. Instantly, three other creatures were on him, pulling and biting. He disappeared in a shower of blood and limbs. A third kind of creature appeared, heavier, with platelike bones covering its vulnerable joints. These beasts lumbered slowly through the swamp, pausing to spit balls of green material from their upper mouths. A ball impacted at the feet of another Fed, exploding in a shower of horrible acid. He dropped his weapon and clawed at his Kevlar-covered legs, screaming in pain as it burned through to his bones.

They were everywhere.

We struggled toward a patch of higher ground. It was only a clump of mud, but it was the most defensive position we had. Milo began to shake horribly, as if he were having a seizure. "Poison," he said through gritted teeth. "Drop me."

"No, you can make it!" I shouted.

"O-O-owen. D-d-drop me," he ordered. His beard was running red with the blood coming from his mouth and staining his teeth. The powerful poison was tearing him apart. I did as I was instructed. Milo fell against a tree, and slid to the ground, pulling up his rifle. "Tell Shawna I l-l-love her," he gasped.

Julie tried to turn back for him, holding out a hand, pleading for her friend. I grabbed her by the arm and continued toward the high ground. There was nothing that we could do. Milo raised his carbine one-handed and fired, keeping the monsters at bay so we could escape. His AR emptied, he tossed it aside, shakily drawing his 1911. We kept moving as the shots echoed behind us. Several fast-moving demons descended upon the red-bearded man, and the last I heard was a thunderous chain of explosions as he detonated the grenades on his vest.

"Bastards!" Julie screamed as she stroked a demon to the ground with the stock of her rifle. I put my boot on its carapace and forced it down, as she put a finishing shot into the struggling thing's throat. We were both sprayed with yellow bile.

I passed Albert Lee's dismembered body, killing the distracted monster that was tearing at his flesh with a single shot to its pulpy brainstem. I loaded a fresh grenade and launched it into the horde following us. It killed four of them and barely made a dent.

I saw Skippy disappear under a pile of the creatures. His brother Edward jumped in to save him, blades singing through the raindrops. I had never seen any living being move with such fluid grace and deadly speed. Claws and heads were severed away in a remarkable dance of destruction, spraying orange fluids high into the air. Edward screamed an unearthly battle cry as he hacked through the beasts, spinning, ducking, always swinging and killing. The severed limbs and twitching corpses began to pile up.

Finally a spine appeared in Edward's back, and then another in his thigh. The orc began to falter. I fired a magazine into the fray, killing a demon with each shot, but it was too little, too late. Edward kicked a monster off of Skippy's body, and stood over his brother protectively. Shouting at the onrushing creatures, he slashed at them until finally he was washed away in a tide of crimson bodies.

The brothers died with great honor.

We reached the high ground. Our Alamo. Our Thermopylae. A twenty-foot pile of mud and sticks. There were only a handful of humans left. I could actually hear Lord Machado's laughter.

But the damned die hard.

CRACK. BOOM! A pile of the thick-set armored demons exploded as Holly's RPG struck amongst them, throwing heavy limbs and bone plates high into the sky. "Take that, you miserable sons a bitches!" she shouted as she tossed the spent launcher aside and pulled a grenade from her vest. She pulled the pin and hurled it into the swamp. At this point the enemy was so thick that we did not need to aim. It erupted in a shower of sparks and fragments.

A nearby Fed was pulled from his desperate hiding place in the crack of a tree trunk. He was dragged screaming into the horde, and violently pulled apart. He spasmodically jerked the trigger of his rifle. The stray bullet struck Holly Newcastle in the forehead, yawed and tumbled violently through her brain tissue, and exited at the base of her skull. She fell to the ground in an instant lifeless heap.

I crawled up onto the mud, shooting the closest demons, blasting a fast mover as it leapt toward us. Julie was still by my side as she struggled to her feet and tossed another frag. I instinctively shot an incoming acid bomb out of the air as if it were a clay pigeon. The remains showered down amongst the creatures. Julie began to pull and toss grenades from my webbing as I kept shooting.

As I reloaded, I saw Trip curled up near the summit. Torn and bloodied from dozens of claw marks, he jerked violently as the poison in his body finally stopped his great heart. I screamed in vain, flipped my shotgun to full-auto and sprayed the onrushing horde. Out of 12-gauge shells, I dropped Abomination and pulled my STI.

Sam Haven stood at the top of the hill, roaring like a berserker, a Fed rifle in each hand, pointing in opposite directions and firing downward into the throng. He was surrounded by a cloud of spent brass and a stream of profanity so creative and vile that it was destined to travel up to the heavens and pervert whole other worlds. The brave cowboy was silenced in the flash of an acid grenade.

Harbinger appeared out of nowhere. He flung his empty Tommy gun aside, hard enough to shatter the head of an armored demon. "Julie!" His eyes flashed yellow. Multiple spines had been driven deep into his back and sides. "Julie!" He drew his revolver, dropped six monsters in less than a second, and reloaded another moon clip in a blur of motion. He fought his way toward us, batting aside a leaping demon with a bare fist. "I'm sorry!" he shouted as he reached us, a veritable wall of monsters at his heels.

"Don't worry about it, Earl," she answered with a slight smile as she tossed our last grenade into the alien horde. "I always figured it would be something like this."

Harbinger only nodded. He dodged under a swinging talon, grabbed the demon by its lower jaw and wrenched its head until the twin spinal columns snapped. Hurling the dead thing back into the crowd, he roared for more.

Franks pulled himself up to the top. Blood was streaming down his lacerated face, and his armor was smoking and burning with acid. A spine pierced his bicep. With no display of emotion he grabbed the shard and wrenched it free in a splash of red. The injured arm hung limply at his side. He drew his Glock and nodded at me. "Die with dignity," he stated simply. Behind him the last of his men looked around in panicked bewilderment, put his pistol in his mouth and pulled the trigger. Franks cringed as his last charge died. "Not like that." The dark Fed fired into the masses, dropping onrushing demons with unflinching accuracy.

There were only the four of us left.

Lord Machado laughed. His physical body was hundreds of miles away, but his spirit, his presence, his consciousness was there with us. He laughed in triumph. He gloated. His pride swelled at the defeat of his greatest enemies.

We drew back to back at the top of the little mud hill, stepping over the lifeless bodies of our friends. Franks' slide locked back on his Glock. He calmly dropped the magazine, placed it in the crook of his lifeless arm to hold it, grabbed another mag, inserted it, snapped the slide closed, and went back to shooting. A launched spine struck him in the wrist, traveled up his arm, and exploded out his elbow, opening his forearm like a gutted fish. The gun dropped from his deadened hand.

"Oh well," he said, both arms hanging limp, drizzling blood, at his sides. With no hesitation he charged downward into the horde, kicking a monster back with his heavy boot, then shattered another's mandibles with his forehead. He kicked another in its package of eyes, but a lashing claw opened up his inner thigh and femoral artery. He fell on his back and was dragged under the orange horde.

I emptied the STI into the demon wall, sending a beast back to hell with each shot. But for every one that I dispatched, another flaming hole would open in the sky, dropping another creature into the back of the throng.

I am sorry, Boy. This is end.

I speed-reloaded and continued shooting. I felt Julie by my side. She was also down to just her handgun. Time was running out. Acid exploded nearby, and scalding droplets scorched us. I heard an inhuman scream of rage from behind me as Harbinger ripped into the demons with his bare hands, crushing their alien bones, and flinging their husks back into the mass.

"I love you, Julie," I shouted as my slide locked back empty and I went for another mag.

"I love you, Owen," she answered.

Too bad I was about to die.

A demon hunched down directly before us, a subcutaneous membrane opening on its back, spines aligning to launch at Julie's chest. I stepped in front of her.

The alien spear pierced through my armor just above my sternum, shearing through the top of my heart and piercing out the muscles of my back. Incomprehensible pain slammed me, heat and pressure beyond all imagining. I fell to my knees, and rocked backwards in the mud.

I looked upwards at Julie as my life blood flooded out of me and onto the ground. Rain poured down into my unblinking eyes.

CHAPTER 23

My body lay lifeless on the ground, legs bent, arms spread wide, an alien spear protruding from my chest, and a puddle of blood spreading under gravity's power.

I stood above myself. Above the battlefield. Demon horde rampaging against the final two Hunters. My spirit moved between the sluggish raindrops. Time had slowed down, and I watched as the last few seconds of the battle stretched into eternity. Julie was only a few heartbeats from certain death. Earl Harbinger stood at her back, torn asunder with wounds, bristling with spines like a mutant porcupine, bleeding from countless injuries, but still fighting beyond any human capability.

Mordechai Byreika stood by my side. I could feel the Old Man's sorrow.

I am sorry, Boy. You fought much hard. Braver Hunters the world never has seen.

What now?

Is over. Battle is lost. Tomorrow Cursed One destroy world.

Above the battlefield was the presence of Lord

Machado. I could see it now. A sprawling evil blackness, roiling in the clouds. His laughter continued.

No.

Is not possible, Boy. You are not stuck. Move on you can. Not like me.

No.

The Cursed One was visible to me now. Of course, I was not bound by the limitations of my human sight. The gash that he had torn into the world was visible. The tear that went to the other place, the rift to the other world. The world that served as a temporary repository for the minions of the Old Ones. The ancient artifact of evil stood above all. It was the key. It was the bridge.

No.

The power was not ready. It was not time yet. Lord Machado would not be able to unlock the full power of the artifact until tomorrow at the zenith of the full moon. The demon army standing below was just a partial example of what the artifact could do.

You can go on. There is good place waiting for you. Move on, Boy. Is over.

No.

I watched in slow motion as Earl Harbinger tore the head from one of the demons. In the view that I had now, I could see the demon's contorted spirit disappear from that animated physical body, denied access from this plane of existence. At that exact moment, a rift appeared to the other world, and the same spirit dropped through, cloaked again in a new physical body.

The Cursed One could only control a limited number of spirits.

His powers were still limited.

No.

I headed directly toward the evil blackness, passing into the realm of the dark one. I aimed my spirit at the artifact. The artifact was the key. The artifact was the key to control the power of time and space.

Boy! Wait. Do not face Cursed One like this. You will become stuck like me!

No.

Lord Machado regarded me idly. I could see the link back to his physical body. His slime-coated form knelt in a dark cavern, surrounded by his sleeping vampire minions and a fresh host of undead servants.

YOU HAVE FAILED, HUNTER.

No.

THIS WORLD IS MINE NOW.

I willed myself to approach the artifact. With the veil removed from my eyes I could see the true evil of the ancient thing. It dwarfed Lord Machado. It dwarfed us all. Its power was incredible. Incredible and dark and old and unspeakably evil. I could see the legions of dark forces waiting to move hungrily into this world should its power be unleashed. Black glistening octopus things, bigger than skyscrapers. Ancient triangular crustaceans the size of freighters, floating weightless through the void. Pale saucer eyes searching for a fresh world to plunder and intelligent souls to enslave.

No.

And I looked upon the glory of the legions of goodness and light that stood ready to do battle against them. A vast host of the noble and great ones. I could have given up and moved on and joined them. They urged me silently onward.

YOU HAVE THE STRONGEST MORTAL SPIRIT I HAVE EVER BEHELD.

I ignored him. I continued toward the artifact. I had to reach it.

YOU SHALL BE A FINE SLAVE.

No.

TOMORROW I SHALL RAISE MY QUEEN. YOU WILL BE HER SERVANT.

My consciousness strained against the evil barrier, pushing onwards toward the horrid power. Far below my surviving friends battled onward. More spines and claws pierced Harbinger, but still he fought on, rolling and splashing down into the ranks of the evil minions, smashing them, tearing them with his teeth and claws, more holes opening in the sky as the spirits of the alien warriors were recycled. Julie stood alone, blade in one hand, alien spine wielded as a club in the other. They fought on.

I reached the artifact. It glowed before me like a black sun, epic and deadly. Finally Lord Machado realized what I was doing.

YOU ARE MAD. YOU CANNOT CONTROL THE POWER OF THE OLD ONES. ONLY I MAY DO SO. YOU WILL BE UTTERLY DESTROYED.

I knew that he spoke the truth. He was not just talking about losing my life, but losing what I really was. The artifact was that powerful. Below me, my love fell to the claws of the alien army.

No.

I touched the artifact. Stretching across a thousand billion years of space and reality, time, matter, imagination, power. I put my will against the meager hold the Cursed One had upon it.

NO.

He rose to battle me, but he had been unprepared

for a challenge. I focused my will upon the dark object as it assaulted my mind and my sanity, bombarding me with strange images and alien memories of a thousand dead worlds. I wrested it from the tentacles of the Cursed One.

The tenuous link across the rift was severed. The tunnel from the world of the Old Ones to an obscure swamp in Mississippi was destroyed. The alien army disappeared in a flash of light and fire.

NO!

The Cursed One screamed at me. We drew face to face for the first time, or as much as was possible since neither one of us currently had a face. His power surged against me, forcing me away, striving to ensnare my spirit and destroy me forever.

The carnage of the epic battle was strewn below. The remains of dead Hunters were spread across the fetid swamp. The dark spirits of the blighted region wandered amongst the bodies, celebrating the victory. My brave friends had been scattered and killed, the life ripped from their bodies. Only the changed Harbinger remained alive, and only barely, and even he would succumb to the lethal poisons shortly.

Trip, Holly, Milo, Sam, Lee, Skippy, Edward, even Franks and his men.

And Julie.

Her body lay still, and from my vantage I could see that her time was up.

I wished that I could turn back time.

Yes.

Lord Machado screamed in rage. Wrath crackled across the universe as his will was subverted.

NOOOOOOO . . .

❖   ❖   ❖

The power of the Old Ones was tapped. Ancient wells of evil were utilized, and for the first time in eons, the true power of their ancient artifact was unleashed. Incomprehensible energies were set free, battering the foundations of time and space, subverting natural order, and crackling across the universe.

For five minutes, linear time was broken.

My spirit was reunited violently with my body and the breath of life filled my lungs. I gasped in pain and confusion. The horrible cleaving pain in my chest was gone. I choked, and the sour swamp gas smell of Natchy Bottom was in my mouth. I watched as concentric rings of water moved backward upon the surface, formed globules of water, and reversed themselves against gravity and rose into the air. As time stabilized, the raindrops froze, and then fell like normal.

I was lying in the mud, shotgun readied before me. The others were spread out over the same patch of ground that we had been defending five minutes before.

"Aarrrgghhh!" Sam shouted, continuing the noise that he had been making when the acid bomb had killed him. Holly aimed at the spot of ground that the first alien had jumped from and wildly emptied her rifle into the water, splashing mud, wood bits and water, but no monster. She dropped the rifle and grabbed her forehead, finding no hole. She then probed under the back of her helmet looking for the exit wound.

Harbinger stood up and looked around in confusion. Gradually the others did the same thing until the whole group was standing, bewildered and confused. Except for me, of course. I lay in the mud and wept, my cheek pressed into the stock of my weapon.

In the distance some of the Feds panicked and detonated their claymore mines against the empty swamp. Shouts of confusion echoed through the trees.

The Hunters checked themselves for extra holes, and found none. Milo walked a few feet away, set the flamethrower down, and then fell to his knees and folded his arms to pray silently. Trip did the same, crying while he did so. Skippy and Edward removed their hoods, revealing their tusked faces to everyone. They both took small, dried-lizard necklaces from inside their clothing and began to bat them with their foreheads and gesture toward the sky.

Julie flopped down next to me. She grabbed the drag strap on the back of my armor and tugged hard. I pushed myself up. She grabbed my face in her hands and kissed me passionately. I responded. She tasted like swamp mud, but it was still great. It was good to be alive.

"I would be mighty appreciative if somebody could tell me what in the hell just happened?" Sam said.

"I died," Lee stated quietly. "I got bit in the neck." He pulled his glove off and ran one hand over his throat. "I left my body."

"Me too," Holly added. "I don't know what got me."

"Fed shot you in the head," I answered.

"Stupid bastard," she said coldly.

"It was an accident. He was getting eaten."

"Still . . ."

"All of us died." I slowly stood up, searching for the

words to explain what I had seen, what I had done. "I . . . When I got killed . . ." I stabbed my thumb to my chest. "I saw the Cursed One. I fought him for control of the artifact. I made a wish . . ."

"You did this?" Julie asked, stunned. She ran one hand down my filthy face. "How?"

"I just don't know." I was way out of my league on this one.

Harbinger had not said anything yet. He slowly sat down on a stump and scowled, deep in thought.

"You seriously made a wish? Like Aladdin and the magic lamp or whatever? And brought us back from the dead? And made all of those *things* go away?" Sam said.

"I guess."

"Bullshit," he spat, "just ain't no way."

"He didn't bring us back from the dead," Milo said, still kneeling, his back toward us. "We never died."

"I don't know about you, Milo, but I got my damned brains blown out," Holly said.

Milo stood and faced us. "Not what I mean. Yes, we died, but that was erased. That has not happened yet. It would be happening shortly, but it got reversed. Turned back to right now. What we just went through never happened."

"Sure it did," Sam said. "It just happened."

"When?" Milo held up his watch.

"Uh . . . in the future?"

"Right. So it has not happened."

Sam thought about it for a moment, head cocked sideways as he stroked his walrus mustache. "Screw it. I need a drink."

Franks drifted into our area, his crack federal agents

following slowly behind him. They were not moving swiftly now. Rather, they looked as shell-shocked and confused as we did. None of them even reacted at the sight of the unmasked orcs. Compared to what they had just gone through, what were a couple of tusk-faced humanoids?

"Hey, guys," Milo said cheerfully. "Let me guess, you all got killed by orange monster insect demon things too?"

"Yep," Franks answered.

"Oh good, at least we're all on the same page."

The dark Fed just held up his thick arms, looking down at where they had been pierced and shredded by whistling spines. He made a fist and cracked his knuckles, then slowly lowered them.

Harbinger finally spoke. "See, Franks, I told you we should have stayed put."

Franks shrugged. He keyed his radio. No longer disrupted by the unnatural rift in the area, we made immediate radio contact. Myers' voice sounded shaken.

"What's going on out there?" the radio shrieked.

Franks scowled as his straightforward brain tried to figure out how to explain our situation. Harbinger keyed his mike and interrupted.

"It was a trap. Ray Shackleford set us up. We were ambushed by a horde of transdimensional demons. We all got killed. Then time ran backwards. We all woke up alive. And the monsters are gone. Request immediate evac. . . ." He let that hang for a moment. "Over."

"Uh, yeah," Franks concurred.

"Air evac is on the way. What caused the time effect?"

Harbinger looked at me through squinted eyes, but did not betray my secret to the Feds. "Unknown. Suspect it was caused by the Cursed One's artifact. We went back in time approximately five minutes."

"I know," Myers responded. "It wasn't just you. We felt it too. It was 2:39, and then it was 2:34."

"How widespread was the effect?"

"Hold on . . ." The radio went dead.

Forty quiet Hunters stood packed together in the pounding rain, taking no small amount of comfort from the nearness of other real people. The emotions displayed ran the gamut from confused, to terrified, to shaken, to ecstatic, but mostly to blank thousand-yard stares while our human brains tried to process the impossible. And we were Monster Hunters, either governmental or private, and every one of us was no stranger to the weird or the unexplainable. Shivering from the cold, I put my arm over Julie's shoulder and pulled her close. Slow minutes ticked by. We all waited for Myers' response.

"Sorry . . . I was told to turn on the news."

"How widespread was the effect?" Harbinger asked again.

The radio crackled.

"Um . . . Reports are coming in now . . . the whole world."

"Say again?"

"Earth. Every person on Earth felt it."

We stood in the Monster Control Bureau's giant tent command center, dripping from our showers, stinging from the leech removal process, and aching from the bevy of antibiotic shots given to us to combat the rancid waters of Natchy Bottom. The flat-screen televisions had been changed from satellite imagery to several different cable news channels.

"—continue to drift in. We can now confirm that India, Australia, Bangladesh and Finland also experienced the phenomenon and—"

"Large scale rioting has broken out in Los Angeles, New York, and in several other cities in the continental—"

"Yes, Diane, the President will be addressing us live from Air Force One in a matter of minutes—"

"—the Prime Minister's office has issued a statement for all to remain calm until—"

"—repent sinners! The hour of judgment is at hand! I'm sorry I cheated on my wife, I'm adulterous slime. It's all April the weather girl's fault. Evil slut. Wait . . . you can't take me off the air . . . damn you, Harry! Repent, you heathen bastard! It's the end of the world! The end I say—"

Some of the media people were holding it together better than others. The same could be said for us.

"Maybe it wasn't caused by this artifact," Myers contended.

"Yeah, and maybe I'm Elvis," Harbinger shouted back.

"It could have been a coincidence," the senior agent pleaded.

"Sure, a rift in time just happens to occur as we're fighting the minions of something that we were warned was going to try to control time? Give me a break, Myers."

"I'm the one that has to talk to the President, damn it. I need to give him more than conjecture.

I need proof! This is the biggest thing that has ever happened."

"Hell, I'll talk to the Prez," Sam added helpfully. "He's a Texan. He'll understand."

Harbinger ignored his teammate. "Myers, there hasn't been an attack of transdimensional forces since '95. That's a rare enough occurrence as it is. It has to be connected."

"There was the Vanni Fucci incident in Dothan a while back," Julie offered.

"Isolated case," Harbinger said.

"I know that, and you know that. But I need to explain this all to people who don't know a damn thing about monsters. They were already prepared to go all the way to 'final option' to stop Lord Machado; what are they going to do now? Preemptively nuke the whole state into a sheet of glass?"

"That'll alienate the Southern vote for sure," Milo said.

I started to speak. I could tell them exactly what had happened. Julie kicked me in the shin. She shook her head in the negative.

The news continued to babble:

"—UN General Secretary has just called for a unilateral ban on time travel—"

"—I'm telling you, Ken, space aliens are behind this. I talked about it in my book, *The Coming Gray Invasion*, this is just phase one of their colonization—"

"—does not appear to be as much widespread panic on the other side of the world, since many people appeared to have slept through the disturbance—"

"—just in, there are reports of . . . this can't be right . . . vampire attacks in Alabama and Georgia?

Vampires? Uh . . . eyewitnesses are reporting that the dead are walking? What is this shit?" The screen went blank, and then to a static display that said they were experiencing technical difficulties.

Myers smashed the screen with his boot. Sparks flew from the sides of the TV. "Enough! Get out of here! Go take care of your local outbreaks! Just get out of my headquarters!" he shrieked at us. His phone rang. "Take Me Out to the Ballgame." His face blanched. Looking like a deer in the headlights, standing in the path of a truck with no brakes, he slowly answered it and listened, his eyes rolling back into his head. "Yes. I will hold for the President . . ." He covered the mouthpiece. "Lieutenant, get these civilians out of here!"

The National Guard soldiers herded us out of the tent. We stopped outside. The rain had thankfully stopped, leaving us with a pale overcast sky. Harbinger sighed in relief and pulled out a cigarette. He offered one to the soldiers, who gladly took him up on the offer.

"So, Mr. Harbinger, is it . . .? Is this really the end of the world? Demons and all that?" one of them asked.

"Not if we can help it," he answered as he walked away, Monster Hunters trailing behind. Our group headed for the parked chopper. Skippy and Edward were busy "liberating" fuel and prepping for takeoff. Our mud-soaked gear was already stowed, and we were ready to go. Harbinger stopped before the hulking chopper, taking a long drag from his cancer stick. "Mount up, crew. Let's get out of here. It's been a strange day."

"We got company." Holly nodded back toward the command tent. Agent Franks was following us, as stoic and impassive as ever. He trudged through the damp grass, hard eyes fixed on our group. He had been busy caring for his men, and had not yet had a chance to change out of his mud-drenched, and surely leech-and-tick-infested armor. He stopped, hands awkwardly at his side.

We waited while the emotionless soldier found the words.

"Thanks."

He snapped a hard salute, ramrod straight, and parade-ground perfect. Harbinger, Sam and Lee instinctively returned the gesture. The rest of us stood there stupidly. Franks made eye contact with each of us, squinty and cold, held his arm rigid for a long moment, and then let it fall. He spun on his bootheel and stalked back toward the tent.

"So does that mean we're friends now?" I asked.

"Hell if I know," Julie answered. "At least he didn't slap you around again."

The others moved for the chopper. Harbinger grabbed me. "Not so fast. Me and you need to talk for a second." He gestured over his shoulder and we walked away from the others. I saw Julie watching after me, looking concerned, and then she was gone into the vehicle's interior. Skippy fired up the turbines, and the powerful engines began to whine.

"What's going on?"

"I really don't know."

"You don't need to keep secrets from me. We're a team."

"You should talk."

He shrugged. "No big deal. I have some issues, sure, but I don't have the ability to twist the laws of physics like you seem to do. Care to explain?"

"Damn it. I told you what I know, Earl." I flushed with anger. "If I knew how to put an end to this, I would tell you. If I knew how to kill that slimy son of a bitch, I would do it."

"Can you find him?"

"I haven't been able to so far. The Old Man doesn't seem to be able to tell me."

"What about when you saw the vision? The road sign? When he got here?"

"The one that almost killed me? You want me to try that again?" I asked incredulously. Not that I had not already thought of it myself. It was a desperate ploy, but we were running low on time.

"If we can't find him, then we're all dead tomorrow anyway. You saw those things. Imagine them crawling over the whole world. Billions of them. Hundreds of billions of them. Orange shells as far as your eye can see, and squid things that look like blimps floating overhead. And that will just be the first wave. Then the big things will come."

"You've seen them too?" I asked in surprise.

"Yes, I have. I might not have magic powers or whatever the hell it is you've got going on up there." He poked me in the forehead. I was too stunned to react. "But I've been on the other side. I've seen that place."

"In '95. You went into the rift to pull out Julie's dad . . ."

He nodded slowly, the memories of the red-skied alien world eternally burned into the dark corners of his mind. I had at least one person who understood what was at stake.

"They're coming, Earl. I don't even know if the Cursed One realizes it or can see it. I don't know if he knows what's waiting for him to use that box, that thing . . . I'm scared," I admitted.

"I am too. And at this point, I'll be honest, I didn't think there was much out there that could scare me anymore." Harbinger was not lying or trying to appear tougher than he was. He was telling the truth. He had moved past the concept of fear, operating instead upon animal cunning and self-preservation instincts. Until now.

"We have to stop him," I stated. "I'll do whatever it takes."

"Find the Place. Find out where he's hiding. I don't care if you have to beat it out of that ghost. Get me a name, a town, something, anything. And we'll teach this clown not to mess with MHI."

"I will." I had no idea how I was going to do it, but I knew that the responsibility fell on my shoulders, on me alone, and perhaps on an old Jewish Hunter who had been dead for half a century.

"Let's get out of here then." He started toward the chopper. "I would wish you sweet dreams, but honestly, I hope you have horrible ones. I hope you see this evil thing and get his address, 'cause I'm personally gonna kick his ass."

I sat by Julie for the chopper ride back to the compound.

"How are you doing?" I struggled to communicate over the internal engine noises.

"Not real good." She patted my hand. "Just when I thought that maybe my dad wasn't as evil as I thought, he sets us up. He sent us all to die. He covered for that evil bitch." She spat. "I believed him."

"Well, he's gone now," I assured her. I suppose that we should not have been so surprised at his treachery. He had been willing to risk everything to bring his beloved back. Of course he would be willing to merely lie for her.

"At least we know he's dead. The Feds *must* have cut his head off and burned the body by now."

"Most likely."

"One down. One to go," she said angrily.

I tried to change the subject from her death vendetta against her parents. Almost any subject was lighter than that. "So, can we technically consider today a first date?"

"I guess. Next time, how about we do dinner and a movie?" She laughed as the tension broke.

"Ha. What girl wouldn't want to crawl through a haunted swamp, get killed, and travel through time? That's one heck of a date."

"You must have dated some strange women."

"Actually I haven't dated very many women at all. I haven't had much luck."

"Why?"

"They usually think I'm weird." That much was true. Slightly strange, kind of big awkward, and ugly—I was no charmer.

"Me too."

"You think I'm weird?" I shouted over the noise.

"No, I mean that people have always thought that about me. You know, crazy girl, always talking about monsters. Spends all her time shooting, building bombs, or practicing how to chop things up. Hangs out with a bunch of crazy people. Paranoid, delusional, lives in a compound, that kind of thing. It takes a real toll on relationships."

"See, I think that sounds perfect."

"You would." She leaned against me.

Across the troop compartment, Holly made gagging motions. Julie and I both flipped her the bird. She winked at us and went back to harassing Trip.

"Sorry to interrupt you lovebirds," Harbinger said over the radio, "but we've got business. Julie, see what other teams you can contact and find out their status. Owen has something he needs to do too."

"I need to get some sleep," I told her.

"I know, it's been a tough day."

"That's not what I mean. I need to make contact with the Old Man. I need to find the Cursed One. Tomorrow night is it."

"Are you going to try to see through his eyes again?"

"I don't know," I answered. "I've got to do something."

She looked out the window and sighed, shuddering slightly.

"Be careful."

"I will."

"Come back to me. I can't lose anybody else."

"I promise."

"Boy! Much has happened," the Old Man exclaimed. "What have you done?"

"I turned on the artifact, I guess," I answered.

"Is as I feared. This is terrible. Much terrible." He shuffled toward me, hobbling on his cane.

"Hey, we're all still alive. It sure beats the alternative."

"No," he answered. "Not better at all. Not for you."

"Hey, I'm the one that had a spine sticking out my aorta."

"Better to be dead than be cursed tool of the ancient evil."

"I'm nobody's tool," I said angrily. I was getting really tired of everybody treating me as if I was stupid. "I did the best that I could."

"No, Boy. Now is much worse than before." His bony hand grabbed me by the arm. "Come, hurry. One last memory to show."

I stopped him, pulling away. "No, Mordechai. I don't have time to screw around. Just give me a straight answer for once. Where is he, and how do I kill him?"

"You not are ready for such things." He looked at me, his hard eyes drooped in sadness. "Boy, to do such a thing would make you dead for sure. Not just dead. But maybe worse. Much worse. Cursed like he is even."

"But I'm not evil," I said defensively.

"No. Surprised I have been by you being so good." He lifted his cane and thumped me in the chest. "Good, but sometimes stupid. Brave, but proud. Too proud for own good. If not more careful, pride will kill you and blow up world. Think you can solve problems, but no patience to learn. Want to rush. Do things now." He puffed himself up and did a very poor imitation of me. "I am Boy. Now, now, now. Hurry, hurry. I can do everything. No need to learn first!"

"You would need about two more of you to do a good impersonation of me, you old midget," I told him. "Plus I don't sound like that at all."

"Bah. You are good boy. But no longer can you worry about what you are. You are Monster Hunter. Your father, he made you warrior. Do not—how you say?—pretend to be something else. No time for doubt. No time for 'normal'." He spat the word.

"You know about that?"

"I live in your head. What? I not pay attention? Now I ask one thing. Just one. Do this for me. I promise before time run out I show you new vision. At that time, what do have to lose? Your brain probably pop, serve you right. But world is destroyed right after anyway."

"Fair enough. What do you need?"

He thumped me over the head with his cane. Hard. "Shut up your big mouth and pay attention!" he snapped. "Last memories while Cursed One was still just man." He put his hands on my head. "We leave quick before he makes change. To be in his head at time, surely you die."

I rubbed the bump on my head. I just did not get much respect around here.

"Let's do this," I said.

Lord Machado's memories.
Were of dirt. Brown dirt.
I woke up. Facedown in the mud. Lying crumpled in my armor at the base of the mighty pyramid. I must have tumbled the entire way. The rain had

stopped, and the jungle sun burned down upon me. I staggered up, heaving against the weight of my plate. Crusted blood coated my body, and wept from my many wounds.

My artifact.

I crawled up the stairs, pulling myself forward on my hands and knees, so very weak, and the pyramid was so very tall. I pulled, gasped and kicked, raggedly crawling my way ever higher.

I blacked out repeatedly, only to find that I had climbed higher without knowing it. My skin burned in the sun and my delirium and thirst increased. I began to crawl past bodies, past the torn remains of my soldiers who had so bravely fought the stone guardians. I cursed them for their betrayal. I cursed Captain Thrall.

Finally at the top, I kicked away the giant feasting buzzards. My ax was embedded through the back of the captain's now-empty suit of mail. His body was gone.

The artifact was gone.

I screamed at the sky. Cursing everything, swearing vengeance upon all, I tore my blade free, shaking it overhead. I vowed to regain that which was mine.

The body of the priestess Koriniha was facedown in a puddle. The carrion birds had pulled her open and eaten freely. Her fine robes were crusted with dried red, stained with her spilled organs. The buzzards reluctantly hopped away as I approached.

She was the key.

I had to bring her back.

We were two weeks from the city, a hard trek through dark jungle paths. I could not carry her weight all that way, especially alone, wounded, and without provisions. I knelt beside her, and with my ax, carefully stripped the flesh from her bones, breaking joints as necessary to reduce her to her component parts. When I was done, I bundled the broken skeleton into a soldier's cloak, and tied it tight with a belt. I slung it over my back and stumbled down the pyramid, in the direction of the city. Surely one of the remaining dark priests would know what to do. If I could bring back my concubine, she could reunite me with the artifact. Nothing was going to stop me.

Days passed.

Delirium increased.

I ate bugs and small animals raw, crawling, dragging myself ever onward. Fever rushed through my body. Eating away at me. Burning me. Killing me. I did not sleep. I pushed onward, through the darkness, strange beings and spirits watching me along the jungle paths, urging me onward toward my destiny. I did not abandon my armor, nor my ax. They were symbols of my authority, and I would not give my enemies the satisfaction of abandoning part of my birthright to rust in the never-ending rain of the hated jungle.

My first sign of the city was the towers of black smoke and the clouds of milling vultures.

It was a city of the dead.

A month had now passed since my expedition had left. The bodies of the people were mostly in their homes, on their sleeping mats, pustules open on their decaying forms, taken by a fever.

I walked down the empty streets. The brilliant songbirds had starved in their cages. The only movement I saw was the carrion animals inside the doors and openings as if they were the new owners. In a way they were. Stray dogs, brought here by my men, prowled the streets, fattened by the vast stores of available meat.

Fires had caught, and now burned out of control, with no one left to fight the blaze. The air was thick with smoke and ash. I did not know if any of the people of the city had survived, but if they had, then they had fled this cursed place.

I made my way to the temple. The priestess had taken me deep beneath it, far down into the bowels of the earth, where strange things lived, and the very walls were alive. She had shown me the ancient obelisk and its prophecy. Surely there I would find my answers.

Infection had set into my wounds, dripping green pus and leaving a trail upon the paved road. My body stank like the corpses in the surrounding buildings. I was aflame with fever, yet shivered because I was so starkly cold. I could not remember my trek to the temple, nor the long deep descent to the ancient unnatural cavern. I do not know how much time passed on my journey down the endless stairs and tunnels.

I found myself in the cavern, reduced to crawling like some pathetic forest beast. The damp bones of Koriniha rattled on my back. I pulled my ax along, dragging a trail through the soft living floor. Now, so close to death, I pushed myself along by will power alone. I had no torch, so I moved through the dark. Strange things skittered over my body, or slithered over my hands. I crawled, hopelessly lost, pushing onwards toward where I felt the obelisk to be. The air rushed and changed direction overhead, as if the cavern itself was breathing. It stank of rotting fish, but I could barely smell it over the stench of decay coming from my own flesh.

At last my quest ended.

The black obelisk was there—still impossibly thin, and disappearing into the darkness above. The ancient writings of the prophecy gave off a faint light of their own. My swollen fingers struggled to uncinch the remains of the priestess from my body, and after much effort I was able to spill her bones upon the patch of floor where I had taken her to consummate our pact.

"Old Ones. I have come," I croaked through my parched throat, barely able to produce any sound. "I demand you return your Priestess Koriniha to life."

Nothing happened.

I lay gasping and heaving on the floor. I forced myself upwards, knees buckling, I fell against the obelisk, barely holding on.

"Old Ones. I am he whom you prophesied." The writing was there before me, glowing, providing scant illumination. It was still in Latin. I read the words again. Surely it was I.

"I have done what you asked. I have fulfilled my part," I demanded. "Give her back to me. Give me my power."

The giant breathing continued, each exhalation brought a greater stink of rotten ocean. Nothing responded. I grew angry. I found the strength to push myself away from the obelisk, standing shakily on my own feet. I pulled my ax into my hands.

"It is mine! Give me my power!"

The breathing continued.

"Damn you then." I found the strength to lift my ax. I swung it into the narrow obelisk. Obsidian chips flew as I struck. "Damn you!" I struck again, finding strength in my fury. Lines of the prophecy winked out of existence. "I do not need you!" Bits of the obelisk embedded themselves in my skin as I hammered it. "I am the one!" The narrow thing cracked and shifted from the roof. More lines disappeared. "The power is mine!" A final blow turned the center into powder. "I curse you, Old Ones!" I spit on their prophecy.

The obelisk toppled, the lower part shattered, and the top hung suspended for a long moment before detaching from the unseen ceiling of the cavern and falling, exploding like glass on impact. I was left alone in the dark, gasping, heaving. Dying.

We must go now, Boy. Hurry.

The cavern shifted. I had drawn the attention of the Old Ones. Shapes dropped down around me, somehow visible as darker than the shadows.

Come. Must leave his mind.

What's happening?

He has—how you say?—pissed them off.

Ten thousand glowing eyes opened on the cavern walls as the giant tentacles encircled me, suckers piercing and ripping into my rotten flesh, lifting me upwards through the cavern, into the gaping gelatinous maw of an Old One. I screamed, but acid filled my mouth and poured down my throat, burning, tearing.

Darkness . . .

Pain . . .

I was once again my self. Owen Z. Pitt.

Thank goodness.

The memory was fading away as the Old Man pulled me back toward light and sanity.

I saw Lord Machado as he was cruelly twisted into the Cursed One. His human form was stripped away, replaced with the foul organic materials of the ancient alien trespassers. His mind was probed and tortured, shattered and pulped against incomprehensible forces, pushed beyond the breaking point of any mortal being. The torment lasted for a hundred years.

Finally satisfied at the punishment, or perhaps growing bored and tiring of it, the Old One dropped the pulsing mass of black tissue back to the floor where it landed with a wet splattering.

Somehow his spirit survived the unspeakable torture, driven by hate, anger and lust for power. Those things were his anchor, keeping him from being absorbed completely into the ancient beast. The inky mass slithered away into the darkness, husbanding its strength.

Planning for its return.

The Polish village was silent. I shuffled through the snow, making my way through the rubble of homes and businesses, looking for the church, what I knew now to be the chosen Place of Power from the winter of 1944. My feet were bare, but the jagged stone, shell casings, and broken glass did not harm me.

"Mordechai!" I shouted. "We need to talk!"

I found the church. The steps were barren. I hurried up them and through the entrance.

"Byreika!" I bellowed, cupping my hands over my mouth. The Old Man was nowhere to be seen. I kicked over a damaged pew. I did not have time for this. "Where are you?"

"Greetings," called a voice. I turned to see a man, a stranger, approaching down the aisle. He was short, dressed in an archaic steel breastplate and plumed, rounded helmet. A yellow and brown family crest was emblazoned upon his chest. His goatee was black and grease-slicked down to a point. His eyes were small and dark, set deep into a face tanned like leather. He glared at me from under bushy eyebrows. "Your friend will be along shortly." One arm hung at his side, lazily holding the handle of his battle-ax, the blade dragging a furrow through the ash and snow on the church floor.

I realized he was speaking archaic Portuguese. The language of Lord Machado's memories.

Not good.

"Lord Machado," I said over the lump in my throat.

"We have never been properly introduced. You have plundered through my memories. My precious things. You have delved into my power and tried to take that which is mine. You have ruined my plans and stolen the glory of the ancients, an honor which is rightfully mine. And yet, I do not even know who you are." He stopped, only a few feet away. The artificial construct of the Old Man's world shifted violently as the Cursed One intruded. The fabric of the surrounding town rippled as if it were fluid. "Who are you?" he hissed.

I somehow found the courage to respond. "I'm the man that's going to kill you once and for all."

Snapping his head back, he laughed—the same evil laugh from the memories. "How naïve. I cannot die. I am eternal. Far greater things than you have tried to take my life. I refuse to die."

"We'll see about that."

He raised the ax slowly, taking it in both hands, balancing it, feeling the weight. He inspected the blade, carefully running one thumb over the edge.

"I've killed thousands of men. I could kill your body now as you sleep. I could take your spirit and chain it to the artifact like your guide. Do not be insolent with me," he threatened. "It would bring me much joy to rip the heart from your chest."

"Try it."

He did not move, merely stood, cradling his ax, smiling slightly, as if my bravado amused him.

"Are you going to sit there, or are we going to do this?" I asked, preparing to fight. How did you battle an immortal being in your own dreams? I was about to find out.

"Nay," he answered. "For in this place you are safe. I am but a shadow, a message, a warning. I am here but as a friend. I come to offer you a pact of peace and cooperation."

"Fuck off."

"My young friend, you have much to learn." He planted the ax head solidly into the floor and leaned upon the shaft. "Tomorrow I will rule. That much is already determined. Those who stand with me will be greatly rewarded. Whatever you so desire, power, riches . . . You wish to have the vampire's daughter. I can see to it that the two of you shall live together for eternity . . . in return for your allegiance. It is within my power to give you whatsoever you wish. I will need captains for my army, great men such as yourself. Think of the glory."

"Real tempting," I answered. "But how about I just find you and shove that stupid ax up your ass?"

"Those who stand against me will be crushed. I shall kill you for eons. I will wear your skin as my cloak, I will grind your bones into powder, I will drink your blood, and I shall chain your soul to the artifact forever. A token trophy of my victory." As he spoke he began to change, features becoming blurry and darkening, as if he was cloaked in smoke. He grew, widened, black-glistening tissue protruding through the seams of his clothing and creases of armor. The ax thumped to the floor, no longer fitting in the fleshless hands. "I shall take every one that you have ever loved. I shall turn them to me, or I shall swallow their souls. I shall make them suffer as you do, and they shall know, as their flesh burns and their skin is peeled away, that it was you who caused this suffering. That it was you, through your foolishness, which caused them such pain. And they will curse your name through eternity."

The Cursed One's voice changed, as if the sound was traveling through water. The flesh of his face sloughed away, leaving a skull, and then black tendrils sprang from under his helmet and out of his mouth, coating his face in a withering mask. "I shall take your family, your father, your mother and your children who are not yet born. They shall feel my wrath and know of my eternal rage. I shall take this woman you love, the vampire's daughter, and I shall inflict savagery upon her such that your pathetic mind cannot comprehend. Once she is broken I shall give her to her mother, and she too shall join my legions."

The transformation was complete, and the true form of Lord Machado towered above me, bones cloaked in a slime-coated mass of moving tentacles: pure black hatred made manifest into a physical presence. The armor remained, only now dented and rusted, bracketed in filth and ooze. The mass slapped wetly against the wooden floor, black fluids dripping through to eat away at the ground below. The helmet dipped down, burning eyes gleaming in my face.

"Choose now. Choose your fate. Serve me or serve eternal pain."

Incomprehensible fear grasped claws around my heart. I knelt down before the billowing wall of evil. The Cursed One began to laugh, echoing through the shattered church, secure in his power and greatness.

"I choose neither."

The pulsating mass that was the Cursed One's head tilted slightly, betraying the still-human reaction of disbelief. My hand closed upon the polished handle of the ancient ax as I heaved myself upwards. I swung the massive blade into the black flesh, slicing through the flailing darkness.

The Cursed One roared and struck.

CHAPTER 24

Light.

Confusion.

Pressure on my chest. Hands restraining me, holding me down.

I lashed out, knuckles colliding with something soft. Strong fingers landed on my throat. I reached upwards, grabbed the person and flung them aside. Something struck me, grabbed me, lifted me through the air and slammed me painfully into a rock-hard surface.

"Wake up, damn it!" Harbinger shouted into my ear.

I gasped. I was alive.

And being crushed painfully into a cinderblock wall. Harbinger held me up by the straps of my armor, feet dangling several inches from the ground. He shook me violently, took one hand away and slapped me silly.

"Hey!" I shouted. "Cut that out."

"Okay. He's back." Harbinger released me and I dropped to the ground. The much smaller man had flung me around as if I weighed nothing. "Sam. You okay?"

Sam Haven stood to one side, rubbing the side of his head. A slight trickle of blood leaked out of his nose and strained through his enormous mustache. "Kid's got a punch all right. Like getting kicked by a horse."

"Sorry," I said.

"Jeez, I was only trying to help. You were flopping around like a fish," the big cowboy said.

I looked around in bewilderment. We were by the hangar, back at the compound. The Hind sat nearby, blades still slowly turning. The team stood around me, looking concerned. I felt nauseous and weak. I slid down the wall and sat. Julie squatted down beside me.

"You were having a seizure again. You started as we came in for a landing." She pressed her fingers to my neck and took my pulse. She glanced at her watch. "Your heart rate is crazy."

"The Cursed One was in my dreams," I gasped.

"Did you get us a location?" Harbinger asked.

I shook my head sadly. "Sorry."

"Shit," he sputtered. "Nothing?"

"He made me a job offer," I added. "Great benefits package. Eternal life, that kind of thing. All I've got to do is help him conquer the world. Or he's going to boil my soul for eternity or something." I did not say what he had said about Julie. I was going to make the slimy son of a bitch pay for that.

"Okay, let's get inside," Harbinger said. I tried to wobble back to my feet. Julie gave me a hand up, and Trip silently put my arm over his shoulder and helped me to walk. Holly picked up my shotgun. "I've summoned every team back to the compound for the night. Pitt, you're going to need to debrief all of us. Maybe somewhere in there is a clue that we need to track him down."

"Aren't the others taking care of local infestations?" Holly asked.

"It's suicide to hunt vampires in the dark. I've got a few team leads who're brave enough to try though, so I ordered them back. So now we regroup, check our gear, and tomorrow we head out again. We have one day left to find the Place."

"I can try again, Earl," I said shakily. "I can do it. Byreika promised he would show me before time runs out."

"You looked like you were going to die back there," Trip said, with concern in his voice. "You sure you want to do that again?"

"You got a better idea?"

He thought about it. "Nope . . . The Lord helps those who help themselves."

"I wish he would send a miracle our way then, 'cause we sure could use one," I said.

"Maybe he has," Trip suggested. "Maybe you're our miracle."

"If that's the case, we're screwed," Holly said. "No offense."

"None taken. Hell, I agree."

"No, serious. Think about it," he told the group as we approached the main building. I never thought that I could be so glad to see the ugly old fortress, but I was. With the sun setting in the distance, the compound looked almost heavenly. "You talk with ghosts. You see visions. You even managed to turn back the clock. Explain that if it isn't a miracle."

"Trust me on this. If you had seen the evil crustacean monsters that this artifact comes from, then you wouldn't be talking about the backwards-in-time experience as if it was a good thing." I shuddered when I thought about their giant saucer eyes floating through space. "You had best put your faith in something other than me."

"I don't know, man. I think you've got a job to do. I think when that werewolf killed you, you got sent back with a mission, and Byreika is your guide."

"Whatever, dude."

"Actually, there might be something to that," Harbinger said. "I'll have to ask Milo, since he's our religious expert, and see if anything like that has happened before. But right now I've got him and Skippy putting the guns and rocket pods back on the Hind."

"What about the Feds?" Julie asked. "They specifically told us not to arm it."

"Screw 'em. World's probably going to end tomorrow anyway. What are they going to do? Prosecute us? It's the least I can do for Skip. The guy has been itching to blow something up for a long time."

Several different vehicles were parked in front of the building. Mostly they were plain Suburbans or large passenger vans. We were not the first team to return. The reception desk was empty. There was a brief note from Dorcas saying that she had gone, in her words, up to Forestdale with some of the kids "to do some killin'" and that there were some pudding cups in the fridge. The chocolate ones were hers, and she promised painful death upon anyone who ate them.

The other Hunters were gathered in the cafeteria. I had never seen most of them before. They were an interesting crew. Most of the heavy suits of armor had been ditched as soon as was possible, and the Hunters were trying to get in the small bit of relaxation that they could. A few had not taken theirs off yet, mostly the ones who had been lucky enough not to be splattered with undead juices during the day's activity. In addition to the infamous horned happy face there were several other team logos present. Some were cartoonish: a fire-breathing warthog, Scud the Disposable Assassin, Samurai Jack, and one that appeared to be a cross between a shark and an octopus. Others logos were more serious: a skull with vampire teeth and a knife through it, a highly stylized dragon, crossed Kalashnikovs, and a version of Munch's "The Scream." All of the patches were black and olive drab green.

Some Hunters were eating, scarfing down whatever calories were available. A large group were clustered around the TV watching the news as more reports trickled in about the worldwide panic caused by the missing five minutes, but the majority of the Hunters were cleaning their guns or sharpening edged weapons. Someone had plugged in a CD player and was playing classic rock.

"Earl!" a ponytailed man in a Harley Davidson tank top shouted. "Hey, everybody! Harbinger's here!" The Hunters dropped what they were doing, jumped up and crowded around us, many of them asking questions.

"Calm down," Harbinger boomed. "As soon as everybody's here, we'll have a full debriefing. Status? Who're we missing?"

The biker-looking fellow started to tick off names on his fingers. Apparently he at least knew everybody. "Nobody called in any casualties today. Most of these vamps never knew what hit them. We stacked up piles of the bastards. Boone is here, but his guys volunteered to be perimeter security for now. VanZant, Paxton, and Mayorga's teams called in and are on the way. Eddings just crawled out of some mine, said he didn't get the message to pull out before dark. So they should be last ones in."

"Didn't get the message, my butt," Julie said angrily. "You don't stay in a vampire hole after dark."

"Crazy bastard," Sam said with admiration.

"Where's my . . . the Boss?" Harbinger asked.

"Called about fifteen minutes ago. Him and the Newbies kicked some serious ass up in Forestdale. They're coming. The Boss sounded really happy on the phone."

"No surprise. He hasn't got to kill anything in years. Thanks, Phillips." Harbinger slapped the man on the back. He raised his voice so that all of the assembled Hunters could hear. "You scumbags best not have eaten everything. I'm starved."

"Fred's making up some dinner—he used to be a chef you know—but right now there's pudding cups in the fridge," said one, as he spooned Dorcas' precious chocolate into his mouth.

"You poor condemned fool," muttered Sam under his breath. For that Hunter's sake, I hoped that Dorcas had had a chance to use up her daily quotient of violence against vampires.

"Whoa there, chief. We're dying here," the man named Phillips interjected. "Rumor has it that you had something to do with that five minutes. What was up with that?"

"Where'd you hear that?"

"It was all over the Feds' encrypted channels. Something about a demon massacre in Natchy Bottom," a female Hunter said. I loved the fact that breaking into the government's secure communications did not cause anyone to bat an eye.

"Yeah, man, that was some freaky shit," said a short man. "Whole world is going crazy out there."

Most of the others nodded in agreement. In the background the news video was showing huge crowds of demonstrators gathered in front of the White House. The scrolling information across the bottom warned of the condition-red terror warning, and the declaration of martial law across the Southeastern U.S.

"Well, I'll address that. But I'm going to wait until everybody's here. I'm tired and I ain't telling that story more than once." He pulled out a cigarette. Three other Hunters whipped out lighters. Every person in the room respected or admired Harbinger far too much to argue. "Somebody scare me up something hot and made out of cow. And that's an order." He leaned in, lit the end of the cigarette from one of the proffered lighters and inhaled greedily. "It's been a hell of a day."

I agreed fully with that sentiment. Harbinger's team dispersed, greeting and conversing with old friends. I dropped my bag of gear on the floor and went to scrounge up something to eat. I was starving, exhausted, sore, aching, and missing a considerable amount of blood from the leeches and thumbnail-sized ticks. However, I was still a gentleman.

"Julie, can I get you something from the kitchen?"

"Hang on. I'll come with you." She set her equipment next to mine, and hurriedly made her way through the double doors. I followed, stomach rumbling, already salivating at the smell of something being fried. I stumbled zombielike in the direction of precious food. But Julie grabbed my hand, led me off to the side, waved quickly at the few Hunters cooking and scrounging, and pulled me through a small side door into the hallway.

"What's up?" I asked, glancing back longingly toward the kitchen. At my size and level of physical activity, I had to eat 4,500 calories a day to keep from getting cranky. She led me quickly up the stairs to the top level. I had not been up here much. I followed stupidly.

"We died today."

"Yeah, I've done that a couple of times. It don't get any easier."

She stopped, glanced down the hall to make sure we were alone. Satisfied, she turned and looked me in the eyes. "It really makes you think. Coming that close. Doesn't it?"

"I suppose," I answered, slightly embarrassed.

"You saved us. I don't know how you did, but you're something special. I can't explain it."

"You're the special one. I've known that since I first met you," I told her sincerely.

"I had the same reaction. I just couldn't explain it at the time."

"Really?" That took me by surprise.

"Yes. Really. Look, I know this is sudden, but what you said back there . . . in the swamp . . . right before you . . . you stepped in front of me . . ." I thought of the alien spear that I took for her piercing my heart. "Did you mean that?"

"I . . . uh . . . well . . ." I stammered, afraid to answer truthfully.

She responded quickly. "Because if you didn't, I totally understand. It was a really intense moment . . . and I don't want to move too fast . . . or anything like that. And there has just been so much going on . . . with my family . . . and . . ." She did not mention the missing Grant, but the look of guilt was obvious on her face. "It's just happened so fast, and I wasn't expecting anything like this. There has been something about you, ever since we met. And then when Grant abandoned you on the freighter . . . We fought about that. I couldn't believe he did that to you. And then he disappeared, and I know how I feel about you, and I should feel guilty because he's probably dead or worse, and so much has happened, but you're here, and I just don't know—"

I cut her off. "I meant it." I screwed up all of my courage. Compared to this moment, vampires, werewolves, undead, gargoyles, demons, giant sky squids—they were nothing. I would rather face legions of monsters than have her reject what I was about to say.

I held both of her hands as gently as a brute like me could manage. Her expression was unreadable. "I love you," I stated simply.

She did not respond immediately. I felt a nervous weight form in my stomach, threatening to drag me through the floor. I swallowed involuntarily as all of the moisture left my mouth. Finally she smiled, a little smile at first, and then gradually it spread into a wide grin.

"Me too."

"Really?" The weight lifted. Lightning crashed. The heavens opened and choirs of angels sang.

"Yes. Now quit squeezing my hands, you're gonna break them."

I hurriedly let go. "Sorry."

"No problem." She leaned in close and we kissed. Her lips were warm and soft. She broke away and nodded her head toward one of the doors off to the side. "That's the room that I use when I work late and end up sleeping at the compound." Julie sounded slightly short of breath. "I figure that we have a little while before the other teams get here and anybody notices we're gone."

Dinner could wait.

I had not thought that anyone had seen us slip quietly back into the cafeteria. I had been as stealthy and nonchalant as was possible. Julie had winked at me one last time and moved off to coordinate with the other teams and take care of business. The room had almost filled with Hunters, and only one team was still missing, but was due at any moment. My gear had been pushed to the side. I picked up my bag, spotted my friends sitting at a table in the back of the room, and made my way over. The cafeteria had taken on an almost party atmosphere as Hunters who had not seen each other in months or years were reunited.

"Hey, dude. What you been doing?" Trip said, sliding over so I could have room to sit.

"Uh . . . nothing."

"Whatever," Holly said as she pushed a plate of now lukewarm pasta toward me. "We saved you some food . . . Stud." She winked evilly. "Best eat. Keep your strength up." Very few things slipped past Holly Newcastle.

"Thanks," I mumbled and immediately began to eat. The meal was delicious. "Wow, they sure did use a ton of garlic."

"The guy that cooked it, Fred, said that it might help when we fight vampires tomorrow," Trip explained. "Maybe they won't want to bite us if we stink like garlic."

Holly snorted. "That's just an old wives' tale. Vamps aren't scared of garlic."

"Hey, up until yesterday night we thought them turning into fog was just a myth too," I answered. "So until then, load me up, baby."

The final team arrived with a flourish. They were beleaguered and their armor was still splashed with undead fluids. Their logo was Smoking Elvis. Their leader waved to the crowd.

"Sorry we're late, but we killed twenty bloodsuckers. Let's get this party started." Shouts of "Showoff!" and "About time!" rose from the Hunters. But it was all in good fun.

"Will somebody hose these guys off? Damn, Eddings, your crew smells like vampire shit!" Sam bellowed.

"Love you too, Sam," he shouted back.

Harbinger cleared his throat. "Get your guys cleaned up, and grab some grub. We need to have a meeting." At that, the newcomers immediately complied. The rest of the room went back to its heated conversations and raucous laughter. Holly watched them go. After a moment's hesitation, she sprang to her feet and ran after them, grabbing the team lead by the arm.

"Excuse me?" she asked as he turned around. I was close enough to hear the exchange over the noise of the room. "Are you the team out of Las Vegas?"

"At your service." Eddings bowed slightly. "I don't think we've met, miss?"

"Newcastle, Holly Newcastle. Yes. Yes, we have met." She surprised all of us by embracing the filth-coated Hunter, hugging him tight, and holding him there. He looked bewildered. Finally she let go of him. He studied her curiously for a minute.

"Ahh . . . I remember now. Wow. Good to see you. You look a lot better. You've gained a bunch of weight," he said that as a compliment. "You must have put on thirty pounds."

"Thanks," she answered proudly. I looked at Trip and shrugged. That was not something I was under the impression you could say to Holly, or any woman for that matter, without getting shot.

"Earl told me he was going to try and recruit you. I'm glad to see you took him up on it. How do you like Monster Hunting?"

"Honestly, I hated it at first, but I felt like it was something I just had to do. Face my fears, you know . . ."

"Yeah. I understand that, after what you went through."

"Now, though?" Holly laughed. "I love it."

"I told Earl you would be perfect . . . Look, I've got to clean up before he skins me for being late."

She hugged him again. This time I could tell she was crying. I did a double-take at that. I was not aware that Holly was capable of producing tears. He whispered something in her ear, and patted her gently on the back. Eddings finally broke away and hurried after his men. Holly wiped her eyes and returned to our table.

"What was that about?" I asked.

"Uh . . . nothing." She mimicked me perfectly. "Now shut up and eat your spaghetti." She sighed and watched them leave, gradually returned to her food and ignored the rest of us.

"Ladies and gentlemen, I'm glad that you're all here. We have a bit of a situation on our hands."

That was an understatement.

Harbinger paced back and forth at the front of the cafeteria. The conference room was too small to fit the assembled humans and orcs, so the large maps of the South had been brought downstairs and leaned against the wall. Many of the red tacks had been replaced with yellow tacks, but there were many new red ones dotting the map. It looked like Alabama had the measles.

Every single member of MHI was present. The ones that I knew were a small minority. Julie sat by her grandfather and a young man who must have been her little brother. Boone's guys had come in from the perimeter and were standing toward the back. Mead had waved happily at me when he had entered. The orcs stood by themselves, slightly separated from the rest of us, packed tightly together, hooded heads kept down, shoulders slumped, not used to being surrounded by so many humans.

"The team leads were sent a brief synopsis as to where we stood a few days ago. But we have had some new developments. At 2:39 today, time backed up for five minutes. This was felt by every single person on Earth."

From the brief snitches of news that I had caught, billions were caught up in hysteria over the event. Some were in a panic, others in a religious fervor, and some were in denial. Thousands of babies had been born twice. Hundreds of people had died of natural causes twice.

"Yes. Those five minutes were in fact related to this case, and it goes to show how serious this one is. This is it, folks, this is the big one. Our real enemy is one General Joao Silva de Machado. We like to call him the Cursed One. He's five hundred years old, and in case you're wondering how you'll recognize him, he's the one that's a blob of black slime wearing conquistador armor. He's armed with some sort of ancient artifact that will be activated at the zenith of the full moon tomorrow night, giving us"—Harbinger glanced down at his watch—"approximately twenty-two hours. This artifact was the cause of the . . . glitch. And that was just a sample of the freak show to come. When this thing really goes off, it's the end of the world."

"What do you mean by 'end of the world'?" a Hunter asked.

"Literally. End of the world as in kiss your ass good-bye." The crowd murmured. MHI had faced some strange things before, but never anything like this. "The artifact must be used at a specific Place of Power, but we don't know where that Place is."

"Like the Christmas party in '95?" the man named Eddings asked.

"Correct," Harbinger stated. "Speaking of that, the Cursed One has killed Ray Shackleford." He stopped, counted on his fingers, and then added for clarity, "The fourth."

The Hunters erupted in confusion.

"Settle down. It gets worse. They tracked him down looking for information. They got him because Susan Shackleford, who is now a Master vampire, knew right where to find him."

If the news of Ray's death had upset the Hunters, the idea of his wife being a vampire stunned them into silence. You could have heard a shell casing hit the floor across that cafeteria. I glanced over at the Shacklefords. The Boss was as stoic as ever, arthritic hands steepled in front of his emotionless face. Nathan Shackleford resembled his sister and mother, but had the hulking build of his father. He was a handsome young man, but at the moment he looked tired and forlorn. Julie put her arm over her brother's shoulders as he hung his head down and stared at the linoleum.

"Yes, people. One of our own is one of the seven. Every trick we know, she knows. She helped make them up. Apparently she 'persuaded' Ray to lie to us. Ray told us where to go, and we went there blindly, in order to intercept the Cursed One." Earl paused to light a cigarette. I noticed his hand was shaking slightly as the flame of his Zippo wavered. He noticed the tremor as well, and snapped the lighter violently shut.

"Working alongside the Monster Control Bureau agents,"—most of the Hunters and all of the orcs started to grumble—"we went deep into the swamp, right into an ambush. It was the creatures from the Christmas party." Harbinger waited for the shouts and swearing to die down. Probably half of the people in the room had been survivors of that night. "The ones we fought at the rift were just drones. These were soldiers. My team and all of the Feds were killed, but when the artifact was activated, we started right before the ambush, only the creatures had been sent away."

"You can't die, Earl!" someone shouted. "That's impossible!"

"Nothing can kill Earl Harbinger!"

"Quiet down," Harbinger ordered. "Y'all know that isn't true."

"But—"

"Shut up!" the director roared. The Hunters instantly complied. "It's possible, because it happened today." He waited a moment before continuing. I did not know what had caused that outburst. Harbinger was a legend amongst the Hunters, but as I had seen back in the swamp, even he had his physical limits. "The artifact was the key. It summoned the creatures. It has power over time and who knows what else. It's a little stone box about the size of a deck of cards. And you'll know it when you see it because it holds a world of hurt, and we're probably going to have to pry it out of the claws of something really bad.

"On this case we have already lost two good Hunters. Jerry Roberts is dead, and Grant Jefferson is missing—either dead, turned or being held captive to be used as a sacrifice tomorrow night. If he's still alive, we're his only hope. So now we're going to listen to a story. It ain't over yet, we still have us a secret weapon . . . Owen."

The room was still. I gulped. "Yeah?"

"Tell us all your story. Don't leave anything out. Hurry up."

I stood awkwardly and walked to the front of the room.

"He's only a Newb," somebody said. "How does he know what to do?"

Harbinger held up his hand. "Listen up. This is Owen Pitt. His team calls him Z. He killed a werewolf with his *bare hands*. In the last week he has saved the lives of my team members on multiple occasions. He's killed vampires, wights, gargoyles and demons. He went head to head against Jean Darné. He alone has seen the Cursed One. And for those of you still doubting, he has fought Agent Franks. Twice. And even managed to kick him in the balls once."

"I would rather fight the demons!" someone shouted.

"Me too," I answered.

"Hunters—treat this man like you would treat any member of my team. Some of the things which you are about to hear are going to sound weird, but I personally believe them, so take that for what it is worth. Some of the things which you are going to be told can never leave this room. If this story was to get back to the Monster Control Bureau, then there is no telling what they would do to him. And know this, if anyone here ever speaks to the Feds about what Owen has seen, I will find out. You can know that of a surety, and I swear upon all that I hold holy, I will track you down to the ends of the world, reach down your throat, and pull your spine out your mouth." Nobody in the room said anything. They knew that he was deadly serious. My secrets were safe with this crew. "Owen, tell us everything."

I stood before the room of brave souls. Men and women who in the eyes of some were no better than mercenaries, but whom I knew to be heroes. I was one of them, and I was proud to have their respect, but humbled at the same time.

I shared my story. I told them about the Old Man, from the first encounter with him after my near death at the claws of Mr. Huffman. I told of the dreams. I spoke of Lord Machado and his failed expedition. I tried to convey his greed, his insane ambitions, his hate, and the inhuman desire that kept him alive when any other mortal man would have just been broken and consumed. I spoke of the Old Ones, slime-coated evil from beyond time, and I spoke of their prophecy and of their search for the unwitting fool with the power to unlock the gate and let them in. I warned of the Tattooed Man, the ancient captain, cursed to protect an artifact of unyielding darkness, and his solemn promise to take my life.

Haltingly, I told the Hunters about our deaths in Natchy Bottom. About my battle against the Cursed One's incorporeal self, and my blind luck in triggering the power of the artifact, surprising him, and temporarily wresting it from his control. Finally I spoke of his offer, my loyalty in exchange for a place in his kingdom, and I spoke for the first time about his threats against the others, especially Julie. I searched her out, making eye contact. She nodded slightly, understanding my fear, but her will was like iron, and she was not afraid of his curse.

Nathan Shackleford interrupted my speech. "This Machado asshole is going down!" The young man rose to his feet, fire in his eyes, fully prepared to defend his family from any further attacks. "I'll stake the son of a bitch myself!"

"Shut up, Nate," the senior Shackleford calmly ordered. "And watch your language around the womenfolk. That ain't polite."

"Sorry, Grandpa." He sat back down. Julie smiled in sisterly pride.

"Thank you, Mr. Pitt," the Boss said. "Is that all?"

"I'm afraid so, sir." I spread my hands in apology. The Hunters began to speak amongst themselves, team leads turning around and telling their troops to quiet down. "I'm sorry."

"No need for an apology, son. You've done your best." He pointed his hook at me. "That is all that any man can do."

"Yes, sir."

Harbinger stood back up. I started to return to my seat. "Stay right there, Owen. This is question-and-answer time. We have about five hundred years of collective monster-killing experience in this room, and I want to take advantage of it. We may be able to cobble together a couple semifunctioning brain cells out of this crew and figure out this puzzle."

Questions came from the crowd as the assembled Hunters picked my brain looking for a clue, something that we had missed. Something—anything—that could point us in the direction of the bad guys, and allow us to exercise our gifts for violence. Monster Hunters by nature tended to be a direct and straightforward bunch, similar to human claymore mines with big signs that warned FRONT TOWARD ENEMY. I uncomfortably tried to answer the questions as best as I could, but it was hard to recall every little thing from the heavily fragmented dreams. I could feel myself growing light-headed. It had been a long day.

Harbinger summed up our scant information. He stood in front of the map, back to the crowd. "So we know he's in Alabama, or at least he was a couple of days ago. Owen saw him underground, but we don't know if he's in a cave, a mine, or even a basement."

"The Elf Queen said that she saw him near water," Milo added.

"Now if we lived in the desert that might help," Sam said sardonically.

I leaned against the wall. I was not feeling very good. It was probably the stress. I closed my eyes. The pulse in my head was pounding, my heartbeat was elevating. My lungs constricted. I felt like I was going to be sick.

"Owen saw the Tattooed Man with Montgomery in the background. He's going to be looking for the Cursed One as well." Harbinger waved his hand over the area representing central Alabama. "But by now he could be anywhere . . . Owen, was he coming or going? And could you tell what direction? Owen?"

I could not answer. My mouth had suddenly dried up, leaving me unable to speak. My legs had gone numb, and I slid down the wall, flopping to the floor. My vision was fading.

"Owen!" Julie shouted.

"Aw hell." Harbinger hurried to my side. Squatting down, he grabbed my head. "Hey! Stay with me. That's an order." He shook me. "Owen!" Behind him I could see the blurry forms of the other Hunters rising to their feet in alarm.

I tried to apologize, but I was fast slipping into unconsciousness. I felt Julie's hands on my neck as she took my weakening pulse.

CHAPTER 25

"Sorry. Is best can do," the Old Man whispered.

"Where are we?" I looked around, but our surroundings were pitch-black and revealed nothing. I could feel his presence standing besides me.

"Shhh." His frail hand landed on my shoulder. "You want him to hear us?"

"Okay." Since I was not actually here, I could not really understand how whispering was supposed to help anything. "I think I'm dying."

"No, you be fine. Unless mess up I do. Then get dead for sure."

"That's supposed to make me feel better?" It was discomforting to be in the darkness. There was an absence of sensation not limited to just vision. I could not hear anything other than my companion. There were no scents, not even the feeling of the air on my skin. I missed the battle-damaged village. In comparison to the sensory deprivation, the shelled-out bunch of rubble might as well have been a plush resort.

"Where are we?"

"Same as before, town was just last thing I see, so is what have to show in your head. Takes effort to make like real. And Cursed One found it. So now we sneak in for look. I promise to show Cursed One's place. Other way not work now. Cursed One has shielded his mind. Blocked his memory. We try this way. I think might work perhaps . . . maybe."

"Mordechai, I swear that if you screw up and kill me, I'm going to be pissed. If I end up a ghost, I'm gonna be kicking your ghost ass for eternity."

"Ooh. Tough talk for alive person. Haunting is much hard work. Kids today not work hard enough to do such things. Now be ready. Is much danger . . . I try to show. Then we go away before catches us he does. He knows about me now. He is ready to stop me. Ready to fight you."

"What happens if he catches us?"

"You get stuck like me."

"And what if he catches you?"

The Old Man did not answer. I felt his hand tighten on my shoulder.

"What happens if the Cursed One catches you?"

"Not know. But must try." There was a slight trembling in his raspy voice.

"What are you going to do?"

"Like first time I show. You leave body. Go quick so nothing comes and lives in you. We take look. We get out. Hard to explain. If something bad happens, you go. Go away fast. Go back to self. Just wake up. Should be safe when wake."

"We don't need to get so close. Can't we just float overhead or something? That's all I need. No need to get all up in his face, or tentacles, or whatever."

"Not work like that again. Shielded. No. We go right in. Take you right to artifact I can. Then out. Out fast. No try to fight. Without body, you not have chance this time."

"I did okay last time," I lied. Even though I could not see him, I knew that he was shaking his head disapprovingly. Luckily he did not whack me with his cane.

"No, Boy. Not like that. You still not understand what you have done." He sighed. "Here, take these things." I felt something bump against my arm. I fumbled around in the dark until I found his waiting hand. He placed several small objects into my palm and then squeezed my fingers shut. "Maybe you can use."

"What are they?"

"I promised more toys to you. I keep promise. If we not die in next few minutes, still very strong vampires to face you have. Sorry I not can give more, is best can do."

"Thanks." I put the little objects away. "I don't know how they work, but they do a number on vampires." I remembered the look of shock on Susan Shackleford's undead face after she had burst into flames. I would be glad to have more of the little killer toys.

"I not know really, but think maybe have idea. Long time ago, before I got calling, like you got short straw . . . before I hunt monsters. I was—how you say?—craftsman. I build . . . I build things with hands." He sighed again, sounding very sad. "I think now, the memory I have left, is all I have. I make things again. I know are rough, but has been long time for me. I send you back with them. I send back to real world with these things I create. Back you go to the world, with these little bits of me. Bits of who I was. Maybe even who I am still now."

"I don't know if I understand."

"Holy things when used by faithful person is much powerful. Why? Not because of little metal star or little wooden cross. No, because of belief. Belief that good beats evil, because of strength that is inside people. For me, not believe—know. These little things, they are all I have left to give."

"Thank you," I said, and I meant it. The toys were physical manifestations of the Old Man, created from his memory and translated into the real world through unknown means. The little objects were like bottled faith.

"Boy . . . glad I have been to be stuck in your head last little while. Gives me hope for future . . . if world not get destroyed of course. Then short future that would be. You are good boy. Proud. Stubborn. Sometimes stupid. But always try to be good. Heart means to be good. Makes me glad that other one chosen is good man. No matter what happens. Promise . . . promise you finish this. Even if I not there to help."

"Of course. But don't talk like that. You aren't going anywhere."

"Bah . . . is much danger in this thing. Promise me."

"I promise I'll finish this."

"Good. Now remember things you have seen. Remember things I have show you. Is up to you, many things which I not could tell, I have show you. Remember them, and all will be fine." He patted me on the shoulder.

A grim feeling of dread hovered around us. I tried

to steel myself in preparation for our raid. The odds were not in our favor.

"It's been an honor," I stated solemnly.

"Me too, Boy. Me too. . . . Now let us go and look. Make no sound. Try not to think so loud. As you say, let's do this thing."

A sensation of sudden movement. An abrupt stop. Dark. Cool. Damp. Musty.

I could sense the spirit that was the Old Man near at hand. There were other things in the dark as well. Not quite living, but refusing to be dead. The presence of the ancient and powerful vampires was thick in the cavern, as well as the oily taint of the Cursed One.

There was no light, but since I was not seeing through eyes, it did not matter. We were in a cave. A mammoth opening in the earth. Pillars of rock stretched from floor and ceiling, most of the stalactites and stalagmites far longer than I was tall. Banks of harsh artificial lights had been smashed and kicked over, leaving only shadow and broken glass.

I could feel the seven Masters. Not all were in the cave itself, but rather they were hunting or feeding in the night above. A few remained on guard, hanging suspended, invisible in the tangled rock overhead. The sense of their power was overwhelming. Susan Shackleford was there. Far younger than the others, but in my current state I could perceive just how dangerous she was—strong beyond all expectations for a vampire so young. The others were older, and some had even been alive when my ancestors were living in mud huts or paddling canoes across the oceans.

For a moment I was able to glimpse into their twisted minds. Their leader, Lord Machado's lieutenant, was the one known as Jaeger. He was also young. Not even undead for six decades, hated and feared by the others, he led them through his unnatural strength, granted not in the traditional manner of the vampire, but rather by the power of the ancient artifact—a tortured gift placed upon him at the moment of his human death, bound to the artifact, and sealed into the service of the Cursed One.

There were humans present as well. Several were being kept in a hole, too steep and slick to crawl out of. They were snacks. Grant Jefferson had been bound and tossed in a corner. Judging from his appearance he had been savagely beaten, but he was still alive. The Cursed One had his sacrifice.

The vampire leader, Jaeger, knelt at the rear of the chamber, a fearsome thing of awe-inspiring strength, now relegated to a mundane chore. He held an ancient conquistador's helmet and polished it, his narrow hands moving like a belt sander. The breastplate and ax that I had gotten to know so well sat on a cloth before him. He was a squire, preparing the colors of his knight before the final tournament. The feathered plume had long since turned to dust.

Something moved at the rear of the great chamber. A tear appeared in the solid rock and light seeped through the crack. It was similar to the rifts that the demons had used in Natchy Bottom, a hidden passage carved through space to someplace else, unnaturally grafted onto the walls of this cave long ago. I could see and understand the portal clearly in my disembodied state. The rift gradually widened as a glistening shape pushed its way through and slapped wetly onto the floor. The temperature dropped from chilly to freezing in seconds. The helpless humans whimpered in fear.

Lord Machado had returned.

I had a brief glimpse into the portal as it disappeared back into the rock. Dark sky flickered in the distance. It was the Place of Power.

The vampire bowed his head and presented the helmet to the waiting master. The withering mass reached down and plucked the antique from his servant's hands. The tentacles gently lifted the steel pot and set it on the skull-shaped protuberance, a crown upon a blighted brow.

The thing that was Lord Machado towered above the tall vampire. Still vaguely man-shaped, twisted and hardened bones formed the supports for the black pulsating tissues. Several tentacles dangled from where the arms would have been, and legs had been replaced with a veritable platform of withering limbs. Every inch of black flesh moved like a bucket of worms.

The creature paused. Then slowly rotated toward us.

I tried to shrink back, an impossible feat in my current condition. The helmet cocked to the side as the burning eyes zoomed in on us. I heard the Old Man's thoughts.

Run.

I willed my spirit away from the Cursed One, back through the huge cavern. Jaeger screamed and leapt at us, his movement too fast to discern. It felt as if a wall of evil slammed into me, pinning me down, capturing me and holding me. I fought against it, but I was not strong enough. Lord Machado oozed across the stone, compressing his body between narrow paths, tentacles reaching forward, driving his will like a spear.

I could not flee. I could not escape. Master vampires detached themselves from the ceiling and dropped around me. The Cursed One was closing. As hard as I pushed, I could not break away from the will of the evil thing. I could feel him pulling me toward him, sinking hooks into me and reeling me in.

I was doomed.

Flee, Boy!

The spirit of Mordechai Byreika did not pull away. Instead he hurled himself against the onrushing vampires. An explosion of blue sparks lighted the cavern as his presence collided with Jaeger, smashing the vampire backwards across the cave in a brilliant display that blinded all of the undead. The vampire struck a stalactite with a resounding crack.

Take that, Nazi bastard! Payback is bitch!

The will of the Cursed One bore down upon Mordechai. The Old Man faced his adversary in a futile but noble gesture. For a brief instant the ghost became visible, holding his cane in his arthritic hands like a weapon, narrow shoulders hunched, eyes hard and jaws clenched. He swung at the onrushing blackness.

And was swept away.

Mordechai! No!

The will of the Cursed One was temporarily diverted. The snares that held me snapped. I remembered the Old Man's admonition. Every instinct told me to fight, but I fled. A sense of pain engulfed me, but it was not mine. It was Mordechai's. It filled the cavern, drowning out all other sensations.

I saw his death.

The Polish winter. 1944. The rubble of the shelled-out town. The burned and blackened church. The Old Man tied to the altar. The incorporeal presence of the Cursed One hovering nearby, hungrily waiting, but already knowing that his calculations had been in error. Jaeger, then merely a human in the black uniform of the SS, holding a gleaming blade high. Bitten by a vampire far earlier in his forgotten youth, the curse of the undead waited in his veins for his suicide and inevitable return.

Sounds of gunfire coming from the village. Multitudes of German soldiers cut down by the immortal Thrall.

The artifact, black energy swirling, sitting by the Old Man's head. He did not fight, for he knew this battle was over. The blade flashed down, cutting sluggishly through Mordechai's narrow chest. Blood splattering over the church, over the ancient Place of Power.

The heart held high, pumping blood down the Nazi's arm. The ritual failed. The time had not been right. The black energy of the artifact dying. The light in the Old Man's eyes dying at the same time.

The sacrifice bound to the artifact. Mordechai's spirit was chained and enslaved to the ancient box, decades passing, as he was trapped, helplessly bound to this world.

Until he found me.

He screamed as he experienced the pain of death all over again.

I knew I had to wake up. I fought my way forward, pushing away from the Cursed One, like a swimmer with lungs burning for air struggling toward the sky.

There was a large tunnel out of the great cave. It was round corrugated metal. It was angled toward the surface.

Behind me the ghostly scream was cut short. The Cursed One returned his attention toward my fleeing spirit, searching, grasping. Energy slung past me like cracking whips. I knew that if I could reach the surface, if I could reach the air, I could return to my body and wake up.

It was close—the surface. I raced onward.

Then suddenly a silent conquistador stood in my path. Blocking my way.

No. Mordechai's sacrifice would not be in vain. I pushed forward.

The conquistador did not move.

It wore a silly cartoon grin. It had a big, stuffed, fake head.

What in the hell?

I broke through, the Cursed One raging below. My spirit soared into the night sky and tore across the horizon at impossible speeds. I was free.

"Owen!" Julie shouted in my ear. "Are you with us?"

"Ack," I coughed, choking off my shout of freedom. "I'm back," I gasped.

"Are you okay?" All of the Monster Hunters were clustered around me.

"Mordechai is dead."

"We know. He died in 1944," Julie explained soothingly as she ran her hand over my face. "You're going to be okay now."

I struggled to form words. "No . . . Just now. He's gone. He gave himself up to save me from Lord

Machado." I lay still. I could feel my heart hammering in my chest. It had to be at least a hundred and fifty beats a minute. I could feel sweat pouring out of my body, and every inch of me tingled in pins and needles discomfort. My hands were clenched into shaking fists. I forced them to open.

Several small wooden toys fell from my hands onto the floor.

Holy shit.

Harbinger was still squatting at my side. "What did you see?"

"Grant's alive. He's the sacrifice." Several of the Hunters began to murmur. It was one thing to have one of our own killed in action. It was another thing entirely to have one of our own in the hands of the bad guys.

"Where are they?" Harbinger pounded his fist into his palm. "Where?"

"A big cave."

"Where?"

"I don't know."

Harbinger gestured at some of the others. "I want to know every cave in the South. Now! What else?"

"It was huge. Lots of rock formations. Kind of pretty. Real tall. Taller than this building. The interior had to be at least a hundred yards wide." It was hard to guess scale when you were not in your physical body for reference. "You had to take a big metal tunnel to get into it."

"Big caves!" Harbinger shouted. "What else?"

"Uh . . ." I thought back to the final thing that I had seen. "There was a conquistador. At first I thought it was something to do with Lord Machado, but it wasn't. It was stuffed. Like one of those big fake heads people wear at amusement parks."

"What the hell?" Harbinger said. "Get me caves with conquistadors."

"Friendly Fernando?" Milo interrupted.

"Who the fuck is Friendly Fernando?" Harbinger snapped.

"Oh my . . ." Milo said, "Earl, some of us went there last year. Friendly Fernando is like the mascot. It's a tourist place. Biggest cave in the state. I can't believe you haven't been there, since you're from here and all. They even have a little theme park with some rides, and a water balloon tower, and a maze, kids love it, and a gift shop, and . . ."

Earl stood and grabbed the red-bearded Hunter by the shoulders. "Focus, man!"

Instead Julie answered, almost as if a light bulb had gone off over her head. "DeSoya Caverns. Lord Machado is in DeSoya Caverns."

We broke to prepare for our assault. Teams formed up. Weapons were readied. Intelligence was gathered.

"DeSoya Caverns Park is in Childersburg. Near Sylacauga. About seventy-five miles from here up the 231." Julie pointed at the map. The team leads were gathered while the rest of the Hunters were busy preparing for the mission.

Harbinger looked at his watch. "If we leave in three hours, we can arrive about the time the sun comes up. Gives everybody a chance to catch a little sleep, and some of our teams have been up for twenty-four hard hours straight. Tired Hunters make stupid decisions. And the last thing I want to do is land on this place when the Masters are awake and prowling."

"Can we just drop a bomb on it? Bury those bastards?" Boone asked.

"I don't think so," I answered. "The Cursed One was in something else. There's a hidden rift to somewhere else in the back of the cave. The cave itself isn't the Place of Power. It's just the entrance. If we blow the cave, we're probably doing him a favor, and he's going to be sitting fat and happy wherever that rift goes to."

"It could be a pocket dimension," Julie explained. "There have been cases of them in monster hunting history. Basically a bubble outside of the regular world, but attached to a fixed point. So if it is a pocket dimension, even if we smash the cavern, it won't touch the dimension, other than to bury the entrance."

"Then we go in after him," Harbinger ordered. "What do we know about this place? What makes it so special?"

Julie started to list off factoids. "Twelve stories tall. Football field wide inside. Lots of onyx and marble. First major cavern discovered in this country. During the Civil War, the Confederacy used it to mine saltpeter for gunpowder. During prohibition it was a speakeasy called the Bucket of Blood."

"So I'm guessing we won't be the first people to put some bullet holes in it," Eddings said.

"Nope. Plenty of people have been plugged in that cave. Before the Europeans showed up it was an Indian burial ground for at least two thousand years."

"So now we have a theme park and tourist attraction on top of it. Makes perfect sense," Mayorga pointed out. "The-two-thousand-year-old holy site explains why this is the target."

"I'm telling you, it's just the gateway," I insisted. "The Place is on the other side of the gate."

"Can you find the hidden gate and open it?" Harbinger asked pointedly.

"I don't know."

"Well, if you can't, plan B is to blow the whole place to hell."

"Do we have the munitions to do something like that?" a Hunter named Cody asked. "I know we have evil genius Milo and whatnot, but even he can only do so much."

"Actually, I was thinking that if we don't stop the CO before the moon is up, we call the Feds. They'll just nuke the place."

"Good plan. Just give us time to get out from under the mushroom cloud first," Cody said. He was a big grizzled man. Other than the Boss and Dorcas, he was probably the oldest Hunter present. He turned to me, expressing some curiosity. "Hey, kid, is your dad Auhangamea Pitt?"

"Yeah," I answered, surprised. "You know him?"

"One of the baddest Green Berets to ever walk the face of the earth. He kept me alive when I was just a scared kid stuck on a firebase in the middle of nowhere. You look like him. Big and ugly."

"Thanks."

"And from what I've heard tonight, you take after him too. So when we get in there, I've got no doubt you're going to get that rift or gate or whatever open. Right?"

"I'll try," I answered, not knowing if I could live up to my father's legend.

"Trying isn't going to cut it. Because if we have

to fight our way through seven Masters, I can guarantee we won't all live through it. And if some of us get killed, only to get in there and not be able to open the gate, then that is just stupid. I say we just blow the whole thing and bury them," Mayorga said, "Calculated risk."

"No," Julie snapped, "you're forgetting Grant. He's captive. We have to get him out of there."

"I don't want to lose my whole team for one person," he retorted. "I vote we blow the cavern from a distance."

"Come on, May, nobody lives forever." Eddings grinned crazily.

"This ain't a democracy," Harbinger said. "I decide. . . ." Mayorga looked at him sullenly. Harbinger turned back to me. "Owen, for the last time. Can you open this rift?"

I thought back to the vision. I was still shaking from it. Finding the spot would be easy. I did not see how it was opened, but somehow I felt that I could. But if I was wrong, a whole bunch of Hunters might die in vain. I answered carefully, "Yes. I can do it."

"Okay, we go in," Harbinger decided. "Julie, gather all the intel you can on this place."

"Speaking of which," a female team lead, who's name tag read Paxton, interjected, "this place had to have come up on the Feds' radar for potential sites. They've got to have guards stationed there."

"I know folks in the National Guard here," Boone said. "I'll make some calls and find out what's stationed there."

"We can assume they're dead or turned. Probably at least bitten, and enthralled so they can still check in on the radio. We'll just have to assess when we come to it."

"Should we contact the Feds first? I know they're a bunch of dicks, but we're talking about the fate of the world here," VanZant asked.

The Boss spoke up for the first time. "No. We hit it at dawn. If we fail, then we call them. I would really prefer to see this handled without an atomic bomb used on my home state." He poked a hole in the map with his hook.

"If we pull this off we are going to be rich," Hurley said.

"Or dead," Mayorga muttered.

"Tell your teams what's up. Grab some rest. We hit DeSoya Caverns at dawn," Harbinger ordered. The team leaders quickly dispersed, excited or nervous at the thought of another mission. Julie gave me a little smile before picking up her laptop and leaving. Harbinger looked at me. Steel blue eyes unblinking. "Well, this is it."

"I guess so."

"Sorry about your friend."

"You would have liked him, Earl. He was a good man." I thought of Mordechai throwing himself at the Cursed One to give me a chance to escape. I remembered my promise to finish this business. I intended to keep it.

"Well, what're you waiting for?" Harbinger asked as he removed a cigarette from the pack in his pocket.

"Huh?"

He flicked his Zippo and ignited the flame, taking his time in responding. "Brief your team."

"But . . ."

He took a long drag. "I've got three Newbies that seem to think you're their leader. Trip, Holly and Albert would follow you anywhere. Whether you know it or not, you're a leader. That's good enough for me. Consider this a promotion."

"But . . . I'm no leader."

"Yes, you are. I know none of you have a damn clue, so I still want y'all attached with my team. But they answer to you, and they stick with you. No matter what. Do what I tell you and you should be fine." He held out his hand. I shook it. He almost broke my fingers. "Don't screw up."

"I won't let you down, Earl."

He only nodded. Gave my hand one final bone-crushing squeeze, and then moved on, leaving me alone in front of the map. Alone, except for my doubts and uncertainty. I hurried to find my team.

Milo Anderson crashed into me. He excitedly pushed a loaded five-round Saiga magazine into my hand. He had an insane gleam in his eye, as he seemingly did whenever he had the opportunity to harness whole new forms of destruction.

"Think this is going to work?" I asked.

"Not a bad idea. They were oversize, so I had to trim them a smidgen. Hope that don't mess up the mojo. Lucky for you I had the reloading bench already set up for 12 gauge," he answered as he tugged absently on his beard. "If this works, it should be awesome. If not?" He shrugged.

"If not, at least my death should be relatively spectacular."

"That's the spirit." Milo grinned. "Lightweight projectiles. Low powder charge. This is short range only, like conversational-distance short range. Accuracy is going to suck. Penetration is going to be negligible. Probably won't have enough pressure to cycle Abomination's action. So plan on going manual."

"Can do. Thanks Milo."

"Good luck, Owen. I've got to go grab some spears and my garlic wreath. Catch you on the flip side." The strange Hunter ran to take care of his team's supplies.

I contemplated the magazine. I sure hoped this worked.

The convoy of mismatched vehicles tore northward at dangerous speeds, dawn fast approaching. I sat in the passenger seat of one of the MHI Suburbans. My armor was still damp and cold from Natchy Bottom. You can't just drop twenty pounds of Kevlar and Cordura into the drier. I had my shotgun clenched between my knees. Over a dozen magazines of assorted 12-gauge ammunition and 40mm grenades rode in pouches on my chest and sides. I was wearing both of the STI .45s that Julie had given me, along with several magazines of silver bullets. My ganga ram was strapped across my chest, and several sharpened white-oak stakes rode in a pouch on my back. I had smoke, frag and incendiary hand grenades. And just for luck, on my ankle I was wearing the little .357 which I had used against Mr. Huffman.

I had used our last few hours to get some much-needed sleep. I had not dreamt, and I felt a chill loneliness. I was certain now: The Old Man was gone.

The wipers beat rhythmically. The rain was increasing, running almost like rivers down the road. The wind was howling and the big vehicle rocked as strong gusts hit us. Being the only one of us who had lived through any hurricanes, Trip assured us that this storm was not far behind in intensity. The sheets of falling water were so thick that I could barely see the tail-lights of the vehicle ahead of us.

The storm had come out of nowhere. It had the mark of the Cursed One on it. I worried about Julie, buckled into the Hind with the rest of her team. Surely Skippy would get them through.

The Newbie team had been crammed into the overloaded Suburban for the trip. Holly had taken to calling us the rainbow coalition team, since we had one white female, and males of the Black, Asian, and Other categories. All we needed was a lesbian and a guy in a wheelchair and we were ready to salve even the biggest liberal's angst. The others were sharing the second row of seats, and the driver was a talkative little Hunter named Gus, out of Hurley's team in Miami.

"Yeah, you guys should have seen it. Little town outside of Pensacola. Vampires nested all over the city works building. We're ready to go in and hit them fast and hard. We get stopped by the mayor for—guess what? You guys ain't gonna believe it . . ."

"What, Gus?" Lee asked in exasperation, not wanting to egg him on, but seeing no other way out. Gus had talked nearly nonstop since leaving the compound. Everybody dealt with the stress of an upcoming mission in their own strange ways, I supposed.

"She was a big Anne Rice fan. She wanted to 'reason' with them. She just thought that they were misunderstood. She wanted to open a 'dialogue.'" He took his hands from the wheel long enough to make quote motions with his fingers. I started to instinctively reach for the wheel as we began to hydroplane.

"I hate that sensitive romantic vampire bullshit," Holly said.

"Yeah, exactly. You wouldn't believe how hard killing undead got after those damn books came out. Every love-starved housewife out there started thinking of them as tragic homoerotic Fabio-looking things. Morons. Well, anyway, so the mayor goes and gets eaten and Hurley says to us—"

The radio cut him off.

"This is Harbinger. We've got to land the chopper. Storm is getting too bad to fly—even for Skip. We're putting down before Sylacauga." The radio went out.

"So, anyway, Hurley says to us—" Gus was cut off again.

"Pick us up. Clearing at the end of the road right before town. Skip will stay with the Hind. Hopefully the weather will clear enough that he can take off and provide some air support later."

I saw brake lights ahead. Gus swore and slowed down.

"What's the problem?" Holly asked.

"Shh," Trip hissed. He rolled down his window, letting rain in.

"What are you doing?" Holly asked.

"Hear that?" he asked.

"No," I answered. But it was no secret I had the worst hearing of the bunch.

"What is that?" Lee asked nervously.

"Tornado sirens."

"What's that mean?"

"It means we have a tornado warning. Weather is weird for them so it probably isn't just a warning on conditions. Means some have been seen in the area."

"How will we know if one is nearby?" Lee asked.

"It'll sound like a million freight trains. You'll know," Trip warned.

I noted with some concern that the clouds had turned green, a sick deadly color.

Other noises could be heard over the rain, thumping against the roof of the Suburban. Small round things were smacking wetly against the window.

"Now, that's different," Gus said as the wipers knocked away the blood and meat on the windshield.

"Dude, roll the window up!" I shouted.

"Oh, gross!" Trip exclaimed as something hit him.

It was raining frogs. Thousands of tiny amphibians were striking us, bouncing off of the hood or road. Some were falling faster than others, hitting hard enough to explode in little red puffs.

"Isn't this from like the Ten Commandments? Let's get out of here before the plague of locusts show up," Lee suggested nervously.

"Well, actually, it's not an unknown phenomenon to have it rain frogs," I said. "Tornadoes or water spouts can pick them up and drop them someplace else. Fish too."

"Not the time for trivia, Z," Holly said.

I bit my tongue. My attempt at explaining the phenomenon was rather lame. We all knew what this meant. This was the day. One of the frogs examined me through the glass before the wiper batted it aside, leaving only a red smear.

❖   ❖   ❖

MHI assembled in the parking lot of a small grocery store. We were only a few miles from the caverns, and Harbinger did not want us to hit the site until the sun was fully up. Not that I thought it would do much good; the clouds and rain were thick enough that it might as well have been night.

"How much light can a vampire stand?" I asked.

"Very little can cause them pain. A direct hit and they catch on fire. And maybe we'll get lucky and get a little sunshine," Julie answered.

"At least it quit raining frogs," Sam grunted.

A large contingent of us had assembled under the store awning, making last-minute preparations, asking questions, or just stretching our legs before the final fight. Some extremely curious locals had ventured out of their homes, trying to figure out what the large group of paramilitary-looking folks were doing in their small town. Considering the things that had happened over the last few days, we were not that weird in the grand scheme of things, but we still must have been a sight.

Sam nudged me and pointed across the lot. A local teenager in a yellow rain slicker approached one of our parked vehicles, a three-quarter-ton pickup hooked to a gooseneck horse trailer. It belonged to our orc contingent. Overcome by curiosity, the kid peered over the side door, only to stumble backwards and fall into a mud puddle when something large slammed into the sheet metal and growled.

"Hey, kid! It ain't polite to poke your nose in other folks' business. You trying to lose a hand?" Sam shouted.

"What was that? Who are you guys?" the kid shouted, suddenly afraid.

"It's your momma. And we're the circus. Now scram!" Sam let his duster jacket open to reveal his armor and .45-70.

The kid pulled himself up and ran back toward his home, probably trying to figure out what exactly it was that he had seen in that horse trailer.

"Sam! Quit scaring the children."

"Sorry, Julie," Sam said as he grinned at me from under his mustache.

"Boone? You got anything about who's on guard?" Harbinger demanded.

"This one was high priority. Word is at least a squad of actual Feds on the cavern. Local guardsmen blocking the road. They've been checking in on a regular basis, so they're still alive," he answered. "We've got authority to deal with local infestations, so the soldiers should let us through. The Feds, on the other hand . . ."

"If they are on site, figure that they've been turned," Julie said.

"You mean I might get to stake a Fed?" Sam asked with far too much eagerness. "Oh, that would be fricking awesome."

"Easy there, big fella. Only if they're dead," Harbinger warned. "This is it, folks. Any questions?"

The group was silent. Our radio channel was open so the Hunters still sitting in the running vehicles could hear. No one asked anything.

"Fine then." Harbinger cleared his throat before continuing. "Whatever happens, I want y'all to know that I'm proud. Most of you know how long I've been doing this, and you know I won't lie. This is the finest group of Hunters MHI has ever assembled. I

mean that. You know what to do. You're the best of
the best. I would take this crew against the gates of
hell themselves if God would give us the contract.
With these teams we could collect PUFF on the four
horsemen of the apocalypse. It's an honor to have
led you into battle, the greatest honor I've ever had.
Like the memorial wall says, *Sic transit gloria mundi.*
We're mortals, but the deeds we do are the stuff of
legend, and your courage will live forever. Know that,
and be sure. You're the modern versions of Beowulf,
of St. George, of Odysseus. You're Van Helsing with
firepower. You're Jack and the Beanstalk with automatic
weapons. We're walking in the valley of the shadow of
death, but we shall fear no evil! Because evil is about
to get a stake put through its black heart because we
are the baddest mother-fuckers to ever set foot in the
valley!" he finished in a roar.

A cheer rose from the Hunters. I pumped my
fist into the air and shouted. All of the horns were
honked. The wargs in the trailer began to howl. I
was surprised that nobody started shooting into the
air. That was probably just because they wanted to
save ammunition.

Harbinger paused, looking out into the rain. A
malicious grin split his face. He finally continued.
"Good hunting. Move out."

CHAPTER 26

The lead Suburban braked before the National Guard checkpoint. An old M113 armored personnel carrier, basically a bulletproof box on treads, blocked the road. The soldiers had been driven under cover, sitting in their vehicles trying to stay out of the horrible rain, lashing wind, and scattered frog showers. They regarded us warily as our convoy approached. One of the soldiers manned the big .50 mounted on the armored personnel carrier and swiveled it in our general direction.

Boone and Harbinger exited the lead vehicle and approached the soldiers, hands held wide, indicating that they were no danger. After the events of the last few days, the soldiers weren't going to take any chances. I noted that having the APC parked in the center of the road was kind of redundant, since the storm had blown several large trees down, forming a very effective roadblock right behind their position. Some smart NCO had some of his men spread out into the trees.

"Poor guys. Stuck out in this weather. What are they supposed to do if a tornado hits? Hide under that tank?" Trip asked.

"It's their job. They're doing what they have to do," Lee said. I felt his hands pull on the back of my seat as he tried to get a better view. "I hope they let us through."

The radio crackled, "Pitt. Come up here. Just you."

"Roger that," I answered. "Be right back, guys." I pulled my black raincoat tight and stepped out of the warm vehicle into the screaming rain. The coat was bulky and long enough that it hid Abomination. I wasn't about to go anywhere this close to the Cursed One without my gun. I struggled to hold my hood down as the wind tried to tear it away. Branches tumbled across the road. It was raining sideways. I splashed down the road, past several other vans and SUVs, Hunters inside looking out at me from their relative comfort. I reached the roadblock.

Boone was speaking with one of the Guard. They appeared to be arguing. "What's going on?" I shouted to be heard over the wind.

"Boone's trying to bluster his way through. He just barely got out of the Guard himself and these are his people. They still won't let us through without permission from the Feds stationed at the cavern itself, and they ain't responding on the radio."

"Figure they're dead?"

"Something like that," he answered. "Do you sense anything?"

"I'm not psychic, Earl."

"Do me a favor and try," he ordered. "You have a

connection with this thing. We need to exploit every advantage. It's worth a shot."

I pulled my hood low, trying to block the rain. I closed my eyes. Balancing in the road as the wind rocked me, coat billowing, I listened. Cold moisture leaked around the openings of my protection and down my armor. How was I supposed to sense them? I concentrated, remembering how I felt at those times when I had viewed Lord Machado's memories.

Then I felt it. A growing presence. Darkness. Age. Power. Masters. I could feel the alien thoughts—the confidence in their strength and their combined ability to crush any number of humans. I could hear their voices, their communications, almost as if they were shouting;

Fools. You have slept so long. You do not know the power of the Hunters' modern weapons. Return and protect our Lord.

We fear no human, Jaeger. I have seen their puny "cannon."

We shall crush them and feast. Calm thyself, young one.

I was one of them. Y'all don't know what you're getting into. Things have changed since your day, you old bastards.

Silence. I have no time for your cowardice. Hide in your cave, female, for we walk in the daytime. Now is our time to reign.

Fine. Underestimate them and see what happens.

As Trip was so fond of pointing out, pride comes before the fall. Most of the vampires ignored the admonitions of Jaeger and Susan warning them of the dire power of our modern weapons. These Masters had slept through the last few centuries, and they held no fear of man. They were coming up the road, heading right toward us, no subtlety, not even rushing, taking their time and savoring their assured victory. We only had a few minutes.

I opened my eyes and the sensation vanished. Heck, maybe I was psychic.

"Earl, we've got company coming." I pointed down the road. "I think it's the Masters. At least a few of them. But they don't understand what they're up against. They're old and cocky."

"Okay. Better to fight them in the open than underground . . . Suckers." He looked plaintively at the sky, but there was no sunlight to be seen. Harbinger approached Boone and tapped him on the shoulder. I drew closer so I could listen. The soldier on the .50 tracked me. "Excuse me!" Harbinger butted in. "Gentlemen, we're about to be attacked."

"My name isn't 'Gentlemen,' it's Lieutenant McNab. And you need to back this convoy the hell up and turn around. This here is a secure area, and no civilians are allowed on this site. Move back or I'll order my men to open fire."

"Lieutenant McNab, sir, we have authorization from the Federal Government to access this area. There's an undead outbreak inside the cavern complex. It's imperative that we get in there," Boone said.

"Undead? Like *Dawn of the Dead*, booga-booga zombies?" The lieutenant laughed. He was very young, and could not have been doing this for very long. "That's the stupidest thing I've ever heard. Back this convoy up now or I'm authorizing the use of force." The nearby soldiers looked around nervously. An older soldier in a camouflage rain poncho stepped behind the lieutenant.

"How much time?" Harbinger hissed at me.

"Maybe a minute or two," I responded.

He shook his head slightly, and cracked his knuckles under the sleeves of his raincoat. "We're gonna have to fall back and let the vampires slaughter these poor saps."

"Excuse me, sir?" the other soldier said. He tapped the lieutenant on the shoulder.

"Yes, Sergeant?" the young man responded.

"I know this man." He nodded at Boone. "This is Sergeant Jay Boone. Nineteenth Special Forces. I worked with him in Afghanistan. He's one of us."

"How's it hanging, Gregorius?" Boone asked.

"Pretty good. Did you get a medal for Kandahar?"

"Yep, and a purple heart, and my medical discharge. Now I'm back to monster hunting."

"Sergeant, what is this nonsense?" shouted the lieutenant.

"Sir, if this man says that we are about to come under attack, I believe him. We'd best let these folks through to do their job."

"I'm under orders, damn it!" he shouted. "Nobody goes through here unless the FBI says so, and they aren't responding!"

"They ain't responding because they're dead," Harbinger answered. "Boone, Pitt, let's fall back while these guys get killed. Good luck, Sergeant. Have your men save their last bullets for themselves."

"Wait," said Gregorius, "Boone, you said undead. Like that thing we found buried in Bagram? The one that ate Chris?"

"No, sorry dude. Way worse. Master vampires. That thing we found was just a pussy ghoul."

"Dang. Hold on." He chewed on his bottom lip for a moment, deep in thought, before turning toward his men. "Defend against the park, enemy is incoming. Prepare to fire on my command." The soldiers complied instantly to their seasoned NCO. Harbinger immediately clicked our radio twice. Doors opened and Hunters spread out, many sloshing across into the trees. Sunroofs were rolled back and belt-fed machine guns or MK19 grenade launchers were lifted into their mounting brackets. The armed Suburbans rolled forward, and pulled off to the sides, forming a front.

"What are you doing? There's no such thing as vampires."

"Shut up and grab your rifle, sir. If we live you can put me in for a court-martial. Boone, what should we do?"

"What do you have?"

"Two squads, the track here, and a 60 on one of the Humvees. But these guys are admin pogues. I'm lucky they gave us live ammo."

Harbinger stepped in. "Hold this center position. Control their fields of fire. We've got a lot more hardware than you. And with these things there ain't no shame in running, so retreat if you need to."

"Sergeant, I order you to arrest these men! That is a direct order. Oh my . . ." He stopped speaking when he saw the door of the trailer drop and the first of the wargs jump free. The giant wolves, as big as horses, limbs squat and heavy with muscle, snarling and nipping at each other, really were an impressive sight. The black-masked orcs quickly found their mounts, slung themselves bareback onto the creatures and readied themselves for battle. "Oh my." He started to draw his pistol, but I placed my hand firmly on his.

"Those are on our side. The bad guys are coming from the other direction." I pointed.

"Oh my," he said again as the pack of wolves and riders wheeled about and headed for the treeline, ready to flank into the enemy. The lieutenant looked like he was about to vomit.

"And that's what we alcoholics like to call a moment of clarity," Boone quipped.

I noted that the orcs had taken the time to put white handprints on their masks and helmets. It was a nice touch. They must have loved the *Lord of the Rings* movies too.

"Edward, this is Harbinger. Hold your wargs in reserve. You're our cavalry."

"Unter . . . stand . . . Harb Anger."

The road stretched ahead almost three hundred yards before disappearing over the top of a lush hill. The Hunters had spread into the forest on both sides. Strange that Harbinger had spoken of a valley of death, and now we found ourselves in one. I turned and found my team waiting, loaded down with heavy weapons, looking to me for guidance. I looked to Harbinger, he nodded to one side, and I went. The others followed. He continued to bark orders into the radio, giving each team lead an area of responsibility, and most notably telling VanZant's team to, "Dig in the big guns."

We set up in a small ditch off of the road, with a good view of the approach and a small amount of

cover. Once again I was waist-deep in water, this
time from the flash floods. Just once I would like to
hunt monsters someplace dry, but as a good rule of
thumb, if you could get lower, you do it. Lee threw
down the tripod, and Trip dropped the FN MAG
machine gun onto it. I was pleased to see that they
did it exactly how Sam had taught us, quickly and
surely opening the feed cover and sliding in the belt
of silver .308. Lee hunkered down behind the big
weapon. Holly handed me an RPG. The heavy tube
was reassuring in my hands. Everyone dug down into
the ditch, prepared to fight. Nervous but competent.
Scared but professional. We were ready to put some
smack down. Not bad for an accountant, a librarian,
a schoolteacher, and a stripper. Not bad at all.

"Ready, guys?" I asked.

"We got a choice?" Lee asked over the stock of
the Belgian machine gun.

"Not really."

The rain ceased. The wind died. The clouds turned
an even brighter green. It was eerily still and the
energy could be felt in the humid sky. Many Hunters
glanced hopefully upward. Unfortunately there was no
sunlight. The ancient evil approached.

"They're here," I said, my voice echoing in the
now silent valley.

Four figures appeared over the hill, walking purpose-
fully down the road. They had to know that we were
there, but they did not care. They were Masters.

Two clicks came over the radio—the signal to get
ready. Harbinger would wait for them to close into the
most efficient kill box before unleashing our fury.

The four vampires continued to approach. They

looked like regular people, out for a nice bit of exercise. Three males and a female. They were dressed in normal attire, nothing fancy, nothing archaic, just regular everyday clothing. Most likely taken off of some of their recent victims. They were graceful and beautiful even from here, but they could not hide what they were from me. I could almost taste the evil.

I wasn't the only one. "Man . . . I would give my left nut for some sunshine right about now," Trip whispered.

"It isn't like you're using it for anything anyway," Holly retorted.

"Will you shut up?"

"The Cursed One isn't going to let it happen." I glanced up at the unnaturally moving clouds. This was his storm. "The sun won't shine until he's finished."

"We get in that cave, I'm going to put a grenade where the sun don't shine on him," Lee promised.

Banter was good. It kept the mind off of the palpable terror that was at two hundred yards and closing. I raised the RPG, sat it on my shoulder, pushed off the button safety, and checked that the hammer was back. I had not shot one of these before, but the sighting arrangement was very straightforward. I centered the vampires in the aperture marked 200.

The radio crackled: One click, two clicks, three clicks.

Fire.

The Hunters opened up. Hundreds of bullets struck first, followed almost instantly by rockets and grenades, and only a few seconds later by the massive explosions generated by our 81mm mortar team's nine-pound shells. Weapons ignited all across the valley. I squeezed the trigger of the RPG. It was a simple tube that directed a rocket-propelled chunk of high explosive. The concussion was amazing. If this hadn't been so deadly serious it might possibly have been the coolest thing I had ever gotten to shoot. I found that I was smiling as the area around the vampires disappeared into a cloud of smoke and dust, with gouts of flames leaping into the air and chunks of dirt and asphalt raining down for hundreds of feet.

It was beautiful.

The ancient ones had underestimated their human foes. They were unprepared for the power of our modern weapons. Pound after pound of high explosive ignited in their midst. Multiple belt-fed MK19 launchers dropped a stream of grenades onto their heads. Walls of shrapnel tore them asunder and their bones and flesh were charred by phosphorus, thermite, napalm and towering pillars of flame.

"Yee haw!" Trip shouted, watching the clouds of smoke rise, and the almost slow-motion falling of debris. It had been a spectacular display of firepower.

Harbinger came over the radio. "They ain't done until you cut off their heads. Watch out. VanZant, keep that mortar on them. Pile it on!"

I tossed the empty tube down. Behind us the mortars continued to thump. I could not see anything moving besides the smoke. "Trip, Holly, grab some more rockets. Go."

"Movement. Vamp on the right," the radio said. Gunfire and rockets flew from the treeline on that side. A burning figure emerged into view, only to disappear again as the dirt around it exploded upwards into a volcano of flame. The shells continued to pepper the area, each one flattening a massive space. There wasn't going to be anything bigger than a microbe that was going to survive the punishment we were putting into that area.

"How much damage can these things take?" Lee asked.

"Beats me," I replied. I saw something emerge from the front. "Vamp in the center. On the road." Lee let loose with a burst of .308, stitching a path of impacts and tracers up the road and into the jerking creature. The flaming vampire ran toward us at impossible speeds, seemingly twisting between the bullets, then disappearing as an RPG landed in its path. The smoking body landed a moment later, crashing down to the pavement, and instantly popped back up out of the crater. They healed too fast.

The vampire was engulfed in a thunderous explosion as something roared from the center. The blast from the Spig recoilless rifle shook us all. It made me glad that I had taken the time to help Julie haul it up from her basement. The smoke cleared long enough to see that the vampire was gone. Holly jumped back into the ditch with arms full of rockets. She thumped me in the shoulder and pointed upwards.

I tracked in on the movement. The torn remains of the vampire were just reaching the apex of their arc, and began descending rapidly toward the earth. The biggest piece of the creature splattered onto the road not fifty feet from our position. The supernatural was no match for the laws of physics and some well-directed artillery.

"Yes!" I shouted. They were killable.

I choked off my triumphant shout when I realized

that it was still moving. The head, one claw, and the torso was trying to pull itself toward us, twitching and splurting fluids from its burned flesh. If it regenerated enough to regain its faculties, it would be able to shape-shift and live to fight another day.

"No way, man!" Lee shouted as he directed a stream of tracers into the body. The heavier rounds from the National Guard Browning .50 began to pepper the carcass as well, kicking up gouts of dirt and vampires bits.

"Edward. Go! All teams hold fire along the front," Harbinger ordered. He was still standing by the National Guard, and he personally made sure that they ceased fire.

A dark shape exploded from the trees, leaping in huge bounds across the burning grass and rain-swollen ditches, claws tearing up plumes of mud and vegetation. Edward hugged low to the mane of the mighty warg as it moved with predatory speed toward the downed Master. Edward drew a sword from his back as he leaned low, hanging barely above the ground as they approached their target. The orc's arm flew upward, like a scythe ready to harvest wheat. It swung down, pushed not just by the power of the orc, but by the speed of the seven-hundred-pound beast driving him forward.

Edward's masterful aim was true. The ancient blade sang through the air. It met little resistance from the charred and ashen flesh, and it crashed against the hardened vertebra with a clang that every Hunter could hear. *Did he make it through?*

The warg passed by, screeching to a mud-soaked halt, before spinning around, red tongue rolling like a giant dog, tearing at the earth and charging back at the vampire. Edward sheathed his sword, hung low, and dragged his fingers through the grass. He swung up, returning to the back of his stead, a trophy held triumphantly above his head.

It was a blackened skull.

Lightning crossed the sky from every direction. Thunder crashed. A gust of wind tore through us, pushing to the north. The skies protested as the ancient vampire's spirit was finally forced from this world. The Hunters began to cheer. The warg bounced back into the trees, Edward still holding the vampire's severed head extended for all to see. The mortars began to fire and drop more explosives into the valley. Only I could hear the mental screams from the other Masters.

Fools. I warned you of the humans' modern weapons. Flee. Protect our Lord.

The burning. It will not stop burning.

No time . . . to heal . . . too much damage . . . so weak . . . need blood.

They have destroyed Gurgo. Sythak is dying. I shall avenge them.

See, I told you so. Assholes.

My lord, use the artifact. Place me into their midst so that I may tear the life from their hearts. Their weapons require distance to work against us.

IT SHALL BE DONE.

"Oh, shit!" I exclaimed, turning from the battlefield, looking over my shoulder back the way that we had come. I keyed the radio. "Earl, vampires are going to gate in close, too close for bombs."

"Where?"

I concentrated, but the moment was past. The

voices were gone. I narrowed my eyes on a point to the side of our parked convoy of vehicles. For some reason it drew my attention. It was almost as if I could see the invisible energy forming, swirling in preparation.

"Behind us, thirty yards off the road. South side!" I shouted as I surged out of the ditch, sprinting toward the spot as fast as I could. Abomination slammed back and forth against my chest. My boots were sodden with water and seemed to weigh hundreds of pounds. My breath came in gasps as I closed the distance. I was never a good sprinter. If the vampires could appear in our midst, we were as good as dead. They moved far too quickly to be stopped with the weapons that we could use at close range.

There was a crackling noise as the rift opened. A red line appeared out of thin air, and then spread wide. I reached under my raincoat and pulled one of the sharpened white-oak stakes from my load bearing gear. I held it low at my side as I ran forward. It was going to be close and ugly.

The creature appeared through the rift, stepping lightly onto the grass. Blood-colored eyes blinked, adjusting to what was, for it, brilliant light. It had already shed its human appearance, ready for battle, looking like a twisted, gray, hulking bat-thing, all fangs, muscles and claws. It saw me.

Too late to do it any good. I jerked the stake upwards, bellowing, my weight and momentum carrying me forward. Crashing into the vampire was like hitting a brick wall. I pushed the stake with all of my might, coming under the rib cage and stabbing into the pulsing black heart. The vampire shrieked so painfully loud that my hearing protection momentarily shorted out. It grasped my hand, trying to pull out the stake. Its jaws opened wide enough to fit my head inside the maw. I continued to push the sharpened wood deeper into the creature's black heart.

A stake through the heart would kill any living thing. It would instantly paralyze any regular vampire. On a Master, it seemed to merely weaken it. At its normal strength, the creature would have been able to break me in half, now it was almost as if I were fighting someone only twice as strong as a normal person.

The creature swatted me across the chest. I flew back, airborne for what seemed an impossible time, landing hard on the hood of one of the SUVs, shattering the windshield, and sliding down until I fell on my hands and knees onto the pavement. The vampire struggled to pull the stake free. Trip and Lee barreled into the creature, hacking wildly at it with their blades, trying desperately to take its head off. The monster shoved them away, but not before Trip fiercely planted his tomahawk into the base of its skull.

With a wrenching squeal, the stake was torn free. The creature roared in triumph, but only for a moment. Its eyes widened as the grill of a Suburban smashed into it at thirty miles an hour. The tires bumped as Holly gunned it over the fallen vampire, crushing it beneath. She slammed it into park, with the thing still trapped, opened the door and hopped out.

"Keys were in it!" she shouted as she turned and pulled a grenade from her armor. "Run!" She pulled the pin, the spoon popped off with a clang, and she tossed it into the front seat of the vehicle. I pushed myself up and ran for my life, trying to get as far away as I could before the five-second fuse went off. If that vehicle had been as loaded down with munitions as ours had been, this wasn't going to be pretty. The vampire bench-pressed the SUV off of itself and rolled the vehicle onto its side. It stood, broken bones quickly knitting, looking for prey.

I dove behind one of the vans and tried to get as low to the ground as possible. The initial detonation of the grenade was relatively mild. The pressurized napalm tank it ignited was not. The crate of 81mm mortar rounds that went off next was downright amazing. The van I was using as a shield rocked up onto two wheels and every window shattered under the pressure.

Once the thunder had died, I slowly lifted my head. I peered around the edge of my scorched cover. The Suburban was reduced to a burning pile of distorted scrap lying sideways in a freshly dug crater. A chunk of metal landed in the grass a few feet away. I realized that it was a door. A burning tire rolled past.

"Wow" was the most articulate thing that I could think of to say.

"Think we got it?" Holly shouted from under the warg trailer.

"I hope so." I lifted the rifle and approached the wreckage. "Trip! Lee! You guys okay?" In the distance the mortars continued to fire.

"Pitt! Status?" Harbinger's voice sounded in my ear.

"I think we got the vampire. I can't find two of my guys."

"This is Mayorga. One of them has broken through. It's in the trees on the left. *Puta* got Abe."

"This is Cody. Got one on the right too."

"Earl," I said into the radio. I kept my gun up,

pointed toward the burning vehicle. "There's only one left in the valley. And it's badly hurt. It can't regenerate until it gets blood." Holly extricated herself from under the trailer, and I tossed her rifle back.

"How do you know?" he asked. "Shit, never mind. VanZant, stop the barrage. Edward, clean up in the center. Phillips, roll right. Paxton, reinforce left. Now they're up close, but we've hurt them, so they're gonna be weaker and slower. We can take them. Pitt, my team is coming your way."

I did not respond. I scanned the surroundings. No sign of the vampire. No sign of Lee or Trip either. "Hey guys? Anybody hear me?" I shouted.

"I'm okay," answered Lee. He approached from the other side of the wreckage. His armor was smoking. He struggled with the FN MAG in his hands. It was almost as big as he was, and the exposed belt of ammo hung to the ground. "That was one big-ass fireball."

"Have you seen Trip?" He shook his head in the negative.

"Oh no . . ." Holly trailed off. "I killed him."

"You don't know that!" I shouted. "Trip! Can you hear me!"

Nothing.

"Look." Lee gestured with the machine gun barrel. I turned quickly, hoping to see my friend. Instead I saw that the flickering rift into the cavern was still open. It floated a few feet above the ground, a door out of nothing, but I could clearly see that there was something on the other side. I lifted Abomination warily, clicked on the flashlight and shined it into the shimmering gap. The powerful light pierced the darkness and illuminated a rock wall.

"Grant!" I exclaimed. Grant Jefferson was lying bound and gagged on the cavern floor, seemingly only forty feet away. "Earl! Earl! We found Grant. We've got a back door into the cavern!"

"On the way," he responded.

"We better hurry before it closes," Lee said.

"How do we know it isn't a trap?" Holly asked. "What if it closes while we're halfway through?"

"I don't know." Wild gunfire crackled through the forest as the other Hunters battled the two Masters. "We've got to try." I reached into a pocket and pulled out a handful of glow sticks. "I'm going in. I'll try to grab him and bring him out. Cover me." I cracked the sticks, shook them, and tossed them through the rift. They landed and scattered across the cavern floor, providing a soft green glow. I couldn't see anything else moving.

"Good luck," Holly said, "you big brave idiot."

I ran toward the rift, no use screwing around. I closed my eyes right before I hit it, only to open them to find myself barreling into the cavern. I had not felt a thing. I gulped in the moist cave air. I turned around, and the rift was still there, only now it showed the valley and the ominous green storm clouds overhead. My remaining teammates were waiting for me.

"Hurry up!" Holly shouted.

That was good advice. I swung my shotgun around, letting the light shine on the damp walls and the slick stalagmites. I did not see any threats. I shined the light on Grant. He moaned softly when the brilliant light hit him.

"Come on, buddy, let's get out of here." I knelt at his side and pulled the gag away.

"Pitt?" he gasped. I heard something shuffle in

the darkness. I spun the light around. Wights. Lots of them.

"Yeah. Time to boogie." I grabbed him by the straps of his armor and, with a grunt, hoisted him over my shoulder. I sprinted for the rift, ignoring the two hundred pounds of extra weight. The wights began to scramble over the rocks toward me. One stepped into my path, only to be nearly decapitated by a burst of Lee's machine-gun fire. Apparently bullets went through the rift just fine. I passed the falling creature and jumped through the portal.

I was back outside.

And the wights were right behind. Lee ripped off the rest of the belt into the portal. Holly stood at his side, blasting any undead that came too close.

"We could use a hand, chief!" Lee said as he dropped the huge gun, pulled his pistol and fired at an approaching wight.

I roughly tossed Grant on the ground, tugged a pair of grenades off of my webbing, pulled the pins and chucked them through the portal. "Off to the side!" The others responded, moving out of the path of the shrapnel. They exploded at the feet of the wights, blasting them into bits of pulsing tissue. A cloud of gravel fell from the cavern ceiling.

"Owen!" Julie called. Her team and several other Hunters were approaching quickly. "I don't believe it. You found Grant!"

Harbinger nodded in approval. "Sam, Milo, cover that rift."

"My pleasure," Milo answered, pushing past Lee, and shooting a rising wight through the spine with his AR10 carbine. "Wow, cool magic portal thingy!"

I drew my knife and cut the cords binding Grant's wrists. His eyes looked wild and frightened. "It's okay, dude. We got you. You're safe."

"Die!" Grant screamed. He grabbed me by the throat, trying to crush my windpipe. I grabbed his hands and tried to pry them away.

"Grant! What are you doing?" Julie cried. "Stop that!"

"Acckkkk . . ." I said, trying in vain to get some oxygen.

"Die, interloper!" Grant shouted, crazed eyes bulging, spraying spittle into my face. Either he knew that I had moved in on Julie or he was insane. Either way, it totally hurt.

"He's enthralled," Holly said simply. "Susan must have bitten him."

Julie stood over him, calmly raised the butt of her M14 and cracked him sharply alongside his head. He was out like a light. "Grant, honey . . . I think we need to start seeing other people."

I rubbed my throat. "Damn, that hurt." On the bright side, it was strangely satisfying to not only rescue my competition, but have the woman we were competing for give him a concussion.

"Is he going to be okay?" Lee asked.

"The enthrallment will wear off pretty quick. But when he eventually dies, no matter how long it takes, he's going to have to get his head cut off, or he's going to come back as one of them. The undead curse is in his blood now," Holly explained. She knelt and pulled Grant's armor open at the neck. There was a ghastly wound on the top of his chest, now caked in dried blood.

"That sucks."

"Yeah, pretty much. But you get used to it," she answered.

"The rift is holding," Harbinger said. "Let's go get the CO." The gunfire continued in the distance. "Now that the vampires have closed the range, we've got a hell of a fight on our hands. Maybe if we kill him, this cloud cover will disperse."

"Roast them bastards good." Sam spat, noticed something moving in the cavern, aimed his rifle and fired. "Let's get some." He levered another mammoth shell into the action.

"Okay, I'm on point. You guys stick behind me . . ." He paused, his nose twitching. Harbinger began to spin, but the Master vampire rising behind him was too fast. It grabbed him by the straps of his armor and hurled him through the air at an insane velocity. Harbinger struck one of the SUVs, crumpling the frame around him as if it had been in a high-speed collision and shoving the massive vehicle several feet across the road.

Nobody could have lived through that.

"Earl!" Julie cried as the Hunters opened fire.

It was the Master from the rift, the one that Holly had blown up. It was fully healed now, and no longer encumbered by a stake in the heart. Bullets struck to no effect. It lofted something in one gray claw, and launched it toward us in a blinding flash. Lee's leg exploded in a shower of blood as Trip's tomahawk head pierced his thigh. He screamed as he toppled to the ground.

The Master moved too quickly to track, dodging and weaving toward us as silver bullets dug divots into its muscled flesh. It swooped onto Gus. One claw stabbed out and impaled the Hunter through the throat, unleashing a spray of arterial blood. The vampire held him there as it licked its lips. I aimed around Gus's twitching form and shot the vampire in the mouth. The slug exploded out the back of the creature's skull. The wound closed instantly. Enraged, the vampire pulled its bloody talon free, leaving Gus staggering, gagging and choking, hands at his throat, trying to stop the bleeding. The Master lashed out with one arm, and I instinctively dodged aside as Gus's head flew past.

The vampire had moved ten feet before the headless body had even begun to fall. It charged the next Hunter in line. Sam was struck in the arm, and the sound of bones snapping could be heard across the valley. The big cowboy roared in pain, somehow dodged under another swing and fell to the ground. He worked the action of his lever-gun with one hand, letting the weight of the barrel carry the weapon down, and then flicking the action closed with his wrist. Sam extended the muzzle and launched a silver bullet up through the vampire's head. It did not even slow the thing down.

I fired as fast as I could, putting shell after shell of silver buckshot into the thing to no avail. It kicked at Sam as he rolled away, claws tearing a hole in the pavement. Milo stabbed his now-empty rifle forward like a spear. The vampire tore it from his hands and batted him backwards through the rift into the waiting wights. Milo disappeared with a cry of panic.

I grasped for the special magazine that Milo had given me and slammed it home, dropped the bolt, and looked up in time to see the Master bearing down on me, blood-red eyes filled with rage. I pulled the trigger.

The vampire stopped, confused. Pain was an unfamiliar sensation for the ancient creature. It looked down at the hole in its chest, then opened its jaws and screamed. It tore at itself, trying to somehow pull the burning agony from out of its insides. Thrashing, screaming, falling to its knees, claws tearing into the ground. Blue flames erupted from the hole, spilling through the vampire's ribs, igniting internal gasses, spitting and crackling. The vampire let out an unearthly wail as it tried to tear open its own belly.

"Take that!" I shouted as I pulled the trigger again. Nothing. Of course. Milo had warned me that the specialty rounds would lack the power to cycle the action.

When I had woken up after Mordechai's death, I had been able to get a good look at his little carvings for the first time. They were simple little tops, or dreidels as he called them. Traditional little Jewish toys, each side carved with a Hebrew letter that I had no idea how to read. They were rather small. And fortunately for us, with a little judicious carving, Milo was able to cram them into a 12-gauge shell.

I cleared the malfunction, and chambered another round. I put the glowing holographic site on the vampire. "Mordechai says hi!" It was a stupid thing to say, but I'm not really eloquent at times like this.

Blue flame flashed on the vampire's head as the toy splintered across its skull. The vampire screamed again, rolling across the ground, driving its head into the mud, trying to put out the flames.

The toys seemed to hurt them, but they weren't strong enough to kill them, and I only had three left. Gradually the blue flames died, and the shaking vampire stood, snarling at me, baring its teeth. The distended mouth struggled to form English words. "You shall pay for that, mortal," it hissed as smoking tissues sealed together.

"Vampire!" someone roared. "Pick on somebody your own size!" The vampire turned, looking for the challenger. Harbinger slowly pulled himself from the wreckage of the SUV, blood streaming from dozens of cuts. He gingerly reached over his back and yanked out a blood-stained chunk of steel, which he then casually tossed to the ground with a clatter. "If you think you're tough enough." He stretched, and bones audibly cracked back into place. "Well, come on then, you stupid thing." He unfastened the armor from his torso and arms and took it off. In the flickering light of the burning Suburban, many holes and injuries could be seen on his wiry body. They gradually puckered closed. "Come on, vampire! I'm giving you a challenge!"

The vampire stopped. Flexing its long limbs. "*Loup-Garou*," it hissed. "Yesss. I accept your challenge. Your kind are nothing to the *vampire*."

Harbinger looked past the creature, locking eyes with me. It was the look of a desperate man. "Go! Kill the Cursed One!"

Harbinger began to change, throwing his head back as if he were in great pain, and then twisting it from side to side. He fell to his knees, hands scraping along the pavement. Bones twisted, flowed, and re-formed. His spine pushed up and out along the top of his back. Skin stretched and ripped as pale hair exploded from every pore.

The others did not wait to watch the transformation. Instead they sprang into action. Sam jumped into the rift after Milo. Holly threw a tourniquet around Lee's leg, and Julie ordered the other Hunters to drag Lee and Grant to safety. I stood transfixed like an idiot.

The transformation continued as the vampire waited, patiently readying itself for a great battle. Harbinger opened his mouth and razor-sharp teeth thrust out of his extending jaw. His pants ripped as his knees reversed direction. Claws exploded through the ends of his boots and he kicked the useless things away. When his eyes opened, they were a predatory gold. He fixated on the vampire, and howled, the sound echoing for miles. Harbinger surged to his feet, clawed arms thrown wide, the last vestiges of humanity disappearing to be replaced with pure animal power. The howl continued, growing in intensity and bristling rage.

If Mr. Huffman had been a normal werewolf, Harbinger had to be some sort of mutant super werewolf. I could sense the power, every ounce of his human form turned into a perfect killing machine. Coiled strength, steel masquerading as muscle. I slowly reached up and felt the scar on my face. It was the most terrifying thing I had ever seen.

Harbinger launched himself forward, leaping into the air. The Master did so as well. The two titans collided in midair with a crash like thunder, nearly twenty feet above the ground. They plummeted to earth in a spray of mud, claws and fangs flying, impossibly fast, shadows spinning and lashing out, backlit by the fire. Red blood and black ichor sprayed as they tore into each other's flesh. It was a contest of wills, immortal speed and primal strength.

"Owen!" Julie shouted. "We've got to move!" The others had already jumped through the rift. A moaning Lee was being fireman-carried back toward the National Guard. I hurried after her, turning one last time to watch the magnificent battle: Harbinger suspended in air, tearing down at the vampire, and the Master driving its claws upwards into its foe. It was an astounding display. Julie grabbed me by my armor and pulled me through the rift.

DeSoya Caverns were quiet. The last of the wights were twitching on the ground—shot, chopped or pulverized into nondangerous pieces. Sam extended his good arm and hauled Milo to his feet. Holly was splattered with Lee's blood, and there was far too much of it.

The rift closed behind us. I swore and jumped aside, just barely missing being caught as it scissored shut. I did not want to dwell on what would have happened if part of me had still been on the other side.

"Well, we're committed now," Sam grunted, holding his broken arm tenderly.

"Earl's a werewolf?" I blurted.

"Well, yeah, I'll explain later. What's our status?" Julie ordered, settling subconsciously into command mode. She scanned her flashlight across the vast interior chamber, illuminating the huge area beyond the pale glow of the light sticks. The stone glimmered wetly.

"Heck if I know," Milo wheezed.

"Lee was hurt pretty bad. I tried to stop the bleeding, but he's going to need a real doctor real fast," Holly said. "Poor Gus. His head just came off . . ."

"I know . . . but we can't do anything for either of them now. Holly, are you okay?"

"Fine. I'm fine."

"Sam, how's that arm?"

"Done broke it," he said. "Stupid vampire. I ain't broke a bone since I gave up bull-riding."

"Can you fight?"

He snorted. "I got a spare." His forearm dangled in such a crooked direction that it made me slightly ill just looking at it. Sam had to have been in horrible pain, but he ignored it.

"Let's sling it up at least so it isn't banging on things. Milo?"

"Sore, but otherwise all right. Lost my carbine though," he answered as he wiped the blood from a cut on his shaved head.

Sam tossed over his .45-70. "Not gonna do me much good with one arm anyhow. Careful, that there's a man's gun. Got recoil that'll put hair on your chest. I still got my pistol."

"Owen?"

"Good to go," I answered. I saw from the still-twitching remains that the wights had once been federal agents. I picked up an FN SCAR off of the floor and checked the chamber. The government guys got all the cool new gear. It was loaded. Full mag in the gun, 20 rounds of their composite silver .308 on tap. The mounted flashlight worked as well. I kept the Fed gun in hand and let Abomination hang. I only had a few of Mordechai's magic shells left and I wasn't about to waste them on a wight. If we were to run into one of the Masters, I wanted to have some of the good stuff available.

"Where's Grant?" Milo asked as he quickly shoved extra shells into Sam's gun.

"Still on top with the others," Julie said. "Probably safer up there . . . unless Earl eats him . . . Where's Trip?"

"We lost track of him when we had that big explosion," I answered. I hoped that he was still alive, but I was starting to have my doubts.

"I think I killed him." Holly spoke quietly.

"It isn't your fault," I snapped. "You did what you had to do, otherwise that thing would have done to all of us what it did to Gus."

"I just wish that I hadn't been so mean to him. . . . He was such a sweet guy," she muttered. "Damn it. He deserved better."

"No time for that." When the chips were down, Julie was all business. "We need to hurry. Owen, which way to this secret portal?"

I glanced around, getting my bearings. Everything looks different when you have eyeballs. "That way." I gestured. "I'll take point," I said as I started between the rock formations.

She hesitated, probably thinking about having somebody else do it. Being the tip of the spear was the most dangerous position. "Just don't get killed," Julie admonished. "I would miss your charming personality."

"Why thanks," I replied.

"Plus we need you to open the door."

I went forward, stabbing the light ahead and also occasionally upwards, looking for any suspended vampires. There were millions of spots in the cavern where danger could lurk. Visions of Gus's tottering headless corpse flashed unbidden into my mind. I stepped over the smashed remains of a historical display and kicked the severed guide ropes out of the way. The five of us moved quickly but cautiously. Every pass of the flashlight illuminated new formations, age-old deposits, twisted clumps of rock and sediment. Every strange shape that revealed itself caused me to jump. The walls shone as our lights struck smooth surfaces.

There was something ahead, a darker shadow on the already dark floor. I held up my fist, the signal to freeze. The rustling of armor let me know that the others had responded. I gestured ahead with my flashlight. There was a hole in the ground, a pit. It was a natural formation, and the guide ropes that had surrounded it to keep the tourists from falling in had been torn and tossed aside. I leaned forward, letting the Surefire illuminate the gash in the rock. I was struck with a sense of foreboding.

"Oh no . . ." I gagged as the smell of torn open bodies hit my nostrils. "Oh no."

Julie drew alongside and shined her flashlight into the hole. She grimaced. "Vampire pen." A look of disgust crossed her face as she stared into the pile of corpses. "Poor things."

I recalled the patients of Appleton Asylum. One of the survivors in their sharing circle had spoken of such a thing. Human captives held in a hole, serving as a vampire larder. Fed upon until they were almost dead, but then being left barely alive, as the undead rotated through their food. Allowed to regain their strength just enough to be bled again. There had to be ten people crammed in the hole, though they were all obviously dead now. The vampires must have feasted in preparation for this day.

Holly shoved her way past me, looking downward, biting her lip.

"Are you okay?" Julie asked her softly.

She held her glove under her nose to block the smell, then stayed focused on the bodies as she slowly spoke. "You have no idea what it's like."

"No, I don't."

"The weakness, the fear, the pain, the humiliation. You just want to die. Most folks do after the first couple feedings. They just give up. Then the fuckers pull the body out and chop it up and send it back down to you, and the thing is by then you're so hungry you don't care. You can't see. You don't know how long you've been in. No light. No air. Strangers pushing on you." There was a small crack in her hard emotional shield, but instead of sadness, there was only anger. "Trying to hide when they come down to feed. All of them scared, just cattle, stupid meat. And when they bite you, it hurts so bad. But at the same time you can feel them, and part of you wants to join them, you want to be them, and that's the worst part of all."

"But you're okay now," Julie assured her. "You made it out."

Holly removed an incendiary grenade from a pouch on her armor. "Damn right I did." She pulled the pin and tossed it into the pit. "And when I eventually die—" The grenade exploded with a puff of flames, spreading out over the corpses, igniting their clothing and hair, burning skin and crackling fat, destroying them beyond the point of return. "—I'll need you guys to do this for me."

So that was Holly Newcastle's story.

"Good luck, friends," she whispered.

I patted her gently on the shoulder. She grimly

hoisted her rifle and stepped away from the edge as oily smoke began to fill the cavern.

We pushed forward, away from the smell of burning hair and bone, deeper into the cavern, moving faster as nothing appeared to attack us. The portal was near. I could feel it. The section that we were entering had been roped off from the public, and it looked as if some sort of excavation had taken place. I illuminated a small information plaque.

I scanned the words. Some of them caught my eye. "Well, I'll be damned," I exclaimed. "Check this out." The others drew close.

Sam read the inscription aloud: "This section of the cavern is believed to have been a burial ground for the ancient peoples of the region . . . Blah, blah, blah, over two thousand years old, yada yada, great significance, evidence of ancient writing that may be an indication of an even older civilization . . . excavated in 1984 by, no shit . . . Dr. Jonas Turley and a team from the University of Alabama."

"That's what the seven were looking for. That's why they attacked his home," Julie said. "Of course . . . Dr. Turley probably found the portal, but didn't know what it was or how to open it. The Cursed One must have known about this place all along . . . but then why did they need my dad?"

"Hello there, honey." A sweet voice sang from the darkness.

I spun around and shined the flashlight on the spot. Nothing.

"Mom," Julie hissed. She swung her M14 around in an arc, searching for a target. Milo, Sam and Holly

did likewise. Five sets of lights crisscrossed the cave.
I could not hear anything over our nervous breathing.
"Come out and fight!" she shouted into the dark, her
voice echoing over and over.

"No. I don't want to fight you." The voice came
from one side. I thought that perhaps I had caught
a tiny bit of movement as the light flickered past.
"You're my daughter. We don't need to be enemies."
Now from the other side. I swung back around. *Damn
Masters are fast.*

"What do you want, then?" Julie demanded. Milo
cracked more glow sticks and tossed them into the dark,
giving us a little bit larger circle of illumination.

"I want us to be a family again, me and you and
little Nate. I know he's up there, too." Her voice came
from the ceiling above our heads. Holly cranked off
a shot into the rocks, it ricocheted across the cavern,
and Susan's laughter rose behind us.

"Wait until you've got a target," Sam ordered.

"All of us, even your daddy. One big happy family,"
Susan said pleasantly. I began to shiver as I felt her
probing our minds.

"Too late for that. You killed him. The Feds have
probably already burned the body." Julie's eyes narrowed as she searched the shadows, cheek resting on
the stock of her rifle.

"Oh, honey. Once again, you think you know what's
going on. You always thought you had everything figured
out. Do you really think somebody like good old Myers
would cut your daddy's head off if he thought that there
might be some information in there of use? I've known
Myers since he was a Newbie. He was always a cold-
hearted son of a gun. Always practical. You know your

daddy trained him, right? You would think he would be sentimental just once and would have done his old mentor a favor and finished him off."

"What are you saying?"

"Your daddy's *alive*." She put the accent on alive, almost as if she was singing it. "Well, not really *alive*, as you know, but something so much better."

"Lying bitch!" Julie shouted.

"Wait, there's more," Susan laughed. "The Feds were expecting some easy-to-handle, wimpy, new creation . . . A weak new vampire. You had your daddy for two nights. I visited him the first night and you never even knew. He was so happy to see me. He would have done anything I asked of him. He even partook of my blood. You know what that means, don't you?"

"I'm going to stake you if it's the last thing I do," Julie vowed.

"You didn't answer my question, but of course you know. As soon as he died, he rose again, far stronger than they expected. He's already escaped. He's returning to me as we speak. His mind will heal. He'll be whole again. Isn't that wonderful, honey? One big happy family." There was a whoosh of air, and then Susan's laughter sounded from back the way that we had come.

"Owen . . . find that gate," Sam whispered. I turned back to the wall, desperately running my hands over the cool rock, looking for some indication of the Place of Power.

"Oh, my darling Sam. I can hear you. No need to whisper. That's impolite amongst friends. I always loved you for your heart and your courage. You can come with us too. Join my family."

He scowled and spit tobacco juice on the ground. "Susan, you were a mighty fine woman when you were alive and all, but personally I'd rather be gang-raped by giant, rabid, syphilitic porcupines, than join your shithead, hippie-commune, undead family, you scrawny-ass, vampire skank whore." He wiped his good arm across his mustache. "It's gonna be a cold day in hell before you've got the balls to come down here and take an ounce of red American blood out of Sam Roger Haven, you slack-jawed, hare-lip, monkey-humping pus bag."

"So be it. Still stubborn as ever. And Milo. Faithful Milo. So loyal. So creative. I have a place of honor set aside for you."

"Uh . . . what Sam said, and stuff," Milo answered bravely. "Leave us alone. We aren't here for you. We just want Lord Machado. You don't want the world destroyed."

"Honey, my world is going to be just fine." She sounded closer now, right outside our circle of glow sticks, somehow evading the beams of our flashlights. She was coming for us, and soon.

I continued to rub my hands over the rock. I needed a seam, a crack, some carvings, anything. The portal had to be here somewhere. I could feel it. In my dream it had just opened right up for the Cursed One. Julie glanced at me anxiously. They were counting on me.

"Last chance, kids." Susan sang. "I'm getting tired of screwing around."

"Z! Hurry!" Holly pleaded. "We need to go!"

"Working on it," I answered.

"Here she comes," Sam said, raising his Sig and

aiming it into the dark. Mist swirled around the beam from his pistol-mounted M3 light. The mist coalesced into the form of a woman. She was too close. We wouldn't be able to put her down in time. Other shapes began to emerge from behind her, shuffling slowly toward us, red eyes coming into focus. Wights. At least a dozen of them at first, and then more, lots more. Red eyes seemingly winking into existence all across the cavern. They were bristling and snarling, held at bay only by the Master vampire's command.

"Susan! Don't make me hurt you!" Milo said as he stepped in front of the others. "I know the real you has to be in there somewhere. You can still repent of your evil ways. It's never too late. Don't make it come to this!"

"Milo? Get out of the way!" Julie ordered as she pushed around me, looking for a good angle.

"You want to test your faith against me? What, do you think this is a Dracula movie or something?" Susan's dark silhouette laughed as she batted her glowing eyes. "I'm way out of your league, honey."

Milo Anderson closed his eyes and bowed his head, the lower half of his face disappearing into his bushy beard. He appeared to be praying. He did not move as Susan slowly walked toward him. Not even a tremble of fear, nothing.

"Open the gate! Hurry!" Julie pleaded. "Milo, run!"

"Dude! Get down!" Sam shouted. "Move, you idiot!"

The faithful Hunter raised his head, smiled at us and winked. "Don't worry, guys. It's going to be okay. You had better get that portal opened, 'cause it's going to get real exciting up in here." He raised one arm as if to wave good-bye.

Susan charged forward, her black shape disappearing in a blur as she surged toward Milo. He said something quickly as the vampire reached for him. There was an explosion of bright light, blinding all of us, searing right through our eyes and into our brains. I saw Milo's skeleton through the flash. Good versus evil. Light versus dark. The cavern shook and dust and rock fell from the roof. Cracks appeared in the columns. The earth shook and I was thrown backward into Julie. Susan screamed, a great and terrible wail of pure hatred and evil. Lightning crackled across the chamber, tearing up chunks of rock.

I swear that I heard Milo's voice say; "Ooh . . . Pretty colors."

The wights, released from their psychic bonds, charged. The ones that ran too close to the clashing powers exploded in showers of sparks and flying meat. The others were going to be on us in seconds. Julie, Sam and Holly started to shoot. Our backs were against the wall. We had nowhere to go. I kept scrambling, looking for the exit. A wight leapt over a rock formation and landed directly in front of us. Sam shot it between the eyes and then kicked it backwards, impaling the creature on a sharp rock. He holstered his now empty pistol, unable to load fast enough with one hand, and drew his massive knife. With a roar he tore into the undead, slashing and hacking, cursing and swearing. He was an amazing fighter, somehow dodging the claws and fangs, while stabbing and cutting furiously at the horde. There seemed to be hundreds of undead, black teeth extended, claws raised. They kept coming.

The black cyclone that was Susan Shackleford

crashed back under the curtain of light. Milo's faith had been far more powerful than she had expected. More wights burst into flames. Julie screamed in pain as a wight reached her, slashing across her side with its paralyzing claws. She fell limply to her knees as her limbs went dead. I reached out and grabbed her by the drag strap on her armor and pulled her away from the creature. Shielding her with my body, I lashed out and kicked the beast in the chest, crushing its ribs and sending it flailing back. We had to get out of here fast.

Damn stupid door. I wish it were here.

A thin crack of red light moved down the rock in front of me. The portal gradually widened. All I had done was desire it to be there and it had worked.

That wasn't so bad, I thought to myself.

The cold tentacles of the Cursed One exploded through the rift, encircled Julie and me, and jerked us violently through the gate.

CHAPTER 27

The writhing tentacles were wet and oily. They pinned my arms to my side. I struggled against them, but it was like being ensnared by a giant boa constrictor. I was momentarily blind inside the portal itself. There was no light in the tunnel to some other dimension. The air was thick and damp, and between that and the pressure on my lungs, I could barely breathe.

We were dragged through the other side and it slammed shut behind us, leaving only blank white sky. Julie's paralyzed form was roughly thrown onto the snow-covered ground. She rolled a few feet before stopping, seemingly unconscious, at the base of a tree.

I was spun around violently, only to come face to face with the Cursed One.

I had seen him in my dreams. I had seen him in visions. I had seen the world through the eye of his memory. I had felt his pain, fear, anger, lust and pride. I knew him better than he knew himself.

But none of that prepared me for actually meeting him in person.

I was frozen in terror. Rivulets of sweat turned into ice crystals. Every fiber of my being ached. My joints hurt to move. My eyes grated in their sockets. My teeth chattered compulsively as my body began to have involuntary convulsions. Here was pure evil. Hate beyond all human comprehension. I dangled above the ground, held by a thick tentacle that extended from under his robe where an arm should have been. I struggled helplessly in his grasp. The ancient helmet slowly lifted, and the crimson eyes bored into me.

YOU.

The word pounded inside my skull like a sledgehammer. His face was like a skull coated with cords of moving muscles that seemed to be made out of dirty congealed oil. He had no mouth.

I SHOULD HAVE KNOWN IT WOULD BE YOU.

He swung me through the air. The tentacle relaxed, releasing me, sending me flying. I had time to scream before impact. I rolled painfully through the thick underbrush, scattering snow, crackling roots, and breaking branches. We were on some sort of hilltop, and I slid and crashed violently as momentum and gravity took me down. I finally slid to a stop, lying in a pile of wet slush. I was in terrible pain. I rolled over onto my back, staring up at the trees of the winter wonderland.

JAEGER. TAKE HIM. WE ARE IN NEED OF A NEW SACRIFICE.

"Yes, my Lord Machado."

The final Master approached. He still wore the leather trench coat as if it were a uniform. I flashed back to the image of him in his Nazi regalia, cleaving open Mordechai Byreika's chest to pull out his beating heart.

I wasn't going down like that.

There was a branch dangling overhead. I grabbed it and used it to pull myself to my feet, showering cold snow down on me. All of my weapons were still strapped into place. It was time to drop the hammer. The Fed prototype ENSCAR .308 was the most convenient. I flicked the safety off and brought it to my shoulder.

"Freeze, asshat. That's a nice coat. I'd hate to put some holes in it."

Jaeger stopped and ran his long fingers down the seam of his coat. "Yes, it is made out of children. Very supple leather, and such a lovely fragrance." He smiled slightly, revealing his fangs. His hatchet face began to blur and shift into his true form.

I NEED A LIVE SACRIFICE. DO NOT KILL HIM.

Jaeger's transformation stopped, and he once again appeared human. "Pity." He moved toward me.

I put the sight at his groin and pulled the trigger. I leaned into the weapon, controlling the recoil, driving the gun, stitching the vampire in one continuous twenty-round burst. The Feds' composite silver ammunition penetrated a few inches of flesh before exploding in a violent cloud of powdered metal. The bolt locked back empty.

Jaeger stumbled in the snow. His flesh was ripped asunder, his clothing hung in tatters, and black fluids spilled onto the white ground. Almost instantly he was whole again and striding my way. His hatchet face was a mask of fury.

I dropped the smoking, hot FN and lifted Abomination. Jaeger appeared before me, having covered the distance in an impossible amount of time. The

Saiga barked as I fired the special shell into his open mouth. The wooden projectile shattered and splintered in his throat, every bit of it instantly transforming into burning energy as it touched undead flesh. Blue fire burst from his face, coming out of his eyes, his ears, his nostrils and mouth.

I worked the bolt and shot him again, piercing his abdomen. I grasped the charging handle, pulled it back, ejecting the smoking plastic hull into the snow. The last of Mordechai's shells entered the chamber, and I immediately launched it into Jaeger's chest. His screams echoed through the trees as his entire body turned into a blue torch.

I released the silver bayonet, lifted the shotgun like an awkward spear and slammed it through his throat, twisting and sawing against his ironlike spine. I had to take his head off. It was my only hope. He punched me in the chest. Distracted from the fire burning inside his brain, it was a weak hit for a Master, but still threw me back into a pine tree.

I lay with my back against the cold bark, gasping for breath. The snowy branches settled around me, giving me the illusion of a quiet shelter. I reloaded Abomination just as Jaeger's burning skull face appeared through the branches. His eyeballs had melted, and were dripping down his cheeks. I flipped the selector to full-auto and let him have it. Abomination emptied itself in a split second, pumping his chest full of silver. Undeterred, Jaeger grabbed me by my shoulders and pulled me from my shelter.

I drove Abomination forward, slamming the silver blade between his ribs and through his heart. Jaeger screamed as fluids erupted like a split hydrant. He lifted one fist overhead, ready to crush my brain. I could see my death looming in his burning sockets.

ALIVE, JAEGER. I WILL NOT WARN YOU AGAIN.

The vampire threw me away. The snow broke my fall as I tumbled further down the hill. I slid on my back, almost like I was sledding, until I toppled over the edge of a small crevasse and landed in a pile of fluffy white. I was up in an instant, lifting my feet, and trying to move through the heavy substance. Jaeger was above me, still disoriented, but coming around as the painful fire died. I lifted Abomination and aimed at him. At some point in the struggle my holographic sight had been broken. I estimated instead and fired the 40mm grenade.

It impacted in the snow behind his feet. The concussion tore through him, sending him sprawling forward. I started to reload the grenade launcher when Abomination violently jerked from my hands. The Cursed One stood at the top of the hill, looking down. Just my luck, Lord Machado was telekinetic. He moved imperceptibly and my weapon was yanked away, the sling tearing into my neck, slicing into my skin, before ripping away and disappearing into the trees.

Jaeger was up and moving. I drew the STI, falling instinctively into my regular isosceles stance and opened fire. Jaeger leapt toward me, soaking up round after round. He knocked the gun into the snow, but I immediately drew the backup .45 and shot him some more. I was struck in the head. My helmet was torn off and sent flipping into the trees. He hit me again, lightly, just trying to capture me. I felt the muscles inside my chest tear and I gasped in agony. I fell back into the snow, still firing. He swatted the pistol away, and my left wrist snapped. I screamed as pain like an electric current moved down my arm. I kicked him in the knee. I might as well have kicked a brick wall. He caught my foot, and twisted it casually to the side. I almost passed out as my ankle broke.

"I've obtained the sacrifice, my lord," the vampire proclaimed loudly. Lying flat on my back, I brought my knee back to my chest, lifted my pant leg and pulled the .357 from my ankle holster. Jaeger looked down at the little muzzle in wonderment.

"How many guns do you have?" he asked in exasperation.

"Lots." *CRACK.*

I stroked the trigger, five times fast. He ignored the impacts, the wound channels were knitting closed before the bullets had even left his skull. He grabbed the little Smith and wrenched it from my hand. I cried out in pain as my trigger finger broke. He clapped his hands together and smashed the snubby into pieces.

I tried to move. The vampire kicked me. For him it was a light blow; for me, agony. He pummeled me, smashing me in the stomach, in the ribs, in the arms and legs, and finally in the face. His limbs moved in a blur. He pounded me down into the snow. I felt other bones break. Tendons tore, muscles ripped, blood vessels ruptured. I tried to defend myself, but he was too quick. He could hear my heart and my internal workings. The hammer blows continued to rain down. He knew exactly how much punishment he could dish out before I would die. He took me to that edge and left me there.

The beating finally stopped. Jaeger pulled back and smiled, satisfied that his work was done. His sacrifice was secure. I coughed up a gout of blood, rolled my head to the side, and watched the red spreading on white. I passed out.

"Owen? Owen? Can you hear me? Please don't die."

Agony. The worst pain ever.

Julie was whispering. At least it sounded like Julie, but it was hard to tell over the ringing in my ear. The other ear did not seem to be working. I don't know if that was because it was clogged with a blood clot, or if the eardrum had ruptured. I lay on my side, facing away from her. I tried to move, but my body was too tired and broken to respond. I forced myself anyway.

It hurt so bad that I almost passed back out.

"Oh no. Owen." Julie sounded horrified. I had to look like shit. "Can you hear me?"

I grunted, blowing red frothy bubbles from my lips. "I'm . . . fine . . ." I lied. The words hurt over my broken teeth and swollen tongue. I could not see her. My eyelids were matted closed with blood, and I could not force them open. I tried to reach a hand up to rub them, but my arms did not want to respond. All I could feel was horrible nerve-racking fire coming from my limbs.

"I'm so sorry," she said.

"Can't move," I replied. I wished that I could see her.

"No. Hold still. You're hurt bad."

I figured that had to be pretty obvious.

"I would try to help you, but I'm tied up." I heard the clanking of iron as she tugged on her bonds.

"How long?" I gasped.

"Hours. You've been out for hours. I don't know

how long. My watch doesn't seem to work here. The moon has got to be nearing its zenith." We were running out of time. And I was not in any shape to do anything about it.

"Others?"

"I don't know. Nobody else has come here."

"Where?"

"We're still in the pocket dimension."

"Bad guys?" I mumbled, and then coughed up blood. That was better. Breathing seemed a little easier.

"Oh, Owen . . . I wish I could help you. Bad guys, they're over there on the pyramid. They've been ignoring us." She sounded distraught. I concentrated on her beautiful voice. I needed something pleasant to keep my mind on. "I'm chained to some ruins. Um . . . Looks like there used to be some sort of ancient temple in this pocket, it almost looks Assyrian."

"Did they . . . hurt you?"

"A little. Nothing like you."

"How bad?"

She hesitated, before finally deciding to give me the truth. "You look awful. I think he broke just about everything on you. There's so much blood. They didn't even bother to chain you. And your face . . ." I could tell that she was crying. "I'm so sorry."

"Not me." I breathed in, trying to will myself to keep speaking. "I was worried about you."

"Oh, Owen," she sobbed. "I'm fine. By the time the paralysis wore off, he had me wrapped up good. Really, I'm okay."

"Keep talking. . . . I'll rest." I was so very tired and confused.

"Okay. Uh . . . the Cursed One and that Nazi are a

couple hundred yards away. They're preparing some
sort of altar. They're at the top of a small pyramid,
hard to tell what it looks like since it has so much
snow on it. They have that little box. I don't know
how this dimension thing works, but the sky above is
our sky. I can see our stars, and that's our regular old
moon rising. So I think that we're still in Alabama,
in the cave, only in someplace that's not really in our
world. Maybe just kind of outside of it, but still connected. It must have taken some serious magic to build
this thing. I wonder who did it? It has got to be at
least two thousand years old." Her historical curiosity
started to come out. "Sorry, I'm rambling."

"No . . . Your voice . . . is pretty."

"Will you quit trying to be so nice? You're about
to get sacrificed. We've got to think of a way out of
here. We need to disrupt the ceremony, or escape,
or something. If we can open the gate from this side,
maybe the other Hunters are waiting to charge in.
We have to think." Julie was desperate. She did not
give up easily.

"Hurts to think," I answered. My body was wracked
with so much pain that all I wanted to do was lay
still and die. "Sleep now."

"Owen, stay with me. Just hang in there. I'll think
of something."

She kept talking, but I was fading fast. My body
had simply taken too much punishment to stay awake
for long. My thoughts began to drift. This was it. My
befuddled brain could not see any way out of this.
The journey was almost over. The Cursed One was
going to win.

Julie tried her best to keep me engaged, to keep

me focused; but I continued to drift. If only I could open my eyes to look at her one last time. I had never been the kind of man to fall for someone, but I had fallen hard for her. I loved her. I'm not by nature a romantic, nor am I very eloquent when it comes to things like feelings or emotion. A few months ago if someone had told me there was such a thing as true love at first sight, I would have laughed at them, and probably taken their lunch money. But if I ever knew anything, it was that Julie Shackleford was my soul mate. If only I could do something to save her . . .

Why was Julie chained here anyway? Why did they keep her alive? They had their sacrifice. But I knew the answer, and to deny it was to lie to myself. I remembered the Cursed One's promise when he had invaded Mordechai's dream world. I remembered his offer in the ashen rows of the blasted church. He was going to hurt her as punishment against me, and after he destroyed her, he was going to give her to her mother to be turned and enslaved. She was doomed. My Julie was doomed to a fate literally worse than death.

But it wasn't just her. If the Cursed One completed his ceremony tonight, then everyone was doomed. Every person that I had ever loved. Every person that I had ever met. Every person in the world. That might not be what Lord Machado's goals were, but I had seen the ugly truth. The real evil was out there, just waiting for the beachhead to be established. In the world of the Old Ones, there would be no room for puny, sentient mammals, other than entertainment or, if they were lucky, food.

They were out there waiting. And once and for all, it was going to be finished tonight.

"Julie . . ." I interrupted her desperate scheming. "I promise that I'll stop them."

"He must have hit you harder than I thought. Is your brain swelling?"

"Don't worry. It'll be okay."

IT IS TIME.

"He's coming," I said. "Whatever happens . . . I love you, Julie."

"I know," she replied. "Owen, it's the vampire. Get away from him, you son of a bitch! Leave him alone!"

I could sense the presence of the Master vampire. The already winter temperature dropped a few degrees. I hated that precise German accent. "Such flame. Lord Machado will enjoy breaking you. Now silence, *Fraulein* Shackleford. You will get your turn." I felt cold hands encircle my neck and pull me painfully to my feet. If I had been able to, I would have screamed.

"*Herr* Pitt. Your time has come. It is a great honor to serve in such a fashion."

I tried to spit in his face. I failed miserably, it was more of a sputtering noise through my swollen lips, and the bloody saliva dripped uselessly down my broken face. He laughed and dragged me away from Julie. She shouted after me.

"Don't give up, Owen! Don't give up!"

I felt the cold snow drifting over my legs as the vampire pulled me along. I began to feel a humming in the air. It was the artifact. I had never been so physically close before. It was a tangible thing, the power. It called to me.

We stopped. I could no longer hear Julie. "I've waited so long for this," the vampire said with obvi- ous pride. "I ended my mortal life in shame when the ceremony failed last time. Little did I realize the blessings I would receive for my dedication . . . the opportunity to live and serve once more. I took great pleasure in cutting the heart out of your *Juden* friend, and I will greatly enjoy seeing Lord Machado take yours. Such a remarkable time, indeed . . . Look upon your end, Hunter," the vampire crowed.

"Can't see . . . dumb ass," I croaked.

"That just won't do." I felt something cold and wet drag across my eyes, moistening the blood. Then Jaeger brutally cracked my eyelids open with his long thumbnails. "Hmm . . . your blood is delicious. I will feast on your corpse once the ritual has been completed. I need to regain my strength. I will admit, you put up a good fight. You should be commended."

It even hurt to blink. I was able to see again, out of one eye at least. My right eye must have been blinded, put out in the beating. We stood at the base of a small pyramidal structure. Snow was thick in every direction, coating what appeared to be an alpine forest. The entire world seemed to be small. The horizon visibly lifted only a short distance away, as if we were in a small valley, and the sky seemed bowed. When I had first been tugged into the pocket dimension, I had fallen down what I had thought was a hill; rather, it was just the curved boundary of this small place. It was almost as if we were the occupants of a snow globe.

The ruins were in the center of the dimension—obviously the focal point. Jaeger dragged me up the stairs, my legs thumping up each stone step. I left a small trail of blood in the snow.

I tried to move my arms. Nothing. They were too badly broken to do anything other than quiver and hurt.

One of my legs responded a bit. I was still wearing my armor, but I could not tell if I still had any of my weapons. I had lost all of my firearms, but maybe I still had a grenade on me. If I could get the pin out of a frag, that might put a kink in their ceremony. From what I had seen, it might not work if they had to scrape up the sacrifice with a spatula.

"My Lord Machado. I present the sacrifice."

PREPARE HIM FOR HIS FATE.

I was hoisted up and tossed violently onto the frozen block of stone. I lay on my back, looking up at the shallow gray sky. Jaeger broke the buckles on my armor and ripped through the Kevlar covering my chest. I heard a clatter as the vampire tossed aside the tool that he had used. I looked over. Bastard had used my own knife. My wrists were shackled and chained to the stone. Not that I could have done anything anyway.

The Cursed One stood hulking a few feet away. He was a massive shambling thing. The helmet and armor had been polished to a mirror shine. The flowing robes were opulent red silks, but under them the flesh was a twisting mass of oily darkness. He just oozed evil.

"You will fail," I said calmly. "Just like you failed sixty years ago."

NOT NOW, BRAVE HUNTER. FOR THIS IS THE TIME.

His thoughts stabbed into my brain, causing mental pain equal to the physical. What had Mordechai said? He had told me to remember the things that he had shown me. I had to think of something. I tried to recall the hazy memories. I was grasping at straws.

The Old Man surely couldn't have foreseen a way for me to get out of this.

"You don't know how to finish the ceremony. Thrall killed your priestess. You don't know what to do. You'll fail again."

The black thing shook. Trembling beneath his robes, bubbles rising through the space that should have been his face, splattering congealed fluids onto the snow—he was laughing at me. I had amused him.

BUT IN THIS PLACE, MY LOVE RETURNS TO ME TONIGHT.

The helmet dipped, nodding toward Jaeger. The vampire bowed, always subservient, and placed a rolled-up bundle of cloth on the ground at the base of the altar. The vampire untied the rope that encircled the package, and unrolled it on the snow.

It was a skeleton. An ancient, dried and brittle heap of broken bones, still chipped from where an ax blade had been used to peel the flesh away to ease Lord Machado's burden.

"Koriniha," I gasped. "No freaking way."

DO NOT TAINT HER NAME WITH YOUR FOUL MORTAL LIPS. IN THIS PLACE, WITH MY POWER, WITH THE ARTIFACT OF *KUMARESH YAR*, SHE SHALL RETURN TO ME.

The artifact was removed from under his robes, coated in black goo He kept it inside his body for safekeeping. As it was revealed, a jolt of power surged through the pocket dimension. I felt it down to the core of my being. I had seen the artifact in my visions. When I had died in Natchy Bottom, I had touched it with my spirit. It had shown me things, things which no human should have seen. It was not of this world.

It did not belong here, in our time, in our space, in our plane. It was a token of the evil of the others. The Old Ones. The forgotten trespassers.

The artifact called to me.

The Cursed One gently set the box down amongst the bones. The pyramid began to shake. The stone beneath started to radiate heat. Water formed as the edges of the snow started to recede, revealing the structure's construction. Within seconds, rivulets of water were running off, snow swept away. The pyramid was not made of stone at all, but blocks of organic ivory. Each stone was larger than a man, carved from the tusks or horns of some impossibly ancient thing. Truly this was the Place of Power.

The bones started to shake by themselves. One by one, they rotated and moved, pulling into position, organizing the bits from chaos, taking form. The skull rolled a few times, righting itself as individual vertebrae formed a chain beneath. The jaw opened and closed. The finger bones curled together, clenched spasmodically, and scratched tears in the fabric of the ancient cloth.

"And the knee bones connected to the leg bone, and the leg bones connected to the hip bone," I sang stupidly. Jaeger cracked me alongside my face for interrupting their sacred moment.

The skeleton was whole. Lying on its back, twitching and rattling. Everything in place, but without ligament or tissue to hold it together. The Cursed One glided until he stood over the skeleton.

MY BELOVED, I GIVE TO YOU OF MYSELF. SURELY MY LOVE WILL SATISFY THE PROPH-ECY OF YOUR MASTERS.

His back was toward me. Almost gingerly, the withering base of tentacles covered the bones. The red cloak was flared wide, covering them as the Cursed One slowly lowered his form to the floor. The cloak settled, concealing the huge lump of oily tissue. There was a horrible squelching noise, like a plunger dislodging a clog. There was a heavy smell of sulfur. The vampire looked on in rapture. The winter air hummed with the power of the artifact. Finally the shape was still.

Man, what I would have given right about then for the use of my arms and a hundred pounds of C4.

Two separate shapes moved under the robe. Jaeger fell to his knees and prostrated himself on the floor, crying out to his master in joy. The Cursed One rose. He did not seem as massive as before. The red cloak was loose, and he was now not much larger than a man. One tentacle reached downward, almost gently, to be offered to another thing. It sat up from the puddle of gore, one arm extended. The tentacle encircled it and pulled upwards. The priestess had returned.

She stood shakily, wobbling slightly, not used to having a physical form. The bones had been coated in the black ichor of the Cursed One, flesh, tendon, and organs replaced by the unnatural mass. She was a human female in shape and structure, but not in texture or material. I could even almost recognize her from the visions, the memory of her flesh had been so perfectly replaced. The cloth that had held her bones stuck to her back, splattered and stained. She tore it away with one hand, then realizing what she had done, brought the hand up in front of her face, slowly opening and closing the fingers, turning it at the wrist to examine herself. Her eyes were crimson pits. She ran her hands over her body, the gelatinous mass twitching and moving.

The Cursed One encircled her in a horrible embrace, their faces melding together in what had to be their version of an impassioned reunion. Tentacles withered and slapped wetly against the ground, splattering me with oily droplets. He pulled away, her arms leaving black stains on his robe, his armor no longer gleaming, but now coated in slime. She stroked her fingers through the front of his face, his tissues parting as she touched the teeth of his yellow skull.

The dead flirt ugly.

MY PRIESTESS. I HAVE DONE AS YOU ASKED. I HAVE CROSSED THE IMPOSSIBLE GAP TO RETURN YOU TO THIS WORLD.

Surprisingly the priestess spoke aloud. Her voice was horrific, bubbling up from fluid-filled sacks, sounding like pouring tar. "My lord, you have done the impossible. Truly the prophecy has been fulfilled."

The conquistador helmet dipped toward Jaeger. The vampire moved in a blur and appeared before its Lord, presenting the ancient battle-ax. The monster took it, wrapping it tightly in its tentacles, and glided closer to me. The artifact was placed on the altar near my head. This was the closest I had been to the device, and I could hear it whispering. Deep inside I could sense the trapped souls, the Old Man, and hundreds—no, thousands—of other trapped sacrifices.

A sound came from the priestess, a horrible noise. It turned into a gurgling chant. The words were familiar and I recognized them from the memory.

The concave hills began to quake and the curved sky began to shimmer. The moon was fat and bright overhead. The device rose until it was floating above the altar. It began to slowly rotate. Ancient runes could now be seen on the simple stone as they took on a black light of their own, detaching and floating in air. They formed a sphere of energy that began to grow, approaching my head. I could feel the electricity licking my scalp as the priestess continued her chant. The words made my remaining ear burn, and it felt like somebody was pushing an ice pick into my skull and twisting it.

"Machado. They're using you. You're just a pawn. The Old Ones are just waiting for you to open the path," I shouted. His crimson eyes looked down upon me, but he ignored my feeble attempts to prevent my death.

Koriniha stuttered briefly in her chant, but continued.

"They're going to come through and take over."

The Cursed One readied himself, the blade was lifted, held awkwardly in the tentacles. I screamed in pain as the black energy of the artifact crackled over my skull.

Now remember things you have seen. Remember things I have show you. Is up to you, many things which I not could tell, I have show you. Remember them, and all will be fine.

The words of the Old Man. I focused on them, trying to blot out the pain, the visions, the flashing cruel energy, the upraised blade.

Yet every five hundred years, a man will be born, a mortal with the power to use this device and bend it to his will. You are this man, you are the one who has been prophesied by the Old Ones. The words of Koriniha. In the vision she had looked into Lord Machado's eyes as she had spoken, but had she been speaking to him, or was it a message for me five hundred years later? The thought disappeared as a black whip of energy wracked across my body.

Control of time, space, energy, matter, that kind of thing. Anybody who tries to use it dies, unless you are one of the special people. Albert Lee had spoken about some of the things in the Old Man's journal. But I had used the artifact. I had unleashed a tiny bit of its power in Natchy Bottom. I had destroyed the flow of time, taken five minutes of history and made it as if it had never existed. And though I had been dead at the time, I had lived.

Thou knowest not of thy fate? Of thy place in this world? The question from the Tattooed Man, Thrall. What was my place? Why was I special? Why had he vowed to kill me?

The memory of Lord Machado, enraged, dying, body wracked by wound and fever, attacking the black obelisk, destroying the lines of the prophecy with his fearsome ax. Each glowing line appearing, only to be swept away in a crash of ax blade against obsidian.

> He will come
> Son of a great warrior

Auhangamea Pitt. The Green Beret legend. To his children he was just a normal man. A stern and distant father. Yet a display case over the family hearth held his Congressional Medal of Honor.

Taught in the skills of the world

The very first time I had met Julie, she had read from my file. *Top of your class, passed the CPA exam the first time.* I was an accountant. A man of numbers and spreadsheets. Facts and figures. Audits and accruals.

Yet drawn to the sword

But I was far more comfortable with a gun in my hand than a calculator. I would rather be in a brutal full-contact fight than fill out a 1040. The glowing line of the prophecy exploded as the ax hammered home.

His very name taken from
The weapon of his fathers

Owen. An obsolete piece of Australian scrap. A cheap stamped sheet-metal 9mm bullet hose. But it had kept my father alive while he had stayed one step ahead of the communist patrols.

Given a quest by the crown
To defeat an impossible foe

The Elf Queen had spoken to me. *Dreamer. One last thing. Ya'll got a mission. Don't screw up. Or we all git dead. This here is serious, and I ain't just funnin ya . . . As Queen of the Enchanted Forest, I order ya'll not to fail. Kill the bad 'un, or it's all over.* I had accepted her quest. It was my quest to stop the Cursed One that had landed me half-dead on this altar.

Possessor of visions

My brave friend Trip, now probably dead. *You talk with ghosts. You see visions. You even managed to turn back the clock. Explain that if it isn't a miracle.*

Leader of men

Earl Harbinger, smoking, trying to hide a slight smile, confident in his wisdom as the most experienced Monster Hunter in the world. *I've got three Newbies that seem to think you're their leader. Trip, Holly and Albert would follow you anywhere. Whether you know it or not, you're a leader. That's good enough for me.*

Ally of dark forces

The Wendigo loomed in my mind. Billowing skins under an antlered skull. Special Agent Franks, still in mud-covered armor, snapping his hand to his forehead in a salute of honor.

Friend of monsters

Skippy and his tribe dancing and rejoicing. A mighty werewolf tearing with fang and claw as he battled the undead.

The line of text shattered in the darkness.

I knew now.

The artifact spun, shrieking, casting off insane energies, piercing screams inside my head from the trapped souls within its prison. It was not just a key. It was a manifestation of all that was bad. It had been forged by a being of unnatural law. Placed here as a tool of invasion. Held in place, waiting for that one mortal with the will to use it. The Old Ones were patient. They were smart. They had steered their pawns into place, taking thousands of years, and generations of human toil to bring this meeting about. It recognized me. It welcomed me. It called out to me.

I called back.

The priestess shrieked out an alien command. I was fully engulfed now in the whipping black energy. Lord Machado swung the weapon. The ax blade descended, screaming down toward my unprotected chest.

"No."

Time jerked spasmodically. There was a thunderous explosion and the ax was blasted spinning into the air. The Cursed One was flung across the top of the pyramid, slamming wetly against the ivory blocks.

I was in control now. I felt the power of the Old Ones coursing through my body. I could move again. Strength surged through my limbs. With one tug, the chains binding my wrists were shattered. I rose, forcing my way through the walls of black energy, a taste for violence in my mouth. I had been pushed too far, and now I was pushing back.

The Master vampire screamed in rage. Somehow I had harmed his lord, and now he descended on me in its full wrath. Jaeger twisted into his killing form, surging toward me at hundreds of feet per second. Claws descended in a flash of speed sufficient to turn rock into powder.

I blocked the claw, smashing the hardened bones of his arm into splinters. The vampire halted in shock. I wrapped my hands around his neck, spun him around and shoved him into the altar. Cracks rippled across the structure as I forced him down. He hit me like a freight train, hammering me with unbelievable force. I tried to tear him apart, but he was the strongest of all vampires. I could not destroy him.

There was a presence. I could sense it coming from the artifact. One of the prisoners, desperately calling my name. I stuck one hand back into the energy and felt something heavy and solid land in my palm.

It was Mordechai's cane.

I roared as I slammed it through Jaeger's chest. It served as a mighty stake, piercing the black heart. He screamed in impossible pain as the cane began to burn in blue fire. For six decades this thing had reigned nearly supreme in his world of undeath. Cursed with powers beyond comprehension, yet bound in servitude to another. Before that he had been just as evil, just as brutal, only in human form he had been a mere cog in the machine of death that had been his calling. He was a murderer, a tyrant, a king of evil. We stood face to face as the vampire tried to pull me into the conflagration. I slammed him back into the altar, again and again, gaining in strength and velocity. I crushed his form into the ivory, pulverizing it into bits.

He tried to crawl away, withering and burning. The flames of the cane would not allow him to change form. There was no escape. I snatched up my ganga ram, lifted the mighty weapon, and brought it down on the vampire's neck. The heavy blade struck true, and driven by my new strength, the hardened spine shattered on impact. His head landed at my feet. Black lifeblood streamed down the pyramid. His eyes looked up at me in confusion as his mouth tried to form words.

I kicked his head into the woods.

The energy release from the artifact was growing in intensity, far greater now than it had been during my vision. I walked through it, unfazed by the lightning. Stepping over the smoldering body of the vampire, I headed toward the Cursed One. The artifact lifted into the air, higher and higher, until it was suspended at the midpoint of the tiny little world. The roar of the unleashed power was deafening. The winds picked up the snowfall and spun it like we were in a blizzard.

"Machado!" I roared. I was whole again. I could hear. I could see. I could move. "Machado! Face me!" I tore off the remaining scraps of my armor and threw them aside. I strode toward the fallen form of the Cursed One. It ended now.

Boy. Wait. You must stop.

Freed from the bondage of the Cursed One, his murderer destroyed, the Old Man reached out for me, trying to help. I ignored him. I was filled with rage. Lord Machado had attacked me again and again. He had threatened my loved ones. He had threatened my world. He had tried to take our lives. My blood thundered and I demanded vengeance. His death was inevitable. I demanded it.

The energy grew in power relative to my anger. It spun high above, now a solid globe of black, so thick and great that the trees were bending, breaking and being sucked upwards. I walked through the fury.

Stop. They use you. Use you like pawn.

Lord Machado appeared out of the whirling snow. He bombarded me with his power. Telekinetic forces striking against me, trying to invade my body, rupture blood vessels in my brain, clamp down the valves of my heart, or pop my lungs like a balloon. He had the power to kill with his very mind.

Nothing.

His powers could not touch me. He belonged to me now. I lost control, washed away in a river of fury.

"Die!" I shouted as I slashed my blade through his neck, spraying oil high. He lashed out with a tentacle. It struck me like a whip, burning me. I swung as it withdrew, taking the end off and leaving a trail of black. He encircled me, whipping and tearing, trying to ensnare me. I snarled and cursed, swinging the heavy blade, chopping through the flesh of the Old Ones. The armored bulk crashed into me, knocking me backwards. A tentacle lashed around my wrist and yanked my blade away as I fell.

I landed next to something—Lord Machado's ax. It was embedded in the ivory. Surging to my feet, I dodged as tentacles crashed into the ground, and wrenched the blade free. The polished wood felt natural in my hands, as if it belonged there. I twirled it overhead, and brought it down on his limbs, severing them in a smear of ichor. The black flesh tore at me, trying to pull through my ribs and into my heart. If I had not had the power of the Old Ones coursing through me, I would have died instantly. I grabbed the slippery tentacle with one hand, and tugged the Cursed One toward me. I slammed the spike of the ax forward, driving it between the crimson eyes. The scream echoed inside my skull. He may have been immune to all normal weapons, but there was nothing normal about his family's battle-ax.

He pulled away, knowing fear for the first time in centuries. I followed him, driven forward in a berserk frenzy. I brought the ax down, chopping, hacking and stabbing against the withering mass. Overhead the black sphere was growing, now filling the whole center space of the world. I drove the Cursed One back, until he balanced precariously at the edge of the pyramid. I swung the blade up, tearing through the face, striking the ancient bone beneath, and launching the helmet into the air. It disappeared upwards, engulfed in the maelstrom of the artifact.

The Cursed One was defeated. Limbs severed, fluids pouring out, shattered skull dangling, he stood on the edge. In the distance the walls of the world were shaking. The created dimension had come loose from its anchor, and we floated just above the surface of Alabama. The ground behind the Cursed One faded away, trees and rocks dropping toward the earth below as the created world began to disintegrate.

The armored breastplate was a target. It beckoned me. I was sure in my knowledge that the organ keeping the unnatural thing alive was beneath. I could feel it beating.

HOW CAN THIS BE? IT WAS MINE. MINE TO CONTROL. YOU HAVE TAKEN IT FROM ME. I HAVE BEEN BETRAYED.

Boy, stop please. Control your anger. You know now who you are. This is not way to finish this. This is what she wants. This is what Old Ones want.

SPARE ME. PLEASE.

The blade impacted the ancient armor and easily pierced through. The pump that served as Lord Machado's heart was cleaved in two. I tore the ax free. An explosion of gas and liquid erupted out of the hole in the armor, spraying me in the face. I gagged as some of the stuff entered my mouth. Lord Machado toppled, and rolled down a level, landing in an oily clump. Some of his blood drifted upward, caught in the pull of the artifact. The droplets disappeared into the mighty sphere.

No. What have you done? Mordechai cried. *You doom us all!*

The words of Earl Harbinger, *Hunters can't lose control. Got that? You never lose control.*

I had said it to Trip myself the night he had talked me out of quitting. *When I get mad, when I lose control, people get hurt.*

I was the one. I tasted the foul blood in my mouth just as Lord Machado had tasted the copper in his own five hundred years before . . . What had I done?

"The sacrifice is complete," Koriniha said, her voice now clear.

I spun around, ax in hand. The priestess stood at the opposite end of the pyramid. One black arm encircled Julie's neck. A ceremonial dagger was pressed into her throat, unleashing a thin trickle of blood. I began to move forward, but the priestess pressed the knife harder and Julie cried out.

"That will be enough, Hunter," she said. The power of the Old Ones evaporated from my body. Suddenly I was dizzy and weak. Stumbling, I went to my knees, feeling empty without the power. "You've had your taste."

"Let her go," I ordered. Julie was frightened but angry. She fought against the priestess. Her chains had been broken, but she could not break free of Koriniha's steel grasp. The priestess was still a patch of oily darkness, but her features had changed to the point that she looked almost exactly like she had in the memory. The red eyes had been replaced with the cunning human eyes that I remembered. She was looking at something behind me.

There was a bellow, sounding even over the hurricane above, the battle cry of an unstoppable force. I turned just in time to see Abomination's blade tearing toward my throat. There was no way I would be able to move in time.

Koriniha's eyes fixed on the bayonet.

It stopped instantly, the edge pressed into the flesh above my jugular. Abomination vibrated, the silver blade dissipated friction heat from the sudden stop into my skin. The Tattooed Man looked at me, pitch black eyes wide in surprise, then down at the shotgun in his thick fists, then at the priestess. She glared at him, and suddenly he was slammed backwards as if hit by a truck. He rolled across the pyramid, instantly springing to his feet near the vampire's now skeletal corpse. Thrall lifted my shotgun, the skull image on his face twisting into grim determination. The black lines on his body moved in unison with the crackling energy above. He began to walk toward me.

"What took you so long?" the priestess asked nonchalantly.

"T'was a mighty werewolf about. There was a great battle to gain entrance to this foul place. Who art thou?"

She laughed. Julie cringed as the knife twisted against her neck. "Do you not remember me, Captain Thrall? It was I who led your general to his fate."

"Thou evil thing. I took thy life once. I shall do so again." Thrall's voice raised in volume and intensity. He changed direction away from me, now heading toward the priestess. "Thou stole the artifact from my hands. Thy minions left me buried beneath a mountain, but I will not die. I have vowed to keep the power from all. I have vowed upon the spirits of my Jarl ancestors. I have—" Koriniha's eyes narrowed and the Tattooed Man was again hurled through the air.

"Fool. I tire of you. Your use to us has ended," she hissed. He landed with a sickening thump. Abomination bounced out of his hands. "We needed you then. We needed a protector for the *Kumaresh Yar*, but no longer. Lord Machado had to work for it. He needed a nemesis. We could not just give him the artifact before the time was right. Thank you for your services, good Captain."

Thrall surged to his feet. He must have retrieved all of my weapons from the snow. He drew both of my .45s from behind his back and pointed them at the priestess, fingers seeking triggers. The priestess pushed them aside with a thought. Bullets struck the pyramid and ricocheted harmlessly into the distance. The STIs were torn from his massive hands and sent spinning away.

The unkillable man charged her with a roar. For five hundred years he had protected the device from any mortal who would dare to unlock its powers. He had sacrificed his life, always in hiding, constantly in battle, always struggling to protect the object from the minions of the Cursed One. It had been stolen once before with the help of the Nazis, and he had regained it. It had been stolen from him again by the hands of seven Masters. He was here to get it back, and destroy any who thought to use it. He was the Guardian.

But the Old Ones no longer required his services.

He stumbled to a halt, clutching at his face in alarm. "What foul sorcery is this?" he bellowed, and then roared in pain as the twisting magic tattoos were ripped from his body, taking parts of his flesh with them. "No! ARRGGHH!" He gnashed his teeth together in agony as his skin was torn off. The black curling lines snaked upwards, crackling into the black sphere, returning to their home. His clothing rustled as the blood-stained lines searched for an escape, poured through the fabric, leaving it clinging to the now blood-soaked form. He went to his knees, twisting and convulsing as he was peeled like a piece of fruit. I had to look away. I had never seen anything so horrible.

He fell onto his face, now all visible sinew and twitching muscle, barely conscious in a spreading pool of red.

"It must hurt. To be a mortal, and to be branded with such glory. Immune from age, sickness, death—" Koriniha appeared to be enjoying his suffering. "—only to have it all stripped away."

"What art thou?" Thrall gasped through his gash of a mouth, white teeth glistening in the pulped mass. The black had been torn from his eyes, and the things were now huge, milky orbs, quickly covered in blood. Eyelids gone, he could no longer blink it away.

"I have been known by many names. You knew me as Koriniha, but that was just a part to play. Oh, how I tired of that act, fawning over your Lord Machado. He should have been the one, but he lacked the will. I have lived a thousand lives. I have trespassed upon this world since the beginning. I am Unwelcome, Uninvited. O mighty Captain, your people knew me as Azgeroth. The tribes that conquered your people thought of me as Hel." She turned to glare at me, her oil-slick face dripping onto Julie's hair. "I am a thing of legend. To your mentor, the ghost, to his people I was Lilith, though they have the story all wrong. To the nation that carried them away into captivity I was Zaltu, daughter of Tiamat. Temples have been built in my honor across this world, all forgotten now. I am a false god in your pathetic mortal pantheon. You sad apes have made idols of me for ten thousand years. I have waited patiently while you fools were sacrificing slaves and forming cults in my name. But who I am is not important. All you must know is that I am the one who prepares the way for the return of the Great . . ." she hissed an impossible sound that hit my brain like a sledgehammer. Julie cried out in pain and tried to lift her hands to cover her ears. The name of her master left me nauseous and stupefied.

"Do you understand now? In your visions, I was not speaking with that fool Machado. I was speaking to you. You are the one. Infinite power is at your fingertips. You are the rightful ruler of this world. You are destined to be a prince of . . ."

The impossible sound again. I clamped my hands over my ears. Julie screamed.

"Use your will to unlock it. All you have to do is wish for it." She glanced upwards at the roaring sphere. "Do it now or I will kill your love." She pressed the tip of the knife in deeper. Julie cringed.

I understood now, understood more than the priestess thought I did. I knew what was waiting on the other side of that gate. They could not exist in a plane like ours. They were outside time. They needed the fabric of the universe twisted into their image, and that was something that they were not able to do on their own. If I were but to will the sphere to open, then the Old Ones would descend on this world to rule. It was a trick. It was all a trick. Lord Machado had just been a pawn, a man used and broken by them to lead events to this moment. A pawn like me.

"Don't do it, Owen. Let her kill me," Julie shouted. Koriniha tightened her arm around her hostage's throat. Julie was undeterred. "Do it, you whore. I dare you!"

"I won't open that gate."

"That is up to you. You are the one. The one prophesied by the great ruler itself. You can control time and matter. You have been tested before and you have proven yourself ready. Now all that remains is for you to satisfy the rest of the prophecy."

The last lines appeared glowing in my mind, obsidian chips flying, ax madly descending.

> Only he will have the will
> And the power
> Through his love of another
> To break time and the world

The final part of the prophecy disappeared in a shower of shards and dust.

Koriniha drove the knife home. Julie's eyes widened in shock. Her mouth opened, but no sound came out. Her eyes met mine, conveying pain, pleading for help that I could not give.

"Noooo!" I screamed, charging forward, ax held high.

The priestess relaxed her grip and let Julie fall. She went slowly to her knees, her hands rising to her neck, futilely trying to stem the tide of blood. It slipped through her fingers, showering down her arms. Her life was pumping out.

My world died. I hurled the ax, sending it hurtling end over end. Koriniha did not move as it sped toward her face. The ax froze in midair, and then fell uselessly down. She glared at me and the power of her mind knocked me to the ground. I rose, only to be smacked down again, and then a third time. This time she put me into the pyramid hard enough to crack the ivory blocks. I clawed my way forward, trying to reach Julie.

The priestess let me. She stood, waiting impatiently, her sleek black form still dripping. She glanced up at the rift like a human would glance at a wristwatch. "Hurry this up, Hunter."

I pulled Julie into my arms. I sobbed. Her hands fell away from her neck as she slipped into unconsciousness. The wound was still spurting, but it was weak now. I pressed my fingers into the gash and tried to clamp the artery shut. It was too slippery. I could not lose her. Not like this.

"For love, human. The last piece of the puzzle. Your pathetic weak little instinct. It is the one thing that your kind can experience sufficient to power the *Kumaresh Yar*. Your hate is almost enough, but not quite." The black sphere crackled above her. I could see things moving inside, pushing, anxious to begin the invasion. "You can save her. You have the power. All you have to do is call upon it. You have the will. All you have to do is wish for your birthright, and it will be yours. Your female will live. You can serve the Old Ones. She will be given to you. They will show mercy upon you. Those that you . . . *love*"—she spit the word out in distaste—"will be spared, and allowed to live forever. You and yours will prosper for eternity. Your every desire will be granted. All you have to do is wish for it."

I held Julie in my arms and rocked back and forth. I knew that she was telling the truth. All I had to do to save her was to will it to happen. She would live. I would be granted power beyond my wildest dreams. Julie would live forever at my side.

"Make your choice quickly. It does not matter to me. Know this, our coming is inevitable. If we fail tonight, we will return and try again, as we have tried before. Eventually one of you mammals will make the right choice. It might as well be you. If you make the wrong choice, then I will bind your soul to the *Kumaresh Yar* so that you can suffer for eternity. Let me give you a little idea of what that will hold."

Pain so exquisite that I cannot explain. Suffering stretching on for infinity. Black icy solitude racked forever with hurt so great that there were not words for it in any language. The split second that she exposed me gave me a window into the unfathomable horror of it.

"And not just for you. Your love will share your fate." Julie convulsed as her unconscious mind was exposed to the horror. "Make your choice. Free her, or condemn her."

I held Julie and cried. I could not fight Koriniha. She could kill me with her thoughts. There were two paths before me. If I refused her, then Julie and I would be banished to an eternity of pain. If I did as she said, if I made the selfish choice, then everything I had ever wanted would be given to me. No more pain. No more suffering. The incredible feeling that I had possessed moments before would be mine forever.

I could see myself doing it, Julie by my side. The Old Ones coming seemed inevitable anyway. Why not? Julie's life was draining out while I hesitated. I would be king, and she would be my queen.

I would be king.

Of a dead world.

"I've made my choice."

Koriniha sighed, slowly shaking her head. "You fool, human. I can see it in your eyes. Five hundred more years on this stinking rock, having peasants sacrifice chickens to little statues of me. Damn you. Your punishment will be the stuff of legends." She focused in on Julie and me, drawing together the energy to cast us both into the black sphere. "Insolent little air breather."

I had to try something. I could not just let her condemn us without a fight. If only I could access the power just enough to fight her and save Julie. I had controlled time once before. Maybe I was strong enough to hold back the Old Ones.

"Yes. You are the strongest one yet . . . you can control it," Koriniha whispered. "I feel your mighty will. Surely you can do it."

Maybe I could . . . Maybe I had a third option . . . I had defeated every other monster that this world had thrown at me. I could defeat these as well. Koriniha licked her oily lips in anticipation. The sphere above her roared, huge now, a world of its own, blotting out the storm-drenched Alabama sky. We stood at the intersection point between two spheres. When they connected, a new world would be born.

I stopped, realizing what I was about to do. The Old Man had warned me about this, only I had been too ignorant to understand. *Good, but sometimes stupid. Brave, but proud. Too proud for own good. If not more careful, pride will kill you and blow up world. Think you can solve problems, but no patience to learn. Want to rush. Do things now.*

That was what she wanted. She wanted me to fight. The Old Ones would eat my soul for breakfast. She waited for my move, so intent on subverting my will and destroying me the instant that I unlocked the gate that she did not see the tentacle slither past her feet and slowly wrap around the battle-ax and drag it away.

"I can beat you," I lied.

"We shall see."

BETRAYER.

The ax blade exploded from out of Koriniha's chest. She shrieked in rage. The broken Lord Machado rose behind her, encircling his tentacles around her form, lifting her upward, and tearing the blade free. He slammed it into her again.

I lifted Julie in my arms and carried her away as they battled. Lord Machado hoisted Koriniha over his shattered skull, the black tissues of both creatures separating and tearing up into the sphere, drawn irresistibly home. The energy pulsed and surged. Growing larger by the second, the wall approached us, shapes twisting and clawing at the other side.

My boots slipped in the puddle of blood from Thrall. We landed next to him. He was still and his lidless orbs stared into the distance. I began to lift Julie. We were too close to the whipping tentacles, and without the power of the Old Ones upon me, one furious strike would be certain death. I heaved her up into my arms.

Suddenly a red hand grasped my wrist.

"Wait—" Thrall croaked through his lipless mouth. I struggled to hear him over the storm. "—was wrong. Thou truly art a warrior without guile." His grasp was still amazingly powerful and he pulled me closer. "So much death . . . I give thee back one life . . ." He held up his other fist. Squirming between the muscle of his clenched fingers was a tiny bit of black energy, the last vestige of his unnatural immortality. It struggled to escape. He opened his hand and pushed it against Julie's neck. She gasped, her eyes suddenly flared open, then she passed back out. The ancient captain uttered one last thing, "Until Ragnarok . . . my friend."

The hand fell limply away. The last bit of power flew home like a bolt. I turned Julie's head. It was a blood-soaked mess, but I could no longer see the entrance wound. Thrall's lungs rattled as he gave up the ghost.

"See you in Valhalla," I whispered.

The sphere was only a few feet over the pyramid now. It blotted out the sky in its terrible majesty. Lord Machado and Koriniha still battled, more and more of their ichor being stripped away by the second, leaving only filthy bones and angry souls.

"Machado! I curse you!" Koriniha's skull screamed as her face was torn off. "Curse you!" She struggled in his tentacles as he forced her toward the sphere.

TOO LATE FOR CURSES . . . MY LOVE.

He thrust her body upwards. She broke the surface of the rift. The last bits of alien tissue were stripped away. Her skeleton quivered, and then exploded, the winds whipping bones about like missiles, snapping out into the forest and embedding into the trees. A jagged femur pierced the ivory next to my head.

Lord Machado's voice screamed inside my brain. His limbs were extended into the rift. It was a fatal connection. His flesh was stripped, withering, disappearing into the maelstrom. I covered my eyes as the black light began to sear my retinas.

There was a roar, followed by a wet explosion, a concussion of sound and fury. Bits of the Cursed One splattered across the pyramid, showering us in gore, and then all was quiet.

I opened my eyes. The sphere was gone. The night sky was bright and clear, and I was lying on a pyramid, in the middle of a little forest valley, which appeared to be floating unsupported several hundred feet above rural Alabama.

Julie was breathing, though it was shallow and her pulse was weak. Her wound was closed, sealed by Thrall in a final act of mercy. I stood up. Amazingly enough, I felt fine, no broken bones, no blindness, no shattered eardrum. The breeze was natural and clean. The moon was descending over millions of stars. It was beautiful.

Something moved from where the Cursed One had last stood.

"Oh, give me a break," I muttered. I looked around for weapons. I found both of my pistols, put the thumb safeties on, and shoved them in my waistband. Abomination was still where Thrall had dropped it. Empty, but it still had a good bayonet. I walked toward the shape that was moaning in the pile of burnt garbage that had been my enemy.

I held the shotgun like a spear, silver blade extended. Kicking aside the charred mess, I searched for the movement. The remainder of Lord Machado's body had turned to ash, and was slowly blowing away in the wind. I saw small glints of the armored breastplate sticking out from under the cinders. It rocked slightly. I readied myself.

Slowly, shakily, a person emerged from the remains. He was a short man, and his features were hard to distinguish beneath the soot. He was naked except for the remaining armor, and a few tatters of the once opulent robe. He struggled weakly to his hands and knees, a tiny creature amongst the ruins of his former body.

I waited.

He spoke slowly, not used to forming words. The medieval Portuguese was still very familiar in my mind.

"The curse is lifted. I am a man again. Human at last."

"Yup."

He looked at his hands in wonder, and brushed the ash away from his skin. He began to cry, tears rolling down the soot. "Five hundred years of torment. I am free. You have freed me from my curse . . . Somehow it is broken."

I tied Abomination's tattered strap over one shoulder and drew the full-size .45 from my waistband. The click of the safety was eerily loud. I carefully put the front sight in place and placed my finger on the face of the trigger. He looked up at me warily. "But . . . but I have been redeemed."

"I'm not in the redemption business."

BOOM.

A hole appeared in his forehead. The silver bullet mushroomed perfectly through his brain tissue and ruptured out the back of his skull in a spray of red and white. The single brass case bounced on the ground. A thin line of blood fell from the entrance wound. Lord Machado's eyes rolled slowly back into his head and he flopped into the ash.

I kept the gun on him. His leg kicked spasmodically a few times. There was no magic. He was not coming back.

Lord Machado was dead.

I slowly lowered the gun to my side. It was over.

The pyramid shook violently. I stumbled, but somehow managed to stay upright. In the distance the edges of the little valley began to disintegrate, collapsing as the unnatural force that sustained the pocket dimension began to dissipate. Trees dropped through the ground, disappearing in showers of dirt and snow. Gravity was a jealous bitch.

I sprinted for Julie. I lifted her into my arms and looked around. The spot where we had entered the little world was gone. The portal was no longer there. The rocks that had supported it were now plummeting hundreds of feet to the earth below. It was shrinking fast, and the ground was falling away, forming a boundary that was heading quickly for the ivory pyramid.

If only I had a parachute.

Hell, I didn't even have a shirt. I might as well

have wished for a rocket pack. I wasn't exactly James Bond here.

We were going to die. The artificial ground was gone now. Only the ruins remained. My footing slipped as the pyramid began to shift wildly, the last vestiges of ancient magic fleeing. The structure dropped for what seemed an eternity, only to slam to a halt, shiver and quake, and then drop again. This halt was especially violent, and I knew that it was our last.

Blocks of ivory broke away, cracking and slipping into the darkness. We only had seconds left before this whole thing fell apart and we were dumped into the air.

Something clanged against the ivory, bounced a few times, and then stopped. *The artifact!* The pyramid jolted again and it slid toward the edge.

I started after it. If I could reach it, I could use it to get us out of here. I surged forward, one hand holding Julie's limp form tight, the other grasping for the little stone box.

My fingers stopped an inch from the artifact. I froze. "Nice try, you evil bitch."

Koriniha's voice echoed through the night air. "Pity. Now I have to put up with five more centuries on this shitty planet." Her spirit drifted away on the winds and was gone.

With a groan the pyramid began its final disintegration. A seam split open between my feet. The artifact slid over the edge and disappeared. The corpses fell away. The last blocks began to plummet, hurtling toward the ground. The top tier was all that remained, and we began to fall. It was a sickening feeling. Air rushed past my ears, deafening me. This was it.

Blinding light. *What the hell?* The spotlight veered away, and something metallic clanged against the ivory. In the split second before the block beneath my feet dropped, I realized it was a chain ladder. I extended one hand and grabbed it. My foothold was gone. I held onto the rung with all of my strength. Julie and I fell. My arm wrenched painfully in its socket. My fingers popped. I cried out in pain as I struggled to hold on. I kicked my legs wildly, panicking, trying to get one foot on the rung. The Hind jerked wildly above as Skippy tried to get us safely to the ground.

It had been an amazing feat of piloting. The clumsy Russian chopper was not known for its precise handling, yet he had managed to match speed with the dropping pyramid long enough to snag us.

I clamped Julie's unconscious body tight against my chest. She threatened to slip away. I could feel the rung trying to pull out of my hand. Instinct told me to drop her and use my other hand to hold on. Screw instinct. My hand was on fire, but I held on. We were losing altitude quickly. I tried to get a foot through another rung, but the ladder was whipping wildly in the wind. Finally, by some miracle, I was able to get the toes of my boot through the chain to brace myself. I held on for dear life.

Ground. Blessed ground. It came up frighteningly fast. Skippy flared the chopper upward, slowing us at the last possible instant. Almost gently he lowered us until the ladder was dragging in the grass. I hopped off, covering my eyes as the blades tore up a mighty cloud of debris. Hunters moved quickly from the woods, swarming toward us. I waved happily. I had no idea what was going on down here, but the Cursed One was dead. The

Old Ones' plan had been foiled. No matter what, we had won. I was briefly illuminated in the spotlight of the Hind as it quickly banked up and away. I grinned like an idiot and gave everybody a thumbs-up.

The final rung of the ladder struck me violently in the back of the head. The last thing I remembered was a bunch of flashlights shining in my eyes and somebody hollering for a medic.

CHAPTER 28

I had to be dreaming. Either that or I was dead.

The field stretched as far as the eye could see. It was the same unnaturally beautiful place where I had first met the Old Man. Only now, the sky was clear. The storm had passed. The crops that had resisted the winds had survived. Their roots had been anchored deep. Now watered and tested, they would be much stronger than before. I felt the moisture under my bare feet. It was a peaceful place.

"Hello, Boy!"

I turned around. The accent was familiar, but the voice was wrong. It was far too young and happy. "Mordechai?"

"You look surprised to be seeing me, you do." He grinned. I suppose I couldn't call him the Old Man anymore. I still recognized him, but instead of being arthritic and frail, he was in the prime of his life. Young, handsome, and strong. Probably what he looked like when he had first started Hunting. He was not even wearing glasses.

"You're alive?"

"No. Am still dead of course. But no longer stuck. You killed the Cursed One. Prison was opened. Now free I am to go."

"Go where?"

"I not know. Have not been to next place before. Have been stuck for long time."

"What do you know about it?" It could not hurt to ask.

"My friend. You find out that for your own self some day." He held out his hand to shake. I pushed his hand aside and engulfed him in a bear hug. I easily picked him up and squeezed. "Ugh . . . Easy, Boy. Respect your elders!"

I put him down. "Thanks for everything," I said. "Sorry about your cane."

"I not need it any more now." He quickly stomped his feet to demonstrate. "Is better used up killing Nazi bastard son of bitch. No, I thank you. Free because you did good, though for second, I thought we were, how you say . . . screwed. But heart was good, and made right choice. I thank you. In fact, many others want also to thank."

"What do you mean?"

He nodded his head off to the side. There was a crowd of people assembled who had not been there before. Men and women, all of them young and fit and strong, much like Mordechai. They were all of different races, and were dressed in many styles of clothing. Robes, furs, silks, even mail armor. A tall man with a curled Babylonian beard saluted me with his bow. The others followed suit, one by one, rais-ing their spears, swords, axes, a musket. I recognized one of the men. He had been the Brazilian Hunter sacrificed by Lord Machado in the memory. He raised his obsidian-tipped club overhead and gave me a nod of approval. There have always been monsters. And as long as there are monsters, there will be some who dare to hunt them. These were my people. I bowed to the ancient Hunters.

One by one they began to walk away. Slowly they became transparent, and began to fade. Within a moment they were all gone. The sacrifices were free.

"Prison is broken, so now they go. Only one of us could break away to contact the one from prophecy. I got to be one to teach you, because mine was the best English speaker." He sighed contentedly. "Sorry I could just not tell who you were, but it was not allowed. Only some things I could see, others I could say. Rules were different. But it is all good now. For me, work is done." Mordechai patted me tenderly on the shoulder. "You probably should be waking up now." He turned and began to walk quickly through the crop, running his hands through the rain droplets clinging to the leaves.

"Wait. What do I do now? Is it over?"

He paused, and looked up as if he was enjoying the sun. "My friend, you still have much work to do. You still have calling. Short straw you have drawn, and you not done until you end up like us. What to do now? Hunt monsters of course. For you, is never over."

I raised my hand and waved. "Thanks, Mordechai. Without you we would have lost. The whole world would have lost. Thanks."

"Silly Boy. Wake up now. Pretty girl is waiting for

you. Be nice to her. Is brave and shoots very good."
He winked. "Not find girl like that very often. Good-
bye, friend."

He walked away with a spring in his step, ready
to embark on his final adventure. Mordechai Byreika
had been one of the greatest Hunters of his day. He
had risked all to stop the storm. He had been my
mentor and my friend. He turned one final time to
grin at me, eyes twinkling, excited to continue on.
He faded from sight and disappeared.

"Hey, guys, Z's awake," said a voice. "Dude, you've
got to be the clumsiest, most accident-prone oaf I've
ever known. I'm amazed you've lived this long."

"Trip?" I asked, trying to rise up so I could look
around. My head ached, and I did not need to touch
the back of my skull to know that there was a huge
lump. "You're alive?"

"Can't kill a brother that easy." He laughed, and
began to cough. His armor had been cut away and
bandages encircled his chest and most of his head. One
leg was propped up and had been tied to a splint. We
were lying on blankets, set under the shade of a tree.
The morning sun was rising in the distance. Several
other wounded Hunters were also resting here. "No
thanks to Holly," he joked.

"Shut up, dick," Holly said from the other side. "It
was a good idea at the time." She was kneeling next
to an unconscious Hunter that I did not know and
applying a clean bandage to his arm. She appeared to
be fine. "Besides, one little hit on the head and you
sleep through the whole battle, while me, Sam and
Milo get to kill like half a million wights."

"I'm just lucky that kudzu broke my fall," he mumbled.

"Sam and Milo are okay?" I asked. I slowly sat up. I was awfully woozy.

"Yeah, but the worst injured have been evacuated to the nearest hospital. We'll be trucking everybody else there in a few minutes. Sam got busted up. At the end, he was killing wights with his teeth since everything else was paralyzed. And Milo? After his little light show against Julie's mom, they're calling him Saint Milo now."

"Told you not to make fun of religious folks," Trip said.

"Julie?"

"Fine, she's wandering around here somewhere."

"Lee?" The last I had seen he had been hit pretty bad.

"He's going to live. But he's probably going to lose his leg. Gretchen did her best, but she wasn't sure." She sounded sad. "He was one of the lucky ones."

"Who else?" I asked. The others grew somber.

"We lost fifteen Hunters. We have another couple that are critical and might not make it. And then we have about twenty wounded. Once the Masters closed the distance, it got ugly. I guess they finally used the wargs to quickly evacuate everybody out of one side of the valley, so they could bomb the hell out of it. Then they concentrated on the last vamp."

"Are they all destroyed?"

"According to Julie, you killed the German, so we got six out of the seven," Trip answered.

"Let me guess." It was too much to hope. "Susan?"

"Yep. My mom got away," Julie said. She appeared in front of me, hands on her hips. Surprisingly, she looked fine, a little pale, but fine nonetheless. Not bad considering that I had watched her throat get cut only a few hours before. She extended her hand to me, I took it, and she did her best to pull me up, but failed miserably. I pulled her down with me. Despite the news of her mother, she laughed when she hit the ground.

"I'm glad to see you're okay," I said.

"Yeah, and you have some explaining to do. How the hell am I even alive? The last thing I remember is the pain, and then I started losing blood, and I was out. I woke up down here."

"Thrall saved your life. The last little bit of evil magic he had on his body, he gave to you. He held it on your neck and then it flew away."

"That would explain this." She brushed her hair aside. The side of her throat was still red and tender, but there was now a thick black line across the side, almost like a tattoo. "I'm not really into the whole body art thing, you know."

"Does it hurt?" I asked.

"Not really."

"Does it feel . . . evil?"

"Not that I can tell. If I get the sudden urge to drown a bag of kittens, I'll let you know."

"Well, let's not knock it then." I moved in for a kiss.

"Slow down. You've got Cursed One and vampire blood all over your face. No offense, but I'm not kissing that."

"Holly! Canteen." I snapped my fingers. "This is a medical emergency."

"Going to have a medical emergency when I shoot your ass," she answered as she tossed me a canteen.

I unscrewed the lid and poured the cool water down my face. It felt good to scrub off the disgusting dried mess. I wiped my face on my arm.

"Okay, now I'm kissable."

"Whoa." Julie's eyes betrayed her shock.

Holly leaned over to see. "Holy shit!"

I raised my hands to my face. What was so surprising?

"What? Let me see!" Trip said.

My skin was smooth. It felt normal. Too normal. My scars were gone. The thick ridge of tissue that had stretched from the top of my head to the side of my nose was gone. I poured some of the water on my chest. All of the scars from my battle with the werewolf Huffman had disappeared. The still-healing road rash on my arms was gone. I probed my molars with my tongue. The missing teeth had returned. My body had been totally repaired.

"The Old Ones . . . When they fixed me so that I could fight and sacrifice Lord Machado . . ." I did not know what to say. I had grown used to the scars and injuries. They were all fixed. It was amazing.

"Wow . . . It's like ancient evil ultimate makeover," Holly said.

Julie caressed the side of my face, then she leaned in and kissed me passionately. Her lips were soft, and it felt good to be alive. Thankfully the others refrained from any snide comments.

When we had come up for air, I had to ask. "I thought chicks dig scars?"

"Right now, I could care less. I'm just glad we're still alive."

"Me too."

◈   ◈   ◈

We cleared out the rest of the wounded. Between the chaos of the mighty storm and the undead-inflicted carnage across the state, most of the hospitals from here to Birmingham were working around the clock. We still had a lot of cleaning up to do, but for today, MHI was done.

Gretchen had ridden up on the back of a mighty warg. She had taken one look at the back of my head and pronounced me something incomprehensible. I did not know if it was good or bad, but the other orcs had laughed at me, so I took that to be a good thing.

Harbinger was still missing, so Julie and her grandfather had effectively taken control of the chaos. Her brother Nate stood protectively nearby. I barely knew the kid, but he was not going to let any of his remaining family out of his sight. I could respect that. Once the wounded were safely gone, the rest of the gear was packed into the surviving vehicles, and then finally the dead. It was a somber duty, but we were not going to leave our dead in the hands of the local authorities.

I helped to lift one of the shrouded bodies into the back of a van. It was Chuck Mead. He had fought hard, and died bravely. But in the end, even the bravest of us would eventually buy it. We had trained together, and I was going to miss the big, simple Ranger. He had been a good man.

Priest said prayers over the bodies of our fallen. He stepped around the corpses, one arm coated in dried blood and slung to his chest. He ignored it. He had work to do. Our comrades would be taken back to the compound where we could perform a proper

Hunter's funeral. It was grisly business, but in our line of work, having your friends cut your head off was the final sign of respect.

"It seems bad, but considering what we were up against," the senior Shackleford stated, "we did good. We did very good."

"Grandpa, has anyone seen Earl since last night?" Julie asked.

"'Fraid not, dear," he answered quietly. "Some of VanZant's boys saw him go past the mortar emplacement after he killed that Master. They said he looked mighty tore up. He was heading into the woods."

"I hope he's okay," she said softly.

"Um . . ." I was sorry to intrude on the family moment, but I had to know. "So Earl's a werewolf. I mean, I'm cool with that. It isn't the first time I've had a werewolf boss, you know."

"Yes. He's a werewolf," the Boss answered, using his hook to tap me on the chest for emphasis, "and that information doesn't go outside of MHI. When that bastard Myers quit and joined the Feds, they found out about him, and he had all manner of trouble. The Feds wanted to kill him."

"And it was only through a whole lot of legal wrangling that he was given a special status," Julie said. "Earl is the only non-PUFF applicable lycanthrope in the world. And even then he is kind of on probation."

"But I thought werewolves were crazy, and violent, and just killed people at the drop of a hat," I said. I unconsciously rubbed my hand on my face, only to realize that my scar was no longer there. I lowered my hand, feeling stupid. "But he seems so in control."

It all made sense though. The way he had defeated Darné so easily on the freighter. The way that he had fought in Natchy Bottom.

"Well . . . he's had a lot of time to work on it," the Boss said. "He has more control over his abilities than any other one that we know about. On the full moon, he still has to lock himself up, because he ain't got no choice but to change then. On the full moon, he just loses it, and it's all animal. He tears the hell out of things, but by morning he's fine. We got us a concrete room with a steel door in the basement of the compound. Built just for him."

"On holidays Milo throws a cow in the cell with him," Nate added helpfully, "kind of like a special Christmas dinner. In the morning we just hose it down."

"He used to lock himself up at the family estate. We had a little building out by the old slave quarters," the Boss said. "Had to build the new cell when he started to wear it out. He didn't want to get loose and hurt somebody when he wasn't in full control."

I knew exactly which little building he was talking about. It had given me the creeps at the time. All of those marks that I had thought had been made by a tool, they had been frustrated claw marks. "But there were millions of scratches in there," I blurted. "It had to have taken hundreds of hours to do all of that."

The three Shacklefords looked at each other, trying to decide what exactly to say. Finally Julie started to speak.

"Not hundreds of hours, but almost that many years."

"Huh?"

"Julie!" Nate said, looking over his shoulder to make sure the other Hunters were not in earshot. "You can't tell him about . . . that."

"Sorry, bro. In the last few days Owen has almost destroyed the universe twice to save me. I'm guessing that he can know about the family secret," she said politely. The Boss nodded for her to proceed.

"Earl isn't just *a* special case. He is *the* special case. As far as we know, he is the oldest living lycanthrope in the world. He is, quite literally, the king of were-wolves. He was bitten back in the 1920s. Over the last eighty years, he has aged maybe twenty years. It took him a real long time to get the hang of it, and to keep from flipping out and killing people like a regular werewolf. That's probably why he smokes so much. When he doesn't get his cigarettes, he gets cranky. When he gets cranky, people get eaten."

"Gives a whole new meaning to nicotine fit," Nate quipped. His grandfather groaned. It probably wasn't the first time that joke had been made in the family.

"He changes his name every generation, always trying to keep his secret safe. Only a handful of us know who he really is. My family has protected him the whole time."

I thought back to the Shackleford family estate, and more importantly the wall of family portraits. There had been only one missing, conspicuous by its absence.

"Raymond Shackleford the Second," I said slowly.

"Yep. You're pretty quick for a bean counter. I like this young man, Julie, much better than your last boyfriend, but I digress. I was only a young man when he was bit, but we stood by my daddy," the Boss said. "Shacklefords take care of their own." The other two nodded. He pointed toward the road where some other vehicles were arriving. "Well, looks like we got some company. Come on, Nate, let's give these two a moment." He shuffled away, grandson in tow.

"So let me get this straight." I took Julie by the hand. "You hang out with your great-grandfather, who's some sort of mutant super werewolf. Your mother is a vampire. Your father was a mad genius who almost destroyed the world. Your grandfather is a half-crazed Monster Hunter with one eye and a stainless steel hook for a hand, and he's the normal one of the bunch." I took a deep breath. "Is that about it? Is there any other family weirdness that I need to know about?"

"No. That's pretty much it," she answered, looking a little sheepish. "Can you deal with that?"

I pulled her close. "Julie, at this point you could tell me that you sprout butterfly wings and a third eye on every second Tuesday, and I would still be in love with you."

"Good," she said with a grin. "Well, there's still my Uncle Leroy, but that's complicated . . . so that story is going to have to wait." She pointed at the horizon. There were several black shapes approaching. Helicopters. The Feds had finally arrived.

The Blackhawks set down in the blasted valley. The Apaches circled over the area. The Feds did not speak as they fanned out into the forest to stake out the fallen blocks of ivory debris. There were only a handful of MHI staff left at the scene, as almost everybody else had packed up and left. We found the Boss arguing with Agent Myers near the original

National Guard position. The Guardsmen were mostly still there, though their lieutenant had locked himself inside the APC and refused to come out. Agent Franks stood off to the side, listening intently to the radio traffic as his men scoured the forest for anything of interest.

"It's over, Myers. We done killed the damn thing. Biggest PUFF bounty ever!" the senior Shackleford shouted. "See, we didn't need no stinking government help."

"Whatever, you old coot," Myers retorted. "This is our scene now. Turn in your paperwork to the PUFF office for approval. I don't care." He saw me approaching. "Mr. Pitt. What happened to your face?" Agent Franks looked up and scowled at me. Once again he was the ugliest man in our line of work. *Haha sucker.*

I ignored the comment. "It's over, Myers. The Cursed One is dead. His body's out there with the rubble. Along with that artifact." I pointed in the direction I thought most of the pocket dimension had landed in. "If you find it, I suggest you don't play with it. Just put it some safe place, and leave it the hell alone."

"That's our business now. Don't you worry. It'll be in good hands. Now get out," he ordered. "This scene is our jurisdiction."

"Fine, but I'm warning you. That box is a lot more than you can handle." I nodded at Franks. "A bunch of your men were killed in that cavern. Turned into wights. You had best see to them."

Franks nodded in understanding. I think that we had come to terms.

"Earl!" Julie shouted. She pointed toward the trees. "He's alive."

Sure enough, Harbinger came walking through the trees. Dirty, caked in mud, grass and leaves, dried blood matted over most of his body—he was totally naked, but did not seem to care. He walked past the Feds, most of whom stepped away from him, slightly fearful. He strode directly up to us, stopping only a few feet from Myers.

"Hey, Myers."

"Earl."

"Got a smoke?"

Myers nodded nervously, took out a pack, and handed over a cigarette. The senior agent handed over his lighter as well. Harbinger took a drag, and sighed contentedly. He looked like a nightmare wild man of the forest, but he did not care in the slightest.

"It's good to have lungs that regenerate," he said. "So, Myers, we've done your job. The threat's dead. The vampires are dead. I suppose right about now MHI is on your bosses' good side. I'm guessing we're square."

The Fed hesitated, not really wanting to answer. "I suppose so."

"Full access to fulfill our contracts?"

"Agreed."

"My teams can move freely?"

"Fine."

"Call off OSHA, the EPA? Fish and Game? ATF?"

"I'll see what I can do."

"IRS?" Harbinger removed the cigarette and blew smoke out his nose. He absently scratched himself. "I bet some certain committee heads are loving us right about now. Probably even the senators who need to approve the appointment of the next head of the Monster Control Bureau."

Myers looked like he had a foul taste in his mouth. "Fine. I'll call off the heat. You're golden for now. But when your people screw up again, your asses are mine."

"Buddy, you should never tell a naked man that his ass is yours," Harbinger said, totally deadpan. Franks snorted. I think it was almost a human laugh. Myers whirled around and glared at his subordinate. "I've just got one question for you."

"What?" Myers snapped, visibly agitated.

"Once the battle started, and everything went down here, how come you guys didn't just nuke the place to be sure?"

"Who says we didn't try?" Myers answered cryptically. He turned his back on Harbinger and stomped away.

"Hey, Franks," Julie called out to the silent Fed.

"Yeah?" he grunted.

"I heard that you guys didn't cut my dad's head off. I heard that you let him turn, and that he escaped." Julie asked. There was a current of anger in her voice. "Because if that was true, I would be . . . disappointed. So, is he still alive?"

Franks took his time composing an answer. His cold eyes studied us.

"No." He nodded grimly, and then followed after his boss.

We watched him go.

"Think he's lying?" I asked.

"I don't know," Julie answered. "I'm sure we'll find out soon enough."

"I know one thing for sure," I said slowly. The others waited. "I know we need to get Earl some pants." The king of the werewolves laughed.

We stopped by the National Guard soldiers to thank them for their help in the battle. Sergeant Gregorius was offered a business card and invited to come see us if he was interested in a lucrative career in beating down evil. Turns out that Boone had already done the sales pitch, and the big soldier had already volunteered for the next Newbie class. I was not surprised. For people like us, Monster Hunting was a calling.

The compound was somber that day as we held fifteen funerals. The fallen were decapitated, cremated, and their remains sent back to their families along with whatever the made-up excuse was for that particular Hunter. Sometimes having a job that had to be kept secret from most of the world was a real bummer. The team leads had to make the phone calls, and I did not envy them at all. The next few days were quiet ones. There were far too many new plaques on the wall.

We watched the news anxiously, just like everybody else in the world. Gradually the panic over the missing five minutes died down, and people, being people, moved past it. Cults were formed, wars were started, nut cases blew stuff up, books were written, theories published, and everyone came away with their own interpretation of the events. As for MHI, we just kept our big mouths shut.

Milo's wedding reception had mutated into one heck of a party. The compound had been decorated and looked pretty festive for a paramilitary fortress hidden in the backwoods. It was good to have many of the MHI staff united again, this time under much happier circumstances.

The Amazing Newbie Squad sat around a table off to one side in the boisterous cafeteria. Holly was in the process of getting wasted. Trip was frowning in disapproval. Lee was tapping his cane on the floor in time with the music. The dance floor was crowded, and Milo and his new bride appeared to be dancing a cross between the hokey pokey and the funky chicken.

"So are you going to take Earl's offer?" I asked Lee, shouting over the noise.

He sighed, distracted from the spectacle. "I suppose. I've been on exactly three missions and been injured on all of them. Doctor Nelson says my leg is going to have permanent nerve damage." He held up his cane and shook it. "I can't be out there beating monster ass with you guys anymore, so I would be a sucker not to take it."

"Good. You're the best man for the job. The archives will be in good hands," Trip stated. He looked strange with the shaved head, but the dreads had to go to make room for bandages after the battle at DeSoya Caverns. Personally I thought Trip looked better. Apparently Holly thought so as well.

"Trip, you sexy geek. Damn it, let's dance." She stood up and grabbed his hand. He began to protest weakly, but he was no match for a determined Holly. I had to laugh as she dragged him out on the dance floor. They made a weird couple.

"Hey." I felt a hand fall on my shoulder. It was

Harbinger, looking slightly inebriated and unusually happy. He tossed a small object on the table. "Here."

"What's up, Earl?" I asked as I picked it up.

"It's official. Grant's turned in his resignation. Moving to Hollywood to consult on a big horror movie or some nonsense." He snorted. Grant had not been his usual cocky self since his kidnapping, and he had never spoken about what he had seen or experienced while in the vampires' clutches. I was not surprised to see him go, but I was surprised to discover I might actually miss him. Almost. "Sam's heading out to set up the new team in Denver. So I'm really shorthanded."

I studied the little flat object. "And this way you can keep an eye on me?"

"Promise not to destroy the world or anything and we shouldn't have a problem." He winked at me and left. I twirled the patch between my fingers.

I would wear the green happy face with pride.

It was a few months later, right after Harbinger's team had returned from a difficult contract in the Philippines. Julie and I were at the Shackleford ancestral home. I had volunteered to help her work on the renovations to the old house. I was not particularly skilled at home repair, but I could do manual labor with the best of them. Mostly I loved the opportunity it gave me to spend time with her. I had bought an engagement ring, but so far I had not worked up the courage to actually ask her. Wrestle with ancient evil, fight aswangs, blow up lindwyrms, or fish for luskas? No problem. Ask the woman I love to marry me? Terrifying.

We were sitting in the formal living room. The paint

was drying, and I had to admit that it was going to look great. We had returned the missing portrait of Raymond Shackleford Jr. to its spot on the wall. We weren't expecting guests, and having the blank spot kind of ruined the symmetry. I had joked that we should just paint a beard and glasses on Earl's picture so that we wouldn't have to worry about taking it down when company came over. I could tell that Julie had been tempted.

It was about 11:00 P.M. when there was a loud knock on the door.

"Somebody's here," I said stupidly.

Julie was startled from the couch. She reached above the mantle and took down the hidden shotgun, tossed it over to me and, without thinking, I caught it. She took down a carbine and checked the chamber. "Perimeter alarm didn't sound," she said quickly.

"Aw hell." I pumped the 870 and started for the front door. "What now?"

The front entryway smelled of wood glue and sawdust. I approached the door, and signaled silently for her to cover me. Julie moved to the side, and took up a position behind one of the interior columns.

I unlocked the five heavy deadbolts. The ornate doorknob was unusually cold under my fingertips. I kept my right hand on the grip of the shotgun and kept it ready. I turned the knob and yanked the door open. I stepped back, ready to fire.

Nothing.

I sliced the pie, slowly cornering around the opening. The porch was clear. I shined the weapon-mounted light into the darkness. I could not see anything in the yard or in the parking area.

"Did we just get doorbell ditched?" I asked.

"Wait, there's a note." Julie approached cautiously. A small white envelope had been shoved under the door. She cradled the carbine in her arms as she tore it open.

"Careful," I cautioned.

"Don't be such a wuss."

She unfolded the note, adjusted her glasses, and read silently. Julie frowned, her pretty features drew into an anxious knot, and she absently rubbed the unnatural black line on the side of her neck, a habit that she had picked up when she was nervous.

"What is it, honey?" I asked. She passed the note over.

The letter was handwritten. There were two separate messages on the single sheet of paper, with two very different writing styles. The first was almost perfect calligraphy.

> *Dear Julie,*
>
> *We just wanted to drop you a note to let you know that we are doing fine. Your daddy is adjusting to his new lifestyle rather well. He has a real flair for it. We have been traveling, and seeing the world, just like we always talked about doing, but never found the time. Now we have all of the time in the world.*
>
> *We want to offer a truce. I hope there are no hard feelings about the little incident we had. As a mom I just want what is best for all of my children. Now I see that you need to live your life on your own and make your own decisions, no matter how foolish*

they may be. You need to learn from your own mistakes.

I wish that I could be at the wedding. I like this Owen. He is a good man. He will be a good husband. If you are wondering what wedding, silly me, I have to realize that you can't read minds. Your poor boyfriend broadcasts his thoughts so loudly that I could pick them up from Mexico. The ring is in the armory. It is rather pretty. Congratulations.

One last offer, as you grow old and approach your mortal end, or if your health is fleeing and creeping sickness overtakes your body, if you choose not the cold embrace of death, call upon me, and I will come. You are my daughter and my offer of immortality still stands. Until that time, if you avoid us, we will avoid you. Search for me and I will kill you and destroy everything that you hold dear with a vengeance terrible beyond your imagination.

Love,
Mom

P.S. I love what you've done with the old place.

The second message was shorter. The writing was blocky and erratic.

Hey Kids,
How's everything going? I hope y'all are well. I'm doing good. Susan is doing good.

We are having lots of fun. I'm still real sorry about the whole thing with the lying and sending you to your deaths in Natchy Bottom, but I had to do it. I hope you understand. No hard feelings. See you around.

Love,

Dad

P.S. Kid, treat my girl good or I'll rip out your heart.

I folded the note, stuck it in the envelope and passed it back. Julie crumpled it into a ball and threw it out the door. I slammed it closed.

"And to think that regular people bitch about their in-laws," I said. "I figure I've got to hold some sort of record on this one."

Julie set her gun against the wall. She fell into my arms with a sigh. I held her tight. "Do you still think normal people suck?" she asked me.

I thought about it for a moment. "Yes. Yes, I do. Normal people suck. Monster Hunting is where it's at."

"Good. I agree." We kissed, vampire mother-in-law be damned. "So where exactly is this ring?"

"Downstairs," I replied nervously. I had had it for weeks. The thought of her saying no was terrifying.

"Owen . . ."

"What, Julie?"

"Yes."

EPILOGUE

Special Agent Dwayne Myers, interim head of the Monster Control Bureau, had in fact called in his "final option" when they had discovered through the actions of MHI that the Place of Power was just outside of Childersburg, Alabama.

As the moon had approached its zenith, the B1 bomber on station over Alabama had been ordered to release its payload of a single low-yield tactical nuclear device. It was only a five-kiloton weapon, but it would have been of sufficient strength to slag the area immediately around the DeSoya Caverns Park. Had "final option" gone according to plan, it would not have stopped the Old One's plot, since the pocket dimension was separated from the normal world until the final close of the ceremony.

When released, the bomb had a clear path to impact. It was programmable to air burst for maximum surface devastation, or to strike the ground first, for more penetration. Since Special Agent Myers believed the target to be inside the underground cave, he had ordered the bomb to strike as deeply as possible before detonation.

By the time the bomb had traveled its course, the rift between worlds had been prepared. The sphere of evil energy had grown to mammoth size. The Old Ones could not cross the rift into our world, but matter from our world could enter into theirs. The five-kiloton nuclear weapon passed cleanly through the rift and entered the plane of the Old Ones.

The resulting explosion split the individual atoms of a legion of the Old Ones' elite troops, and the edge of the blast singed the carapace of the Overlord itself. This was a grave offense.

It called upon its minions to sally forth and destroy the human world utterly, but in those final moments, the rift closed, cutting off entrance for another five hundred years.

Greatly offended by this slight, it called upon its many servants, demanding an explanation of how the feeble mammals had been able to actually cause a small bit of harm to an Old One. The 10,000-foot-tall crustacean commanded them to discern the cause of the explosion.

The minions searched, trying to discover what foul creature could do such a thing. Though their contact with the human world was limited, they were able to piece together a few clues. They were mostly incorrect and confused, but they were happy to give their Dread Overlord an answer, hoping to keep from being flayed alive for eons. It did not take kindly to failure.

They reported back that the attack must have come from a lone human. It was a single mammal who had dared to launch a feeble atom weapon into their plane of existence. The Dread Overlord was joyous to hear that the perpetrator had been identified, so it only devoured a few dozen of its minions. They were digested painfully for an eternity. It ordered a message sent to the world of the humans. There were still ways to send information, and there were a handful of servants on the human world able to listen and obey.

The message was sent across space and time:

To all minions of the Overlord. Find and utterly destroy the human Hunter known as Owen Zastava Pitt.

ABOUT THE AUTHOR

Larry Correia is hopelessly addicted to two things: guns and B-horror movies. He lists his occupations: gun dealer, firearms instructor, accountant, and writer, and was until recently part owner of a company specializing in firearms and movie props. He shoots competitively and is a certified concealed weapons instructor. Larry resides in Utah with his very patient wife and family. He has also designed a special patch for the agents of Monster Hunter International, Inc. As he puts it, "If you don't look good while you're killing stuff, then you're not really a monster hunter."